I0735078

DONALD PETERS

THE IRAN AFFAIR

WORKBOOK PRESS LLC
187 E Warm Springs Rd,
Suite B285, Las Vegas, NV 89119, USA

Website: https://workbookpress.com/
Hotline: 1-888-818-4856
Email: admin@workbookpress.com

Ordering Information:
Quantity sales. Special discounts are available on quantity purchases by corporations, associations, and others. For details, contact the publisher at the address above.

Library of Congress Control Number:

ISBN-13:   978-1-958176-95-5 (Paperback Version)
                978-1-952754-04-3 (Digital Version)

REV DATE: 08/31/2022

THE
IRAN AFFAIR

Third Book of 'The Mark Taylor' Series

Donald Peters

By the same author:

Covert Decisions

The Gatekeeper

Donald Peters
www.donaldpetersbooks.nz

'If words don't add up, its' usually because the truth wasn't included in the equation.'

The Central Intelligence Agency suspects that the recent Iranian involvement in the drug trade is just a cover for a plot to assassinate a leader of an African country.

The President of the US overrides his advisors, who have suggested that it is not their business, and insists that the US should take some action to protect anyone who may be targeted. With the CIA reluctant to get involved, Mark Taylor and his team are recruited to carry out a covert mission to find out what is really happening and to prevent any assassination.

Mark travels through Africa and beyond following the trail of drugs.

A complex plot emerges involving a drugs and honey-trap operation by Iran targeting members of the diplomatic community and putting pressure of the US security services.

It turns out that these operations are just a more elaborate cover for what Iran really wants and brings the two countries to the brink of all-out war.

Mark fails to convince the CIA of the real purpose of the Iranians and rushes back to Washington DC to see the stunning conclusion that no one expected.

Chapter 1

Where It All Started

Somalia is a country in the Horn of Africa well-known in international circles for all the wrong reasons. Conflicts had plagued it for decades. Its population of fifteen or so million predominantly Sunni Muslims finally began to see something resembling peace in 2012. But there were still remnants of various terrorist groups looking to distract the fledgling government from the road to a more stable economy.

Especially in the latter years of the 20th century, terrorist cells were springing up worldwide – especially in countries with or without recent civil wars.

The government of Somalia had to spend a good deal of its time and a majority of its scarce resources trying to keep such activists under some form of control.

And - to be fair - they have been more or less successful.

The economy of Somalia is primarily dependent on agriculture. The country has few natural resources that could attract the attention of overseas investors. Non-the-less it has tried to play its part on the world stage as members of the United Nations, the Arab League, the Non-Aligned Movement, the Organization of Islamic Cooperation, and the African Union.

Being a sovereign state, Somalia had to have an intelligence service. In this case, the organization was called the National Intelligence and Security Agency (NISA). While not part of Somalia's military, this agency worked closely with its uniforms colleagues to protect the country from any form of interference in its affairs.

The United States Central Intelligence Agency also had a cell in Mogadishu -the capital city in Somalia. The workload performed by this CIA office was nothing like what it had been a few years earlier when it was probably the busiest cell on the continent of Africa at the height of the troubles in the region. Now it was more limited to keeping track of Somali pirates working on the east coast of Africa. It occasionally got involved in negotiating peace deals between the various factions involved in these irritating skirmishes. Even this activity had lessened in recent years as the actions had been repressed by the United States and allied Navy's and by the training given to merchant seafarers. It had taken time. But the owners of the big ships that sailed these waters had finally realized that it was in their best interest to spend money on self-defense and keep flowing.

However, the CIA cell in Mogadishu was staffed by professional spooks. Consequently, they did all the usual things expected of agents in the field.

And they reacted when something unusual occurred.

One unusual thing that had occurred recently was the arrival in Mogadishu of an Iranian who went by the name of Mohamed Haji. This particular gentleman had been flagged as a person of interest on the USA's terrorist watchlist. He was listed under the name Mohamed Haji and linked to the various aliases he had been known to use. The basic profile said he was of olive complexion, black hair, blue eyes, five feet six inches in height, athletic build, and weighing about one hundred seventy pounds. He was known to appear in various disguises – often with his facial hair moving from a full beard to multiple shapes of the mustache to being completely bald.

So – overall the profile described him as having similar characteristics to about half of the male population of Iran,

And probably the male population of several other middle eastern countries as well.

It was not as though Haji was necessarily known to have links to any of the well-known terrorist groups such as ISIS – the Islamic State of Iraq and Syria - or al Qaeda and other wannabe organizations that littered the middle east. However, it was a remarkable coincidence that he had been linked with various events in the recent past where certain prominent people had ended up dead. Investigations into these deaths firmly pointed to a terrorist influence by their very nature. They had been performed with a callousness that defied belief and showed little regard for what the Americans would call collateral damage.

However, attempts to find a motive behind the killings did produce some interesting information. All of the deceased had been linked to activities in which the Ministry of Intelligence of the Islamic Republic of Iran - known by the short name VAJA - had played a significant role. Consequently, the conclusion was relatively easy to reach. Haji was working for Iranian Intelligence.

Since the United States regarded Iran as a sponsor of terrorism and since someone like Haji was on the terrorist list – in addition to being considered a nasty piece of work - the Mogadishu CIA cell reported his presence to their masters at the CIA headquarters in Langley, Virginia.

The CIA has over twenty thousand people labor, although the actual number was a not-so-well-kept secret. What was known by anyone who cared to ask, the exact number of spies in the organization was considerably less than the twenty thousand personnel aforementioned. The CIA is officially tasked with gathering, processing, and analyzing national security information worldwide. The methods that they employ to get that information is secret.

As are the people who acquire it.

However – the CIA is a bureaucracy.

Bureaucracies the world over have at least one major characteristic they all share.

They grow exponentially irrespective of the workload.

This characteristic is pretty easy to understand when it is borne in mind that many are government agencies. Therefore, they report to politicians. But it is not just one amorphous mass. A bureaucracy is typically made up of various cells – many of which have a life of their own. Such cells can and do survive irrespective of what may be happening elsewhere in their organization. And they have been known to defend themselves against encroachment from other cells from within the same organization.

And the bureaucrats who make up such cells occasionally put a finger up to remind people of their importance.

To understand this phenomenon more fully, you only have to look at a particular cell at the CIA by an example of what happens.

The CIA has offices – or 'Desks' - for different regions of the Earth. There is a desk for every part of the planet. So – within the CIA headquarters, an office called MENA is responsible for the Middle East and North Africa. That office has specialists who cover particular countries within that broad area. In addition to regional distinction, there are also specialists in cultural and religious groups. In the case of Muslims, which would require different specialists for Sunni. Shia and Kharijite Muslims. In a conflict occurring within a region, the desk would have to be expanded depending on whether that conflict was between cultural groups, religious groups, or war within a group. Such expansion at CIA headquarters would be reflected elsewhere.

During the Somali Civil war in 1991/1992, the Somali desk within the Mogadishu office was expanded to cope with the increased intelligence gathered from the field. And the intelligence which was flooding into the office from elsewhere. In CIA terms, the locally acquired intelligence was defined as HUMINT - or Human Intelligence. External forms of intelligence gathering such as SIGINT (Signals Intelligence run by the National Security Agency), IMINT Geospatial-Intelligence run by the National Geospatial-Intelligence Agency), or MASINT (Measurement and Signature Intelligence run by the Department of Defense) all require vastly more resources to gather the intelligence. And fewer people. But they need considerably more people to carry out the analysis.

When the United States decided in 1993 to send troops to Somalia to cope with the aftermath of the war and to deal with other problems that arose – including but not limited to terrorist groups, famines, displacements, and refugees - that cell was expanded again to cope with the expanded reliance on Intelligence. Therefore, an expanded group within the CIA continued to grow both in Mogadishu and at CIA Headquarters Langley Virginia and developed a level of ability that would be hard to replace.

Different groups would be involved in the conflict in

the years that followed. That meant that varying levels of expertise were needed. The existing people could not be replaced or retrained. They would be added to.

That is when a group such as this cell develops and assumes a life of its own. As the situation in Somalia stabilized, there would be far less activity in the cell. But there is a significant time lag. The office, which was expanded exponentially to cope with the increase, would not decrease exponentially.

It probably would not decrease at all.

What is more, those in the cell now with little to do would jealously guard whatever intelligence came their way, fiercely proposing to anyone else in the organization who was within earshot that their expertise was not only required but was critical.

When the recently gotten snippet of information that placed Mohamed Haji in Somalia came to light, two things happened. Firstly - that snippet of data was analyzed to death. Secondly - to justify the existence of the analyst, it was insinuated that there was more to the story than was first thought. And on a quiet news day could be worth mentioning in their daily report to remind people that the cell was still alive and well.

In summary – Haji, who is a known associate of Iran Intelligence – a man who has turned up in various places where important people have been killed - turns up in Somalia. The timing is significant. It is shortly before a meeting of the African Union to meet in nearby Sudan. And he is seen talking to a bunch of Somali thugs.

It could have all ended there were it not for a curious mix of events that had occurred half a world away.

A couple of weeks before the arrival of Mohamed Haji in Somalia, a gentleman from Saudi Arabia by the name of Muhammad Hadi had appeared in the United States. The origins of the business that Hadi engaged in primarily concerned the Saudi Stock Exchange – or Tadawul. Since most stock and financial transactions worldwide usually involved having access to a computer keyboard (and not much else), he probably did not need to fly halfway around the world to meet with his associates. However, the amount of investment by both countries in the other shares markets made the occasional face-to-face meeting inevitable. Added to that, the friendship that the Americans had for the Arabs – based entirely on strategic considerations and not much else – guaranteed that visitors from Saudi Arabia were welcome in the land of the free.

Other factors were, of course, in play. While relationships between the two states may be friendly, that did not stop the posturing of lobby groups on behalf of both sides involved in the game.

Another factor that would affect Hadi's visit was that the United States was at this time in the middle of a Presidential election campaign when it was doubtful whether anyone would be interested in whatever it was that Hadi would want to talk about, being politely dismissed as unimportant at the moment, or he would entirely be dismissed by the derogatory term of *Raghead* by the bigots.

Which position suited Hadi admirably because very little of his business during this visit would have much to do with stocks and shares. The less attention that his visit attracted, then so much the better.

Of more interest were a couple of subjects which had been years in the making.

After visiting New York City and doing the compulsory visits to the New York Stock Exchange Wall Street in the financial district of Lower Manhattan, Hadi hired a car and drove south to Washington DC. There he checked into the Four Seasons Hotel on Pennsylvania Avenue – a venue that was not exactly the cheapest place he could have chosen - and set about organizing himself to manage the real reason he had come to the United States.

The first reason concerned a gentleman named Asif Fisk.

Asif had joined the Department of Homeland Security as a young man intent on becoming a Secret Service special agent and gaining an exciting career in the service of his country. Well - Not his country of birth, of course. But it was the country that had provided a home to him and his sister. They had lost both of their parents in the Gulf War and been adopted by US Sergeant Adele Fisk in the aftermath of that conflict and brought to America to make the family that she and her partner would never otherwise have had. And Asif Fisk had done well, being rapidly promoted, and finally assigned to the Secret Service detail to protect one of the contestants in the upcoming Presidential election.

This made for an exciting prospect in the life of the young man. Should the person he was assigned to protect win the presidential race, and Fisk continue to perform his duties to a satisfactory level, then the odds were that Fisk would become an integral part of the Presidents' protective detail.

His ascendancy in the Secret Service had meant that Fisk had been thoroughly vetted and his background exhaustively checked by the security services. But even the rigorous and intrusive nature of such checks can fail to grasp every event in the life of a young man.

While at Georgetown University undertaking study of

Political Science and Governance, he had met and befriended a lady called Catherine Kirby who seemed to have interests similar to his own. She had come to the United States from a remarkably similar background. The only difference was that her foster parents had insisted on her changing her name completely in an endeavor to put the sad part of her earlier life behind her.

That was fine until she invited Fisk to her home to meet her parents. He took the invitation to be an encouraging sign for their future together. And in the interests of impressing them with his ethnicity, which linked him with Catherine, he proclaimed that he had also been fostered as a refugee from the Gulf War.

And that was the end of that relationship.

The young Fisk went through a period of intense depression in which he even contemplated ending his own life. But then he crawled out of the depths of despair and reassessed his position. While the United States had offered him a home and an education far exceeded anything that he could have had in the country of his birth, it was still the country responsible for his being an orphan. It was still a country accountable for the death of his parents.

And it was still a country filled with bigots like the Kirby family.

An intermediary had arranged the meeting between Asif Fisk and Muhammad Hadi, and it was made to look like a chance encounter in a bar at the Four Seasons. Very little was said other than to establish that Fisk, in his role of a protector of an important man, would be privy to some subjects that could be of value to Hadi and that Hadi was in the unique position of being able to assist Fisk in any way that his plans desired.

The other area that Hadi had an interest in was much more critical and complex, albeit largely beyond Hadi's ability to control. This was because most of what he had to achieve would be dependent on the outcome of the forthcoming Presidential election. And, at the same time, it would be influenced by his political masters back in the middle east.

The political system in the United States was bad enough. While democratic, the US system still left many people in the world bewildered as to how it all worked. The fact that the United States could elect a Democrat as President did not mean that the resultant Government of the United States would be Democrat. This was because the Senate was filled with two Senators per state, who favored the Republicans. In addition to that, Senators are elected for six-year terms. Members of the lower chamber are elected for two-year terms. The President is elected for a four-year term. So - who knew how you figured out whether a change of government had occurred?

The current Presidential election campaign was trending towards the Democrats. That would suit Hadi. Such a result would make the governance of the United States more difficult – at least for the next four years. Non-the-less it was what it was. Most foreign countries trying to do business in the United States had to be aware that any influence they may have developed with departments of state could be turned on its head for no apparent reason. Apart, that is, as a result of a handful of votes going one way or the other.

Hadi had developed a working relationship with some middle-level management staff in the Department of State, resulting in a steady flow of largely innocuous but useful information without anything being revealed that would cause repercussions at an international level. However, if the election outcome went the opposite way to trending, the new President would be a Republican. He would then need to replace the left-leaning Secretary of State with someone more in tune with the policies of his new administration. An even worse scenario was that the new President would probably appoint a new Secretary of State from amongst his closest supporters, selecting someone from within the Department with more right-leaning views. It was to be hoped that Muhammad Hadi could influence that choice, but for the moment, all that he could do was ensure that he had contacts on both sides of the political fence.

Again, the Four Seasons Hotel meetings had been arranged by intermediaries. The political affiliations of the participants were unknown to Hadi, and he did not care. All that he knew was that his longer-term relationship with one of the men would cease dependent on the pending outcome of the election. There was nothing formal about the conversation. After a casual chat that lasted less than one hour, the two men shook hands as is the way in western cultures to signify an understanding between them.

After that, he had a similar conversation with the opposition.

Then they shook hands and left.

Hadi headed for Dulles International airport.

The first flight took Hadi to Frankfurt, Germany, rather than a more direct flight to Saudi Arabia. The reason for this was that two-fold. Firstly, Muhammad Hadi had booked a nights' accommodation in Frankfurt. Secondly, the following morning, he would present himself back at the airport for a direct flight to Teheran on Iran Air.

On this flight, he would use another passport.

That one was under his real name - Mohamed Haji.

Chapter 2

Ethan Khatami

Mahmoud Khatami was now seething as he stared at his television in disbelief. Initially, he had watched the United States Presidential election results with almost detached interest. All the popular polls had expected and confirmed that the Democrats would win the election in a landslide. And such a result would only be good for the Islamic Republic of Iran. It would also be suitable for the many other countries subjected to political abuse and penal restrictions imposed by the previous Republican President - the so-called leader of the free world.

But – No. Against all the odds, BJ Thomas and the Republicans Party had engineered another victory. Now America would continue with its relentless shift even further to the right. Isolationist when it suited them. In favor of free trade, but only if it served them. Spreading the message of peace but only when there was nothing to be gained by continuing their bully tactics.

It was not as though Khatami could have cared less whether Republicans or Democrats held sway in the United States government. The American political system had numerous twists and turns that many people barely understood within and without the US. But, in the end, the Americans still had an eat capitalists controlled. No amount of political involvement, democratic or otherwise, could change that.

But – No. The man himself – BJ Thomas - that Mahmoud Khatami had grown to hate.

And it was personal.

Under the earlier US administration, then-Senator BJ Thomas had been at the forefront of an aggressive movement that sought to impose a set of crippling trade sanctions on the Islamic Republic of Iran. The pretext for these sanctions was the Iranian insistence on its sovereign right to develop *nuclear* facilities in a country with few alternative means of generating electricity. However, the very mention of the word nuclear meant that the western world believed that Iran would have the means to enrich uranium, which was, of course, true. And from that position, Iran would have the means to develop nuclear weapons. Which was, of course, absolute nonsense.

Well – Maybe!

There were, of course, other forces at work. It was a fact that Iran had friends that were not on the US government's Christmas card list. That was a good enough reason to impose sanctions on all sorts of trade and products, including Oil. This policy had been sold to the American public based on the false understanding that the sanctions would not impact the lives of ordinary citizens of the target country.

But they did.

Khatami had been the President of Iran for the last two years and could expect to remain in that position for another six years - a total of eight years which was equal to two terms of four years - the maximum allowed under the Iran constitution. That is on the assumption that the body remained in place. And on the more likely, and essential belief that he stayed true to the Supreme Leader Ali Khamenei. The Supreme Leader was, of course, appointed for life and could, if he so desired, terminate Khatami's position both figuratively and literally. However, if Khatami's only fault was that he hated the new President of the United States, that would only endear him to his Leader for eternity and beyond.

Mahmoud Khatami had a younger brother – Ethan Khatami. Ethan had been dependent on his elder brother since the death of their parents in an automobile accident when Ethan was still a teenager. The younger brother chose a different path in life than the older and the more ambitious Mahmoud. At the age of eighteen, Ethan had qualified for entrance to the University of Tehran and had embarked on a physics course to become a scientist. After graduating with a degree with honors, his immediate aim was to travel and enhance his experience and knowledge before settling down to improve the lot of his fellow Iranians.

That plan was brought to a shuddering halt when he complained of headaches that no traditional medicines seemed capable of fixing. On seeking advice from various doctors and then being referred to specialists, he was finally diagnosed with a tumor in his brain.

In the opinion of the head doctor, the tumor was potentially cancerous, malignant, and inoperable.

But Ethan Khatami was encouraged not to give up hope. The doctor had expressed an opinion as to the worst-case scenario, and Ethan had the right to seek a second opinion, which he did.

Cancer had been initially defined as Glioblastoma

grade 3 on a scale of 1 to 4, with grade 4 being the highest risk. However, after further analysis, it was decided that an operation to remove the tumor was out of the question because of the aggressive nature of his cancer, the size of cancer, its location, and the observed speed of growth of the mass. An operation carried out by the very best surgeons in the world would not make any difference when faced with these issues. The doctors in Tehran correctly concluded that Ethan had less than a year to live unless some of the new cancer drugs and treatments developed by pharmaceutical companies in the USA and Europe could be utilized.

In the more advanced economies, experiments were well advanced in gene therapy, but that would be too late for this case. More hopeful was the progress in immunotherapy and vaccine therapy which looked to strengthen the immune system to fight cancer of various types. The problem with immunotherapy was that it paradoxically caused chaos with the body's immune system. Consequently, there were serious risks with this approach. But these risks were reduced considerably if the person being treated was young and fit. And if the cancer was found early enough in its development. And provided private funding for such treatment was assured that it was too early in the development cycle for any such treatment to be publicly funded.

Since Ethan was the brother of the President of Iran, funding for such treatment would not be an issue.

So, the doctors had concluded that there was an excellent chance that Ethan would resume his everyday life after receiving treatment.

And that was where the sanctions imposed on Iran by the United States came into play.

All because of the bill put forward by one man - BJ Thomas.

Despite the considerable efforts of President Khatami and the Iranian doctors, there would be no access to the new drugs to treat the younger Ethan as long as the sanctions remained in place.

The next hope was to get Ethan to either the United States or Germany, where any money would be supplied to get him treated. But the prospect of that happening ran into all sorts of problems, not helped because the US Embassy in Teheran was closed. The Swiss government taking care of US interests in Iran did not have the mechanisms to facilitate such a plan. The speed with which bureaucracies move was not the problem here. In this case, the problem was getting a decision.

The escalated hopes of the young man came crashing down, and all that Mahmoud Khatami could do was to watch his brother waste away,

The younger brother of President Khatami finally committed suicide rather than face the prospect of a rapidly deteriorating and painful existence and eventual death.

It was probably at the funeral gathering that the elder Khatami felt the most pain. The people were in the mosque's courtyard listening to the kind words being spoken by the Imam. But the President wasn't attending. He was watching the grief-stricken wife of Ethan as she clung to her daughters, trying to reconcile the fact that life had to go on without him. Mahmoud recalled an earlier time when Ethan had first been diagnosed, sitting with his family, and looking expectantly at his elder brother. Then the wife had a look of respect and trust on her face as she heard assurances that everything would be Ok. The daughters did not understand the impact of sanctions. All that they knew was that their father would receive the very best of care. They were in a very privileged position. Uncle Mahmoud would assure that position.

Then Mahmoud's thoughts moved on to a later time when he began to realize that things would not be quite as he had wished. The look on the wife's face became one of pleading. The daughters were concerned that their mother was upset.

And their uncle was the cause of that.

Now it was the funeral of a devoted husband and father. And the wife would not even look at Mahmoud, fearful that he would see the hate she felt. But the daughters could. Knowing no better, they stared at him, tears streaming down their faces and their feeling were plain and simple. And in plain sight, for all to see. They were accusing him of abandoning the family and robbing them of their father.

It did not matter to the distraught girls that it was not his fault.

President Khatami decided there and then that he would do something to avenge the death of his brother,

It was not as though the US sanctions on Iran per se had much to do with it. It was the perception that counted. Doctors and Pharmaceutical firms had to choose their test patients carefully to ensure that they did not conduct the tests on patients who were likely to recover anyway fully. Or, more significantly, did not carry out tests on patients who would inevitably die irrespective of the treatment, if for no other reason than that it would be a waste of money. And, after all, it was money that drove the system.

Testing to find out who should be in the test group was in itself a time-consuming task, and even some patients who were only marginal cases would miss out because of resource considerations. Against these odds, when people made it into the test group, there was a need to keep a constant watchful eye on their patients undergoing experimental treatment with the consistent ability for the doctors to adjust therapy. So, it would have been impractical if one of the patients was thousands of miles away in places like Iran. Being treated in the land of the infidels was the obvious choice for Ethan, but the problem was, how did you justify moving Ethan to the US, which in itself would at least be seen as a means of getting around the sanctions. And, at worst, be seen by Americans as favoring a foreigner over one of their own. Being treated at home in Iran would have been an option because that would have involved sharing research with the doctors in Iran, making the sanctions pointless. Irrespective of these factors, a medical opinion in the US was that the condition of the patient would have given any treatment at best a five percent chance of succeeding, which did not meet the cut-off point for acceptance,

But lesser misconceptions have been the cause of world conflicts in the past.

After the conclusion of the US elections had been confirmed, President Mahmoud Khatami summoned his closest advisors to a meeting to discuss what position Iran should take in the light of the latest developments in the leadership of the western alliance. At this first meeting, the Iranian Intelligence service – known as VAJA – revealed (erroneously) that BJ Thomas, the new President of the US, had a similar illness to that suffered by Mahmoud's brother.

Khatami greeted this piece of information with some pleasure. But he went further than just taking pleasure in the BJ's misfortune. Khatami decided that he would use this forum to obtain revenge on the man who was the cause of his grief. This, of course, met with immediate agreement, especially from the clerics among the inner circle members.

It was decided that Iran would need to do a couple of things to commence Khatami's plan on revenge. They would have to activate their sleeper agents in the United States and get them prepared for involvement in a program of harassment to put unrelenting pressure on America and their President.

The Iranian Ministry of Intelligence was wrong in diagnosing the US president's illness would not affect what happened.

Chapter 3

Fun and Games

It was unusual, but then it had been that sort of a day.

The briefing session in the Oval Office at the White House would typically take place as early as was possible in the day. After all – you could not have the leader of the free world starting the day without being fully and adequately informed of what was happening before he had to make crucial decisions that may affect, or be affected by, what was going on in the world. But it just happened that way due to a peculiar set of circumstances.

President BJ Thomas had been at Camp David for the weekend after being at his hospital for what would become his regular monthly checkup. Because it was his first checkup since taking office, and because it was known that the President did have some health issues, it had been decided that his physician would accompany him to Camp David for *observation.*

Since leaders of the world were supposed to function like robots and be constantly available to the media and everybody else on the planet, the President was not allowed to be ill. So, the story was that he was retreating to Camp David to study some vital briefing papers in the peace and tranquility that the Catoctin Mountain Park could provide. Located about sixty miles northwest of Washington DC, at least technically, a military installation and security at the site were second to none. In addition to the President's protection provided by the Secret Service, the camp was staffed by United States Navy personnel plus an undisclosed number of United States Marines. These personnel were heavily armed and took the job of protecting their President seriously, irrespective of their personal view of politics.

And politicians.

The facts of the matter were that the President *was* ill. Security of Camp David allowed his physician to observe, without anyone in the media – and therefore the public - being notified.

There were, of course, several people who already knew. There had to be. Even so, the majority of the lesser people at Camp David did not know precisely who the bearded and bespectacled gentleman was, other than that he was referred to as 'BC,' which was sufficiently close to BJ to cause no end of confusion to the staff. However, it did not take a rocket scientist to discover that BC was from the medical fraternity.

This man had been collected on Friday afternoon from the Johns Hopkins University School of Medicine by a Secret Service detail and brought to Camp David. No one at Hopkins would have been aware of where he was going, who he was going to see, or why. That had to be so because Hospital communities are like a family. So, people talk – in the strictest confidence, of course. And the staff at Camp David were also like a family, so they spoke as well. Except in the case of the Navy and Marine personnel who staffed the place. What they talk about is a tightly held secret. That is if a secret can be kept among staff more than one hundred who often changed depending on what was or was not happening and who had met their principal for the first time since his election.

The President's sixtieth birthday on Monday did not improve things.

It made things worse.

BJ Thomas had been suffering from what the medical people called MDD – technically Major Depressive Disorder. While that was manageable from a strictly clinical point of view, the doctor had other things to consider—namely, the attitude of his patient. There was nothing that this President would not do to avoid an admission of his illness. That was even though the stigma had long since gone. President Abraham Lincoln is remembered as a President who was assassinated and the man who ended slavery suffered from depression. Almost every other man who had filled the office of President since. The possible exception would have been President Ronald Reagan about who said that he was never awake long enough to know whether he did or did not suffer from anything other than boredom.

Professor of Neurology - Bryce Caldwell - had yet to figure out the history of the current President's illness, and that was why he had spent the weekend at Camp David. Depression usually affects people at a much younger age. So - was this depression, not depression, but the early onset of Dementia, Parkinson's, Alzheimer's, or Huntington's disease? Or should BC refer the case to one of his colleagues in the Psychiatry Department and get the hell out of here with his reputation intact?

The first lady was the person who had insisted that the President get some treatment. Who else could?

As a consequence of that first analysis, the doctors

had concluded that he was suffering from a form of Melancholic depression – which may or may not have been something that all women complain about in their men who can no longer get it up as age wearies them. The net result was that the President was resigned not to seek a second term.

As it turned out, that was the least of his problems.

There was more bad news on the way once various tests were completed.

They gathered in the Oval Office at five o'clock on Monday afternoon. The team consisted of the five members of his inner circle that the President had brought into government, plus two other members he inherited from the previous administration. In theory, this group of seven should have been reasonably settled given that they had all maintained a friendship amid the chaos that existed in the Washington political scene during an election campaign that could best be described as brutal. On both individuals and companies. But then – the fact that they had now been called upon to serve at the higher level of Cabinet rank could make for strange events and complications that no one had predicted. And at this level, there probably would appear some bias or previously hidden agendas where individual ambitions got in the way of group cooperation.

There would undoubtedly be a fair bit of juggling for a position at the feeding trough during the first few weeks of the new administration, but that could be expected to settle down in due course. While most of the men were personal friends, or at least they had been before the election, some would fall by the wayside as friendships became strained, or they discovered that they lacked the enthusiasm in the face of public scrutiny.

Or BJ found that personal friendship did not equate with loyalty. Or that the expected dedication did not work both ways.

The Secretary of State, who went by the name of John Scott, was the highest-ranked member of the cabinet behind only the President and the Vice President. His appointment was subject to a confirmation hearing by the Senate. Still, as the Republicans held a majority in the Senate and the Congress, the confirmation was regarded as a mere formality. The position was equivalent to that of the Foreign Minister in other countries. The State Department would have control of all US diplomats. Scott would be responsible for shaping US relations with other countries for at least four years. Or at least for as long as Scott remained in that position. He was a large brute who regarded most people around him as little better than doormats. He could be the most charming man they would ever wish to meet to those he had to negotiate with at an international level. To the defeated Democrats, he was a man they hated for many reasons – some political, others more personal.

The Secretary of Defense – Barry Crammer – was a quiet and thoughtful little man who nonetheless could and did manage to oversee the rough and tumble of dealing with the military people and their ambitions rather well. During the selection process, the president was pressured by various lobby groups to nominate a retired Army General to the position. However, there would have been problems with the work effectively made Crammer the Deputy Commander in Chief of the mighty United States military., One of his jobs was to maintain *civilian* control of the military. Consequently, there were restrictions on the appointment of ex-military people. BJ did not want to battle with an even partisan Senate to get a General he had never heard of appointed to the position.

The Attorncy General – Mike Fischer from the Department of Justice – was the oldest among the new team members. He was a lawyer by trade but few who could become a competent administrator. And he regarded all politicians as people to be tolerated but not trusted. That was because of the role, and the US constitution said that no one was above the law. Fischer was responsible for the enforcement of the law and the administration of justice, and he could not envisage two tasks further removed from the antics that went on in Washington. The Department of Justice was the agency responsible for several vital institutions – particularly the FBI – the Federal Bureau of Investigation – and the DEA – the Drug Enforcement Administration. Nothing that went on in these institutions had anything to do with politics. Whether their work had anything to do with politicians would, of course, be dependent on individuals and circumstances.

Nicolas Harrison was the White House Chief of Staff, and he was in a unique position among the group. The President appointed Harrison. The work did not require Senate confirmation, and his role could be whatever the President decided. And for as long as the President agreed that Harrison could continue. As a general rule, the job had been a private Secretary – just making sure that the White House functioned smoothly and efficiently. But there was more to it than that. Harrison could influence and control what others could, or could not, do, and he probably had more contact and closer contact with the President than any other man on the planet. He was, therefore, in a position that could make or break anyone else. Although Harrison was still to find out how much he could exercise any control over anyone else. Although Harrison was still to find out how much he could exercise any control over anyone. His job was akin to that of a shepherds' dog. He was supposed to control the sheep, but occasionally, that would result in someone being bitten.

The Vice President who had almost single-handedly gotten BJ elected was Roger Warren, a white-haired, tall, thin man from Texas who thought everyone else was on this earth solely for his benefit. He was a man of questionable morals. But no one could question his dedication to whatever project he elected to pursue. And so, by fair means or foul, he had bulldozed the American public into supporting BJ Thomas as next President of the United States against seemingly overwhelming odds which polls had suggested the Democrats would win at a canter. Latterly in the campaign, BJ had realized the kind of man he had as a running mate, but it was too late to do anything about that. The only consolation now was that, should BJ elect not to seek a second term – as after his latest session with his doctor was reasonably certain to be the case - he was equally sure that the American public would see the error of their ways and would not support Warren in his bid for President. That, in turn, could mean that it was equally sure that BJ's successor would be a Democrat. Still – it was too early to get too far ahead.

The two members in his inner circle that BJ Thomas had inherited from the previous administration were the National Security Advisor – Bruce Aderholt – and the Director of National Intelligence – Peter Fairfield. They had both been retained because BJ could not think of anyone he could trust with such critical positions among his friends. And they were probably the only two amongst the seven men who knew anything about the business of translating intelligence into some action that was necessary to run a government.

The National Security Advisor was another position that the President could fill without getting the appointment confirmed by the Senate. That had the effect of placing BJ in a quandary - caused by the simple fact that BJ knew nothing about intelligence matters. Consequently, he was being asked to appoint someone as an *advisor* without having sufficient knowledge to judge whether or not his appointee would know what he was talking about. So – BJ took the obvious way out. He did nothing to change the NSA, and he made sure that he had a counter by also keeping the existing Director of National Intelligence.

Well - there was only one small change that he did make – he made sure that the DNI would be a part of his inner circle.

The original position of Director of National Intelligence had been set up as a response to the 9/11 terrorist attack on the United States based on the mistaken assumption that there had been a failure in the US security and intelligence services. The establishment of a DNI did add another level to an already crowded – some would say cumbersome – field. It also added a stumbling block between the principal intelligence source – the Central Intelligence Agency - and the President. Nonetheless, Fairfield held a reasonably powerful position in the inner circle, calling on the expertise of the sixteen influential organizations that made up the top tier of the US intelligence community.

The net result was that, even though all seven of these men owed their present positions at the feeding trough to BJ, the gathering was not exactly cordial, and the President was unsure why.

They were all professionals, experienced, and dedicated

Republicans, so what was the problem?

There might have been two problems. The first could be due to their all being supported by vast bureaucratic structures irrespective of their personalities. The second was that there was now a new administration to deal with. These two factors, taken together, could result in paralysis. In the early stages of the administration, getting any report out of the bureaucracy could result in a conflict between the stated current position and the assumed new position. That would result in attempts to adjust everything, not to release anything until every last 'I' had been dotted and every previous 'T' had been crossed. In the interim, their masters were either bureaucrats or politicians, and they tended to act like a flock of sheep, one following the other, wherever they were led.

Or pushed.

The President seemed much better from his rest. So, the members of his inner circle were quite content to discuss matters of state. However, this gathering was not intended as any formal cabinet meeting, and it would be unusual for any decisions to be made at this time.

And since it was the Presidents birthday and outside regular office hours - at least for some - they had a drink of something a little more substantial than the regular coffee.

No questions were asked of what each would drink. The Navy steward could remember the favorite drink of each of them despite only having met most of them once before today. Except, for the President himself, the steward would be more cautious. Well – the steward could remember what the President favored. But he was also aware of the medication he was on. Consequently, the older man got a weird concoction of non-alcoholic mixes, which were lemon, lime, and bitters for today, which did not improve the mood of the President.

Then, amid all the idle chatter and apparent friendship, the National Security Advisor Aderholt dropped a bombshell.

'We are hearing whispers out of Africa of a plot to assassinate one of the leaders before the meeting of the African Union scheduled for Khartoum next month. The CIA is tracking it through contacts close to the various ISIS and al Qaeda groups in the region. It is still early days – but it looks as though our friend Uncle Robert of Zimbabwe is the chief focus of their attention.'

And the National Security Advisor took another sip of his Bourbon and Dry.

The Vice President did not help. Roger Warren would have known that Mugabe was the leader of Zimbabwe. He probably knew that Khartoum was in Africa. Possibly knew that it was the capital of Sudan. He may have been aware that two countries shared the name Sudan. But that would have been the extent of his knowledge.

He asked a simple question.

'Do we care?'

No one answered at first.

The Secretaries of State and Defense and the Attorney General just sat staring into their glasses. They had seen the stunned reaction from their President, and they knew that he was about to explode. All three of them believed that the only reason why Aderholt was still in his office was that the President had not gotten around to replacing him. They thought that the world of spooks was just blown up out of all proportion. And they also knew that the Vice President was someone that the President loathed based on the guy's morals – or rather lack of morals.

BJ Thomas had only gone along with having Warren as his vice president because BJ Thomas would not be the president without Warren.

Now BJ was stuck between a rock and a hard place – and it was all his fault!

Dumb ass!

The President groaned. Maybe he should have listened to Bryce Caldwell, the smart-ass doctor from Hopkins, who had tactfully advised him to step aside. He had told him that his health was more important than any job! No matter that, over two hundred million Americans would do anything to be in his position and would crawl over broken glass to stay there!

The President had laughed when he told the first lady the night before of the opinion of Professor of Medicine Bryce Caldwell. He had asked her – *What is the difference between God and a Doctor? Answer – God doesn't claim to be a Doctor.* Ha, fucking, ha.

If the President was to take that advice and resign little more than a few weeks after being elected, that meant that the next President of the United States would be the current Vice President. At least, that is what the Constitution of the United States said should happen. That was something that the President had never envisaged happening. And, in all fairness, neither had the vast majority of the voting public lost in all the hype of a fiercely contested first pass-the-post election fight with the Democrats.

'We should do something!' the President finally responded. 'We cannot have a bunch of thugs from ISIS or al Qaeda going around the world killing Presidents.'

BJ laughed at what he thought was a joke. No one else in the room laughed. Because in this age – threats to kill Presidents were genuine. And the mere mention of a threat was sufficient to have the Secret Service officers automatically increase their alert levels. Archie Williams was head of the President's detail on this particular day, and he exchanged a nervous glance with the only other member of his staff who was standing like a statue at the other side of the room. The secret service personnel would generally be regarded as little more than furniture by the esteemed company in the Oval Office. And people in this office talked freely about all sorts of matters that the media, and any foreign government on the planet, would pay with their lives to be privy to. The secret service personnel were assumed to be oblivious to all they heard or saw. They were focused simply on protecting the one man they had sworn to serve.

But were they?

The President frowned.

No one reacted to his joke! Why was that? *The next President to be attacked could be me!* - BJ mused – but did not say.

That was another reason to get out! Then maybe the next one to be lined up for assassination would be his Vice President. Now that was a thought ……

As one of the senior members present, the Secretary of State thought he should add his thoughts before this conversation got out of hand. In addition, John Scott had reasons why he would not want this group of goons pushing their noses into matters that did not concern them. Or, if the truth is known, he would be pretty happy to be rid of some of the world leaders who could be the target of such a plot. There were two reasons for this view.

Firstly – it would make running the countries diplomatic services so much easier.

Secondly, it would make the job of his President much

harder.

'The question is the extent to which we can get involved.' Scott began. 'We can inform the governments of any country of the intelligence information that we have. Then leave them to make their arrangements for their security. I believe that is as far as we should go.'

Crammer, the Secretary of Defense, had a quiet smile to himself. He thought that he knew where this was leading. And he was glad that the subject was well outside his area of responsibility. Well - until the shit hit the fan and, as usual, it then became a military matter for his men to have to sort out. Yet again! Meanwhile, the NSA Bruce Aderholt went apoplectic as he addressed the Secretary of State.

'You are not suggesting that we do any such thing – are you? We cannot simply spread information around like confetti on the off chance that something constructive would come of it. We would risk giving up our sources of intelligence. And the boys down the road at the CIA would not want that to happen. You would also risk drying up any information we might get in the future. If there were a threat of revealing our sources, people would not talk to us.'

So - *'shove that up your ass,'* the NSA did not say.

But Aderholt had been suckered into making a statement that he would have been wiser to have avoided.

Peter Fairfield, the DNI, nearly choked on his drink as the discussion became more intense. Fairfield now faced the problem that would continue to be the case as long as there was a National Security Advisor. The position of the Director of National Intelligence had been founded after the debacle of September 11th, 2001. The event had led to a situation in which many people blamed it on a failure of the security and intelligence services. That was probably grossly unfair. But it had led to a knee-jerk reaction to try - yet again - to get some coordination and cooperation into matters of national security and intelligence. Now, with the benefit of hindsight, all that had achieved was to impose another layer to an already multi-layered organization.

Which made the job of National Security Advisor that much more complex.

The Central Intelligence Agency had been principally responsible for overseas intelligence, and the Federal Bureau of Investigation managed domestic intelligence. Anybody who believed the matter was as simple as that was a few sandwiches short of a picnic. At least fourteen other organizations were part of the US security and intelligence network. The National Security Agency, responsible for electronic surveillance and intelligence, was the largest single organization involved with security. With its headquarters at Fort Meade, Maryland, it belonged to the Department of Defense. The Pentagon controlled the largest intelligence-gathering organization on the planet. Unfortunately, the Pentagon and the CIA were not strictly speaking terms with each other. Any number of other organizations fed into the mix would not change that.

The State Department was also involved in intelligence gathering in every conceivable part of the world, and it did – because it had to – cooperate with the CIA. The head of that department - the Secretary of State - sat in on virtually every meeting of the power brokers, and the DNI was pushing shit uphill with a fork trying to penetrate the workings of the crowd down at Foggy Bottom.   And now the National Security Advisor had admitted that the CIA could still call the shots on the simple question of what they did with the information they gathered without even bothering to inform the DNI.

'There should be a way we can do this without being seen as directly involved!' the President interjected, trying to lead rather than be led. This President did not like the term *'Deniability'* because that term ran counter to the principles that he had stood for. After all, the United States was supposed to be the leader of the free world. That meant transparency. That suggested that you could not deny the truth. However, what he was proposing still amounted to the same thing. A situation in which the US could influence world events without seeming to have been involved. Or have had any prior knowledge of what had, or had not, happened. And if, or when, things turned pear-shaped, they could deny all knowledge.

The DNI saw an opportunity in this dichotomy to recover the ground he had lost in the earlier exchange. However, that just resulted in him making matters worse.

'You could authorize a covert operation citing a threat to our national security. After all – while we are not directly involved with the African Union – we have still been invited along as observers. And this business does involve a threat to all the world leaders. That could create instability in the region which we do not need right now. And it is not too large a step to envisage that ISIS, al Qaeda, and similar terrorist organizations could target people in our own country!'

The DNI had raised several critical issues that would cause concern.

Firstly – the President was obviously in favor of doing something, and he had the power to do it irrespective of what his advisors may think. The so-called plenipotentiary power of government officials – particularly Presidents of the United States – had been around for centuries.

The only problem in a real democracy such as the US, which had a powerful Senate and a Congress to worry about, was that someone else was supposed to know what it was to be used for and why, preferably before the event happened.

Secondly, the president's organization for such an event was the only one under current United States law to conduct covert operations. That organization was the CIA. If someone were to target heads of state, then interference in the perpetrators' plans would presumably mean killing them. However, contrary to popular belief, the CIA does not have that much experience killing anybody.

Thirdly – and the overriding issue was – did the United States have the capability to, in fact, launch such an operation?

Discussing these issues presented severe problems that the DNI did not want to raise. Apart from capability and resources, the most significant of them was – Did the CIA want to mount such an operation?

The DNI knew what the CIA wanted to do about the alleged plot.

Nothing!

The Attorney General had kept quiet during this exchange, happy to let the Director of National Intelligence dig for himself into an even more giant hole. Meanwhile, the Department of Defense and the State Department dicked around trying and failing to score brownie points off those above.

The Federal Bureau of Investigation for which the AG was responsible would not be involved. Even so, Mike Fisher's advice to the President, had it been sought, would have been to do nothing.

Before this meeting, Fisher had discussed this very situation with the Director of the CIA, and, in a rare display of cooperation, they agreed. They were as one. Stay out of it!

However, this President had recently shown that he did not take too kindly to any advice that countered his thinking. The DNI had been correct in saying that the President could authorize a covert operation. While strictly speaking, the whole matter would eventually have to be reported to Congress, by the time that happened, the process would be either completed, curtailed, failed, or the person responsible for the decision would not be around. Fisher knew that there was a definite threat. Otherwise - why were they even discussing it? And they knew what was bugging the President.

The United States, under BJ's leadership, had done and said nothing to alleviate the constant demands for action on any number of fronts. Therefore, the US was on a downwards spiral in terms of international influence, and the longer he delayed, the worse the situation would get. Something had to happen sooner rather than later. The Attorney General knew because Bryce Caldwell had warned him that time was running out for BJ, and he would want to do something – anything – to lift his flagging standing while he still could.

Well – not precisely warned.

The Professor himself was also in a spot of bother. So, Caldwell had turned to the Attorney General for advice on a straightforward subject – What to do about the President?

In the judgment of the Professor, the President would be lucky to still be alive at the end of this week if he continued at his present level of stress.

BC had seen many similar cases. The first diagnosis had concluded that the President was showing signs of old age with the usual mixture of depression and forgetfulness. For some people, there was a solution – it could be treated with drugs. If the problem involved plumbing, then that was a different story. Even if you concentrated on physical symptoms that could be managed, the patient's mental state was up to the task.

Blood tests, computed tomography scans, and other observations were analyzed over the weekend. They had revealed that the President had suffered a series of minor strokes referred to as TIA's or transient ischemic attacks over the previous few months. Now there was something a little more sinister going on, and a CT scan – just part of the routine check-up for one so important as the President – had revealed what it was.

The President had suffered a partial bleed into the brain. Depending on where the bleed was, that was survivable. Sometimes operable. But the area in which it had occurred was also an area where he had, not one, but potentially two aneurysms. The prognosis coming from the leading neurologist was not good unless *"urgent remedial medical intervention"* was undertaken. Because of the position of the aneurysms, surgery needed to be performed at once. That could be done either to surgically clipping them (assuming that was possible), insert stents (thinking that was also possible), and then coiling. It was a fairly standard procedure. But the risks were enormous. Like – there was a 60/40 chance that the patient would die while on the operating table. So - the President wanted to think about it – and that was fair enough. It was his body. It was his life. That should be fine as long as he did not leave it for more than a couple of days. And then, because of the ongoing risk even after surgery, this President should quietly go off into the sunset.

Mike Fisher had to put those deliberations aside for the moment.

There was a country to run.

'I think we could look at employing a similar strategy to the one recently employed to sort out that mess at the CIA,' the Attorney General began. 'As you will recall, the Drug Enforcement Administration had a couple of guys go to Afghanistan to track a drug problem, and I understand that they did an excellent job. We could use a similar strategy here. With a little help from the Pentagon, it would be a simple matter of inserting them between the leaders and the terrorists, then having them point out the terrorists to the local security people, and then duck!'

The Attorney General could not help but laugh at his joke. Although, on reflection, it was not all that funny.

But what he had done was quite clever. It was hardly necessary for the AG to mention that a senior member of the CIA and a junior FBI agent had killed themselves because of that action, but that was a side issue. Fisher had got his President out of a hole that he did not want, or need, to be in. The AG had also intimated that the Pentagon should be involved rather than the CIA, which meant that the whole scheme was several steps removed from the awkward and legally complex business of exercising plenipotentiary powers.

If this advice was taken, all that would now be left to do was for this idiot, who claimed to be the Director of National Intelligence, to get his thumb out of his ass and organize something that might, in fact, work. For a change. All the DNI had to do was work out whether to leave the whole thing to the Pentagon – which he should do – or work out how to coordinate things with the military – which unfortunately he would do.

The President had to ask an obvious question.

'Who were these people?'

The DNI was the one who would be expected to answer that question, but in a true bureaucratic style, he avoided the real question. There are matters that even the President could not be exposed to, and the naming of participants in covert operations was one such matter.

'The Drug Enforcement Administration organized that, and the group was covert,' the DNI replied, avoiding the question while disguising the fact that the CIA had been the real instigator of that little escapade. And it was effectively passing the buck back to the Attorney General.

The AG sighed.

'I will have that looked at by my people. We should be able to organize something for the DNI to work with.'

The President sensed that he had an opportunity to achieve something from this discussion and had got two of his organizations working together instead of against each other.

'I do not want to know the specifics, but you seem impressed with what they achieved. We could award a medal to the leader of the team. Something like a Silver Star – that way, we do not have to relate it to a specific event, act, or service.'

The President looked quite pleased with himself. He smiled and took another sip of his lemon, lime, and bitters.

'Yes! Well - that is all agreed then!'

No one else said a word. No one yet had sufficient confidence in their position at the feeding trough to risk contradicting the President's decision. Of the eight men in the room, only three had a department behind them, and they would carry the can should something go wrong. They groaned in unison. Only one of them because he would need to change his plans.

The Secretary of state, John Scott just shrugged. Barry Crammer from Defense would be the one under the most pressure.

The Attorney General raised his hand to summon a

steward to get him another drink but thought better of it. Fisher had enough of this meaningless chatter and just wanted to get out of the place.

The only member of the group who thought that something had been achieved was the President.

BJ shook hands with his Attorney General as they all got up to leave.

'Keep me informed of progress – you will have my full support!'

Chapter 4

Strange

It was surreal. Despite it being nearly six years since he had left the military service – the United States Special Forces and Delta Force, and all the hype that went with that - Mark Taylor still had that sixth sense that told him something about this picture was not quite right.

On this particular day, he had left the office later than usual. That had two effects. Firstly - the traffic was less congested than it would typically be. Secondly - it was now dark.

Consequently, it did not require a rocket scientist to discover Mark followed. The pattern of the headlights following him was too distinctive. The people who drove the two vehicles that Mark had seen following him were good at their job. They stayed about two or three vehicles behind him. When he turned a corner, the first car went straight ahead while the second car turned and followed him around the corner. Then the first car would magically rejoin them and repeat the whole process all over again with the two vehicles having changed positions.

It was a game that Mark had played on his way back

to his apartment every day. But, before today, he had noticed nothing out of the ordinary. Maybe it was a "macho" thing. Perhaps a longing for the more exciting time in his life. While surveillance and counter-surveillance were taught in all the police schools and some schools where people from the intelligence and security were taught their craft, there was no substitute for experience. Whether genuine or not, what would become a routine for the followers became a pattern recognition exercise for those being followed. Mark had experience in places far less organized than New York City. Areas in which being aware of someone on your tail could be a matter of life or death.

On occasions – the same could apply in New York. It was just that Mark could not think of any sane reason why they should apply their craft to follow him.

Mark was returning home to an empty apartment. There would be no wife or girlfriend waiting to greet him. There would be no one with who he could share his thoughts with one to share his bed. There would be no "Fridge" – the cat – who would rub his body against Marks's legs until he got fed. The cat had died. Well - it had been murdered by the people who had kidnapped his girlfriend. The "girl" friend at the time of that death was away in Sudan, Africa. She was trying to save or at least trying to help the poor, the misplaced, and the oppressed. Doing anything that she could do to avoid living with the man she loved. For reasons that Mark ultimately failed to comprehend,

Now, Mark Taylor was all alone in his little world. He had his work to keep his mind occupied. That only partially compensated for the abject loneliness that he felt every day.

The company that he owned and worked for – Taylor Software - had done very well. There had been the odd hiccup as was to be expected for a start-up computer software company financed totally out of his own pocket. During the six years that the company had existed, he had lost two of his assistants. A rogue FBI agent had killed the first one. Despite his earlier experience, Mark had learned one of life's lessons in that event. Although anxious to protect her, he had dived towards the agent with the gun instead of towards the girl. Was that a mistake? Or was it training that said – first get the gun! The other one had just left because she could no longer stomach the stress of working and living with the boss. It was not that Mark could be held responsible for that stress. Or that anyone would claim that he was a bad person. Quite the opposite. It was just that Mark had tended to put himself in harms' way while trying to complete missions on behalf of others. It was hard for someone who loved him to accept that as usual for someone who was supposed to be simply running a computer software company.

In an attempt to deal with his loneliness, the staff of Taylor Software had tried to help. The senior person on Marks's small team was a hacker who used to work with the Central Intelligence Agency Directorate of Science and Technology called Brad Morgan. And Morgan was very much aware of the emotional plight of his boss following the departure of his last PA – Debbie Peterson. So, he and his girlfriend Shania had taken steps to alleviate that problem.

Shania, who worked for the FBI and who, like Brad, was Afro-American, had suggested that Mark employ one of her friends in the role of his Assistant until Debbie Petersen could be coaxed to return to civilization. Mark had agreed to go along with this without revealing his suspicion that there was a little more to it than that of simply meeting his obvious need for a PA. There was nothing wrong with the lady. Annabelle Jackson was attractive, efficient, and a great personality around the office. It was just that Mark was very good at reading body language. In this case, he may have read more into it than was there. However, Mark believed that Annabelle was intended to do more than push papers around the office and count the paper clips.

A couple of years before the events that were unfolding now, the offices of Taylor Software had been broken into. While no one had suffered any injuries in that occurrence, later events had led to some people being killed. At that time, Brad had been working in Taylor Software as an undercover CIA operative – a fact that Mark was oblivious to at the time. But that raid had freaked Brad out. His experience was with computers, not with the shadier side of operations.

Brad's now girlfriend - Shania - would know that Mark Taylor could take care of himself with all his experience in the military. But she would not be so confident with Brad. He was not exactly a nerd, but he was too engrossed in his computers to have any time to worry about trivial matters. Such as defending himself. So, Mark had a theory that Annabelle was there as protection for the company and Brad, and she had a look behind those smiling white teeth framed by her ebony complexion of someone who could take care of herself.

And those around her.

That was fine with the boss.

It certainly could not have been that Shania wanted Brad to be watched if he might stray. The two of them were like they had been joined at the hip, and they spent every moment together whenever Shania was not chasing criminals, and Brad was not bum-up in some technical stuff.

Mark was financially very comfortable thanks to a couple of his major clients – the Augem Group and the Styris Group. A subsequent deal had been done with the government; Taylor Software was now a computer *consultant* being paid by the United States Drug Enforcement Administration, which somewhat paradoxically involved the government security systems. This latter arrangement gave him extraordinary access to information held by various other government agencies, including the FBI and the CIA. Therefore, it made him a potential target – of the people he was working for and the people his clients were working against. This deal had been very carefully set up and was known only to a few selected and mighty people.

However, like all secret deals, there was always a risk. An off-hand comment, by some official, wanting to impress, was all it would take for the whole house of cards to come tumbling down. And the threat of exposure was not limited to people outside the beltway.

Taylor Software was being paid to investigate the systems employed by the very organizations that Mark worked with during his time in the military. The particular emphasis in the current *consultancy* was on security. Consequently, some people would be understandably pissed at an outsider becoming involved—especially government was paying to ensure that their security could not be breached. More so by those from other organizations – mostly from offshore – whose sole *raison d'etre* was finding security ways.

It was not dissimilar to that of Marks' father – Harold Taylor. The senior Taylor was the Assistant Inspector of the CIA, and that had the added problem that Harold had ex-CIA staff working for him. As is the way in any bureaucratic organization, secrets were hard to keep secret once they were shared with just a second person. Add to that; there was the father-son personal relationship., There was a further complication in the relationship between the CIA and the DEA. There was a potential marital/relationship between the Assistant Inspector – Harold Taylor - and the Director of Intelligence at the DEA – Karen Marshall.

In some respects, the prospect gave Mark a massive advantage. When all else failed, he had personnel contacts in very high places. And in other regards, it had the potential to provide him with a significant headache.

Mark was cautious. Some would say even paranoid. So, he played his little games ever on the lookout for potential attempts to penetrate the security around his and others' affairs. But behind all of that paranoia, there could be deadly intent. So, he was prepared for the almost inevitable disruption to his everyday life.

Mark pressed the remote, which opened the door into the basement, and he entered the underground car park of the building where he had his home. Neither of the vehicles he seen following him made any attempt to follow him into the building as the door automatically closed behind him. So much for dreams. He was not being followed.

But he would not let matters rest there. Just yet!

He got into the escalator, road the car up to the fourth floor, and entered his cold and lonely apartment.

The sound of a knock came sometime later.

That was after he had turned on the television and switched it to CNN to find out what had happened to the real world. He had spent the day sorting through the myriad of problems in the computer world, which was a different place than the real world. He had managed to place a TV dinner in the microwave. He had passed by the answerphone as he had entered the apartment. There were no messages. And there would not be a message that he cared about until the end of the month when Debbie Peterson would make her call. It was something to look forward to and then something to dread. He loved to hear her voice. He hated it when she had to say goodbye.

The knock was a mere distraction. No one else could have access to the building. And what friends he had tended to revolve around his work. It was probably one of his neighbors.

Mark went to the door and looked through the spyhole to see who was calling. The two men standing on the other side looked harmless enough. One of Mark's skills during his formative years was reading body language. It had never let him down – but there was always a first time! In this case, he did not see or sense any threat. He opened the door.

The two men standing there looked like they were government. They were immaculately dressed in identical dark blue suits, white shirts, and plain ties. No expression registered any character or interest in life beyond their current task. Or any emotion. They had a job to do. They had been told what to say. While in the movies, bad guys always looked angry and untidy, and the good guys always looked – well, like the two men standing in front of Mark - in reality, it was different.

The difference was in their body language.

'Are you Mark Taylor?' the tall and very fit-looking man asked.

It was more of a statement than a question.

'Yes - I am Mark Taylor,' he answered. 'Who wants to know?'

Mark had long since ceased to be intimidated by officials. Standing six feet four and with a body that he kept in shape, Mark could take care of himself from all those years in the United States elite military group. To be sure, he had in his waistband his favored Smith and Wesson pistol – a gift from his friends when he had retired from the military. And he knew how to use it with ruthless efficiency. A man with a gun could always beat a man without one, no matter how much training and experience the latter had. Mark had a straightforward rule – Don't give any advantage to the opposition.

It would not be necessary this time.

'Our Deputy Director would like to meet with you. Would now be a convenient time?' the older of the two men asked. Again, it was not a question. And there would appear to be no question of negotiation on time.

'Deputy Director of what?' Mark replied, half predicting the answer. Something to do with the CIA, the DEA, the FBI, or any one of several security and intelligence organizations that used three-letter acronyms. All of them had more Deputies and Assistant Deputies than you could count. They were, after all, bureaucracies. The growth of such organizations depended on starting from the ground up, and that growth began with the lowest ranks requiring an assistant or a deputy. And that process continued to the top.

'Of National Intelligence! Sorry, I did not clarify that the government official replied in his cold, emotionless, and matter-of-fact tone.

Mark sighed. Getting a straight answer out of bureaucrats was always tricky. They were so entrenched in their little world that they often failed to realize that ordinary folk had no idea what they talked about. He could think of at least sixteen agencies involved in US national intelligence. They all had similar structures. But it did give Mark confidence for the simple reason that anyone who wanted to cause him harm would have done their research and would have given a more complete - if fictitious - full story.

'Ok,' Mark replied. 'So – we are playing a guessing game - are we? Tell me who wants to see me, or I close the door and go back to my dinner. You have more than a dozen directorates to choose from, including some not well-known. So - which one is it?'

The man smiled!

'Ok – so you know your stuff. It is the Assistant Deputy Director of Intelligence. But don't ask me to go beyond that because I have no idea. It is way above my paygrade.'

Mark thought of his dinner in the microwave. It was lasagna. It had once been his favorite, but even favorites can pale into insignificance if repeated often enough. He switched the microwave off, returned the lasagna to the fridge, and the three of them left the building.

They traveled in a large black SUV. An identical SUV followed them with a lighting system similar to one of the vehicles that had followed Mark from his office to his home.

Mark did not ask the men how they had gained access into the building. Later he would have a word with the building manager because that was not supposed to happen except for firefighters, or in the case of a national emergency, the police. Or for these men if they were not entirely truthful about their paygrade!

They made their way through the evening traffic until they arrived at what Mark assumed was a temporary safe house. He was unaware of the NSA having a branch in New York City. And they were headed in the opposite direction to that which would have taken them to the local

FBI headquarters. It would be a safe house - because that is what people in the intelligence business have all over New York and probably every other major city on planet earth. Temporary – because no attempt was made to hide where they were going, Mark could only assume that it would not be used again. Unless that is, these men had tremendous faith in the integrity of their guests.

While that faith would have been well-founded, the chances of that being the case were remote. Nobody in the security and intelligence business could afford to trust anybody.

Maybe that was a question that should be added to the list of things that Mark should look at in his day job.

Mark was greeted politely by a lady dressed in a black trouser suit that did nothing to hide a shapely body beneath it. Although she was small, she was petite standing at the side of Mark - she was very fit and did not appear either intimidated or intimidating. She had dark brown hair cut to shoulder length, high cheekbones that suggested native Indian or Asian blood, and sparkling brown eyes. Mark could see the worry lines around the eyes, but they did not detract from a handsome face and very much alive eyes. And calculating.

She smiled at Mark as she introduced herself as an Assistant Deputy Director of National Intelligence. Mark knew that there were several Assistant Deputy Directors but assumed that she would reveal which one she was when the time was right.

It happened that her name was Stephanie Gompert, and she had the official and somewhat overbearing title of Assistant Deputy Director of National Intelligence Analytic Mission Management. Not that it mattered. Such titles were invented for the bureaucrats to use. They did not necessarily have to make any sense to ordinary people, like those who contributed to their wages.

Mark could not avoid smiling as he thought - it would have tasked the bureaucrat responsible for making a name tag of ADDNINSAAMM, but they needed something to make their day more enjoyable.

'Please take a seat, Mr. Taylor. I have heard a little about you!' she said as she sat down in an opposite chair. 'Having Harold Taylor as your father must have been something of a problem for you. He has asked you to do extraordinary things in the recent past! You seem to have coped with them quite well?'

Mark had to smile yet again.

'My father is dedicated – I'll say that much for him. I do not believe that others could not have done the jobs that my father asked me to do. But I can understand his logic in asking me' Mark replied with a shrug.

'You should not be so modest!' Gompert responded. 'Some people have been very impressed with what you achieved. Even the President is now aware of your various roles. And the President thinks that we should use you to do another little job for us.'

Mark said nothing.

'Are you interested?' Gompert teased.

Now Mark had to think about that. He had recently done a job for his father – or rather his country since his father was the Assistant Inspector at the CIA. The DEA had picked up the tab on that job. The job had taken him to Afghanistan. While in that country and during the aftermath back in the USA, that *job* had almost cost him his life. Not once, not twice – but three times. OK – he had come out of that mess alive. Taylor Software now had a very lucrative contract doing computer system security work for the Drug Enforcement Administration and other government agencies. That was on the back of an earlier mission undertaken when his father had been the CIA Head of Station in New Zealand. That *job* had taken him to various other parts of the world, including New Zealand, Australia, and Papua New Guinea. This job had resulted in the death of a couple of his friends, and the experience was hardly likely to encourage him to seek a repeat.

Despite all the drama that had occurred during those two missions, he had ended with his company being relatively stable and with an assured source of income for the foreseeable future. However, as a businessperson, commonsense would suggest that he should avoid getting involved in any further extra-curricular activities. The fact was that he did not *need* another job either from a work perspective or from a financial perspective. Add to that the overriding question – Did he *want* to risk his life doing work that, in his view, any number of people were equally – if not more – qualified to do?

So - the question could be - Did he want another job?

Mark knew that the mention of the President – presumably of the United States of America – was just done for show. Any task involving the National Security Agency office would also affect the Director of National Intelligence and should have been thought through and well planned before the President heard anything about it. The President would only know what he needed to know. Or as much as the NSA/DNI thought was necessary – which would not be very much. So, the NSA would have handled connecting the dots. The President would have agreed if Mickey Mouse had been suggested for the role – such was the power of the NSA. Long gone were the days when the President knew all the players or had any real say in what went on in the murky depths of the intelligence world. Mark was sure – at least as confident as he could be – that the recently elected President would not know the details of his prior involvement in matters that concerned the organizations that Mark had worked for. And it was doubtful that the President had any knowledge that he was still working as a consultant.

All that aside, Mark was stuck between a rock and a hard place. He could say *no* to the job. And where would that leave him? He was almost sure that the President would be unaware of his current role with *his* government. However, it would be a mistake to make any assumptions. The NSA and DNI almost certainly would be aware of his involvement. So, what effect would him saying *No* have on his consultancy role with the DEA and the rest of the vast security and intelligence network?

Most likely, it would bring his involvement to an abrupt and premature end. The fact that Mark had signed a contract that guaranteed him a very comfortable income for the foreseeable future did not mean that the contract could not be canceled - albeit with a nice check and a commitment to silence for the rest of his life. But then there was the cost to his business and the loss of stature in the cut-throat world of the particular niche of the market that Mark had chosen. Taylor Software was a minor player in a huge market. That market was concerned with computer systems security. The President, the NSA, the DNI, and powerful men who formed the new administration's inner sanctum could not have given a rats' ass what Taylor Software did for a living. But they could sure as hell make certain that Mark Taylors market opportunities could disappear in a New York. Minute if they so decided.

'What is the job?' Mark heard himself ask.

It was now Stephanie who smiled.

'I cannot tell you that - yet. I can say that it will need a team of about eight men. You get to choose them. The job will be in an African country for about seven to ten days. Fly in, do the job, fly out.'

'So – Why do you need me?' Mark asked.

Stephanie again smiled. But this time, the smile did

not travel to her eyes. She shrugged.

'The people that we would normally use for such a mission do not appear to agree with our political masters on the need for our involvement. Or to be more correct, we cannot afford any internal bickering between Defense, State, and Security about whose territory this is in. Rather than go down the road of trying to resolve that thorny issue – which would take too long in any case – the Director of National Intelligence and the President want the matter resolved now. The decision of whether we go or not is out of our hands. The question is simply one of who we send.'

Mark looked as though he was about to leave before Gompert continued.

'I can tell you a little of what is involved. There is a meeting of heads of state in a few weeks. We have intelligence that suggests an attempt may be made on the life of one of them. The President wants all the leaders to be there and not distracted by the demise of one of them!'

Gompert teased with another shrug of the shoulders. Her body language indicated that she did not care one way or the other. Mark had no way of knowing whether that was because of who the person was that was the supposed target or whether that was because she was on the side of those questioning the entire operation.

It was comforting that the President and the DNI did not want anyone to get themselves killed. Whoever that was.

At least – not now.

At least - not until after the meeting.

'So let me summarize what you have said. You want me to take a team to an unnamed African country, to conduct an unspecified job that will ensure that some un-named leader can attend an as-yet-unspecified meeting in a few weeks. Is that about all there is to it?'

Mark could not avoid the sarcasm clear in his voice and body language.

Stephanie Gompert held Mark's gaze.

At least she was still smiling.

'Your father knows you better than I thought, probably better than you thought! He said that you would say exactly that. Well!' and she laughed.

'He put it in slightly more colorful language than that. Or was he emulating your friend Archibald Miller?'

She looked at her watch while not missing the reaction that she got to the mention of Dusty's name.

Then she continued.

'I can tell you that an attempt is to be made on someone's life. We want your team to prevent that. We will give you first-class support in the theatre. And you will be well paid for your services. But first, we want two things. First - we want a team that we can vet and approve. If we approve, then that team will be sworn to secrecy. Then, and only then, comes the second - we will tell you the details of what is going on. The mission is relatively straightforward - the information is just politically sensitive. The mission will be clandestine or covert, whichever terminology you prefer. But we have to have absolute secrecy. I can tell you that the President has already approved the mission in principle. We need to sort out the details. Fair enough?'

Mark should have said *No*.

He heard himself say 'Yes.' At least he added a condition. At least he knew how these games were played. No one in the security and intelligence business ever volunteered information if they did not have to.

'I need to tell the people that you expect me to recruit something of the mission! The kinds of people we are talking about are not silly. If they do not know where they are going, they will answer no. And that means your covert mission is a non-starter.'

'Ok – I can tell you a little more detail.' Gompert continued without missing a beat,

'The meeting is a meeting of the African Union where all the leaders will attend. At this early stage, the code name for the mission is Steel Tiger. Your security code from day one will be an alpha-numeric representation of that name. The security code will change daily using an algorithm explained in your mission instructions. Because of time zone differences, you will have a period of grace – six hours – to allow for the time difference between Washington and Africa. The instructions are for your eyes only. Once you have read the instructions, they will be destroyed. So, commit the code and the algorithm to memory. Now, do you have any questions?'

Yes! Mark wanted to ask any number of questions.

Like - Who came up with these stupid names and numbers? The DNI and the National Security Agency must have a whole department that had nothing better than inventing security access systems. He had dealt with such issues before. Mainly with the CIA and their cumbersome way of doing such things. He knew what the risks were when systems collapsed. Or rather, what the potential costs were to the people out in the field. Simple things like – What happens when the only person who knows the codes and the mechanism by which they are changed is killed? Or were they incapacitated? Or cut off?

In these circumstances, you can have a situation where the mission is effectively cut off from its support because no one on the mission team knows the code or algorithm to talk to their people! And the whole concept ignores the fact that the men may be in danger and need help when the least of their worries would be a password-style code. Meanwhile – the entire bureaucracy continues working in full knowledge of the mission, merrily randomly updating the regulations, and efficiently advising the likely change recipients.

And wondering why they never hear from anyone!

Mark just said - 'No questions - that is fine. Lets' do this!'

He would be telling his team members what the code arrangement was. And what the procedures were for changing it. And he would be programming the logic into their satellite phones. And he would ensure that they could call for help when they needed it - at the push of a button.

Mark was taking men in harms' way, so he owed them that much.

To take men into harms' way, he had to trust them.

And they had to trust him.

Otherwise, the DNI and the President would have to find someone else.

Chapter 5

The Team

Mark had been given forty-eight hours to choose his team and report back to the office of the Director of National Intelligence. That timescale was about forty-seven hours longer than he would have needed to select his people. He could have even saved the other hour if that had been necessary. But Mark was dealing with a bureaucracy, so paperwork was to be completed, partially explaining the time allowed.

The simple fact that Mark had been chosen for the job meant that they would trust his judgment on selecting the men. It was doubtful that any of his men would be challenged. Still, they were dealing with a government. They would have the final say on who Mark was allowed to take with him because that was the way the system worked.

The critical thing about selecting a team was that they would need to work together. However – there was one overriding criterion—everyone involved in the selection process had to be aware that the people were human. There would be times when the whole team was quite simply not available. Like – they had to sleep! That meant that it was necessary either to build redundancy into the choice or to select people that were at least readily interchangeable.

Mark chose the latter.

Mark had been given several forms that each man had to receive, read, inwardly digest, append a signature, and return. That task could take the whole forty-eight hours of frantic email activity and assumed that the men were sitting by their computers waiting for the unexpected. However, only Dusty Miller had the legal qualifications to understand all the gibberish and would have spent any of that time reading the documents. The rest of the team would rely on Mark and Dusty to have read it, and if it landed them in the shit, they then had someone else to blame.

Cutting the team down to the eight people required from the dozen or so that would nominally be on the shortlist would be the first step. That did not take long. It was just a matter of getting the correct balance in the team – a mix of powerful men to do the heavy-lifting and thinking men to do the planning. The fact that three of these men were currently serving as members of the United States Special Forces would make their acceptance by the NSA pretty automatic since they were part of the defense fraternity. At one time, the government employed the rest of the people Mark had in mind either in the Special Forces or in related agencies, making their nomination relatively simple. So – it was a question of who to leave out. That was, of course, assuming that all the men on the list were willing and able to take time out from their regular day job,

From Mark's limited knowledge so far of what would

be needed, it was plain that the team would need to be fit, preferably single, proficient with weapons, and be able to think quickly and effectively in times of stress. Precisely the kind of person that Special Forces training produced. The only other critical thing was that they would need to get on well with each other. Therefore, being either Irish or Afro-American in origin had to be a plus for whoever Mark chose. This aspect may have caused some misgivings in the higher echelons of the National Security Agency, which was not known as having a bias in favor of either group.

On an earlier mission, not that long ago, Mark had experienced problems where one team member did not meet the criteria that Mark would have used. While there had not been any racial bias in play in that particular case, and it was not a selection that Mark had been responsible for, it had demonstrated the problems that could occur when just one member of a team did not fit in. So, this was the deciding factor. If the NSA did not accept the team that Mark was putting forward or proposed someone, not on Mark's list, they could find someone else to do the job.

It was not Mark who would have to convey that message to the President.

As things turned out, the NSA had almost to a man anticipated Mark's choice for the team's makeup. The only difference between the two groups was that Mark included a father and a son combination that, in all fairness, there was no way the NSA could have predicted.

As head of the team, Mark was ideally suited, and that is why he had been chosen by the President and whoever had dreamt up the scheme.

Mark Taylor was in his fortieth year, six feet four in height, with a trim figure that he kept in shape by regular visits to the gym and taking punishing runs at every opportunity.

He was single. His earlier marriage to the nymphomaniac Helen had ended five or so years ago at approximately the same time as he had left military service. Probably because his presence at home would interfere with his wife's extra-curricular activities, he had tried two relationships since that time. They had been with ladies he had met through his work at Taylor Software. One had ended abruptly when a rogue FBI agent had killed Annette Kovic. The other had ended when Debbie Petersen had gone to look after the sick and needy in Africa. Debbie may come back. But for that to happen, Mark would have to cease his involvement with the US intelligence community. Or rather, he should avoid getting talked into carrying out missions on their behalf. The other choice was that Debbie would have to stop being so paranoid, as mentioned earlier, or cease being so scared every time Mark set foot into the world.

All of these situations were a possibility

All were unlikely.

Mark had entered the Marines and came through that, finishing his training with his body almost intact and his mind sharpened. That led to service with the United States Special Forces and the Delta Force, which sent him to places few knew about. Doing things that no one ever talked about. And doing it to people who few knew existed. Those years left him with a view of the country's intelligence services that was not exactly complimentary. So - he had left the military. He had moved to New York City and formed a computer software company specializing in security. His business limped along until two things would change his life once more.

The first thing that happened was that he got a contract to develop a system for the Augem Group, specializing in Insurance and financial services. That led to them buying a system worth perhaps a hundred thousand dollars for ten million dollars. That led to the second event.

His father, who at the time turned out to be the Central Intelligence Agency station chief in far-away New Zealand, got him involved in a joint FBI and CIA fuck-up. That situation threw Mark's respect for the security and intelligence services further into question. When his father was later promoted to Assistant Inspector of the CIA, he had Mark get involved in yet another episode, this time involving drugs and the CIA.

That episode nearly cost Mark his life.

Mark came out of these experiences as probably the only person still alive on planet Earth who had twice fought against rogue elements of the CIA and won.

Now he was taking on this latest mission proposed by the Director of National Intelligence, being run out of the office of the National Security Agency and authorized by the President of the United States! That was assuming that the story he had been fed so far was accurate. It was not a mission that involved the CIA.

But why not?

Could he be venturing into a mission with excellent reasons why the CIA did not want to be involved? Or had the CIA been deliberately excluded? In which case, his mission would lack support from the one organization designed to provide it!

On a more positive note, Mark had scored a contract with the Styris Group, which kept his business afloat. He had also scored a significant agreement with the government that ensured he was well aware of what went on in the depths of the security and intelligence services. This would ensure that he could quickly check on any personnel the DNI attempted to impose on him. The ability to do that would have been handy before his last overseas mission.

But hindsight can be a wonderful thing.

When it came to selecting men for the mission, several of these factors could have a bearing. None of the men would have any interest in the financial standing of his company. However, it was handy to know that the team leader had access to funds independently of their sponsors.

Mark had one fear in selecting men from the same background as his own. The fear of PTSD – Post Traumatic Stress Disorder. The men would have been through the rigors of training, having been hand-picked by the Special Forces management. They would have then endured the pain and suffering of the activity itself. That would have killed most men. Then they would have gone on missions on behalf of their country. Most of which no one would ever know about. All of which they could never talk about. But they were still just men.

In their roles, they were called upon to do things that most men – even experienced soldiers – could never have anticipated or even envisaged. Such missions were short and sharp engagements.

They were followed by day after day of relentless training, knowing that they would remember lessons learned from the experience whether they had won or lost.

They would often return from such missions with memories of the brutal reality of life and death. On many occasions, they would return without one or more of their comrades who had made the ultimate sacrifice. Worse than that - they often had to return without the bodies of their fallen comrades. They were surrounded by men who went through the same things during their service and understood and could share their thoughts and experiences. But when they left the service – some of their own free will, others because of injury, others because they could not take it anymore – they lost that support.

That is when the nightmares started. The self-doubt. The self-criticism. The inevitable questions. If only I had reacted quicker? If only I had known this or that? In vivid flashbacks, they would re-live the life they had been an integral part of. Not the months of training. Not the happy times with their mates. Not the excitement of being a part of an elite team. What they would see is the slaughter of friend and foe. There would be no fear as these men performed their duties for which they had been trained. The fear came after the events. And no man, no matter how strong and brave, could avoid bursting into tears at the waste of human life. And the thought that the next bullet could have his name on it.

Mark could see himself suffering from the same symptoms. He had his thoughts of how to deal with it. Focus on the positives. Look to the future. Don't dwell on the past.

Even so, when alone at night, the human mind is free to roam through all the experiences from the past.

The mind did not care too much about the accuracy or otherwise of such recollections.

The first person that Mark would choose to have in the team would be Archibald Miller - otherwise known as Dusty – ex-Marine, ex-United States Special Services, ex-Delta Force, now a Lawyer. Dusty had known Mark for many years, first when they had both been serving their country. They had worked closely together through the business for the last five or so years. He had been a Master-sergeant, and Mark was a Major. Dusty was an Afro-American, built like the proverbial brick shithouse, proficient in all weapons, and one who did not take fools lightly. He had been responsible for getting the troops he had served without many a sticky situation and someone who you would very definitely want to be on your side rather than that of the opposition. He had traveled to Afghanistan with Mark on his father's latest caper. Apart from almost losing his life to hypothermia, he had performed exceptionally well.

Unbeknown to Mark, Dusty had a girlfriend. It was impossible to know why Dusty kept it a secret from his closest friend. He had had a girlfriend many years before, which had ended in tragedy. A drug dealer had killed the lady. The drug dealer had been put out of his misery by Dusty. That was before Dusty joined the Marines. After that, he had completed a very distinguished military career. Now he was probably scared that someone would try to take his latest girlfriend away from him, or at least would attempt to cause her harm.

So, it was a secret.

That was Dusty's other essential attribute – he could keep a secret.

The second person Mark selected was Brent Shannon, also Special Forces and currently attached to the Delta Force group at Fort Bragg. Mark did not know Brent all that well. He had met his father – the Irishman Elliott Shannon – during an earlier dust-up with the CIA and FBI. Mark was initially torn between whether or not to take both father and son. Eventually, he decided that he would need both of us for entirely different reasons.

In the earlier encounters, Brent had probably saved the lives of both Mark and his father, Elliott Shannon. Mark had been very impressed with the young man. Their lives and careers had followed a similar path. Both of their fathers were in the CIA. Both of the younger men had joined the Marines and gone onto Special Forces. It helped Mark check through the military database that he had access to, courtesy of his role as a "Consultant" to the DEA. Brent's military record was impressive, albeit interspersed with the occasional misdemeanor. Such misdemeanors usually involved some snotty-nosed officer having his nose put out of joint by this tough but likable young man. Brent inherited a few things useful from his father, including the Irish sense of humor, cynical regard for fools, and a commitment to see justice done.

Elliott Shannon would bring a different set of values to the team. He had spent his working life in the Central Intelligence Agency. He was first trained as a field operative and then served in many different locations. In his later life, he found himself behind a desk at Langley, Virginia, trying to make sense of the kind of information that he used to collect out in the field. He had never made it up the ladder to a Chief of station or a head of the desk, probably because his nature would not allow him to play bureaucratic games. Now he had retired, but Elliott had a clear understanding of politics and would be very useful in balancing the team. He would also provide a source of valuable advice for the leader.

The fourth person on the list was Blake Whittaker, who had also previously been with the Special Forces and, like Dusty Miller, was an ex-senior sergeant. Blake and Dusty were very similar. Born of an Afro-American father and a Mexican mother, Blake had been brutally efficient in the military. Simultaneously, the Latino side gave him a tremendous sense of humor and a no-nonsense approach, making him an ideal friend. But someone you would not want to have as an enemy. He had married as a young man – probably too young – but loved his wife and adored their twin daughters.

And then tragedy.

His wife had been killed in an automobile accident. It was as senseless an accident as anyone could imagine.

Driving through a red light, the vehicle had smashed the car that his wife had been driving. It had traveled at such a speed that she had been taken the full force of the impact and had no chance of survival. The attorney for the defense had a job to do. But Blake would not forgive the callous way in which he had tried to have the charges brought against the defendant dismissed because he had been abused as a child. The druggie driving the vehicle had to come out of prison someday, and then he would need to answer to Blake.

Since the accident, Blake had left the service he loved to spend time with his daughters. But he could not turn his back on his country. So - he was working with an obscure branch of the FBI under the Assistant Director for Facilities and Logistics Services to try to develop some drugs that could be used to render criminals and druggie's incapable of putting up a fight.

The FBI had belatedly realized that they would never win the battle with public opinion over force in apprehending felons. Nor would they win the battle of convincing them that someone high on drugs did not necessarily respond to a polite request to come down the station for a chat. This was not quite the career path Blake would have expected, but he was now heading in the right direction. And no one had said that it was necessary that this fight had to be fair.

If Blake had not joined the Marines, he would have made an outstanding chemist or a good drug supplier. He had the knack of being able to get almost anything – no one knew how. But he always came up with the goods in double quick time no matter where he was. Mark needed someone as a "Gofer." Especially since this mission was being planned in such haste, Blake was the ideal man, and despite his wish to be close to his children, he would leap at the chance for some action.

In any case, it would only be for a few days!

The fifth person was Mike Gilroy. As the name suggested, he had his origins in the rolling green fields of Ireland. He had joined the Marines because he could not get any other job. Since he had made that decision, he had loved every minute of every day. He volunteered at every opportunity and had been to almost every part of the globe where the United States armed forces had ventured. First as a Marine "grunt" and later in the Special Forces as a sergeant. He had been involved in two missions into Colombia in which Mark had taken part and had escaped with his life despite the efforts of others. Like Mark and Dusty, he knew the shortcomings of the US intelligence community. Unlike Mark and Dusty, he said that he did not blame anyone. That was life! But in reality, Mike did have another string to his bow. He was a Marine!

The last time he had crossed paths with Mark was some months before in the little-known Battle of Ghazni in Afghanistan. Like all experiences in military life, there were brief moments of intense and frightening activity, followed by long periods of doing nothing. He had seen Mark for one day at Ghazni, had no idea what Mark had been doing, and then they parted to meet again sometime, somewhere, whenever.

The problem for Mike would come when he was too old to continue in the life he had chosen. First - he would end up at a Marine training facility, trying to impart his considerable knowledge on a new breed of recruits. But then had to bend to the inevitable and go out into a suspicious world where there was not much demand for someone with his particular set of skills. He joked that he would find himself a rich wife, but deep-down was fearful that he would waste away, drinking himself into oblivion. Meanwhile, back at Fort Bragg, another job was coming up, and he would volunteer. Except that this time he had already been volunteered. And that was cool.

The nomination of Mike made the next person that Mark selected very simple. That would be Hamish O'Dea. Hamish and Mike were almost inseparable, having followed identical paths through the Marines and the Special Forces. Practically virtually as though an umbilical cord attached them. They had fought together in all parts of the world and, apart from a slight hiccup in Afghanistan when Hamish had been injured, looked likely to continue. Hamish was the quiet one. Happy to follow along, always with a grin on his face, taking all the shit that life dishes out and never complaining. But ruthless when it came to dealings with the bad guys. That is what got him injured. The first into battle, the last to withdraw. If it came to a choice between Mike and Hamish, Mark would have had to go for Hamish. Except that they were inseparable. So - someone else would have to miss the fun.

That just left one place to fill, and the man who got the nod was Ben Chapman. Ben met all the criteria. An Ex-Marine and Ex-Special Forces was another quiet one who let his deeds do the talking. His job now was as a greenkeeper on the Washington National Golf Course. The Manager came from the same background. Ben had never let anyone down. But he had blown a few up! He was an expert with explosives, and although the criteria for this team did not require his particular expertise, it was better to have it than to regret it.

Mark had to call each of these men in turn, hoping that none of them were otherwise occupied. He had confidence that none of them would refuse without good reason. But men still had their lives to lead, and he suspected that none of them would be sitting around on the off chance that someone like Mark would ask them to join him on an overseas trip.

His first call was to Dusty Miller. It must have been a quiet day. Dusty was almost polite. Mark explained what had occurred in his discussions with the NSA – without bothering to explain the ADDNINSAAMM handle. The response he got was in the affirmative. Dusty did not comment on the short notice, having immediately dropped into his sergeant's role receiving orders from his officer. Just a – *please tell me what you need me to do* - and that the first of his seven calls done and dusted.

Mark would not tell Dusty or any of the others the whole story – well, what little he knew of the entire story. Mark would leave that until they were in the air and on their way to Africa.

His next call was to Blake. Mark felt that he had dialed the wrong number when a young girls' voice answered the call. And then he had a pang of guilt when he realized that it was one of Blakes's twin daughters. He chatted to her for a few minutes. That was after she had referred to him as *Uncle Mark*. Mark had to choke back the tears as he realized that the respect evident in her voice could only have come from her father.

Reluctantly, he had to ask if he could speak to her dad. The girl seemed reluctant to hand over the telephone, but eventually she did.

'Hi Blake – it's Mark Taylor.'

'So soon! I haven't heard from you for years, and two calls in as many months. What gives?'

Mark hesitated for just a moment too long. Blake had helped Mark before, but that had not been overseas. A bit of flattery would help, but at least it was truthful.

'I have a small job to do over in Africa – and I need someone with your skills and experience. You want to come?'

Blake hesitated for just a moment too long before he

answered.

'What kind of job? Are you working for the CIA again?'

Mark laughed at that. Mark had never actually worked *for* the CIA. He doubted that Blake would be any difficulty getting time away from his job in the FBI, and deep down, he knew that Blake would want to be part of this team. But he wondered how the explanations would go when it came to getting him away from his daughters.

'I need to know for the moment whether you are in or out. I cannot tell you too much. Otherwise, I'd have to kill you.' Mark laughed.

The laughter did not travel to his eyes, but he was on a telephone; that did not matter. He had a feeling of dread – a feeling that he could not explain. He wondered whether that feeling had come across in his voice. He could almost feel the shrug on the other end of the telephone.

'Ok. When do we leave?' Blake replied. 'Just need to make sure the girls will be ok.'

Mark bit his tongue.

'Look, Blake – if you cannot get away, I will understand – the girls must come first. I can always get someone else!'

That was the trouble with people who had been in the Special Forces. Once they had heard of a mission, it became *their* mission. Mark hoped that nothing he had said during this conversation had influenced Blake as he had not intended to apply any pressure. But he would know that the pressure was there, and he could not do anything about that. So – it did not come as a surprise that Blake sounded annoyed.

'Mark – the girls will be fine! I will sort it!'

And that was the end of that conversation.

Those were the first two tricky calls out of the way.

Dusty was a given. And the good news for Mark was that he did not have to put up with the usual banter that generally would come from his best friend on the way to agreeing with whatever Mark proposed. But – Blake was a very different story – brutal to read even for someone with Mark's ability to read body language. This time, Mark sensed some issue that eventually both men would confront. However, there was a mission and a team to set up, and Mark could only focus on matters within his ability to control.

Three of the remaining men on Marks' list would be at the military base of Fort Bragg, North Carolina. He would imagine that they would be only too pleased to get out of there and away from the almost brutal training regime. The training was always worse than being out on a mission!

The specification as 'Special Forces' was not given lightly. It meant that anyone who was part of that Force was the elite amongst a military that could otherwise put the fear of God into any opposition. That did not mean that dedicated as they were to the training regime that kept them at the peak, they preferred to be home instead of out in the field.

Brent Shannon was surprised to hear from Mark but sounded pleased when Mark briefly told him the same story, he had told Blake.

'I'll do anything to get out of this incessant training!' he laughed, 'and it sounds like fun. I assume you have cleared it with my boss?'

'That will be taken care of,' Mark replied.

Brent did not ask who by.

Mark did not mention Brent's father, Elliott. While Mark did not expect any problem down the track, now was not the time to get involved in any family business. Or to get involved in the inevitable father/son conflict of who was or wasn't fit for purpose.

Mark got the same response from Mike and Hamish when he finally managed to track them down. The pair had recently returned from a tour of duty in Afghanistan – Mike on rotation and Hamish because he had been injured. There was some doubt whether Hamish was one hundred percent recovered from that battle. But, as Mike bluntly put it, he would rather have Hamish at less than fully fit, rather than any other plodder.

In any case – the mission as so far explained - was not expected to be that difficult – was it?

The next call was to Ben Chapman. In some ways, that call was the most difficult. Mark knew Ben's Manager from his days in the Special Forces, and he knew why Ben was a greenkeeper on his golf course. There had been several break-ins at the golf club in recent times, and on one such occasion, the Manager had been beaten as he tried to prevent a bunch of lowlifes wrecking the shop. Since the arrival of Ben on-site, there had been no further break-ins. Two attempts, then word had got out in the criminal fraternity that it was just not worth the risk. Now – while Ben would be keen to take part in Mark's team – the boss would not be too pleased with losing his security.

'Hi, Ben – Mark Taylor. Still working on your handicap?'

'Yeah – it's getting up there' came the reply.

'I have a little job to do for our government over in Africa. Time seven to ten days. You want to come?'

'Ok.'

It was like having a conversation with Dusty Miller. Talking as an officer to ex-sergeants from the Special Forces was always a one-way conversation. Apart from trying to read anything into Yes, no, or ok was problematical even for someone with the personal skills that Mark had. In Dusty's case, Mark could always come up with some abusive comment which would be a sufficient distraction. In the case of Ben Chapman, any such distraction would have been a waste of time. Mark had to conclude the conversation.

'Good. I will be in touch shortly. You can tell your boss that I will have someone keep an eye on the Club while you are away. Ok?'

'Ok.'

It was almost a relief to cut that call and try to get hold of Elliott. There was always the risk that the elder of the Irishmen would be somewhere out in the Chesapeake Bay and just sailing. As luck would have it, the yacht was at the marina for maintenance, and Elliott answered the call immediately.

'Mark! Good to hear from you again. Still trying to get yourself killed – or have you finally given up?'

Brent Shannon was still talking to his old man because that was the only source Elliott could have heard of Marks' earlier exploits. That is – unless Elliott still had sources within the CIA that Mark was unaware of!

'Hi, Elliott. I was about to invite you to join me on my next attempt. You interested?'

That caused a pause in the conversation before Elliott replied.

'What would you be up to now?' came the delayed and hesitant response.

There was also hesitancy on Mark's part. He did not expect this latest mission to be as life-threatening as the last one. But he was about to ask a man who had given everything to his job for his adopted country and was now entitled to some peace in his retirement to come on a mission that younger men would be expected to do. It was only on a whim that Mark had judged that the experience and judgment of the older man would be helpful. In all fairness, the benefit would be to Mark and not to the likable

Irishman. In addition, he was about to drop another piece of information on Elliott – that his son would be a part of the team. On the other hand, Mark's current job was to find the men who could best perform the mission, not to worry about what would be in the best interests of the individuals.

Mark did not know how Elliott would react. He decided to tell Elliott the truth on the spur of the moment, not knowing whether that would influence his decision. Elliott would see how the system worked. So, he would probably be more hesitant than the rest.

'The DNI has asked me on behalf of the President to take a team to Africa to try to prevent an assassination.' Mark told the Irishman. 'Included in the team I have contacted so far is your son – Brent. I want you on the team because I expect that mission could involve some diplomacy, where we will need your experience and knowledge. I will understand if you decline but, in my judgment, you are the best person for this job. And I don't want any hangers-on getting in the way.'

Elliott laughed at the flattery.

Mark knew then that he had his man.

Now, all that Mark thought he had to do was sell this team to the office of the Director of National Intelligence and the NSA.

As it turned out, neither the NSA nor the DNI cared.

They had already more-or-less correctly expected who Mark would choose! They thought of questioning the inclusion of an older man in the squad.

But they could not question the logic behind the choice.

Chapter 6

Decision

The next meeting between Mark Taylor and the US security and intelligence services were held in the same Safe House as their earlier meeting. That was convenient for all concerned. This time, Mark had Dusty with him - Mark as the boss - Dusty as the sergeant.

There was a good reason why Mark had asked for *permission* to have Archibald Miller accompany him to this meeting. Dusty was a lawyer who represented both Mark as an individual and Taylor Software as a legal entity in his civilian life. There was also another reason. Dusty was unlikely to tolerate the usual bullshit that bureaucrats brought with them.

The NSA representatives were supplemented by a gentleman who claimed to be a personal assistant. This was both misleading and probably untrue, except that anyone could argue that status if the mission were to be set up on the specific instruction of the same President. Mark was over all the drama of letting public servants play their silly games but was glad that he did not have to listen. That is why Dusty was there.

The gentleman introduced himself as Phillip Fergusson. According to Marks' information, Fergusson was from another prominent five intelligence agencies member. This information said that he worked with the National Reconnaissance Office, a defense intelligence organization reporting to the Director of National Intelligence and the Secretary of Defense. The NRO – as the name would tend to suggest – was involved with surveillance satellites and had not been known to be involved in operations as mundane as that currently being envisaged for Mark and his team.

Even so, for a covert or clandestine mission of this type, the DNI had to hook into an organizational structure. That ploy seemed possible since the NRO has the largest budget and the smallest number of people of the extensive five US security and intelligence services. And there was a certain amount of wisdom in this choice since the President had said that he wanted to monitor the mission. The DNI had no way of doing that without the help of someone with access to resources such as were available to the United States military through the NRO.

The methods that the NRO would employ and be responsible for with this mission monitoring would not be known to the participants. On both sides! The good news was that any kind of electronic monitoring would be unknown to whoever would be regarded as the opposition. The fact that any satellite monitoring for a mission that employed only eight men would be next to useless would not, of course, be made known to the President.

For the man himself, Phillip Ferguson reverted to type. The National Reconnaissance Office representative brought a new meaning to the word serious. But one thing was obvious – he had no clue what they were asking this team to go into or how it would carry out their mission.

The meeting skated through the personnel that Mark

had chosen. There was, of course, the question of getting three of the team released by their current military units, which would require mention of the fact that it was to meet a *request* from the President. Mark had checked that all three were in the country and had checked that they were all prepared to go – even based on the flimsy information that he had been able to provide them with. It was simply a matter of the trust that existed between Special Forces people – a faith that could never be understood by the cretins who looked to use them in pursuit of often questionable goals. As for the matter of their release by their units – Mark had, correctly, assumed that decisions of this nature would be made at a sufficiently high level to make it a fait accompli. There was just no point in dwelling on matters that someone would take the time to go through with so fine a toothcomb and get all the paperwork in order. The men who had been selected were tough. Sure – some of them were a little on the rougher side of downright nasty with those who deserved it. But none of them had ever crossed the line between doing bad things to people who deserved it and therefore did not matter and people who did matter.

It was Fergusson who held the floor. He addressed himself solely to Mark and Dusty, which may or may not have meant that the other people present in the room already knew the details of what he had to say.

He was nonetheless thorough.

'Nothing I have to say is to be repeated outside this room, except in conversations between you and your men necessary for this mission. You have signed the forms that we gave to you. You have read the terms and conditions of this mission, so you will know the penalties that will be incurred if any one of your team should step outside them.'

Fergusson barely hesitated, but he had to ask.

'Can I go on? Are you satisfied so far?'

Yeah – sure! The men that Mark had chosen had not bothered to read the documents before signing them because the forms were all bureaucratic bullshit. They were drawn up by a legal team who were probably worse than the bureaucrats they worked with. Dusty Miller – being a Lawyer – may have understood what was implied. Mere mortals had no chance. Since the men had every intention of doing the job they were asked to do, the agreement they had signed would only be used if they failed.

Or if information about this mission was leaked. In which case, all bets were off.

If the men failed in their mission, the probability is that they would all be dead, so it would not matter one way or the other. They could, of course, have challenged the agreement because it was so one-sided. The government did not offer anything of any importance to the participants. It also did not in any way restrict what the government could do. Or instead – it had a variety of conditions that would be believed to occur so that they could wash their hands of the whole deal should they so choose. And it threatened hell and damnation to the men if they as much as farted at the wrong time.

All that the government was doing was protecting its backside and ensuring that it could deny all knowledge of the mission if it chose to do so. That was more likely to occur due to political considerations, which the men could also not have given a rats' fart about.

Mark just nodded. Fergusson continued.

'Right. Now for the mission itself. A few weeks ago, we received word that an attempt was to be made on the life of the President of one of our African friends. We believe the group responsible is an offshoot of al Qaeda working out of Somalia and with links to another group operating in southern Sudan as part of ISIS. They also have set up links with several other groups in several other African nations, and we understand that they have got together with one particular group to plan the attack. Our information is that planning for the attack is well-advanced. We want that attack stopped, or at least we want the President unharmed.'

The man paused, so Mark took the opportunity to ask the obvious question.

'Is this attack to occur in Somalia or Sudan, or am I missing something here?

Mark had attended numerous briefings with NSA, CIA, FBI, DEA, NRO, and other officials over the years, and they were all the same. Some official had his moment in the limelight and wanted to make the most of it. So - he wanted to be sure that everyone knew how important he was, and the best way to do that was to keep everyone guessing. Then he would spring the critical facts at the final moment for maximum impact. Nonetheless, neither Mark nor Dusty was expecting the reply that they received.

'No. It is in Zimbabwe.'

'So – the President is....'

Fergusson cut Marks's secondary question off with his answer.

'That is correct – President Robert Mugabe.'

To say that Mark was stunned did not do justice to the situation. Sure – Uncle Robert had every right to live as much as the next man. And, in this age of peaceful co-existence, you couldn't have people attacking a President of a sovereign state! Although some people would even dispute that in the case of Robert Mugabe. But why did the United States involve itself at all in a matter which was none of their business?

And in a practical sense, the removal of President Robert Mugabe by whatever means would appear to resolve many more issues than the alternative of having him stay alive?

Was this then the reason why the US security and intelligence services were having difficulty finding people from within their ranks to carry out this particular mission?

Mark phased his next question very carefully.

He could not disguise his voice or body language despite his best efforts.

'Are you saying that you want us to foil a plot to kill the President of Zimbabwe? Why would the United States want to do that? Or even want to be involved?'

Did Mark detect an air of embarrassment? He was aware that there were politics involved, but this was politics gone mad! Was there disagreement here? Nonetheless – Fergusson was sticking to his story.

'You have to understand the delicate political balance that exists in Africa. There is trouble brewing in North Africa – a fight between the Muslim communities and those fighting for less autocratic democracy. To the south, we have problems in Sudan. We have significant issues in Ethiopia and Eritrea in east Africa. In Central Africa, we have problems with the Congo. In South Africa itself, we have a nightmare scenario where there is still tension between the black and white populations, which could explode into violence at any moment. Throughout the region, we have the massive problem of Aids and HIV, not to mention Ebola in the Congo, which all attempts to solve have failed, and the problem is getting worse by the day. With all this, we cannot afford an al Qaeda plot to be successful in somewhere as far to the south as Zimbabwe, irrespective of how we might view Mugabe. Now we have a political problem amongst our allies. The British, French, Dutch, and Belgians cannot agree on taking. They all have – or should I say had – a significant influence on how Africa has evolved in recent years. They are all part of the

European Union. The current President of the EU is Germany which adds another complication.

Fergusson paused, maybe expecting some comment. And did Mark sense that he was reluctant to get involved in any political discussion rather than technical?

There was no comment, and so he continued.

'There is a bi-annual meeting of the African Union in Khartoum Sudan in a couple of weeks. We hope sanity will break out at that meeting, and we can start to get to grips with the outstanding issues in that part of the world. The Union was formed in July 2002, and at least it gives the nations of Africa a sense of power, albeit masked by the inevitable bickering in such forums. Over fifty countries in Africa are most unstable and politely described as *developing nations*. There are problems in Zimbabwe too, but those problems pale insignificance compared to the north's broader issues. But if Mugabe, or any head of state, is killed before this meeting, then nothing will happen if indeed, as a consequence of assassination, the meeting happens at all. That is just a fact of life in the crazy world of politics!'

Everyone in the room was tense. As the representative of the DNI and the President, Fergusson had effectively said that he was not concerned about what would happen if Mugabe was killed *after* the meeting! So – was it assumed that the United States would not object if he were dead after the meeting? In which case - what was it that happened at the meeting that the US was so concerned about?

Or had the world gone mad?

Mark probably should have avoided getting into a discussion on the politics of Africa. However, he felt that he needed to be clear on the intentions of the President before he finally committed his team.

'Surely – the USA has nothing to do with meetings of

the African Union!' Mark pointed out. 'You are not suggesting that the position has changed simply because someone has the plot to kill one of their leaders and because none of the European countries wants to take responsibility?'

As soon as he said this, Mark realized that he should have kept his mouth shut. Ferguson did not exactly say that it was none of Marks' business. The NRO statement that he was not fully briefed and therefore was not authorized to discuss policy matters said the same thing.

But - was that helping any? Mark decided to move on. The plot unfolds while they are sitting around discussing politics. He had a plane to catch.

'Ok – so tell me about this group. Who are they?'

The NRO guy looked relieved. African politics was not his strong point. Also, he had just painted a picture of a whole continent that was riddled with problems - not to mention disease. And sitting before him were two of the men who were being asked to go there to protect one of the most ruthless and hated me on the planet! And the NRO official had so far did not provide any justification at all for why the United States government had chosen to get involved.

'The group which is to carry out this attack is from Somalia. We believe that their leader is a gentleman called Mohamed Haji. Now Haji is an Iranian. He is a very nasty piece of work - and we believe he will lead the actual attack. We understand that he may be traveling on an Iran Navy frigate down the east coast of Africa. He will then be transferred to a Somali fishing boat carrying the rest of his group. We understand that they will land on the coast of Mozambique. Once there, Haji will travel to Mutare on the border with Zimbabwe, waiting for all their resources to be in place. We plan to follow the group on the Zimbabwe side of the border. When we have evidence that they are going after Mugabe, we either pounce or leave the cleanup to the Zimbabwe authorities. We prefer the latter of these options. Mugabe and his henchman can claim that they have foiled the plot rather than reveal any involvement by the United States. The judgment of how you do that will be dependent on circumstances – so it will be yours to call.'

Mark was again genuinely puzzled.

'Why not just alert President Mugabe to the plot and let his people take care of it? I hear that they are quite good, originally trained by the Brits. Why do we need to be involved at all?'

Mark did not have to add – *'Being trained by the British makes them quite ruthless and far more likely than we are to bring the matter to a quite rapid, vicious and deadly conclusion,'*

There was an exchange of looks between the various NRO, DNI, and NSA representatives, which was that the NSA got the right of reply.

'President Mugabe has a couple of other problems that, according to our information, he as yet knows nothing about. You will know that not everyone in Zimbabwe is impressed with their dear leader. He has upset quite a few people, especially since his attempts at shared power turned out to be a sham. Now there are rumors that there is friction within his government. The CIO – Zimbabwe's Secret Police or Central Intelligence Organization – is the organization that would normally be tasked with sorting out any plot. However, the reliability of that organization is suspect. It always has been. Back in the days when the country was called Southern Rhodesia, the CIO was infiltrated by the Israeli Mossad, among others. And the situation has hardly improved since. These days just about every country interested in that part of the world has some source of information or input, be it from political sources or from within the so-called public service.'

'So. Our problem is that we may have people in the CIO who may not be as loyal to their President as they appear. This plot could excite such people to believe that they could use it for their purposes. Therefore - we cannot take the risk of their CIO becoming involved in the early stages for two main reasons. First - it would alert them that we have sources of information that gave us knowledge of the plot that we are talking about. Second – various people within the CIO may not even know of the plot, but they could pass any information that we may supply on to the Iranians. So - we have no choice - we have to deal with it ourselves. At the very least, we need to get to where Haji makes his move. Then it will be too late for any dissident group within the CIO to do anything other than close it down.'

There was another exchange of looks. Except for Mark and Dusty, every head in the room nodded wisely. But - did Mark detect the fact that the NRA had made a slipup in pointing the finger at Iran? That was a nation outside Africa but not on the US government Christmas card list? And was the involvement of Iran the real reason why the US was concerned? According to Mark's reading of the body language, everyone in the room was not necessarily in agreement despite their apparent unity. That meant that at least three out of the top five security and intelligence organizations did not agree. The conclusion to all of this was that the decision to go ahead with the mission had been made. And had been made without having all the facts, or intelligence, or both.

And had been made at such a high level in the United States government that it did not matter,

And that – as they say – was that.

'So – what can you tell me about Mohamed Haji – do

you know what he looks like?' Mark asked.

The DNI guy replied to that question with a shrug of the shoulders.

'We have a couple of photographs which will not tell you very much. You are welcome to have copies. He is in his mid-forties, average height, and weight; he normally has black hair and a mustache, but that is not used. He has several aliases and access to various identities and passports. Which means he can, and does, change his appearance. The only thing we know that he cannot change is physical. He was involved in a car crash last year – when the CIA very nearly caught him. He escaped, but we understand that the crash destroyed the kneecap on his right leg. So - he walks – at least when last seen he was walking - with a pronounced limp.'

'Ok - How do we get into the country?' Mark asked. If this job was to be done very shortly, there was some traveling to do and a hurry.

A United States Navy guy wearing the uniform and insignia of a Captain took over. He was more into Navy Air than Navy Sea from his markings, which was scary. He did not introduce himself, which suggested to Mark that he was Navy Intelligence. Nor did he do anything to alleviate the feeling of apprehension that Mark was beginning to get.

At least the Captain smiled.

'Our information suggests that a team led by Mohamed Haji will be landing on the coast of Mozambique sometime shortly. Where exactly? – we do not know. Where will they go from there? - we also do not know. We expect that they will travel inland and then head north. So – we need to get your team close enough to be able to follow them.'

Mark did not say anything. His body language said it all. And the Captain correctly read Mark's skepticism.

'You ever landed on an Aircraft Carrier?' the captain asked Mark.

When he got a negative shake of the head, he continued.

'Ok – not many people have. We have the USS Carl Vinson steaming off the coast of Mozambique at present. She has been there on an exercise which is quite convenient. The plan is to fly you to Cape Town, South Africa, as civilians' which description he used without the usual mocking attitude of his army and air force friends.

'From Cape Town, you will fly up to the Carl Vinson by cattle truck. Once there, you will be outfitted with everything you need and then transferred to land by Helicopter. Oh! - I forgot to mention – the landing on the Carl Vinson and your land transfer will occur a night.' And with that, he again smiled, closed his folder, and sat down.

It was now the turn of a squat Army Lieutenant Colonel who had the look of someone who had seen his fair share of scraps. He did not introduce himself either. It was either a part of a plan or just something that caught on. Whichever it was, Mark was distraught when the Army started to speak. There were now many people who knew all about it for a project that was supposed to be secret and a mission that was supposed to be covert, even if some of it was to occur under cover of darkness.

Mark was aware of the need to know the basics involved in all schemes of this nature. He was also aware of the ratio between men in the front line and men to support them. It was a figure that would make even the most ardent fan of bureaucracy blush with embarrassment. It was reassuring to some people to know that there would be hundreds of support staff for every single man who went out into the field. But Mark and his carefully selected team were the ones going out there. All the support people and the resources they represented would disappear in a New York minute when the shit hit the fan.

The Colonel unfolded a more detailed map than any maps Mark had previously seen. It was created using satellite imagery and gave quite an incredible amount of detail and sharp relief.

'The Helicopter should set you down about twenty klicks away from this position – to the northeast.' He said, pointing to a position inland from the east coast of Mozambique and in an area devoid of anything resembling civilization.

'There you will be met by a couple of our people who will provide you with transport. This map area to the west shows the most likely crossing point. It is dangerous to cross, but it has a couple of things in its favor. First – it is not heavily patrolled by either side. Second, we believe that Mr. Haji will make his crossing. You and your men all have Special Forces experience, so it should be a cakewalk for you. You will have GPS locators. The GPS positions are marked on the map. I'll leave it with you. Good luck.' And the Colonel faded into the background, having done his job.

Well – not quite.

'Ok – how do we communicate, and who do we communicate with?' Mark asked.

Mark had been on covert missions before. Covert meant that the enemy should not know of the mission's existence. But communication by the team was essential. It was critical. From the point of view of the people in the field, all of the time. From the point of view of the support personnel - at least until the job was done. Or until they decided that the job was concluded. Or until someone in charge decided that the usefulness of the men was no longer of any interest.

The Colonel managed the question. His body language said he was not too happy with something, but he answered the question anyway.

'You will be issued with satellite phones when you get to the Carl Vinson. They will have a speed dial that will directly link you to the Intelligence Officer onboard the ship. Depending on what you are communicating, they will either deal with it or patch you through to an office in Washington. You will also have a speed-dial number you can call in an emergency. That will get you in direct contact with our counter-terrorist people.'

'Do we have a name?'

The Colonel still looked unhappy. Maybe he had been out in the field himself – then he would understand.

'The name of the mission is Steel Tiger. You will be given a security code which you will always quote in all communications. The communications port will be worked around the clock, so there will be a variety of operators. But I get your point!' he said with a worried look on his face. But he continued.

'The operators will not know much about your mission. Their job will be to function as a conduit and will pass you on to the right people - unless the shit hits the fan.'

'Ok – that all seems quite simple.' said Mark.

It was to be the usual setup. Less than half of the people involved would know less than half of what was going on, so it would be unlikely to be of much use.

When all the talk about the mission was concluded, the DNI guy took Mark into a separate room for the final briefing. Mark would have preferred that all the people had remained on the basis that they all knew enough to bring the whole operation to its knees. However, the gentlemen insisted.

'For your ears only,' he began. 'Our President has given the go-ahead for your mission, and his instruction is obvious. You have full authority to do whatever you deem appropriate to accomplish your mission. Should circumstances require it, you have the authority to go anywhere and do anything. The rules of engagement are open-ended and are left to your judgment. Let me explain that. We have reason to believe that a plot to kill our friend Robert Mugabe may be only the tip of an iceberg. Having Mohamed Haji running the show only tells us that someone has to keep control of the more erratic and irrational thugs that are likely to be used. And Haji should not be underestimated – as you have been told – he is a nasty son-of-a-bitch. But we believe that there may be someone else involved or something else going on. Any direct involvement by Iran in African affairs would be a cause for concern, but we have no information to tell us what that involvement may entail.'

Mark was surprised by this, but the body language of the gentleman told him much more.

The DNI guy was scared of something.

Mark could not think of anything else to say.

So, he just asked another question.

'Ok - How do we get back?'

Chapter 7

Kuwait

The United States Ambassador to Kuwait was recently taken seriously ill and rushed back to the United States for urgent medical attention. This situation left Lawrence Johnson as Acting Ambassador, which the young man was certainly not prepared for. Kuwait is a tiny emirate at the northern end of the Persian Gulf squeezed in between Iraq and Saudi Arabia. It was relatively insignificant other than by its location and its GDP. Johnson had only recently been appointed as head of the Political Section in Kuwait by an administration keen to show the world that the United States was moving away from the old era of international politics and starting to get some youthful enthusiasm back into the game.

Although Kuwait did not figure high up the totem pole of overseas appointments, the thirty-five-year-old man was still young to have been appointed to head of a section. He undoubtedly was far from ready for total ambassador rank.

On the other hand, Johnson had been through the US Foreign Affairs Institute in Arlington, Virginia, and passed nearly at the top of his class. So academically, he was well suited to the role. All that he lacked was an experience.

With time, that experience would come.

A quiet place like Kuwait was viewed in US diplomatic circles as the best place to get valuable experience. The problem for Johnson was that trouble could come at any time in the business of diplomacy. And could come from a direction that was not expected.

But there were a couple of other problems.

Many of the staff in the Kuwait embassy were old and had been dumped there while the government tried to get some younger blood into the more challenging embassies in the neighboring countries of the Gulf states. That was particularly so in Saudi Arabia and Iraq while the US dealt with the ongoing dilemma posed by the Islamic Republic of Iran. The Secretary of State had decided that Johnson could do an adequate job. He had pointed out to the minions in their comfortable and safe offices at Foggy Bottom that there was not much happening in Kuwait since the war with Iraq. And it was an excellent opportunity for the young man to gain much-needed precious experience at minimal risk.

Many people have pointed out that mistakes increase your experience, and experience decreases your errors. We have been getting a lot of experience lately.

At the same time, Secretary John Scott assured his minions that the appointment had nothing whatsoever to do with the Johnson family name or that LBJ still had pulling power when it came to donations. That was even though the 36th President of the United States had been dead for over forty years. The other pertinent fact was that LBJ had been a Democrat rather than a Republican, which seemed a little at odds with the present administration.

But Johnson's appointment as acting Ambassador to Kuwait did come at a cost to the man himself and the United States.

Lawrence Johnson had a young family, and when his wife Janine became pregnant with their fourth child, she decided to return to the United States to be closer to her mother. And, as she put it to her husband in unequivocal terms - closer to *existing* medical facilities. That conclusion was understandable to a point. Their third child had been born prematurely and, although the hospital facilities in Kuwait were excellent, she would not risk going through the drama again.

That left Johnson somewhat lonely, in a foreign country, as far from home as it was possible to get, and without the comfort of a friendly bar to console him. He would only get limited support from his fellow Americans at the US Embassy, most of them from a different generation, and resentful of the young upstart who had leaped ahead of them in the pecking order.

One thing led to another. Johnson got on with his job as best he could. To entertain himself, he befriended other people in the diplomatic community of a similar age group and with similar interests. He met some of the chief players in this part of the middle east.

And some who were not so chief.

The problem was that Johnson was far younger than most of his peers at any formal gathering he attended; after the initial diplomatic chatter, there was just nothing about which he could confidently talk. So, he tended to drift off and find himself in the company of people who may have been in his age group but were in a different position at the feeding trough.

One such occasion appeared to happen by accident. At a reception that people went to because they had to, not because they wanted to, Johnson got involved in a conversation with a lady called Perim Koytak. She claimed to work for the Turkish Embassy, although she did not explain what she did. Nor did Johnson ask because to ask such a question would have been undiplomatic.

And that association should have ended there.

But it did not.

Koytak's command of the English language was excellent and spoken with barely a trace of an accent. Being in the same age bracket as Lawrence Johnson, her interests were more compatible with his own. The subjects of her conversations were more exciting than those of the droll businesspeople. Diplomats and businesspeople alike talked non-stop, repeating the same comments as everyone else in the hope of getting attention to some notion that was perceived as being necessary for this special reception.

Perim was lonely too. She was single and far from home, in a country that lacked the nightlife she had been accustomed to back in her homeland. Here she was, amongst a group of older people – mostly older adults - who had no compatible interest outside the orbit of their tedious work, apart from getting into her pants which was not going to happen.

At the end of the more formal proceedings, Johnson offered Perim a lift from the Millennium convention center where the gathering had been held to her residence. She claimed that she lived in a flat in a gated community by the Kuwait International Airport. Initially, she was reluctant to accept the offer, claiming that it would be inappropriate. However, she finally took the offer when getting a taxi from the venue proved difficult. And Johnson had reasonably pointed out that her flat was on his way south where he had his accommodation.

When they arrived at the place that Perim had navigated him to, it turned out that she had a unit in the Safir Airport Hotel, which she laughingly explained away as temporary while her flat was being renovated. She invited him in for a drink because, being at an international airport, it more than adequately catered for the needs of foreigners.

They sat in the lounge for about an hour, where their conversation meandered from business to the opposing conditions in their respective countries of origin. That is where Perim asked the young diplomat if he had ever tasted Raki. She explained it as a Turkish liqueur, traditionally known as Lion's Milk. With a laugh, she further explained the Turkish belief that Raki was supposed to do such colorful things as to ease the pain of a job loss. Or the end of a relationship. The traditional Turkish toast amused Johnson – *en kotu gunumuz boyle olsun* – meaning - *may our worst day be like this!*

In the absence of anything else to do and facing the prospect of another lonely night, he accepted the invitation and saluted his host with the same toast.

Johnson had, by and large, bypassed alcoholic beverages since his arrival in Kuwait because it was just inappropriate in the Muslim state. However, the combination of his loneliness and the prospect of a dalliance with another culture appealed to his sense of adventure. He had to admit; the lady was good company. And she was not exactly unattractive.

They left the lounge bar and retired to her room on the hotel's sixth floor.

Once inside the room, they sat on a two-seater couch sipping on their drinks of Raki and continued their conversation as though they had known each other for years. The room was quite palatial by any standards and had a magnificent view of the whole airport, although it was pretty quiet at this time of the night. Nonetheless, Johnson gained the impression that this young lady would have to be more than just an assistant at the Turkish Embassy. But he was too polite to ask. He was just content to enjoy her company. And to take the opportunity to gain knowledge of another culture that he was unlikely to get from anywhere else. As well as to taste the Raki. The aniseed flavor disguised the alcoholic content, and the Raki lulled him into a feeling of contentment.

When thinking about this experience later, Johnson could not be sure who had first raised the subject except to acknowledge that the conversation did turn to talk about drugs. The young Johnson had never been a heavy user of recreational drugs but admitted that he had tried cocaine and heroin in a strictly social environment. And likewise, Perim laughingly admitted having dabbled with these drugs when her low income could afford her to *dabble.*

One thing led to another. Perim excused herself for a moment and came out of the bedroom with a small bag of cocaine. At first, she playfully explained that there was only really enough for her, but they both had a sniff in the end.

With his mind relaxed with the Raki and the euphoria brought on by the cocaine, Johnson could not remember a time in recent history when he had felt so content, relaxed and comfortable. And out of control.

Perim was a lovely lady. Johnson began to realize that she had enchanted him. She would have been relatively tall even without the high heels that she had worn at the reception. She had sparkling blue eyes and a generous mouth that framed glistening white teeth against her tanned skin. When she removed the ties, her long auburn hair had flowed down over her shoulders. Perim was the kind of girl that most men could only dream about being alone with. She was dressed in a dark green business suit and a white blouse that probably had a few buttons left undone. This allowed a tantalizing pcek at what the rest of the blouse covered. She probably wore a bra. It was of such material that it hardly contained her nipples if she did. And, indeed, did not prevent them protruding invitingly to the young man's eyes.

In the end, Johnson could not resist the temptation to touch her.

His first tentative move was to slide his hands down her hair onto her shoulders. And then, in his mind, he cupped her breasts in his eager hands before continuing down to her slender waist. She did not object as she leaned towards him for the obligatory kiss.

At that moment, his hands returned to her breasts as though they had a life of their own.

For a moment, he froze in anticipation of rejection as he ran his hands over her body. He need not have worried. She reciprocated by guiding his hands. The more he caressed her; the more aroused she seemed to become, and before long, they were wrapped in each other's arms.

Now there was nothing to stop the inevitable from happening. Lawrence Johnson watched in awe as Perim removed the rest of her clothes and was temporarily distracted by her beautiful body. But Perim urged him on. They both ended on the rug while he struggled to remove his trousers.

Johnson could not recall who made the final move as they thrashed around on the floor.

He had never experienced such a wild encounter as she pinned him down on the floor and climbed on top. And then she furiously kissed him as they clung to each other arms.

Exhausted. But content.

Johnson would never forget that wonderful experience.

And neither would someone else.

The United States Ambassadorial tenures are generally for three years, after which time people were reassigned – in the case of professional diplomats – or retired – in the case of political appointments. Sometimes one or other such events could depend on what happened in Washington DC. That was politics at play. Suppose a particular Ambassador did not fit the political perception of the then President. In that case, they could be reassigned, retired, or otherwise sent off into the wilderness with the clear message that their services were no longer needed.

In the case of the Ambassador to Kuwait, the combination of diplomacy and politics made for an exciting situation. The official Ambassador was absent on sick leave. However, he would have been in a somewhat precarious position had he stayed having views that did not align with the new administration. The acting Ambassador – Lawrence Johnson – had political views aligned with the new President despite his family links to President LBJ. However, he was woefully inexperienced. Therefore, the heads at Foggy Bottom need to consider his position seriously. But there were other things to think about in the early days of the new administration, so that would have to wait.

A couple of things happened, almost simultaneously, that had a significant bearing on the way events unfolded. And they had nothing to do with politics.

The first thing that happened was that Johnson had a telephone call from his mother-in-law. She informed

Lawrence that he was again a father. His wife and his new daughter were both well. And she had another piece of news. His wife had decided to stay in the United States for the foreseeable future. Lawrence was elated at the birth of his daughter. But he was not so pleased that the mother of his new daughter and their other three children had not called him herself. The explanation that she was sleeping but would call him later had to be accepted for what it was. It was an excuse for putting off a difficult conversation that probably would end in tears.

The second thing that happened is that Johnson had a telephone call from his masters at Foggy Bottom. That call informed him that the official Kuwait Ambassador was too ill to return any time soon. Therefore, the call had been made that Johnson would continue in his role as acting Ambassador in Kuwait until a more permanent arrangement could be made.

On querying that message, he was informed that no decision would not be made on the eventual replacement of the Ambassador in the foreseeable future due to three considerations. Firstly - there were far more critical things for the new administration to think about than an appointment to the State of Kuwait. That appointment was one of more than two hundred seventy overseas posts, and it was not a high priority. Secondly – there were a couple of meetings coming up shortly where it would not be appropriate to have a new person lacking local knowledge representing the United States. Thirdly – the Secretary of State (which could or could not mean that the staff at Foggy Bottom agreed) had every confidence in Lawrence Johnson.

These two calls gave Johnson added stress to add to what he was already under. However, the call from his mother-in-law took a lower priority than the call from Foggy Bottom.

The role of ambassadors anywhere in the world is to keep the government of the nominating country aware of any developments in the host country that may affect its interests. They could be trade, politics, immigration, humanitarian issues, foreign aid, military, and business intelligence, and any one of several other things. Of course, an Embassy had different sections to deal with all these things. But the ultimate responsibility rested with the person at the top.

Excited as Johnson was at the prospect of moving up the ladder in his chosen profession, Lawrence needed more than ever to get release. And he needed to share the good news with someone he felt comfortable with.

In the absence of his wife, he decided to give Perim a call.

And – Yes – it was good to hear from him again.

And – Yes – she would be glad to see him again.

Their second meeting was a much less formal occasion than the first. They met at her Safia Hotel apartment in the late evening. This time, she appeared in a dressing gown that Johnson could only assume meant she was prepared for whatever might eventuate. She did not seem to care that it barely covered her thighs. Or that when she leaned forward, her breasts were almost totally exposed.

There was no hurry this time.

Without bothering to ask Lawrence, she split a small plastic bag of what looked like heroin into two equal amounts, sniffed once, and then invited Johnson to do the same with the other. Which he willingly did.

They followed that with a drink of Raki.

They discussed what each had been doing since their last meeting.

He did not mention his mother-in-law or the subject of her call. He did say the call came from Washington DC. He tried to impress his host by slightly embellishing that call by confirming his position as US Ambassador to Kuwait. He did not go into the detail of the temporary nature of the appointment - not wishing to spoil the euphoria of the moment.

Which resulted in Perim leaning forward for a congratulatory kiss.

And things went rapidly downhill from that point.

Several weeks after this event, Johnson had to go to the Iranian capital Teheran on one of many memorable meetings. The United States tried - and failed - to get closer to the ruler- the Supreme Leader Ali Khamenei.

The US Embassy in Teheran closed in 1979 following the Iran hostage crisis. The Iran Embassy in Washington DC was also closed, and so, at least technically, the United States and the Islamic Republic of Iran were not talking.

In practice, these behind-the-scenes meetings were quite common. However, it was unusual for such arrangements to occur in the tyrannical Iranians' capital city rather than neutral ground. The United States was represented by a couple of professionals whose job was to get some sanity into the never-ending negotiations on the use of nuclear power. And to prevent that developing into the ability to enrich uranium to a level suitable for making a bomb.

At all such diplomatic meetings anywhere in the world, breaks enabled both sides to retire, discuss and regroup before the next session of the talkfest. It was not unusual for delegates to be 'paired' at such sessions. Someone on each side of the negotiations was *paired* with someone on the other side. This was not a *formal* arrangement nor one that either side would acknowledge. But it was an accepted part of conducting diplomatic dialogue. It was an integral part, and that was the primary purpose of having diplomats like Johnson present.

In this diplomatic dance, each partner's job was to find anything to shed light on what the other side was thinking. Or even what the other side was talking about.

The situation was that, despite the abundance of translators and assistants, the formal talks rarely made much sense to anyone outside of the chief negotiators on either side. The chief negotiator would repeat themselves, changing only a few words through their various iterations until someone died of boredom. Or they latched upon a few words to indicate something resembling progress. Or that something had changed in the stated position of one of the parties.

The other minions at the meetings then had to search out a compromise on matters on which the talks would otherwise stall. Or it was used as an opportunity to pass on some message outside the confines of officialdom, where someone thought there was a chance of helpful something happening.

All in the best interest and spirit of the meeting - of course!

The reality of the situation was that Lawrence Johnson was simply an observer at this meeting, and everyone on both sides knew it. In fact, from the myriad of people at the meeting, only two people did any talking. The talks were orchestrated, each taking his turn to repeat what had been saying before, barely acknowledging what was told by the other side. And the meeting continued throughout the morning, boring the onlookers to distraction —the occasional change in a word here and there to show that someone was awake. There was an obligatory delay to enable the translators to catch up. That was even though the meeting could just as efficiently have been conducted entirely in English. That was because the two speakers were both well versed in that language. It was just that no one had quite figured out that either side would lose no face in any such compromise.

It was known as diplomacy. And that had a language of own language.

Because of Johnson's status at these talks, he was assigned to a low-level gentleman who went by Hossein Ahmadi. Both Johnson and Ahmadi were bored shitless, and at the next break in proceedings, Ahmadi suggested that he and Johnson take a walk.

They went a fair distance from the meeting hall and entered a room that looked more like someone's home. No sooner had they entered the house than a gentleman wearing long flowing trousers, and a very ornate shirt came in from the opposite side of the building. He was accompanied by a lady dressed in a long coat and had her head covered in a scarf. Johnson did not recognize the man as anyone he had seen at their meeting or who he had met previously.

However, despite the attempt to cover her head, Lawrence Johnson did recognize the lady.

It was Perim Koytak.

The man was relatively calm and polite.

'Please sit, Mr. Johnson. I believe that you know this young lady, so there is no need to introduce her. I also think we have something that we should talk about.

Lawrence Johnson looked at Perim, half-expecting a kind of greeting, But - there was nothing. No smile. No acknowledgment. Just a cold blank stare.

Or was that a look of resignation?

Or was it a look of fear?

'What is this all about?' Johnson asked, looking first to Ahmadi, then at Perim, and then at the man, who had yet to introduce himself.

The reply that he got chilled him to the bone.

'You must be aware that we do not tolerate the kind of behavior that I am informed you have been involved in this part of the world. In your western culture, it may be tolerated, but I am sure your employers, the United States government, or indeed your wife may not be quite so accommodating.'

The man sat at the table opposite Johnson, and at the flick of his fingers, Perim – or whatever her name was – should do the same.

'Now – let me introduce myself. I am Ramin Madani. I am speaking on behalf of the Iran security and intelligence service. VAJA, I believe your people call it. So, do we talk? Or do we let things take their course? Do we see the end of a promising career? Do we see the end of your marriage? Do you want to discuss how we may help each other? It is your choice.'

Johnson's first reaction was to protest his innocence. After all, if his evening rumbles back in Kuwait hadn't been consensual, then Perim had been a brilliant actor. His second thought was just to let things take their course. So – he had been caught with his pants down! He would not be the first diplomat - or the last - caught in a honey-trap. As Madani correctly said, western cultural norms were not the same as Iran's. So – in the worst-case – bite the bullet and look for a new job. KFC was always looking for people who had the brains to ask customers if they would like ketchup with their fries.

His final thought was to plead for mercy.

None of these options appeared likely to result in anything good. Especially given the coldness of the lady who had joined him a few weeks before – in fact, in his opinion, had been the primary instigator - in that passionate and explosive encounter.

His shoulders sagged, and his head bowed.

'What do you want?'

'Oh – nothing much!' replied Madani. 'We may need information from time to time. You have no fear that we would look to ask that you commit any crimes against your own country. No - we require a little cooperation – we may need to know about your President – what he is thinking rather than the rubbish we hear in his official statements. Now that should not be too hard – do you think?'

'That is not possible!' Johnson protested rather too dramatically. 'I am only a low-level bureaucrat in a little place. I have never met the President and am never likely to! Whatever makes you think that I could supply any such information?'

Ramin Madani looked compassionately at the young diplomat, concerned that Johnson still had not got the message.

His voice was cold as he replied.

'You will provide us with as much as you can! And - never fear - we will know if you are lying. Should you try to deceive us, you should be aware that we do know the whereabouts of your wife and family, and we will have no hesitation in bringing them up to date on your extra-curricular activities should that be necessary. If things become more serious, we could always harm them. We do not want to involve your children if we can help it, but that is entirely up to you. Just to let you know that we would have no hesitation in taking action if you were to compromise our agreement. Now - there are things that you will know that we don't know, and all we ask is that you tell us. Even your Embassy in Kuwait will be briefed on United States policy in this part of the world. Normally we get such information from CNN, but you must know how unreliable that is! So - we would like to know what the policy is. And that cannot be too hard, can it? And it barely meets the threshold of being disloyal to your masters, does it?'

Johnson looked at the Iranian in disbelief before the meaning of what Madani had conveyed slowly dawned on the hapless American. He had a choice. He could become the conduit for intelligence out of his Embassy and thereby avoid the disgrace of his behavior being revealed to his masters - and his family – and the end of his career.

Or he could fight!

But how?

Madani took the nod of his head to be Johnsons' acceptance of the inevitable.

'Now – we will even make this task much more pleasant for you,' Madani began.

'Firstly, although our religion does not approve of their use, we will provide you with all the drugs you and your associates need. This will be excellent quality heroin sourced from Afghanistan. There would be no need for you to deal with any nasty drug dealers. Secondly, although we disapprove of adultery, we will let you continue your relationship with this lady! In return for these generous favors, all that we ask of you is that you report to her at least once a week. You will only have to supply the information that we need. In return, she will supply you with all the drugs you and your friends require.'

The horrible truth of the whole situation dawned on Johnson.

He was trapped.

Perim Koytak – or whatever her real name was - would

be his minder. Not his lover. Given how the trap had been set and exploited, he could not envisage ever wanting to make love with this woman again!

And another truth dawned on Johnson.

Koytak was not Turkish. And she had probably never had anything to do with that country.

She was probably a fully paid-up member of the Ministry of Intelligence of the Islamic Republic of Iran.

Colonel Madani's next meeting was with President Mahmoud Khatami in his Teheran office. There was an air of anticipation in the room. Madani could sense that his report on his meeting with the young American had far more meaning to his President than he thought would be the case. And so, he felt that he had better keep what he had to say as brief as possible.

'The United States Ambassador to Kuwait is now completely under our control. Lawrence Johnson will do exactly as we say. He has little choice! Despite what he told our agent, our information is that Johnson is only the acting Ambassador, which plays into our hands. He has been well and truly compromised, and he will have nowhere to turn! Our agents in America confirm the whereabouts of his wife and family and will add further pressure should he make any attempt to escape from our clutches. We also have people in various parts of their administration who will report to us any attempt he may make to alert the Americans to his plight.' was all that Madani had to say.

That statement caused the President to hug the Colonel, who was not used to displays of affection from his President. As part of the Islamic Revolutionary Guard Corps, Madani was quite suspicious of any show of even friendship in the murky world of security and intelligence services. Unlike the US Central Intelligence Agency, his agency was almost entirely military in its membership and administration. And they had a reputation for brutality that made the CIA look like a child-care center. In Iran, where one man effectively controlled everything, even the President would think twice before crossing the VAJA.

That situation arose because, for several years since the Shah was overturned in 1979, Iran had been run by an oppressive theocracy headed by the Supreme Leader Ali Khomani. And the Supreme Leader has control of the military. And the military has control of the security and intelligence services. There are elections in Iran every four years to elect a civilian President, a legislature, and various representatives down to the local level. But the facts are that they are all ultimately controlled by an Islamic theocracy.

Still, a hug from his President did say that they had done something right.

'Now we can move on to the second part of our plan' was the only other comment from President Khatami before dismissing the Colonel.

Madani had no idea what that meant, but he assumed that he would eventually be told.

Then he would have to apply his professional expertise again to sort out the ranting of this amateur.

When Madani had last checked, the Supreme Leader of the Islamic Republic of Iran supported President Khatami and his plans. At least for now.

So, what choice did he have?

Chapter 8

Somalia

The three fishing boats chugged away from the beach as the evening approached, and the sun began to sink behind the mountains to the west. As is the way with anglers the world over, there was the hope that they could scrape a living out of the sea. With luck on their side, two of the boats would return the following morning with enough fish to feed their families. And some fish to sell to others so that they could try to crawl their way out of this life of poverty.

There was not much hope of that.

It was all an illusion anyway.

The three boats had left together, but one of the flotillas had no intention of fishing.

One of the fishing boats would head to the south with a much more deadly purpose.

The theoretical place that the boats left from was the port of Kaambooni. This ramshackle seaside town was at the southernmost point in the country of the Federal Republic of Somalia. It was located on an outcrop of land that to the north of the peninsular was part of Somalia and to the south was part of the Republic of Kenya. Technically speaking, the boats should have left from the northern side of the peninsular, but no one cared that much in this barren and desolate part of the world.

The boat crew that headed south stood to make more money from this voyage than they could ever hope to make in a lifetime of fishing. That was, provided that they strictly followed their instructions.

They had to transport some guests to be at a specific place at a particular time. Then they had to collect one specific person and deposit the group in a particular spot on the shore. None of the crew knew the real purpose of the trip other than that the boat was carrying packages which were to be off-loaded at the same time. The assumption was that these packages held drugs. But the sum of money that the crew had been offered for making this trip was much more than they could expect to make from selling drugs in the quantities likely contained in the packages.

Most of the crews of fishing boats that plied these waters were well versed in the art of concealing all sorts of things from prying eyes. Be it drugs, weapons, fish, and even people. The most common method of concealment on the boats was to use a false bottom which made searching for contraband at sea a somewhat hazardous occupation for the searchers. For this trip, the crew had been instructed to *hide* a couple of weapons in the bilges hoping that any search would find them and then leave them alone.

The crew of this boat had also been requested had to construct a couple of different storage places which would conceal the packages in a place where no one would think of looking.

Again, the sum of money offered ensured that the crew

would happily comply with this *request.*

The boat had initially come from the northern port of Harardhere and had since been re-named the *Nadifa El Aziza.* The boat had been renamed many times during its' long and violent history. Its latest name was the combination of the given names of two of the daughters of a now-dead pirate. As with all names, they had a meaning. Nadifa meant *Born between seasons,* while Aziza meant *Beloved* or Gorgeous. The irony of that situation would be lost in the chaos that surrounded the port of Harardhere. It was the home to some of the most vicious pirates that the world had ever known.

The new name of this boat was meant only to confuse anyone who might stray into its path on its journey south. It was no longer intent on attacking merchant ships the plied these waters of the east coast of Africa. It was not that the boat had any distinguishing features that would identify it from any other. But, even in these troubled times, the naming of a boat was an essential factor to the crew. And it did mean something to the master.

The master of the boat was the brother of the dead pirate.

In addition to the master, the fishing boat had a crew of two. The passengers on this trip consisted of five men under the Muslim Hussein Samatar. He was not and never had been a fisherman, and neither had any of the four men he led.

On this part of their journey, the destination was the seaport town of Quelimane, sixteen miles from the mouth of the Roi Dos Bons Sinais - or River of the Good Signs - in Mozambique. The trip was scheduled to take them about seven days. During this time, the passengers would discuss their plans, exercise to stay fit for the task ahead, and pray. None of the five men expected to return to Somalia at the end of their journey. At least they were not yet committed to dying.

The plan was to join them by another leader somewhere in route south, but Samatar either did not know who the leader would be or where or how to join them. Or he could not or would not say. The passengers talked about this man as though he were a God. The crew would believe anything as long as he brought with him the funds to pay the price that they had been promised.

Back in the Somali capital of Mogadishu - weeks before they had got to this stage - the plan had seemed to be relatively straightforward. The terrorist cell to which all five of the men belonged had been formed as an offshoot of the powerful al Qaeda movement. The government of Somalia was weak and the rule of law almost non-existent so that the cell, and many like them, could flourish in this wild and war-torn state. When someone had called for volunteers to carry out this brilliant plan, Samatar and his four followers had eagerly put themselves forward. It was not that often that people from their backgrounds had the chance to travel and to do the work of Allah.

The foreigners who had recruited them had stressed that it was vital to work as a team. And that was fine. They could not produce any references because all the people who could have made such documents concerning the effectiveness of this cell were all dead. Their first task had been to find a vessel and a crew to take them south, and that they did quickly and efficiently with all the criteria met. The essential criteria were that bands would not be missed because they were unlikely to be seen again.

The recruiter had decided that this was adequate proof

of the talent and aptitude that he needed.

Now that the job had been explained to them and they understood the size of their task, they were apprehensive. Some would say that they were afraid. But in the world in which they lived, and many had died, that fear was acceptable. The fear could arise from the magnitude of the task itself.

It could have arisen from realizing the type of people they had committed to working with.

The five men were indeed not new to the business of death. Apart from Samatar, who had the benefit of having a cause to fight for – albeit slightly extreme - and the money to be able to do it - the rest of the group were just plain out and out ruffians. They would fight for any cause as long as the money was good. However, to survive in the complex world of terrorism, they had to adopt an attitude that showed dedication to *The Cause.*

An almost complete lack of education helped.

As did Drugs.

Although drugs - particularly the illegal kind – were the antithesis of Islam and the Muslim faith, they were a fact of life. They were in every religion. Especially those religions that looked to advance their cause through terrorist activity. This was because there was so much money involved in the drug trade. And since there was a place called America which had an almost inexhaustible demand for drugs.

And an equally inexhaustible supply of money.

The five men all came from similar backgrounds. They were all Somali, born in or around Mogadishu, and all had been made orphans at the wrong age. Not that there was an excellent time to be orphaned. Four men were orphaned at the age of fifteen, victims of the wars that ravaged their country. The fifth was orphaned at the tender age of thirteen – this one was a victim brawl between competing gangs. The result was that they were all resentful of anything that did not go their way, which accounted for most things.

So, they became street thugs.

Later, they got a bit smarter. They realized that they could sell their street smarts to the highest bidder who happened to need their particular skills. And there was plenty of demand for such skills in war-ravaged Somalia and surrounding countries.

The Somali group had to travel many miles by sea to reach a pre-arranged point in Mozambique, and then they had to travel overland to reach their ultimate destination. The men were murderers. So - the assumption was that they were on a mission to kill. The contract such as it was said that they were to be paid when one man said that they had fulfilled their task. They were told they would receive their ultimate orders from that same man. Therefore, only one man would decide who lived and who died. And who got paid. That was fair enough.

There were five of them – so they could and would handle the paymaster when the time came.

At this time of the year, the seas off the east coast of Africa were not particularly treacherous, and the weather patterns were favorable. The waters were patrolled by ships – well, actually warships – belonging to the United States Navy and their allies. Even though these were international waters, these warships did have the annoying habit of stopping and searching any vessels or boats they came across. Any ship or ship had every right to be there, but that did not stop them from being susceptible to the military.

But the warships could not be everywhere.

The Nadifa-El-Aziza would be carrying nothing that would alert the suspicions of any crews who happened to be a member of a boarding party from one of these warships.

One possible problem was that the Nadifa would be far from where it would usually be expected. The crew took solace that even this was nothing to do with the infidels.

Another possible problem was that their current leader - Hussein Samatar - was well known to the Americans. At least the name was. After the Somali civil war in 1991, the US had kept a small force in Somalia. They were continuously harassed by groups who did not like the then-current Government for one reason or another. Or who objected to the presence of foreigners in their country. Or any particular problem that people available for hire as mercenaries would be prepared to align themselves with.

However, although the name Samatar was often mentioned in intelligence reports, it was doubtful if any American had ever seen him in the flesh. In any case, to the fresh-faced young Navy sailors who would make up any boarding party and who would be too young to remember the Somali conflict, one Somali thug would look like any other.

In any case, this time, he was traveling under another name.

The Iranian Navy IRIS Sahand – a Moudge class frigate built in the Gulf port of Bandar Abbas - traveled south, parallel to the African coast and following a similar course to that of the Nadifa. She was sitting just below the horizon and avoided contact with other vessels. At least her commander believed that he had avoided detection by the US and allied Navy vessels in the region. Not that it mattered. The Iranian Navy rarely came out of the Persian Gulf and did not want to draw any attention to the ship's ventured this far south. It was not as though the ship did not have the right to be there – after all, she was in international waters. But the Americans owned the sea, and the Iran Navy could not hope to compete.

Before the Sahand had left the base at Bandar Abbas on the southern coast of Iran on the Persian Gulf, her commander had a visit from Rear-Admiral Khanzadi, who gave him his sealed orders and stressed the covert nature of the mission. They were to stay out of trouble and avoid contacting friends or foes. When the time came to execute their orders, these were to be conducted under cover of darkness, and then they were to immediately return to their home base in the Straits of Hormuz. When the commander had pointed out that his ship's passage was unlikely to escape the attention of both the Americans and the British Navies, the Rear Admiral had smiled and wished him good luck.

The ship was carrying a passenger whose occupation was unknown to the Commander or anyone in the ship's company. The Commanders' job was to land the man on another boat.

Not to start a war.

The British navy ship HMS Lancaster - a Duke Class Type 23 Frigate - was sailing north along the east coast of Africa after having been on a ceremonial visit to Cape Town, South Africa. She was to rejoin the British Navy contingent, spread from the south of Mozambique to the northern part of the Persian Gulf, intent on protecting merchant ships as they passed through those waters. The major problem for the Navy was pirates off the coast of

Somalia and the vast nature of the area in which they operated. The major problem with the Somali pirates was that they did not care.

Life was tough in Somalia, and there was little chance of gaining meaningful employment in a country whose economy and infrastructure had long since been destroyed. The residents of that land had to watch as ships owned by or hired by the capitalists in the west plied their trade between the oil-rich Gulf states to the north and the all-consuming western world.

And made their fortunes while the people of Somalia starved.

Fortunately for the Somali pirates, most of the ships traveling between the Gulf states and western economies were too large to travel through the Suez Canal. So, the pirates had plenty of opportunities to plunder and pillage.

Albeit there were risks.

The sailors on board the Lancaster had enjoyed the stay in a friendly port, and they were now dreading the return to normality – the boring but essential normality of checking every craft that they came across—knowing that any one of them could be loaded with hostiles. They knew that it was not unknown for the pirates in the event of a fight. To abandon their ship, having set their boat on a direct collision course with whatever Navy ship happened to be around. And then they would inexplicably rely on the same ship to rescue them.

Knowing that the boats crewed by Somali pirates were poorly maintained and lacked any respect for safety did not improve the Navy's response!

Most of these boats carried drums of fuel as deck cargo. Most of the crews were addicted to smoking cigarettes or other more exotic drugs. Added to the danger, the Lancaster may have to escort the pirates to a *safe* harbor where the frigate would be more vulnerable to the peculiarities of the wars that were raging there. That was not a pleasant thought.

As the frigate sailed off the east coast of Kenya, the forward watch reported something in the water to their landward side, and the ship went from being in cruise mode to being at active quarters. The Commander grinned as he ordered the ship to battle stations. There was a first time for everything. And such action broke the monotony of the patrol.

As a training exercise, the skipper – Commander Rory Bryan RN –ordered her Lynx HMA Mark 3 Helicopter into the air to investigate. When the aviator reported that he had found what appeared to be a Somali fishing vessel heading south, the skipper decided to turn his ship to port and then to launch two inflatable boats, each with a crew of two sailors and six heavily armed marines; the inflatables were jammed with more than sufficient firepower to deal with any threat posed by the fishing boat. The helicopter kept station to the leeward side, careful to stay out of range of any small arms on board the fishing vessel but well within striking range for its weapons. The Lynx was an anti-submarine weapon. In normal circumstances, it could be armed with Mk 46 torpedoes, Sea Skua missiles, depth charges, 70mm rocket pods, and two 20mm cannons. None of these was more than adequate for dealing with the odd fishing vessel. In addition to that show of force, the Lancaster had anti-air and anti-ship missiles, anti-submarine torpedoes, as well as an array of other guns that could blast the fishing boat out of the water if the Commander felt so inclined.

The fishing boat did not try to slow down and appeared to ignore all the naval activity completely.

Until a warning shot was fired across her bows.

The marines from one of the inflatables climbed on

board the fishing boat and began their inspection while the other one circled with weapons selected to be safe for the moment. Only one of the British sailors could speak Somali Arabic, and then not very well. And there was no guarantee that they would speak Arabic since it was not the natural language for Somalis. Consequently, there were moments of tension as the two groups tried to communicate with each other. In the end, sanity prevailed.

While the vessels were well to the south of the Somali coast, they were still in international waters, so each had every right to be there. Pirates had been known to work as far south as the southern coast of Mozambique, so the American and allied forces still checked. In this case, the marines who were probably unfamiliar with vessels of this type could find nothing which would indicate any wrongful intent. There appeared to be no arms on board other than a collection of AK-47 rifles, which were poorly maintained and not of much use. There seemed to be no drugs on board. There was certainly no fish. There were the usual drums of extra fuel, but that was understandable.

And even the Royal Navy could not arrest people for simply being surly.

The Commander of the Lancaster ordered the two inflatables to return to their ship, along with the helicopter, and the ship stood down to general quarters.

As is the practice in the Navy, a record was filed and duly transmitted up the command chain, to be filed, and probably ignored in some innocuous pigeon-hole. It read:

Boat @ N03 43 40/E40 23 06 @ 15:30 EAT 11/04 Nadifa El Aziza, no record of registration. – recommend checking. They are believed to originate Harardhere Somalia.

7 crew or passengers. Limited personal weapons- no threat. Equipped for Fishing – no fish apparent. Fuel on deck suggests some time at sea. No immediate action is intended. Query number of crew. Query destination. Also, detect warship east of our position. Unknown. I will investigate further. Ends.

Hussein Sadamar spat into the water as a mark of defiance as the British pulled away. He had nothing but admiration for the British Royal Navy. Not so for the Americans. He had fought against the United States forces in Mogadishu, and he would not forget the cruel way they had carved up his fellow revolutionaries. Even though, in the end, his side had been victorious, and the Americans mainly had been pushed out of the country, he still hated them. Now their lackeys thought they had the authority to query everyone's right to travel on the high seas. And they felt that people should travel without any means of protection against the bandits who did not care who they harassed. Well - Sadamar and his men were better prepared than the average pirate. They had guns, but the allied forces would never find them without dismantling the boat.

That was the problem with the overwhelming power the allied forces hoped to project. It was all very well for politicians to boast about what they were doing to protect shipping in this violence-riddled part of the world. And indeed, the fragile boats that cruised these waters hoping to catch sleepy oil tanker captains unawares were no match for the might of the Navy vessels that also sailed these waters. But the men who conducted the policing work had more practical problems to deal with. Back on land, they could take their time and worry about any set of issues to death until they found out the truth. At sea, it was a very different story. They had to make on-the-spot decisions with what they had before them. So – faced with a boatload of ruffians a thousand miles from where they would logically be expected to be, communicating in Swahili, with no clear intent and no weapons which would at least indicate some hostile intent – they had to make a choice. Either to bring the warship - probably worth more than half a billion dollars - to a shuddering halt in the middle of the ocean while every apparent misdemeanor was investigated or to take every boat in tow to get them back to a safe harbor. Or to sink them. Or to settle for a slap over the knuckles and return to the task that the Navy was built and trained for.

The HMAS Toowoomba - an Australian Anzac Class frigate - was steaming south down the east coast of Africa under the command of Commander Andrew Quinn, headed for Salisbury Island Durban – where the South African Navy had the repair facilities to fix her problem. A strange concoction of events had led to this situation, and the Aussies were furious about it. While patrolling off the south coast of Somalia, the ship had been rammed by a merchant ship that they were supposed to be protecting. In the dash to intervene between pirates and the MS Liberty Belle, the master of this ship had turned to port instead of starboard. The reason for this fundamental blunder had been the drunken state of the people on the bridge of the Liberty Belle.

More would be heard about that in court.

But that did not help the Australians.

After a heated conversation between the people on the ship who knew what was going on, and the people in Canberra who did not know what was going on, it had been decided that the South African option was the best way to go. So, with temporary repairs to her rudder, the

Toowoomba was sailing along, barely able to maintain twelve knots without the vibration becoming a pain. That was still sufficient speed to catch up with and pass the Nadifa-El-Aziza, making heavy weather of traveling along the coast of Tanzania at between eight and nine knots.

The Australians were bored and resentful, and since at the respective speeds of the two vessels it would take them quite some time for the fishing boat to drop out of sight, they decided to take a look. The captain first dispatched their Sikorsky S-70B-2 Seahawk Helicopter. When that radioed back that they should investigate what looked like a Somali fishing boat, he ordered two inflatable boats into the water—the same procedure as had several days earlier been conducted by the HMS Lancaster. The Australians had two of their people who could speak passable Arabic. Although that was not the same as the language spoken by the majority of the people in Somalia, most people in Somalia understood Arabic, When the leading inflatable reached the boat and queried what the boat was doing so far south of their regular *Fishing* ground that brought the usual response. Silence.

Rather than give up, one Arabic-speaking Australian Chief Petty Officer tried a different approach. In Arabic, he instructed his men to prepare to sink the fishing boat with all hands and return to their ship. The fact that his crew had not the faintest idea what he was talking about was irrelevant. But his message was understood by the master of the fishing boat, as proven by his angry reaction before he realized that he had been conned.

However, there was nothing that the Toowoomba could do. Even though a boarding party was allowed to perform a cursory inspection of the Nadifa, the boat had freedom of passage. There were no clear signs of any criminal intent. While the boarding party suspected that weapons were on board, their first search had failed to find them. The investigation had also found no signs of any fish. The Chief did manage to elicit one piece of useless information. The master of the boat had muttered something along the lines that the sooner *Abdul Nadir took over,* then so much, the better.

The message that was sent out from the Toowoomba made the frustration felt by the Australians clear:

Nadifa-El-Aziza. Boarded @ 12:45 EAT east of the coast of Tanzania. Suspect intent. Fishing boat – no evidence of fish. 7 Crew. 5, not anglers. The captain of the boat is not the leader. Request search on backgrounds of Hussein Samatar on board and Abdul Nadir mentioned in discourse but not thought to be on board. Samatar claims to be Somali but wrong dialect, possibly Yemen or Saudi. Slowing to monitor until further instructions.

New subject. Unknown warship to the east of our position. No visual. No threat as yet. Req. Clarify. Ends.

The response they received shortly afterward was not unexpected, as was the spelling of the ship's name. The message had come from the US Navy.

Ack Toowoomba. Maintain position until relieved by USS FFG-58 – approx. 24 hours. Limited commercial traffic is expected in your area. Has been diverted to the west of your position. Warship to your east is Iranian frigate Sahand – source US sat. Samatar has known contacts in Mogadishu. More follows. Investigating unknown Abdul Nadir. Probably alias. Ends.

The USS FFG-38 was the USS Samuel B Roberts, a

United States Navy Oliver Hazard Perry Class guided-missile frigate belonging to the US Fifth fleet. For the last few days, a small task force had been involved in exercises in the Straits of Madagascar between Mozambique's coast and Madagascar's island. This exercise had intended to evaluate the ability of the allied naval forces to seal off an area between two bits of land, as a precursor to closing down areas of the Red Sea, the Gulf of Aden. or the Persian Gulf to the north in the event of hostilities in those areas.

It was probably just as well that the exercise was conducted out of the watchful eyes of people in the Middle East because the activity had not been all that well planned and was poorly implemented. But they did learn valuable lessons. The most important lesson was the dependence on the aircraft deployed by the USS Carl Vinson – a nuclear-powered United States Navy Nimitz Class super-carrier that was part of the task force.

Because the gap between the two coasts was at its narrowest - a distance of over two hundred miles - and at its broadest often extended out to over a thousand miles, the planners had cheated. On their charts, they drew a rectangle from the narrowest point in the north up to and including the islands of Comoros and down the coast of Madagascar. This satisfied the aims of the exercise, and with modern GPS technology, this was not a problem. However, it also meant big trouble for anyone who happened to be passing through this area of the sea.

The Carl Vinson carried a flight of Boeing F/A-18E/ F Super Hornets, which had the range, the maneuverability, and the speed to make hiding from them nearly impossible. The Americans kept the exercise area as far as possible away from the east coast of Africa. However, that still meant that all shipping still had to traverse the northern-most and narrowest point of the exercise area. And as part of the exercise, all ships were noted, recorded, and investigated where appropriate.

The Nadifa-El-Aziza entered the rectangle of the exercise area. It was identified as a fishing vessel. Pending further clarification of her status, she was noted as hostile. The USS FFG-38 watched the passage of the Nadifa as routine as the various bits of data came together. A check with HMS Lancaster and HMAS Toowoomba logs confirmed that this particular vessel had been checked and cleared. A message was then sent to the control center onboard the Carl Vinson as a consequence of which the status of the ship was changed to noncommercial miscellaneous – no further action required.

For reasons that a communications specialist on the Carl Vinson did not know, he posted the change in the classification of this vessel to a website., The classification was picked up by the IRIS Sahand and conveyed to Mohammad Haji.

Onboard the Nadifa, Hussein Samatar began to feel nervous. While it was typical for a naval exercise in international waters to be notified to all and sundry, this did not include unregistered fishing boats from another land that just so happened to be in the area at the time. Consequently, neither the master of the vessel nor Samatar were aware of the exercise and wrongly assumed that they and their colleagues were the focus of attention. The further the boat penetrated the exercise area; the more Samatar became aware of the presence of warships. And, to make matters worse, there was also the occasional presence of aircraft, and they were of a type that suggested that they had been launched from an aircraft carrier. It was not until they had sailed down past the Natiquinde Cape and then started to hug the African coast that they began to see the less naval sea and air activity.

The crew could begin to relax.

It appeared that whatever was going on off the coast of Mozambique had nothing to do with them.

They were wrong.

The United States forces had, along with their allied forces, taking a particular interest in the Nadifa-El-Aziza. Apart from the fact that it was a fishing vessel without any fish, it had traveled a great distance to the south of where it should have been, without giving any plausible explanation of what it was doing. The allied forces had often intercepted similar vessels on the high seas with equally unexplained motives. Usually, they turned out to be either harmless enough or beyond the ability of western intelligence analysts to make any sense of. But this one was different. This boat's crew seemed to be resolute in reaching a particular objective. It did not call at any of the many coastal towns and villages along the way.

And then there was the name Abdul Nadir.

Investigation into the background of Abdul Nadir initially turned up blank. However, further investigation through the countless records the western intelligence services kept eventually turned up a possible link. Of course, many people shared that name, from the innocent Gastroenterologist going about his business in Phoenix, Arizona, to any number of good and bad guys in all parts of the world.

The name Abdul Nadir would not usually be associated with Somalia. It was more likely to be a name more readily associated with Pakistan. But by the wonders of modern search engines, the security and intelligence services found that the name had been mentioned before in

Somalia. It was a name that had been used by a nasty piece of work who went by the name of Mohamed Haji. Further investigation of this name showed that this gentleman was someone the Iranian intelligence services had used on several occasions. And he had been implicated in several events where people had died. He was on the move if they were talking about the same Haji. If this was so, then things were either getting too hot for him in his recently adopted hometown of Mogadishu, Somalia, or he was moving to cause trouble somewhere else.

And, whichever the case, that was a matter of concern. The problem was – Where the hell was he now?

The CIA had a file that held stories – really a collection of rumors - that Haji and his friends had been communicating with other groups throughout Africa seeking support for a broader range of plots and terrorist events. In Somalia, the United States forces had largely been withdrawn. There was not much left for the terrorists to do in that country other than to harass the local population, the government, or each other. That was meaningless in the grand scheme of the global Jihad, and it was not felt that Haji had any particular axe to grind as far as religion was concerned.

Similarly, ISIS and other al-Qaeda-derived terrorist organizations had penetrated throughout North Africa from Morocco in the west to Egypt in the east, and central Africa down through the Sudan and Chad, and even onto the Congo. Again - that was all about power and influence and had little to do with any religious intent. But the terrorist groups had not had any luck in penetrating further south, and that had become the focus of their attention. The rumors were that that was not only their next goal. Haji was inextricably linked to their plans and was very much a person of interest in this regard.

Mohamed Haji was born in Saudi Arabia, but both parents were from Yemen. They had been working as contractors in Saudi Arabia for so long that they had long since abandoned any plans to return to the place of their birth. That was until their eldest son had got into trouble mixing with Osama bin Laden sympathizers. While Osama had lost his Saudi citizenship and his wealthy family had disowned him, there were, and still are, quite a few his followers in Saudi Arabia. The Saudi authorities do not exactly tolerate them, but it is time to call it in when a Yemini starts ranting about his al Qaeda network. So, first Mohamed and then his family returned to Yemen.

Once he was back in Yemen, Mohamed got bored.

Seeing much more action occurring across the Gulf in Somalia, he once again left his home and went to join in the fun. There he came to the attention of the United States forces by his ruthless and vicious murders of ethnic Somali people who disagreed with his particular brand of the Islamic faith. Or instead, that was used as an excuse for the murders. Towards the end of the United States action in Somalia, the CIA had a price on the head of Mohamed Haji. Unfortunately, Operation United Shield saw the withdrawal of United States troops from Somalia and the end of their influence in the country before the money could ever be collected.

Although that was way back in 1995, Haji would never forget.

And neither would the Americans.

Chapter 9

Deployment

The NSA had briefed anyone who cared to listen that their mission was of the highest priority, yet no one seemed to be in any particular hurry. The United Airlines Boeing 767 flight 918 pulled away from the Dulles terminal Gate 11 thirty minutes later than was scheduled. No reason was given, although there were plenty of questions about the people on board. The flight was supposed to leave at 6:05 p.m. Washington time and arrive at Heathrow London at 6:20 in the morning local time. The connecting flight to Cape Town, South Africa, could not be expected to wait for them, but for reasons best known to British Airways, or the NSA, they would have a twelve-hour plus wait between their flights, so that would not be an issue. Again – the urgency seemed to have been lost. Still – that was for someone else to worry about.

Mark thought that there were far quicker ways to get to where they were going in the circumstances. However, he wasn't picking up the tab.

Or controlling the operation of Steel Tiger on behalf

of the President of the United States, so that was that.

The eight men who made up the team had made their way to Dulles in four groups– Mark and Brent, Dusty and Blake, Mike and Hamish, and Elliott and Ben. There was no special reason for this particular grouping other than that it was comfortable. They were all dressed for the occasion, wearing business suits, and looking like other businesspeople taking off for a couple of days in Britain. And as was appropriate, they were all flying in business class.

The last person to board the airplane, and the assumed cause of the delay, was a short, wiry man who brought a whole new meaning to the term harassed. But that did not fool Mark. He was a CIA agent. Whether or not this gentleman had anything to do with the business that Mark and his team engaged in did not matter.

The man would need to be watched.

Mark had been briefed that the CIA had their noses out of joint, so he would expect that they would seek to find out what was going on. That is – if they did not already know. Mark's team at least had an advantage. They were split into four unrelated groups and could see from different angles and perspectives. By a series of eye contacts and innocuous hand signals, they could converse as they had done many years before while serving in the US Special Forces.

The fact that the target of their attention appeared to sleep during their entire trip did not distract their attention. It at least gave them something to do.

The trip across the pond went without incident, and with a following wind, they made up for any time lost on departure from Dulles. That just meant that they would need to spend more time at Heathrow.

Mark had been told that he would meet with someone in London called Etheridge. Again, that was for someone else to worry about. How this *Etheridge* would find, and contact Mark had not been stated.

The arrival hall at Heathrow was typically crowded with people rushing to get to where they wanted to go after having stood in queues for hours waiting to get by check-in, immigration, security, and customs. While airports the world over tried to make life easy for the traveling public, *easy* was still hard. Mark watched from the transit lounge with dispassionate interest. They were patiently waiting for contact with the illusive Etheridge.

After the first boarding call had been made for their British Airways flight BA59, someone finally approached Mark. It was a young lady. Dressed in faded jeans and a formless sweater, a rucksack on her back, the lady caught his eyes and asked if he was Mark Taylor. It was more of a reaction to Marks' body language than acknowledging his reply. She just disappeared back into the crowd to be replaced by a gentleman who looked like he was fresh out of spy school.

He fell into step beside Mark as he walked across the departure lounge.

And he did not say much.

'You have a tail – watch it!' he said, looking casually around, his eyes never resting on any particular spot.

'Everything is on track, but you will need to hurry once you get to your destination.' And with that, the elusive Mr. Etheridge – if indeed that was his name - melted back into the crowd. But not before he had brush-passed a piece of paper into Mark's hand. It was all very cleverly done, and it was doubtful if anyone had noticed anything at all. Except that Mark had been unaware that he had a tail.

That gave him something else to worry about.

The gentleman they had under surveillance on the flight from Washington had vanished on arrival at Heathrow.

But that did not mean that he could not have been replaced by someone else. And it was too late to contact the rest of his team to check.

Instead of continuing towards the departure gate, Mark stopped to fiddle with his carry-on bag while taking a furtive look around. Not seeing anyone paying him any attention, he had that sinking feeling that he was once more in a situation where he was out of his depth. He had been through all this kind of shit the last time he had traveled overseas – worrying about surveillance and counter-surveillance and not having a clue of what the rules were. For sure, Mark had some experience in such matters. But he could not pretend to have the ability to counter the professionals. Etheridge had given him a wake-up call, and now was the time when he would need to at least get his shit together and hope that he was good enough to survive in the world of spooks!

The flight out of Heathrow Airport took off on time. As soon as they started to settle down at the aircraft's cruising altitude, the flight attendant indicated that passengers could move around the cabin; Mark went to the toilet. Like Etheridge, the piece of paper that Mark extracted from his pocket did not say much. It just had a name of a contact – Banga Matsikenyeri. But that was all that Mark needed. That was the man's name that they would have to trust in Zimbabwe and who would provide them with some form of transport. Mark had assumed that Matsikenyeri was tied up with the British Secret Intelligence Service, otherwise known as MI6. But he could be the CIA.

The CIA and other United States-based intelligence organizations – not for want of trying – had failed to make headway in Zimbabwe to set up a base for gathering any useable intelligence. And for that matter, they did not have much success in South Africa either.

The reason for this strange situation was probably more to do with Zimbabwe's dependence on Britain dating back to the time when the place had been called Rhodesia than with any distrust of the Americans. However, in the case of South Africa, this situation was purely due to suspicion. So, the Americans had to play this card and depend on the British MI6.

Mark and his team had to have someone they could rely on once they were on the ground in Africa. Or if, or when, the shit hit the fan.

As things turned out, it did not matter.

Their flight arrived at Cape Town International Airport just before nine o'clock in the morning. Having traveled at night-time for the last two nights, all team members were well-rested. And since the flight to South Africa barely involved any change in time zones, there was no issue with jetlag. The team was looking forward to doing something worthwhile.

Mark had failed to pin anyone on the flight as being a tail, but that was just another problem that he would have to deal with later – if at all!

None of his team members had any checked-in baggage to worry about. They were met by a United States Navy Commander, whisked through the transfer lounge reasonably quickly, and then driven in an SUV up to the northern end of the airport. There they were shown into a windowless room and devoid of any character where they discarded their suits and put on fatigues that were provided for them. After the very briefest of delays, they walked out onto the tarmac to begin the next stage of their journey. The flight up to the aircraft carrier - USS Carl Vinson.

The aircraft they would travel in was a Grumman C-2A Greyhound designed to deliver mail, other things, and occasionally people to the US Navy Carrier fleet. It was an ugly-looking plane – more like a flying tube –but then the Navy wasn't too concerned about what it looked like. It was patiently explained to the passengers that they would stop at the King Shaka International airport at Durban to refuel, which should be - just – sufficient to get them to the Vinson.

That was the last comment before the engines – twin Allison T56 turboprops– burst into life, and then any further conversation was impossible. Mark and Mike were in seats that had some means of communication with the cockpit – *"in case of emergency,"* it was explained with a grin that said there would not be one. Well – not one in which this means of communication would be of any use. The Greyhound had no windows other than those required by the pilots, nor did it have much in the way of creature comforts. The seats were not cushioned, and it was clear that this aircraft was not supposed to have any passengers as the facilities were minimal.

But it did have earmuffs.

And the security at the Cape Town airport was one way of ensuring that Mark and the team were not followed.

The stopover at Durban was uneventful. The pilot explained that the airport could not take the lar, ger Boeing, so they had come via Cape Town. The runway length was undoubtedly not a problem for the Greyhound. And as far as Mark could see, the airport appears to handle all the flights that came and went without any issues. So, the pilot was on a fishing trip. They were trying to find out what?

And why?

The Greyhound finally arrived at its rendezvous position with the USS Carl Vinson just after seven o'clock in the evening. It was pretty dark, and the weather had deteriorated by this time. The wind was blowing at over forty knots, and the cloud cover was down to about three hundred feet. Not that either factor presented any more than a challenge to the pilot. Landing an airplane on an aircraft carrier requires great skill. But the landing itself is just a partially controlled crash in the best of weather. Landing at night with variable winds made it that much more exciting.

There are usually four arrester wires stretched across the carrier's deck at intervals of roughly fifty feet. The aircraft has a hook on its tail, and it is simply a matter of this hook catching on the arrester wire, and then hydraulics systems on the flight deck do the rest. Pilots rarely try to land on the first wire because it is the closest to the edge of the carrier deck and, therefore, likely to result in a real crash – into the ship's stern. Carrier pilots usually aim for the third wire – since that was the safest. That did not leave much room for error if they missed.

As the Greyhound lumbered towards the deck, a sudden gust of wind slewed the plane and made things a little dicey with the pitch and roll of the Vinson. The pilot had to abort his first attempt to land and go round again. Now things were getting serious. If the pilot were to be believed, they had cut their fuel reserves to the absolute minimum, and this time around, they would have little choice but to land on the carrier deck. Or to ditch into the sea.

In the interests of harmony, the pilot – a young United States Navy Lieutenant who looked like he was fresh from flying school – cheerfully explained the two options to his startled passengers and tried again. The fact that neither Mark nor Mike, the two who had communications with the pilot, had any idea of the significance of what he had said was probably a good thing.

The Greyhound once again lumbered in towards the heaving deck. The wind again slewed the plane on its final approach to the flight deck. The pilot decided to risk landing at a thirty-degree angle to the flight deck. He almost snagged the third arrester wire and fearing that he would also miss the fourth and last wire, he cut all power to the engines. The aircraft belly-flopped onto the flight deck. The hook caught the fourth and final wire.

Whether the young pilot felt any relief, it did not show in his demeanor. Or in his words of welcome.

'Welcome aboard Cell Block 70!'

This was a derogatory reference to the ship's code of CVN 70. The captain of this floating city would have preferred using the Vinson's more popular nickname of 'Gold Eagle."

Since his passengers could not see anything of the heaving deck or their dramatic landing, they could not understand what all the fuss was about.

Or they were just scared shit-less.

Peer pressure alone would ensure that they admitted nothing.

That was about to change.

While this was not the first time that any of Marks's team had been onboard a United States Navy vessel, they were still disoriented by the mass of narrow passageways, pipes and stairs, and the constant noise. A Chief Petty Officer was assigned to take them down to an area where they would be acquainted with their gear and equipment. The Chief patiently waited while the landlubbers struggled with the pitch and roll of the vessel, but eventually, they made it into the briefing room. The room was laid out more like a classroom. When they were in this room, the Chief closed and locked the door and introduced himself.

'Ok. I am Chief Petty Officer Howard Morton, and I don't want to know who you are!' he said with a smile.

The implication was clear to all.

Chapter 10

Intrusion

Banga Matsikenyeri was not delighted with the job given to him by the MI6 head of station in Harare.

Matsikenyeri was a native of Zimbabwe and had served their British *associates* for the last thirty years. This was done with the full knowledge and agreement of the Mugabe administration, who depended on the British MI6 probably more than they relied on their secret police – the Central Intelligence Organization.

With this job, that reliance was even more critical.

Under normal circumstances, it would be expected that a request for support of an American mission would come from the CIA and be directed to the Zimbabwe CIO. But this request had come from the US Department of Defense and had been directed via MI6 in London. Not that being able to trust the Zimbabwe CIO would surprise anybody. What surprised MI6 was the sign that US Defense intelligence chiefs did not trust their own CIA?

It was probably the latter that caused MI6 to agree to provide support, even if they did not know what they agreed to. Disputes between various factions within the US intelligence and security community were not exactly rare. Although it was rare for MI6 or any other organization on the planet to know what the dispute was about. Or if there was a dispute over whose territory someone was stepping into!

But, in this case, the dispute had been laid bare, and MI6 was only too keen to assist in any way they could to find out what the hell was happening.

The job itself was pretty simple.

The timing and location of the job weren't.

A small US force was to be inserted into Zimbabwe at a place and at a time yet to be revealed. The aim of the US force was to follow an equally small bunch of thugs.

The origin of this latter group had not been stated.

The objective of this bunch of thugs was either unknown or was also not stated. They would be entering Zimbabwe from Mozambique. It was not known if they would cross the border legally or illegally. On the assumption that they would at least try to make the crossing legally, it had been concluded that the entry would be in the region of the Zimbabwe city of Mutare. That meant that this group would have to assemble near Machipanda as that was the only place close to the Mozambique-Zimbabwe border and the town of Mutare.

Based on these assumptions, it, therefore, followed that any force employed in following this group would need to pick them up at the border. However, the Americans had specified that their party would be landed by helicopter in Mozambique – somewhere close to the town of Chimoio - and would follow the thugs over the border. Therefore - their simple requirement was to obtain some form of transport.

And that is what made Matsikenyeri so pissed.

Getting hold of a couple of trucks in the out-backs of Mozambique would be complicated at the best of times.

Getting a couple of trucks that worked would be an entirely different and more complex mission.

However, the Americans did have a couple of things in their favor. Firstly - Money would not be a problem. Secondly – their force would have access to the latest GPS equipment. So, all Matsikenyeri had to do was find a couple of trucks, know the GPS location, and then either he went to them, or they came to him.

Matsikenyeri and two of his associates left the Harare British Embassy in a Jeep devoid of any markings to indicate where it came from. They traveled east to the border town of Mutare. While in the town, they scouted the border crossing points and discussed procedures with the officials to ensure that they could accurately brief their American visitors on what they could expect. They then crossed over into Mozambique with all their papers in order and continued heading east towards the town of Chimoio. The roads were not exceptionally well-maintained, but they covered the distance in under two hours and then searched for a couple of rental trucks.

The vehicles required by the Americans specified that they should be unobtrusive as this mission was clandestine. They should also be as self-contained as possible. They should be able to cross the border into Zimbabwe without raising any issues.

Matsikenyeri headed to the nearest Hertz yard. There he was able to hire a couple of campervans using the story that they were to meet up with some British tourists in the Gorongosa National Park. Their subsequent journey would see them cross the border into Zimbabwe and end up in Harare. The payment was made in US dollars and was supported by a letter from the British Embassy, which confirmed the story. And made the British responsible should there be any problem – like if the hire period exceeded the two-week term.

The group then moved to the outskirts and checked into a motel on a per-diem rate to await the next move. That move was over to the Americans. In theory, another group of men would land by helicopter and at night, in the general region of Chimoio. Matsikenyeri would be contacted and told to bring the transport to a specific GPS location where the handover would occur.

That should be the end of MI6 and Banga Matsikenyeri's participation in the operation of Steel Tiger.

And it would be. Although in not quite the way that they intended.

The organization of transport for the Iranian group who would be entering Mozambique was presumed to be somewhat different.

CIA Intelligence reports had indicated that the team headed by Mohamed Haji would be landed on Mozambique soil at, or near, the seaport of Quelimane. That port was four hundred five miles northeast of Mutare on the Zimbabwe border. The selection of Quelimane was presumed to be based on the availability of people to assist with the landing and subsequent transfer of the men to some other form of transport. It was probably also based on the ability to land people without drawing too much attention to what was going on. Logistically and logically, the preferred alternative would have been to land the men at the port city of Beira. This was further south than Quelimane and only two hundred miles from where they intended to cross over into Zimbabwe. And gave them access to better roads than would be found up north.

However, the decision would have been relatively

simple despite its logic and the extra distance they would need to travel over-land. Beira did present a significant problem in assuming that the group intended to remain covert. Beira was a busy port responsible for serving the central region of Mozambique and providing the main port for access to land-locked Zimbabwe. The chances of the men being able to land their boat undetected would therefore be remote.

In the northern part of Mozambique, a group of Jihadists had established themselves after being forced south during the Somali war. At the end of that conflict, remnants of the group had remained and had slowly been increasing their influence in an otherwise peaceful country. In recent years, they have attracted Iran's attention. That had resulted in support. However, their power had yet to extend further south than the Zambezia Province. Therefore, the decision had been made to land the men in the seaport of Quelimane – where there would be plenty of support. And the very layout of the river port would make it easy to land the boat undetected by any authorities.

The choice of transport was not so easily explained.

Whoever was organizing the transport for this group had little experience traveling in this part of the world. The jeeps that were to be used were two open deck utility vehicles. On the assumption that there was a minimum of six men in the party, which meant that each car would have to carry at least one of their numbers on the open deck. In Mozambique, the temperature rarely falling below 60 degrees Fahrenheit and often rising above 90 degrees did not seem like a good idea.

The CIA did not like to make assumptions.

However, in the case of the Iranian group, their assumptions were pretty close to the mark.

Not that it mattered.

Chapter 11

Insertion

Now Haji had another mission to fulfill, and yet again, that was sponsored by the Iranian government. The Iranians wanted someone who could not be directly attributed to Iran but was sufficiently adept at killing people. And they needed someone skilled in the art of covert operations.

This mission did involve big players on the international stage.

However, on its face, the current mission had little to do with the Americans. At least not initially.

They had to get Haji into Zimbabwe. The best way to do that was by land because the all-seeing Americans could track anyone, anywhere, through the booking systems universally used by the airlines and travel industries. Also, the Iranian plan needed a bunch of thugs to accompany Haji on this mission with the same ruthless attitude and the same main characteristic – they could not be traced back to Iran.

The answer was to use a group from either Yemen or Somalia, where Iran associated with any number of groups that met their criteria. They settled on the group from

Somalia because they would have less distance to travel and would at least have a plausible reason to be somewhere off the east coast of Africa. This group would sail south in a fishing boat. They just would not be doing any fishing. Then the plan was to have Haji on board an Iranian Navy ship, which would shadow the main party as they made their way south and then insert Haji immediately before they made landfall.

The main problem here was that it would not stop the US and their allies from harassing his colleagues on board the fishing boat. The Iranians could not risk Haji being seen on that ship. They believed – incorrectly - that the CIA knew what he looked like. They would undoubtedly remember the price that would be paid for the capture of Haji, but that was not the same thing. Nor had anyone on board the boat been told the man's real name who was to join them. They had simply been informed that Abdul Nadir would join them. This was an alias that Haji had used before and probably unknown to the Americans. However, the Iranian plan required that the team enter Mozambique to tie up with other necessary resources and then travel over-land into Zimbabwe. That required that Haji join the team before the boat made landfall. So, the basic plan was quite simple.

The Nadifa had to endure the harassment until the Americans gave up on any serious monitoring of the boat. The Iranian Intelligence had a plan for that. They had a source that would advise them when the fishing boat was no longer of interest to the Americans.

Then Haji could join the boat.

Haji could then take command of his gang of thugs.

In the planning stage, the Iranians hadn't counted on the Americans running a significant exercise in the area off the African coast through which both the boat carrying his team and the Iranian Navy warship carrying

Haji would have to pass. But now it was too late, so they would just have to cope.

Under cover of darkness, the Iranian frigate Sahand launched her Sikorsky CH-53 Sea Stallion helicopter displaying flying skills not expected of the Iranians. They flew at wave height towards the Nadifa. The arrival of a helicopter, although expected, was a frightening wake-up call to the men on the fishing boat, but they managed to receive the man who was winched down onto their deck. As quickly as it had arrived, the helicopter disappeared back to the east.

They now had a new leader. Mohamed Haji was now on board, but until the group had made landfall, he would continue under the name of Abdul Nadir.

As a matter of routine, the US forces were checking all activity in the area, which accounted for almost everything on the east coast of Africa. They continuously tracked the Nadifa and the Iranian frigate and noted the Sikorsky flight. They also followed the Sikorsky to a position that coincided with the Nadifa.

They had no way of knowing what had occurred when it got there.

That piece of apparently useless information was passed to the Naval Intelligence guys to give them something to worry over while the monitoring returned to the more exciting stuff. Like - why, after the return of the Sikorsky to a position which placed it back where it had come from, had the Iranian frigate begun to turn to port and start a slow circular path which would have her heading north. That information was also passed to US Naval Intelligence. It did not appear to make any sense. But – that was someone else's job to worry about.

Since the Navy could not make any sense of it either,

it was first passed up to the next level to military Intelligence weenies at the Pentagon, and secondly to the CIA at Langley, for them to sort out.

That is where the information had an impact.

The office of the DNI was informed. That started a flurry of activity, including a message back to the fifth fleet instructing them to seek out further information on the passage of the Nadifa.

To discreetly follow and observe.

Surprisingly - Instructions were issued that the Navy was not, under any circumstances, to interfere with the passage of the vessel.

Eighteen hours later, the USS Samuel B Roberts – an Oliver Hazard class-guided missile frigate - shadowed the Nadifa until it entered the river mouth of the Rio dos Bons Sinais. From there, it was presumed to be heading up the river towards the port city of Quelimane.

Darkness began to descend. Because the risks were too significant in the shallow waters and ever-changing sandbanks that made up the river estuary, the Samuel B Roberts launched an inflatable boat with four men aboard.

The frigate stood out to sea to await developments.

The marines in the inflatable benefited from night vision binoculars and could follow the Nadifa up the channel. The senior chief on board initially thought of following the target vessel without showing any navigational lights in the gathering gloom of sunset. However, he decided against that choice. There was sufficient traffic around despite the late hour, and he did not want to be rundown by any other boat or ship which would not know the rules of the sea as well as he did.

Then things got interesting.

Instead of sailing into the port at Quelimane, the Nadifa continued up the Cuacua river and eventually hove-to where that river was joined by another river - the Licuare. Once there, they just waited until darkness had fallen completely.

Things then began to happen.

The Navy saw an exchange of signals between the Nadifa and someone on the bank on the eastern side of the Licuare river. They could not see who the return signal was from. After receiving the call, the boat could drift slowly towards the shore. The boat hove to probably because they did not know the water depth closer to the riverbank. The crew of the Nadifa then launched a small run-about which was rowed to the shore by one of the men. It had no sooner reached the edge than two men, dressed in what looked like military fatigues, clambered on board. The runabout then returned to the Nadifa and was tied up alongside. All three passengers climbed on board the Nadifa.

The American observers still had no clue of who the two men were.

But their arrival certainly changed the atmosphere onboard the boat.

The Nadifa had drifted back into the center of the river. Again, the observing Americans had no clue whether that was intended or just because the crew was otherwise occupied.

It was a still night with not a breath of wind, and the sound carried over the water. The Americans could hear an argument going on below deck on the Nadifa conducted in a language they could not understand. However, the discussion ended abruptly with firing two shots that sounded like they were of a low caliber. Probably fired from a pistol. Shortly afterward, four men could be seen struggling with two packages on the deck, which were slid into the water. Judging by the posture of those handling them and the apparent weight and size, the packages looked suspiciously like they were contained two bodies.

Whether it was the bodies of the two men they had picked up from the shore or two of the people already on board, there was no way for the Marines who were watching the whole process to tell.

Although the inclination of the American marines would have been to do *something*, having just witnessed the apparent murder of two fellow human beings, they had been instructed not to interfere. So that was the end of that.

Onboard the Nadifa, two men then tried to lower an anchor. From their hopeless struggles, it became plain to the marines that there was now no one left on the boat who knew much about nautical matters. Four of the men then climbed down into the run-about carrying what appeared to be rifles and a couple of packages. Again - the American observers had no clue of what they held. The runabout once more headed towards the shore.

There did not appear to be any people on the shore waiting for them. There was too much vegetation to be sure of that, and the fuzzy green outlines produced by the night-vision binoculars were inadequate to get a clear image.

After off-loading three of the men, the run-about returned to the Nadifa. The remaining four men, clambered onto the run-about, complete with an assortment of weapons and packages his time, the load seemed a little too much for the boat with the water lapping over the sides. However, they eventually made it to the shore without getting too wet. Once there, the men quickly disappeared into the bush, leaving one man to tie up the boat to the beach before disappearing into the undergrowth.

No attempt was made to hide the vessel, which suggested either they had no further use for it or some or all the men would return shortly.

As it was, the eight men joined up and headed west along the riverbank and turned to the north and disappeared into the darkness.

Initially, the Chief onboard the Navy inflatable did not know what to make of this activity. He could reasonably speculate that the two men of the original crew of the Nadifa who knew how to sail were now dead, but the boat was still there sitting unattended in the middle of the channel. So, he radioed a report back to the frigate and waited. That message was first relayed to the Commander, then onto the Carl Vison, from there on to the Pentagon, on to the office of the DNI, and finally into the office of the NRO. The reply came back remarkably quickly.

We need more information! Investigate and report. Stay Covert. ROE remains as before.

Well - that was sweet.

Some dickheads back in Washington DC had decided that the Navy with its four marines manning the inflatable should now find out what was happening onboard the Nadifa-El-Aziza. Although they had no idea who they would find, they should stay covert. The Rules of Engagement were to remain as they were – basically that they could not shoot anyone.

After a brief discussion among the marines, they agreed that they would ignore that part of the message related to the ROE. If threatened, they would need to shoot first.

Based on the original advice from the Intelligence officer back on board the frigate, they believed that they had accounted for all the men who had been on board the boat. That was provided the two dumped packages had been the bodies of two of them. There was no sign of anyone being still on board, no lights, or anything that would suggest that their logic was wrong.

But they had to be sure.

The RHIB inflatable had twin engines that could boost their speed to well over forty knots, but, of course, they made quite a noise in the process. The Chief feathered the engines as they drifted to the seaward side of the Nadifa and used a couple of grappling hooks to tie the RHIB to the side. Then two men armed with sufficient firepower to deal with any resistance and still wearing their night vision gear climbed on board while the other two covered them. Working as a pair, they began a slow and methodical search of the vessel, never letting one man get out of sight of the other. It was quiet and tedious work. They had to be careful that no one was hiding and armed. They had to be sure that there was nobody left on board.

They found nobody.

But they did find something.

Aft of the wheelhouse was a compartment that looked like a place to store life jackets or other ready-use equipment. It was empty. Yet the marines did not know of any men who had left the boat wearing any life-saving apparel. More significant than there was a slight dusting of white powder that the marines took as a drug. They took a sample for later investigation back on board the frigate.

They had just seen the start of a twist in this outrageous plot.

They did not know anything about the plot, so they had no way of judging the significance of what they had seen.

The Chief radioed in his report and asked for instructions. That message went through the same channels as the previous ones, so that it was quite some time before he got an answer.

Return to your ship. Ends

When the inflatable finally returned to the Samuel B Roberts, the boarding party was tired and puzzled. They were de-briefed by the executive officer and recounted again what they had seen. They could shed no light on where the man called Abdul Nadir - but probably called Mohamed Haji - and the rest of his gang had gone. They guessed that the two fishermen were now dead as the most likely outcome but could provide no proof that they were the "packages" that had been dumped into the river.

One of the problems faced by the captain of a lowly frigate is to sort out the difference between taking the initiative and suggesting a course of action and merely passing information up the chain of command for someone else to make the decisions. Fortunately, Captain Bruce Lindsey USN, the commander of the Carl Vinson, had high regard for the commander of the Roberts – Angel Cruz – otherwise, the matter may have ended right there.

At the dawn of the following morning, two things happened.

The first thing that happened was repositioning a satellite to pass over the area where the so-called Abdul Nadir was believed to be. That was no trivial thing. The satellite traveling through space thirty thousand miles away would require a minor and temporary adjustment to its flight path to move it to no longer overfly Somalia. As with all bureaucrats, the sudden loss of information was an irritation that would not go unnoticed. That was even though they had failed to get any meaningful pictures for several months. The satellite was under the control of AFSCN – the United States Air Force Satellite Control Network - but in the complex world that is the United States security and intelligence network, they were really under the control of the National Reconnaissance Office or NRO.

This satellite's information was filtered through all sixteen intelligence agencies but primarily used the NSA and the CIA. Both of these organizations were advised of the temporary realignment but were not informed of the reason. The office of the DNI had the power to do just that, leaving the CIA particularly pissed. Consequently, various rumors started in the communications group, and the stories did not end there.

The second thing that happened was that four F/A-18E/F Super Hornets under the command of Lieutenant Commander Brett Rivenski took off from the USS Carl Vinson and headed towards the coast of Mozambique and then inland. The cameras which each Hornet carried were capable of taking ultra-high-resolution photographs of anything on land, irrespective of the cloud cover. All they had to do was localize anything worth taking a picture of.

It was a matter of coordinating information from the satellite and the intelligence services who had been following events occurring in this part of Africa, with information that they thought they knew from events in Mozambique. And one of the Hornets got lucky.

At a place about three miles short of the border between Mozambique and Zimbabwe, just outside the town of Manica, two jeeps were photographed meeting up with a truck that had made its way across the border from the west.

All the disparate bits of information had come together. Something was about to happen, and they now knew exactly where it was to start.

But what the hell was about to start?

And what the hell could they do about it?

Chapter 12

The Followers

Chief Morton knew that the people he was dealing with were experienced professional warriors and so wasted little time introducing the men to the gear laid out before them. Despite his earlier comment about not knowing these men, he did know who they were.

And where they were headed.

'Shortly, I will bring in our Intelligence Officer, who will brief you on the current situation as far as we know it and on what happens next. Meanwhile – you will see your gear laid out for you. I suggest you check it very carefully – because after you leave the ship, you will be on your own and there will be no coming back. You were issued with visas back in Washington, which should be sufficient to deal with any border issues.'

The Navy certainly knew how to plan. Everything was catered for. Mark just hoped they did not need all the gear but, having been on similar missions in other parts of the world, he knew that you had to carry all you may need – just in case.

Each man in the team was outfitted with full combat

and survival gear. They also had a complete set of electronics, including a satellite phone, recorder, GPS unit, camera, and spare batteries to power a small town. There were also a few extras, including an Entrenching Tool (a collapsible space), a can of tear gas, and a collection of drugs – mostly pain killers and sleeping tablets. They did not expect to use the latter.

The net effect of carrying all this gear would be to make the men much bulkier than before. And Mark realized that the extra weight would be a significant factor if they had to travel on foot. All the men finished getting dressed in silence, stowing the gear into the many pockets and holsters provided before settling down around the table. Mark also took a seat in a chair - more to stop his constant swaying from the ship's motion than for a rest.

A knock came on the door, and the Chief unlocked it and let in a guy dressed in the uniform of a Lieutenant Commander. You would expect him to be of far higher rank from his age. He had the tired body language of someone who had not had much sleep recently. But he was pleasant enough and all business. And Mark very quickly decided that he was indeed from Navy intelligence.

'Gentlemen! I am Commander Pat Lewis. I will be your liaison officer for as long as we can be of any help to you on this mission. We have been tracking the people that you wish to meet up with. At present – as far as we know – they are holed up on the border. Waiting for what? We just don't know. Your Helicopter will fly you to a point about twelve miles from that position.'

That said, he unrolled a map on the table and the team, including Chief Morton, gathered around. The Navy had never really got into the Army habit of talking in klicks – meaning kilometers – except for some people who wanted to sound impressive.

'The Vinson is currently steaming towards Mozambique and should be in position by about 22:00 hours,' he said, showing a position that seemed dangerously close to the shore. 'The bad guys are here,' he continued showing a place in the middle of nowhere but very close to the Mozambique-Zimbabwe border. 'And this is where one of our Helicopters should land you. I am sorry that it cannot be closer. Helicopters tend to be noisy and draw attention to themselves, and we do not want to risk alerting the people you are to follow!' was the only explanation he gave. He then looked at Mark and waited for any questions.

'So - the guy we are hoping to catch up with is called Mohamed Haji? Do you know that he will be there, or is that a guess?' Mark asked, which resulted in a smile and a shrug from Lewis.

'Fair question!' he replied. 'No – we cannot be sure of that – but this is the group that we have identified as having been assigned to whatever the Iranians have in mind. The man who is apparently in charge claims to be Abdul Nadir, but our intelligence would have us believe that he and Mohamed Haji are the same. Haji had a reputation for being one of the more extreme members of a movement called the Ogaden National Liberation Front or ONLF, which has origins in various so-called Fronts that have been part of the emergence of Somalia. We believe that he has since joined another group with closer ties to al Qaeda. Although he now operates somewhat independently, we suspect that he has connections with the Yemen Houthi, which means he works with Iranian intelligence. But – we don't know. Or should I say – I have not been provided with that information – so that is just speculation on my part. But you get my drift. He seems to align himself with whatever group is at the forefront of terrorist action.'

Mark did not think from what he already knew that Lewis was far off the mark. The Navy was telling him something they thought was critical information despite the instructions they would have received from their masters in Washington DC. It was typical of the security and intelligence services the world over. Mark was quite familiar with not providing the troops in the field with all the available information. Sometimes with disastrous results. And the real worry was – who had provided the information? For reasons that he did not understand, Mark was inclined to trust the Navy intelligence rather than the CIA or whichever non-military intelligence unit was providing the analysis on which the mission would have to depend.

Still – he could not do anything about that now.

'Thanks for that,' Mark acknowledged.

'Now, I was given to understand that we may have some assistance from the locals. What do you know about that?'

It was hard to tell whether the Navy knew much about that, but the Commander tried to make it sound positive.

'We believe that you will be met by a small team of our intelligence operatives under the leadership of a gentleman called Banga Matsikenyeri, who is from our office in Harare. He will provide you with your vehicles and anything else you might need on the ground. He will also provide you with a briefing on what you have been doing in Mozambique. I understand that you will be named as part of a UN survey looking at national parks. So, I suggest you google the Gorongosa National Park in Mozambique and the Nyanga National Park in Zimbabwe and learn something about them. We did try to have that part of the plan changed because there is a risk that they might fail to turn up – or more than likely turn up in the wrong place,' Lewis added with a sarcastic smile.

Mark had to say something.

'It is not exactly covert - is it? I thought we would be better sneaking across the border rather than presenting ourselves so blatantly at two border posts. The border cannot be strictly controlled outside the areas where there is a designated crossing!'

Lewis was again reticent.

'Our instructions are that they do not want to risk the Zimbabwe authorities finding out about the mission. Therefore, they erred to take the more cautious approach and do everything by the book. The Risk was that if you were spotted getting into the country illegally, the mission could be blown before you even started. I will go with your approach if you want my personal opinion.'

Mark was still not convinced.

'Surely – Haji and his team will not be going through the border posts. That would be suicide for them – not so much on the Mozambique side – but on the Zimbabwe side. I presume we do not know what they are masquerading as, but it seems unlikely that they could be trying anything as elaborate as our plan.'

Lewis was becoming frustrated – probably because he had had similar discussions with the DNI representatives.

And had no success.

'Mark – the issues that you raise are noted. There are several areas in which there are various options. But we have to take what we have because of time constraints in setting up this whole mission.'

It was Marks's turn to be frustrated, but he deferred to the Navy.

'The timing is the issue!' Lewis continued. 'Timing is dependent on what Haji does. And that is unlikely to be what the CIA thinks he might do! We were overruled on several issues - but to be fair, it comes down to what we know of the environment' Lewis concluded with a shrug of the shoulders.

Mark could not recall anything about the United States presence or any operations in Mozambique, and he doubted that the CIA had much interest in this part of the world. He also suspected that the CIA did not have much say in this business, but the Navy and Commander Lewis probably did not know the complete logic behind the situation.

The US Embassy in the capital Matupo city of Mozambique was well to the south of where the team would start their journey. If they had been dragged into this mission, it was more likely that a couple of junior staff members would have been assigned to take care of their transport. That would have involved a logistical nightmare. The area they would need to travel through would involve a six hundred miles journey, which because of the lack of roads and any population of note, would take them at least fifteen hours even in the best of circumstances. Presumably, that was why a decision had been made to use the embassy in Harare.

That did not change the timing issue that the Navy was so concerned about.

It was Marks's turn to shrug his shoulders.

'Okay - What do you know of the terrain between our drop-off point and where you believe Haji to be? And more particularly – where our transport will be?' Mark asked.

'Okay. It is fairly rough country but nothing that should worry you too much. There are very few people in the area and plenty of cover. If you follow this road, you should be alright but be careful – there are other dangers other than Haji and his goons.'

Lewis traced his finger over the map. As far as Mark could see, nothing on the map that showed a road existed, but the commander appeared very confident in his positioning.

'But be warned – it is not exactly an interstate highway.' He traced a path that was far from straight. However, it did eventually end up at the border with Zimbabwe.

'Fine,' said Mark. 'In your estimation – how long will it take?'

The Commander thought about that for quite a few moments. He looked at the team and was impressed with what he saw – they all looked fit and lean behind all the muscle – and all the gear they carried in their packed clothing. And unlike earlier briefings that he had given over the years, these men were all attentive to what was being discussed. A few months before, Dusty would have been the only one who was overweight and would seemingly be out of step in this group. But not now. Not since his recent experience with Mark in Afghanistan when both were close to death from hypothermia.

Lewis hesitated before answering the question, which caused Mark to take a note of yet another piece of this mission based on the inadequate intelligence and looked to be heading south. 'About three or four hours.' The Commander finally said.

He was wrong on this piece of intelligence.

Not that it mattered.

By the time the Vinson was approaching her station, despite her size, she was beginning to pitch and roll more than she had when Mark and the team had landed on board. The Navy prepared the last meal for the eight men as though it was a banquet for a dozen men and fed them in their cocooned room below decks which made the pitching of the Vinson seem even more pronounced.

That would generally have put many men off the food that was being served but for two factors - Firstly, the Chief had said that this was the last *real* food they would get for several days - Secondly, the food was excellent after two days of intermittent airline plastic-wrapped meals.

Chief Morton finally ushered the men onto the deck. The atmosphere had changed, which was explained by the alarm that had sounded about a half-hour before. The carrier crew was at their battle stations – not as a show of force to their visitors – but because of the threat from attacks from the shore. Ever since the raid on the USS Cole in October 2000, the US Navy would never risk letting any suspicious vessel within miles of the ship. The Vinson was, therefore, at maximum alert. Despite the atrocious weather, the flight deck was busy having launched four F/A 18C Hornets – known as Stingers - to monitor any ships that might be foolish enough to try to get through the barrier provided by the various vessels that made up the carrier's escort.

On the vast deck of the Vinson, the helicopter looked frail as the wind continued to blow, and the carrier heaved its way into the swell. The men were to be transported to land in a Sikorsky MH-60 Seahawk multi-mission military helicopter, which ordinarily would have been quite intimidating. Now the lights flashing on the side of the aircraft were the only thing moving. Mark had to ask.

'Will this thing be able to fly in this atrocious weather?'
What he meant to ask was – *how safe will my men be?*
The Chief just grinned.
'He will be able to fly and get you to where you are going. The pilot is not so lucky - he may not have enough fuel to return. That is why there are a couple of jerry cans

of spare fuel on the flight deck. So – just a tip – if the chopper looks like it is going to crash kick the jerry-cans out the door – that way we will be able to know which body is which without you being burnt beyond recognition.'

The Chief laughed.

So - Mark did as well – not sure if he should.

They clambered on board one at a time and settled into the seats that were arranged at right angles to what would be their flight path. They were again issued with earmuffs to deaden the noise coming from the twin General Electric T700 GE401C Turboshaft motors. When the helicopter lifted off the deck the noise would increase so their chances of having any meaningful conversations were gone. Although the crew held a conversation with someone in the control tower they may as well have been talking in another language entirely. At the end of a quite serious exchange, during which neither the pilot nor his navigator smiled, they simply gave a thumps' up to the loadmaster and the helicopter lumbered as it lifted off into the sky.

The Sikorsky struggled to keep an even keel as it fought to escape the turmoil created by the vast bulk of the carriers' superstructure, as though reluctant to leave the safety of its host.

Eventually, it did get clear of the Vinson and settled into a nose-down trajectory path as it headed towards the land.

There was nothing to be seen and despite the earmuffs, the noise from the rotors made any conversation impossible. The men sat there staring at the bulkhead lost thought.

And contemplating what was to come.

The rolling country that was Mozambique had few people who could afford the luxury of such simple things as electricity and there was very little vehicular traffic on the ground, and fewer roads. Their flight path was mostly determined by the electronic navigation system and the pilot rarely looked up from the instrument panel as they drove on into the interior.

The helicopter had crossed the coastline of Mozambique south of the port city of Beira where the land was sparsely populated and then turned north-west passing over bush-covered land following the course of the Pungwe River. Then they approached an area where a couple of tracks through the bush crossed, and some lights came into view indicating that there was life after all. Finally, the navigator turned round in his seat and gave a signal to Mark – five minutes to touch down.

Except that they would not touch down – the eight men would need to jump. There was no point in risking a 43-million-dollar helicopter by touching a land-mine. It could ruin the whole day and even though there was no record of mines in this part of the world there was just no point in taking any chances.

For the return flight, the crew would need to land the helicopter to enable them to top up with fuel which would entail them having to land on a road where the risk would be minimized. And at that stage, there would be no point in staying covert so they would just have to deal with any traffic.

Men jumping down into the undergrowth would also need to be carefully judged. Where and how they landed was crucial lest they sprain an ankle or worse. It wasn't the pilots' job to worry about that. The pilot had enough of his problems – like where could he hide a helicopter until daylight if their fuel reserves should prove inadequate when – hopefully - someone would drop him some more fuel so that he could get back to the ship.

Mark's team was tapped on the shoulder and one by

one they had jumped for the ground. No sooner had the last man jumped down than the helicopter was gone. Silence quickly descended on the group. They were alone in a foreign country, where they were not supposed to be, heading into another country where they were also not supposed to be, and following another group who had even less right to be there. It was a familiar situation to all the men who Mark had picked for this mission. They were fully aware of the dangers that they would face.

The problem was that they were now in unfamiliar territory.

As the noise of the helicopter receded and their ears adjusted, the absolute quiet in the jungle-covered hill country was somewhat weird to the men who have spent the last two days on four different types of aircraft and moving at a frantic pace through various countries.

Now they were on their own, in a foreign and unfamiliar country, following people who were nothing less than thugs, and they were dependent on other people to get them to where they needed to go,

The only thing familiar to the men was the weather. It was not cold, but the precipitation that had started as a drizzle turned to rain.

Using their GPS units there was little chance of their getting completely lost. Even though they could barely see more than a few yards in any direction, they knew precisely where they had been dropped and precisely where they should be if they reached their objective.

The Global Positioning System is a global navigation satellite system – or GNSS – that would supply accurate location and time data anywhere on the planet. And in all weather. Which was just as well considering the atrocious conditions that they found themselves in. Each of the men had their device and so, at least theoretically, there was no risk that anyone would get lost should they become separated.

The GPS units gave them the position that they needed to get to. What the GPS unit could not tell them was the best way to get there. They had not been given any means of contacting Matsikenyeri. They only knew where he was supposed to be – at a position, the coordinates of which were 19.0659S / 33.5296E.

In a city in the United States, it was simply a matter of loading the right map, naming the starting and finishing parts of the equation, and off they went. Now they were in the boondocks of Mozambique where there was very little sign of any movement, few roads, no lights, and no evidence of life. From a satellite map, they could download an image of the terrain, but their device was not sophisticated enough to do that in real-time. In any case that was not quite the same thing as being there.

They set off heading west on the edge of a track that showed evidence that the vehicle had used it sometime in the previous hundred years. Mike took the point position for two reasons - firstly he was the best tracker in the group, and secondly - he spoke a little Portuguese – which was the official language of Mozambique. If they ran into any people, the chances were that these people would be natives. Such people would not be overly concerned with what was official and what was unofficial. Such people may be alarmed at meeting a bunch of soldiers carrying weapons but that was more than likely to cause them to flee rather than to stop and debate what these men were up to.

Mozambique is described as a multi-lingual country which unfortunately did not mean that everyone spoke or understood more than one language. Any people they met this far from civilization would likely be Bantu tribesmen who had their language, and, within that, each had their dialect. It was just hoped that at least they should have some understanding of Portuguese.

If not, Mark and his men were all carrying M16 assault rifles. That should settle the matter.
However, if it were at all possible, they would seek to avoid any human contact. The team certainly had no desire to get involved in a firefight.

About a half-hour into their journey the track began to wind up the hill and, as it did so, they had little choice but to follow the actual road because of the denseness of the foliage on both sides. On two occasions they had to scramble off the track to avoid an approaching vehicle but, in both cases, the undergrowth was their friend. Both events passed without incident, and in this, the weather conditions would have helped. The vehicle's windshield wipers were going flat out to keep up with the incessant rain and the people on board would have barely been able to see more than fifty yards in front of them> They would certainly have had no time to take in the scenery.

Or to see the lethal firepower that the bush was hiding.

The journey continued at a brisk pace but despite this Mark could see that the three hours that they had allowed as a consequence of their briefing aboard the Carl Vinson would not be met. Judging by their present rate of progress, they would be lucky to get there within six hours. And that presented a problem. Soon they would be approaching a position where Matsikenyeri and their transport were waiting, and they still had to catch up with Haji and his gang of thugs.

The theory was that Haji, and his men would wait until the early morning before heading west. The configuration of the land meant that Mark and his men would need to travel through that same area to gain access to the border entry point that both teams were heading for. The transport that Mark's team was to use should have arrived in the same broad area and he could only hope that the people who were in charge of that part of the plan would have been aware that all of the natives would not be friendly. Another concern was that they would arrive at that place as the sun came up behind them, rather than in the dead of night which would have been Mark's preferred choice.

There was some good news though.

The one thing that was in the group's favor was the weather conditions – they were atrocious. What was not in their favor was that the position they were aiming for was only known by the coordinates, so they had no feel for the lay of the land or what exactly was in front of them.

As they approached their immediate objective – at least according to the GPS coordinates - the rain started to reduce to a few showers, and the sky started to lighten as the early sunrise struggled to break through the clouds.

At the stage where they came into the approximate area where their transport should have been, they split up into four groups. While Mark had every confidence in the CIA or whoever had organized this, he had to be sure. And he was not about to take any chances this early in the mission. Of most concern were the birds. Mark would have expected the early morning chorus to be in full swing.

But there was only silence.

Mark and Dusty approached on one side of the track with Elliott and Ben on the other side, Brent and Blake took off at a trot to outflank the area on the left, and Mike and Hamish took the right. Using a series of hand signals, they maneuvered into positions where they had the area reasonably well covered. It was an area that backed onto a hill. That gave them the disadvantages because people looking down could spot their movements. On the other hand, the sun was beginning to filter through and that meant that people would be looking down into the darkness of the bush below them.

Mark's thinking was that Haji, and his team would have long since left this area heading due west towards the border with Zimbabwe but that did not tell him enough about the actual route that Haji had taken. If Matsikenyeri was up with the play, and if he had been suitably briefed on the likely movement of other people through this area, he would have avoided any confrontation.

Still, Mark did not want to take any risks.

Finding no evidence that anyone else was in the area, the team closed in on the GPS location.

The briefing back aboard the Vinson had said that they could expect at least two campervan-style vehicles plus a means of transport for the original drivers to get the hell out of there when their job was done. In a clearing that the team now surrounded there was only an old beaten-up Jeep and no sign of anything else.

There was no sign of any men.

And there were no other vehicles.

An exchange of signals with Brent on Mark's left arranged for Brent to move forward and investigate the Jeep. The others arranged themselves prone on the ground to provide covering fire as Brent crept, ever watchful, towards the Jeep. There was an eerie silence that was unusual in this part of Africa. Normally they would have expected that their movements would have disturbed the animals and birds awoken by these intruders as they faced another day in the endless struggle for survival in this inhospitable land.

But there was not a sound.

Mark watched, his feelings a mixture of anticipation and dread, as Brent approached the Jeep. He had his men covering the surrounding area weapons drawn and all switched to single-shot mode.

The rules of engagement were quite simple.

Anyone who moved would be shot and questions asked later.

Brent had all the patience that had been drilled into him in the US Special Forces and despite his size and all the gear he was carrying, he moved with all the stealth of a cat.

He eased himself into a position on the left side of the Jeep just to the rear of the driver's door where he had a good view of the vehicle and its seats. And there was a man. He was sitting in the drivers' seat asleep at the wheel. Silently Brent moved forward towards the door that was not fully closed and he eased it open using the barrel of his M16 rifle. Brent showed no reaction as the man, slowly at first, and then with a final rush fell silently from the cab onto the ground.

The man was dead.

The method of his death was clear. His throat had been cut so viciously that it had almost severed the head. His shirt was drenched in blood and the fact that some blood was still dripping from the body suggested that death had occurred within the last hour. Cutting someone's throat was not the recommended method of termination because the human body in the throes of death could make an extraordinary amount of noise as the plumbing fought to continue its work while waiting for a signal to stop. The person or persons responsible for the dead body did not know that because they could not have avoided being covered in blood.

Or they did not care.

At a signal from Brent, Mark crept forward and joined

Brent at the Jeep. From there both men surveyed the surrounding area peering into the surrounding bush for a hint of someone watching. They finally nodded their agreement. They were alone. Mohamed Haji, or whoever had been responsible for the dead body, appeared to have left the area.

They could not be certain of who was responsible.

Nor did they know who the man was in the jeep.

A further signal from Mark brought Mike to the Jeep, leaving the others still in the undergrowth guarding their flanks. There did not seem to be much point in continuing to creep around, but Mark still did not want to take any risks. Blake and Hamish dived further into the bush and made their way around the Jeep and ended back on the track two hundred yards further up the hill before finally signaling the all-clear.

The rest of the team now stood in the clearing while still holding their M16s at the ready. They examined the Jeep looking for some indicator of who the vehicle belonged to and who the dead body belonged to. The vehicle itself seemed undamaged and it still had the key in the ignition.

That caused Mark to signal that Ben should come forward to investigate the next possible problem. An intact Jeep with keys in the ignition and a dead body in the drivers' seat suggested only one thing.

The Jeep was booby-trapped.

Ben was used to blowing things up, but he would also be the best man to find any bomb without blowing himself up in the process. The rest of the team retired a suitable distance away and watched as Ben got to work. He did not take long before he turned and gave the signal to Mark.

There was no bomb.

Why then had the Jeep been left here with the body?

The only conclusion that could be reached was that it had been left because the people were alerted to the pending arrival of Mark and his team and had to leave in a hurry. Or had the jeep and the body been left as a warning?

But a warning to who?

And a warning about what?

They found a partial answer to some of those questions after searching the pockets of the dead man who now lay on the ground beside the Jeep.

Although he had nothing on him that would identify him as a CIA agent, he still had a drivers' license.

His name was Banga Matsikenyeri.

The team had not even begun their task of following the Haji group and they were already in trouble.

And Mark was an angry man.

Whoever had arranged for Matsikenyeri to deliver their means of transport had effectively signed his death warrant because he was ill-equipped to manage the task. But there was another far more important issue. The mere presence of Matsikenyeri and a couple of empty vehicles could have given Haji ample warning that there was a plan to find him and to follow him on his mission into Zimbabwe.

According to the briefing, the group that Marks's team was supposed to be following would consist of eight men. On the balance of probabilities, Mark would back his team of eight highly trained Special Forces men against the disorganized rabble of Haji's group in any straight-out shooting match.

However, Haji did have a massive advantage.

Mark had no clue of his whereabouts.

Mark had to call it in and the only connection he had

was with Commander Patrick Lewis on board the Carl Vinson. And Lewis was the man who had indicated only yesterday that he had been opposed to the method of organizing their transport.

It was too late now but Mark should have reacted to that comment and arranged things differently.

Mark took out his satellite phone and made the call using the codes that he had been given. There was a moments' delay while the phones were synchronized and then he heard a voice ask how he could be helped. Although the words were in English, they were generated by computer and delivered in the monotonous tone normally reserved for commercial help desks.

He replied 'This is operation Steel Tiger reporting in. We need help. Over!'

'What is the nature of the assistance that you require?' came the inevitable response.

There was a pause in the conversation while Mark thought of a polite response. How do you respond to a computer-generated voice?

Mark ended the call.

He did not have time for this shit!

Dusty, being a lawyer by trade, had been searching in the surrounding bush and finally found what he had been looking for. He called Mark and Elliott over to the spot where he was focused on what lay on the ground. The knife had been thrown from the Jeep by one of the men involved in the murder. They did not care to take it with them. Or they just could not be bothered cleaning it. Or they had plenty of other knives.

While Dusty did not have anything as sophisticated as a forensic evidence collection bag, he placed the knife in a wrapper and placed it in one of the many pockets in his jacket. Maybe he would get the opportunity to present it as evidence sometime in the future.

The team dug a shallow grave on the side of the track and buried the body of Matsikenyeri as best they could. On the advice of Elliott, they sprayed the ground with some tear-gas (or CS Gas - technically Chlorobenzalmalononitrile) to try to keep animals away until the body could be recovered. At least they hoped it would be recovered. Special Forces hated the thought of leaving any bodies behind but there was just no way they would be able to take it with them. There were eight men in the team that had to fit into a Jeep that would normally carry four.

They did not mark the spot. Even in a third-world country, there were the curious who would be unable to resist the temptation to dig up the body. While Banga Matsikenyeri was probably born somewhere in East Africa, he was employed by the United States government – or so they thought. His role had been to help the infiltration of a group of men who were on a covert mission without the knowledge of the Mozambique authorities. And the burial alone would point to the presence of foreigners or someone who was not supposed to be there.

But the team made certain that they had precise GPS coordinates of the grave and would report that to those that they could trust to do something about it.

And when they caught up with Mohamed Haji and could prove that he or his men had been responsible for this murder there would be a reckoning!

Chapter 13

Iran

The Embassy of Iran in Harare was just like any other office in Belgravia and, it was there to deal with such things as documentation and visas for travelers and not much else. The Head of Mission was a gentleman named Ahmad Erfanian and naturally enough he was a member of the Iranian diplomatic service. However, there was another part of the Iran government services that did not fall within the orbit of Erfanians' official duties. They were some services and functions that were not run from the same office.

There were two reasons for this.

Firstly, there was a vast difference between diplomatic services which were concerned with keeping cordial international relations, and the security and intelligence services which were concerned with gathering information on matters of interest to the home office which may, or may not, help with the former. Secondly, the two service functions – one of projecting a diplomatic image and the other one of protecting a political image - were often opposed to each other.

The Ministry of Foreign Affairs of the Islamic Republic of Iran had little choice but to meet the expectations of the world and conduct affairs of state in a reasonable and civilized manner. If they did not meet at least the minimum expectations, then their diplomats would be declared persona-non-grata and be expelled from the countries where they had hoped to maintain a presence. The Ministry of Intelligence and Security had no such restriction. But so that intelligence personnel could gain entry to the various countries around the world where Iran chose to do business or had *interests*, these people had to have the same security and clearance as diplomats. It was just a part of the game played by all countries and, generally speaking, it worked.

Most of the time.

In the case of the Iran Intelligence service and its operations in Zimbabwe, the arrangement had recently been interrupted by pressure from the British Foreign Intelligence Service who took exception to some of the antics of the Iranians. That was fine with the government of Zimbabwe and its President Robert Mugabe who had for years relied on the influence of the earlier colonial rulers of his country to hold other nations in check. However, this did result in an unintended consequence. It meant that the people who had previously been under surveillance by the British were either replaced or changed their modus operandi so that their activities were much harder to follow.

It would have been a big mistake for anyone to underestimate the capability of the Iran intelligence service. It was true that they lacked the sophistication of the likes of the American CIA and the British MI6 which were each supported by massive bureaucracies and by equally large – if unspecified – budgets. They also lacked the sheer brilliance and ruthlessness of the likes of the Israeli

Mossad or the French Direction Générale De La Securite Exterieure or DGSE. On the other hand, the Iranians did have an army of people who individually could foot it with anyone at least in terms of their dedication to their country. Of even greater significance was that - and, unlike their American and British counterparts - they were an integral part of the Iran military organization.

This latter attribute gave the Iranians a massive advantage. They could – and did – resort to physical violence because their aptitude and training were designed to do just that. So, any intelligence operations tended to be planned with military precision.

And the normal measure of the success or failure of any military operations that were undertaken was usually the body count.

Now the Iranians seemed to be up to their old tricks planning an operation that was of particular concern to the British. Although the MI6 had not been specifically informed by their CIA associates that there was an issue, they had nonetheless heard from other sources that the CIA had discovered a plot to kill Zimbabwe President Robert Mugabe. That piece of information had its origins in the Somali branch of the CIA and the specialists at Langley Virginia had somehow concluded that it presented a serious threat. This analysis did not quite fit in with what other sources and MI6's analysis was telling the British Foreign Intelligence Service. However, it was of sufficient importance to raise the alert level in the Zimbabwe office and the MI6 Africa desk in London.

The resulting confusion between the two western allies suited Iran intelligence just fine.

The Iranians were expecting a group of men under the command of Mohamed Haji to enter Zimbabwe and to make their way into Harare. They understood that Haji had given the slip to a group of Americans who had been planning to follow him. In the process of that, Haji had murdered four of the men and taken control of their transport on the other side of the border with Mozambique. That was unfortunate but you could expect collateral damage in an operation of this kind. Especially since the Haji group was not exactly made up of professional soldiers, lacking in training and almost every other desirable attribute. None of the Haji men were Iranian. They were a bunch of ruffians, The role of the group in the scheme was simply to ensure that Haji got to Harare in one piece, and he delivered what he had been asked to do. It was doubtful if the group would survive much beyond this early stage of the exercise. Haji on the other hand should survive provided he did what he was supposed to do.

As far as Iran intelligence could tell, the CIA had only a very limited knowledge of their intentions in Zimbabwe, and they would probably screw up their response anyway.

That was the problem with intelligence services throughout the world. You can gather as much information as you like and have that information analyzed by a team of experts. But that would be a waste of time if either the information was incomplete or incorrect or the information was deliberately supplied – or leaked - to ensure that you reached the wrong conclusion.

The dilemma was not dissimilar to that faced by police in a criminal investigation. Once a theory has been established, more attention is focused on any snippet of new information that tended to support that theory until eventually the theory is taken as fact. The difference with intelligence gathering was the fact that any *theories* became the subject of political interference at a much higher level than police work such that they took on a life of their own.

In the political world, you have the added problems of spin, bias, or just plain political gain. Once the much simpler question of whether or not the analyzed data would be accepted had been answered all bets were off. Much effort would have gone into presenting a case that recommended a particular course of action – otherwise what was the point of the exercise? And that came down to the question of whether the theory just happened to be politically acceptable, or if the theory fitted in with someone's preconceived idea of how things should be.

There was of course the other issue.

How smart were the final decision-makers?

Contrary to popular belief that intelligence people do not rely on assumptions when coming to any conclusion based on whatever data they had, what choice did they have but to do just that? Unless the information that they gathered was gleaned from God himself their story would – by simple definition and except in very extraordinary circumstances - be incomplete. So – they would need to fill in the gaps – or to use the term commonly used - connect the dots - by making an intelligent guess based on experience, prior knowledge of the past performance by the players, and conventional wisdom which predicted the future. It is difficult to describe this process as anything but an assumption.

If the decision-makers were smart enough then they could make their assumptions. And they did make assumptions even when they weren't smart.

And there was yet another issue. Albert Einstein is credited with the saying -*The definition of insanity is doing the same thing over and over again but expecting different results.*

However – there are circumstances where that incisive logic does not necessarily apply. In the medical world for example researchers would run the same tests over, and over, and over again in the hope that they would get the same result. But then cynics would correctly state that the tests were not the same because the tests are conducted on different people. So – that would be to say that the whole matter had to depend on something – and that something would be the individuals involved.

In this Iran Affair, the main individual involved - although the President of his country - was not a trained intelligence officer.

Nor was he necessarily smart.

At a more practical level, the Iranian Intelligence office in Harare Zimbabwe knew that they had a potential problem. Haji had reported that he had encountered a small force over the border in Mozambique and had eliminated it. But not before extracting a few important details from the men they had captured – and then murdered. This force – thought to have come from the CIA office in the Mozambique capital of Maputo – claimed to have the simple role of providing transport for a much more lethal group that had been landed further to the east by the US Navy and which was making its way towards the border. Haji, in true belligerent style – and acting like a terrorist rather than an intelligence officer - had simply commandeered the transport, disposed of the bodies, but left their leader's body behind as a warning to the following force.

The Iranian Intelligence head of station in Harare was not too pleased with this action. While the CIA was not particularly active in this part of the world, and the United States people were not exactly friendly with their Iranian counterparts, it still did not pay to piss them off with no obvious gain to be had. Nonetheless, they had been instructed by their masters in Teheran to supply whatever assistance Haji and his team should ask for. They were not informed of the purpose of Haji's visit to Zimbabwe. Therefore, they were also not informed of the methods that Haji would employ to achieve whatever his true purpose was.

They only knew from what little they did know that the order to support him had come directly from the President of Iran and that the President had the backing of their Supreme Leader.

It would therefore be a very brave man who would question the mission.

Or a very stupid man.

Chapter 14

Conflict of Interest

Ever since that horrible day of September 11, 2001, the United States Central Intelligence Agency had felt somewhat left out of matters of national strategic importance and the decision-making that resulted from the deliberation of such matters. It was not as though the role of the CIA in the United States Intelligence and Security Services had changed all that much. It was just that the head of the CIA no longer got to brief the President daily as had been the case before 9/11. Sure, the CIA had a major input to the analysis that was presented, but others took all the credit especially when the analysis was believed to be on point. Now the defenseless CIA would be blamed for everything that went wrong even though their role was to simply provide an analysis of information that others would present or act on. And receive no credit for anything that went right.

However, the latest decision had been made, not at a scheduled *Briefing*, but at what could only be described as an informal gathering of the presidential inner circle. Unlike the more formal meetings, there would be no official record of what was discussed or how the decision had been arrived at. Certainly, there would be a recording of who said what as was the way with any conversation in the White House. That record was only used by the security people and would probably never be replayed – unless the President happened to be assassinated on that particular day. This situation would suit the leaders of the security and intelligence agencies who were present at the meeting because they could rightly claim that the decision had been reached without the full facts and proper analysis. The President had made *his* decision on that basis.

With the benefit of hindsight, the DNI and the NSA should have pressured those assembled at the meeting to pause before agreeing on the course of action that they were now committed to.

Now that a decision had been made to do something and how that something was to be carried out, there was another complication. The CIA, which had been responsible for producing the information on the subject, was not to be involved in this mission.

And there was another complication.

Why anyone in his right mind would want to protect the life of President Robert Mugabe of Zimbabwe was beyond comprehension to most of the members of the intelligence community. There may have been some underlying political motive that favored Mugabe staying alive, but none sprung readily to mind. And on balance, Mugabe should have been dead already. At least the new CIA Assistant Deputy Director Intelligence thought so and he had at least the tacit agreement of his Director James Schlesinger.

The CIA had plenty of data still pouring in from all parts of the world, and their vast bureaucracy still included some of the best analysts on the planet. Any intelligence activity in which the United States was involved had to affect the work done by Langley. So, it was no surprise that they had been to the fore in getting information out of Somalia concerning a person of interest - Mohamed Haji - and a band of followers who had been drawn like moths to a flame.

By any definition, Mohamed Haji was a terrorist. Haji had appeared several times in the past in reports from various parts of the world. Nothing in these reports suggested that anything but a thug for hire.

It was believed that he had been born in Saudi Arabia to Sunni Muslim parents. That would have suggested that he would be anti-Iranian although a gambler would not put his house on it. However, he had featured in several missions believed to be conducted on behalf of the Iranian Revolutionary Guards which meant that he was associated with Iran Intelligence. As a consequence of this, he had made it onto the US terrorist watch list and his movements would be monitored by the CIA and every other intelligence organization that had half a brain.

Now – what was he doing in Somalia?

While the CIA had a lesser presence in Somalia than had previously been the case, it still had a network of informants in that country. The information coming from these informants was not exactly the most dependable, but it did have a curious consistency. Apart from miscellaneous groups that had simply been formed to fight whoever became the government, there was a core of groups that had relationships with terrorist organizations throughout the middle east. Of these the Al Shabaab military group – an offshoot of al Qaeda – was keen on claiming responsibility for any event that could gain headlines in the world news for all the wrong reasons. So, it had its informants that then fed information to anyone who would listen.

From this shambolic background, it was no surprise that the CIA had first had a sniff of the reason why Haji had suddenly appeared in Somalia. Then that had rapidly grown into a plot to kill an African President. Careful analysis of their information by the CIA.s East Africa section had concluded that the most likely target was President Robert Mugabe of Zimbabwe. They had based this conclusion on intelligence sourced in Somalia from what remained of their sources dating back to the 1990s when the United States had led a United Nations Task Force – UNITAK – to try to sort out the Somali civil war. Although the CIA would admit that these sources were pretty ragged and somewhat unreliable, they had other intelligence *sources* in Zimbabwe which were reliable. Well - as dependable as any intelligence information could be.

Intuitively that deduction made sense.

If you were to try to assassinate a President, it may as well be someone well known. Even if that fame was for all the wrong reasons.

The US government, since their withdrawal from Somalia, had no specific policy on this part of Africa. It had very little interest in the health, or otherwise, of the erratic dictator of the country of Zimbabwe. It was not a subject that figured much on the list of things that the CIA had to worry about.

Against this background, all that the CIA could do was simply monitor the situation. It could assist when needed. Or run interference. Or take other more drastic – although admittedly covert – measures, depending on what, if anything, was required.

The CIA Head of Station in southern Somalia was a man called Jared Hackett who was a very experienced agent and not the type to raise any issue without just cause. He had recorded the apparent departure of Mohamed Haji and flagged his report as *Urgent Attention Required*. He had three very obvious reasons, and one not so obvious, for the urgency flag. Firstly - Mohamed Haji was very much a person of interest having been identified as a suspect in several deaths or disappearances in both Somalia and elsewhere. Secondly – it was believed that he was heading for Zimbabwe, a place where the CIA had no record of his having been before and had no valid reason that the CIA agent could think of to go there now. Except! Thirdly – Haji was rumored to be aiming to kill someone by way of assassination and the talk was that his target was a President of an African country. Since the only President who would be in Zimbabwe for the foreseeable future was Robert Mugabe, it did not need a rocket scientist to work the rest out.

The other reason – and overriding all the afore-said reasons - was the known relationship between Haji and Iranian Intelligence and the fact that Haji was still on the list of wanted terrorists. The fact that he was on the move should alone be sufficient information to raise a red flag. And do something about it.

The CIA Somali head of station was not surprised to receive a response from Langley which indicated that the journey of Haji would be checked by the United States and allied Naval forces that were patrolling off the east coast of Africa. What he could not see were the messages that were passed between Langley and their masters, or the reaction to them. The CIA was told that the matter was being dealt with by the office of the Director of National Intelligence and that they were to continue monitoring the situation and sending any further information as they saw fit.

The CIA was not pleased with being left out of the action even though they doubted whether any action could be taken that would affect the outcome. But, in any case, they could do nothing about it.

Luck is a factor in all walks of life. The Irish Republican Army – the infamous IRA - one of the most ruthless terrorist organizations on the planet and - being Irish – factored *Luck* into every mission that they ever planned. However, most other organizations, on both sides of any conflicts between good and evil, try not to depend on it. They believe that good analysis and good fieldwork should eliminate luck from the equation - both good and bad.

Sometimes the shape of the bureaucratic structure tends to get in the way of that. But this time it did play a role in what happened next.

In the CIA Intelligence Division, they have an Assistant Director for Asian Pacific, Latin America, and African Analysis and he has a separate section to deal with each area of the world that lay within this vast region. The section head for Somalia Affairs was a young – but relatively senior - agent by the name of Ralph Kovacevich, who had previously been with the section that dealt with Afghanistan affairs. In another part of the CIA organization under the Deputy Director National Clandestine Service, they have the Counter-Terrorism Centre and in that division, they had an attractive young lady called Lindsay Berquist, who had previously been with the Counterintelligence Division. The fact that these two disparate people from different parts of the vast bureaucracy that made up the CIA got together could be attributed to either luck or lust.

Or both.

Both of these parts of the CIA organization had a task, amongst the myriad of things that kept them busy, to keep a watching brief on the antics of Iran as they affected their particular areas of the world. This meant contacts with the likes of Mohamed Haji.

Whatever the reason, Ralph, and Lindsay while they were out on a date could not get their heads away from their work, Kovacevich happened to see Mark Taylor who he vaguely knew from his earlier position on the Afghanistan section entering a safe house on the outskirts of town. And Berquist happened to recognize Stephanie Gompert who was entering the same house. Kovacevich knew of Mark Taylor from a mission into Afghanistan not that long ago. Berquist knew Ms. Gompert before she was transferred to the office of the DNI. It may have been completely coincidental. But then why were Taylor and Gompert - two people from very different backgrounds - meeting at all?

The following morning this unusual meeting was mentioned at their respective staff briefings. For no other reason than it sparked the inquisitive nature of the CIA, a case officer was assigned to look further into it. They were particularly curious about the involvement of Mark Taylor since his last involvement with CIA matters had resulted in one of their senior officers being arrested - and subsequently dying. Well –being killed. It was not as though they felt any allegiance to the dead officer. Stephen Rodriguez got what he deserved. But still, the circumstances that they had happened upon did seem to be unusual.

What if Gompert and Taylor were now involved in the same thing.

It is not unusual for one part of the vast US intelligence and security services to spy on another part. Although it was unusual for the CIA to get involved in such nonsense on American soil. But these were extenuating circumstances. And it was good training for CIA personnel.

The safe house was placed under surveillance. Nothing happened at all on the first day, but on the second day, there was a flurry of activity that involved a very powerful team being assembled, including the two aforesaid people Taylor and Gompert.

The wonders of modern science made the task quite easy. Photographs were taken and transmitted to Langley and the results fired back to the agents, and upstairs to the seventh floor. As a consequence of that, another two agents were assigned with the specific task of monitoring the movements of Mark Taylor. Although the previous mission that Mark had been on was legitimate – at least some people thought so – he was nonetheless regarded as something of a pariah in certain quarters by the CIA. There was obvious disquiet at having someone effectively spying on one of their fraternities – even if it turned out that the spying had resulted in the revelation that one of their senior members was not exactly working in the best interest of the CIA or the country.

When it became clear that Mark Taylor was to embark on an overseas trip, arranged at very short notice in collusion with the DNI, the CIA operations directorate asked for authority to continue monitoring the situation even if that meant that they had to employ other resources to assist. The answer they got was that they should continue on the condition that their actions were to be covert and that the task was to be handled entirely in-house.

That told the agents part of the story. Mark Taylor was once again off on a mission that may or may not involve their department. The part of the story that they were not told was that their bosses were pissed at having been cut out of the mission. The CIA had gathered the information that had initiated the decision to proceed. And the CIA was the agency within the government that had the authority and the means to implement a mission. The only problem was – the CIA had no idea what that was.

Well – they would take steps to see what could be done about that!

When Mark Taylor arrived in Cape Town South Africa the local CIA agents received a surprise. Instead of continuing to use commercial airlines, Mark and his group switched to a United States Navy replenishment aircraft –the Grumman C2-A Greyhound. That made it quite clear where they were headed. The Greyhound was designed for Carrier onboard delivery. It had a range of about 14 hundred miles. The closest United States aircraft carrier was the USS Carl Vinson which was sailing off the east coast of Africa. If that was the destination, it would require the Greyhound to refuel before it got there. It did not require a rocket scientist to work out that from onboard the Carl Vinson they could, and probably would transfer to a helicopter and head for land somewhere on the east coast of Africa.

And the minions at the CIA did not take long to relate two simple facts. Mark Taylor was heading towards the east coast of Africa, and their intelligence reports showed that he was headed in roughly the same direction as the Iranian-sponsored Mohamed Haji.

It was the speed with which everything had happened which attracted the particular attention of the CIA Operations Division. Together with other intelligence, they reached the logical conclusion that this may be the basis of a mission to prevent Mohamed Haji from killing President Robert Mugabe.

Then they heard of a curious request made by the

Department of Defense for support for an operation in Mozambique. That request reached the US Embassy in Matupo which had a Defense attaché but no formal CIA representative. The Defense attaché was unable to help, so he contacted the Embassy in Harare which did have an official CIA cell. The CIA station chief who had very little experience in any physical work passed the request onto the British MI6 who were far better equipped to handle it. In doing so he stressed that the job was relatively simple and was not particularly important. Because the British regarded Zimbabwe as their patch and did not see why the American CIA would involve themselves in this part of the world they agreed. The job was given to a gentleman named Banga Matsikenyeri – a native of the country but on the payroll of MI6. His briefing was to find out what the CIA was up to. And at the same time, to arrange a couple of trucks.

The people at Langley were not too pleased with this turn of events which had the effect of lessening their involvement. However, they had to admit that they just did not have the resources and had to accept the arrangement. What they could do was to escalate their interest from merely running surveillance operations to running an active mission. The people in the CIA had a history of acting independently from their political masters when a particular set of events did not quite suit their purpose. Or rather – what they perceived to be their purpose.

The role of the Central Intelligence Agency is to make national security intelligence assessments as directed by the President. But Presidents change from time to time. There is a much wider picture than would be a Presidents view of the world. And there is a much longer-term view of events than could be envisaged by a man thinking in four-year blocks of time. If this all meant that for the CIA to meet its objectives, they would need to take a different course of action, then so be it. The CIA, and indeed most organizations in the security and intelligence business, rarely embark on missions that involve murders, assassinations, or simulated suicides. That is not to say that they never got into situations that involved where some people got killed. When they did get involved, it was usually in situations where their involvement was clandestine or covert. Or their involvement could be denied. Or at least could not be traced back to them.

Or could not be traced back to their political masters.

In keeping with the rules and traditions of the CIA, this would have to be a *Black Operation*. The CIA is the only organization that is legally allowed to conduct a covert action, under United States law. And then there is so much oversight involved that you would wonder why they bother trying to keep anything secret. If the mission is covert, that means it is deniable – the sponsor is concealed. If the mission is clandestine, that means the whole operation is hidden from both friend and foe. But to legally conduct a *Black Operation,* then that had to have the approval of the President. And that would require knowledge by the US House Intelligence Committee – admittedly after President approval. That is where things could get messy because the involvement of politicians and secrets was just asking for trouble.

So, in this case, to conduct a mission that was both covert and clandestine, and to ensure that there was no leak of their intentions, the CIA would not seek permission until after the event.

It was no big deal as they were unlikely to incur the wrath of their masters. If the mission resulted in President Robert Mugabe living, then the CIA would just forget the whole thing and write the time spent on this job as training. If Mugabe died then the CIA, who had already identified the plot, and had been told by the DNI to keep out of it, could justifiably say that they were just conducting a passive role to witness the inevitable but were prevented from interfering by instruction from no less than the President himself.

The CIA team was increased to four by the addition of two men from the South African State Security Agency. This had to be agreed to by the CIA and its sister organization in South Africa but that turned out to be a mere formality when it was explained as a training exercise.

The South African security organization came about as a result of the joining of three separate entities – the South Africa Secret Service known as the SASS, the Defense services National Intelligence Agency known by the acronym NIA and the South Africa Police Service known as SAPS. The resultant chaotic organization rarely, at least officially, dabbles in matters outside of Africa. Apart from the passive role of monitoring what their neighbors were up, rarely got involved in matters outside the country.

But could not resist the opportunity to dabble in this one.

The South Africans enjoyed a reasonable relationship with Zimbabwe at the administrative level, despite the fractious nature of the relationship of their leaders. The South Africans were anxious to project themselves as a leader in the African Union but there were more practical considerations. They could not hope to compete in the security and intelligence stakes with the likes of the American CIA, the British MI6, Chinese MSS, or the Russian FSB. However, on the African continent, all countries had some form of a security and intelligence organization and they all looked to jealously guard their little bit of territory. But – *and it was a rather Big But* – in the modern era they just had to make arrangements with other countries, both within the African community and elsewhere if they were to have any hope of trying to keep up with the play. With a collection of over fifty states involved from a diverse collection of cultures and religions, it was a miracle that someone had been able to get them all together in the first place.

The CIA team from South Africa was assembled in Pretoria just to the north of Johannesburg and about two hundred fifty miles south of Zimbabwe. They were assigned an Army helicopter for the early part of their journey. That made life much easier for all concerned. Instead of trying to get up to Mozambique and then follow Mark Taylor who in turn would be trying to follow Haji they would work their way up to the border between South Africa and Zimbabwe. From there would be assigned a couple of all-terrain vehicles, GPS gear, and communications equipment which would keep them in touch with their controllers in Pretoria.

Then, they would wait for things to happen.

Chapter 15

Harare

The road that Marks team were traveling along was not very wide but at least it was relatively flat and straight. Mark had tried to keep as far behind the jeep and the campervans in which Hadi and his team were traveling to avoid them being recognized as having any interest in the visitors from Somalia. That task was made easier by the binoculars that had been provided by the USS Carl Vinson. They were Steiner Military Marine 10 x 50 – and could make a target many miles away look as though it was only a few feet away. There was a small price to pay. The magnification was so good that it was hard to hold the image steady enough to see what was going on. But, in this part of Zimbabwe that did not matter all that much. That was until they could see the skyline of the capital of Harare in the far distance.

After the disaster where Mark and his team, were supposed to have been provided with vehicles by Banga Matsikenyeri they had little choice but to crowd into the Jeep and head for the town of Chimoio. There they managed to procure a couple of campervans from a rental company that had connections across the border in Zimbabwe. Nonetheless, the Manager was not overly impressed by the prospect of his trucks disappearing over the border. He also seemed to be concerned that his stocks were running low due to an earlier and similar request that he had received from a Zimbabwean. Mark ignored that and produced a bunch of American dollars, and that seemed to settle the deal. The Manager was bemused by the men and the gear that was loaded into the campervans but held his peace.

Mark thought about sneaking his team across the border without using the official crossing. However, that proved more difficult than he had envisaged. For the most part, the border between Mozambique and Zimbabwe is designated by markers rather than an actual fence. But finding a place where they could cross in broad daylight without having to travel a reasonable distance with no roads to speak of was just too difficult. The problem was that their contact was to have provided them with a briefing on the border crossing. That now would not happen. Their choice now would be to request help from the US Embassy in Harare.

Time was the issue. It would take at least four hours for an official or a set of documents to travel from Harare to Mutare and in the intervening period, Haji and his gang could be anywhere. And at the same time, the Embassy staff would be concerned about the news that Matsikenyeri was dead. While they would still be prepared to help – did Mark have the time to get involved in explanations? The important thing was to find Haji.

Still – in this case, Mark was only the messenger.

Mark had no choice now than to call on the NRO to work their magic and try to identify where Haji and his men had gone. In this respect, they had a couple of advantages.

The NRO had two satellites that had originally been assigned to the Navy for surveillance of the waters off the east coast of Africa during their recent exercise. One of these was in a geosynchronous orbit twenty-two thousand miles out in space permanently checking activity off the Somali coast but at that distance, a small correction could change the focus by many thousands of miles back on the Earth. This could be used to instruct other satellites to take high-resolution imagery. The other one was an LEO (Low Earth Orbit) satellite - and was routed to the west to cover what was happening anywhere along its flight path and could take detailed photographs of anything happening on the ground. Between the two satellites, it was simply a matter of a temporary realignment of cameras for a few minutes and then coordinating the results and the computers did the rest. And there wasn't that much traffic in the border area.

Imagery had located a jeep which appeared to have been abandoned only a couple of miles from where Mark had found the body of Banga Matsikenyeri and suggested that they would not be going anywhere anytime soon. They also located a jeep and a couple of campervans that had traveled from the same location and were now located in the city of Mutare just inside the Zimbabwe/ Mozambique border. While this information involved a certain amount of speculation it was nonetheless quite solid. But it still required to be verified and there was only one way to do that. Mark would need to get his team to Mutare before the campervans left.

This was all based-on assumptions.

But there was another assumption that had Mark puzzled.

Why did it appear that Haji was waiting for them to catch up?

The team had split into three with Brent and Blake taking the lead in the jeep, Mike, Hamish, and Ben in the middle, and Mark, Dusty, and Elliott bringing up the rear as they raced to the border. Putting aside his paranoia, Mark did not expect to have much trouble crossing from Mozambique to Zimbabwe. It was presumed that the documents that they had been provided with would have the correct visas. None of them were carrying anything illegal. Guns were allowed in both Mozambique and Zimbabwe - provided the carrier could prove just cause. Drugs were not allowed.

However, the civil war that had been going on in Mozambique in one form or another since the country gained independence from Portugal in 1975 made the border guards on both sides reluctant to let anyone pass without a long - and largely pointless - exercise in repetition.

Their cover story had been organized by the US State Department and involved security checks on the consular offices in both countries. Even so, it beggared belief that the checks that were conducted were needed for travel overland. For not the first time Mark discovered that the distribution of a few United States dollars seemed to clear up any confusion on the Mozambique side of the border and the team was free to get on with their journey.

When they arrived in Mutare, Mark was surprised to find the campervans carrying Haji and his team were still in the city. Mark had a difficult task in trying to rationalize how Mohamed Haji had managed to convince the guards on both sides of the border to let him and his thugs through. Then he had answered the riddle by his own experience. Assuming that they did not have the same kind of documents as Marks team – with the support of Iranian Intelligence, Haji would also have had access to the greenback.

Mark had confirmation of his original suspicions that the Haji team had been waiting for Mark to catch up. No sooner had Mark and his team been cleared through the border post into Zimbabwe than they left on the road to Harare.

At the most, the distance between Mutare and Harare was about one hundred seventy miles which would take little more than four hours to travel even considering the state of Zimbabwe roads.

There was very little traffic on the road and so Mark's team kept some distance behind Haji – this time with Mark and Dusty in the lead vehicle in an attempt to at least add some variety. Maybe Haji knew they were there. It did not matter. It did seem farcical to be following at least two vehicles that had been hired by the US government. And there would be a reckoning on that score as well in due course.

They could tell where the jeep and the campervans were by the dust, so it was not too hard to follow.

As they got closer to the capital, could see another trail of dust. This one was coming from the direction of Harare and towards them. At first, Dusty, who was driving at the time, made a mental note that he would have to remember to keep to the left since the last time he had been behind a wheel the people had driven on what he regarded as the correct right side of the road.

But then a strange thing happened.

As the vehicle approached the jeep that was leading Hajis team, it slowed, flashed the headlights, and then pulled off to the side of the road. The jeep also slowed and pulled off and stopped about twenty yards further up the road. The driver of the Jeep got out of the vehicle and walked towards the new arrival. Mark immediately got on his satellite phone and told Brent who was following Dusty to keep going while he stopped to investigate. He then told Dusty to pull over while he focused his binoculars on the meeting.

The vehicle that had come from the direction of Harare was a standard black Ford station wagon – not what would normally be seen outside the city. The driver was a white man of about six feet tall, thin, bearded, and looked to be in his 50's. He wore a grey suit he was all grey – suit, hair, beard, skin – only his shoes were black, and they were polished so that he looked as though he had just stepped out of an office. From the distance, it was impossible to tell what was being said even with the binoculars.

However, it was not difficult to read the body language. The man who Mark had assumed to be Haji was the man in charge. But the man in a grey suit had some conditions to add to the discussion to which Haji reluctantly agreed. That discussion resulted in Haji returning to the jeep, picking up two parcels, and returning to the place where the white man was standing and handed the parcels over. Before Haji got back, Mark had the opportunity to get a good view of the grey man. He got an excellent picture of the man using the long-range camera given him by the Navy that he had never thought would be useful until now because it had been a bit on the bulky side. It was a combination of technologies taking the sniper scope Leopold Mark 4 and combining it with the Canon F1 SLR Navy camera. It made for distortion depending on the light and atmospheric conditions, but neither of these was a factor here.

The two men exchanged a few more words while Mark tried to get both of them in the same picture but that attempt failed. Then they shook hands which event Mark did record and the two men retreated to their vehicles. Both vehicles then left heading in the direction of Harare.

Mark again called Brent.

'Can you follow that Ford? I want to know where he goes. We will continue following Haji.'

He then turned to Dusty.

'Ok – we had a better close up the following distance. We are getting near the capital, and we have no idea what will happen. We do not want to lose them! Brent should be able to pick up the old man.'

Mark and Dusty followed the jeep and the two campervans into the city and were surprised that they turned south and then west, and then ended up stopping outside a house in Bishops Gaul Avenue. Which was about as far from the President's residence in the north of the city as you could get and still be in the same country.

No sooner had they stopped than Brent came through on the satellite phone.

'You never guess where our friend ended up. He has driven straight into the United States Embassy.'

The time difference between Washington DC and Harare is six hours, So, calling Harold Taylor at three o'clock in the afternoon Harare time should find him in the office and just getting his feet under the desk for a full days' work.

Harold's line lit up, but there was no message to say who the caller was, so he ignored the call. A minute later, the secretary to the CIA Assistant Inspector came through and simply said 'It is your son Mark calling from Harare. He insists on speaking to you!'

That came as a shock.

Harold had heard that Mark had been recruited by the President to undertake a mission in Africa. That was none of his business. In the true spirit of compartmentalization and *need to know*, he had taken no interest in what his son may be up to. However, Harold concluded that it would be nice to talk to Mark and find out what his fellow bureaucrats down the corridor probably would not know.

At least for now.

So, he took the call.

'Good morning, Mark – or should I say afternoon where you are. And to what do I owe the pleasure of this call?'

The relationship between Harold and his only son Mark had always been a strange one. Probably because the father had always been a spook. And probably because Mark had, at least until recently, been in the US military who had a somewhat jaundiced view of the civilian intelligence organization that paid Harold his salary. For all of that, the two of them often relied on each other when it mattered.

'Father – good morning to you. Now – have you got your machine switched on? I want to send you a photograph of a person who I need you to identify.'
Harold had to smile. Sure – Marks's knowledge of computers was, and always would be, far superiors to his own. But – Yes – he did know where the on/Off switch was!

'Ok – send it through.'
The grainy picture of the man who had been standing by the road into Harare slowly came through pixel by pixel onto Harold's screen. Because of the problems of getting the picture from the camera to the laptop, the image came through feet first, which gave them time to talk.

Even that was silly because, while Harold did not like to interfere in matters that did not officially concern him, he still had the old craving to know what was happening out in the real world.

Harold Taylor's job was to investigate the CIA people who had strayed or had committed some demeanor that the powers that be thought would bring the CIA into disrepute. And investigating that kind of stuff was not half as exciting as the life of a spook.

So, it was a delayed reaction,

But a reaction that shook both of them.

'Where did you get this from?' was the immediate response from Harold when the face in the photograph became clear on his screen.

'It was taken by the roadside outside of Harare. I just need to know who that is. Do you know him?'

Harold was still being cautious although it was fairly evident that he knew the man.

'Mark! Why do you need to know?'

Mark was used to his father's pontification,

But Marks's patience was starting to run a little thin.

'Father, do you know him or not? Or do I have to use my sources? You do know that it is very unlikely that he would be someone that my other job for you guys would exclude me from. I do have not time for that but if I have to, I will try another line. You presumably know who I am working for, but I cannot trust my normal channels of communications – as per bloody usual!'

'Ok. He is Nigel Checksfield. He is CIA Head of Station in Zimbabwe.'

Checksfield had not had the most distinguished career in the CIA and that was why he had ended up in Zimbabwe.

It was not as though he had done anything wrong. It is just that Checksfield had never done anything to make him noticed by people in authority.

When the position of Head of the Political section Zimbabwe became vacant, Checksfield was appointed to it more by default than by qualification. And that was just another job. In Harare, the Head of the section simply meant that it was another desk to fill because there was no staff in the office save for a young lady who answered the telephone - and did the filing - and not much else. However, it did make life easier for the Ambassador because with this appointment he did not have to *pretend* that the CIA Head of Station was something else. Now he could happily introduce him as a legitimate head of a section rather than a Cultural Attaché or whatever nonsense the CIA came up with when nominating some diplomatic title that served to hide what Checksfield did. Which was not very much anyway. Sure, half a dozen agents were running around to spy on other governments rather than on Zimbabwe, who Checksfield was responsible for. But rarely did anything come up that anyone could get too excited about.

Then Checksfield did something quite silly. And totally out of character.

It wasn't entirely his fault. His office lady was working late after a flood of mail had been received by the Embassy as a result of the Zimbabwe elections. Some people in the local media seemed to think that the United States Embassy's opinion on that subject would be of interest to their readers. Which it wouldn't. And the US had virtually zero interest in something that would be a foregone conclusion. That was even though the result would be reached more by manipulation of the vote count rather than by the vote itself.

On this particular day, the bulk of the staff at the

embassy had been invited to *drinkies* at the British Embassy. And someone had forgotten or omitted to invite Checksfield., He decided to help with the paperwork. At the end of this menial work, he and his lady assistant decided to have a quiet drink on their own since neither of them had much else to do.

One thing led to another. The lady who was a US citizen by the name of Julia Benkovic had come to Zimbabwe to be with her husband who was a businessperson with interests in gold bullion and other precious metals. It turned out to be more than just precious metals that attracted him to Zimbabwe. He had dumped Julia in favor of a South African lady who had proved more attractive, And, she had important contacts in Zimbabwe that Julia lacked.

Julia Benkovic did not dare to return to her home in California and to face the ignominy of having been abandoned by her man. She just stayed on in Zimbabwe and lived a lonely life in a flat with only a housekeeper for company.

And no one to talk to.

Checksfield on the other hand had a wife back in the United States who he could not convince to come out to Zimbabwe. Her latest excuse was that their two boys were about to embark on university education, and it was important that they had at least one of their parents on hand to support and encourage them. The fact that the boys were at university on the west coast of the United States and their home was on the east coast told Checksfield that their marriage was dead in all but name.

On this particular day, the problem for Checksfield started when Julia began to cry, probably because it was so long since anyone had bothered to listen to her. And, by way of consolation, he was able to sympathize with her predicament at being abandoned so far from home. Checksfield began to get emotional because he could not remember when anyone had confided in him on so sensitive a subject as their failed married life. He placed what he thought was a fatherly arm around her shoulders and she dutifully placed her head into his chest and continued to cry. Eventually, Checksfield offered to drive her home because he judged that she was in no condition to drive herself. Which offer she gladly accepted.

Once they arrived at her modest home - actually an apartment - which was not that far from the Embassy - she begged him to come in for a meal and some company. Having nothing better to do and still miffed at having been abandoned by his fellow workers, he gladly accepted. Although Zimbabwe has a little-known wine business Checksfield managed to find a couple of local bottles of Cabinet Sauvignon which Julia was quite partial to, and they enjoyed a pleasant meal each drowning their particular sorrows in red wine.

Then things got slightly out of hand. Nigel Checksfield ended up staying most of the night. It was not exactly rampant sex since neither of them had much experience in such matters, but they did make love. And more than once since their first fumbling attempt at lovemaking turned into a bit of a mess.

Rumors have a life all their own. During the following weeks, the two people had several evening liaisons a couple of which extended to overnight stays, and one of those was witnessed by Julia's housekeeper – a Zimbabwe local called Tanya. And the story could have ended there had it not been for a casual conversation between Tanya and her friend Sanjaya who engaged in the same trade.

To make the story more exciting Tanya mentioned

that the lady she serviced worked at the United States Embassy. And to add some intrigue she guessed that the man looked like he was someone important and worked for the same Embassy. The whole point of this exchange of irrelevant chatter was that Sanjaya was a cleaner at the Iran Embassy and Tanya merely wanted to show that she too had friends in high places.

Sanjaya thought nothing of repeating the story to one of the ladies who worked in a senior position at the Iran Embassy – well she was a filing clerk – for a bit of a giggle. That casual conversation was overheard by the First Secretary who happened to be a member of the intelligence community and who had as one of his assigned tasks to seek to disrupt the US consular service.

And this presented him with a unique opportunity to meet this requirement without needing to do very much at all.

When Checksfield next called in to see Julia at her home, he was met by a young man who at first seemed lost and simply asked for directions. That delay was just to allow time for his colleague to make certain that they were not being followed and that they had the right man. Then they invited Checksfield to take a ride around the block while they had a chat. It was not that they wanted Checksfield to give them any secrets or to betray the oath that he had sworn to defend the constitution of the United States et cetera. All that they needed him to do was collect drugs and pass them on to people of their choosing. And that would be made easy for him because those people would be identified with each shipment and most of them – although not all – he would be meeting with anyway as he moved around in the diplomatic circus. And just to assure him that it was all legitimate, no mention would be made to the associates of his affair with Julia.

Just so long as he behaved himself, of course.

Mark had to have a plan but whatever he had thought of on the drive from the Mozambique border was thrown into disarray by the revelation that the CIA in Harare could be compromised.

A plan had to be simple and could only make limited assumptions about what the other players would do. The aim was to try to prevent the assassination of President Mugabe. That meant that they had to find out what Mugabe's movements would be for the foreseeable future and from that where and when he would present an opportunity for someone to kill him. As a general rule, Mugabe would be safe while he was at his residence. He would be surrounded by his security guards. He would be protected by extensive electronic alarms which would make an attempt on his life at that place a suicide mission for whoever tried it. Not that a suicide mission would be out of the question. And that was of course assuming that an attempt would be made without inside assistance. If that were the case, there was nothing that Mark or anyone else could do about it.

So, the question was - Where would Mugabe be vulnerable? Leaving aside cooperation from someone inside his security service, and assuming the same security arrangements would be replicated wherever he went, there would be few opportunities. Assuming an external agent such as Mohamed Haji would be the person to carry out the attempt, the answer was that he would be vulnerable while he was on the move. And probably in the time at which he was transiting between his mode of transport and the place he was arriving at or leaving.

The next question was – just how capable were Haji and his team?

The answer to that question was complex. Haji had a reputation of a killer. It could therefore be assumed that he was at least capable of organizing a killing. As for the rest of his team – you had to assume that they could kill. After all, they were thugs. But would they be any good at killing? And would they be able to plan a killing in Zimbabwe, which, despite the disorganization, was not the same shambles that they would be used to in Somalia?

The next question was – What means would be used?

Based on the history of assassination conducted around the world, it was probable that the weapon of choice would be a rifle. That assumption was in turn based on another assumption. You had to assume that the killer – or killers - would want to go undetected. And they would also want to escape the ensuing chaos without being detected. To achieve these objectives there would need to be a certain amount of planning that went into the business of finding a suitable. There were practical considerations. You would need to have a good view of the target. You would need to avoid the crowds. It would be preferable that the position of the shooter be elevated. The shooter would need to have a clear path to get out of Dodge when he had completed his task. And, of course, there was an even more practical issue – the target needed to be there or thereabouts and in plain sight at the appointed time.

Then came the question of who would the shooter be? Mark had a cynical view of that. He doubted that Mohamed Haji would be the shooter. From what he knew of the man, Haji would be the type of person who lets others do his dirty work. That way he could take all the credit for a successful killing. And blame someone else if it failed.

The theory was that Haji was conducting a mission

on behalf of Iranian Intelligence. In that respect, he would need to be careful that the mission met their criteria. That could both simplify and complicate the issue. The reason for this was simple. Despite the high-powered briefings that Mark had attended and the extraordinary lengths that people had gone to getting him this far - no one appeared to have answered the question – What was the motivation for the killing?

It could be that the role of Haji was simply to deliver the assassin to the right place and then do his usual trick. He would simply disappear! That meant that everyone in his gang had to be watched.

And there was another issue. The normal rules of an assassination plot may not apply in this case. Haji may not care a toss whether the shooter would escape or die in the attempt. Then there was the more obvious situation. The attempt may be planned as a suicide mission. Then the shooter would not give a toss either!

Back on board the USS Carl Vinson, it had seemed like a straightforward mission. They had to follow Mohamed Haji and to interpose themselves between him and President Robert Mugabe and that was about it. Now there was an added complication. Well, two complications.

Since he had arrived in Harare, Haji had not gone anywhere near the Presidential residence. He had however gone near the last people that he would have been expected to contact – the United States CIA!

This meant that for Mark to have any chance of achieving anything he had to watch three people and he only had three vehicles and eight people in his team. The rule that he had always exercised on missions of this nature was that you operated in pairs. Which was fine if everyone stayed awake 24/7.

Since saving money would not be high on the list of priorities the first thing Mark did was to hire another vehicle.

But - he could not go out a hire another couple of men, could he?

Mark allocated his first team – in this case, Blake, and Dusty - to watch the Mugabe residence. His second team – in this case, Mike, and Hamish - to watch Haji but with two vehicles because Haji had a total of seven people in his team. And they could go anywhere as a group or individually at any time. His third team – Mark, and Brent - would watch the US Embassy. At this early stage, Ben and Elliott were in reserve and were instructed to work out some kind of roster, before things got too complicated.

Of course, Mark was assuming that all the aforesaid people they were watching had remained in place while he was getting organized.

In the case of President Robert Mugabe of Zimbabwe, they did not even know if he was in town, let alone in residence. In the case of the US Embassy, Mark had no idea how many people worked there. In the case of the Haji team, they could all be asleep.

All the vehicles were finally in place and all the people were under observation.

And then nothing happened.

For something to do to pass the time Mark made a couple of phone calls. The first one was to the US Embassy in Harare. He could of course have merely walked to the door since he was parked less than two hundred yards down the road. Such are the wonders of modern technology! His call was answered by a receptionist who was aware of what the code that Mark used was all about and showed due respect. However, she had to explain that the Ambassador engaged in some other business and could not be disturbed. That translated into the situation that Mark, despite having a code that was supposed to carry with it the full authority of the White House, was about to be shuffled down to a lower level. At least that was to a level where someone knew what was going on. The lady named Julia offered to put him through to a senior person who would deal with his problem.

And so, Mark Taylor became connected to Nigel Checksfield for the second time today.

'Good afternoon – can I help you?' came the formal response.

'Yes – good evening more like! We are in Harare and understand that you have a house that we can use for a few days' Mark replied.

'Ok – what is your code number please?'

Mark told him. He could hear the clicking of keys on a computer keyboard and then Checksfield came up with an address. He repeated the address and then asked if the caller needed any further assistance. Mark was going to ask about the likely movements of President Mugabe but thought better of it. It would also have been useful to get directions to the address since this was Marks's first, and probably his one and only, visit to this city of Harare. However, Checksfield seemed preoccupied. And Mark was a little perplexed at the apparent lack of interest.

Mark terminated the call.

The next call Mark made was to their controller who was presumably at sea somewhere off the east coast of Africa but could have been anywhere knowing the way the US services worked. As it was, a lady answered his call with the inevitable question *'Can I help you?'*

Mark again gave his code and then asked if she could shed any light on the likely movements of the President.

And Mark had to give the lady, officer, ensign of whatever she was, due respect – she knew which President he was referring to. And she avoided suggesting that he contact the US Embassy in Harare. She would be unaware that he was sitting within spitting distance of the main gate to that establishment, but she was aware that he would have a reason for not taking that option.

'The latest information we have is that he is due to leave Harare for Khartoum at 10:30 am tomorrow on an Emirates fight.'

Hmm... thought Mark. So, President Mugabe was not planning on being killed today. And the odds appeared to be in his favor based on the activity that had occurred so far. But you never know!

'Ok – we should plan on going with him. Can you possibly book seats for four of my team on the same flight? The other four will stay on the ground in Harare just to make sure he does get on board. The four leaving will be Taylor, Miller, Chapman, and Whittaker.'

'One moment please.'

There followed a couple of minutes of mumbled conversation and the clicking of keys before the lady returned.

'There are no seats available on that flight. Do you want me to arrange an alternative?'

Now that was interesting. The *no seats available* statement probably meant that Mugabe had booked the entire Emirates flight for himself and his motley crew of henchmen. In a country where almost everything was named after the man himself, there was little doubt that he could do that! The *do you want me to arrange an alternative* probably meant the US Navy would need to rapidly arrange something. But that was what the US Navy was for wasn't it?

Mark replied, 'Yes please!' and that was that.

The conversation with the Navy was just completed when the gates to the Embassy opened and the black Ford that Mark had seen on the road into Harare emerged. Checksfield was behind the wheel. Without appearing to take any notice of whoever may be watching he turned left and headed east as though he was not in any particular hurry. However, Mark had identified another vehicle that was parked on the opposite side of the road and whose driver was taking an inordinate interest in the goings-on around the Embassy. The driver was just too casual and there was just no reason for him having stopped where he was. Mark had not noticed the vehicle before the emergence of Checksfield, so whether the vehicle had been intending to observe or follow Checksfield or Mark there was just no way to tell.

Or was Mark just being paranoid?

'There were two vehicles which left the Embassy immediately before the Checksfield Ford – one turned right, the other went this way' Brent said as he started their vehicle and eased into the traffic heading in the same direction as the Ford. They had no difficulty blending in with the traffic and following the Ford for two miles before it turned right and came to a stop outside a block of flats. Brent drove past and then pulled into the side of the road and stopped in a position where he could see in the rear-vision mirror what was happening without being too close to be noticed. The other following vehicle seemed to hesitate, then drove on past where Brent had stopped, and then pulled over further down the road.

That told Mark what he needed to know.

Mark was the one being followed.

A vehicle was parked in the carport at the side of the block of flats and Brent noted that that was the vehicle that had left the Embassy earlier. The driver of the Ford got out of the car and there was no doubt that it was Checksfield. He walked briskly to the door of the bottom right apartment. His ringing of the doorbell was answered by a slim lady very nicely dressed, about five feet five probably aged in her forties with long brunette hair. Body language said that the lady was not related to the man, as she greeted Checksfield with a kiss. They both went inside and closed the door.

Mark was surprised. At no stage was there any evidence of any concern by Checksfield of who might see him or follow him or any other precautions that he might expect a CIA Head of Station to naturally do when wandering around in a foreign country. While Zimbabwe was not the wild west it was still best described as an under-developed country where the rule of law was not exactly to the forefront, and you would expect a certain amount of caution. That was unless the guy was extremely skilled in the arts of surveillance and counter-surveillance. Even then, he would not be expected to take any risks. And there was just no time in the short distance they had traveled from the Embassy for Brent to have considered an attempt to avoid detection even if Checksfield had been the least bit interested.

That caused Mark to get on his satellite phone and call Washington DC.

'Father – good evening or good morning. How is your day?'

Father sounded flustered. Mark had probably woken his father up or even may have interrupted whatever else his father got up to in the bedroom. Harold said that he was Ok.

'What can you tell me about this Checksfield character?' Mark asked. 'Like – is he married, and can you describe his wife?'

'Sure!' came the response. 'I am not at my office at the moment but as I recall - Yes - he is married. His wife is blond – natural or not I do not know - about the same age as Nigel, a little on the plump side, five feet nothing – lives up in Baltimore I believe. Not the brightest lady from what I have been told. Why do you ask?'

'Because I think that either she just dyed her hair brunette, lost a few pounds in weight, grew about six inches in height, and is a long way from home, or she has been replaced!'

The NRO had the easiest of jobs. They had been asked by the DNI to monitor the progress of the mission in Zimbabwe. The problem was that they did not have a satellite that could be assigned to that task full time. Despite the number of military satellites that they had under their control their first task would have been to identify a satellite that could perform the task required of it. That was after they had first eliminated those satellites that were either out of service, Decayed, Retired, Deorbited, Failed, Decommissioned, or presumed to be any one of the above.

They had two satellites that flew over the east coast of Africa at various times of day or night monitoring mostly activities around the east coast of Somalia. With a small tweak in the flight path, USA-290 could have been scheduled to pass over Zimbabwe but that would have resulted in howls of protests from the military people. Why this should be was debatable – after all the military had thousands of satellite photographs daily and since there was no war going on in this part of the world at the moment the takes were all archived – mostly in digital form - being of no immediate use to anyone. Consequently, the nearest they could get to monitoring activities on the ground in this irrelevant part of the world was by re-focusing one of the many cameras to gain a distant view of the capital Harare which told them that the weather was fine and not much else. Those cameras could of course be instructed to zoom in on any spot and take a close-up picture of any individual on the ground sufficient to tell whether or not the person had cleaned their fingernails. But – first of all, someone would need to request such action and would then need to tell them where their target would be.

Had the NRO been able to monitor activity on the ground they quite possibly could have found a small group of four CIA agents trying to follow the movements of the eight members of Marks' team, who in turn were trying to follow the movements of Haji's group of seven men, who were supposed to be tracking one man. And that one man – the notorious President Robert Mugabe – was holed up at his official residence and going nowhere anytime soon. Of course, even if they had a more accurate definition of their overhead take, the NRO would have been quite unable to determine that there was a CIA group involved.

They would have found no particular evidence of their existence in Zimbabwe because the group did not make any contact with the resident CIA official. And that would have been made more difficult by the dumb decision that was made by the CIA half a world away in Washington DC to split their team into two divided into racial lines. That meant that the two US agents who were both white stood out like dog's balls while the two South Africans who were both colored could easily blend into the background,

And the problems did not end there.

The team that Mark was leading was working in four groups and the two following four just does not work. In addition, the leading CIA agent decided that he should watch the Mugabe residence leaving his allies to try to watch the other three groups. Consequently, the South Africans watched as an unknown US Embassy official, dutifully followed by Mark Taylor, simply go home to have dinner with his presumed wife.

Tinashe Machingarufu was puzzled by the goings-on in the Embassy. He had been recruited by Nigel Checksfield as a trainee field operative working for the US CIA just two years ago. After spending six months in Harare learning about the US and its position in Africa he had gone on a course at Camp Perry Virginia – otherwise known to the CIA as the farm – learning how to become a spook. There was still a long way to go but that is what it takes. He had returned to Harare for further training under guidance from Checksfield before his scheduled graduate training back at the farm – hopefully in a couple of months.

So, he was not yet qualified.

But that did not mean that he was dumb.

Personal security was not something that his boss was good at. Coupled with that Checksfield had a habit of criticizing any decisions made by his bosses at Langley. Consequently, it was general knowledge within the inner sanctum of the branch that the CIA had cocked up on a plot to kill President Robert Mugabe.

So, Machingarufu had a number of questions for his boss. Like – Even though the CIA was not directly involved in moves to prevent that happening why would you not want to *assist* those who were? And why, having had a simple job delegated to MI6, had you not followed up to make sure that the job had been completed satisfactorily. Or to put it another way, why had you not heard from MI6 about the outcome? And why would there be another group of CIA operatives from South Africa active in your territory without having made any contact with the local Head of Station?

There had to be a simple explanation irrespective of the competence or otherwise of the man himself. And that was a worry. One possible explanation could be that news had reached the powers that be at Langley Virginia that Checksfield was having an affair. This would cause them to suspect that he may have been compromised. That would cause them to lose faith. But – why had they not taken some more decisive action?

There were few secrets in an office the size of the Embassy in Harare. The number of times in recent weeks that Checksfield had vacated his office shortly after his female assistant had vacated was bound to raise the odd eyebrow. And body language can be very revealing. Around the office, Julia Benkovic had been much brighter than was usual. At the same time, Nigel Checksfield who was a dour sort was suddenly talkative and cheerful. When the two of them were together, there was a chemistry that had not been there before.

So, it did not require a fully trained spook to work out what was going on. It did take a partially trained spook to decide to do something about it. And his reason for acting was simple self-preservation. If there was a problem in his Embassy that would reflect badly on all the staff because as he had been taught – this was a team effort - everyone watched everyone else's back.

Machingarufu recalled verbatim the words used by his first instructor on his first day at the farm *'Our highest principles guide our vision and all that we do: Service, Excellence, Courage, Teamwork, and Stewardship!*

He decided that he needed to talk to someone.

He also decided who among the players he would talk to.

Mark had to think about getting their accommodation organized. It had been a long day and before long fatigue would begin to take a toll. Before he could do that, his phone chirped. It was Hamish, who was watching the Haji household.

'We have movement at the house – though not what we expected. Haji has just had a visitor. It all looked very friendly – Haji gave his visitor four parcels. As far as I could tell nothing else was exchanged. Mike is following the car to see where it goes. Shit – hang on! Haji just came back out of the house and is getting into his jeep with one of his dudes. I will have to follow. Talk to you later.'

'Ok – nothing is happening where we are, so we can come down and join you. Over and out!'

Mark called Dusty to see what was happening at the Mugabe residence while Brent navigated his way through the traffic towards where the Haji team were. Dusty sounded bored shitless. He reported that the grounds were crawling with security guards. Which at least meant that there was someone important in residence! But he did have something of interest. A vehicle was parked on the opposite side of the road containing two white men whose focus of attention seemed to be the residence. They were not part of Hajis group. In the absence of anything other conclusion Dusty assumed that these men were either from a private security organization or were from some intelligence organization – possibly MI6 – probably CIA. With little else to do, Dusty would watch them.

Mark chilled when he realized that the two men that Dusty had seen were not the only unexplained people around. He had found a vehicle that also had two men on board that was following the vehicle that he and Brent were in. Mark had noted that they could be locals since they were both dark-skinned. But they were not from the

Haji group. Since nothing else appeared to be happening he asked Brent to stop at the side of the road and explained what he wanted Brent to do.

Brent got out of the vehicle and walked down a side street. Mark got into the drivers' seat and moved off down the road taking a turn down a side street on the left and then stopped again. The following car turned left also and then appeared to be confused by the situation. They drove on past.

Mark had established that he was the one who was being followed.

He reversed back to the main road collecting Brent and immediately took the next right-hand turn and then completed a block circle which brought them back to where they had started. It took a few moments before the other vehicle appeared again.

Mark blocked the road and Brent waved the jeep to a stop.

Mark could have carried a weapon but that seemed to be over-dramatic. He just walked to the drivers' window.

'So – do you want to tell me what this is all about?'

The man spoke excellent English so had no problem communicating. And Mark had to give him full credit – he was able to adapt to his situation.

'We work for a Security Company and have the job of looking after staff from the US Embassy. We were interested in your following a couple of their members is all.'

Mark could also adapt.

'Well - that is strange! We have the same task – except that we are paid by the US government and were unaware that in Zimbabwe there are any contractors employed. So – do you want to try again?'

The fact that both of them were lying caused the man

to laugh and Mark could see the funny side.

'You have only been in the country for one day. I do not believe you!' the man replied.

Mark had his turn. 'And you are South African and have probably been here about the same length of time that we have. Am I right or do you want to carry on the charade?'

The two South African citizens looked at each other and came to a decision. They decided that there was no point in continuing with their surveillance since they had been spotted and could no longer carry on their covert mission.

'Ok – it seems to me that we are actually on the same side. We will leave you alone.'

As the two men disappeared up the road, Mark called Dusty again.
'Guess what? We have just had a chat with a couple of guys who were following us. They were South Africans, but I would wager that they are working for - or with - the CIA. Now what say the two mystery buddies out near the Mugabe residence are from the same team?'

'Yes – that makes sense.' Dusty opined. 'The CIA have their noses out of joint not being involved – so they have their team snooping around. Do you want to tell them or should I?'

Mark had to laugh.

The thought of two CIA agents being approached by the large Afro-American in the middle of the Zimbabwe stakeout somehow appealed.

'Ok – off you go! Leave your phone on record. I would like to listen to this!'

Dusty got out of his vehicle and walked a few yards across to where the two interlopers were parked. As he approached their vehicle the man in the passenger seat was engaged in a somewhat terse conversation over his satellite phone. Dusty approached the other side.

He put both arms on the roof of the vehicle and in an exaggerated Brooklyn accent simply addressed the startled men.

'Has the CIA nothing better to do than waste taxpayer dollars watching Uncle Robert? You do not have to worry about us – we won't tell. You do need to worry about the rest of your team – your South African friends are out of business.'

At first, the men were speechless and then the passenger killed the conversation he had been having on the phone and asked.

'Who the hell are you?'

Dusty grinned. 'If you have to ask that then you are in the wrong job. Stay if you must. We have already reported your presence to our masters in Washington DC, so you do not need to do anything. I would expect someone will be on the phone shortly to discuss what you do now. Good luck with that!'

Dusty strolled back to his vehicle – trying hard not to burst out laughing.

No sooner had Mark finished his conversation with Dusty when Mike called.

'Hamish would have told you that I was following the visitors that Haji had. Well, guess where they ended up? I will give you a clue – the flag on the building is green, white, and red with a Lion and Sun motif in the middle! The Embassy of the Islamic Republic of Iran!'

'Ok, Mike' Mark replied. 'Can you stay there and see what happens next. It is no surprise that the visitors should be Iranian. What it would have been nice to know is - what were they carrying back with them?'

'Looked like drugs to me. But – what would I know? I will be watching but I would not expect much else to happen!' replied Mike.

Then it was Hamish on the phone.

'I might just do the same as Haji! He just picked up a feed from the local KFC and it now appears he is heading back to where he came from. Do we have anything to do other than to babysit these guys or can I go get a real job?'

As the leader, Mark had to decide before his team lost the plot. It was not as though these men were not dedicated and had – and would continue to – support and follow Mark. But even men of this caliber knew when they were wasting their time. He had a team of highly trained Special Forces troops who had traveled many miles through some pretty tough country, following a man who had the reputation of one of the most vicious killers on the planet. The exercise had aimed to protect another man who made the mistreatment of his fellow citizens into an art form. Now they had proved that the target – the President of Zimbabwe - was ensconced in as secure an environment as was practical and surrounded by enough armed guards to start a small war. The only man who posed any threat to him was probably watching the Simpsons on TV and eating KFC. And the chief CIA official in the country was probably oblivious to the antics of both Mugabe and Haji and was bonking his secretary.

Mark called them all. They would maintain a single watch on the Robert Mugabe residence which they would cycle through the team at intervals of two hours with Dusty taking the first stint. They would do the same with the Haji residence with Hamish taking the first two hours session. Provided nothing else happened, the rest would take a well-earned break.

Mark found the house that had been assigned to them. It was located on a large section and had ample space all around so that they could see anyone approaching from any direction. The house itself did nothing to impress. There were four double-tier bunk beds in one room, a table and a couple of couches in another, a kitchenette where it would have been difficult to fit two people and was devoid of anything resembling food, and a combined toilet and bathroom. It looked as though nothing had been cleaned this century. Blake went to get food and drinks from one of the local shops while the others set about trying to tidy the place, leaving Mark to report in.

The reception was excellent. The conversation was not so good.

Having battled his way through the Navy security system he got to talk to a person.

'We have absolutely nothing to report apart from the accommodation' Mark began. 'You should ask the President to come to Zimbabwe and instead of staying at the Holiday Inn, he could stay here with us. It's the pits! And we have been followed by a couple of goons who we managed to lose. The Mugabe residence is being watched by someone else, but we can shed no light on who they may be. They look like intelligence types but whose intelligence we have no idea. If you want an opinion - they are CIA.'

The person on duty had no respect for people on a mission at the behest of the US President.

'What is your report on the status of your mission?' was the response.

'We have nothing to report!' was the reply.

Mark ended the call.

The tapping on the door caused Mark to regret not having set up some form of surveillance on the property that they were in. He had assumed that a safe house would be *safe*. And that the chances of anyone bothering them were remote.

He signaled to Ben and Elliott to take up positions covering the door, weapons at the ready. He had a loaded pistol in his waistband as he approached the door.

Surprisingly, the door did have a security chain and a viewer. Mark attached the security chain before putting an eye on the viewer.

It was hard to tell whether the man standing at the door was alone. He was of average height and built like an AFL offensive guard. Body language said that he was no threat. However, Mark and the team had zero knowledge of the locals. And this man was definitely a local.

Mark did not open the door.

'Who are you? And what do you want?'

The reply to his questions surprised Mark, both for its candid nature and its eloquence.

'I am Tinashe Machingarufu. I work at the US Embassy. I would like to talk to you if you can spare the time.'

Mark opened the door allowing the man to enter and ushering him towards one of the crude chairs.

Ben and Elliott were not too sure and kept their guns on display.

'Ok – what do you do at the Embassy?' Mark asked the visitor.

'I work for Nigel Checksfield – he is head of the Political Branch' came the easy reply.

Mark held the gaze of Machingarufu.

'We know who Checksfield is. So – what do you do for Mister Checksfield that would cause you to want to talk to us?'

Beads of sweat started to appear on the forehead of the visitor. He was either lying or he was out of his depth. Mark guessed that it was the latter. And he was proved correct, as the poor man let it all out.

'I am on the payroll as an assistant to Nigel – really as a junior CIA agent. But I have been let down by my boss. This so-called safe house was allocated to a team that is being run by the DNI in Washington DC to try to prevent an attack on President Mugabe. I don't know whether he is acting under instructions from Langley or whether Checksfield was upset that he was not involved. He has done nothing to support you. Rather than use our resources, he even asked the British to arrange for your transport out of Mozambique. He has also done nothing to support a team of CIA agents who are in the country to monitor your progress. He has also....'

Mark had to interrupt. This guy was way out of his league. But he was blurting out facts that concerned covert operations. Stunningly accurate – but which would not normally be shared with a junior agent. It was too late to do anything about that. Having come this far, Mark wanted to know some other facts, before deciding what to do with the young man.

'What do you know about our transport from Mozambique? It could have a bearing on issues that we may have with your boss.'

Machingarufu composed himself before he replied.

'As I understand it, MI6 was to arrange to hire a couple of vehicles from a hire company in Chimoio. I presume that was organized Ok – well you are here!'

The atmosphere in the room had become tense.

Mark exchanged glances with Elliott before he asked

his next question.

'Have you heard from the agent since he went to Chimoio?'

The CIA agent looked puzzled by this line of questioning but answered. Then asked a question of his own.

'No. Is something wrong?'

Mark was unsure how to go ahead. Something was wrong. He just did not know how to tell this young man what it was! Elliott came to the rescue.

'Do you know the name of the man who went to Chimoio?'

Finally - Machingarufu realized he was talking about something that was supposed to be secret. At least he had been told that the mission was covert. But he was talking to the men who were already involved. He took a deep breath. He had to go on now.

'His name was Banga Matsikenyeri – like me, he is a trainee agent here in Harare – but he works for the British.'

Elliott exchanged glances with Mark. He got the nod that said to go on.

'How well do you know Banga?'

'Very well. We have excellent relations with the Brits and at our level, we often get together for a chat. He has been associated with our cell since the previous administration. At times he has been the 'Go to' guy when Checksfield wants something done on the quiet. He has always seemed very capable. You are not suggesting he has let you down in any way – are you?'

'I am not suggesting anything' Elliott replied. Again - the nod from Mark told him to go on.

'There is no easy way to tell you this. Banga Matsikenyeri is dead.'

The effect of this news on Machingarufu was profound. He sat in the center of the room speechless. He looked from Mark to Elliott as though appealing to one or the other to tell him that was not so. Then he sat there, stared into space, and muttered.

'You must understand that Banga and I were both born in Zimbabwe. Only last week we were at a barbeque with his wife and kids. He asked me to be the godfather to his youngest daughter – the fifth of five beautiful girls. What am I going to say to his wife? They were devoted to each other!'

And then Machingarufu had another thought. His look changed from one of intense grief to one of anger.

'Does Checksfield know about this? Why has no one been told?'

Mark stepped into the conversation. Now was not the time to say too much about what the team knew about Checksfield. He did not think that Machingarufu was into drugs, but it was too early to tell. He also did not know whether he had prior knowledge of his boss's infidelity.

'Checksfield may not know – yet.' he said as gently as he could.

There were tears in the eyes of the young man. He was too stunned to say anything. Mark continued.

'You could help us catch his killer – if you want to!'

Chapter 16

Not Dead Yet

At least the following morning had the semblance that normality would return the mission.

Mike Gilroy had been watching the Haji household and he reported in at 6:30 am that a whole lot of the residents had piled into their vehicles and were heading out.

Mike told Mark of this development and then followed Haji at a discrete distance. He was excited at having something positive to do. And he was nervous that Haji was about to fulfill his mission.

However, the vehicles that he was following traveled, not towards the city itself, but they turned south. After continuing through the morning traffic, it soon became clear where they were headed.

They appeared to be heading towards the Harare Robert Gabriel Mugabe International Airport.

Mark summoned Brent and Hamish from their bunks in the safe-house and they scurried to head out to join Mike on his surveillance.

Elliot and Blake, who had been watching the Mugabe residence, reported in shortly afterward. A motorcade was forming up outside the residence. Judging by the amount of activity it looked likely to leave very shortly.

At 8:45, the motorcade, with President Mugabe buried somewhere amid an army of guards and a flotilla of vehicles, left as a convoy. And there was an energy and purpose about the convoy that suggested they were on a mission. Police along the route stopped all other vehicles to allow free passage for the dear leader of this impoverished country.

They were headed in the direction of the International Airport.

Mark did not know what was going to happen now as he reviewed his plans and assessed the risk to Mugabe. Was this how and where an attempt would be made to assassinate the President?

Mark had accurately judged that the area of greatest vulnerability was when the President was transferring from one mode of transport to another. He had also correctly assessed that nothing would happen at the Mugabe residence because that location was too heavily defended. And anyone trying an assassination would have about zero chance of getting away in one piece. That explained why Haji and his team had stayed well away. Now a situation was developing in which there could be a real chance that there could be some action.

Was Mark's theory about to become reality?

Could an attempt be made on the life of the President while he was transiting between the motorcade and the airport terminal? The most likely plan for such an event seemed to be a sniper attack since there was not much chance of getting close to Mugabe in any physical way. The question would therefore be - Where could a sniper position himself to be able to get a shot at the President? And where would he be able to escape undetected? Or more correctly – How could the whole team get out of town before they, and their role, be identified.

There were so many security people around Mugabe that they would descend on a man with a rifle like a plague of locusts. The only way that a shooter could avoid detection would be to immediately abandon his weapon and just blend into his surroundings. That was assuming that the shooter was not on a suicide mission. And there was no way of knowing with terrorists. They often thought only of killing the target. They probably did not even think of why the target had to die. In such circumstances, they rarely thought of what happens next.

However, in this case, they were dealing with Mohamed Haji. Based on the limited profile that Mark had of the man, Haji seemed to have had a remarkable ability to survive. That made it clear that Haji would not be the shooter. He would be the organizer.

This raised the question – Did Haji care whether his nominated shooter would have a practical escape plan or not?

The answer was – probably not.

Overriding all of this was a great unanswered question.

What was the motive?

Mark called his controller to inform he, she, it, or them that it looked as though they were, at long last, about to get some action.

The reaction that he got from the controller was similar to a reaction of someone told that the sun was due to rise the following morning.

Mark had another call. He was surprised by the speed

with which the young Machingarufu had acted after their conversation of the previous evening.

'I have found out that Banga hired two campervans from Hertz rentals in Chimoio and I now know the registration numbers of the vehicles. What do you want me to do with this information?'

Mark knew that he could not let things play out any other way.

'You will find those vehicles at the Airport. We are heading that way now. Things may get a little rough, but I suggest you join us out there.'

While Mark was on the phone, Dusty grabbed all their gear and the two men headed out to the airport relying on the other members of the team to keep them informed of what was happening. As they approached the airport Mark contacted Mike to find out what had happened to the jeep and the campervans being driven by Haji and his men.

'I am at the airport terminal.' Mike answered at once. 'As far as I can make out Haji's group has split up. I have found the vehicles – they are in the short-term carpark - but I cannot find Haji. I need some help. Where are you?'

'Ok – Brent and Hamish should be with you shortly.' Mark replied. 'The rest of the team are not far behind them. Stay where you are until Brent arrives then start searching leaving Hamish at your vehicle until we arrive. The airport cannot be very busy. See you soon.'

Hamish came on the phone. 'We have been held up. This motorcade has blocked off the roads leading to the Airport. I don't suppose it would be a good idea to show them my naval expeditionary force medal to let me through!'

Mark had to laugh.

Here they were trying to prevent President Robert

Mugabe from being killed and two of the men who were best qualified to do that were held up by *his* motorcade. It would be ironic if that motorcade's passage would allow Uncle Robert to ride - uninterrupted by hordes of his citizens - to his death.

'Just wait where you are and follow the motorcade when you can. Dusty is going to turn off the access road and hopefully go around through the cargo area. Talk to you shortly.'

Things were starting to look dicey. The team was rapidly losing contact with the people they were supposed to be following. Mike was the only one who was close and even he had lost contact with the most dangerous Haji. But even if that were not the case, they could hardly go rushing through the terminal waving their guns in the air. Mugabe was surrounded by his bunch of security people and as they came into the airport terminal, they were most unlikely to hesitate in shooting anyone carrying a firearm.

Mark's team all had Beretta M9 semi-automatic service pistols and between them, they had three Heckler & Koch 416 assault rifles. Mark and Dusty had one as did Hamish and Brent, and the other one was with Blake. These were good weapons to have for normal operations. But they were no match if they were up against a person with a sniper rifle. The sniper would be well hidden. He would probably be elevated. And they had no idea where he might be.

The preference that the team had was to use only their pistols. That would require that they had a target. And that would require that they were close enough to that target to be effective.

Mark and Dusty got to within two hundred yards of the terminal building when their progress was blocked by trucks and there was just no way through. They had no choice but to abandon their vehicle and continue on foot. They contemplated taking the assault rifle with them. But there was no way that they could carry it without it being obvious. And therefore, making them a target for both the trigger-happy security force and the sniper.

They rushed towards the terminal and arrived at the same time as the motorcade screeched to a halt at the departure drop-off area.

No sooner had the motorcade stopped than security guards flooded out onto the concourse. And they were everywhere.

Mark had to make a decision. He pulled an old DEA identification badge out of his pocket. He held it high above his head and marched straight to the security perimeter that Mugabe's men had quickly established. There he spoke to one of Mugabe's guards. At least the guard had the look of the man in charge.

'I am Mark Taylor. I am working with the United States CIA. I have reason to believe that there are people in the terminal with guns!

That got an immediate reaction.

Fortunately, the security guard that was closest to Mark could speak English and got the message loud and clear. Also – fortunately – he had no recognition of what was or was not a CIA identification badge. Or if indeed CIA agents carried a badge. Which they don't.

A more senior officer rushed over and in all the excitement he just accepted Mark for what he had said he was.

'Do you know what the gun carrier looks like? Where specifically is he? And what is his name?'

Mark pulled out a crumpled-up copy of a faxed photograph of Haji.

'This is the man who leads the team. His name is Mohamed Haji.'

The security guard got on his cell phone and rapidly issued instructions, At the same time, he signaled to one of his colleagues to keep the doors closed on Mugabe's limousine. Then he turned back to Mark.

'You had better not be dicking us around! Come with me.'

Whatever Mark may have thought of their Presidents' security detail before, he could only admire the speed and efficiency with which they executed their reaction to potential danger. The terminal was locked down within minutes. Nobody and nothing were moving.

That is, except for an Emirates flight that was already rumbling up the runway and lifting off to the east before slowly turning north as it climbed to its cruising altitude.

Mark spotted Mike Delaney standing by the entrance.

Mike rushed over to join the group as Mark asked him.

'Where is Haji?'

'Not a clue!' was the simple answer,

'Ok – so where are their vehicles?' was Marks' next question.

Mike pointed out towards the public carpark where the jeep and campervans were parked in the middle of a large space. It was supposed to be a short-term carpark. The problem was that not many people in Zimbabwe had cars to park. Those that did had no reason to park at an airport where there were not that many flights either in or out. Few people in this rundown country could afford to travel. That meant that the carpark was virtually empty.

Mark grabbed the nearest security guard and pointed him in the direction of the carpark, and the vehicles that had carried Haji and his bunch of thugs to the airport. And two of the vehicles that should have carried Mark and his team from Mozambique judging by the registration plates.

Again, that worked surprisingly efficiently and effectively. The occupants of the jeep were completely unaware of the action by the Zimbabwe police and the security agents. As two police vehicles entered the parking area from opposite sides and blocked the jeep from going anywhere Mugabe's security detail flooded the area. The driver of the Jeep got out and could be seen protesting his innocence. He has quickly turned around, cuffed, and thrown to the ground. The police got another five men out of the other vehicles and had them spread-eagled on the ground while other officers searched all three vehicles.

There were enough weapons to start a war.

There was no sign of Mohamed Haji.

It was no use trying to get any sensible information out of the men who had been arrested. Most of the security forces had Shona as their native language but spoke passable English. The people they had arrested had as their native tongue the Somali language and spoke no English.

Mark told security that there should be at least two other men. And one would be the most dangerous among the group. But – where were they?

The easiest way for the security detail to communicate was to shout.

'Where is Haji?'

That go no response. Possibly because none of the men spoke or understood English. Possibly because Haji had used one of his aliases. Probably because all the men were trussed up.

Mark tried the gentle approach. He had identified by

reading body language the one man who was likely to be in charge of the men in the absence of the elusive leader. And the one man who clearly understood the first question but chose not to respond. Therefore - the one who understood English. He pulled out his pistol and held it against the man's temple.

'Where is your leader? Point to where he is. Otherwise, start saying your prayers!'

Again, it was the eyes that answered Mark's question. The wild flickering of his eyes from the gun to the airport departure area told Mark all that he needed to know. The place where Mugabe was still sitting, and fuming, in his car. He was safe in the car. It had bullet-proof windows and was built to withstand an attack from assault weapons of a type that would have been beyond the resources available to Haji and his men.

At least that was the theory.

Mark and the security detail rushed back into the terminal building and frantically looked around for Haji.

There was no sign of Haji.

But Mike had intercepted a man coming out of the restrooms dressed in the same drab uniform as the men in the carpark. And while twisted against the wall with his arm up to his back he made a mistake. Mike had suggested in English that he should not bother struggling or he would end up with a broken arm. The man replied that Mike should 'Get Fucked!' which told Mike all he needed to know about his command of the English language.

There was a loud crack as the arm was forced out of its socket.

Even Mike squired as the Mugabe police took over the interrogation and brutally slugged the man until he answered their questions.

It was not the answer that Mark wanted to hear. No

shooter was hiding in the airport. And there was no Haji. The man had stopped in the restrooms and was taken completely unawares as he stepped out into the arms of Mugabe's security.

After he had seen Haji board his plane and fly off.

There were enough guns in the vehicles in the carpark to have started a small war and in the absence of their leader Haji to try to explain their purpose, the men were doomed. These men would be going to jail after a brief but brutal interrogation by the CIO – the Central Intelligence Organization - the Zimbabwe secret police who were not renowned for treating people kindly. Especially since the men they held were foreigners who could speak neither Shona nor English. And they had unfortunately been caught at the Robert Gabriel Mugabe International airport with all those weapons at the time when the dear leader of the same name was boarding a flight out of the country.

Tinashe Machingarufu arrived as the men were being bundled into a police van. Armed with the details he had obtained from the rental company he was able to explain to the police the origin of the two campervans. Not that the Zimbabwe police were the least bit interested in how the men had got into their country. They would just make certain that they didn't get out anytime soon.

As the police left the scene when Dusty pulled a small package from one of his pockets.

'This is the knife that we believe was used to kill your friend. Here are the GPS coordinates of where we buried his body – it is on the other side of the border with Mozambique. We have reported as much as we know of what happened to our controller and explained that we were in no position to bring his body with us. Can we rely on you to take this evidence and the coordinates to MI6 and arrange retrieval of the body? I would imagine that you would want to go to Mozambique – but that is your choice.'

Tears again welled in the eyes of Machingarufu as he grasped the knife.

'What are you and Mark going to do now?' he had to ask.

Dusty placed a hand on the shoulder of the distraught man as he tried to console him.

'Our mission is to follow the man we believe was responsible for Banga's death. We will do that. Your immediate job is to ensure that Banga's body is recovered. That is the most important task. It will help bring this evil man to justice. Trust me – in my other life I am a lawyer - without a body, we can't even begin the process. Now – can you do that?'

For just the briefest moment, the young man looked at the knife and then looked around the carpark as though expecting Mohamed Haji to magically appear so that he could kill him. Then he focused his attention back on Dusty.

'I will do this. All that I ask is that you inform me when you catch the bastard!'

When the police gave the all-clear, President Mugabe came through the sliding doors of the terminal surrounded by security guards. Mugabe stood at a height of about five feet ten inches. All that Mark could see of him was the bobbing head amongst a sea of heads all of about the same height and color.

Mark was about to turn towards the exit when he saw the crowd swerve in his direction.

The President appeared from the crowd and came

towards him with his hand outstretched.

'Mister Taylor - I believe I need to thank you and the United States Central Intelligence Agency for dealing with a difficult situation. Thank you – and please convey my thanks to your President.'

Mugabe was a man in his eighties but seemed remarkably vigorous for someone of that age. He did not seem to be the kind of man who would control such a brutal regime and Mark could understand why people referred to him as Uncle Robert. What he could not understand was how was this going to be explained to the CIA?

They would get credit for an event that they – at least officially - knew nothing about.
Mark shook the hand that was offered before Mugabe was whisked away towards the departure gate, lost in a sea of bodies.

Since the last flight out had been an Emirates aircraft and the staff were still clearing the departure gate Mark was able to question the people while the passengers would be fresh in their minds. They confirmed from the photograph that Mark had shown them that a person resembling Mohamed Haji had indeed left.

The flight was heading to Khartoum Sudan.

There was no one on the flight with a name resembling Mohamed Haji.

There were other problems for Mark to worry about as his team all of a sudden was reunited in the middle of the Harare airport. Half of the team had not had a clue of what had just happened. The major problem was a riddle. Why had Mohamed Haji gone to all the trouble of coming into Zimbabwe by what was probably the most difficult route possible only to leave on an airplane having achieved – What?

It was probable that his group had been trafficking drugs. But surely that did not demand that amount of complexity. Surely that did not require someone with the experience – as evidenced in the profiles that Mark was aware of – of Mohamed Haji.

The only thing that had happened which could be seen as unusual was his connection with the CIA Head of Station in Zimbabwe. And even that was assuming that Haji knew that Checksfield had anything to do with the CIA.

Now the situation was that Haji was on the way to Khartoum.

That was the same destination that Mugabe was headed for.

The team that Haji had left behind was just a group of common or garden criminals. It was unlikely that they would supply any information on what Haji was up to. For the very simple reason that they would most probably not know.

The only clear thing was that Mark had to get to Khartoum to try to solve another riddle.

If the original CIA theory had any truth to it, and if Robert Mugabe was the President who Haji was to assassinate, then where was that to occur? And as if he did not need a reminder – Mark now had the major players on the way to Khartoum leaving behind the team that had been tasked with preventing an assassination.

Mark called his controller wherever he or she was but presumably still onboard the USS Carl Vinson somewhere at sea to the east of Africa. In this instance, it was a lady but not the same one that Mark had spoken to the day before. After going through the inevitable exchange of codes he conveyed his report and got what he wanted.

A Navy Grumman C-2 Greyhound twin-prop plane was already sitting at the Harare airport waiting for them. It had landed at Harare with apparent electrical problems which Mark was assured would disappear the moment it was confirmed that it was required to fly again. While the Greyhound was not exactly suited to flying passengers around it would do for the short flight to Khartoum. In any case, on this particular trip, it would only be carrying troops although there would now be eight of them on board instead of the four that Mark had originally booked.

Mark also asked the controller if they could convey a request for assistance from the US Embassy in Khartoum. He had to have someone who could check on the arrival on an Emirates flight from Harare. Specifically, they would need to locate a passenger known as Mohamed Haji – possibly known as Abdul Nadir – or possibly known under any name you cared to think of - and, if possible, find out where he went when he got there. Mark presumed that the controller had codes that would ensure that these instructions were carried out but frankly he was starting to get pissed off with the whole business.

The task would be assigned – or should be assigned – to Chief of Station or COS of the CIA office, and if they were in the same mode as the CIA representative in Harare then Mark did not hold out much hope of success.

Mark and the team had to wait inside the terminal while everything else was shut down while the President went through check-in, immigration, and security with very little in the way of checks and was then whisked onto the waiting Air Zimbabwe Boeing 737-800.

Although Robert Mugabe had reserved the entire

aircraft for his use it was still full when all the security and support staff had taken their seats.

No wonder the people of Zimbabwe resented the excesses of their leader! Then again, he was the leader of the country and even the Presidents of other countries – like the United States – liked to travel in style!

Chapter 17

Confusion

It was a strange combination of things. Power and ego were important elements of that combination.

Even so, the resulting decision came as a surprise. The new Presidential administration was still feeling its way into how it was supposed to conduct the affairs of the state. A critical part of this was the communications system that it relied on. And that had still to come to grips with the people involved and their respective places at the feeding trough.

The first real challenge arose when the Secretary of State had to go out to Saudi Arabia for an urgent meeting with the Saudi leader Mohammed bin Salman. The Arabs were getting more than a little concerned about the antics of the Islamic Republic of Iran both on the international stage and much closer to home in the Straits of Hormuz in the Persian Gulf.

At their narrowest point, the Straits were technically within the territorial waters of two sovereign states – the Sultanate of Oman to the south and Iran to the north. By international agreement, there is a "shipping" lane which is two miles wide in the middle of the Straits in the Persian Gulf which allowed trade to flow in both directions. So technically speaking Saudi Arabia was not involved. But the Saudis and their traders used the Straits, and the closure or disruption of the shipping lane would have a major monetary effect on all the Gulf states, and a major effect on international trade.

The Saudis had more money than anyone else in this part of the planet. They also had more land than other nation-states in the area – albeit mostly desert. However, it was what was underground that mattered the most. Iran knew these things, but, since the two antagonists had a history of conflict, the Straits of Hormuz was as good a place as any to cause trouble.

The Americans had recently been tied up with an election. That had featured the usual protectionist and nationalistic Republicans against free international trade Democrats. Consequently, the American public would be ready for a bold first move by the Republican who had been elected with less than fifty percent of the popular vote. In these circumstances, Saudi Arabia was keen to test the resolve of their western ally. As indeed was Iran.

Both of these countries were of course predominately Muslim.

Iran was Shia Muslim.

Saudi Arabia was Sunni Muslim.

While on paper the Saudis were more than capable of managing any threat coming from Iran, they still needed reassurance that the United States would come to their aid in the event of hostilities. The US had already poured billions of dollars into the Gulf state which assured that the Saudis should at least have the military bits and pieces to fight a successful war.

What Saudi Arabia appeared to lack was the aptitude for the fight being adept at enjoying their wealth but not so adept at defending it if needs be. Strangely, this played into the hands of their American allies and the hawkish policy of the new administration.

For years, the Saudis had skillfully avoided attempts by the United States of America to establish military bases in their kingdom. This was despite in recent times having been involved in battles with Iraq in which it was probably only the presence of US forces in the Gulf that prevented a bloody invasion of Saudi Arabia. Latterly the Saudis were embroiled in their conflict in Yemen which involved Iran and its terrorist allies, and it was only managing to hold that war at arms' length through the use of advanced US technology. That scenario was looking brittle as the war in Yemen intensified and seemed to have no end in sight.

While the Kingdom of Saudi Arabia was by far the largest and the richest of the Gulf states most of its land was in fact desert. But that did encompass two key components – the cities of Mecca and Medina.

That made it a critical place in the eyes of the Muslim world and sooner or later there would be a showdown between the major players about who had control of these two cities. Since the cities were both in Saudi Arabia, that raised a simple question.

Who would be the other *major* player?

The US strategy was to use diplomatic pressure to force the issue and ensure that, when the dust had all settled, the status quo would remain.

This strategy had nothing to do with supporting either the Shia Muslims or the Sunni Muslims. It had everything to do with oil without which Saudi Arabia would be finished.

Iran also had oil – plenty of oil – and that was at the moment being restricted by sanctions imposed by the United States with the backing of most of its western allies.

While the US had no desire to enter into another war in this area of the world, there were more practical matters to consider – influence, money, and oil – in no particular order.

Saudi Arabia was a major producer of oil.

And so was the United States.

In the best of times, the Saudis and the Americans did not compete with each other. They just agreed on what the market could take in terms of volume and price. And they got on with the business of having the rest of the world – that is the vast majority of the countries who had no oil - pay. But what would happen if say the world demand fell. Or if someone else – be it Iran, Russia, or even Venezuela where the only inhibition to their increased output was political – became a more significant player on the supply side. That could reach a point where one of the established suppliers had to take a fall in revenue?

If that occurred, then self-preservation would become the overriding issue and existing friendships would become irrelevant.

With all this in mind, the US President had offered his aircraft to fly the Secretary of State on this trip out east. It wasn't *his* aircraft. It was dedicated to him as President for as long as he held onto his job. Whenever the President flew in it the plane was known as Air Force One. When he was not flying in it, the plane was just a normal Boeing 747 with the call sign SAM27000 or whatever number the Air Force thought to attach to the Special Air Mission tag. Well – as normal as you could describe a Boeing with several added tons of communications gear on board.

One theory freely circulating in Washington DC was that the use of the aircraft in this way was to impress the Saudis by having Secretary John Scott arrive in Riyadh in a private jet. Or to at least emphasize to the Saudis the importance of their relations with the US.

The other theory - which was probably closer to the truth - was that the Secretary of State had been tapped as the likely replacement for BJ Thomas if the President could not serve out his full term. So, that begged the question – What would happen to Vice President Roger Warren who by the US Constitution should succeed BJ?

Non-the-less the plane did have every conceivable electronic and communications gadget on board and could get all manner of intelligence – both official and unofficial – from anywhere on planet earth. Consequently, whoever was on board at the time could be kept fully informed on all matters from the latest episode of *The Simpsons* to who was winning or losing in the latest war. So, it was surprising that the Secretary of State was not fully briefed on what was happening in the world when the plane landed at Khartoum Sudan for a brief stopover. This was simply to talk to the US Ambassador to Sudan about what he should or should not, observe at the upcoming and relatively unimportant (to the United States) meeting of the African Union.

The United States and some other favored nations from outside the continent of Africa were invited to attend the meetings as observers. Such countries would have no speaking rights of course unless they were specifically invited to speak on a subject of particular interest to the official members of the African Union. That aside, they would be excluded from some sessions which were restricted – in other words, those sessions at which the Union members would talk about matters that were confidential or embarrassing. Like when they wanted to criticize the aforesaid observers.

Or - like when they wanted to criticize one of their members.

One of the peculiar things about meetings of the African Union was that the local and international media were allowed to attend all the sessions while the countries which were attending as observers were not. This situation begged the question of the validity of press credentials because it was a well-known fact that some reporters were fully paid-up members of their respective countries Security and Intelligence services. In the case of some countries, the press may as well have been an official section of their governments such as their alignment with its policies.

The United States of America for one would not of course dabble in such subterfuge especially since that would circumvent United Nations resolutions on the subject of the press and what member nations should, or should not, do to protect their freedom.

Except on occasions when it was the only way to get critical information.

Nonetheless, there were important matters that could concern the interests of the United States and so the Ambassador would attend those sessions where the main players were in attendance. The Deputy Ambassador would attend the rest. A representative of the US intelligence and security services would make sure that nothing that occurred went unrecorded.

Because the US Secretary of State was not directly involved with the meeting of the African Union and because his time in Khartoum had nothing to do with the Sudanese government, John Scott was met by the Ambassador and taken straight to the United States Embassy in Soba. The meeting with the man who was only ranked as a Charge d'affaire could just as easily have taken place at the airport, except that it allowed John Scott to see the city. And more importantly, for the peasants to see him.

After a brief introduction to the senior Embassy staff, they went into the formal reception area where they proceeded to discuss matters of very little importance.

The Deputy Chief at the Embassy soon got bored with the idle chatter and she decided to ask a question.

'What is going on in Zimbabwe? We have been asked to help a team of mercenaries who are working for the United States. We had no prior knowledge of any such operation.'

Hmm. The Secretary had been briefed that this lady was also the acting CIA Chief of Station in Khartoum. And it was the CIA who had alerted the United States to potential trouble in Zimbabwe. That bit of intelligence had come from Somalia and made its way up the chain of command to be brought to the attention of the DNI and then onto the President. Whether it had then filtered back down the chain to become common knowledge throughout the vast network of CIA agents, Scott could not know. What he did know was that the President had authorized a team to come to Africa. And that team had been arranged without CIA involvement.

But what had that got to do with Sudan?

So - he dismissed her query.

'That was a matter that was to be managed in Zimbabwe. The latest information I have is that the mission is all over.'

But then he could not resist the temptation to appear on top of the situation. He felt it important to impress this lady and the CIA with his grasp of matters which may on the face of it appear to be outside his purview while keeping what little he knew of the mission to himself.

'What help would they want from you in Sudan?' he asked.

The CIA officer recognized the opportunity to reciprocate by impressing the Secretary of State with her command of matters which obviously would be beyond his ability to understand.

'Apparently, a gentleman by the name of Mohamed Haji is in or is coming to, Khartoum. He is a Shia Muslim and operates under several aliases. We have been asked to observe and monitor his movements. The claim from the team is that - whatever their mission is – they have the authority of our President. This all seems rather weird particularly since neither our office here in Khartoum nor the Chief of Station in Harare has been informed.' She mused.

John Scott had his reasons for not wishing to continue this conversation but thought better of just dismissing the lady's disquiet. Probably she was just pissed off because a mission had been undertaken without the CIA involvement despite the intelligence data having come from CIA sources. Whether she was aware of the details of that origin was beside the point. Word travels through any bureaucracy and a particular attitude becomes part of the culture. The Secretary of State could do nothing about that. It was the same with the Department of States' intelligence people – they thought that their work was more important than diplomacy. The Secretary had his problems to deal with and this issue was not high on the agenda.

Like many people in the western world, John Scott had little real understanding of Islam. The fact that Haji was a Shia Muslim and Scott was going to Saudi Arabia to meet with Sunni Muslims was almost irrelevant to his way of thinking. If Sunni Muslims thought the teachings of the Prophet Muhammad were more important than what the local Shia Ayatollahs had to say was just politics – religion style. That was like saying that the Bible was more important than what the Pope had to say! So, you take the writings of people from two thousand years ago about what they thought their God's message was instead of listening to the man who was the same God's representative today. The fact that Islam appeared in the seventh century made it newer than Christianity – but that still meant that basing beliefs on writings in the Koran in this modern-day and age was something that John Scott had trouble understanding.

In the same way, he did not understand what the difference was between sending a bunch of CIA agents into Africa and sending a bunch of *others* on a wild goose chase. He oversaw the United States diplomatic service and that took precedence over spooks playing their silly games.

The Secretary of State decided to play it safe.

'Well – I can say this much. There was an operation underway in Zimbabwe which had the blessing of the President. According to the latest information I have, that mission will be ended shortly. I do understand that the group has some flexibility as to the duration and direction of its mission. However, I do not think that they have the authority to demand support from other parts of the United States government. So - I would suggest that you ignore the request.'

Which suggestion the United States Deputy Ambassador in Sudan and the CIA Chief of Station in Khartoum was quite happy to take.

The CIA would do nothing to find and follow Mohamed Haji.

And the US Secretary of State would be pleased that she did nothing.

Chapter 18

Khartoum

The US Navy Grumman arrived in Khartoum sometime after the Emirates flight carrying Mohamed Haji and just behind the Air Zimbabwe plane carrying President Robert Mugabe and his entourage. It did not take long for Mark and his team to clear immigration and customs courtesy no doubt of their official security status conveyed to officials by the Navy crew and by-passing any interference from the US Embassy.

The man they were here to protect had to wait while his staff was scrutinized in some detail by the Sudanese officials. They had no wish to recognize the President of Zimbabwe as anything other than another visiting dignitary amongst many who were visiting their city at this time.

However, once Mark and his team were clear of the formalities, other people wanted to see them.

The team was met in the airport arrivals hall by two representatives of the Sudanese General Intelligence

Service – or NISS as it was known – the National Intelligence and Security Service. Mark had the impression that these people were more meeting them out of curiosity than anything else. They did not press too hard to find out what the team was doing in Khartoum. However, they would be aware that the timing of the visit would have some relevance.

The African Union was having a meeting in that city during the next few days, and it was reasonable to expect that the NISS would want to make sure that there was no trouble. Or troublemakers.

Mark would have preferred to have avoided the meeting with the NISS, but the reasons soon became clear. The team was invited into a room on their way through the warren of passageways at the side of the airport terminal where there was someone else waiting to meet them.

The Deputy Chief of Mission of the US Embassy in Khartoum rose to meet Mark as he entered the door. She made no effort to acknowledge the presence of the rest of the team.

She quickly acknowledged that they had lost sight of Mohamed Haji shortly after he had arrived in Khartoum. That was hardly delivered as an apology which told Mark a couple of things. The Deputy Chief of Mission was the CIA Chief of Station in this part of the world. It also told him that either something had changed in the way this mission had been set up, or this lady was pretty pissed about something. Mark decided that he would hear out what the lady had to say before he left the building.

'I was very disturbed to receive an instruction from the USS Carl Vinson that we were to follow your friend Haji' she began as though discussing a request to pick up a kid from school. 'You must understand Mr. Taylor that you are in Sudan now and we are only working in this city with the forbearance of the Sudanese government. The NISS people that you have met are somewhat disturbed that they have eight people coming into their country for no apparent legitimate reason. They have enough on their plates looking after the heads of state here for the meeting of the African Union. My Embassy has been asked to vet your credentials and frankly, we have no information from Washington DC that enables us to do so.'

Mark was surprised by the ladies' attitude.

He felt like saying *'So ring the President!*

But he would not do that - Yet. Instead, he asked a question.

'Are you saying that the authorization codes under which my request that someone in Khartoum track Haji does not apply in your town?'

'What I am saying Taylor is that this Embassy takes its instructions from the Secretary of State and until we get that instruction then nothing will happen!'

'So – you did not lose track of Haji. You did nothing – is that about the sum of it?'

Dusty – who had listened to this nonsense without comment. He was about to comment. A signal from Mark calmed him down.

'Well - you have a telephone. So - you can call the Secretary of State now! Better still - here is a satellite phone – use that!'

Mark fixed the lady with a steely glare.

'If your secretary happens to be too busy, get your message patched through to the President, or do you not have the balls to do that. Or you could call Langley whose switchboard you would no doubt be more familiar with!'

The lady blushed.

'You cannot talk to me like this! We have to ensure that we maintain a good working relationship with the Sudanese government. As part of our commitment to the

the country, we have to verify any US citizens that step across their border. In your case, we are at this stage unable to do so.'

Just then her cell phone rang. She should have excused herself and taken the call outside. This time her face went quite red as she killed the call. It took her several seconds to gather her thoughts before it was her turn to fix her glare on Mark. She looked as though she was about to burst into tears.

'Now I understand that you have been posing as CIA officers! What is the meaning of this?' she managed to blurt out.

Mark almost laughed but managed to control his reaction.

'So – now that we have proven who you are, I can tell you that this is not true and once again the CIA is making an assumption based on what? So - how did you come by this piece of wisdom?'

'Because the fucking President of Zimbabwe has called the White House and thanked *OUR* President for having the CIA save his life. And he mentioned you by name!'

Now Mark did laugh.

'As I recall what did happen - President Mugabe thanked me and the CIA as he left the Harare airport on his way here. He was mistaken in naming either myself or any of my team as CIA. I correctly judged that it was not in the interests of our government in correcting the President. You may have a different view to which you are entitled. But you were not there. I was. And judging by your reaction I would think the CIA is the last organization we would want to be associated with. But that is how it is.'

Now the lady was mad.

And irrational.

'Well, Taylor – I can tell you that you will not be entering Sudan today if I can do anything about it!'

Mark then got serious. Now the gloves were off.

'Ok – if that is your position you must excuse me while I make a couple of calls.'

'Fine – I will leave you and return when you start to show respect!'

She stormed out of the room.

'What the fuck is that all about?' Dusty summed up the feeling of all the men.

Mark was somewhat stunned by the performance but had to smile.

'I don't know. I guess that we are running into a bureaucratic nightmare. I would assume that the CIA has not been kept up to date with the play. Understand that they were the ones who came up with the theory that someone wanted Mugabe dead. He was, according to their information, supposed to die in Zimbabwe. But he didn't. Now that the focus is on Sudan that involves another department. But don't ask me to understand what goes on. Hang on and let me try to sort this out.'

Mark called the USS Carl Vinson. He talked to his controller and insisted on being referred through to the person who could sort this out. He was immediately patched through to the commanding officer of the ship Captain Karl Thomas, quickly explaining the predicament that they were now in. He did not mention that the Deputy Head was also the CIA Chief of Station in Sudan. His concern was that Mohamed Haji was somewhere in Khartoum and that no one had done anything about finding out where he had gone.

It turned out that Thomas already knew the staff at the Embassy in Khartoum. At least he knew that the lady was only the *acting* Chief of Station.

'Ok, Mark leaves it with me. She wants a secretary to talk to, does she? I cannot get the Secretary of State, but the next best thing. I will have the Secretary of Defense call her now. If I cannot get him, then I might up the ante and get my father to deal with her. She may listen to BJ!'

Chapter 19

Haji

Mark and his team finally got settled in the City Flats hotel apartments in the city by six o'clock in the evening. Mark did not know who had spoken to the Embassy after their confrontation with the CIA lady at the Khartoum airport. Whoever it was had certainly cleared the air.

The two people who came into the room at the airport after their confrontation with the Deputy Ambassador were the men from the Sudan National Intelligence and Security Service. The senior of the two - a NISS gentleman called Ibrahim Mustafa - had come to welcome them into his country. He apologized for the earlier misunderstanding. And he seemed sincere. Probably because he had very little respect for the CIA. At least their representative in Khartoum.

Mark's understanding of the Sudanese Arabic language was limited to *Salam Aleekom* which translated to *Hi!* Fortunately, the two Sudanese gentlemen spoke passable English. The reading of their body language said that Mark could trust the guys.

He decided to tell them a little of the reasons why he

had brought his team into this part of the world.

'We are looking for a guy called Mohamed Haji' Mark began. 'Wc have followed him from Zimbabwe. I doubt whether he would have used that name on his travel documents and his passport is false. Here is a photograph of the gentleman – I am sorry it is a little fuzzy. He is believed to be traveling on an Iranian passport but most of his recent activities have been in Yemen and Somalia. We do not know why he has come to Sudan although we doubt it would for any good reasons. With the meeting of the African Union due to start tomorrow, he may be up to mischief regarding that. Frankly, we just do not know anything specific about what he plans to do while he is here. We did ask the US Embassy to track him when he arrived in Khartoum, but they were unable, or unwilling, to do so.'

The other members of the team took no part in the discussion although they would know where Mark was coming from. There was a very good reason for not revealing that the person who would be the focus of Hajis attention would be President Robert Mugabe.

Mugabe was probably more hated by the Sudanese than he was by his people. So - it was better to have the NISS believe his target was just some other – any other! – a member of the Union. Mark had also made mention of the assumption that Haji was Iranian. The vast majority of the Sudanese population follow Islam – but they were Sunni Muslims. Whether Haji was Sunni Muslim or Shia Muslim Mark did not know. However, if he was working for the Iranians, it was safe to assume that he was Shia. There was also little point in informing the NISS that there was a conflict between the CIA and any otherwise normal visitor from the US, although that should have been clear from the earlier confrontation.

Mustafa took the photograph and showed it to his

colleague. They switched to talking in Arabic for a couple of minutes and then appeared to reach a consensus.

'Ok – we will find him for you!'

Mustafa had made the statement as though he felt that it should be a simple task. Mark was not so sure – although it could have been a simple misuse of his second language.

'Can we keep this photo?' Mustafa asked.

'Sure!' Mark replied with a shrug.

All members of his team had a copy although they would not need it. They were getting to a point where they would recognize Mohamed Haji without a second glance. While they had yet to get close to him, they had the benefit of the Navy-supplied high-powered binoculars. And, as far as they knew, Haji did not know that he was being observed, so he did not try to hide his face. Or his limp.

'Just one more thing' Mark said – not so sure if it was worth raising.

'While we don't intend to get in any firefights, as you know we arrived in your country by a US Navy airplane and brought small arms with us. Do you have any objections to my men carrying?'

That brought a smile from their host.

'Our gun laws restrict who can and who cannot carry arms. They are meant to restrict arms to those like ourselves who may have a legitimate need to use them. But – this is Sudan. While you are in Khartoum you will see little evidence of people carrying guns. Anywhere else in this country you would not want to step outside without a gun. In theory, you are supposed to have a firearms license and I can fix that if you are concerned about it. Your men are proficient in their use so that should not be a problem, however, I doubt that you would get agreement from your Embassy if the CIA had anything to do with it!' Ibrahim finished with a laugh.

That meant that the NISS knew that the Deputy Ambassador in Khartoum that they had met earlier, was the CIA Chief in this part of the world and that was interesting. Whether Langley would be aware of that Mark could not know. After this meeting was over Mark would take steps to find that out because if the NISS already had that information then that would be ample reason to have the lady removed. But now he had a further question

'Are you saying that, when you find Haji, you could arrest him for the fact that he is carrying? That is apart from him being in breach of your immigration rules.'

That brought another smile from Ibrahim Mustafa.

Mark quickly got his team organized. They needed four vehicles, and these were organized with the airport Europcar rental firm. It wasn't ideal because the rental terms would restrict their flexibility but until they sorted out what kind of support they could get from the US Embassy, they would have to do. They picked up a couple of maps and headed into the city.

Mark had booked them into the City Flat apartments for two reasons. Firstly - there was little choice with the hotels being full of people attending the African Union meeting. Secondly - because that is what Mustafa had recommended.

It also suited Mark because their movements in and out of the apartments would be noticed by no one. There would not be the usual monitoring found in a hotel. And it would make things a little more difficult for people who would wish them harm.

They again split the team into four groups. Mike and Hamish were an obvious choice for one group, and they had Ben and Elliott following as they went out to look at the hotel where Robert Mugabe and his massive team of hangers-on were supposed to be housed.

He sent Blake and Brent to cruise around and check out the Corinthia where the conference was to take place the following day.

There seemed to be little point in assigning anyone to specifically look out for Haji. All of his team would do that anyway. Their chances of finding Haji in a city as chaotic as Khartoum were remote. That task was best left to the NISS – after all, it was their town, and they would at least have some idea of where to look. Meanwhile, Mark had a couple of things that he needed to check. He delegated one task to Dusty. The other task he would do himself.

Mark called Harold Taylor at Langley.

It was now four o'clock in the afternoon in Khartoum, so the timing was good. His father would have had a couple of cups of coffee. And it was too early for him to be contemplating having lunch.

Mark called on Harold's private line but even that required him to go through a secretary. However, it did mean that he did not need to say who he was!

'Hi, father. *Keif Alhal*?'

If that greeting was meant to impress Harold Taylor with Mark's increased knowledge of Arabic, it failed.

'I am very well! So - what are you doing in Sudan?'

Mark did not bother to point out that Sudanese did not like to have their country referred to with the prefix 'The,' so he got straight to the point.

'We have had a degree of difficulty getting any cooperation from the CIA in this part of the world. Don't your people have any respect for someone who is working on behalf of our President?' Mark said, with sufficient sarcasm that he thought he was bound to get a bite out of his old man.

That did not work either.

'Let me guess' Harold replied laughing. 'You have crossed swords with a lady called Margaret Laws – she is the Deputy Chief of Mission in Sudan. And you are quite right – Well almost right. She was temporarily made CIA Chief of Station when Wallace quit after being spooked by some scandal. I suggest that you bypass Laws and talk to the Ambassador. His name is Anthony Luxton. He is a good bloke. Just don't call him Tony!'

Who the hell was Wallace? What kind of scandal he had become embroiled in? Why would a guy named Anthony not want to be referred to as Tony?

Mark had no idea what the answer would be to any of these questions. And could not have cared less.

He just needed to move on, and as usual, he was beginning to get a little pissed at having to put up with the ramblings of his old man.

'Yeah – sure! I just roll up to the Embassy and demand to see this Luxton character.' Mark surmised. 'Would you like to suggest how I do that?'
Harold was not the least put out by his sons' testy response.

'No problem – give me a number where he can contact you and I will get Anthony to call you.'

Dusty also had good news from his call to the States. His call had gone to Taylor Software, and he did not need to go through any Secretary. Brad Morgan answered the call himself.

'Hi Dusty – where the hell are you now?'

Brad used to be employed by the CIA Science and Technology Division before coming to work for Taylor Software. He was a whiz with computers and anything else that had buttons on it. He and Mark also worked together on a recent contract that they had with the US Government which was so cloaked in secrecy that very few people knew about it. Dusty, as Marks's lawyer and most trusted friend, was one of the few.

'Hi, Brad. The boss wants you to do some looking around for information. We are in Khartoum and hit a blank wall when we met a person who was believed to be the CIA Chief of Station. Mark wants to know who she is and what the fuck she is doing in Sudan. Hang on a minute!'

Dusty had a quick chat with Mark who had finished talking to his father and then came back on the line.

'Ok – Mark tells me that the lady is called Margaret Laws. He also wants to know who this guy Wallace is. Or was! And why he quit as Chief of station in Khartoum. Can you do that?'

Ordinarily, such a request for information would turn up a blank response. But there were a couple of factors that changed that. As part of the contract with the US Intelligence and Security Services Taylor Software had limited access to some government databases. That access enabled Mark and Brad to go deeper into the data than the contract envisaged. Certainly, deeper than the CIA had envisaged. And probably deeper than what the DEA, who had been responsible for the contract, thought possible. But that was being picky. Brad was a professional hacker. When Brad had to access information beyond the scope of their authority, he had to use a clever piece of software that was disguised as a maintenance update. It was most unlikely that it could ever be traced. Nonetheless – this request was relatively simple. Brad assured Dusty that he would have the answers within a couple of hours.

He did not disappoint the team.

By the end of the day, Mark was beginning to get the information that he needed. Brad had called back with probably more information than was needed. Wallace Perriott had been the CIA chief in Khartoum who had fallen on his sword after getting caught having an affair with a lady who was of unknown origin but was believed to be from somewhere in the middle east. It was suspected that he had been caught in a honey trap arranged by an as-yet-unnamed country. The evidence so far was pointing to a likelihood that the country was Iran on the basis that they had previously employed similar tactics. That investigation was still in progress.

Perriott was being held at the Naval base in Anaconda with the suggestion that he could be the target of an attempt on his life. That was made more difficult by the fact that the investigators had failed to get Perriott to talk openly about his predicament. Other than to curse himself. Maybe out of fear for his life. Maybe out of embarrassment for what he had done.

However, the view of the FBI profiler who was investigating this case was that there was something more sinister going on. It remained to be seen whether this had involved Perriott passing sensitive data to a foreign power. However, the FBI was confident that there was nothing that had crossed his desk in recent times that would have been of any interest. Perriott was certainly being used as a drug mule and it was being assumed that this would perhaps lead to further indiscretions. Therefore, the FBI was following two lines of inquiry. The first one concerned the other staff in Khartoum. The second one concerned other diplomatic staff stationed in Africa.

As it turned out, the FBI would have been wise to spread their inquiries a little further.

The story on Margaret Laws was far more straightforward. She had been seconded from her normal duties in the diplomatic service to take over from Wallace Perriott while an investigation was conducted into whether the whole CIA cell in Sudan had been compromised. Information showed that she had been trained by the CIA but not at a level that would qualify her as a professional spook. Reports on her file said that she lacked the necessary initiative and aptitude. The theory was that with a little help from people with experience in the field she could overcome what was termed as these *obstacles to her progression.* Khartoum had been chosen as the place to send her to get that help being a country where nothing was happening to interest the CIA. And that was fine until the Perriott affair turned all the theories on their head.

Anthony Luxton called Mark on the evening of their first day in Khartoum. As Harold Taylor had alluded to, he seemed like a nice bloke. Luxton apologized for the reception they had received from Ms. Laws and offered the services of his Embassy to meet any requirements that they may have. Which effectively told Mark not to bother calling the CIA any time soon.

Mark would leave the matter of Law's cover having been blown to a later date. And after he had checked the extent to which her position had spread to the rest of the diplomatic community. It was not a matter of any great concern that her position was known to the NISS. They were just doing their job. But it would be a matter of serious concern if it had spread elsewhere after such a short time in the position.

It was a game played by all diplomatic communities – trying to find out who was actually who despite their various official titles. It was just a pity that Laws - who on paper would have been the ideal choice for a covert Chief of Station - had blown it at the first hurdle due to inexperience and arrogance – mostly the latter - rather than due to lack of initiative and aptitude.

Mark did have one immediate request that he hoped Luxton would be able to meet. His team needed to gain access to the conference of the African Union rather than being limited to hovering around outside. Since the United States had been granted the rights as an observer at the conference, he felt that his request should not have been too difficult to meet.

Initially, Luxton was reluctant to meet this request. because that would limit access by Embassy diplomatic staff. While nothing was going on that would cause a major headache, Luxton still had reports to send to his masters at Foggy Bottom. And, despite the innocuous nature of the conference, the Secretary of State had indicated that he would be none too pleased if the reports turned out to be inaccurate or incomplete. However, Mark talked him into it after explaining that the whole purpose of his team being in Khartoum was to be able to protect someone who was involved in the meeting. To do that, whether they succeeded or failed, Mark had the support of President Thomas.

Mark wanted to, but did not, speculate that meetings of the African Union were usually a forum for the leaders to make statements in a less conflicted environment which would be of little importance in the grand scheme of things.

Because even the United States was restricted on how many diplomatic people could attend with observer status, Luxton got around the restriction by giving media passes. Which arrangement turned out to be fine despite being contrary to the normal that rules that governed international diplomatic activity.

The African Union had distributed more media passes than those given to diplomatic staff. There were more US-based media organizations than anywhere else in the world, and the actual allocation was left to the Press

Attaché at the American Embassy. The problem that the African Union did not envisage was that very few international media organizations would accept the invitation. Therefore, the subterfuge was not that difficult to arrange just so long as their presence did not conflict with genuine reporters. It was therefore simply a matter of knowing which organizations were not represented. Then all they would have to do was try to ensure that the media organization that they claimed to represent were sufficiently obscure to escape the attention of others in the press gallery.

The reasons for Mark and his team to attend the conference were exactly why other media organizations would want to be there.

If only they knew!

With that matter settled, the next task was to work out exactly what Mark and his team were going to do now.

The current meeting of the African Union was being held in Khartoum Sudan. The main office and conference center of the Union – or Commission – was based in Addis Ababa Ethiopia and it was rare for the meetings to be held in any other city. That was probably because it was just too difficult to organize a sort of roster which could keep all the leaders happy while they dealt with the major problem. Many countries in Africa just did not have the facilities to stage such a conference. Even if they did – it would be extremely doubtful if they could provide the security necessary for hosting the leaders of all fifty-five leaders.

So – this rare meeting place was merely symbolic.

The goals of the Union were also symbolic.

Those lofty goals included such things as promoting

unity and solidarity, eradicating the remnants of colonialism, and aiming to achieve a better life for the people of Africa. But the Union had other more immediate problems to address. They wanted to diminish conflicts on the African continent, particularly those that involved interference by other countries in affairs that they saw as their own. They wanted to bring an end to the corruption – and that was endemic to many of its members. They wanted to boost democracy at the expense of some of their members whose rule was best described as authoritarian or dictatorial. They wanted to set up a mechanism that would ensure the credibility of the leaders both within the Union itself and on the world stage. All four of these lofty aims would be appropriately directed at the government and the leaders of the Republic of Sudan. So, even if the leaders failed to look into a mirror, it was likely to be an interesting next two days at the meeting.

There were rumors that some countries had infiltrated the bureaucracy that supported the African Union over the years that the Union had been in existence. These rumors were probably true. The purpose of such activity was unknown.

Mark decided that the best they could do was to monitor the meeting and not worry about any side issues. They would keep one eye on Mugabe and look out for anyone who might wish him harm. At the same time, they would watch for any move by Mohamed Haji, or Abdul Nadir, or whatever name he had adopted. The latter part of this task was hopeless. They could not be proactive. They could only be reactive.

However, that was the task that they had been recruited for.

It was not ideal – but it was what it was.

The first day of the meeting passed without incident. When all the delegates had left the conference and returned to their hotels, all that was left to do was to set up a roster to monitor Robert Mugabe. They had few worries about his security while in his hotel where he would be surrounded by his minders. What they did worry about was what would happen if he moved away from that security blanket!

They had however detected that something was going on around the meeting that may or may not have something to do with their primary task. Mark could not have been expected to know the intricate norms of surveillance, but he did have his training with the US Special Forces to fall back on. Each man on his team had the back of everyone else. Consequently, they were all continuously checking who was watching who. They very quickly concluded that the Sudanese NISS was in evidence everywhere – whether they were on the lookout for Haji or had other things to worry about they did not know. The CIA was there and stood out like dogs' balls – whether they were watching the US contingent of observers or were on the lookout for something else Mark and his team neither knew nor cared. There was another group of people who were also watching and that was the group that got Mark's attention.

This group seemed interested in one man.

And it was not President Robert Mugabe of Zimbabwe.

It was Mark Taylor.

Chapter 20

Changes

The gentleman was beginning to annoy Mark.

He was sitting in the lounge area in the lobby of the Corinthia reading a newspaper. He must have been a very slow reader because he was not turning the pages. But what he was doing was forever looking in the direction of Mark and Dusty. Body language said that the guy was nervous. Shit scared was the more proper description that Dusty gave. If he was on a covert mission to see what Mark and Dusty were up to then he was either not very experienced or was not doing a very good job. There were other people around the lobby all of whom seemed innocuous compared with this guy.

Finally, Mark could stand it no longer. The mission that they were on was about as exciting as watching paint dry, so he had to do something to lighten the day.

Mark walked over to the guy and towered over him. Not knowing his nationality Mark could only guess where he had come from. The newspaper was an English language edition so that gave Mark the confidence to address him in English.

'Do we know each other?' was all that Mark had to ask.

The hands holding onto the newspaper began to shake. The reply to his question surprised Mark.

'Can we talk? Somewhere not so public. Shit! I need some help!'

Mark was about to sit when the guy jumped to his feet, roughly folded his newspaper, and stuttered.

'I have a room on the ninth floor – room 910 – please come upstairs and we can talk! and then he left the lounge and scurried off heading for the elevators.

At first, Mark did not know what to do. He ambled over to where Dusty had watched this strange episode.

'That guy looks like a fruitcake! He said he was going upstairs to his room – and I have no reason to disbelieve him. But it could be a trap. He said that he wants to talk – what about he did not say. You stay here while I check it out - and watch my back to see if anyone else is likely to be involved. I will go outside and check that nothing is going on, then I will join you shortly.

With that said, Mark walked out of the hotel.

He crossed the street to a news vendor and bought a newspaper which he flicked through while looking around. Nothing seemed to be out of the ordinary. He had a quick chat with Blake who was wandering up and down the entrance and asked him to cover the foyer while he dealt with this problem. Satisfied, he walked down the street and crossed the road again, around a corner until he came to a loading bay of the hotel where a delivery truck was being unloaded. The two staff involved were too busy to notice as Mark slipped through the doorway and back into the service area of the hotel.

Mark climbed the stairs to the ninth floor and looked through the window on the access door. Along the corridor, rooms were on both the left and right sides – even numbers on the right, odd numbers on the left. Mark cautiously opened the door at the end of the corridor. A lady was walking down the corridor away from where Mark stood, but he could not tell whether she had come from a door or was going to a door. So, he waited patiently until she stopped further down the corridor, and then she entered the elevator and disappeared. Then, with the corridor now empty, Mark quickly stepped into the alcove which was the entrance to the apartment numbered 910.

The door was unlocked.

Sitting on the couch was the gentleman that Mark had briefly met in the downstairs lounge. He was blubbering uncontrollably and made no sense. Dusty sat on a chair opposite him, and he did not look impressed. As Mark entered and locked the door behind him, Dusty just spread his hands.

'He had said nothing – just sat there crying like a baby - other than that he wants to talk to you.

Mark had no idea what this was all about but was in no mood for any funny business. He just walked up to the man, slapped him on the face, and barked 'Get a grip of yourself! Now what is your name and what do you want? We have more important things to worry about at the moment. I do not have time for this shit!'

'I am Lawrence – Lawrence Johnson. I am the United States Ambassador to Kuwait' he stammered. 'And I have done a stupid thing and need your help!'

The tears started to flow again as Mark and Dusty looked at each other in total confusion.

The mood that Mark was in did not improve.

'I find that hard to believe! Then what are you doing in Khartoum? You had better start telling the truth!'

'I was Acting Ambassador at the time – until notice came through that I had been bumped up!' the man claiming to be called Johnson almost shouted. And that was said with a certain amount of pride, Mark noted.

'So – what is the US Ambassador to Kuwait doing in Khartoum?' Dusty asked. 'And why are you talking to us? You should be talking to your Embassy in Khartoum – they tell me that Ambassador Luxton is very good!'

Johnson looked almost embarrassed as he replied in almost a whisper.

'Our Secretary of State decided that I needed the experience, and so I was sent here as an observer at the conference of the African Union. Anthony is aware that I am here in Sudan and of my reasons for being at the conference. And, of course, the Ambassador and I are in constant communication about the conference and other matters. But that is not what I want to talk to you about.

'Ok' said Mark, beginning to realize that this guy Johnson could be wanting to talk about something of a more personal nature. That was usually the case when someone admitted to having done something stupid. But Mark and Dusty were not employed as members of a citizens advice bureau.

'Before you tell us what the hell you are talking about – you had better explain why you specifically want to talk to us? We have nothing to do with the US diplomatic service. And only a very loose affiliation with anything to do with the African Union. So – unless you can explain why we should not leave now this meeting is at an end.'

'Well, you are Americans – and I assume you are here in a security role – but not a part of the CIA or anything like that!' Johnson blurted out.

Mark and Dusty again exchanged glances. Then Mark gestured towards the door.

'No matter what you think we are associated with, whether we are with any official American security detail, is none of your business Mr. Johnson. Yes - we are here on legitimate business but that has got nothing to do with you, and the last I heard that business did not involve babysitting the likes of you. So, unless you have something else to add, I think this meeting is over.'

Johnson looked as though he was at breaking point, but he desperately tried to stop the two new friends from leaving.

'Can't you at least hear what I have to say?' he began, sitting forward on his chair. 'I believe that I have stumbled into something that is of extreme importance to America and could be quite damaging if it is allowed to go ahead. Because of the various factors involved, I cannot use my usual resources to report this to a higher authority. That is why I came to you. I have been watching you during the day and formed the view that I could trust you.

Mark pulled a chair close to where Johnson was seated and leaned forward addressing the young man.

'I haven't got time for this crap! I can tell you that we do have connections to people in places far higher than you envisaged. So – you now tell me what is really bothering you, or I will leave now and lay an immediate complaint with your bosses at Foggy Bottom. I guess that the so-called *various factors* concern the *stupid thing* that you or your associates have done. So – how about the truth? What have you done?'

And out came the long and sorry story, in all its detail.

'I have been caught in what I think you people call a honey trap. It was not meant to happen this way – I thought – no that's not right – I did not Think! You cannot know what it is like in Kuwait.'

Both Mark and Dusty stood to leave. They had heard enough. And did not want a bar of it.

Johnson almost screamed – 'Please hear me out! If you cannot help then so be it and I will have to go elsewhere, All I ask is a few more minutes. Please!'

Mark sat but Dusty remained on his feet and went to

the door, opened it a peered left and right down the corridor. Then he returned to the room, locking the door behind him. And took out his Beretta.

Dusty then walked up to Johnson grabbing him by the throat and almost lifting him out of the chair.

'If this is some kind of game that you are playing you are in more trouble than you think. We are in Khartoum to find a killer. If he gets to kill someone while we are here listening to your crap, I will be pissed off – and believe me that will not be good for either of us. Either you get to the point now or we are out of here. And just so that you do understand – as Mark said - we do know people in high places and when they are made aware of our conversation so far, your honey-trap problem will be the least of your worries!'

Dusty dumped Johnson back in his chair – but he did not sit down. Dusty just towered over the man from Kuwait, and he still held his gun.

'Now talk!'

'Ok. I met a girl, and we had a couple of drinks. One thing led to another, and we ended up having sex. Then a week or so later I had to go to Teheran for a meeting with the Iranian government. During a break in that meeting – you know how these things work – everyone has a minder from the other side - I was taken to a room where I was introduced to a guy from VAJA – the Iran Intelligence organization. The lady called Perim - that I had sex with - was also there. I had thought that she was Turkish but not. I was advised that I could help Iran gather information on the US or they would inform my government and my wife about the affair and effectively end my career. He said that if I did what he asked I could continue in a relationship with Perim, and they would continue to supply me with drugs. That effectively meant that Perim would be my minder. But the supply of drugs is what has me frightened. They want me to become a supplier to people with the Embassy and the whole western diplomatic community. I don't do drugs – apart from the odd social use. But this is scary. I realize that I could feed them false information although they say that they would know if I did – but CIA would know about all that kind of stuff. But if I supply drugs to the other people in the diplomatic community then things could spiral out of control - And I don't know what to do!'

Mark and Dusty exchanged glances. Johnson had been watching too many movies if he thought he could become a double agent. The CIA would have a fit if they were asked to take him on. And Mark felt it very unlikely that the diplomatic service had the sophistication within its intelligence service to run something as daft.

The honey-trap thing was just bad news for Lawrence Johnson. He would need to come clean with the wife – wherever she was – and take his chance whether that was the end of his marriage. Some women could be very forgiving, but the vast majority of them would kick Johnson out on the basis that they would never be able to trust him again. And Foggy Bottom would take a similar view. Not that having an affair was exactly unknown in diplomatic circles. It was just that Johnson had been caught. As for the drug thing – that was probably a ploy to recruit other people although on its own it could be fatal for anyone involved. The drug business was based on a form of trust. Well – reliability would be more correct. Reliability could be bought. Trust had to be earned. If that trust was broken the retribution could be swift.

In this scenario - Why had the Iranians introduced drugs when they already had their prey on infidelity? The answer was that question was that Johnson would have to have been a user. So - Johnson was a liar as well as a fool.

It looked as though his career was done.

Mark looked at the young man with a certain amount of sympathy. But not much.

'I do not know what you think that we can do for you.' Mark began. 'I could start by asking who the gentleman was from VAJA - but that is almost certainly a false name unless the guy was brain-dead. Then I could ask – Where is your wife? – but she is not in Kuwait. You stuffed up and only you can decide how this plays out. You could have romantic ideas of having the CIA interested in using you as a double play. That means you could supply information to the VAJA under CIA control. That is a very dangerous game. And it only happens in the movies. You need some legal advice – Dusty what do you think?'

Dusty laughed.

'Lawrence - I am a lawyer in my daytime job. What I suggest you do is resign and get the hell out of Dodge City while you are still in one piece. You are dealing with some very nasty people. I wish you good luck. You are sure going to need it.'

Dusty headed for the door.

Mark handed Lawrence a scrap of paper with a number on it.

'Let me think about it for a day. I could talk to some people to ease the pain. There are a lot of factors to consider. None look good from where I sit. And a lot depends on the attitude of your wife. Call me on this number tomorrow. May I suggest that you call your wife first.'

Mark stood to leave.

He did not accept the handshake that was offered.

Mark and Dusty returned to the Hotel foyer and sat well out of the way of other guests so that they could talk in privacy. Neither of them knew where to start to unscramble the tale that they had just heard. There was one very obvious question – Why on earth would the Iranians want to compromise the US Ambassador of Kuwait?

The state of Kuwait was a small emirate – less than 7000 square miles and a population of less than five million of mostly Sunni Muslim religion. At the head of the Persian Gulf, it was surrounded by Iraq to its north and west, and Saudi Arabia to its south. It was located on the edge of one of the driest and most inhospitable deserts on the planet. It could hardly be described as being of any strategic importance to anyone.

It was true that in 1990 Saddam Hussein sent his Iraq forces to invade the country for reasons that the world is still trying to come to grips with. The only motivation was probably greed. Hussein wanted to get his hands on the Kuwait oil reserves. Alternatively - or also - he wanted to gain access to the Gulf which was the highway of the massive middle east oil trade. That invasion of Kuwait was a very short-lived exercise for Hussein. The United States and its allies bludgeoned the inept Iraq forces into submission, sending them back to Bagdad bloodied and defeated. And that treatment was repeated in the Gulf war in 2003 which resulted in another defeat of Hussein.

The suggestion to anyone in the region was not to mess with any country that had a significant role to play in the supply of oil.

The world has changed since the 1990's and the US – Iraq war of 2003. The US has shied away from involvement in being seen as the global police chief. Coincidently, the US had also reduced its ability to project itself as the hammer in any conflicts. Whether that was intended to get other countries to share the costs of policing the world, or was just politics at play, was beside the point. The facts were that other countries and their leaders would see an opportunity to project their power at the expense of others who were weaker and unable to defend themselves. However – getting a young US diplomat in the tiny and almost irrelevant emirate of Kuwait caught in a honey-trap and forced to deal in drugs was not quite the same as an invasion of another sovereign state.

But Mark was beginning to see a pattern in all of this.

For whatever reason, the Kuwait Ambassador was now under the influence of Iran Intelligence. Why Johnson had not taken the simple step of alerting the Central Intelligence Agency was an unknown. The Kuwait Ambassador would certainly know who the CIA Station Chief in Kuwait was. It would appear to have been a simple matter of drawing the matter to his or her attention.

The fact that Johnson either had not, or had not said that he had, raised another issue. Was the CIA representative in Kuwait also in the same predicament as the Ambassador? Mark had seen the Station Chief in the Zimbabwe capital of Harare – five thousand miles from Kuwait - receiving packages that looked suspiciously like drugs. That same gentleman was also having an affair with a lady. The only difference between the two cases appeared to be the origin of the lady. In the Kuwait case, the lady involved had been a professional deliberately introduced to the American by a foreign power. In the Harare case, there had been no need for such delicacy. Checksfield had offered himself up on a platter.

Now they had the situation in which the CIA Station Chief in Khartoum was back in Washington for *consultations* due to some misdemeanor that had yet to be identified. So – had he also been caught with his pants down.

And - Was he also involved with drugs? Certainly, from the information that Brad Morgan had supplied, the

FBI seemed to think so.

It did seem a strange coincidence that Haji had been a recent visitor in two of the cities. In the Harare case, Mark had seen the evidence for himself. Checksfield had been compromised before the arrival of Haji. In the Khartoum case – Warren had also been compromised before Haji arrived in the city. But – Haji had a reputation for being an organizer. And the method employed in Kuwait to trap Johnson – get him involved in infidelity and then get him involved in drugs - was too similar to be a coincidence.

This strange situation left Mark with two things that he must do irrespective of what happened to Robert Mugabe. Firstly - he must find out some more about the so-called murderer Mohamed Haji who he was following and try to find out what he was really up to. Secondly – he must talk with the CIA Assistant Inspector - his father Harold Taylor - to try to find out what the CIA intended to do about it.

The first task turned out to be both straightforward and frustrating. Mark was able to get into several databases hosted by the US intelligence services which had many thousands of *persons of interest* that had come to their attention over several years. And Mohamed Haji was listed in all of the databases that Mark accessed along with several cross-references to various aliases that Haji was known to have used. There were also other names listed that were assumed to refer to the same person. However, the information held against these names was rudimentary and did not shed much light on exactly how Haji had gotten the reputation that he had.

One profile said that he was an Iranian born in 1981 in the city of Mashhad in the remote province of Razavi

Khorasan close to the border between Iran and Turkmenistan. Another said that he was born in the Saudi Arabian city of Jeddah. What was consistent was that his father was a Professor of Economics at the Ferdowsi University in Mashhad which gave credence to the former. The younger Haji did attend the same University for several years, although no one seemed to know what he studied while he was there.

Haji first came to a sort of prominence at the age of thirty when he was a major player in the Iran Green Movement which sought to overthrow the election of the then Iranian President Mahmoud Ahmadinejad. The Green movement is not to be associated with green activists in western countries. Most of the personnel in this movement were ruthless people whose sole purpose was political and violent. They had no interest whatsoever in saving the planet, halting climate change, or any other such peaceful pursuits.

But then, as quickly as Haji had appeared, he vanished.

After a time out of the limelight, he re-emerged in a very different role. He appeared as a contract killer closely aligned with the Iranian Revolutionary Guards and Iran Intelligence. Physically he was a small but broad-shouldered man of under five and a half feet in height and was claimed to have a mop of black hair and a beard.

When he had been first sighted by Mark in Zimbabwe, presumably under one of his many aliases, he was bald and cleanshaven. There was a brief mention of an injury to his right leg which caused Haji to have a limp. Although it was not stated how the injury had occurred it was mentioned that the CIA had attempted to capture him. He escaped and it was after this event that the limp started to appear in his profile. Even so, it did seem a little strange to Mark that the CIA had raised the issue of Haji being the chief suspect in a plot that they had identified based on so little information about the man and in so unlikely a place as Zimbabwe.

Haji was mentioned in passing on reports emanating in Somalia and Yemen that assumed that he had some involvement with groups that were aligned with causing trouble for whoever the Iranians were targeting at the time. But there was nothing specific. That was – if the Central Intelligence Agency had chosen not to share what information they had on Haji with the rest of the intelligence community. Also, nowhere was there any mention of drugs even though he seemed to be now heavily involved in exactly that business.

Mark decided to call his office in New York before he made the call to Washington.

'Hi, Brad! It's Mark – I have something that I want you to do for me. Could you find some more information on the two people that Dusty rang you about earlier? The man we are following - Mohamed Haji – the CIA must have more information than I have been able to find so far. I suspect that he has gotten involved in the drug trade but can give you nothing specific to follow up. Also – we have our man, Wallace Perriott. I need more information on this guy. How did he get caught up with the woman and what information is there on how they came to be an item? Also - how did he get into the drug business? If the guy was recalled to Washington on a *please explain mission,* there must be some information lying around which at least explains what the CIA suspect. In both cases I don't need evidence to take to court - I just need to know what they have been up to. And what, if anything, the CIA going to do about it.'

Brad took to message as though it was an order for morning coffee.

'Ok – I'll get onto it' was all that he said. With the

contract that Taylor Software had with the US Intelligence and Security services, it was not a tall order. And since Brad had been fully trained at government expense in the art of hacking what information he could not get by legal means he would have to exercise some of his other skills.

The next call would be more difficult. Harold Taylor was a very powerful man in the huge bureaucracy. But – as a bureaucrat – he was often tied to following procedures.

'Hi father| It is Mark – I have something that I want you to do for me. There is evidence that the CIA and our diplomatic services in Africa are being targeted with sex and drugs by the Iranians. Before I get too involved, I need to know a couple of things. Firstly - whether anyone in Washington DC is aware of what is happening. Secondly - what either the CIA or those drones over at Foggy Bottom, are intending to do about it!'

Harold laughed.

'You don't expect me to be able to do that do you? I cannot just go waltzing over to the Secretary of State, drop a bombshell that says your diplomatic service is riddled with sex and drugs, and ask for a please explain!'

Mark had neither the time nor the inclination to get involved in a philosophical discussion with his father. But he knew Harold well enough to know that once he had the sniff that something was not right, he would not let it go until he was satisfied with the answers.

And a solution.

So – he just dangled the obvious carrot,

'I will have to leave that with you!' and ended the call.

Chapter 21

Turning Point

It was getting close to ten o'clock in the morning on the final day of the Africa Union meeting before Mark and Dusty had resumed their patrol of the entrance foyer to the Corinthia. By that time most of the delegates had already arrived and were in the conference hall. A quick check with Blake and Ben, who were patrolling the street outside, revealed that they had nothing to report. Brent and Elliott who had managed to talk their way into the main conference hall representing the Los Angeles Times with the small group of international newspaper reporters who had bothered to turn up, sent a message on his cell phone that all was well inside. Mike and Hamish, who had been checking the goings-on with Mugabe's party at their hotel – the Al Salam Rotana – were now cruising around to make sure that most of his entourage were accounted for.

That was one of the problems that Mark, and his team, had encountered throughout the meeting. With forty-nine of the African leaders in attendance, each with the usual contingent of hangers-on, plus the representatives of countries invited as observers, plus the media, there were over seven hundred people in attendance. Many of the delegates engaged in what was termed 'side' events held elsewhere around the city which meant there was a constant stream of comings and goings around the actual conference. In the case of the Zimbabwe contingent, the crowd was so large it was difficult to tell who was, and who was not, in Khartoum for the meeting. Mugabe had the habit of traveling with different people and in a different vehicle whenever he went anywhere. And, whenever he appeared at the front of the Al Salam to get into his car, he was buried in a crowd of security people that made it well-nigh impossible to tell whether he was part of that particular crowd or not.

Amongst this chaotic scene, there were still people who appeared to have nothing to do with the actual conference. People who for reasons unknown were watching the various delegates as they went about their lawful business. The foyer was like a railway station with the constant flow of bodies in and out. But some people were always there. Or to put it more accurately – there was always someone in a position where they had an uninterrupted view of certain people. It was reasonable to assume that the Sudanese intelligence service would be among the watchers but that did not account for all of them.

Mark had full confidence in his team but still, he worried even though there had been no attempt to attack any of the delegates during their stay in Khartoum. There was no sign of Mohamed Haji and Mark had heard nothing from the Sudanese NISS. As Dusty put it – Mark was the boss and so he was the one who had to worry – the rest of the team would just do all the work.

Except those things were about to change.

After the doors to the conference hall had been closed and the meeting got underway, four people came into the foyer and presented their credentials to the staff who were controlling entry to the hall.

Mark was alerted by the way one of the people walking. It was a man, and he had a pronounced limp. It took a double-take to realize that it was the right leg that was causing the problem. He was the right height, build, and every other aspect. Of the four people in this party, two were women – at least they were dressed in headscarves and long flowing dresses, so their gender was impossible to decide. And they could have been carrying anything.

It was only on that realization that Mark noted that there did not appear to be any check at the conference whether anyone was carrying a gun or not. His suspicion that he knew one of the men was confirmed when Blake came into the foyer and indicated in the direction of the four people who were presenting themselves to the lady controlling access to the hall.

It was Mohamed Haji.

Before any of the team could reach the four people were into the meeting hall and the doors closed behind them. That caused Dusty to immediately text Brent and Elliott to warn them that Haji was now in the conference hall.

Mark got on his satellite phone.

He called Ibrahim Mustafa.

'Hi – It's Mark Taylor.' Hoping that the Sudanese NISS would remember who he was. 'We have just sighted Mohamed Haji. He is at the Corinthia and has just gone into the conference hall.'

Mark did not know sufficient Arabic to be able to understand the initial response which sounded like *ibn kiab* –

the Arabic equivalent of the *son of a dog*. He understood the next comment and kept his mouth shut while the NISS officer berated Mark for not taking any action.

'Yeah – well that may be fine with you' Mark replied, probably more forcefully than he had intended. 'But this is your country, Ibrahim. Even in our country, we don't go around waving guns without just cause. We don't know for certain that he intends to get up to any mischief. May I suggest that you get here as quickly as you can? Then we can decide what you are going to do about it.'

Mark disconnected the call, not sure whether what he had said in English would translate well into Sudanese Arabic.

He went up to the lady whose job had been to check on the credentials of people entering the conference hall. He did not threaten her. He just asked with a smile.

'Who was that group who just entered the hall?'

The reply he got startled even Mark.

The lady was proficient in several languages none of which she had perfected. Nonetheless, the message was clear.

'That was the Iran delegation who have been cleared to attend as observers.'

'Do you have their names?' asked Mark, knowing that, even if he got an answer, it may not help him.

The lady was only too happy to provide him with the information.

None of the four people had been named Haji.

Mark next asked if he could see the schedule for today's meeting, realizing as he did so that he should have thought of that earlier. The lady was happy to oblige.

He quickly scanned the paper that the lady had produced, and in his hurry, he almost missed it. That was because Mugabe's name did not appear on the schedule. All that it said was that a discussion on corruption in Africa was to take place under the chairmanship of the Republic of Zimbabwe. That discussion was to take place starting at approximately 11 am.

The time now was 10:45 am.

Mark had Blake go into the conference hall and get as close to the Iranian delegation as was possible without attracting any unnecessary attention. Within minutes Blake texted that Haji was sitting on his own towards the back of the hall and was busy playing with his cell phone and taking absolutely no interest in the goings-on at the meeting. The three other people who had gone with him into the hall were off to the side involved in an animated discussion with one of the staff - apparently having difficulty getting a suitable translation service on their earpieces. That was not surprising since the African Union was not too interested in producing a translator for Farsi.

The Sudanese hosts were even less interested in doing anything for Shia Muslims.

Mark checked his watch. In five minutes, he would need to do something. He presumed that Robert Mugabe would be unable to resist the exposure and would want to chair the meeting himself. With all fifty-five countries in the African Union being represented at the meeting there would be limited exposure for no more than a handful of the leaders. The President of Zimbabwe was far from being the most popular leader at the present gathering, but he either did not know that or chose to ignore it.

Mugabe would be taking his place on the rostrum.

What better place could there be for an assassination?

In the hall, Brent slowly made his way into a position that was closer to where Haji was still fiddling with his cell phone. Like Blake, Brent had a Beretta pistol which despite his training and ability with firearms would be less than accurate at any distance over twenty feet and useless beyond that. He feared that any firearm could be carried by one of the two females. If they were both carrying, then he was as good as dead. It was unusual for someone with his training to ask the question, but he texted anyway.

What do I do now?

Before Mark could reply, Mustafa came into the foyer and rushed over to where Mark and Dusty were standing. He started to speak but was stopped by Mark, who had his plan.

'Whether Haji plans anything or not we need to get him out of there. I do not care about how you do it, but we cannot take the risk. The three people he came with may have nothing planned and may well claim diplomatic immunity. That is as may be. What I do know is that someone with the background of Mohamed Haji has no place in a conference of this kind. I want Haji and the Iranians out of there. Can you do that?'

Ibrahim hesitated for a moment. His country had invested a huge amount of money to host this meeting in the hope that it would reflect well on the international circuit and give much-needed credibility to the Sudanese leadership. For years Sudan has not had the best of luck - shunned by the International Monetary Fund and stuck in the inevitable conflict where it could not generate sufficient funds to invest anything in its future, Now was the chance to prove that it was playing a useful part in the African community of nations. And that could all be dashed by having an embarrassing diplomatic incident.

And it would certainly not do anything to further the career of Ibrahim Mustafa. But he had to make a decision. In the end, he just muttered something under his breath.

'Ok – I will need help, and if this turns to shit, I suggest you leave Sudan before word gets out! How many men have you got?

'There are eight of us – with yourself and your off-sider that should be enough.' Mark replied. 'What do you plan to do?'

'I was rather hoping that you would have a plan. You must have some idea!' Mustafa replied. Which Mark translated into *if he left someone else to make the decision, he at least stood a chance of keeping his job!*

'Ok - we should politely ask all four of the people to join us for a chat outside the conference hall. Let's go and see what we can do.'

Mark, Dusty, Mustafa, and his assistant moved towards the door of the conference room as Mark talked to Mike on the satellite phone. 'Get in here quickly as you can and organize a room where we can interview our guests. Preferably on the first floor – anything that avoids the use of the escalators. Ask Hamish to check it out and make sure it can be secured. Then I want everyone kept out of the way. Go!'

The group pushed past the lady who was staffing the door and went straight into the conference hall. The three Iranians who had been trying – and failing - to get their translation service organized were just about to sit down in front of where Haji was seated. Blake and Brent stood and moved in behind Haji.

At a signal from Mark, they simply said 'you are coming with us' and grabbed Haji by the arms. Mustafa dealt with the Iranians by simply showing them his badge of office and asking them in English to go with him to the back of the hall while he had a chat. They did not understand. Or at least they said that they did not understand English. He repeated the request in Arabic.

They again shook their heads,

Mustafa lost his patience and showed them his gun.

The Iranian man started to protest but by this time it was too late. Mark and Dusty each took one of the women and ushered them towards the door with the rest following behind.

Mike was standing outside and pointed them to the far side of the foyer and a small meeting room with Hamish standing beside the door. They rushed across the entranceway and into the room before anyone in the foyer could even notice what was happening. They all piled in before Hamish and Mustafa's assistant – a man named Abdul Osman – closed the door and stood guard outside.

The Iranians by this time were furious at their treatment but Mustafa simply told them to sit down. Which they did without questioning his language which told Mark that they were all quite proficient in English – and probably in Farsi - and probably Sudanese Arabic as well. Strangely enough, no one protested too much about the behavior of Mustafa. Whether that was because they realized that they were in some sort of trouble, or because of the intimidating presence of men the size of Mark and Dusty it was hard to tell. In Marks's view, it was probably because they were all representatives of the Iranian Embassy, or the Iranian Intelligence service and they knew – or at least thought that they knew – that this would be over very quickly by their claiming diplomatic protection.

Mark started the questioning just to see how far they could go before things started to turn nasty.

'First things first – We believe one of you is called Mohamed Haji and that you are in this country using a false passport. Now we want to know which one of you is Haji'

No one said a word.

'Ok.' Mark continued. 'Well, we will try to sort out who is not Haji!' and he motioned to Dusty who pulled a photograph out his pocket and showed it to each of the four Iranians in turn.

'Now does anyone recognize the person in this photograph?' he asked each of them.

Dusty was not expecting any verbal response to his question. What he was expecting was a reaction to the photograph that showed a grainy picture of a smiling man with a full beard a good head of black hair. And that reaction he got from the man who was now clean-shaven and bald – a flicker of a smile across the face of the person they knew as Haji said much more than any words could.

None of the Iranians said a word.

But Mark had all that he needed to know. He just nodded his head towards the Sudanese contingent.

Mustafa took over from Mark and moved towards the man that Mark had indicated was their target and fixed him with an icy stare.

'Ok – I will tell you what happens now. Mohamed Haji - or whatever name you are currently using – you are under arrest for entering Sudan using a false passport. As for your reasons for this illegal entry – our colleagues in the United States Central Intelligence Agency tell us that you are responsible for a plot to attack one of the leaders in the African Union. We believe that you and your three colleagues entered the conference where you intended to carry out that plot. I am therefore also arresting your three colleagues on suspicion of being accessories in that plot. We do not have a bill of rights in this country as your American friends do, so I will not read you your rights. In simple terms, because you have refused to answer our basic questions, you do not at present have any rights. You will be taken from the Hotel to the Kober prison here in Khartoum. Until you can answer our reasonable questions you will each be held in isolation until you do. You will not be allowed any visitors. You will not be allowed to talk to anyone from a foreign Embassy. On the other hand – if you will supply details of who you are, where you are from, and which Embassy you wish to represent your interests, then we may take a different view. Now - Do you have any questions?'

The man who was the leader of this small Iranian group smiled. Well – it was a smirk. He spoke in perfectly good English.

'This is contrary to international law. My Embassy has every right to know that we are being held against our will. And unless you can produce proof of this preposterous accusation that you have made against my colleagues, I require you to release us at once.'

Then it was the turn of Mustafa to smile.

'I am so sorry I do not believe that you have told us who you are. As far as I am aware this is currently a terrorist matter as well as one that concerns the integrity of a nation-state. Therefore, until we settle the details, you will be detained under Sudan's terrorist law which I might add some countries find particularly brutal. Again, in simple terms, we are trying to protect the lives of our guests and until we can eliminate you and your colleagues as a threat you are being held as potential terrorists. Now let us be reasonable. We cannot advise any Embassy that you are being held because firstly – we do not know which one to advise, and secondly – we do not know who you are - do we? In addition, at least one of you entered Sudan using a false passport. Because no one is saying anything, I can only assume that you are all did the same thing. Now – if you would be so kind as to answer my quite reasonable questions we could move on. But you won't. So – we can't/ Now - Do you need any further clarification of your position. Or can I go ahead with the more formal part?'

Their leader looked confused.

'What are you talking about? You know we are the Iranian delegation. And what *more formal* part of what?'

Again, the smile.

'Now who is being unreasonable! At least one of your group entered my country illegally. Then he tried to get into the meeting either under the same name with which he entered Sudan or yet another name. And anyone can turn up at the conference and claim to be from anywhere. So – we need to sort that out. Meanwhile, you go to jail – as much for your safety as anything else. It should only take us a couple of years to sort that out. And then you will either be released with our apologies or stay and rot.'

Much to the surprise of Mark and Dusty that still had no effect. They did not know whether that was because they had been terrified by what Mustafa had to say. Or was it because they would be in more trouble with their masters? Or did they just not care? Or did they believe that the Islamic Republic of Iran would have sufficient power to be able to nullify any effort by the Sudan NSIS?

Mustafa just shrugged. Sudan had its share of terrorists and Mustafa had dealt with them.

'Ok – one at a time – stand up by the table and let's see what you have. We will take the men first. We may as well start with you.' He indicated the man that Mark knew as Haji.

'You cannot do this!' their leader, who had been named Yazdani on the documents presented to the conference, almost screamed.

'Oh – but I can. Because, as I have already explained, you are going to Kober prison. We need to search you all to make sure that you have nothing on you that our prison would not allow' Mustafa replied. 'It is a formality – if you are carrying something that you shouldn't that is your fault, not mine. It would be better for all concerned that you tell us now – but that is your choice. The sooner we get this over with the sooner you can get on your way, Mind you, I cannot see why you would be so keen to get there. Kober prison does not have a very good reputation.'

Mustafa opened the door and summoned inside two ladies who were dressed in the blue uniform of the Sudanese police. They did not say anything. They just stood inside the door with their arms folded.

The man known as Haji had little choice but to comply with Dusty and Blake standing over him. He emptied his pockets which did not reveal anything useful other than his cell phone. It was the involuntary smile on his face that gave him away as he went to return to his seat. Dusty simply held out a hand to restrain him and then locked his arm up to his back in a vice-like grip which caused Haji to scream.

Dusty ignored the scream. He then grabbed at Haji's waistband. The two men struggled to get control of the pistol that he extracted.

It looked to Dusty very much like a 9mm PC-9-20AF illegally manufactured in Iran as a variant of the Swiss SIG Sauer P226, the pistol would normally have a 10 round magazine but there wasn't time to find out whether it was fully loaded. Dusty was just too powerful. In the same movement, he slammed Haji to the floor still with his arm twisted up his back. Mustafa clamped handcuffs on him before dragging him to his feet and almost throwing him into a chair.

After an exchange of words with Dusty, Mark addressed this evil little man. 'So – where did that come from? And what were you planning to do with it?'

Haji almost snarled his reply.

'Come on! Nobody in this country walks around without a gun!'

That statement had a certain amount of merit except that he could not have entered the country with the gun – unless he also did that illegally. And – since it was (probably) of Iranian manufacture it was clear where he would have acquired it. As had been discussed between Mustafa and Mark back at the airport on his arrival there were still regulations and diplomatic standards of behavior that should be followed. Mustafa could decide just what those standards were,

This whole situation was getting to the point of being an embarrassment for Yazdani if he was indeed an official from the Iranian Embassy.

It was most unlikely that Haji had brought the pistol with him. Airlines were reluctant to allow anyone to fly carrying sidearms even if the ammunition was separated from the gun. Even then it was only allowed with special permission from the captain on the flight deck. Had Haji flown into Sudan by Iran Air he may have got away with it? But not by traveling on an Emirates flight. So – the odds were that the pistol that Haji now had, had been provided by the Iran Embassy or some organization very close to it.

Mark let the matter pass for the time being. It was unlikely that Haji had intended to shoot Robert Mugabe – at least with a pistol. Unless he was an excellent marksman, he would be unlikely to be able to hit a barn-door from more than forty-feet distance, and he was unlikely to be able to get closer to Mugabe given the throngs of bodyguards that were around.

They next searched Yazdani which revealed the inevitable cell phone and very little else of interest. As had been the case with Haji, there was nothing to reveal who or what he was. So, it appeared that the Iranian delegation was intent on remaining incognito. At least Yazdani, or whatever his real name, was not carrying a gun.

Then Mustafa merely nodded his head towards the two police officers, and they went to the first of the two Iranian ladies and commenced a pat-down search. They took their time and ignored the constant stream of protests which sounded like curses in Farsi. The first lady who had a quite indifferent attitude despite her indignant protests produced a similar result to the search of Yazdani.

Nothing.

Then the police officers moved to the second lady who had a quite different attitude to the first of the women. She immediately collapsed on the floor wailing that she was unwell and needed to go to the toilet. Mark was impressed by the reaction from Mustafa and the police officers. They just smiled and waited.

While one of the police officers simply lifted the lady back to her feet as though she were a rag doll and held her with her arms behind her back while the other police officer carried out a frisk-down search unmoved by the whole affair.

This lady was carrying a Heckler and Koch MPT-9 Submachine gun held in front of her dress by a strap around her neck. She also had four cartridges concealed in the left and right sides of her gown. The gun was of German design but this one had probably been made elsewhere under license from the original manufacturers. Most likely in Iran.

The atmosphere in the room changed dramatically.

The Sudan police are not renowned for the treatment of any prisoners especially those apparently about to carry out any form of terrorism. The door to the room was opened once more and blue uniforms of police flooded in. A brief command from Mustafa saw all four of the Iranians gagged and trussed. Without any regard for their prisoners or any casual observers, the four people were roughly moved through the hotel foyer and thrown into a truck that had no windows and the door was slammed shut and locked from the outside. It was all over in the blink of an eye,

In the conference hall, Mugabe carried on chairing his meeting oblivious to what had happened.

As the police drove away with the captives, Mustafa stood in the entrance to the Corinthia looking like a heavy load had been lifted off his shoulders.

He turned to Mark with the inevitable grin on his face.

'Well, that was fun!' he said. 'First, let me apologize for my failure to locate Haji before today. I assume that he was holed up in the Iranian Embassy and would have been out of our reach. My thanks to the CIA for helping us avoid an incident at the conference. You cannot know what it means to my government – so a very sincere *Thank you!* to you and your team. Do you happen to know who their target was?'

Mark had to think before he answered that.

In the end, he just said 'No! we did not know who the intended target was. Just that Haji was involved. Nor did we know of the involvement of Iran. People who are paid a lot more than I am will need to sort that out. You know how this works! – we do all the work – someone else has to develop the spin!'

Both men laughed, shook hands, and went their separate ways.

Chapter 22

Flight

Mark was very relieved to make the final call to his controller. It was the end of yet another successful mission. There were a few things that needed to be done to tidy up a few loose ends. And he had one more thing that he had to do while he was in Africa.

The team had avoided the death of one of the most hated men on the planet. They had carried out this mission on behalf of the government of the United States because the CIA – the people who had come up with the idea that an attempt was to be made on the life of Mugabe - would not, or could not, do it.

Now that it was all over – the CIA would once again get all the credit. The President of the United States had already received a call several days earlier from the man himself thanking the CIA for their role in Zimbabwe. The President would most likely now get a call from the President of the Republic of Sudan thanking *him* and *his* CIA for avoiding the disaster that would have occurred had Haji and his suspected Iranian friends succeeded in their assassination attempt at the conference of the African Union.

Mark made the call to his Carl Vinson. After going through what was now a routine before he got to speak to a human being, he delivered his report.

'Haji is now in prison courtesy of the Sudanese Police. Mugabe is safe and well. I understand he is about to leave for home. It looks as though we are all done here.'

The reply was what he had come to expect.

'Ok – I will pass that on up the line. Could you confirm in due course that Mugabe has left Khartoum and then await further instructions!'

Mark could hardly believe his eyes as he watched President Robert Mugabe enter the International Lounge at Khartoum Airport. For a man who was supposed to have been killed during the previous few days, he looked remarkably fit and seemingly had not a care in the world. But then – Why shouldn't he!

At no stage during his stay in the city of Khartoum would he have been aware of any threat having been made against him. The person who had been tagged as the potential assassin, and who had been the subject of constant and intense scrutiny by Marks team, was in a Sudanese prison. Although there was no evidence - or even a hint - that Haji had any connection with Mugabe, there was evidence that he was armed and in the same hall, at the same time. Add to that - Haji was on a terrorist watch list and had entered Sudan under another name. Therefore, he would be locked up for the foreseeable future. He would no longer be a threat to anyone.

Undoubtedly some people would wish that things had turned out differently. Zimbabwe was reputed to be a democracy and it was true that elections were held there from time to time which gave the impression that whoever held power did so at the will of the people. In reality, President

Mugabe ruled his people with an iron fist and benefitted from corruption as would any other dictator. He did so with apparent impunity and the full support of the international community. And now he could thank the leaders of the free world for assuring that he could continue.

More out of courtesy than duty, Mark thumbed his sat phone and hit speed dial for the number that he had been given to contact his controller.

The robotic voice answered his call with the usual message.

'Yes – How can I help you?'

'Operation Steel Tiger reporting in. President Robert Mugabe is just about to board an Ethiopian Airlines flight from Khartoum to Harare, via Addis Ababa. Requesting instructions.'

'One moment was the reply, followed by a pause and what sounded like a heated conversation interspersed with various electronic sounds, and then the robotic voice returned.

'Hold your position and await further orders.'

The line went dead.

Mark just stared at his phone as he heard the final boarding call for the Ethiopian Airlines flight being called. He had been instructed to check that Mugabe left Khartoum – nothing more, nothing less. He had no idea whether Uncle Robert was going straight home to Harare or was planning to stop over in Ethiopia. And, quite frankly, he could not have cared less.

Mark had other plans while he was still in Africa. Having come this far he could not wait to implement them. He did not want to have those plans messed up by a bureaucrat in Washington DC.

He stared out of the window on the observation deck as the flight made its way towards the main runway. Khartoum has only one runway and so the airplane had to wait for what seemed an eternity for clearance to leave. But eventually, it took off and headed south-east slowly disappearing into the dusty sky that was typical of Africa.

And then all hell broke loose.

An alarm started to sound throughout the terminal and emergency vehicles rushed to the airport runway. Over the loudspeakers, a voice barked in both Sudanese Arabic and English instructing would-be passengers and other people who were in the airport to return to the check-in area and to vacate their departure gates and the observation deck. Once there they were instructed to evacuate the building, assemble in the carpark, and await further orders. As Mark made his way amongst the panicking crowd, he could sense that this was not a drill.

Trying to find out what was going on was impossible.

So, he called Dusty.

'What is going on? We have been told to evacuate the airport.'

Dusty laughed. 'Yeah – news travels fast in this place. We were tuned in to a local police radio. They just announced that a bomb threat has been made on an Ethiopian Airlines flight. The flight is returning to Khartoum. All the available police are rushing to the airport. That is all we know.

Mark froze.

'You don't think that the Iranians had a plan B? Wait until Mugabe was in the air, then blow up the airplane!'

As usual, Dusty was very helpful.

'Mark – if they wanted him dead what better way to do it? There is nothing you can do now. Just calm down and see what happens.'

Mark had to see the logic in what Dusty had said. The fact that his team had followed Mohamed Haji for a long and boring journey without being detected and yet failed to protect the man who had been the target of Hajis' group meant that his mission had achieved nothing. Not that Mark cared about whether Mugabe lived or died. Yet – if he died that would mean that the mission had failed. That was something Mark cared about.

All other flights in and out of Khartoum were canceled until the emergency was dealt with. The only flight that was allowed to land was an Ethiopian Airlines plane. Mark, who was watching from the carpark, correctly assumed that it was the flight carrying President Robert Mugabe.

There followed several hours during which all the passengers on the flight were not allowed to leave the airplane until they had been thoroughly checked by security. Then they were all lined up on the runway in full view of the public as well as an ever-increasing scrum of media reporters – most of whom were hardly in evidence at the conference – together with their vast collection of visual and sound recording equipment.

The threat of a bomb being on board an airplane that was carrying someone of international significance become instant world news. And there for everyone to see was President Robert Mugabe standing impatiently with the rest of the peasants, waiting to identify and recover his bags. Of course, there is a standard and universal procedure for such an event. Everyone on board the flight was to find and then standby their luggage. The problem for Mugabe was that he had never packed a bag himself in living memory and the exercise took on a life of its own. Once that was sorted out, the airport staff wandered between the passengers and their bags with detector dogs at the end of which not one single item had been identified as containing anything that could be remotely called a bomb.

Mark made his third final call to his controller.

He got the usual helpful robotic answer.

'How can we help you?'

Mark answered the question with one of his own.

'The airplane that was carrying Mugabe has returned to Khartoum due to a bomb scare. Do you have any information on where that alert came from?'

There followed the usual background noise and static. After a wait of several minutes, the conversation was taken up by a human, who simply informed Mark that the first phase of his mission was complete and that he should now await further instructions.

Mark was not satisfied with that. He was not aware that his mission had more than one phase. But more importantly – Who had arranged the bomb threat?

So, he asked the obvious question.

'Did your people arrange the bomb threat?'

There followed more background noise and static, and then another person took up the conversation.

'You do not need to know that. Your orders now are to await further instruction. Do you understand those orders?'

Mark was surprised by that reaction.

So, he made the next obvious comment.

'My present orders came from the White House. So, are you sure the order that you are now giving me has that same authority?'

That got a reaction.

The call was disconnected.

Mark got hold of an English Language newspaper - the Khartoum Monitor – and scanned it for any news of what had occurred the previous day. He finally located a few words tucked in amongst articles of local news which indicated to Mark that the events at the Corinthia were being downplayed by the Sudanese. The article simply reported that an arrest had been made in downtown Khartoum and that four people were being detained by the Sudanese police for *immigration irregularities.*

No mention of pistols or a submachine gun.

No mention of Iran.

No mention of a potential diplomatic incident.

No mention of Mohamed Haji.

No mention of the involvement of the CIA.

The rest of the news was of no interest to Mark and doubtful interest to anyone else.

It was now time to stand down his team and to think about getting them home. For the three members of the team that Mark had brought to Africa who was serving in the US Army – Brent, Mike, and Hamish – it was just a matter of arranging their flights out courtesy of the military attaché at the US Embassy. Blake was a little different because he was no longer in the Army and only loosely – for that read covertly - attached to the FBI. Ben and Elliott had no particular attachments, but they could easily fit in with whatever arrangements were made as was the case with Mark and Dusty.

Except that Marks's orders were to *await further instructions.* It had not been stated where those orders were to come from.

Mark made a call to Ambassador Anthony Luxton in the hope that he could sort things out and they could all get the hell out of Dodge.

The government of Sudan was in the process of calling the President of the United States to thank him for the help of his Central Intelligence Agency. The US Embassy in Khartoum was basking in the glow even though the CIA

Station Chief was in Washington on a *please explain* mission and his office had nothing to do with what had occurred anyway.

The result was that Mark Taylor, and his team were the favorites of the month in the Khartoum Embassy of the United States. Except for the Deputy Chief of Mission who was both confused and angry.

Things were a little different in Teheran Iran.

President Mahmoud Khatami was livid and was seeking answers from the Intelligence Ministry. The facts of the matter - as had been reported to the President - were that the mission to destabilize things had been thwarted by the CIA despite careful planning and the allocation of vast sums of money and resources. The attempts to have diplomatic staff compromised had achieved nothing, and the main man who had been assigned to the task was now in a Sudanese prison. Khatami was not overly concerned that Mugabe was still alive because the President of Zimbabwe had always been a side issue. But there had been no publicity at all coming out of the meeting of the African Union. It seemed likely that his equivalent in the US - the man who was supposed to feel the heat - had received nothing but good news as a result of their endeavors.

The only good news was that the Iranian intelligence had reported that President Thomas was in hospital but had been unable to get confirmation of why. The suspicion was that it was on a routine matter and – thankfully – the Iranians avoided any claims of their involvement. Still, that did not please Khatami.

Surprisingly, the intelligence people seemed upbeat despite the failure of their operations. Their belated attempt to cause a bomb scare on Mugabe's flight out of Khartoum and get him back to where they had a chance to kill him also failed because they lacked the resources to conduct such a plan at short notice. Well – it wasn't the Ministries fault that they had been provided with inadequate information on the ramifications of the earlier blunders. It would have helped if – for example – they had been informed that Haji was in prison along with his co-conspirators from the Iranian Embassy.

It still took them some time to calm the irate President who confronted them. But it was not his job to explain it to this amateur what had happened with the plot.

Larijani was not certain.

That was a job for Supreme Leader Ali Khomani.

He just settled for patiently outlining what would happen next.

'Our information is that the US Central Intelligence Agency has had nothing to do with our operations so far and that the Americans are in a state of total confusion. The team of Americans that have been involved in this affair has been stood down and we are checking their movements. In case they should wish to be further involved we are arranging through our contacts for them to be distracted while we implement the next stage of our plans. Our man in Khartoum has indeed been detained by the Sudanese on an immigration issue but that will be resolved shortly. As for our attempt to compromise a couple of their officials – in one case that has resulted in their man being recalled to Washington leaving them vulnerable while in another case we had to intervene when the man contrary to our instructions talked too much and he had to be terminated. But – overall everything is under control.'

Larijani would have a more difficult job delivering his report to the full security council. He could blame Haji.

Or he could claim that he did not know all the implications of their plans. What he did know was that Khatami was not particularly well-liked by the clerical members of the council. So – all that he needed to do was to let them bicker among themselves.

Mark was very surprised to receive an offer of a free trip from Ambassador Luxton.

During the previous few days, Luxton had arranged to go with the High Commissioner of the United Nations Refugee Agency – an Italian ex-diplomat called Lorenzo Ganni - on a visit to the Pugnido refugee camp in Ethiopia. The camp had existed since 1993 and held refugees from the various conflicts in the region but mostly in South Sudan. The United Nations was keen to have the United States get more involved with refugee matters but that was hard to do without threatening a form of blackmail. And an opportunity had arisen recently with a scandal that had involved the Embassy in Khartoum. Lorenzo Ganni took full advantage of that.

Luxton did not think that the UNHCR would have the balls to follow through on their threat to embarrass the United States, but a curious set of events caused that to not matter all that much. He had been informed by the Secretary of State that the offer would be made to accompany Ganni, and he was left with no choice but to follow the wishes of his boss.

The actual conversation with Luxton had a few surprises.

'I have been instructed to invite you on a quick trip to Ethiopia. The Secretary of State informs me that your mother is in Pugnido, and you would like to catch up with her while you are in the area.'

To say that Mark was confused by this would be a

complete understatement.

'What is my mother doing in Ethiopia?'

Mark's response came as a surprise to Luxton and then they were both confused.

'I was just repeating what State said! Well – he described your mother as "the dear lady" so I just assumed...'

Mark could see the funny side.

'Anthony! The *dear lady* that he was referring to is my girlfriend! But – Yes – if the offer still stands - I would love to come, provided I can bring one of my team – we planned on making a trip there anyway.'

The full implications of this action were still not clear – at least to Ambassador Luxton. He had been more or less instructed by his Secretary of State John Scott to have a chat with Taylor about the proliferation of drugs in Khartoum and elsewhere in Africa. And those instructions had clearly said that the *chat* should not be conducted anywhere near his Embassy. The instructions had left the distinct impression that some members – or members! - of his staff were implicated in the drug trade and that was a cause of mounting problems for the career diplomat, Not the least of which was the fact that his boss knew more about the problem than he was prepared to tell Luxton.

Mark Taylor's role in this was much more straightforward. The State Department had indicated that Mark had recently been on a mission into Afghanistan on the trail of drugs. He and his friend Dusty Miller had experience with the US Special Forces where they had been involved with drug dealers and their ilk. So – the Secretary of State's plan was aimed and getting Taylor to sort out another mess. Why the US President could not simply have issued an executive order to reassign the team to a new mission was beyond Luxton to understand. That had been dismissed by Scott as merely a temporary problem. The President was absent from his office – no reason given – and the Vice President did not want to decide on such a sensitive matter.

Or - just maybe - he was waiting for the wheels of bureaucracy to turn, before doing so.

That would explain why Mark and his team had been *awaiting further instruction* in Khartoum pending a decision in Washington.

But it sure seemed a strange way to run a railroad.

Since Mark and Dusty had planned to head for the Pugnido camp anyway, the invitation was accepted for quite practical reasons. Traveling in this part of the world on an UN-sponsored flight that would go directly to the camp would be far better than taking the risk of traveling on a commercial flight of dubious reliability and then having to make a road trip in some of the more hostile territories on the planet.

It did occur to Mark that this invitation was a strange coincidence. He could understand that John Scott would have access to all sorts of intelligence and that could include the whereabouts of Debbie Petersen – after all the location of the lady was not exactly a state secret. But – why had Scott bothered to find out this piece of otherwise useless information?

Mark could only conclude that there was more to this than Ambassador Luxton had said.

Or – Luxton was just as confused as Mark.

Chapter 23

Compromise

Lawrence Johnson sat in his hotel room contemplating his next move. He was supposed to be attending a dinner at the US Embassy but had called in sick. He did not want to sit around with a bunch of diplomats talking the usual crap when he had other more serious matters on his mind.

At first, his meeting with Mark Taylor had left him stunned. He had expected that Taylor would have been sympathetic to his plight. But he had got that wrong on two counts. Firstly – Taylor was not the person that Johnson thought that he was. Or he was not on any official business. Or he was on a mission that was so secret or covert that he could not be distracted from his main purpose. Or he just could not be bothered. Secondly – Johnson had to admit that his request for help was naïve. His was not the first occasion in which a man in his position had been caught with his pants down and he should face that fact and deal with it himself.

He had not heard anything from the Iranians since that fateful meeting in Teheran. He had not seen or heard anything from the lady who called herself Perim Koytak. He had not been approached by anyone looking to provide him with drugs. So, the answer was that he should disappear before there was an attempt to involve him in any of their activities.

What he had done was wrong. He knew that.

And he must take the consequences.

It would mean the end of his marriage. In all fairness, that marriage was on shaky ground even before he had strayed. It would mean that he would not be seeing his kids anytime soon. But he had to admit that he had not been the greatest of fathers. The career path that he had chosen took all the attention. That was the price you paid for ambition and now the cost would be borne by him alone.

Ironically, it would mean the end of a very promising career in the US State Department. The brief adulation that had accompanied his rapid rise to Ambassador level would be gone. So – he would need to start again. It had been done before. He was still young. And he came from a family that had the resources that could, and would, support him.

He smiled as he contemplated his future. He was scheduled to board a flight out of Khartoum in the morning of the following day. That Emirates flight would take him to Dubai for the short connecting flight to Kuwait. Except that he would not be going to Kuwait.

Not tomorrow.

Not ever again.

He would resign his position in the US diplomatic service effective from tomorrow and with immediate effect. An email would be sent to his wife telling her that he had quit and that he would be seeking refuge in an as-yet-unnamed country. He would make it clear that she would be financially supported. His theory was that, out of spite, the Iranians would simply inform his wife of his indiscretions and that would be the end of that. The money would not be an issue. He would back the US financial system to secure his financial future and that of his children. He would back the US security systems to protect them all.

Satisfied that his plans were in place, he helped himself to a generous serving of bourbon and dry from the mini-bar and sat back to do something that he could not recall having done in a long time.

He would watch a western movie.

Lawrence was so engrossed in the antics of the Magnificent Seven that he almost missed the faint tapping on the door. More from annoyance at the interruption, he used the remote to turn down the sound, and there it was again. Tap, tap, tap.

Rising from his seat he went to the door and looked through the viewer. At first, he did not recognize the visitor. It was a lady dressed in a short skirt and a loose top, her hair was in a mess, and she had no make-up on. The red rims around her eyes suggested that she had been crying. She looked nothing like how he remembered the girl that had been the cause of all his troubles.

But Perim Koytak still looked beautiful.

He checked that the security chain was in place before opening the door to the extent of the chain.

'What do you want?' was all that he asked in a tone that he hoped reflected his annoyance.

The answer that he got shocked him.

'Please! Let me come in! We have to talk!'

And the tears started to flow. Heartfelt tears tugged at his heart, as though something terrible was about to happen and only he could do something about it. But – he had decided on his future. It was going to happen the very next day. And – could he trust this girl who he had made love to not that long ago only to see his life turned upside down?

Johnson remained resolute.

'I have nothing to say to you!'

The door started to close.

Perim grabbed the chain and pleaded with him in a despairing tone that could not have been faked. She did not raise her voice – just choked as she whispered.

'Please, Lawrence! I am in desperate trouble. Please help me...'

Perim disappeared from view, as she collapsed to the floor.

Lawrence hesitated.

Then he muttered a tirade of obscenities under his breath. He released the security chain and threw the door open. Looking left and right up and down the corridor, he could see no one. He lent down and assisted Perim to her feet. She clung to him like a leach.

In desperation, he dragged her inside, slammed, and locked to door.

The only thing he could do was to deposit Perim on the couch while he returned to his seat opposite the TV. Reluctantly he turned the sound to mute so that the only sound that remained in the room was the quiet sobbing of Perim.

He looked at the girl more out of pity than anything else. He remembered vividly the first time they had met and the passionate encounter that had resulted from that. He remembered the second time when it had seemed so natural to make love to this girl who had a body to die for.

And then there was the third time!

'What do you want from me?' he asked, biting his tongue as he did so.

Perim finally looked up and sat forward on the edge of the seat. Then it all came pouring out in one long stream interspersed with tears.

'Lawrence – you must believe me! All those terrible things that the man in Teheran said to you. I just so wanted to hold you and tell you that it was nothing to do with me. I do not know how he found out about us. But I was kidnapped and taken to Teheran. I did not know that you would be there. They threatened me that I would be killed if I said one word to you. Since then, I have been trying to get away from them – but they are everywhere! I refused to carry out their wishes. And now they forced me to come to Khartoum where they said that I would find you. And I have! So – you must help me get away from them!'

Perim again burst into tears. She was inconsolable.

Johnson did not know what to say or do.

He wanted to get rid of her out of his room.

Out of his life!

But could he? What if the Iranians had indeed forced Perim into all this nonsense? And what if she, like him, had been sucked in?

Johnson got up from his seat and walked across to the couch. He sat beside her and put an arm around her shoulders hoping to console her. Perim buried her head in his chest and then reached up placing her arms around his neck, clinging to him in desperation. Her skirt rode up her thighs. As his hands move to stroke her back it was obvious that she was wearing nothing underneath the loose top. It took all of his concentration to avoid touching her more affectionately and he had to fight to prevent his becoming aroused.

Except that he kissed the top of her head.

Perim responded by offering her lips which he was unable to refuse.

The Tap, tap, tap, came from the door.

Johnson looked around searching for the source. It

had to be the door.

Another Tap, tap, tap.

Perim smiled up at him.

'I am sorry. That will be room service. I told them that if I did not return, they should bring a drink and a snack. Sorry! I forgot. If you do not want a drink of Raki, I will tell them to go away!'

He had to smile.

He had been so preoccupied with the other issues he had not eaten, and a snack seemed like a good idea. And a drink of Raki seemed rather appropriate.

'It is Ok. I will let room service in and then we can decide what I am to do with you!'

Johnson got to his feet, went to the viewer, and looked out. There were two men. One dressed in chef's clothes carrying a tray and the other one dressed as a bellhop carrying a bottle and two glasses. The bottle looked suspiciously like Raki.

He released the security chain and opened the door. The chef walked straight to the lounge table placed the tray and removed the lid to reveal an assortment of food. The bellhop ushered Johnson back to his chair, placed the glasses on the table, and poured two generous portions. When Johnson asked for the chit to sign for the food and drinks the chef told him that it had already been taken care of.

The two men then turned and retreated to the door.

Except that, they did not leave.

The bellhop replaced the security chain and turned around gripping a SIG Sauer P226 semi-automatic handgun pointing it at Johnson. The chef who was the person in charge sat down next to Perim and smiled.

'Lawrence! Have a drink of Raki – it will probably be your last so enjoy it! Now – we understand that you have done something which you were told not to do. Do you have an explanation?'

'I don't know what you are talking about!' was the only response that Johnson could think of.

The chef again smiled.

'Well let me remind you. We understand that you had a conversation with your security and intelligence people. We would like to know what that conversation was all about.'

Johnson hoped that the indignation in his voice would have the desired effect.

'I still don't know what you are talking about!'

The punch to the side of his head was unexpected and could have been fatal were it not for the fact that he had been sitting at the front of the chair causing him to lose balance and crash to the floor.

As Johnson looked up from the floor at the two gentlemen, he began to realize that this was not going to end well. Perim smiled as she took another sip from her glass of Raki but otherwise took no part in the proceedings. The chef just continued talking to the man on the floor.

'I do not have time for this. You spoke to one of your CIA people. We want to know what was said. Now that is a reasonable request is it not?'

Johnson knew that it was no use protesting. He could have tried a line that as an ambassador he had to talk with all sorts of people. And he could not be expected to remember every conversation. But he knew which conversation they were referring to. And they simply would not believe anything he told them except the truth of that conversation.

He was as certain as any man could be that Mark Taylor would have revealed nothing to the Iranians.
He made up his mind that they would not learn anything from him.

The next blow was to his head and came from the boot of the bellhop.

He had a vague feeling of the room spinning and then everything went blank.

Chapter 24

Iran

It was not entirely true to call the Iran Ministry of Intelligence and Security of the Islamic Republic – otherwise known as MOIS or its Farsi name of VAJA - the Iranian equivalent of the United States Central Intelligence Agency. They were more than just the organization that gathered intelligence around the world. They also had responsibility for domestic intelligence fulfilling the functions of the US Federal Bureau of Investigation, conducting intelligence functions performed through US diplomatic channels, and doing most of the work carried out within the intelligence arms of the US Army, Navy, Air Force and Marines. In addition to that, there was not the proliferation of perceived functions that existed in the US in a mix of multiple organizations including the NSA and NOR. It was little wonder that the US system was confused given that the disparate organizations would look to defend their territories and would only reluctantly share information.

Intelligence matters in Iran are under the strict control of one Ministry. Called by various uncomplementary names by the people of Iran, who almost to a man hated the organization, it has a variety of names by which it was known to the international intelligence community. MOIS was the more formal name, but many now call the organization VAJA from the Farsi – the Vezarat-e ettela'atjomhuri-ye Eslami-ye Iran.

The British Secret Intelligence Service is popularly known as MI6, which had a long history of involvement in the country, still referred to it as SAVAK – the name by which it had been known in the time when the country was referred to as Persia and the Shah was a gentleman by the name of Mohammad Reza Pahlavi. The name SAVAK persists out of sentiment, but *Persia* disappeared off the map when the Iran Revolution broke out in 1979, and Mahammad, the last of the Shah's left Iran going first to the United States for cancer treatment, and finally ended up in Egypt where he died at the age of sixty.

The Intelligence Ministry reports directly to the Supreme Leader. For that reason, the council that controls the operations of the ministry had several senior clerics among its members. But the intelligence organization is an integral part of the military community and military men were not likely to have much sympathy for the religious views of people who were not in uniform. Nonetheless, the Ministry as a unit did wheel extraordinary powers within Iran. It was feared for its ruthlessness both locally and internationally.

Like most Intelligence and Security organizations in the world, VAJA is tasked with collecting and analyzing both internal and external intelligence. The goal is to uncover any activity, be it conspiracy, subversion, espionage, or sabotage, which would threaten the integrity and wellbeing of the state. But the organization had the reputation of doing much more than that. VAJA is probably more adept at causing rather than detecting such activities, although to be fair, usually in states outside of Iran. VAJA personnel, under the title of MOIS personnel, are often attached to Iran Embassies and Consulates to foster terrorism or terrorist recruitment. Such activity is not the normal activity of diplomats.

But the reach of VAJA goes much further than that.

VAJA often places agents in the overseas branches of Iranian state-controlled organizations such as Banks and other seemingly normal and legitimate businesses to extend the influence of the state and the nefarious activities of the Ministry. The annual budget for the MOIS is a secret. But it can be assumed to be huge. Consequently, it is hard to pin down the extent of the organization or the number of people actually in its employment. While some aspects of the true budgets of US-based intelligence agencies are often hidden away in innocuous projects under the guise of almost anything so the American public can see them, at least it is possible to have a reasonable stab at the manpower.

Not so with the Iran Intelligence service.

The weekly meetings of the Iran Security Council were typical of any bureaucratic body anywhere in the world. People were fighting for their positions in the hierarchy and there were many seemingly endless procedural matters taking up most of the time. Eventually, they would get around to talking about important matters and of an intelligence and security nature.

The President of Iran had insisted on Iran's pursuit of a plan that would keep pressure on the United States and, in particular, on the man that Khatami loathed – the US President BJ Thomas. Usually, lesser mortals from the vast bureaucracy would brief one or two members of the council who would, in turn, present a report to the Council. Then, after due consideration, they would convey any wisdom or further guidance to members of the security service. However, in this case, it had been decreed that the matter was too important to take the risk that something would get lost in translation, so the member was invited to attend the Council in person. At least that was the explanation given by Khatami. The probability was that the President would want to distance himself from any failures that may have occurred and leave the security service to answer any awkward questions that would arise from that.

Consequently, the man who had been tasked with implementing this plan had been summoned to this meeting to explain the progress that had been made.

His name was Hormuzd Lajani.

He would have been known to the United States Ambassador to the State of Kuwait – Lawrence Johnson - as Mahmoud.

Larijani would expect several interruptions as he tried to deliver his report for the simple reason that as he was not normally a member of this esteemed body, and those who were members would look to impress or bully the interloper. But there were other more obvious and practical reasons why this should occur. Amongst those reasons was the fact that things had not exactly gone to plan. Another, not so obvious reason, was because it was unlikely that most of the morons responsible for overseeing the many plots and subterfuge that they said that they supported would understand what went on in the world of spooks.

'We now have the CIA under our control in Harare Zimbabwe using the methods that you approved previously. We have a senior CIA agent who compromised and distributed drugs to his friends in the US diplomatic community. Our attempts to infiltrate the United States Embassy in Khartoum were successful. Unfortunately, the gentleman who wc compromised has been taken ill and recalled to Washington and has been replaced by a woman. I have people working on the restoration of the drug network once we know who we can target. You will understand that this lady does not quite fit the profile that you approved for our action. Our attempts to infiltrate the US Embassy in Kuwait were also successful but we faced a setback because the man we targeted committed suicide before he could be of much use to us. He did however enable us to identify the people who the United States Central Intelligence Agency had deployed against us, and we should now be able to have better control of events as we continue. However, the point is that the method of compromising an official and then having him or her introducing drugs as a cover for what we want to achieve was proven and can now be used successfully in other areas.'

The agent sat back having delivered as much as he dared to say. In that process, he had pointed to an area in which their scheming never envisaged the CIA would employ a woman. That was the problem with having an organization that was answerable to a religious zealot who regarded women as lesser mortals! At least from a pure intelligence point of view, his organization had identified the women for what she was which was a major achievement. He would leave the kudos of that sitting in the air, knowing that most of those present would have no clue of the significance. However, the military people would and that was all he cared about!

Another issue that Larijani was uncomfortable with concerned the Ambassador to Kuwait. Lawrence Johnson had been murdered by Iranian agents after having been suspected of communicating with CIA agents was probably well known – or at least assumed - by the entire council, The fact that someone in the MOIS had authorized the killing was hardly likely to be of any concern to these ruthless men despite the episode having been contrary to the rules under which diplomatic relations between countries were supposed to be maintained. Even though there was no direct contact between the governments of the Islamic Republic of Iran and the United States it did not mean that diplomatic rules and norms should be ignored. And there was sure to be a major diplomatic incident when the juggernaut that was the US investigative system found out who had been responsible for the killing.

No one was surprised that the next question raised was on a different subject.

'Where do the drugs come from?' one of the religious leaders wanted to know.

Larijani had to smile at that question. They were embarking on a plan that could ultimately involve nuclear war and this guy was worried about where the drugs which were to be used by infidels were to come from!

'We have a very good source and excellent security on the supply chain. The drugs only need to cross one border and that is well away from the prying eyes of the Americans. But the fewer people who know of such details the better to protect the source. Of course, if you must know you have every right to that information, and I will be able to provide it. Unfortunately, I do not have it with me at the moment.' Larijani lied.

He knew he was on safe ground here, even though he had lied. While it would not pay to cross one of the religious members of the council given that the ultimate boss of everyone in the council was his eminence the Supreme Leader and questioning *him* was like asking if the Pope was a Catholic. In addition, the cleric who had asked the question was already on the outer and would probably not be around much longer. After all, he was well into his eighties and was due to be made to disappear sooner rather than later. Overriding all this was the fact that the Supreme Leader Ali Khamenei could not be seen to be involved with the use of drugs. Although the Supreme Leader had endorsed the plan, *He* did not want to know these details so it was unlikely that question would get much further.

The principle of Deniability was alive and well in Iran just as it was in the western world. So – that was the end of that!

The chairperson, who was a military Brigadier, was somewhat intolerant of the clerics on the council, but he accepted them for what they were. He nodded for Lajani to continue, confident that the interloper had more than adequately managed the situation.

'What happened in Khartoum?' he asked to steer the meeting in another direction.

'In Khartoum, we were able to attend the meeting of the African Union so that we could judge the people we will target next. Several states outside of Africa were invited to attend as observers and the United States representatives from a number of their overseas missions were in Khartoum at the same time as the meeting of the Africans. This gave us an excellent opportunity to meet with them before our next move.'

That was as far as Lajani wanted to go. He could have waffled on as a cover for the fact that his plans had not been implemented by the peasants who had been assigned to the actual task in Khartoum. Any further comment would lead to questions about his next moves and the availability (or reliability!) of his men. He had plans for that, but first, he had to get Mohamed Haji out of jail. And that would be difficult because he had yet to decide how best to continue in the absence of his key personnel. But the council was not about to let him off the hook just yet.

'I hear that a number of your agents were detained by the Sudan police for failing to meet with their border entry requirements. That does not seem to be a good way to progress, does it?'

Again, the same cleric asked the question. And that told Larijani something that he had not previously known. Someone else within the Iranian security and intelligence network must have fed this snippet to the cleric. Of greater significance, someone in the field was checking or observing what was happening. Where he had got this piece of information from, Larijani could not know. However, it was more likely to have come from diplomatic sources rather than from military sources. Consequently, he could reasonably expect that the cleric had not been informed that Mohamed Haji was one of those who had been apprehended! In the past, Haji had been a favorite of the council has handled several missions that were both successful and brutally efficient and he could well be earmarked for advancement at the expense of others. Including Larijani!

However, Larijani had to smile. The trouble with the Iranian intelligence service was that despite its inclusion of everything under one banner it also had many disparate groups. And each group had its agenda. In the western world, it would be referred to as a territorial dispute. In Iran, it was much more serious than that. Each had to defend their territory as if their life depended on it. Which it did. So, there was another report that only the President had seen that placed the blame for the failure in Khartoum squarely on the shoulders of those responsible.

That report would probably be attached to the CV of Mohamed Haji.

'You need have no fear - our strategy did envision this

possibility' Larijani explained. 'They will be released by the end of the week – well the men will. We have a problem with the two women because we do not have the contacts in the female prisons as we do in the male prisons. That is just – as our American friends would say – collateral damage.'

And the *collateral damage* only affected two women so that was the end of that.

The next question came from a Colonel - a specialist in communications and a member of IRGC - the Iran Revolutionary Guard Corps. He just wanted to be heard and to claim some part in the plotting, and a part that he felt had worked. The problem here was that the IRGC had developed a simple communications system the sole aim of which was to confuse the American National Security Agency – NSA. For this to be effective, it was dependent on the continued use of social media. Social media was controlled by Americans. And the brain-dead clerics were insistent on occasionally restricting access to social media as a reaction to US sanctions. This was even though the US government had no control over the social media giants.

What the IRGC also did not understand was that the NSA had long since compromised the Iranian communication system. And that was the whole point of the exercise which made all other factors irrelevant! Yes – the latest attempt to confuse the Americans had been successful because the IRGC *wanted* the Americans to gain access to these particular messages. Being on social media and in plain text, the trick had been to make the messages so obscure as to not attract any attention from the powerful computers that the American NSA owned. They could find the plain text. That did not mean that would be any wiser in finding out exactly what they meant. And the most important thing was finding out to who the messages were addressed. Since there were many millions of possible answers to that question – good luck with that!

'Yes – we believe we have successfully used your very clever method of exchanging messages and they have indeed confused the Americans.'

And that dealt with that.

Of course, Larijani had no evidence that anyone had been confused. Nor did he know if anyone had even bothered to read the messages. But it seemed the right thing to say. For all that he knew the Americans could be reading the messages right now and maybe rounding up the people, they were addressed to. That was the problem with communications. The theory was that you sent a message from one place to another. And you assumed that it arrived and would cause the action that you intended. But you could never be certain that it had not also gone to any number of other people or organizations. The simple answer to this riddle was to make your message available to everyone.

The Brigadier had enough. He asked Lajani the question that he already knew the answer to.

'So - what is our next step?'

'Our next target is in Turkey. We have a target in the US embassy in Ankara who meets our needs. And we also have contacts in the US Air Force base at Incirlik who assure us that we can compromise several personnel there without too much difficulty.'

The comment about the Incirlik airbase was bound to raise a few questions – and it did. The base was used by the Turkish Air Force, the US Air Force, even the British Royal Air Force, and a smattering of other allied forces including that of Saudi Arabia – all of whom were not exactly on friendly terms with Iran. But, of far more significance was the fact that the base was where the United States had chosen to store nuclear weapons. The weapons themselves were old and employed out-of-date technology. They had been there since 1959 as part of the US nuclear deterrent employed during the Cold War with the Soviets But they were still weapons. And they were still nuclear!

'Is it wise to involve us in a potential nuclear conflict in that part of the world?' The question came from the same cleric who had asked the earlier question about the source of drugs. However, while the man had every right to ask as many questions as he liked, the decision had already been made by their Supreme Leader. And *he* had said that, while the council should be informed of the basic plan because it did involve activities on foreign soil, they were not to be told the full details. Certainly, they would not be informed of any plans that involved stealing a nuclear bomb. And they should not be informed of the end game. But they could be informed that it was planned to start a campaign of fake news. Like – that the US government planned to move the nuclear weapons in response to rising tensions in the Middle East. Quite naturally that would be dependent on causing friction between Turkey and the United States. Turkey was a current member of NATO but that could easily change depending on the mood of their leaders. The US was an increasingly reluctant member of NATO but more for financial reasons than anything else. So – generating a conflict between these two powers would be easy to achieve, given the bombastic nature of the current US and Turkish President's various statements concerning each other, each other's stance on a variety of issues, and the world situation in general.

Hormuzd Lajani knew that he was on very safe ground and could just as easily have ignored the question. However, there were reputations at stake. The President needed to maintain his influential position in the council, otherwise, someone else could very easily, at the whim of the Supreme Leader, take his place. And Lajani's position would depend on how he handled this subject. Although the last thing Iran needed right now was to have another interfering cleric involved in matters which were way beyond his ability to manage or even to understand, he needed to be careful. If the Americans got even a hint of the plan through loose talk by a disgruntled old man, then they could be in real trouble. So, he had to steer the conversation towards something that would appeal to something that he could understand.

'We have to gain maximum benefit and embarrass the Americans as much as we can by drawing attention to the base at Incirlik. The American public will want to know – What is the significance of Incirlik? And the US media will do the rest for us. The US President will have to publicly admit the existence of nuclear weapons on Turkish soil, and the Turkish President will have to admit that he has known of their existence for some time. Now, of course, we are not going to start a nuclear conflict, but it makes things so much harder for the US to justify their stance against the peaceful development of our nuclear enrichment facilities at Natanz.'

'You seem very confident in your strategy!' one of the military members commented. General Mohamad Jafari was the commander of the Revolutionary Guard and was probably the most powerful member of this particular group, clerical or otherwise. His comment was not meant as a compliment. He was signaling that the matter should be closed. Larijani was aware that the last time they had discussed a strategic move against the US and its Turkish ally, the very same cleric who had raised such annoying questions had proposed the use of chemical weapons. And he did not want the conversation to head in that direction. He knew that the military was developing such a plan but whether that plan would ever be implemented was way above his paygrade. That plan was top secret, and it would stay that way forever.

Or until it could be presented to the Supreme Leader as a workable option to get final approval.

And then came the question that Lajani was least equipped to manage. It was not that the question was asked with any intent of causing him any embarrassment. Things had not exactly gone to plan so far and that needed to be explained. Or rather – the council needed to be assured that any problems that they had encountered so far would not be repeated. The whole council was happy to blame the American CIA for almost anything and the facts of the matter where that they could be a troublesome enemy. But was it the Central Intelligence Agency that was causing the present problem? Or was it another group or organization – still American but of unknown origin? There was a plan to deal with this group, but it was outside Lajani's ability to control.

And that scared him.

The question was simple enough and it came from one of the younger clerics who had been handed the question by one of his superiors rather than dreamt it up himself.

The question was very specific.

'We understand that a CIA team has been following the movements through Africa. We cannot afford for that to continue during the next phase. How do you propose that we respond?'

Larijani wanted to preempt his reply with a big *'IF'* but stopped himself.

'We have arranged a small diversion which will distract that group away from our actions under the next phase. You will recall that many of our targets so far have used drugs and it was always a part of my plans that they would play a significant role. Now is the time for that to take effect and you will see how that will be played out. Now the Americans will be encouraged to follow the drugs while our people conduct their allotted tasks uninterrupted. Action to implement this is already in hand by our agents.'

One of the problems with all controlling bodies of security and intelligence services is that no one person can know everything. Another problem was that the people who made the decisions at this level were never in possession of all the facts. In many cases, this arose from the simple position that many of the facts could not be known no matter how well and thoroughly you planned. Some events that were to happen were dependent on decisions that had to be made on the spur of the moment by individuals who may not be aware of the overall plan because someone at a higher level deemed that they did not need to know.

In Iran, intelligence matters may have been managed by the Ministry of Intelligence and Security. But the real power rests in the Supreme National Security Council which was under the direct control of the Supreme Leader. The President was also only one of three people who was invited to attend meetings of the Council who thought that he knewa what Hormuzd Lajani's ultimate orders were. The Supreme Leader of course could assume that he knew all there was to know and he would let his fellow clerics know what he wanted them to know. The other most likely font of all knowledge on the council was Major General Hossein Fadavi – the head of the Islamic Revolutionary Guard Corps. But none of them could know everything that had or was about to happen. Nor could any of them predict how others would react to their actions – in the case of those that they assumed to be their enemies – or instructions – in the case of those that they assumed to be their friends.

Chapter 25

Interlude

Despite the short time that Mark and his team had been in Sudan, they had impressed the local Ambassador (actually a Charge d'affaire) Anthony Luxton. Despite the earlier misunderstanding between his Deputy and the team that had come from Zimbabwe, Luxton had accepted that Mark and Dusty were indeed working under orders from the President and that their reasons for being in Khartoum Sudan had been genuine. The resultant comments from the Sudanese government had been a major boost to the standing of the US representatives in their country so that, as they say, was that.

For reasons that he would not divulge to any of the Embassy staff, Luxton had insisted that Mark and Dusty be allowed to go with the US contingent on their visit to the Pugnido Refugee camp in the western Gambella region of Ethiopia. That arrangement had been suggested to Luxton by the Secretary of State and that *suggestion* had come with a condition. The condition that he had imposed on the two Americans was that Luxton wanted to talk to them, and he was very specific about the time that he wished to do that.

The time to do that would be on the return trip to Khartoum.

The Pugnido camp held more than seventy-thousand refugees from the shambles caused by the ongoing fighting in South Sudan. The United States had previously tried - and failed - to get resolution to their plight. The responsibility rested with UNHCR – the United Nations High Commission for Refugees. However, a mix of bureaucratic bumbling within the world body, lack of resources in Ethiopia, a chronic lack of interest in the government of Sudan, disputes between governments about whose responsibility it was, and an ever-worsening political and economic situation in South Sudan, combined to make the task impossible. The trouble with the UNHCR was that it was voluntary cooperation between nations and countries that were elected to its controlling body for staggered three-year terms. The present High Commissioner for Refugees was a German by the name of Zelda Altenburg and the body that she was responsible for was constantly changing. And so were the goalposts as each nation tried to use its influence to affect the focus of attention towards an area that they had a particular affinity with. Or away from an area that they had an eversion to.

Nevertheless – the visit of the UN High Commissioner did allow Luxton to leave his office in Khartoum, and to talk to someone without the prying eyes and ears of those that he thought wished him harm. And his boss had sufficiently disturbed him that he was no longer sure who he could trust.

Luxton was all too well aware that in 1973 a Palestinian Terrorist group – operating under the name Black September – had reputedly murdered Cleo Noel, the then US Ambassador to Sudan, and two other diplomats. The attack had taken place in the Saudi Embassy and the last that had been heard, Black September had not been in operation for at least the last twenty years. But diplomats have long memories and view time through a different lens than normal people. While the present-day circumstances were very different than they were back in the 1970s, Luxton did not want to be remembered for all the wrong reasons.

Mark was not so concerned about the safety or otherwise of Luxton. He had been given a job to do and that job seemed to have been extended to include other matters that he had yet to be advised of. Nonetheless, he would carry out whatever that job was with due diligence and his usual ruthless efficiency.

He was aware that at some stage during this visit to Ethiopia, or more probably sometime during their return flight to the Sudan capital, Luxton would want to have a serious chat. Luxton would wait until they were no longer surrounded by UN officials - there would be none of them on the return journey – which was understandable.

Or members of his staff – which seemed weird.

But there were other reasons why that discussion would have to wait, and these reasons had little to do with either Ambassador Luxton or the people he was accompanied by on this trip.

What interested Mark was the Pugnido camp itself. And one of the volunteers who worked there.

Debbie Petersen.

Not so long ago, back in New York, Debbie Petersen had been Marks' live-in girlfriend. Debbie had left him, not because she did not love him – because she wholeheartedly did - nor because she felt that he did not love her – because he quite clearly did - but because of the overbearing stress that came with living with the man who seemed to take serving his country too seriously. Well — saying just that would not do justice to the man and his commitment. Mark was honest and loyal and once he committed to do something then that was that.

The problem was that the last *job* that Mark had been involved in on behalf of the government of the USA had almost cost him his life. Once was probably Ok given that the job did involve a certain amount of risk and the odd brush with the grim reaper was inevitable. However, nearly losing his life twice was stretching things a little. A near-death experience three times in the space of as many weeks was too much.

Debbie did not try to change Mark. That would have meant trying to change the man that she loved into something different and something that he was not. So, she had just walked away, hoping that maybe someday they could get back together when things were quieter.

The aircraft landed on what is a more civilized part of the world would be termed a goat track and taxied to a bunch of huts that served as a passenger arrivals hall. From there the dignitaries and their hangers-on in the party were ushered into a couple of trucks and left on a drive along roads that were in even worse condition than the airport. Although it was not very far, that drive lasted nearly two hours. They eventually arrived at the remote refugee camp.

The sight that greeted them would have been enough to make anyone who had even the remotest affinity with his or her fellow humans burst into tears. As usual, there were children everywhere and children are always excited when something different was happening. So, the children laughed and called out to each other, or to anyone else who would or could listen. But their elders sat there in absolute silence, with blank looks on their faces. Long since resigned to their fate, clinging to their meager belongings, or what they perceived as theirs.

Dust was everywhere.

Hope was nowhere to be seen.

A couple of their leaders stepped forward to greet the visitors without any enthusiasm.

Dignified but bitter.

Alive but the walking dead.

The vast majority of the refugees in the Pugnido camp had come from the southern part of Sudan where an uneasy truce in the battles between the Army of Sudan and the southern Sudan Revolutionary Front meant that they could not return to their homes. The United States and members of the African Union were powerless to intervene in either the dispute itself or on behalf of the people who had been bulldozed aside.

The disagreements had originally started as a dispute about ownership of the desolate border area between Sudan and Southern Sudan called Abyei. But there were powerful economic forces at play and these factors – better defined as greed by both sides - made the dispute more meaningful. The region of Abyei sat on top of recently discovered vast oil reserves.

There was also an ongoing dispute to the north of Abyei in the Darfur region of Sudan which started as a minor disagreement between nomadic camel herders and pastoral farmers. That dispute ended up being one of the worst conflicts on the continent of Africa. It was the conflicting cultural, ethnic, and linguistic differences that caused the ordinary people of this land to be forced to leave. They simply could not compete with the power and resources that others brought to the table. Initially, the displaced had to find refuge in other areas of Sudan. Eventually, they were forced from their homeland and across the border into Ethiopia.

The result was the Pugnido refugee camp where people were homeless. And their position seemed hopeless.

Mark desperately looked through the dust amongst the thousands of ramshackle tents trying to judge the insanity of it all and searching for just one person amid all the carnage and mayhem. Despite the size of the crowd, he felt suddenly very lonely. Had he made an error in assuming that he would be welcome here?

Mark had never really understood women. The assumption that Debbie would be pleased to see him so far from home in this God-forsaken place could be wide of the mark. Had he made a terrible mistake? Would it have been better to just call her and warn her that he was going to drop by to say hello? But then – how could he have done that? They arranged that she would call him because there was no such thing as a telephone in this place.

His feelings of dread and deflation were absolute.

And then there was a friendly tap on the shoulder by a person called Jeff who he had briefly talked to on the flight in. Jeff was a UNHCR nurse from the Philippines. She was tiny by any standards. Jeff had told him that, before her birth, her parents had desperately wanted a boy. And so, she was named Jeff before she was born. She was Ok with that and accepted it for what it was. And she seemed to accept all that life threw her way.

'I think you need to go to that bunch of tents over to your right.' she said as she gently took his massive hand in hers. She steered him through the teeming crowds of people and towards what was the hospital area of the camp.

'It will be Ok!' she smiled up at the massive frame that

stood beside her. 'Do not worry!'

With Dusty also towering over Jeff, the three of them stood in the makeshift doorway and scanned the chaos that was laid out before them.

The two Americans are hardly able to believe what they saw.

There were bodies everywhere with only half of the patients actually in beds. The other half of them lay on the bare ground patiently waiting their turn to be seen by the over-worked staff. Strangely, in this horrific environment, the patients were un-complaining, seemingly grateful for the care they were receiving, and just thankful for any assistance that they could get.

And, although she had never been trained as a nurse, there amid all this chaos and wrapped in plastic protection gear to the point that it was difficult to recognize one from the other, was the diminutive figure of Debbie Peterson.

Debbie was wearing personal protective gear including rubber gloves, a hair cap, and a mask such that she was covered entirely in blue plastic and the only part of her that was visible were her forehead and her eyes. If people from another planet had witnessed the scene as it unfolded, they would have had to assume that Mark was in love with a blue roll.

But Mark knew that it was her.

An involuntary tear formed as he looked in her direction and he wondered how he had ever managed to live this life without her.

Why had he let her go?

Why had he not changed so that she could still be by his side?

Debbie turned to see what the group standing in the doorway wanted. She was aware that United Nations officials were visiting the camp this day but did not expect that they would be interested in the work that was going on in her tiny area of the camp.

Jeff told Mark to wait by the doorway and rushed over to where Debbie was changing the dressings on a young child. She told Debbie that she would complete the task while Debbie went to deal with the new arrivals.

And only then did Debbie realize who the visitors were.

If she had been completely honest with herself, Debbie probably recognized Dusty first. It was hard to miss someone of his size, and impossible to miss the huge grin on his face.

At first, she hesitated. She had never seen Mark or Dusty outside the confines of New York City or Washington DC and if the two of them were together anywhere else in the world that could only mean that they were on yet another assignment – Mark on another job – Dusty as his bodyguard. But – in the end – she could not contain her delight at seeing the man she loved.

Debbie flew at Mark, reaching up and grasping him tightly around the neck, the tears flowing down her cheeks. It would have been funny in different circumstances. Mark stood well over six feet. Debbie is only just over five feet.

Eventually, she calmed down, sufficiently to ask him if he was alright, and assuring him that she was fine. Neither of them noticed anyone around them as they exchanged a passionate embrace which resulted in a round of applause and laughter from both the refugee patients and the hospital staff.

Then, just as quickly, something resembling normality was restored. Debbie rapidly explained the important work they were doing and lead him by the hand further into the hospital. She introduced Mark to the other nurses and the patients she was caring for as though she was introducing royalty.

Out of the chaos came Estefania Rodriguez the girl who had gone with Debbie on her trip to Africa. Shy at first but gave Mark a heartfelt hug and shed a few tears of her own in the process.

Estefania was the daughter of a CIA official with who Mark had crossed swords recently. That man was now dead and, as far as Mark could tell, the loss of Stephen Rodriguez was not of major importance. Despite the death of that evil man, the ramifications of that case were still being inexorably drawn through the US justice system and were unlikely to be resolved anytime soon, no one missed him.

And neither Mark, nor Debbie, nor even Estefania, could have cared less.

Debbie led Mark to a relatively secluded area where there was a tarpaulin cover over a couple of chairs. They sat down neither able to take their eyes off the other. Debbie still gripped his hand. It seemed incredible that there was such an area in the camp with as many as seventy thousand bodies crammed into an area not much bigger than an American football ground. There was so much to talk about but neither of them could find the words that could adequately express what was going on in their minds. There was no chance that they could be alone - so they just sat and smiled as the children played around them while taking in the awful truth of the human misery that they were in the midst of.

Neither of them noticed at first. Someone wandered into their space. Mark was concerned but did not want to break the spell. It was Debbie who reacted but in a way that humbled the ex-Special Forces Major.

'Hello, Jamal. What is wrong?'

'I am hungry!'

Debbie was talking to a young girl. She was probably

eight or nine years old but had the body of someone far younger. Growth stunted by a poor diet she was impossibly thin. And as she turned towards Debbie Mark realized that was not her only problem – the girl was partially blind. Whether from cataracts, trachoma or macular degeneration Mark could not tell. He had to bite his lip to watch the young girl who seemed oblivious to her condition which would have been repaired if she had been lucky enough to be born somewhere else. She stumbled across to where they were seated and as she reached out to Debbie, she suddenly reacted to Mark's presence.

'It is Ok Jamal. Meet my friend Mark. He is visiting us – just for today. Say Hello to Mark.'

At last - she smiled. The voice was excited at meeting someone new.

'Hello Marak!' she said, converting his name into something she could relate to.

The eyes never focused but her thin delicate hand was raised towards the unknown. Mark gently took it in his. It seemed so unreal. The massive hand of Mark Taylor holding the tiny hand of the diminutive figure of Jamal. The reality of a world in which people have pushed aside so that others could prosper. People who have everything briefly touch those who never will have anything.

Debbie saw that the moment had an impact on this big brute of a man. And she knew now why she loved him.

'Well – we will have to get you something to eat – won't we.' Debbie reached inside the plastic coverall and pulled out a muesli bar. At first, Jamal just did not know what it was until Debbie took the wrapper off. Then her face broke out into another smile when she realized what she held in her hand.

'Thank you, Debbie!'

It could not last.

All the excitement and emotion eventually drained away with the realization of the vastness of the task ahead of thcm. Mark was humbled by the sheer size of a problem that he could do nothing about. He realized that it did not matter how hard Debbie and Estefania worked. There would still be another patient to treat and to care for. Mark did not have the heart to tell them that he had simply come to this place as a guest of someone else and that he was about to leave it all behind to return to ...... What?

He could not tell them what his next move would be after they left this camp. Mark had hoped that it would be on a flight back to New York City and civilization. But at the present, he could not say. His orders could take him anywhere compounding the reasons why his girl had left him.

Heartbreaking though it was, the girls turned away and returned to their work. Mark and Dusty walked in silence back out of the camp. Neither had anything to say. Or – more correctly - they couldn't say anything for fear of revealing too much emotion at what they had just witnessed.

The two men had not seen each other since their flight had landed in Ethiopia, but on the return flight to Khartoum, an already exhausted Anthony Luxton had invited Mark to join him in a vacant part of the plane for a talk.

'I believe that you people have difficulty bugging aircraft with all the extraneous noises so our conversation should not be overheard by anyone!' Luxton laughed as Mark sat beside him.

Mark had to laugh as well. Yes – bugging a plane - any plane – would be a difficult task but there were ways to do that if you had the technical resources of the CIA. Bugging one as ancient as the propeller-driven aircraft that they were in would however be impossible even with those resources. Mark was amused that Luxton had now assumed that he was working for the Central Intelligence Agency despite his earlier dispute with Luxton's deputy. Mark could only assume that Luxton felt that he would be aware that Ms. Laws was not a fully paid-up member of the CIA and so would treat her as an outsider, rather than the other way round.

Whatever the reason or the logic of Luxton's position Mark chose to ignore the implication.

'Yes sir!' was all that Mark said.

'How long do you intend to stay in Khartoum? I understand that you were expecting to be ordered back to the States, but are awaiting instructions from your controller?' Luxton enquired. Which in diplomatic speak translated to something like - *'I haven't a clue, so enlighten me.'*

Or was it? Body language said that Luxton was leading up to something.

The ambassadorial services of the United States were held in high regard throughout the world. Controlled by bureaucrats found at Foggy Bottom in Washington DC, all Americans traveling abroad had the assurance that they could call into anywhere on earth where there were the Stars and Stripes and an American representative and be safe. So, why did Mark feel insecure?

He decided to give a neutral response.

'Yes – I am unaware of the reasons why we are still in Sudan. But you know how bureaucracies work!' Mark replied, not knowing whether Luxton would see the situation as quite as funny as he did.

He got no reaction at all from the Ambassador, so he continued.

'It was very kind of you to allow us to visit the camp – we have a couple of our friends working there and it was good to be able to catch up with them. Not the job that I would choose – but each to his own!' Mark added bitterly. Luxton gazed out of the window.

'So - you are happy that the matters that you were originally concerned with are no longer an issue?' Which in diplomatic speak translated to *You tell me first what you think, and then, maybe, I will tell you what I think – because I think there is unfinished business!*

Mark had to laugh.

He was not a diplomat and was not trained in the protocols of their discourse – or their language. He was aware that diplomats tended to talk in riddles and rarely came directly to the point they were trying to make. It was a miracle that diplomats ever got married because that kind of discourse was, in Marks's limited experience, reserved for females. But reading body language was the same everywhere. And Mark was very good at reading body language.

His reading was that Luxton was on a fishing trip – on whose behalf he had yet to find out. So that would determine his answer.

'Yes sir. Our visit to Khartoum seems to have achieved its objective. So, there is nothing more for us to do here.' Mark replied.

'Hmm – So tell me about Lawrence Johnson. Why do you think he was killed? It does seem strange that he should be killed in Khartoum at the same time as your team was in town.'

Mark was visibly shocked by this piece of news and Luxton must have been aware of that!

'What do you mean? I did not know that Johnson had been killed! How? When did that happen? Mark asked.

Luxton looked at Mark for a couple of moments

trying to assess the implications of what he had just said. Luxton was trying to work out whether the shocked reaction was genuine or was the shock was one of timing and guilt. The look on his face showed that he did not believe that it was the former.

'Come on Mark. You cannot tell me that you did not know. If the media could report it – how come your team of highly qualified men could not know?'

Now that was a different situation altogether. The last Mark had seen of Lawrence Johnson was when Mark had left him in his hotel room with a scrap of paper that had a contact number with instructions to call Mark. Johnson had not taken advantage of that offer and Mark had put that down to the fact that he and Dusty had shown little sympathy for the plight that Johnson found himself in. Was the Ambassador now suggesting that Mark or one of his team was responsible for Johnson being killed?

Either Luxton was fishing, or he was totally out of his depth. Alternatively, Luxton was basing his comments on rumor or innuendo that he had sourced from somewhere in what would be a considerable network that extended up to at least the Secretary of State and possibly beyond. That meant that the information would have had to have come via the intelligence network. Mark knew – or thought that he knew to be fair – that the Deputy Ambassador in Khartoum was acting CIA Chief of Station and he doubted that he would be on her Christmas card list. And there was no way, on reflection, that Luxton could know that Mark was aware of some of the facts that surrounded her appointment to this position. So, either the CIA was, as usual, coming to mistaken conclusions, or the State Departments' security and intelligence service had somehow reached its conclusion. Or that the two organizations had reached an agreement on what had occurred. In either case – why had Luxton invited Mark to go with him to Ethiopia? It did seem a bit of a stretch to invite him for the simple purpose of making such an accusation.

It all made no sense to Mark – unless Luxton had received a briefing that he did not believe and had taken the opportunity to get away from town and find out for himself what the hell had happened. As a diplomat, he would be well conditioned to believing official briefings at the expense of intuitive thinking,

But - he was still human!

Mark decided on the spur of the moment that it was all too much. He had been polite and respectful in calling the Ambassador Sir, even though he was only a charge d'affaire. Now that would change. Now Mark was hurt!

Mark stood and turned to walk away.

'That is the end of our conversation Mr. Luxton. I would have thought that as a diplomat and head of an Embassy you would be better informed. Apparently, that is not the case! I thank you for the opportunity to visit the Pugnido camp. Good-bye.'

'Wait!' Luxton shouted.

Fortunately, the sound was lost in the noise of the aircraft. But the intent was not lost on Mark,

'Mr. Luxton – you can shout at your underlings at your embassy, and you can throw accusations around. But not at me. If you want to accuse me or any of my team of murder, then that is your prerogative. But I do not have to sit and listen to this crap. I would have expected that you would show some respect to the group of men who scored you a few points with the country in which you are representing the United States. But apparently not. So, as soon as this plane hits the ground in Khartoum we are out of here. And good riddance!'

Luxton's voice was reduced, almost to a whisper.

'Mark - please hear me out. I had to be sure! Give me one more minute to explain. Please!'

Mark towered over the back of the seat. 'Ok – your minute starts now.'

'No – Mark please sit down. Just hear me out.'

'Ok – talk. And cut out all the diplomatic bullshit – you only have half a minute left of your time!'

So - the Ambassador talked.

'The suggestion that someone from your team took part in Johnson's death came from the CIA. That suggestion was backed up by our intelligence people who were accompanying the Secretary of State on his recent visit to Khartoum. That, and the fact that our President is in hospital. That is the reason - by the way- why you have been told to await further instructions. I believe that the opinion you are a suspect was colored by opinions held by some CIA officials. As I understand the position - there is resentment of your role in recent events in other parts of the world. I do not understand why that should concern the diplomatic service, but I can understand that our local CIA personnel could have had their noses put out of joint by your involvement.'

Luxton paused for a moment, probably caused by the sardonic smirk that appeared of Mark's face. Mark did not say anything, so Luxton continued.

'The Sudanese police initially said that the death of Johnson looked like a suicide. I doubt that for a variety of reasons, but we have to await the coroner's report. Not that we can place too much trust on the coroner - given that the local ability is not that great. And, in this country, you can virtually write your own coroner's report if you pay for it. So, I have asked for our medical people – and that means the FBI - to check the Johnson case. I have yet to receive an answer on that, so that is another reason for the delay between you and your team. My guess now is that the initial verdict of suicide was just a case of misinformation or could be an attempt to deflect blame. Or it could be an attempt to distract from CIA errors in the past. Anyway – I had one of our medical staff view the body and she said it is the first case of suicide where the victim seems to have kicked himself in the head! So - we are looking for someone who is a murderer. I know a little - very little - about your previous exploits in Afghanistan concerning the CIA and drugs and someone may be trying to get back at you over that. That is worrying. But - a little closer to home - I have another more worrying theory.'

Luxton appeared to stop and gather his thoughts before continuing.

'There has been a lot of noise coming out of Teheran recently, and Iranian intelligence has also been active in this part of the world. I have reason to believe that Johnson somehow got involved with them – probably drugs – and they tapped him because he would not follow their instructions. Or – maybe – he had threatened to expose some plot that they were working on. I do not know. But it does seem very strange that a young man with so much potential, with a young family, and so much ahead of him would risk his career over something so stupid as a drug deal. Lawrence Johnson is – sorry Johnson was – with our Kuwait office and I do not know all of the details of the situation there. However, there has been a noticeable increase in the availability of drugs among the diplomatic community in Khartoum and elsewhere. That is very worrying. And we do not know where they are coming from and how they are being imported and distributed. It is of course possible that they are being brought in by any foreign embassy, but I would guess that it is the Iranians.'

The flight attendant came by to check whether Luxton wanted coffee, tea, or milk, and interrupted the Ambassador.

The lady was quick – and quite rudely - ushered away.

'My instructions from Washington say that the drug issue is not my problem and that it will be dealt with by the Drug Enforcement Administration. And the instructions coming out of the CIA is that the Iran thing is being managed by them, and therefore that is also not my problem. Now I am told that the FBI will take over the investigation into the death of Johnson because it could involve other American citizens. These instructions just do not make any sense. Why would they want to exclude the Embassy in any such matters, unless there is more at play than I have been privy to!'

The two men sat staring out the window for a couple of minutes. Luxton either because he had nothing more to say, or because he had already said too much. Mark because he had realized that this guy Luxton was much smarter than he had earlier given him credit for.

Mark could not confirm any part of what Luxton had said. But the story was in one respect remarkably close to the truth as the now-dead Johnson would have confirmed. And Mark was very suspicious of how things had played out in Khartoum both concerning the CIA Head of Station and the antics of the Iranians at the Africa Union conference.

What Luxton had alluded to was remarkably similar to what Mark would have concluded. But nothing explained why Mark and his team had been accused of being responsible for the death of Lawrence Johnson.

Mark had two different theories of how that had occurred - that was apart from the suicide verdict that the local police had concluded. Either he had been killed by the CIA – which - much as he had reason to dislike his own country's organization - he doubted - or Johnson had been killed by Iranian agents.

The latter seemed the most likely given the rambling

account that Johnson had given to Mark and Dusty for his predicament. And having reached that conclusion Mark felt a chill go up to his spine. Someone else had assumed that Mark was involved with the CIA. Someone else had been following his team. Someone else had probably been aware that Johnson had made contact with Americans.

That trail led directly to Mark Taylor.

'Ok – just tell me one thing.' Mark asked the Ambassador.

'Wallace Perriott – he was the CIA Chief of Station in Sudan. What exactly happened to him before he left?'

Luxton had to smile.

'Yeah – I thought you would put the two together. Wallace told me that he was approached by someone to get him to distribute drugs within the US Embassy and beyond. He refused and promptly left town. He did not say, or he did not know, who was behind the drug deal. But he was sacred. I do not know – but I suspect – that he was having some kind of affair. That is the usual way these things start – isn't it?'

Mark doubted that Luxton was telling him all that he knew on this particular subject. And that was fair enough given what Mark already knew. But it was most unlikely that Perriott would skip town without at least expressing an opinion on who was responsible for his plight, and how he had gotten into this mess.

'Ok' Mark thought it was time that to cut to the chase. 'You did not invite me on this trip because you wanted a sounding board for your thoughts. So – what do you want me to do?'

Luxton seemed to relax for the first time since their conversation began.

'Given your previous experience, I thought it would be helpful if you took your team to Afghanistan.'

The aircraft was beginning to make its descent into Khartoum International. The engine noise that had earlier masked their conversation had died to a whisper so that they could no longer converse in private. Both men stood and shook hands before Mark returned to the seat next to Dusty. They made eye contact which said that they would talk later.

Mark was quiet and lost in his thoughts as the plane descended.

There was a pattern here that was beginning to take the shape of a far more complex plot than was at first thought. The team had been following Mohamed Haji on the assumption that he had a plan to assassinate Robert Mugabe. They had finally been involved in the arrest of Haji and three of his friends – caught in the apparent attempt to execute that plan.

But what if there was something else going on that was far more threatening than that? After all – the death of Mugabe was hardly a matter of great importance to the government of the United States. Or for that matter to the Islamic Republic.

Mark had seen evidence that Iran – if indeed that is the country that Haji was working for - was involved in the introduction of drugs into Harare. He had heard from a man who was now dead about Iran's involvement in supplying drugs to Kuwait. Now there was evidence that someone had tried to do the same thing in Khartoum.

But there was another more troubling element.

In at least two of the cases, there were women involved in circumstances that suggested an element of blackmail – the tradition of the honey-trap. If Mark had discovered these things in the short time that he had been in Africa, how many more cases remained undiscovered? If the pattern was consistent, then the US diplomatic service and the CIA were in serious trouble.

That suggested that something else was going on and Mark did not have a clue of what that might be.

His discussion with Luxton had shown that the Ambassador had similar concerns. But there was a number that was cause for pause. What did the Ambassador know? How much of what he believed to be the truth had he shared with his Secretary of State? How much had he shared with his CIA chief? Or to put that slightly differently – to what extent, if any, had his views been formed by advice from the CIA.

Mark had to smile at the irony of it all.

What if Mark had missed the obvious?

What if Warren Perriott had nothing to do with any of this?

What if Anthony Luxton was having an affair with Margaret Laws?

Mark and Dusty sat through the landing which was somewhat haphazard given the state of the landing strip and the incompetence of the pilot. Khartoum Airport was soon to be replaced with a new one.

That would fix the landing strip.

It would not fix the pilot.

Chapter 26

Porkies

The team assembled in Marks' room in the Khartoum Corinthia Hotel. The men who had been left behind while Mark and Dusty had gone to Pugnido had all changed into more casual gear and packed all their combat gear ready for what they expected to be their return to the United States.

They would be disappointed.

None of the men, except Dusty, were aware that their lives were about to change – again. That is – on the assumption that they would do what Mark was about to ask.

Mark did not want to sound officious, but it came out that way. He was the leader of the team of friends, and he was about to ask them a favor. At least he hoped it sounded that way.

'Ok listen up. We have been asked to continue our mission although the objective has changed. If any of you want to call it quits, I will understand. There is no pressure, but I would prefer it if we stayed together. If anyone wants to leave the team – then say so now.'

Blake was the only member of the team to react and that wasn't exactly in a negative way.

'Where are we going now?' he asked.

'Afghanistan!'

Mark had not slept since returning to Khartoum.

The call had come first from the office of the National Security Agency in Washington DC, and then it had been followed by a late-night call from Ambassador Anthony Luxton in Khartoum.

The first call was almost innocuous.

'Mister Taylor! Its' Stephanie Gompert. You may remember me from a meeting that we had in New York a few weeks ago. I have to say the President is very pleased with the work you and your team have done. I trust that you are all well and are now rested after your endeavors?'

Mark was used to hearing how pleased everyone was.

'Hello, Stephanie. And to what do I owe the pleasure of this call?' Mark replied not feeling indebted to anyone and not feeling any pleasure. 'And how are things in Washington – in particular, how is our President?'

He thought that was the proper way to acknowledge NSA's ADDNI-AMM. He may as well have not bothered.

'He's fine. Have you heard from the Ambassador?'

'Which Ambassador?'

'Why? Ambassador Anthony Luxton in Khartoum.'

'Yes – I have been down to Ethiopia with him and talked to him on the way back. He was Ok when last I saw him!'

'Ok. Well - you will get a call from him shortly. Just thought I would give you a heads-up on what we are thinking in Washington.'

Mark was just coming off a long and emotional couple of days.

'That must be a new experience for people in Washington!'

Gompert laughed.

'You are starting to sound like a politician! Mark - we want you to extend your trip and try to get to the bottom of a problem in the diplomatic service. The President has been talking with John Scott and they are both very concerned about what is happening with drugs in Africa. And the president wants answers – and he wants them now.'

Mark was now feeling the stress of the day as well as the stress of dealing with this bureaucrat.

'Just back up for a minute. My team is not in the business of investigating the diplomatic service. Surely that is a job for the FBI and, if drugs are involved, for the Drug Enforcement Administration. We are just simple soldiers and are much better employed, as we have been, following a bunch of thugs. We can manage people with guns, but we cannot be expected to sort out a bunch of desk jockeys who get their rocks off dabbling with drugs. I seem to be repeating our first meeting but – Why me?'

Gompert was silent for a moment and Mark thought she had hung upon him. Then he heard the quiet voice. It wasn't pleading. She was only the messenger.

'Mark – have a chat with the Ambassador – then call me back. Please.'

The line went dead.

It was an hour later that his phone chirped again. This time it was Ambassador Luxton. He sounded about as tired as Mark. And a lot more worried.

'Mark – have you heard from Washington?'

'Yes - I have.'

'So – what do you think?'

'Nothing – because they told me to talk to you.'

The groan that came over the line told it all, followed by some hardly diplomatic language.

Finally - Luxton recovered himself and told the story as best he could recall it.

'The President and the Secretary of State have got together at last. Sorry about the hold-up with your team - but Scott has been traveling and the earliest they could talk was this afternoon to enable them to reach a decision. I know that you have done the job you were given and that your friend Haji is now behind bars. But the powers that be in Washington are concerned at the ease with which we have been manipulated by these people using drugs and other means. They want that stopped and they regard the matter as critical and urgent. Given your experience with the drug problem in Afghanistan, they now want you to find out where the Iranians are getting the drugs from. Our best guess is Afghanistan. It should not involve the rest of your team. ....'

'Whoa! Hold it there Luxton. Have you ever been to Afghanistan? There is a war going in that country. In fact, there are several wars between various factions. And I hear those things have got a lot worse since I was last there. If you, or some of the buffoons at Foggy Bottom, think I am going back on my own – you need to think again! On my last visit to Afghanistan, I was almost killed, and I do not intend to repeat that experience. So – the answer is No! I will not be going. And may I remind you that we are all volunteers and not a group who can be ordered to do anything!'

For a brief moment, Mark thought that Luxton had disconnected the call until he eventually came back on the line.

'The Secretary will not be very pleased. I will need to talk to him again if there is an issue. Are you sure that I have to tell him that you are refusing to help? The President was a party to this agreement, and he understands that you have been working with our security and intelligence people on several other matters. He would have thought that in the circumstances he could count on your continued cooperation.'

So – that was the way things were! Luxton was adopting his skills as a diplomat as though he was negotiating with another country on behalf of his government where all options were on the table. Mark had to smile. The various contracts that he had with the DEA and they're like to sort out their security issues were to be traded for yet another mission. These contracts were worth a lot of money, not to mention prestige in the cut-throat world that Mark was in. He, therefore, gave the only answer that he could.

'Wish your secretary good luck! My team will be out of here first thing on the morning – heading home!'

Mark disconnected the call.

When Mark received a further call later in the evening, Luxton sounded even more flustered than he had done earlier.

'Mark – I am sorry about our misunderstanding. The Secretary meant to say that you have full freedom to conduct your mission as you see fit and using whatever resources you consider appropriate.'

Just for a moment, Mark thought of letting other issues slide. His team had been virtually accused of responsibility for the death of a US diplomat. At least it had been alluded to by Ambassador Luxton. Mark decided that this issue needed to be settled once and for all.

Mark did not know how to ask the question without sounding sarcastic.

'In our earlier discussions, you conveyed the accusation that I, or someone in my team, was responsible for the death of one of your fellow diplomats. Now you make no mention of that. Do I assume that those idiots in Foggy Bottom have come to their senses? Or have you found out who done it?'

Luxton tried to laugh – and failed.

'You must understand that this has been a difficult time for all of us. The team in Washington has been receiving conflicting advice from several sources. I can only tell you what I now know is the official position. The reason for the hold-up of your team had nothing to do with the unfortunate death of Johnson. It had more to do with the Secretary of State being absent overseas, the President being in Hospital, and his Vice President being unable to decide in his absence. But we now believe that you were not involved in his death. We suspect the Iranians.'

It was Marks' turn to laugh – and he succeeded.

'Has it occurred to any of you morons that the Iranians have got our government in a state of total confusion!'

He would not know until much later how close he was to finding out what was happening.

Chapter 27

Afghanistan

The US Drug Enforcement Administration had arranged with the Department of Defense to administer a couple of FAST units. These were Foreign deployed Advisory Support Teams which were a part of the DEA's Drug Flow Attack Strategy (DFAS). These units aimed to disrupt the Afghanistan opium trade and the flow of drugs into America. These units worked very closely with US Special Forces and were headed by a former Navy Seal.

However, it was a very uncomfortable arrangement. Apart from watching the DEA spend a fair amount of their resources coming up with the acronyms, the Pentagon would have been content to just get on with its job of fighting a war without bureaucratic interference from the Department of Justice.

The DEA would have been content to get on with the job of enforcing the laws on drug use without needing to be constrained by the might of the US military and its bureaucratic structure. Or without the need to resort to physical violence. Still – they were working in Afghanistan - and there was a war going on. And it was never a simple matter to decide who was, or was not, on the same side. So – flare-ups of violence would be inevitable.

Mark had been involved not many months before in trying to understand how the US Central Intelligence Agency had become involved in the Afghanistan drug trade. The outcome of his involvement would have pleased the military who had reasons to distrust the CIA. At the same time, his involvement had put Mark offside with the CIA. While some would grudgingly accept that Mark's work had correctly shown a serious problem within their ranks, there was still resentment that his mission had been carried out without their prior knowledge. Well – that was not strictly true. The father of Mark, one Harold Taylor, was a powerful member of the CIA Inspectorate and he had been responsible for organizing the whole thing together with his ally at the DEA – one Karen Marshall the Director of Intelligence. Consequently, Mark had powerful friends in Washington DC. And he used them now.

Mark called Karen on her private line. He was probably taking a risk calling someone of the rank of DOI, but as she was likely to become his stepmother very soon, he thought the risk was worth it. Since it was 5:15 pm in Khartoum, which made it 10:15 am in Washington, that was too early for Marshall to have gone to lunch with Taylor.

Karen Marshall answered the call almost immediately.

'Well, Mark it is so good to hear from you! I trust you are well?'

'Yes - I am – Over in Sudan at the moment - if a little hot and tired after a quick trip to Ethiopia.'

The mention of being in such a faraway and remote

place got no response from the Director. There again, the DEA probably had agents in almost (but not quite) as many places as the CIA, so the Director was quite used to receiving calls from strange places anywhere in the world. In addition to that, as a consequence of his previous activity on behalf of the DEA, Mark was now employed as a consultant by the DEA to advise on their computer systems. It was not as though the bureaucrats took much notice of his advice but at least this director was on his side.

To try to keep the conversation moving, Mark skipped over recent events, leaving out any mention of why he was actually in Sudan, and who had authorized that trip. It would have impressed most people in Washington to mention that he had come to Sudan on the express instruction of the President, but that did nothing for Marks' ego. And would probably have been of little interest to Marshall. It certainly had no bearing on what he wanted.

'I have been talking to our Ambassador in Sudan and he is concerned about drugs coming into this country and in particular how they are being distributed within the international community. I thought that you could shed some light on where they are coming from. I have been asked to help.'

Ordinarily, a Director in the DEA hierarchy, would not be expected to share what knowledge she had in a casual conversation with an ex-Marine. But their relationship involved more than a possible family link. Karen Marshall was aware that Mark had placed his life on the line, not once but three times, and that made him special in her eyes. And she was well aware of Marks' views on drug traffickers and they're like.

'Ok – I will call you back on a secure line.'

Marshall ended the call, before calling him back a

few moments later. Mark had to smile.

Since Taylor Software had signed a contract with the DEA and other organizations who were tied up with the government security and intelligence networks, things had been different. One of the first recommendations that the Taylor group had made – tighten up on the way officials use their private communications devices and avoid the potential problems that they could cause. Most of the useable intelligence that people gathered came from gossip. And most gossips came from conversations that were believed to be private and therefore not subject to scrutiny by the many prying bodies with which Washington DC was awash. Unfortunately, not everyone in Washington was as conscientious as Karen Marshall, but they had to start somewhere!

'Mark – if you are in Sudan – I might suggest that you hop back to Afghanistan. The military has a meeting with our FAST units in Kabul in three days and on their agenda is a related subject. There is a rumor that drugs are being smuggled out to one of the Afghan neighbors. We do not know who is behind it, where exactly the drugs come from, or where the drugs are going. But it is a new development, and we need to get a handle on it. And sooner rather than later! The other issue is – What are the drugs being traded for? That question could involve factors beyond my area of concern but first things first. I would appreciate your take on how that meeting pans out – that is if you have the time.'

So – that was it! The DEA - or at least Karen Marshall - knew why Mark was in Sudan. And they or she also knew that he could simply hop over to Afghanistan without stepping outside the parameters of his *mission*. The bureaucratic rules of the game were alive and well. Anyone involved in this conversation, be it as a direct participant or someone with even the vaguest connection to the people or the subject, would be able to deny any knowledge. Deniability was also alive and well. As was the Washington game of overlapping territories and power struggles!

Mark sighed.

'No problem. 'But I cannot just roll up to the meeting! How do I get accredited and, importantly, who else is going to be there?'

He knew that getting *accreditation* would be a walk in the park for the DOI. He also knew that he would not be told who would or would not be there, other than a vague reference to what organization they were from. But he asked anyway in the hope that Karen may give him a heads up.

Marshal laughed.

'Well - there will be some of our friends from the CIA which may cause a few issues. But you do not need to worry about that. I will arrange for your accreditation as you call it. Although it is being held at the Bagram Air Base for security reasons, the meeting has been called at our initiative so we can invite who we like. So – for ease of everyone we can tag you as DEA officials – probably consultants since you already have that title if it comes to a pinch. That is the bit that will get under the skin of the CIA representatives. Although your last trip to Afghanistan was successful the CIA may have a different view and there may be trust issues. Anyway, if you need any other people, there who may need visas just let me know. As for costs – well we can talk about that later, but I guess this can be charged to the DEA. I guess you would want me to do the same for Dusty and whoever else you may wish to go with you? So – I had better get onto it – good luck!'

Now – how did she know that Dusty was with him?

However, one thing was clear. Karen Marshall, for a

a future stepmother, certainly was on to it and infinitely better than his actual mother at getting things organized. Elizabeth Taylor had been a rock that his father – Harold Taylor - could depend on while he had been the resident CIA Chief of Station in Wellington New Zealand not that long ago. But, since her return to Washington DC Elizabeth had changed into a real moaning old lady.

And that was even before his father Harold had met Karen!

There was much to do and there was not much time. He just told Dusty they were returning to Kabul Afghanistan and that he needed help getting organized. Dusty had heard half of his conversation with Karen Marshall, so he just shrugged and said - 'tell me what you want!'

Mark had to arrange flights out of Khartoum and into Kabul via wherever flights went to get *from* and *to* these two third-world places and in a hurry. He needed to rapidly prepare his team for a very different environment from that in which they had been operating. He was not going to Afghanistan again without being certain that he had the men and the resources necessary for such a hostile country.

Mark was confident that Blake Whittaker would be able to adapt and his other two recruits Ben Chapman an ex-Special Forces sergeant and Elliott Shannon a retired CIA operative were people he could trust, and there was no issue with their availability for the next task. The three men who he had recruited from active service – Brent Shannon, Mike Gilroy, and Hamish O'Dea – would be keen to see some further action and Mark did not see any point in seeking authority for their release from their units. He had caused enough problems for the President or the Secretary by insisting that his team stayed together, and he had to assume that they could be spared for a few days in Afghanistan. And now was not the time to get involved in another selection process.

Even so, Mark had the feeling that he would need another set of eyes outside the meeting in Kabul and then for whatever eventuated from that. He would need to contact Owen Squires the man who had probably saved his life on his last trip to Afghanistan and get him to Kabul because he had a feeling that this would not turn out to be a simple or an easy mission. In particular, he would need the Welshman's extraordinary skills at getting things out of nothing. But the real benefit of having Squires in the team was one skill that he had in his toolbox – he could speak and understand the local language.

Mark also needed to contact the British MI6 in Kabul to find out if they still had the satellite phones that they had used on their last visit. If they did not, then he needed to contact Brad Morgan in New York City and get him to download the security routine that he had loaded onto the phones that had been borrowed from the British. It was a feature that Mark had not bothered with while the team had traipsed around Africa where the level of surveillance was not overly sophisticated. But Afghanistan was different. There were probably as many Russian agents in the country as there had ever been and that required a whole new level of security. The last thing Mark needed now was to have interference from Russians who would typically be hell-bent on causing trouble – just for the hell of it.

On this trip he might even take the time to explain to Reginald Smith and Mike Robinson – MI6 agents masquerading as the British consular representative in Kabul - why it was that MI6 had been unable to unscramble their previous communications despite their attempts at bugging the phones that Mark had borrowed.

Mark had considered most of the possibilities. Probably not all of them. But he was certain that he was not going back to Afghanistan as unprepared as he had been the last time!

Mark and Dusty talked to each of the team to make sure that they were all on the same page. Most of the team would be employed as security until a decision was made on what would happen next. The last member of the team they talked to was Blake Whittaker. That was because they would invite him to join them as consultants to the DEA in Kabul. That in turn was because of his knowledge of drugs of a more legal nature than those that would be discussed.

Blake just laughed. 'Of course! Did you not know the definition of consultants?'

Dusty raised his eyebrows. Blake had a story for everything. Whether that made any sense to mere mortals was debatable. 'Go on – what sick story have you got now?' Mark had to ask.

'A couple of bulls were standing on the hill in a field contemplating how they could get at the cows in the field below which was separated from their field by a barbed-wire fence. The older bull turned to the younger bull and said *I have a plan!* If we start at the top of the hill and run towards that knoll, that will give us the necessary speed and trajectory to leap over the fence. The younger bull was skeptical, but the urge to get to the cows was sufficiently strong that he overcame his misgivings. They both took off at a fast gallop down the hill, and at the precise moment indicated by the older bull, they leaped into the air, looking to clear the barbed wire. They almost made it. They landed on the fence rather than over it and ripped their balls off on the barbed wire. Ever since that day, they have been Consultants to the other bulls.'

Mark and his team assembled at the Bagram Air Base Afghanistan on the morning of the meeting after a crazy trip from Khartoum. They had been booked on a Turkish Airlines flight which took them to Istanbul Turkey. From there they were taken by a US Airforce transport Boeing C17 Globemaster to the Incirlik NATO airbase in southeastern Turkey, before being loaded onto another Globemaster for the final part of the trip into Bagram.

It had been a hectic three days since Mark had the conversation with the DEA, in particular trying to get hold of Owen Squires. Mark knew that Squires would be somewhere in either Afghanistan or Pakistan but that was where his knowledge ended. By first contacting Brad Morgan in the New York office of Taylor Software he got hold of a couple of possible satellite phone numbers neither of which turned out to be of any use. However, another quick call to the Karen Marshall at the DEA Washington HQ revealed that Owen Squires was once again working with the DEA and one of their FAST teams in Afghanistan. He had not been scheduled to attend the conference but that turned out to be a non-issue. She arranged for him to be seconded to Marks' team for however long he was needed – much to the relief of Mark – and the obvious annoyance of DEA personnel.

Neither Blake, Ben, Brent, nor Elliott had previously met the Welshman Owen Squires and the introduction was in order. He was a small, thin man who walked with a permanent limp and was by far the smallest member of the team. However, what he lacked in size, he made up for inability, and Mark and Dusty were pleased to see him again after their last exploits in Afghanistan. Owen had been single-handedly responsible for rescuing

Mark and Dusty from a certain death from hypothermia in the mountains to the north of Kabul where they had been left to die courtesy of the Afghans. Which was of course courtesy of their Russian controllers.

Owen had nothing to do with the attempts to kill Mark back in Washington DC and he was quite surprised to hear of his exploits. At least, saving his life in Afghanistan had allowed Mark to die closer to home.

It was decided that only Mark, Dusty, and Blake would attend the full meeting at the Bagram base, leaving the rest of the group to attend some of the workshops that would be spread over the two days, before the meeting ended with a 'question and answer' session on the morning of the third day. The accommodation was provided in barracks at the Air Base and allowed the participants to mix in the mess hall without any apparent divisions between the various groups.

The meeting itself was much more pleasant than Mark had expected. Mark did not know any of the CIA representatives, but he did know one of the military people from his days working with the Special Forces, and also knew one of the FAST team guys who had five years before this left the Special Forces and joined the DEA and had subsequently been rostered into Afghanistan.

The animosity that Mark had come to expect between the Military and the DEA group, between the Military and the CIA group, and between the CIA and DEA was not evident amongst these people. That told Mark that the people involved here were at a lower level in their respective organizations, and that meant that they were more concerned with getting things done than the nonsensical bureaucratic power games that others at a higher level looked to play.

The meeting discussed various matters, mostly concerning the increasing influence of the Taliban and other terrorist groups on the drug trade of Afghanistan. No mention was made of the earlier attempts by the CIA to dabble in the drug trade. No ownership was taken of the fact that most of the massive quantity of drugs produced from Afghanistan's opium crop was destined for markets in the western world and particularly in the United States. The focus was on trying to prevent the Taliban and other insurgent groups from gaining income to support their activities in this country and beyond.

But that was where the meeting did not meet the objective of coming up with a plan to kill the drug trade completely. Yes – it was pleasant. There was no evidence of conflict between the various groups. The focus of the meeting was on the biggest problem – the Taliban. But there was no attempt to try to find any link to the reason why Mark and his team were here – the supply of drugs to members of the United States diplomatic service by a foreign power. As far as Mark could ascertain this meeting was intended as just an excuse to get people together to chew the fat and not much else.

More out of frustration than anything else, Mark decided to contribute to that discussion.

'Doesn't it strike you as odd that the Taliban are looking to raise funds for their activities from the very people that they are fighting against?' Mark asked the assembly. 'You could solve the problem overnight by cutting off the demand for drugs in the United States. But - that will not happen because there are neither the means nor the political willpower to crush that demand. Unfortunately, it is not our job to analyze where in our society that demand comes from or where the kingpins in the supply chain are peddling their wares. So, at this level, the next point to look at is the supply chain here in Afghanistan. The last time I was in this country we were concerned with the disruption of supply which was orchestrated by the same people who took part in the sourcing and supply. That was a conflict between rival suppliers. There was so much competition to get control of the supply chain it was a miracle that any drugs made it out of the country. So – those are the people you should target. I was only here for a couple of weeks but, in that time, I was able to find and identify a couple of the major distributors. And as far as I know, they had nothing to do with the Taliban. They were businesspeople – in the trade for one thing, and one thing only. The money. Ok – one of those distributors was killed in rather suspicious circumstances, but the clear speculation was that he would immediately be replaced by another businessman without any apparent interruption to the supply chain or any involvement by the Taliban. So – am I missing something here? Instead of trailing the Taliban – look for the businesspeople who traffic in drugs. Or – look for the people who are funding the trade. Find out how and where and the money comes from and cut it off. If you do that then I am sure that you will find that funding for the Taliban and other groups will suddenly dry up. Worst case, it will force the Taliban to be more active in the market and then, and only then, will your present plans begin to make any sense.'

That invoked a response from one of the CIA representatives called Peter Ross, who was Chief of station in the southern district of Marjah.

'It is not as simple as that. This is not Washington DC. You cannot just rustle up the local branch of the FBI and make a raid on a suspicious house! The growth and the supply of opium have been going on in this part of the world for over a hundred years! It is their way of life. Nothing that we can be done will change that.'

The nodding heads around the table told Mark all

that he needed to know. This lot had already given up. The days that they had spent sitting around a table discussing this difficult question had served only one purpose. It had convinced them that they were wasting their time.

Mark was not about to join them.

'I came to this meeting looking for answers on how drugs are getting into our overseas diplomatic services and, more importantly, who is the supplier? Now what I am hearing is that you do not know and regard the question as too difficult to answer. You are focusing on the Taliban – but for them to be successful in using drugs to fund their activities they need a market. And that market is right in your backyard! Yet, despite the enormity of the problem you plan to do nothing, Well I might as well ask – What is the point of you holding a meeting if the only purpose is to agree on the size and scale of the problem and then to do nothing about it! So – is that your final answer? I will not spoil your little meeting by telling you who I report to back in Washington DC, but I can assure you that they will not be impressed!'

Mark settled back in his chair knowing that the meeting would reach no conclusions that would be of any use to him and would probably not shed any light on what was happening in the countries that he had recently visited. But his comments to the meeting had stirred a thought deep in his soul. What if there was something else at play? The Taliban needed funds to pay for weapons and so they could simply supply drugs in exchange for money.

But why bother with money?

The money would attract people like bees to honey. It would cause squabbles between people anxious to get an ever-larger share of the proceeds of their crimes without a second thought for how the wealth was accumulated.

But barter was even older than the growing of Opium – wasn't it?

The Taliban could trade drugs for weapons.

'**Let us** sort out what we know and what we don't know – and go from there.' Mark was talking with the eight men who now made up his team. They were located in a safe house in the Wazir Akbar khan district of Kabul. According to Owen Squires, the house belongs to the US Drug Enforcement Administration but was available to any of the various United States organizations that had business in the Afghan capital of Kabul. That meant that it was not a safe house in the true traditions of the security and intelligence service. But it was a house. And it had plenty of room even though it did not have much in the way of furnishing and had no means of heating. In any case, Mark did not intend to stay long.

'We know that the bulk of drugs coming out of Afghanistan comes from the southern provinces' Dusty began. 'If, as you suspect, the drugs that we are concerned about are falling into the hands of Iran – that means that they are probably finding their way into Iran through their eastern border.'

'Yes – that makes sense' Owen contributed. 'The western border of Afghanistan is fairly open by any standards. It is a vast and remote area that is hard to police. And it has for centuries been crisscrossed with smuggling routes. On the Iranian side of the border, we would expect stricter control of what goes on than on this side. That is because the borders are mostly under the control of the Iran military, but even they cannot be everywhere. On the Afghan side of the border, there are only sporadic patrols, and the border forces are of doubtful value. Even those who can be relied upon – well the border guards cannot be everywhere - and the smugglers have long since got them sorted out.'

'That leads to the other problem!' Mark mused. 'I

suspect that, although the Iranian culture is against drugs of any kind, there is official government involvement and that means the Iran military in the form of the Islamic Revolutionary Guards is likely to be heavily involved. All that the drug traffickers need to do is to get the drugs to the Afghan side of the border and hand them over in exchange for cash or goods. If that is the case, then we have no show of tracking the drugs any further than the Afghanistan – Iran border. But first – we must establish that the drugs get that far and who the suppliers are. Second – we need to ascertain that it is the Iran military rather than your normal dealers who are receiving them. If it is the military, then all we have to do is to estimate the size of the problem. And we can logically forget dealers because they would surely be looking to supply people in Iran – not to supply them to another country.'

Blake had been following the discussion with only casual interest. His job was to help supply the number of troops necessary for whatever the experts wanted. But he was also not expecting to waste his time in this god-forsaken place.

'So – are you saying that we have come all this way to reach the inevitable conclusion that we are fucked before we start?'

Mark and Dusty had worked with Blake in dark places before and were quite used to his not-so-subtle descriptions. The other members of the team were not so sure. Mark just grinned as Dusty put on his lawyer hat and dealt with it by asking a question of his own.

'Come on Blake! You tell us. You are supposed to be the FBI's resident expert on all things to do with drugs. – so – How do we do it?'

The question that Dusty had asked was on point, and Blake realized that the two men he was talking with had just as much knowledge of drugs as he did. He did not apologize but it was obvious from his body language that he regretted the outburst.

'Ok - If we can find the drugs that are destined for Iran from here in Afghanistan, then we should be able to recognize the drugs that appear on the other side. That is provided we have the right tools to do the job. It is a stretch, but we can do it. Every drug batch will have an element that makes it slightly different – not that the drug users would know the difference and not that those in the trade could care a hoot. But there are differences. It is just the nature of the drug manufacturing process. It is not an exact science and with the somewhat haphazard process of manufacture employed the results would be variable. But we are not looking for evidence to take to court. All we need to do is show that, on the balance of probabilities, these drugs are the ones that are finding their way into a certain market. And that market is pretty specific provided you can get samples of the drugs that make it that far.'

'Ok – that makes sense. Now how do we do that?' Elliott wanted to know.

'Well on the practical side that is quite simple' Mark began with a sarcastic smirk.

'Working backward from the border, we need to find the laboratory that manufactured them and get a few samples. That means that we have to know who the distributors are. Then we need to try and track how they get to the border and who receives them. As a bonus, we should be able to find out what they are exchanged for. That was one of the things that I would have hoped would come out of the meeting at Bagram. Where I have to say, we got no help at all.'

Owen summed it up. 'Ok – so we are on our own.'

'Yes – that about sums it up' replied Mark. 'But - there is another problem that I should mention. What we do not know is what stockpile of drugs the Iranians may have.

It could be that they have stock and that the drugs we are tracking will not make it into circulation in the timescale that we are working to.'

Dusty shrugged.

'Well let's go and find out!'

'Yeah - But first, we need to go talk to the Brits.'

Mark and Owen went to the British Embassy in Kabul to meet with the Deputy Chief of Mission Reginald Smith. They had met with Reggie some months before – that time on the golf course not far from where they were now. At that time, he had been masquerading as a mere Cultural Attaché. But for all the fancy titles and all the deflection, his mission in life had not changed at all. He was still the British MI6 chief of station in this part of the world.

Reggie greeted Mark like a long-lost friend but could not help proving that he was up with the play.

'So, how did your meeting go at Bagram with your American friends?' he asked as he reached across the desk to shake hands with his guests.

Mark had to smile. He had learned earlier in life that the British seemed quite attuned to finding out what their allies were up to. That is apart from their real mission which was to look out for their enemies. But it was all done in the very best spirit of cooperation. Or so it seemed.

'Oh – it was just a get-together to exchange views on how the world was ticking over' Mark replied in what he thought was diplomatic speak for that is *none of your business.*

Reggie did not show any reaction to the clear rebuke.

'Let me get Mike Robinson in – I am getting too old for this, and I might miss something if I didn't have Mike to keep me on point.'

Which was also bullshit. When Mark had called to make this appointment, he had half-expected to be meeting the chief spook at a clandestine place – in the middle of a park, or – heaven forbid back at the golf course – because that would have appeared more dramatic. But no – meeting at the British Embassy meant that the British wanted a recording of everything that was said at this meeting. And that told Mark that MI6 knew something pertinent to either the subject or the personnel at the meeting. Whether they would reveal what that was would depend on how the meeting went.

Mark had a lot to learn.

But he was learning.

'Before we start, I have to ask a favor!' Reggie began. 'Our electronic chaps would like to talk to you sometime about what you did to those satellite phones that we lent to you earlier in the year. You installed some security system that they think is pretty neat. It can be improved of course! But it is something they have not seen before – even on US government phones. So – is that something that is special to the US military – or should I say special to the US Special Forces - or your DEA. Or is it your own?'

So that was the way it was going to be! The security system that Mark Taylor had installed on the satellite phones had been developed in the United States by Taylor Software. Among other things, it blocked any attempt by anyone to listen in on the conversations and overrode any software that MI6 – or anyone else for that matter - may have conveniently left on the device for that very purpose.

Now the game had changed. The proposition on the table was that, if the Americans were to ask the British MI6 for any help on his present mission, there would be a price to pay.

And that was fair enough.

And that could work both ways.

Mark again smiled.

'Yes – it is a neat system developed by my own company – Taylor Software - in New York City. And it has not yet been adopted by any US department either commercial or military.'

Mark hesitated before talking further about this subject. But then – why not? The British had adopted the Stingray machines developed in the United States by the Harris Corporation. The sale of their cellular phone surveillance devices was very strictly controlled and limited to the military and law enforcement agencies (probably because what they did was somewhat illegal). But they had expanded sales into other allied countries and their existence was not exactly a secret. Taylor Software was in the same business and was looking to improve on the Harris model particularly in the area where it was vulnerable to countermeasures – by the development of crypto phones. That was solvable, but Mark would need some help. The devices were an IMSI catcher. And where you were dealing with International Mobile Subscriber Identity the British, amongst others, would be very interested. But before you could get into the business of defeating countermeasures there were other problems to solve first.

Mark decided to open the door but give nothing away.

'I will be quite happy to talk to your technical people, but you will understand I may need to offer it to the US government first. And given the security implications, my government may want to have a say in what happens.'

Both men smiled at that,

While the British MI6 was primarily a covert intelligence organization concerned with matters of strategic (and often military) importance to the Crown, they were still aware of the commercial nature of the world in which they operated. And it would be commercial considerations that decided what would happen despite the military implications.

Mark continued.

'Right now, I want to talk about another problem that you may be able to help us with.'

Mike Robinson had entered the room and at once adopted the role of a senior intelligence officer. He poured cups of tea for the four people in the room even though Mark could not remember when he had last took part in this curious British habit.

He got straight to the point.

'We have been investigating drugs that we believe are traveling from Afghanistan into Africa. In particular, they are finding their way into the US diplomatic community. Because it appears to be specifically targeted, we suspect that it is the work of a foreign power rather than the normal drug dealers. We cannot prove it! At least – not yet. What we are now trying to do is find out what drugs are going where other than the normal flood of drugs going into the United States. To do that we would logically track the drugs from their origin to the point that they leave Afghanistan. However, we suspect that it will be a matter of finding out where the exchange takes place and who that involves. The other issue is what the drugs are exchanged for, but we will cross that bridge when we come to it. For now, we need help.'

Reggie and Mike exchanged a meaningful glance before Mike spoke.

'I would have thought that the meeting at Bagram over the last couple of days would have been the start point for such an investigation. Was that not the case?'

Mark now laughed.

'That meeting did not get down to talking about specifics. So – No! We did not get any help from there.'

Now it was Reggie's turn.

'You have been wandering around Africa lately. Is that where you have concluded that the drugs are appearing? Yes – we have been aware of drugs in Africa – and it is not a problem limited to you Americans – but we have heard nothing specific about them coming out of Afghanistan. Having said that – Heroin is the popular drug, and it seems a long way to bring it from Columbia and Mexico when you can pick it up in Afghanistan'

'Yes,' Mark shrugged – surprised that the MI6 chief would reveal that he knew about their African exploits. He was not surprised that they knew. What he could not know is whether they knew about the shambles that the CIA had organized for their transport in Mozambique. And the death of one of their agents.

'There seems to be a pattern to this – and it is too organized and targeted to be like your normal drug deal. We suspect that there is no obvious money involved – at least to an extent that would interest the normal drug dealing fraternity – so we are thinking that something else is at play.'

'And you claim to have no idea who is behind this!' Mike asked with an air that suggested he was not believing it.

Mark again shrugged.

'I can only tell you what I suspect if you want me to guess. I suspect that the Iranians have a hand in all this. Only on the basis that they appear to have been unusually active in Zimbabwe Africa and now shifted their attention further north to Sudan. And, strange as it may seem, they have been active in Kuwait, although how that fits into the scheme of things I do not know. I have no idea why – and that is what I am trying to either prove or disprove.'

Smith had the look about him that said that Mark was not far off what he was thinking. Or far off what MI6 already knew?

'Yes!' Reggie mused. 'Some weeks ago, we followed the CIA's theory that someone was trying to kill President Robert Mugabe in Zimbabwe. That proved to be a fizzer, but it did point the finger firmly in the direction of Teheran. And the same thing with your experience in Khartoum where there was a definite Iranian involvement in what happened there. And I understand that you were instrumental in upsetting their plans. I am sure the British government will get around to thanking you for your help in Harare! But – what is the aim of all of this? It does not make any sense!'

Mark could not help there. It did not make any sense to him either. And the CIA's latest position – at least as notified to the troops in the field - saw nothing to worry about. The CIA did not think that drugs were the problem. Or they felt that it was a problem but that another department would deal with it! Or – heaven forbid – it was another situation in which the CIA were up to their old tricks in the drug trade.

'So – what is your plan from here?' Mike asked.

'Well, what else can we do?' Mark began. 'As a starting point - we will head down to the Helmand province and try to track any drugs heading west and over the border into Iran.'

Smith seemed to come to a decision. Whether it was the official position of MI6, or the British government, or a decision made on the fly in Kabul - he did not say. And you never could tell when dealing with the Brits.

'We may be able to help you there! We can get our people to contact you when you get down out west and maybe they can help.'

So – the British had people in Afghanistan who were

familiar with the drug trade and who were actively investigating some aspects of it! That was not surprising. The British had a long history of involvement with the Afghans and would be only too well aware of the power of the poppy. And of the culture that surrounded it. But – did Mark detect something else going on? The Brits were either already investigating the subject that Mark had touched on or was determined to piggyback on Marks's investigation.

It was asking too much for the British to tell Mark and his team who they could or should contact. But this was the next best thing.

Back at the safe-house Mark was surprised to receive a call from the US Embassy in Khartoum. He was even more surprised when he realized who the call was from.

'Mister Taylor! It is Margaret Laws calling from Khartoum. Luxton asked me to call you and tell you that two of the prisoners who were incarcerated here in Khartoum while you were here have escaped. I am afraid that is all we know at this stage! We have no idea where they have gone and are trying to get more information from the Sudan police. But we are not hopeful – as you will know, the police are not the most efficient!'

The acting CIA Chief of Station in Khartoum, who was according to information that Mark had was not a CIA officer, actually sounded quite aloof and pleased. That annoyed Mark. It also annoyed him that this lady should refer to her boss by only his surname rather than at least adding his title.

Mark put those thoughts aside as he decided to twist her tail.

'Ok. Do you have any idea how they escaped? And

which two people are we talking about – the two men or the two women? And, more importantly, what is your assessment on where they may have gone?'

The answer that he got was negative on all counts – she did not know how they had escaped, who had escaped, or where they had gone. All that he heard was a long ramble about being short of resources which was a typical bureaucratic response. That translated into the simple fact that the CIA in Khartoum had no clue.

Or, was Ms. Laws being deliberately evasive?

Mark killed that call and put a call through to his other contact in Khartoum - Ibrahim Mustafa at Sudan Intelligence.

'Well word gets around fairly quickly!' Mustafa said, clearly very angry at someone after Mark had asked him what was had happened to the prisoners. 'I have only just been informed myself and am trying to find out how and why this happened. It does not surprise me! Our prison system is not the best or the most secure. And is prone to all sorts of corruption. I am of course sorry that this has happened. At the moment I have no idea where the two men may have gone but we will find them!'

Yeah! And pigs can fly! Assuming the two escaped prisoners were who Mark thought they were. *We will find them* was the assurance that Mustafa had given to the Americans when Mohamed Haji had first arrived in Khartoum. And yet Haji had still managed *to arrive* - undetected - within shooting distance of his target with a pistol and an accomplice equipped with a submachine gun!

'Ok – I would appreciate it if you could keep me informed of how you get on.' said Mark, ending the call.

On the advice of Owen Squires, the eight men in the

team traveled from the capital city of Kabul to the southern city of Kandahar in two vehicles. The vehicles they would have expected to be given to them would have been simple Humvees which were the most common military vehicles around. But they were allocated two MaxxPro MRAP (Mine Resident Ambush Protected) armored vehicles which were not exactly small. They each weighed more than 30,000 pounds. They were more appropriate for going into battle than they were for transporting people between towns. Still – the last time Mark had traveled the road between Kabul and Kandahar they had ended up in the little-known Battle of Ghazni. In reality - with the recent reduction in the US forces in Afghanistan there was a huge collection of vehicles available in Kabul. The US rarely, if ever, took vehicles back to the States when it ceased or reduced an overseas deployment. But, in true bureaucratic style, the vehicles were stored and maintained in full working order in situ and were made available to any quasi-government organization or task. The choice of two vehicles rather than four vehicles was based on the fact that there would be any number of vehicles available in the south of the country.

The choice of two vehicles rather than one was much more practical – if one vehicle was attacked or hit by a roadside bomb there would at least be half of their team still intact.

They traveled south in a convoy which was a little different from the last time Mark had traveled along this road. There were significantly fewer US and allied troops in the defense forces and about the same number of Afghan forces. There was a smattering of other people in uniform throughout the convoy, but Mark suspected that a majority of these men were not any kind of combat troops. They had the look of people who would rather not be traveling in this convoy. They would be of little help should they be attacked by any of the numerous bands of terrorists and other groups that inhabited this land. Mark could remember only too well his previous experience in Afghanistan when the convoy that they were part of was attacked. Five of the current team were in that battle of Ghazni – Mark, Dusty, and Owen following one of the men from the CIA and Mike and Hamish who were on that occasion part of a troop assigned to the convoy. Hamish was the only one of the five that was injured but it could have been far worse had it not been for the timely intervention of British and US helicopters.

This time most of the men being ex-special forces personnel tolerated the cramp, noise, and somewhat uncomfortable driving characteristics of the MaxxPro. For their part, Owen and Elliott just enjoyed the thrill of traveling in a vehicle that felt extraordinarily safer than other forms of transport. If this convoy was attacked on this trip, the International M1224 Maxxpro MRAP was probably the best place to be.

It may well have been the sheer presence of these two frightening vehicles that allowed the convoy to complete the journey without interference. The Taliban and others who would wish to cause them harm would often take on a far superior force that the American military would class as stupid. But not this time.

The Taliban weren't that stupid.

When they arrived in the southern city of Kandahar, Mark's team was thankful for the anonymous mask that the military environment provided.

As he had sensed with the convoy, Kandahar was also a very different place than that which Mark remembered from his recent visit to Afghanistan. At first, he found it hard to decide what had changed, but that soon became clear. The United States forces and their allies, including the fledgling Afghan Army, had previously had control of the city. The local Afghan population simply kept out of their way.

Not anymore.

Now the Taliban, who had always had a strong presence in the city, were everywhere and provocatively carrying their guns in the open. And now the locals stared at the military vehicles with looks akin to fear rather than respect. That was not to say that the attitude of the locals had changed. What had changed was the balance of power.

Kandahar had been relatively peaceful when the Americans were at full strength and the people felt safe – whether they supported the Taliban or not. With the subtle change in the balance of power the ordinary people who wanted no part in any battle between the Taliban and the foreigners were now being forced to take a side in the dispute.

And they felt that the Americans were deserting them.

Amid all this mayhem, there was still the Drug trade.

In the midst of that, there was now a stronger Taliban.

There are two theories about the Taliban. The first said that, as a group, they were opposed to the drug trade and wished to ruthlessly stamp it out. The second theory said that they would tolerate drugs so long as they could control the distribution and the resultant, and considerable, cash flow. The fact was that both of these theories were true in one context or another. That was one of the reasons why the meeting in Kabul had been unable to reach any conclusion. There was just no way of knowing what the Taliban were up to and what they would do. They were and had always been, unpredictable and that was what made the Taliban so dangerous.

With this in mind, Mark led his team into the Kandahar International Airport where the US had established a base back in the days when the mission known as Enduring Freedom was in full swing. That base was still a safe place but for how long would it continue to be?

Although the journey from Kabul had taken about ten hours in which the team had nothing to do except sharing the driving, which in itself was tiring, the constant tension of traveling in this inhospitable land had taken its toll on the team. The men spent a brief time in the mess, not trying to associate with other groups. They had a feed from the galley which was probably the best meal that they had had since leaving the United States – whenever that was! They then retired to surprisingly comfortable quarters for a good nights' sleep.

Before retiring Mark made another attempt to find out what had happened to the prisoners in Khartoum. While the United States government appeared to be satisfied that his team had circumvented the attempts to assassinate the President of Zimbabwe in both Harare and Khartoum, Mark had a lingering doubt that he had heard the last of the people who had planned this affair. But he doubted whether he would get much help from either the local CIA or from the diplomatic service.

He again called Ibrahim Mustafa of Sudan Intelligence.

'That was timely!' said Mustafa on receiving the call. 'I was just about to call you. We have been able to confirm that Mohamed Haji and his fellow prisoner have left Sudan for Damascus by Syrian Air' Mustafa began, clearly pleased that his men could at least get that right, even if that was not what was supposed to have happened.

'We are checking with the airline how that happened and there may be repercussions – but I doubt whether anything will come of that.'

'Ok – that is good that you have been able to clarify how they got out of the country' Mark replied, not sure if it was good or it wasn't. 'Now – do you know where they are going after they arrive in Damascus?'

Mustafa knew that as well and his answer left Mark confused.

Why was Haji going to Turkey?

Chapter 28

The Hajib

The couple came into the restaurant shortly after it had opened the doors for the start of the evening dinner service. They were in the south-eastern Turkish city of Adana, and this was unfamiliar territory for both of them.

This was the time of the evening when the staff would normally be preparing things before guests started to arrive for dinner at around six o'clock. The couple had turned up shortly after five o'clock and that was unusual for people to want to eat so early in the evening. The problem was that they had arrived by private car from the northern city of Ankara, and they simply had nowhere else to go,

Still – business was business, and they were quickly settled at a table. It was explained to the guests that dinner service would be delayed until the Chef got his kitchen organized, and they were quite Ok with that. They chose to sit at table number four by the window which gave an excellent view of the street and the assorted run-down buildings that were the norm in this part of town. And they would have an excellent view of who came in and

Having taken their order for drinks, the maître de retired behind the bar and continued her preparation for the evening trade while she did her usual summation of the guests.

The guests were not residents of Adana. Nor were they Turkish. The receptionist guessed that they were, probably, either Iraqi or Syrian, but they were customers and that was all that she was interested in. However, there was a tenseness about the couple that seemed to permeate the whole restaurant and that was the other unusual thing about this couple.

The waiter came across and added his thoughts. He guessed that they could be two people on their first blind date and had reacted with mutual horror at their first meeting. On the other hand, they could be a couple who had a near-terminal disagreement and were battling to stay together. But why come to dinner so early? In fact, why come to dinner at all?

The man was well presented, in his mid to late thirties, about six feet tall, dressed in a dark-colored business suit, black hair, clean-shaven, and took great care of his body. Despite all this, he was an arrogant son-of-bitch and at no stage was there even a hint of a smile.

The lady was a foot shorter than the man, stylishly dressed in an off-the-shoulder dress, high-heeled shoes, died blond hair, and had a body to die for. Despite all this, she was nervous as hell and looked as though she would rather be somewhere else. Or with someone else. Or both. So, she did not smile either.

The waiter finally surmised that they must be a business couple, but of more importance to him was that there would probably be no tips coming his way from this couple.

That is if they were indeed a couple.

The receptionist and the waiter were both wrong in

their assessments, apart from the waiters' observance of the arrogance of the man and the body of the lady.

Reema Zadeh was the youngest of three daughters born to a middle-class family living in the outskirts of Teheran Iran. Her father was a Doctor of Oncology at the Teheran Milad General Hospital, and her mother was a Doctor of Gynecology at the Ruin Tan Arash Women's Hospital – also in Teheran. The parents had dreamed of their daughters following them into the medical field. The elder two daughters had been pressured into doing just that. However, the younger Reema could not stand the sight of blood or the thought of dealing with sick people and wanted to get out to see the world.

She had studied hard and drifted into, rather than chose, a career in journalism which it turned out she had a natural aptitude for. Her career started as a trainee in the political section of the Teheran Times newspaper where she gained an understanding of the complex world of international affairs. Eventually, an opportunity arose for her to accept an overseas appointment as a press officer in the Iran Embassy in Ankara Turkey. She had leaped at the chance to get away from home, away from the strictly ordered life imposed on her by her father, and away from the restrictions on her journalism which were imposed by the managers of the newspaper who were – at least in her view – controlled by the Iran government.

Life in Ankara turned out to be a little different from life at home. It was controlled by the Islamic faith. She was required to meet the strict wishes of her peers. But once she settled into the routine of pumping out propaganda on behalf of the government of Iran rather than using her initiative and skills as a journalist, she began to enjoy herself as an independent young lady. There was not much in the way of social life because of the strict rules that Iran's diplomatic staff had to adhere to. However, it was different. And there was always the chance of finding excitement in foreign lands.

One thing she did do was to befriend one of the lesser mortals from the diplomatic staff at the Iranian Embassy. He was a young man starting at the bottom of the diplomatic ladder as a cultural attaché. His name was Siyamak Rahmati. Reema thought that he was quite cute. After a few dates that amounted to having coffee together in a local bar they did end up agreeing that there was a serious attraction, and the two of them ended up sharing a flat. And whatever else young people shared when away from the confines and discipline of home.

As they got to know each other better she soon realized that his work at the Embassy had little to do with culture. Nonetheless, although he was very secretive about what he did, she became intrigued with his work and prodded him to tell her more of what he got up to. And as is the way with all young men he could not help but feed her inquisitive nature with snippets of his secret life of a spook.

Most of it was of course bullshit. For the simple reason that nothing was happening in Turkey to get excited about other than the mundane feeding of mostly commercial intelligence to his masters in Teheran – almost all of which would be filed away by some bureaucrat never to see the light of day again.

And then something happened that changed things between them.

Out of the blue, she was summoned to his office for a meeting. There she was introduced to another handsome young man named Babak Mazanderani. He was even more mysterious than her boyfriend. The introduction to his work told her nothing.

'Babak has been asked to do a small job on behalf of our Supreme Leader and he needs the help of a lady to carry it out. I mentioned you as a possible candidate as I thought you would not mind helping us. It would require you to travel down to south-eastern Turkey for a couple of days. Would you be interested in performing this small task for our leader?' Siyamak Rahmati casually asked the girl who only the night before had shared his bed.

Reema was at once excited.

Now she knew that what she had suspected all along was correct. Her boyfriend was running an intelligence operation and was experiencing one of the problems that the Iranian Intelligence service - in fact, most Iranian services of every kind - usually encountered. They rarely allowed women to play any significant role in their activities but there were circumstances where they had no choice. This time they needed a lady to do something for Iran and their Supreme Leader Ali Khomani! And this task would get her involved in real intrigue as opposed to the bullshit stories that her boyfriend had been feeding her with.

Reema was confident that Siyamak would not want her to come to any harm. And he had chosen her because he trusted her.

They would even allow her to go out on the mission without her hijab!

So, she was pleased to become a part of one of his silly little games.

Now that the time had come to carry out the assigned task, her enthusiasm had dramatically waned. As had her regard for her accomplice. Barak Mazanderani, who was not used to having his instructions questioned, put her position in clear perspective. He had quite simply told her that, if she did not complete the task that had been assigned to her, then she would be returned to Teheran.

The way that he said *returned* confirmed what she was now coming to realize. If she did not complete the task, she would be returned to the capital and into the hands of the Iran Intelligence service. Once in their hands she would be subjected to intense interrogation, probably torture, and other indignities that men inflicted on women. Because she could not know the nature of the dreadful crimes that she would be accused of, there would be no defense. She would be found guilty after a sham trial and then banished to the outskirts of the Kavir-e-Lut desert to live out her miserable life.

Or, if she was lucky, she could be executed depending on the mood of the clerics, and the seriousness of the crime.

After the couple had talked intently in whispers for several minutes, which mostly consisted of Mazanderani explaining something to Reema, the male summoned the waiter and asked if they could order a meal now.

It was a little early – but of course, they could!

But, as the waiter explained, there would be a delay because the kitchen was not yet geared up at this early hour. The man did not seem fazed by that and simply asked the waiter what the Chef would recommend. Which the waiter interpreted – correctly – that the man had not had much experience in dining in Turkish restaurants. The question itself could have caused confusion because this Chef did not recommend anything. So, the waiter recommended a pasta dish, his logic being that this couple may not like traditional Turkish food and the only other meal on the menu was a sort of oven-baked fettucine. And that dish avoided any of the meats that – if the couple were either Syrian or from somewhere to the east of where they were now – they may have found offensive.

Both readily accepted the advice of the waiter, and Mazanderani then returned to his whispered conversation with the now frightened young lady.

'So – this is what you are going to do. When the restaurant is busy you will go to the lady's restroom. You had better make sure that you will not need to go back because once you have completed your task, we will leave the restaurant. It is better if we use the female restroom because that is the way that we can guarantee maximum coverage. In this heathen place, women are more likely to deal with their hygiene than men. You have plenty of time to get prepared, just relax and enjoy your meal, and then we can get this done.'

From this point they sat in silence - Reema staring out of the window. Mazanderani flicked through his cell phone and taking no interest in his dining partner.

The restaurant slowly filled with other guests and most of them seemed to be foreigners was excellent for what the two Iranians had in mind. Reema's boyfriend Siyamak Rahmati had chosen this particular restaurant well because that is exactly the target that they intended to reach.

The instructions they had received from Iran Intelligence had been clear. Their task was to infect as many foreigners as possible.

Their pasta dishes eventually arrived at the table. They ate their meals in silence. The food had been very well prepared. Mazanderani attacked the meal with gusto. Reema was too tense to do justice to hers. She merely nibbled at the pasta.

And then came the moment that Reema Zadeh had

been dreading.

Babak Mazanderani asked the waiter for the bill, explaining that the half-eaten meal was due to his partner being unwell and asking for directions to the female restroom. And Yes - he said that he would pay in cash.

Before she left her seat, Reema first made certain that no one else would be in the restroom at the same time as her. Mazanderani accounted for all the people in the restaurant and assured as well as he could that everyone was busy in conversation or eating. He instructed her that the time was right.

Reema nervously got to her feet and scurried towards the ladies' restroom. Desperately prayed that no one else in the restaurant did the same thing.

She clutched her small handbag as she made her way through the tables towards the door. The bag was more a large purse than a bag.

The only item in the bag was a small aerosol can.

One of the problems with bacteria or viruses is that they do not last very long without a live body to thrive on. This particular virus was a vigorous little bugger well adapted to human beings. But once released it could not survive for more than a couple of hours without a host. As Reema sprayed the aerosol over every surface including the taps, the washbasins, and the toilet seats, she was terrified. Back in Ankara, they had both been assured that the vaccine they had been given was fully effective and that they would be safe. That would be fine for Mazanderani because he would be remote from the spray. But for Reema that was not so. The logic that it was better to use the spray in the lady's restroom rather than the men's was plausible for the simple reasons that women were likely to spend more time cleaning and pampering themselves than their menfolk.

But Reema did not see it this way. She saw it as an excuse by Mazanderani to avoid any risk to himself.

She knew something about vaccines and viruses having had to put up with the endless chatter amongst her family back at home in Teheran. She knew that receiving a vaccine was no guarantee that she would be safe.

And being vaccinated did not make her feel any more confident about being alone and in the same room as the active virus itself.

Iran had been quietly developing strains of the coronavirus bug since it was first raised in China in the early 2000s. Now the Iranians believed that they had a massive advantage in biological warfare. They had a weapon that could be applied anywhere, at any time, of their choosing, and no one would have even the faintest idea where it had come from. What is more, they had developed a vaccine, so that when an outbreak did occur, they could protect people of their own choice.

And come to the rescue of people of their own choice.

This time they would not come to the rescue.

At least not yet.

As a reporter, Reema Zadeh had read all the papers where experts had explained their theories about how a virus spread. But - no one knew the full story - did they? Were they transmitted by touching a surface or by breathing or by ingesting? Were they airborne or transmitted by the transfer of body fluids? Or were they transmitted by all of the above?

Reema desperately wanted to wear a mask, but the man had very definitely said No!

So – she was petrified.

Having finished with the spray she carefully wrapped

the now empty can in tissue, placed it back in her handbag, and rushed towards the exit door.

She nearly died of fright as two people came through the door. She struggled to hold back the tears as she realized one of the people was a young girl of maybe eight or nine years of age. They were both European which would be ideal for the mission that she had been instructed to undertake. But the pain that she felt was almost crippling as the girl smiled at her as Reema made to leave the restroom.

Back in Ankara, they had said it was even better if they could infect the young because they tended to be both more mobile and less responsive to restrictions that would limit the spread of the virus with which they had been infected. She hurried through the door before the two ladies could see the tears that welled up in her eyes.

Reema muttered *man mikhaaham ozr khaaahi konan* in Farsi as she left despite having been told to speak English by her minder.

The young girl looked confused as she watched Reema disappear through the door.

'Mum – Why is she sorry?'

The two Iranian nationals drove away from the restaurant and towards the motel where they had a booking, At least - that was the plan that had been described earlier. The relief was palpable. For the first time since their first meeting in Ankara, Reema began to feel the tension draining from her. They had achieved what their Supreme Leader had asked of his team and furthered the cause. Whatever that was.

Despite all the fears that Reema had before, their mission had worked exactly as planned. No one would be able to link them to the events of this evening. Or to whatever would happen next.

But just as quickly doubts began again as her thoughts turned to matters of a more practical nature. Mazanderani drove past the Sirin Park Motel without a second glance. As he continued to drive through what seemed like a maze of twists and turns, Reema began to worry again. She felt certain that they had passed the same point more than once. She thought to ask him where they were going and whether he knew where they were. But she was too traumatized by the events of the evening to risk angering the man.

Finally, after making several more turns, he pulled into a side street in what appeared to be a run-down part of town and stopped outside a house. Without bothering to explain what was happening, he got out of the car and indicated that Reema should do the same. He then pulled a bunch of keys from his pocket, walked to the front door, and slid a key into the lock.

They entered the building which was a large two-story house. The first floor had what appeared to be a large lounge area, a kitchen, and a dining room. Up the stairs were four bedrooms and two bathrooms.

After satisfying himself that they were alone and had not been followed, Mazanderani closed and locked the door behind them, before turning his attention to Reema.

'This is a safe house where we are to be de-briefed when the rest of the team gets here. Up the stairs, the first bedroom on the left is yours. Inside the wardrobe, you will find a dressing gown and a clothes basket. Take off all your clothes and put on the dressing gown. Place all of your clothes, your bag, and everything that you had in the restaurant into the basket.'

'Whatever for?' she asked, fearful of the answer she might receive.

Mazanderani smiled, hoping to calm Reema.

'We have to make sure that all traces of the virus are

removed and that no one will recognize anything connected with what we have just done and where we have been. Your clothes will be burned. I stress, we need to make sure that everything that could identify you or has traces of the virus is destroyed. Your clothes will be collected by a member of our team and taken away. Another set of clothes will be brought to you later.'

A feeling of dread began to creep into Reema's senses. She was about to ask whether the same would apply to his clothes, but she was too scared to say anything. She climbed the stairs and Mazanderani followed her as they entered the first bedroom on the left.

It was frugal. There was a double bed under a skimpy duvet cover, a wardrobe, a set of drawers with a small mirror, a small table, and a lamp. There was nothing else in the wardrobe except for the gown and a basket. The gown was not exactly as it had been described. It was a hospital cotton gown of the type that had three ties at the top, middle and bottom. For a moment Reema hesitated because the gown was both short and about two sizes too small for someone with even her small frame. But she was too scared to protest. In any case, she would soon have more clothes because the Mazanderani had said that was what was to happen.

She had no reason to disbelieve him.

Babak Mazanderani did not try to leave although he did turn his back as he played with his cell phone. Reema just shrugged in resignation and started to take off her clothes, hesitating only when she was down to her undergarments. She then went ahead to put on the gown.

Mazanderani noted her hesitation and quietly issued another instruction.

'All of your clothes Reema!'

She started to protest but Mazanderani just waved his hand in frustration.

'I have my orders – and therefore so do you. Be a good girl and just comply and we can have this thing over with very shortly.'

Reema was at least grateful that he did not seem to be interested in her in any sexual sense. She had heard that girls caught in this position were often abused by members of the intelligence and security service who arrogantly thought that it was their right to take advantage of the situation especially in the circumstances in which they now found themselves.

It was not that Reema was unattractive. Far from it. And she had lovely smooth skin and a perfectly proportioned body that her boyfriend Siyamak Rahmati had been unable to resist.

Maybe she was lucky? Maybe Babak Mazanderani was gay?

Dressed in the flimsy gown she turned away and followed his wishes removing her underwear. She then secured the gown as best she could with the ties that hospital gowns the world over seem to defy all logic. Then she made certain that all her clothes were in the basket and handed it to Mazanderani.

And she breathed a massive sigh of relief as he just turned without a second glance and headed back down the stairs.

As she turned to close the bedroom door behind him there was a disturbance at the front door and two men entered. It was obvious that Mazanderani knew them and rushed down to join them. Reema peeked down the stairs so that she could get a better view just as he greeted the new visitors. Both of the men were immaculately dressed in western styles suits. They both spoke fluent Farsi although she could not hear what was being said. Other than to understand that there was some disagreement between them and Mazanderani.

After this conversation during which the obvious disagreement was settled by the superior rank of at least one of the new visitors, Mazanderani turned to look up the stairs and ordered Reema to come down and join them.

Had Mazanderani known that she had been watching the arrival of the two visitors or that she may have heard what their discussion had been about he did not let on. Or he did not care. As it was, Reema had no clue of the subject of their discussion.

Had she done so she would not have been so compliant?

She came down the stairs and was instructed to sit on a chair by the dining room table. One of the new arrivals left by the rear door with the basket, and Mazanderani went up the stairs. The third man sat on a chair at the other side of the table and pulled a notepad and a pen from his pocket.

He smiled at Reema, but the smile did not travel to his eyes. His gaze glanced over her body, lingering over the shape of her breasts and then down at her fully exposed thighs before he finally spoke.

'Ok - Tell me what happened.'
Reema did not know how to answer that as she cowered in the chair.

She just asked - 'What do you mean?'

Her inquisitor sighed. His tone changed from what had been casual to one of aggression.

'I do not have much time for this. So - I will help you. In the restaurant where you went for your meal — What else did you do apart from eating a meal?'

That is when the tears started, and all the pent-up emotions came flooding back. Try as she may she could not give a coherent account of that horrible five minutes in the restaurant restroom. In the end, she concluded with her description of that poor innocent child.

Her inquisitor merely made a short note on his pad
'Whcrc was your hajib?' he asked.

The sudden change of subject threw her off for a moment. Then the chill of fear came back.

'I was told that I did not need to wear a hajib!' she stammered in reply.

Her inquisitor sneered.

'And who told you that? You must always wear a hajib!'

That was where she began to lose it.

She could not remember who had said what during the discussions back in Ankara. It was probably her boyfriend Siyamak who had mentioned it. But it seemed to her that it was the height of irrelevance anyway. She had been asked to do a job on behalf of their Supreme Leader and as far as she was aware that job required her not to wear a hajib. And here was this arsehole who could only concern himself with her frigging headdress!

He made another note on his pad.

'Did anyone else see you go to the restroom? What was the nationality of the two people who you did meet?'

Reema tried to compose herself.

'No – I made sure that no one else would be in the restroom before I went in. The lady, and a girl that I took to be her daughter, came into the restroom as I was leaving. And, from the way they were dressed, they would have been from the west - probably Americans.'

Reema was relieved that this explanation seemed to satisfy her inquisitor as he made another note on his pad.

However, his next line of questioning first raised her hackles, and then fear gripped her again.

'What happened when you returned here?'

'Why – nothing!' Reema replied not knowing where this was leading.

The man looked at Reema with a cruel smile on his face.

'So – those are the clothes that you wore at the restaurant?'

'Of course not! I just went up the stairs and did as I was told! I took off my clothes and placed them in the basket. Babak said they were to be burned.'

Again - the sigh.

'So - *Babak* just told you to take off your clothes and you just did as you were told? How long have you known him as Babak?'

'Not for very long. What are you saying? Why don't you ask Mazanderani! She almost shouted at this horrible man.

'Are you a virgin?' he asked with a leer on his face.

'No! I mean – what are you talking about?'

'What I am talking about is what happened when you got back from the restaurant? You are telling me that you come into a strange house with a man who you have just had dinner with. A man with who you are obviously on a first-name basis. You then immediately go upstairs and take off all your clothes. And you say nothing happened! Or that nothing was about to happen!'

Her stammered reply was almost incoherent.

'Nothing happened! What are you talking about?'

'Stand up!'

Reema stood, not sure what was happening now. She stood quivering with fright.

The man also stood and moved around the table so that he stood in front of her. She began to tremble out of fear as he reached for the top ties that held her gown in place. As the gown slid from her shoulders, he reached out towards her, and his hand slipped inside the gown caressing her breast. His other hand moved down and rubbed the bulge in his trousers, as he continued to look at her body. Then he grabbed the gown tearing it from her as she stood before him, now completely naked, trying to cover her body with her hands.

The sound of a door opening and closing shattered the moment and saved a situation from getting out of hand. He pushed Reema back into the chair as she scrambled to retrieve the gown to cover herself,

He returned to his seat at the other side of the table.

'We are finished here.' he said as Mazanderani came back down the stairs

The interrogator pulled a pistol from the small of his back and proceeded to screw a crude silencer onto the barrel.

At first, Reema did not react to what was happening. Then she turned to Mazanderani a look of terror on her face and her mouth wide open. No words would come out.

The suppressor made the gun a little unwieldy but for the distance, the bullet had to travel that did not matter. Reema collapsed as the bullet entered her forehead and only just missed Mazanderani as it exited the back of her skull, embedding itself in the wall.

Reema was dead by the time her body hit the floor.

There was no visible reaction from either man to the ending of the young life. The two men just dragged the corpse out of the rear door into the yard where the third man had completed digging a shallow grave. They dropped the body into the ground, quickly covered the corpse, and filled in the hole. The three men trampled the earth so that there would be no sign of any disturbance. The ground was very dry so that there was only the dust on their shoes to show that anything had happened.

Not that it mattered.

There was no way that this house would ever be used again by the Iranian members of VAJA and there was nothing to tie them to this house.

There was nothing that could link the body, if it was ever found, to what had happened in Adana.

The secret of the events in the city of Adana was safe.

The two men walked back inside the house. Mazanderani rushed upstairs to collect any evidence that they may have left behind. The interrogator waited impatiently at the bottom of the stairs believing that his minions could take care of such mundane tasks.

In any case, Mohamed Hajis right leg was giving him pain.

Chapter 29

The Search

After breakfast the following morning, Mark managed to talk the base vehicle maintenance team into allocating them another two MaxxPro MRAP vehicles and then set about planning the next few days. The extra vehicles were insurance. They were justified by the fact that things may require some flexibility in the way he deployed the team. And the use of such powerful vehicles was justified by the increasing hostility in the city of Kandahar.

Unlike on his earlier mission in this country, there seemed that there would be little to be gained by being overly covert. However, there were other issues at play. The most significant issue was the mixture of nationalities that seemed to inhabit the Kandahar airport. Apart from the US Air Force and Army personnel, there were also British Royal Air Force and Royal Navy aviators, French and Belgian Air Force, plus a considerable number of people from the Afghanistan Air Force and Army.

It was the latter that was the most cause for concern.

The Afghanistan culture is an odd mixture that had been developed over centuries during which time the country had been almost permanently involved in many periods of wars and conflicts. All these conflicts had led to a scattering of various ethnic groups. These had simply disappeared or had been seamlessly absorbed into the general population.

The problem stemming from this situation was that it was well near impossible to work out which had group now dominated the culture?

The dominant religion in Afghanistan is Islam and the origins of that were Persian and Arabic. This meant that – although fiercely independent – Afghanistan is more than likely to be siding with its western neighbors than with its south-eastern neighbors. However, the vast majority of people in Afghanistan are Sunni Muslims which explains why the al Qaeda terrorist group with their origins in Saudi Arabia was able to find a home in Afghanistan. While most Afghans speak Dari and Pashto languages many claim that they would speak in Farsi if they had not been forced to speak Dari by the majority Pashtun ethnic group.

Farsi is the dominant language of the Persians.

Persia is now known as Iran.

The western border of Afghanistan is shared with Iran.

And to complicate matters Iran is predominantly Shia Muslim.

Mark had planned to split the team up into four groups and to then begin a grid search of what was viewed as the most likely area of Kandahar in which opium was being converted into heroin. By observing the movement of trucks into and out of the area there would soon be a pattern appear that told them where the majority of drug laboratories were. Then it was simply a matter of narrowing down the labs to find out which were shipping their drugs to the west and into Iran as opposed to those that were shipping them to the north and west.

By Mark's calculation, it should not take more than a week to sort the first part of the plan. Kandahar was not a very large city with a population of only about six hundred thousand, and the area of the city which was most likely to contain drug laboratories only accounted for about one hundred square miles.

With that completed, the second part of the plan should be straightforward. It was just a matter of convincing the residents to talk - and talk honestly - about what was going on in their midst. And to ignore the threats from the Taliban and other dealers who might take exception to the details of their business dealings being shared with the infidels. Add to that Mark had only one member of his team who could speak both Farsi and Dari, and who could understand most of what was being said by people who spoke Pashto.

The other members of his team would have to rely on sign language.

It was little wonder that the team started with a feeling of apprehension, bordering on a lack of enthusiasm. Apart from the enormity of the mission, their chances of achieving anything as quickly as they hoped did not look too bright.

Fortunately, the British MI6 came to the rescue, albeit in not quite the form that Mark had envisaged.

The call came while Mark was just finishing his morning shower.

'Hello – is that Mister Taylor ... Mark Taylor?' the voice asked in a whisper. The voice was that of a lady, who

Mark took to be local judging by her accent and the obvious fact that English was not her language of choice.

And she sounded as though she was scared shitless.

'Yes - this is Mark Taylor. Who is this?'

'I am Larmina. I was asked by Mister Robinson to call you.'

Mark had to think for a moment, before realizing that *Mister Robinson* was Mike Robinson – the assistant to the British MI6 Chief of Mission in Kabul.

'Oh – Ok. Well, when and where can we meet?'

'I'm sorry. English not good.'

'Ok - Hang on! I will get you to speak with one of my team who should be able to help.'

There was no point in trying to cover the phone, so Mark just yelled. 'Owen! – Can you come here please – quickly!'

Owen came into the room to be met by Mark with a towel wrapped around his waist and hanging on to a wet satellite phone. He just thrust the phone at Owen and disappeared back into the shower to finish whatever he had been doing.

Owen initially said 'Hello!' in English and then quickly switched to speaking Dari which the lady seemed to be more comfortable with. He then listened intently for several minutes. By this time Mark had completed his shower but Owen signaled for him to wait until Larmina had finished. He then said something that sounded like *waada meykonom* which his body language showed that he made some kind of promise. Then he killed the call.

'Ok – she wants to meet but it needs to be under certain conditions. She has been working for the British MI6 but did not say under what arrangement' Owen explained. 'And she made me promise that she will be protected at all times. From whom or what she did not say. I suggest that we go to meet her now. Then let us see what happens.'

Mark was not so sure.

'It sounds a little bit flakey to me! Are you sure we want to do this? How sure can we be that this is not a trap?'

Dusty and Blake came into the room looking for someone to go with them to breakfast and joined in the debate. Owen was convinced the lady had been genuine having had a long conversation in Dari. Dusty could not understand why the lady could not come to them in the relatively safe environment of the Kandahar airport. Blake said a flat – No!

Mark had to reach a decision. He was anxious to make progress. The only constructive lead he had was from MI6 – so he wanted to believe it was the thing to do. But at what cost?

He had serious doubts because of his reading from the brief conversation that he had with the lady who called herself Larmina. It was the usual problem of communications. If you could not understand someone, it was hard to judge the person. And over the telephone, Mark could not fall back his reading of body language. Owen on the other hand had the advantage of communicating in the same language with the lady and in some circumstances could have a different view.

In the end, it was reluctantly decided that Blake and Dusty would drive Mark and Owen to this unusual rendezvous in one of the MaxxPro and just see what happened.

They each carried a Beretta pistol and an M16 semi-automatic rifle.

They hoped that none of these weapons would be needed.

The meeting took place in the great hall of the Kandahar Museum. Not that there was much to see in this museum. The building had been closed more often than it had been opened during the last twenty or so years and had been struck with several bomb attacks that made it a somewhat decrepit place.   However, it did meet the criteria as a place to meet. It had very few visitors and was in a part of the city that also had very little traffic.

As he had been instructed in his earlier conversation, Owen entered first and surveyed the scene before signaling that Mark should follow him. The only other person in the same part of the building was a local, and a lady. She was very petite and could not have been much more than five feet in height. She was wearing a dark green dress and pants and a lighter green chador or headscarf.

That was the color of the dress that Owen was looking for.

The lady was walking clockwise around the room, so Owen and Mark walked around in an anti-clockwise direction until their paths met. Then Mark continued walking as the lady and Owen stopped and stared at what Mark could only assume was some landscape painting by a long-dead Afghan artist. They talked in whispers for a couple of minutes and then continued on their opposite circuits making a barely perceptible nod towards the next room. Owen caught up with Mark and while they looked at a painting that looked remarkedly like most of the others, delivered his report.

'Ok – bad news! Larmina Meskin is our contact from MI6. She has been doing undercover work for the Brits, but she believes that her cover has been blown. She and her sister have been tracking Iran weapons that are coming across the western border with Iran and going to the Taliban. Until recently the sisters have been located in the Farah region, which is about 230 miles west of here. She says that they had to get out of Farah in a hurry. She suspects - but cannot be certain - that the trucks that are used to bring in the arms are used to take goods back across the border and into Iran. Those goods – sourced here in Afghanistan - are most likely to be drugs. That is the good news from our point of view because it gives us a lead on where the drugs are coming from, how they get to Iran, and how they are bartered. The bad news is that she won't help us unless we can guarantee safe passage out of this place for her and the sister when our mission is over.'

Mark had listened without interruption. He contemplated why Iran should be complaining about sanctions imposed on them which specifically forbade the selling of arms and the materials necessary to make them. At the same time as they were battling against the sanction, they were shipping arms across the border to the Taliban. That was Shia Muslim Iran shipping weapons to the Sunni Muslim Taliban. That just did not make any sense.

He did not reply at once as another man dressed in a pale blue dress-like cover, pants, and a cap walked by and disappeared into the next room. Mark then asked what he thought were pertinent questions.

'Has she informed the British MI6 that her cover has been blown? Surely the fate of her and her sister is their concern, not ours? And what's with the sister?'

Owen knew that the next bit of news would not be well received. But he was only the messenger.

'The answer to your first question I do not know – she did not say. The answer to your second question is – the sister is only seven years old. I don't know what arrangement you have with MI6 and whether the sister was part of the deal. All I do know is that Larmina does not want her sister to be involved in any of this stuff.'

Blake came into the room before Mark could even groan. Blake looked around the room and then asked a question.

'What happened?'

Mark and Owen exchanged a look not knowing what was happening. And then Owen sprinted as best he could with his gammy leg towards the next room that Larmina and then the man wearing the cap had gone into. Mark and Blake followed puzzled but taking the lead from Owen.

There was no one in the next room.

Blake explained that he had seen a figure in green sprinting from the other end of the building, followed seconds later by a man in blue who was chasing after the green figure. Checking on the color of clothes the two people were wearing it was clear that the first person was Larmina. The following person could have been anyone. But from Blakes's description, he would have looked remarkably similar to the man who had walked by Mark a few minutes earlier.

The three of them rushed outside but there was no one to be seen, except for Dusty who was waiting in the Maxxpro.

Dusty could only confirm what Blake had seen.

Now they had no clue of where this lady called Larmina had gone.

The team had no choice but to abandon the meet and return to the Airport. Mark got on his satellite phone and called Reginald Smith in Kabul and delivered the news to the head of British MI6. Mark was distinctly unimpressed with the reaction he received from Reggie. He just ended the call while the MI6 chief continued to rant.

There was no way Mark was going to become involved in problems that MI6 had with its agents in Afghanistan.

Mark was not about to accept any responsibility for the loss of an MI6 agent who he had seen only briefly and had not yet met or spoken with.

Marks' phone chirped almost instantly. He found himself talking to Mike Robinson from MI6 in Kabul.

'Apologies for that outburst – the boss is having a bad day!' said Mike - and that is a far as he got.

Mark was fuming.

'Look, Mike – we all have our bad days. But your boss's reaction is unacceptable. I appreciate his original offer to help us. And I accept that we have no control over how he does that. You will recall he did say that he would arrange for your agent to contact us in Kandahar – and not the other way around. So - it is not our fault if those arrangements turn pear-shaped. My call to Mr. Smith was simply to inform him of our position and the position that *his* agent appears to have landed *herself* in. If Smith does not want us to keep the British informed on such matters, then so be it. We have enough problems on our plate without having to put up with the tantrums of your boss whether he is the chief guy on the block or not. So, goodbye...'

'Please wait Mark!' Robinson pleaded, 'I will put Reggie back on.'

There was a couple of seconds of muffled conversation coming over the line and the tone made Mark smile. He felt sure that Robinson had told his boss to pull his head in!

'Mark – sorry for my outburst.' Reggie said without sounding at all sorry. 'It was nothing personal. I am going to get our man in Kandahar to follow up on this mess. And we will see if we can get another form of help to you.'

'Reggie – the last thing we need is MI6 running around trying to interfere in our affairs in what started as a fairly straightforward mission. You are starting to act like our CIA. So – no thanks – we will handle this.'

And Mark again ended the call.

No sooner had the call from MI6 been disconnected than Mark's phone chirped again.

This time it was Larmina.

And she sounded more frightened than she had in her earlier call.

Mark did not even acknowledge the call. He just handed the phone over to Owen.

For quite some time Owen seemed to be trying to calm Larmina. And he seemed to be failing. Then he grabbed a piece of paper and a pen and scribbled a note. Owen then disconnected the call saying something in a language that Mark did not understand. It sounded like a curse!

Owen breathed hard a couple of times then looked at Mark.

'Ok – I know that you are starting to lose faith in what the Brits have to offer. But - in my opinion - we need to go get Larmina and her sister. They are holed up in town and their position does not look good. I know it is not our problem – but look at it on the bright side. From what she told me earlier - they can help us! We just need to figure a way to help them out of their current mess. She has told me where they are holed up and is looking to us to pick them up. I thought I knew you – It is not like you to leave them to their fate!'

Owen instantly regretted the barb.

Mark was hesitant, but he could see the logic of what Owen had to say. Now he did groan and then made a decision. Against his better judgment - Yes – they would try to rescue the two girls.

He would get Dusty to do the driving, Owen to do the

navigation. Blake and Ben to supply the heavy stuff.

'Ok – do what you have to do.' Mark instructed. 'Take one of the MaxxPros and go gct thcm. When you come back into the base be sure that no one sees the girls. No one should think to look in your vehicle – at least I don't think they will. If they do, you will need to think of something to distract them. Or shoot them!'

The Maxxpro left the base and headed back towards the museum and slowed to a crawl as it approached the entrance.

Larmina was obviously street smart.

After leaving the museum pursued by the unknown man she had doubled back when she judged it was safe to do so. She had lost the man who was pursuing her in the myriad of alleyways and back streets that surrounded the Museum. There were two reasons for this. Firstly, that was the last place her pursuers would expect her to be - back at the museum. Secondly, that was where she had left her sister.

Her plan was almost right.

The Maxxpro came to a halt close to where Owen had parked earlier in the day but there was no sign of anyone. Owen cursed.

'Now that was fucking stupid! Owen was talking to himself.

'We come to the earlier meeting in a vehicle that identifies us as associated with the United States and looking ready to join in World War III. The people that chased her away would be only too well aware that we were in that vehicle. Then we turn up later in the same vehicle to rescue the same lady presumably from the same people. That is just dumb! Wait here!'

Owen grabbed a rifle, jumped out of the Maxxpro,

and headed into the museum. Blake and Ben armed themselves and stepped onto the concourse not sure if they would be much help. Dusty stayed at the wheel but decided that since everyone else was armed and ready for a fight, he would do the same.

And it was a good job that he did.

Just as Owen reappeared out of the museum ushering a lady and a young girl in front of him, four men armed with what looked like AK47 rifles, and who looked suspiciously like Taliban, suddenly appeared from down the street running and gesticulating towards the place where Owen had appeared. Dusty did not know what was going on, but he recognized trouble when he saw it. Blake and Ben were looking towards where Owen was coming from and could not see the four men because he was blocked by the bulk of the MaxxPro.

Dusty let out a stream of profanities before leaping from the drivers' door and firing a shot over the head of the advancing armed group. That shot certainly got their attention. But it did not slow their progress. They were rapidly approaching a point where they would be close enough to have a fair chance of hitting something if they fired their AK47s.

It is not generally appreciated that from a running position firing a rifle with any degree of accuracy is not the easiest of tasks. Even if they were standing still, even if they were Olympic standard shooters, and even with a significantly more efficient weapon than an AK47, their chances of hitting something from their current distance were remote. But Dusty decided that he had seen enough and was going to take no further chances. He almost casually steadied his rifle on the side of the vehicle, sighted his gun on the leading man, and pulled the trigger. He cursed as the man staggered. Dusty had aimed for the center of the critical mass which would have rearranged the rib cage and splattered the guy's internal organs in a heap on the ground. Instead, it connected with the shoulder spinning the guy sideways into the path of one of his colleagues, and they both tumbled to the ground. The problem had been that Dusty had not previously fired this weapon and the sightings on guns differ. It was several months since he had fired a weapon of this caliber in anger.

But one shot was enough to get his bearings.

Dusty re-sighted on the third and fourth guys. One dropped like a stone and was probably dead before his body had hit the ground, but the other one kept coming forward, as the two men who had stumbled to the ground got back to their feet. They were now getting to be within a distance from which they could do real damage. Fortunately, Blake and Ben who had heard the commotion had worked their way up the side of the MaxxPro and surveyed the scene that was unfolding. Dusty was good with a rifle and would probably have been able to cope. But both Blake and Ben had been snipers in an earlier life and the discipline that the particular skillset entailed had never left them. Blake calmly shot the leading man through the head while Ben and Dusty cleaned up the other two.

Owen, seeing that the immediate threat from the Taliban was neutralized, ran from the museum with the two frightened girls in tow and headed towards the MaxxPro. Blake provided cover on the museum side while Ben covered the area from which their assailants had come. Dusty got back into the drivers' seat and fired up the massive engine.

They had all scrambled onboard their vehicle and were pulling away from the curb by the time an Afghan police vehicle came down the street with sirens wailing.

A US Army MaxxPro versus an Afghan police jeep

would be no contest. Dusty just gunned the motor and left the scene, leaving the local police to scratch their heads and sort out what had just happened.

The Afghan police had four dead Taliban to clean up and no one around to tell them how they had died.

The *way* they had died was irrelevant.

The Maxxpro returned to Kandahar Airport and Dusty managed the security guards at the gate. Although they were entering an area where there was any number of different nationalities, it was still a US military base, although the security was provided by a British civilian security contractor G4S. So faced with a US Army Maxxpro, driven by a huge Afro-American driver which had only recently exited from the base, the vehicle was just waved through the gate.

Blake Whittaker had not had the easiest of lives. Back in the States, he was dedicated to bringing up his twin daughters who had been robbed of their mother – and Blake had been robbed of his beautiful wife – by a driver who had crashed his car into their SUV in alcohol or drug-induced moment of madness.

When Blake saw the condition of the young girl, his mind went back to that sad day on which his world had been destroyed. The girl was distraught from what she had experienced back at the museum and there was no consoling her. Blake carried her in his huge arms into the accommodation block ignoring all offers of help from her sister and the other members of the team.

He placed her in a bed, and then Blake just sat there, tears streaming down his face, trying to assure the girl with words that he was not certain that she could understand, that things would be Ok.

Mark knew the signs. PTSD – or Post Traumatic Stress

Disorder – has different effects on people. Blake had several factors that contributed to his condition, and he had just revisited one of them head-on. He would be Ok – but for the time being Mark quietly ushered the rest of his team, and the elder sister, out of the way and left Blake alone.

Back in the mess, Mark asked Dusty what the hell happened.

'There was a bit of a skirmish back at the museum. It looked like the Taliban but who can tell? They just appeared from nowhere while Owen was bringing the girls out of the building – so we had to kill them. The younger sister seemed to get upset by all the noise and was virtually inconsolable. Blake seems to be good at talking to her – even though they don't even speak the same language – and she now won't leave his side.'

Mark nodded. 'Blake has two daughters who would be about the same age. He is a solo parent thanks to a drugged driver who killed his wife, and he now relies on the help of his mother and the community. Leave him be – he will talk to us when he is ready. Now we must talk to her sister!'

Mark and Dusty wandered across to the table where Owen had been talking to Larmina, alternating between English and Dari depending on whether or not the rest of the bemused team needed to understand what the conversation was about.

Mark was at last formally introduced by Owen to Larmina Meskin.

'She wants to apologize for the trouble she has caused.' Owen started. 'Larmina says that she will help us as much as she can, and we can forget her earlier request to look out for them. When this is over, she and her sister will just disappear.'

Mark looked at Larmina and saw the hurt in her eyes.

He had seen that look before. In western society, it was given a name, and that name had so impressed the media that it was now used to describe everything that someone who had been even remotely connected with an armed and violent conflict would suffer, from a mild fleeting headache to near-suicidal brain-scrambling chaos.

She also had PTSD – but this time it was obvious that the lady was suffering for someone else.

Mark struggled to rationalize the events of this day and the primary aim of the mission. In the end, he settled on the only decision he could make. He turned to Owen and gave him a friendly pat on the shoulder.

'I want you to tell Larmina that we will support and help her, and her sister, in every way that we can. If she doesn't want to help us, I will understand. If she does want to help us, then we need to talk to her about how that can be made work. In her own time - there is absolutely no pressure - except that we cannot wait too long. No matter how we may personally feel, we have a mission to fulfill, and unfortunately, that comes first. But - we have had enough excitement for one day!'

Inwardly, Mark had the feeling that this whole business was rapidly spiraling out of control. He had effectively cut off his communications with the British MI6 when this was the only source of help. Had that been a mistake or was it a good move? The British had the reputation of being ruthlessly efficient at gathering intelligence compared with the US CIA – at least in this part of the world. But they also had a reputation for keeping things to themselves. Except that is when it suited them to do otherwise – as was the case with Mark where they had alluded to a potential deal on his satellite phone software. The British had been involved in a close alliance with the Americans for more than one hundred years. That was the frustrating thing that Mark could not get his head around.

Now, this young lady had presented herself as the only hope that Mark had of resurrecting some form of help. And he had just said that she could just walk away. On the face of it that did not appear to have been a very smart move! But Mark had his conscience to answer to and, on that basis, he could live with the apparent dichotomy. After all - he was no worse off now than he had been at the start of this part of the mission.

However, despite all the drama and frustration, Mark was conscious of one overriding question.

How much time did they have?

He left Owen talking to Larmina and went to discuss their next move with the rest of the team.

After about half an hour of talking with the lady, Owen called him back.

'Ok – she is going to help us. But first, she wants you to understand where she is coming from and her motivation.'

The Meskin family had been wiped out two years earlier when they were caught in the crossfire between a Taliban group and a US expeditionary force that was trying to plug the gaps on the western border with Iran. That battle had been decided by an Iranian group who had ventured into Afghanistan and slaughtered both the US force and the Taliban. And anyone else who happened to be in their way. But it was the Taliban that had started the fighting. The Taliban caused the distraction that enabled the Iranian force to sneak in and kill the Americans and then to slaughter the Taliban and others as they mistakenly welcomed the victors.

The only two who had survived that fateful day were Larmina and her little sister Kaamisha. And that was by pure luck. The Iranian soldier who had found them covering behind a wall had a child of his own back over the border and let them be.

The name Kaamisha had meant a *happy soul*. However, since that day the young lady had barely spoken a word to anyone except her sister. And then all she would talk about was the death of the people she loved and the need to avenge those deaths. Although she was only five years old at the time of the senseless slaughter, she started learning to read. Then she made a notice that she had carried with her ever since. It was a quote attributed to Alexander the Great.

May God keep you away from the venom of the cobra, the teeth of the tiger, and the revenge of the Afghans.

Most people would believe that Kaamisha was still too young to have any real knowledge of what those words meant. But her elder sister Larmina did know. She would do anything in her power to avenge what had occurred in that tragic event and to satisfy her sister's lust for revenge. That meant doing all that she could to prevent the Taliban from succeeding in whatever evil quest they had. She hoped that it would ultimately get the message back to Teheran: That the Iranians, or anyone else, should not interfere in the affairs of others.

It was two hours later that Blake Whittaker came out into the main mess area where the team was relaxing around a table. Kaamisha held onto his hand and did not look likely to let go anytime soon.

Blake did not look in Mark's direction, instead of focusing on where Owen was sitting talking to Larmina. The young girl looked as though she had settled down, but it was clear she was still traumatized from the events earlier in the day. IIe briefly spoke to Owen, who in turn seemed to translate what he had said to the sister Larmina. Mark did not know what was happening, so he just shrugged as Owen left with the young lady and the girl.

The look on Blakes's face and his body language suggested that he was unhappy as he wandered over to where Mark was sitting. Blake sat down and choked as he struggled to deliver his message. It was like a voice from the grave.

And it was bad news.

'Misha is almost blind. She has been since she was three years old. I do not know whether it is permanent, or whether it can be fixed. I guess that if she were living in the States the problem would have been fixed long ago. What I do know is there is no hope for her in this shithole.'

Blake rambled on for a few more minutes and then did not wait for a reaction. There were tears in the big man's eyes as he stormed away.

Mark was jolted by the news. He immediately thought of the young lady Jamal that he had met not so long ago at the refugee camp where Debbie was working. Here was another case of the haves and the have nots. Here they were, in another foreign country where neither they nor anyone else seemed to care about the lives of ordinary people. It was always the kids who suffered the most. But being blind as well must have been emotionally crippling.

Owen and Larmina returned shortly afterward and explained that they had left the younger sister at an American creche where she seemed happy playing with other children of her age.

Mark had been involved in what appeared to be an amicable conversation on his satellite phone with Mike Robinson of the British MI6 and finished that chat with 'Ok – we will see' and disconnected the call.

Mark seized the opportunity to gather his team together and to start planning their next move. Elliott and Ben had been gathering some provisions but were rapidly running out of things to keep them occupied. Dusty and the three Special Forces men had been cleaning their rifles and checking that they all had sufficient ammunition for the next couple of days hoping rather than assuming that the morning's activity was not the norm. All the team looked relaxed. But they were eager to get on with their job rather than sitting around.

By reading the body-language Mark realized that he had to get them moving before boredom set in.

The exception to the relaxed atmosphere was Larmina who looked as though the whole world was about to collapse on her.

'Ok folks – we seem to be about ready to rumble. We have four vehicles at our disposal. Owen – I understand you are not happy with them. Explain please.'

'Well – I think we made a mistake turning up in the middle of town with vehicles of that type. Sure - they project power - and few people would want to take us on in a firefight. But I am not so sure if that is what we want. They draw attention to us like moths to a flame.' Owen surmised.

'Any comments?'

Elliott was the only one who did.

'I think he is right. There are plenty of Humvees sitting idle on the base. I could swap them out if everyone agrees.'

There were just a bunch of nods from around the table.

'Ok – when this meeting is over – would you please arrange that Elliott, but we will hang on to the MaxxPros while we are in Kandahar – this town is crawling with Taliban, and I don't want to take any chances.'

Everyone seemed to agree with that, so Mark continued.

'Now I will split us into four groups which I will explain shortly. If anyone has any questions or wants to make any suggestions sing them out and don't be shy. But first of all, there are a couple of things that I need to sort out. If you want a translation into Dari, I am sure Owen will oblige. Now Larmina - I think you have a sufficient understanding of English to stop the pretext of your having language difficulties. Is that not true?'

At first, the young lady looked at Mark almost beseeching him to not go on with this line of questioning. But that is when the tears started.

'You must understand my English is not good. With my people back in Farah I could not reveal my involvement with the foreigners and speak in your language would draw unwanted attention. No one could be trusted in Farah because they could have links to the Taliban or other terrorist groups. It was just so hard! I have been working with the British and now I am with your group. I do not know who these people are!' she added indicating towards the Irishmen who looked on both amused and confused.

'Ok – I understand that! But spare me the drama!' said Mark, clearly irritated. 'You are among friends here. We have already proved that by bringing you here after my men risked their lives to extract you and your *sister* from a situation that I doubt whether you would have survived without our involvement. We are a team that relies on trust in each other, and we do not have time for this nonsense. We cannot work effectively unless there is trust. So - can we please drop this façade and move on? You are either with us or you are not. So – which is it to be?'

That brought a nod of the head, a look of embarrassment, and finally an apology from the lady.

'Ok – next.' Mark continued – still looking at Meskin – and still irritated.

'Now tell me about your sister. She is not your sister - is she?'

He did not need to wait for a reply. The color drained from the face as Larmina had to face another truth.

'So - Who is she?' Mark asked, trying to be gentle. And failing.

The tears flowed again. Larmina looked at Mark imploring him to back off. But he would not. There was just too much at stake. He had to lead a team in this most hostile environment and that needed the truth among men. Mark did not like doing this, but he felt he owed to the team to have this discussion now and make the relationship clear and transparent to all. He continued to press.

'Larmina – or whatever your name is – whatever you have been through, and tough as that might have seemed to you, you are dealing here with men who have seen far worse. But men who know what it is like to have a member of the team who they are unable to trust. So – I say again - you are with us, or you are not. If we know the truth, then we can help you. If you cannot tell us the truth, then you have no place in this group.'

That did it. It all came out with a rush. Apologies. Explanations. Excuses.

At last, came the truth.

'My *husband,* who was killed by the Iranians at Farah along with the rest of my family, was a criminal.' Those words she almost spat out using the Farsi pronunciation for husband as she composed herself before carrying on.

'I did not know until the very end that he was actually with the Taliban. As for Kaamisha – you are right – she is not my sister!

'Well – Who is she?'

'Kaamisha is my daughter!'

Chapter 30

Ankara

The United States Embassy in Ankara Turkey was in the district of Kavaklidere on a section that was befitting the long relationship that existed between the two countries. The Embassy was one of the grander buildings on the Ataturk Boulevard having been built to US specifications and had the attraction of sitting on a site that was surrounded by native trees. Across the street from the Embassy was a park and the surrounding offices were well spaced to give the correct impression that this part of the city was home to the more affluent members of the Turkish society.

The US military was represented in Turkey by a US Air Force Brigadier General with an impressive staff of senior officers under his command. The most senior of them was an Army Colonel by the name Samuel J Henning who, amongst other things, was responsible for maintaining security at all bases where the US had a presence in the country. In addition to that, Colonel Henning was head of the working group which oversaw the security throughout the Middle East, and on that score, he reported directly to a US Army Brigadier in the Pentagon. This dichotomy could have caused a problem for the chain of command had it not been for the fact that the Colonel spent most of his time away from Ankara. As it was, the only problem that it did cause resulted from the company that Henning chose to keep when he was away from the office. And the fact that the Pentagon was too remote to be able to take any notice of what the Henning was up to.

The Colonel was a married man with two grown-up children – a son who was twenty years old and a daughter who was eighteen years old – both of whom had long since decided that military life was not for them. His wife of thirty years had originally traveled with him on his various postings to various parts of the world but eventually gave up on that idea and decided to stay with their children in Boston. And the marriage was all but over in everything except the name. So - the Colonel was free to do whatever he pleased.

And that would have been fine if it weren't for the drugs.

Colonel Henning was an arrogant son-of-a-bitch, just short of six feet in height and overweight from lack of exercise. He had close-cropped grey hair which partially hid the fact that he was going bald. He also had facial features that caused him to have an almost permanent expression that looked like someone had earned his displeasure. Consequently, it could not be said that he was particularly attractive to the opposite sex.

Back in the States, he had been a bit of a gambler, and at one stage while still a relatively young man he had thought of quitting the military to accept an offer to become a professional poker player. But his equally young and then-pregnant wife had managed to bring some logic to the table and had convinced Henning of the risks inherent in such a career. Now on his own in Turkey, he did go to a couple of Clubs in Ankara none of which were more than a mile away from the Embassy to at least spend time in mixed company. Very rarely, if ever, did he stray far away from the bar and he was not sufficiently confident to enter any games on the quite reasonable assumption that he would have had difficulty reading the locals – and occasional foreigners - at the table.

He did not drink to excess preferring to sit on his drinks for longer than the bartenders would have preferred. But he at least paid for his drinks and did not cause any trouble. And since he was quite obviously an American of some standing there would be no trouble caused by other service-members while this grumpy Colonel sat at the bar.

However, other people would notice him there and who would take an interest in both who he was, where he was from, and what he did for a living.

And why he was always alone.

After these people had watched him and assessed him for a couple of weeks, a man of obvious Middle Eastern origin, but who spoke near-perfect English, opened a conversation with Henning and stayed at the bar, introducing himself as Babak Mazanderani. Nothing of any note happened for a few days, and then the two men met again, and each greeted the other like long-lost friends.

But this time Mazanderani had a different plan to just sitting at the bar in idle chatter.

Through his contacts in Washington and intelligence that he had been able to piece together from his home base Mazanderani had an extensive profile on the Colonel. This mainly dealt with his military career which chronologically traced what, where, and when he had been serving leading up to his present position. Such information was readily available on almost any career officer in the American forces provided someone had the patience to gather it all together. And the fortitude to avoid going mad through boredom in the process.

The part of the profile that was of primary interest to Mazanderani – after having decided that Henning was in a position to be able to help him – was of a more personal nature.

He had gathered that Henning liked to gamble and, thought that he could have made a career as a professional poker player if only he had the guts to ignore the advice of his wife. So, the plan now was to tempt the Colonel to participate in a game with minimum stakes and with people who just wanted to have some fun with little risk of losing their shirts.

They went to a room in the adjacent Hotel where Henning was introduced to two other men. They both claimed to be Turkish, but Henning was not fooled by that. He had assessed that Mazanderani was from further east and could therefore assume that the other two men were of similar origin. However, all of them spoke excellent English, so he assumed that they were connected to one of the other Embassies in this part of the city and were probably just as bored with diplomatic life as he was.

When Henning and Mazanderani arrived, the two men had been drinking the Turkish liquor Raki. When Henning asked for a beer, one arrived as if by magic. They commenced to play a couple of games of straight poker, and Henning soon learned that the other men were not particularly skilled at the game and were no match for someone of his skill level. After a few the games played for small stakes of a couple of lire from which Henning made a small gain, he introduced them to a game of stud poker and then draw poker both of which games they initially had difficulty understanding. But what they lacked in skill they made up for in enthusiasm and they soon got the hang of the basic rules. After two hours of amicable play where Henning came out the clear winner, the group shook hands, broke up, and went their separate ways, agreeing that they must meet again to repeat their amicable gathering.

Henning was quite keen that they should get together sooner rather than later. Not that winning a couple of lire was the motivation. Rather, he had found a group of men whose company he enjoyed and who shared his liking for his favorite game. But he had no idea how to contact any of the men and he had to wait until the end of the week before Mazanderani again appeared at his favored watering hole. And it was Henning who suggested that they reassemble the men for another game of poker. At first, Mazanderani appeared reluctant but after a couple of phone calls, he finally agreed to arrange a meeting for the following Monday evening.

That arrangement was inconvenient for the Colonel because he had planned to travel to Incirlik on a pointless exercise to review the security at the base. But Henning, in his eagerness to meet with his newfound friends, decided that it would be Ok. The Brigadier at the Embassy - who Henning reported to - would be out of the country at that time, and his other boss at the Pentagon in Washington would not quibble about a report which would tell him nothing that he did not already know, arriving on his desk a day or so later than had been planned.

The meeting of the group on Monday evening followed the same pattern as their previous session. Once more Henning had to admit to himself that he was a little bit surprised that none of the others in the game had suggested an increase in the poker stakes, but he again opted not to suggest that himself since he was winning anyway. Henning did try a drink of the Raki liquor that the other men were drinking. He found that the aniseed flavor appealed to his tastes and so he settled for Raki instead of his usual beer.

The Colonel should have stayed with the beer which contained less than five percent alcohol by volume instead of nearly fifty percent alcohol that the Raki contained.

The fact that the American failed to notice the ease with which his winning streak continued unabated you could put down to the Colonel's skill as well as cultural differences between him and these peasants. At least the other men seemed quite content to play the game and did not seem to be the least bit concerned that they were losing.

As the evening wore on, Henning did not require much encouragement to drink more of the Raki and since he was now quite comfortable with the group there did not seem to be any harm in that.

When Henning woke up, he did not know where he was.

His head felt as though it was detached from the rest of his body and his eyes would not focus on anything.

He tried to sit up, but the room started to spin before his eyes, and he was overcome with a feeling of nausea.

So, he rapidly lay down again.

Henning was on a bed although he had no recollection of how he got there. With his head beginning to throb, he was about to close his eyes and try to sleep, when a female voice attracted his attention.

Where had that come from?

It was painful to move his head in any direction. Ever so slowly twisted his head around to the direction from which his fuddled brain thought that the sound had come from, groaning as he did so.

The girl – she could not have been much older than his daughter – was lying on the right side of the bed. Apart from a blanket that was draped seductively over her body, she was stark naked.

Had Henning been able to focus he would have realized that the smile did not travel to her eyes.

'You ready to go again?' she asked, while not showing a great deal of enthusiasm.

'What! Where am I? Who are you?'

The confused words flowed out of Henning's mouth as he realized that he was also naked. Ordinarily, he would have expected his body to react to being so close to an attractive young lady lying so provocatively on the bed next to him. The lady did not attempt to cover herself and even as he watched she started to spread her legs almost willing him to come to her. But, even if the desire had been there, his body did not seem to be functioning properly.

His mind certainly was not.

Before he could clear his head, another noise came from the other side of the room and Babak Mazanderani came through the door followed by one of their colleagues from the poker game. There was none of the friendly chatter that had been Henning's earlier experience with these people.

Mazanderani barked at the girl in his native tongue – whatever that was – and she simply go off the bed and left the room without speaking, with little more than a bedsheet wrapped around her.

'Well – what have you done Sam?' Mazanderani asked in a sympathetic voice.

At first, Henning just stared at him before blubbering his response.

'What the fuck are you talking about?'

But – Henning knew that this was not going to end well.

The other man was collecting a couple of syringes from the table and the remains of what looked like two small plastic bags. Then he moved to dismantle a camera that had been partially concealed by the curtains but pointing in the direction of the bed. So, they had a film of him doing whatever he and the young lady had been up to on the bed. And a film of him or her injecting drugs. Because of the presence of syringes, the drug could only be heroin.

Henning could not even remember how he had gotten here, let alone what he had done while he was here!

He thought of appealing to the man who had befriended him only a few weeks ago but looking at him sitting there he realized that would be a waste of time. However, all was not lost! Despite the fuzziness of his brain, he concentrated his mind on the now. His second thought was that he had to get his clothes on but quickly realized that even that would have to wait. He could not stand for fear of falling over so he settled for straightening his back and tried to get a semblance of dignity and formality to the occasion.

'Ok – What do you want?'

The following morning in Teheran, President Mahmoud Khatami had his scheduled meeting with intelligence chief Hormuzd Larijani and was expecting to hear good news on the progress of his plans.

The President was not disappointed.

'We now have infiltrated the US Embassy in Ankara' Lajani began. 'It turned out to be a far easier task than we had expected. We now have a Colonel who is responsible for the security of the United States bases throughout the Middle East hooked and squirming like a fish on a line. You do not need to know his name.'

'How did you manage to do that?' asked Khatami, clearly impressed with the news.

Larijani laughed because he had come up with the plan and it had been executed perfectly. Well – not really – but there was no need to go into details of the original intention versus what had happened.

'Our research showed that the Colonel was a keen card player. So, we encouraged the Colonel to play cards with a couple of our agents. He had too much to drink and got very amorous with a young lady who is also one of our agents. When he woke up the following morning, we were able to convince him that we had a film of him in bed, having sex with a naked underage girl and taking drugs. And he fell for it1 He is now under our control out of fear that we will send the film not only to the US Embassy but also to his wife. We entertained the possibility of threatening to send the film to the western newspapers. But we decided against that. We will reserve that ploy just in case he does not meet our wishes.'

Khatami needed more information.

'You mean you do not have such a film? Are we not at risk that he will – how do the Americans say? – Call your bluff!'

Again - Lajani laughed.

'I do not think so. The only reason we were not able to film him in a more compromising position was that he was too drunk to – as the Americans would say – have it off with the young lady. And that took some doing! The lady was very professional, and she did her best to get him aroused without any success. However, she was able to simulate the act – in fact, several acts – and our film would be sufficient to convince anyone.'

And the drugs?' Khatami had to ask.

'Same thing – we provided heroin which is most effective when injected. We have a film of his hand on the syringe and injecting the girl with the drug and then of the girl injecting the Colonel. There is no doubt that the film will show everything was consensual. We suspect that he would have no recollection of either event but of course, the film would not show that – would it? However, in the unlikely event that he is tested, there will be evidence of heroin in his system and puncture marks on his body. You know how the Americans work and think!'

But that was the problem. Khatami did not know. Larijani certainly did.

'Their society tolerates sex even if it is in the form of adultery but frowns upon having sex with minors and drug-taking even though the United States is the largest market in the world. The key point is that our Colonel is an official representative of the US government and is in a very senior and responsible position. So – quite simply - he cannot afford for us to release the video of his deeds.'

'And the girl?' was Khatami's next question. 'How sure can we be that she will not reveal what has happened?'

'That we can be sure of! While we may not have the same control over our girls as the Soviet Union were famous for with their Sparrow school back in the days of the Cold War between them and the Americans – our girls are well disciplined and well rewarded for their services. And, of course, we have them on film performing services that they would not want to be published on social media no matter what other inducements may be offered by the Americans.'

But the sad thing was, the simple fact that Khatami had raised the question meant that Larijani would have to change his plans.

Since he had assured his leader that this would not be a problem, he would now need to make certain that that would be the case. So, he made a note on the list of things that he had to do. The girl would have to die. Collateral damage as the Americans would call it. But not until Henning was well and truly under their control. Insurance as the Americans would call it.

'Ok – good report!' the President said. 'So – what happens now?'

Now Lajani would make his leader happy because this

was one of the final pieces coming into place. It may be a trivial one – but one that would have a major impact on the overall plan.

'We have the head of their security compromised and he would not dare to not do as we instruct. This is the good part of our plans. The compromising of the Colonel will enable us to ensure that we can get our people into or out of any United States base in the middle east with the assurance that their purpose would not be detected. As you would know extremely well, the foolish Americans have very tight security, but it is all designed to prevent people getting into their bases.'

Larijani deliberately paused before delivering his final message.

'All we need to do is to get out!'

Chapter 31

Where To Now?

Mark had managed to borrow a printer from one of the US procurement administration offices in the Kandahar base. It was adequate for what he required – it at least connected to his laptop computer. Although the Wi-Fi connection did not exactly operate at the speed that he was used to in the office of Taylor Software back in New York City, he got into Google maps and was able to identify the areas where it was most likely that drugs were smuggled out of Afghanistan. The potential area that could be involved in the drug trade with Iran accounted for almost all the western border of Afghanistan which stretched from the border with Turkmenistan in the north down to its border with Pakistan in the south. That was a total distance of close to six hundred miles. What Mark wanted to do was to identify the part of this vast area that was of the most interest. They could not hope to cover everywhere. They would focus on the region to the north of the district of Farah. This was an area in which smuggling had been continued for centuries.

There were all sorts of things that crossed the border

as well as drugs. And this traffic went both ways from Afghanistan to Iran and from Iran to Afghanistan. As with all such border traffic the world over, most of the traffic was technically illegal but largely ignored by the authorities. Especially when and if it suited the people in power.

There were upwards of a million people of Afghan origin living in Iran many of them having been born there. Therefore, it was not surprising that there would be exchanges of both goods and people across a border. The border itself was both ill-defined and poorly monitored by Iran and Afghanistan for the quite simple reason that there was just nothing there. That in turn was because it was one of the most hostile and inhospitable areas on the planet.

Other areas in Afghanistan were potential crossing points - especially the southern route into Pakistan - where smuggler trails first led south and then west into Iran. However, Mark judged correctly. The kind of trade that was the focus of his attention would seek to avoid the added complication of the more sophisticated border controls that would exist in the south of this country.

Although following trails on Google maps was something new to the lady from Farah, she soon got the hang of switching between different styles of presentation. She was able to narrow down the routes that would have been used by both the Taliban and the Iranians. They were all north and west of Farah. Mark was, at last, beginning to see progress. And he was beginning to see the benefit of having the local knowledge that Mina brought to the team, despite his earlier misgivings about her trustworthiness.

None of the team had questioned Mark about the

way he had managed the issues that bringing the girls into the team had posed. Maybe that could be written off to the normal disciplines that would come from their backgrounds. Or maybe they had discussed it among themselves and decided to let matters rest. Dusty was the only one to ask Mark how he had known that Larmina had a better understanding of English than she had first indicated. And how he had known that Kaamisha was not the sister – but her daughter.

Mark smiled at the question. 'You are worried that I might be able to read minds? He laughed.

'No! I am not that clever. Blake gave me the message. At first, he could not work out why he could converse with a child at the tender age of seven and yet her elder *sister* claimed to be unable to hold an even basic conversation in English. When Blake joked with her that she was smarter than her older sister she laughed and inadvertently told him that Larmina was her mother. I subsequently checked it with Mike Robinson, and he confirmed what Blake had said. There are thousands of kids in this country who have a mother but no father through no fault of their own. Why did Larmina hide it? Mike said that her husband got in with the wrong crowd and that was the reason the Iranians targeted him and his parents. Mother and daughter are lucky to still be alive. But they are and now she doesn't want Kaamisha to have any memories of her father. Bad luck I suppose but mothers do strange things where their kids are concerned, and we cannot criticize her for that! As for Blakes's role in all of this – because of the way that all this unfolded, he was torn between telling me and keeping the secret – but in the end, he believes that he made the correct decision. And I agree with him on that score. Subsequently, he has explained that decision to Larmina and she says that she now understands. I hope she does!'

Mina – as she now preferred to be called – seemed to have got over the embarrassment of Marks's inquisition. Owen – whose knowledge of female fashion ended before it began – had gotten new clothes for her so that she was now dressed more like a man than a woman. Owen had insisted that she wear a Kevlar vest which had the effect of reducing her shape to that of a cylinder, her hair was tied up and locked under a grey turban which was the same drab color as her dress and pants. He could do nothing to hide the beautiful face that sat atop his creation and so he settled for telling her that she would just need to pretend to be a young gentleman rather than a lady.

The young daughter who preferred to be referred to as Misha was transferred from the creche to the base hospital for observation – more as a precaution than anything else. The American doctor was very experienced at dealing with PTSD cases and she had concluded that the best thing for the young lady would simply be to rest. After that, the doctor recommended that Misha spend time with people of her age, but the expression on her face said that she did not hold out much hope of that happening anytime soon.

Mark called his team together.

'Ok – listen up people. We are going out for a short patrol. I want us to get a feel for the town so we will go in a convoy. Ben and Elliott in the first Humvee, Owen, Blake, and Mina in the second, Brent, Mike, and Hamish in the third, and Dusty and I will bring up the rear. Stay together. If for any reason one of the following vehicles is stopped, then we all stop. Remember this is just a practice run so there will be no shooting! Any questions?'

There were none.

'Ok – lets' go! '

Chapter 32

Intrigue

The meeting between the Iranian President Mahmoud Khatami and his lackey on the Security Council was held in the Presidents' office. There was no need to involve the full council because their meeting was just about the routine operations to implement a plan that had the full support of the Supreme Leader. At least as far as the objectives of the plan were concerned. The method of achieving those goals may have received further scrutiny.

'So – tell me – how is our plan going? Khatami asked his friend.

Hormuzd Larijani had a confident – perhaps smug - look on his face as he presented his report.

'The problems we had in Khartoum are behind us.' he began. 'We were able to get our main man out of Sudan and Mohamed Haji is now in Turkey and pursuing our plans to cause havoc in that country. We have started the spread of our virus which will become clear within the next few days. Our medical people were a little vague on the incubation period but as soon as people start turning up at the hospital with symptoms, we can start making our next move. The US Ambassador in Kuwait who we were intending to make use of met with an unfortunate accident that we have ensured will be treated as a suicide. He can be replaced. The team of Americans who were following Haji in Africa have been stood down. We understand that there was some delay in getting orders from the United States due to the US President being ill and there is no one else who can make the decision. So – we have the US government in a state of paralysis.'

'I thought that the African team was under the command of their Director of National Intelligence and as such would be able to act independently of their President. I did not know that the Americans were so dependent on one man. Or is their bureaucracy so inept?' Khatami asked – more to show that the underlings he understood how these things worked. Or didn't work as in the present case.

Again - the smug look on the face of Larijani.

This was an opportunity to show how clever he was. The real juicy part of his report would reveal exactly what had happened.

'Yes – I will get around to that.' he continued, ignoring the obvious question. 'The CIA believed the rumor that we fed to them, that our dear friend Mugabe was to be assassinated. They also believe that they saved his life in Khartoum. Again - exactly as I planned. We now know that, during the delay in getting their instructions, two members of the team made a trip across the border with Ethiopia to the Pugnido camp. I was not able to get into that camp, but our sources tell us that the purpose of their trip was to meet two young ladies. We have people finding out those details. Preliminary information suggests that there is a close relationship between their leader and the girls. If that turns out to be the case, that will enable us to use the ladies to our advantage if the CIA team should become a problem in the future.'

He took a drink of water before continuing. Really to make Khatami wait for the good stuff.

'Now we have reason to believe that our CIA friends have gone to Afghanistan.'

'How did that happen?' Khatami asked.

Larijani laughed.

'It appears that they have been assigned a new mission to get into the business of chasing drugs. Possibly as a result of our activities in Africa and Kuwait. They have been joined in their efforts by someone of unknown nationality but believed to be an Afghan local. Probably as a translator to enable them to understand the local languages. They originally went to a meeting at the airbase near Kabul. From what we know of the other people who attended that was is intended to review progress on US efforts to control the Afghan drug problem. And good luck with that! So - it would look as though we have seen the last of that team. However, we will continue to watch them just to make sure that they are well out of the way of the other stages of our plans. This team is now in the south of the country doing nothing of any substance – presumably looking for drugs and trying to find out how they got into Africa. That should keep them fully occupied and well away from where the action is in Turkey. We have them covered. Should they move from where they are or start to show any interest in what we are doing we will know?'

'How can you be sure of that? Have you got an informer in their camp?' asked Khatami, not certain how his minions had been able to engineer that in a country as unstructured as Afghanistan? He knew that Iran Intelligence had a very good source of information from within the US Government. But there were obvious limits to how much information he could get without revealing position and therefore himself. He also knew that the US government was so riddled with informants acting on behalf of every other country, as well as informants within some departments acting on behalf of other US departments or interest groups, it was a miracle that the United States ever achieved anything.

'Yes – I have an informer.' Larijani said, hoping that Khatami would not ask for the name. Which he didn't.

Instead, he asked a more brutal question.

'I think it is time to get rid of these interfering Americans. They may be out of the way. But that is a loose end that we should not ignore. What are your plans for dealing with them?'

And that was the question wasn't it.

Lajani could not authorize a strategy that would see the demise of foreign nationals. But his President certainly could. Albeit with the final approval of the Supreme Leader. Such approval would be automatic for sure but there was still a procedure that had to occur. And there had to be a back-out clause that would absolve the aforesaid President and the Supreme Leader should things turn out pear-shaped. Organizing such an event would be left to Larijani. He would need to be sure that these two gentlemen were in a position to claim the credit if the situation allowed. Or to disclaim all knowledge if the situation required it.

At a more practical level, Larijani had the same problem as his masters. They wanted something done to rid themselves of the interfering foreigners. However, they did not want to be seen as the people responsible for whatever was about to happen. It was frustrating. Nothing could happen in Iran without the approval of the Supreme Leader. Everyone in Iran knew that. And so did the Americans.

Larijani's expression remained impassive. His mind was in turmoil. His only solution was to remain confident.

'The Americans are in the south of Afghanistan where the Taliban are in the ascendancy. And the Taliban would not appreciate their interference in matters that they consider to be none of their business. I have contacts that could ensure that our American friends do not come out alive if you so ordered.'

Larijani held his breath.

Would Khatami see through his ruse or see his comments as an attempt to escape the blame? He hoped that his presidency would not have the experience in matters of this nature. And would grab at a chance to be seen to be making a decision that others would consider wise.

He breathed a sigh of relief when the man's arrogance won the day.

'Kill them!' replied Khatami.

Chapter 33

Reaction

The Medical Officer at the Incirlik base in Turkey was an officer in the US Air Force and had the task of caring for about five thousand air force personnel men and their families. The air forces personnel of course never reported sick whether due to the arrogance associated with the ability to fly off at super-sonic speed or due to peer pressure. So, First Lieutenant Amy Shoebridge spent most of her time studying to get a real job where something happened when she left the service.

But this day was turning into something different.

A couple of days earlier, a lady on the base who was the wife of a Chief Master sergeant, had come into the medical center with her daughter who had complained of mild symptoms which she believed to be flu. What the mother was more worried about was the listlessness that went with the normal flu symptoms in a daughter that before this bout did everything at break-neck speed.

Shoebridge – ever mindful of the attitude of mothers who had their daughters with them on deployment overseas – decided to assess the mother as well. The young girl was understandable - and stomach pains – which the doctor initially took to be referred pain. However, the mother had the same underlying symptoms. She also had some difficulty breathing. That could be due to a simple respiratory tract infection. And the shortness of breath could be due to the lady being somewhat overweight.

But it was the mother who had symptoms that were a little different from what would be normal with the flu. Her temperature was ninety-seven degrees which were only marginally above where it should have been, and her blood pressure reading was also a little high for both her systolic of 145 and her diastolic which was above 90. That could have been caused by what was known in some quarters as *'White coat Fever'* – the result when someone gets anxious when confronted by a doctor conducting a simple medical test. However, the symptoms that Shoebridge was more concerned about were the cough and the distinct lethargy which could point to something a little more serious.

Just to be certain, she convinced both of these patients to have a blood test. Then she sent them on their way with the usual advice to take paracetamol and plenty of rest – but with the warning that too much paracetamol could itself affect blood pressure.

Shoebridge had now received the results of the blood tests which she hoped would reveal that all her patients had was a simple dose of influenza.

However, they didn't.

The results of the tests suggested that it was not just flu that the two ladies had caught. There was something more serious going on. The indications were that it was most likely to be a virus of unknown origin but similar to severe acute respiratory syndrome or SARS which caused a worldwide epidemic in 2003.

The blood tests were unequivocal – both of her patients had the same disease.

The first reaction was one of panic.

Shoebridge desperately tried to recall the events of a few days ago when she had first taken the blood samples. That recollection just made things worse. She had examined both of the ladies including looking at their throats and doing all the normal things expected like feeling around their necks for any swelling. All done without a mask to cover her mouth and nose. All done without wearing any surgical gloves. So, the odds were that, in her examination, she would have been infected with the disease!

On the assumption that it was SARS, the event presented a major problem for the medical world. And an immediate threat to anyone who had come into contact with those already infected. It was a highly contagious disease. It was very difficult to treat – being resistant to all conventional medicines. Shoebridge felt the fear build up as she contemplated her future. How could she have been so stupid to not have taken the rudimentary precautions that her training had taught her? Tears welled up as she realized the effect of her mistake. Now she could only hope that someone in the medical world had continued the development of a vaccine.

The trouble was - she just did not know.

What she did know was that viruses of this type could rapidly become an epidemic. Or even worse – a pandemic!

She stared at the reports, reading through them again. Looking for something that would give her something to cling to. But the words were presented in the cold clinical medical language. Taking a couple of deep breaths, she realized she had to focus. Her patients came first. Her safety would have to wait.

The first problem was - Where had the virus come from?

And why had it suddenly appeared in a relatively clean environment like an Air Force base? Experience showed that the one major factor that could encourage the spread of viruses of this type was the lack of hygiene. Surely that could not the problem here!

Shoebridge dreaded calling the lady and telling her of the result despite the realization that it was something she just had to do. But first, she would need to fill the hole in her knowledge. Where could she get vaccines and treatment so that she could assure her patient that she would be safe? As was typical of people in her profession, her first thoughts were for her patients. But the awful truth was that the Doctor had seen several other patients while waiting for the result of the blood tests. Other patients who had come to see her may have unwittingly collected an infection from the Doctor! And then passed the infection on to others.

Doctor Mirac Kartal was tired. It had been a long and stressful day in the Turkish Adana Health Center which was less than twenty minutes' drive from the Incirlik base. People chose to come to see him for special reasons. One reason was that he was by far the most experienced Doctor in General Practice at this Health Center. Another reason was that he appealed to the older residents who came to chat rather than moan about a perceived injury or illness. In his fifty-two years in practice, he had lived through the various epidemics, pandemics, and other health-shattering events all of which - if the so-called *experts* on social media were to be believed - could have ended life on earth as we know it.

He was due to be retired in six-months' time. He would

be missed. What he would miss was the daily meeting of new people, listening to their stories of the older ones. And seeing the younger ones beginning their lives.

The doctor's last patient of the day came into his surgery. She was a lady of sixty years of age. She quickly assured the Doctor that she did not want to make a fuss. It was just that this damn flu would not clear away and she was due to fly out in a couple of days to travel to the United States to attend her daughters' graduation from the John Hopkins University.

That got the doctor's undivided attention and most of the subsequent discussion centered on the daughter. She was to specialize in Oncology which was probably the most demanding of callings that she could have chosen. But eventually, they returned to the reason for the mother's visit.

The lady had the flu with the usual symptoms of a higher-than-average body temperature, a headache, and nausea. That could be dealt with by a simple course of paracetamol. He looked into her mouth to make sure that her throat was clear and felt around her neck to make sure there was no unusual swelling. There were no obvious symptoms there. However, at the ladies' insistence, and to make her happy, he gave her a prescription for an antibiotic. That was overkill, but it would certainly clear up any underlying problems. Not before she was due to leave for her daughters' graduation – but it would be Ok.

Since the lady had been his last patient of the afternoon, Doctor Kartal gathered together his papers, placed them in his safe, and made ready to leave for the day. He was just putting on his coat when his receptionist interrupted him. She asked if he could take a call from the Medical Officer at Incirlik airbase.

He had met this young lass a couple of times and he had been impressed with her enthusiasm for all things medical.

But, of far greater importance than that, he had developed a soft spot for this attractive brunette in Air Force uniform despite – or possibly because of - the difference in their ages.

So – he took the call.

'Hi, Mirac – this is Lieutenant Amy Shoebridge from the Incirlik medical center. How was your day?

They chatted for a couple of minutes about what had been happening in the medical world. Until they finally got around to talking about their patients.

'I have just got the results back from a couple of blood tests' Shoebridge began, 'And they both tested positive for - you will never guess what – SARS!'

Kartal felt the blood in his veins turn cold.

Had the call come from any source other than Lieutenant Shoebridge he would have treated it as a joke. But the staff of the Incirlik base was up there with the very best. And although the testing lab was here in Adana he knew of few cases where either the lab or the base had been wrong in their diagnosis.

'You are certain?' knowing that the answer would be in the affirmative. 'Do you have any idea where the patients have been? Have they been overseas recently?' The questions just poured out as his thought process rattled through the various things that he had to check and exceeded his ability to speak fast enough.

He just got the answers that he was dreading.

Yes - Shoebridge was certain,

No - the patients had not indicated that they had been anywhere of note.

No, - as far as she knew, the patients had not been overseas.

Then Kartal had another thought that chilled him even further.

'Amy! Could you wait a minute – I need to check

something!'

'Ecrin!' he almost screamed at his receptionist. 'Can you get my last patient to come back? – Now!'

'Sorry, Amy – I have just seen a patient who could have the same problem as yours. God – I hope not – but I just sent her on her way without thinking! If it is SARS – she has been in contact with other people and she said that she had the symptoms for several days before she came to see me. We could have an epidemic on our hands! And my patient is about to go overseas!'

Lieutenant Amy Shoebridge was a lot calmer than doctor Mirac Kartal.

She just asked the question that had prompted her call.

'Don't we have a vaccine for SARS?'

Doctor Kartal let out a sardonic laugh.

'That is where the whole world was fooled by the outcome of our last SARS experience. Because SARS was brought under control relatively quickly, everyone assumed that management of the virus was achieved by medical science. What happened was that the virus simply disappeared. Whether that was due to what treatments we already had, or due to people simply developing an immunity to it, we never found out. And when that happened, the rush to develop a vaccine also disappeared as pharmacy companies switched to more profitable jobs. They never got to the stage of developing a vaccine, as far as I am aware, and never concluded any clinical trials. Now - I hope that somewhere in the world someone did get to the stage of having a vaccine. Finding that out may be difficult. However – first things first. I suggest you get your patients back in and do a more thorough check on their symptoms. If they are still symptomatic get them into isolation and try to find out where they have been and who they have been in contact with recently. You may have to get those people that they have been in contact with tested as well.'

Now it was the turn of Shoebridge to let out a sardonic laugh.

'Yeah – starting with my office and the fucking Doctor that they came to see!'

Now Shoebridge was not so calm but still, her focus was on her patients.

'What can we do to find out how they got infected?'

Kartal was a professional and he did not like to shout at the young doctor, but he was starting to lose it. After all – he was in the same position as Shoebridge. Despite his many years of experience with infectious diseases and having all the knowledge to follow best practices in dealing with them, he had not done so for one very simple reason. At the end of the day, he never expected to be dealing with a potential pandemic!

'Amy – we don't have time for this. One thing at a time! I will call you back – just give me a few minutes.'

The lady who had been in earlier came back into the surgery having been contacted by Ecrin on her cell phone.

'You wanted to see me? I was just waiting for my prescription at the pharmacy.'

Kartal wanted to project a calm professional image and assure the lady that he only wanted to be sure that all was well, however, it was no use. He put on a mask and donned a pair of plastic gloves before asking his patient to lie on his examination table. He took her temperature and blood pressure again. He was beyond keeping his usual bedside manner as he asked her if she would take an urgent blood test. She sensed the tension in the surgery and was too worried and confused to decline. Kartal had

Ecrin come in while he took a sample of her blood and the fact that the receptionist was wearing a mask and a plastic coat only raised the tension in the room to a whole new level.

The doctor quickly extracted two tubes of blood and he asked her to wait with Ecrin as he rushed out of the door. The two ladies were just as confused as each other and they both burst into tears.

The Laboratory that processed the tests was in the same building, so the doctor did not have too far to travel. It was most unusual for any doctor to request this sort of urgent attention but this one was worked up about something. There were no guarantees. Fifteen minutes was the best response that they could offer for a *preliminary* result.

Kartal left the lab after the technician had assured him that he would be the first to hear the result. He returned to his patient in his consulting room.

Human blood has thousands of different chemicals and molecules. Although blood testing was routine, it was nonetheless complex. There were no shortcuts, and the process could not be rushed. The normal procedure is to put a sample of the blood in a centrifuge to separate the blood cells from the other fluids. That takes time and patience. And even then, that would not necessarily enable a consistent analysis every time. As the saying in the medical fraternity goes *'Treat the patient, not the lab test!'* meaning that it was often necessary to take several tests before a conclusive result could be reached taking account of factors that were pertinent to, and often only known by, the patient.

And, hopefully, the results of the test and the characteristics of the patient could be brought together by the doctor responsible for the treatment.

The patient was near hysterical by the time Mirac

Kartal re-entered his surgery. He had to ignore that and concentrate. He tried to describe her symptoms as simply something that he needed to analyze further before he could reach any conclusion.

His attempts to calm his patient fell on deaf ears.

He urgently needed to know more about what his patient had been doing during the last few days. For 'few days' – read fourteen – because that was the probable incubation period for a virus of this type. He needed to know basic things like, who she may have been in contact with? Where had she been and what other people could she have infected? Where could she have caught the infection? Had any of her friends or the people that she lived with displayed similar symptoms? And he had to ask the most embarrassing question - had she had any physical contact of a sexual nature within the last few days?

The total of all that was to make the lady incoherent.

The first blood test results came back quicker than the doctor had dared hope.

There was evidence of an unusual virus in the blood samples. Further tests were necessary to confirm it. But it was probable that the lady had a condition known as a severe acute respiratory syndrome.

The SARS virus was back!

It was a dilemma that most doctors have to face up to from time to time. Did Doctor Mirac Kartal alert the World Health Organization of a potential epidemic based on only one blood test and the say-so of a lowly Lieutenant? Should he wait until the blood test was completed and care for his patient first?

There was more to it than the simple question of -

Should he alert the WHO? There was also the more direct question of who should do the alerting?

The United States was by far the largest contributor to the funding of WHO. A call from someone of US origin raising the same issue was likely to get more attention than a message from a lowly GP from a place an obscure place in Turkey that they probably would need to do a google search to find where the city of Adana was.

In the end, Doctor Mirac Kartal MD of the Adana Medical Center called United States Air Force First Lieutenant Amy Shoebridge MD of the Incirlik airbase.

'Hi, Amy – sorry to take so long before getting back to you. Bad news I am afraid. My patient has all the same symptoms as do your patients. I have had a preliminary blood test done and the initial results point to SARS. That suggests that the source was either someone in Adana or at least in the southern part of Turkey, or someone at your base. Now I am going to have my patient transferred to the local hospital once I have confirmed that they can hold her in isolation. I am afraid I will also need to isolate as well. And you will need to isolate yourself together with your patients, and quickly. But, before you do that, could I ask you to contact someone at WHO and alert them to the fact that we have the potential of an epidemic on our hands. It would carry more weight coming from you.'

The Lieutenant bridled at that request even though she could see the logic of it. Raising such a matter with an international organization the size and influence of the World Health Organization based on a diagnosis by a lowly Lieutenant was no mean task. Realistically – it would require someone way above her pay grade to make the call. There was just no precedent for an event of this nature. And this was not exactly a subject that would be covered in her standing orders.

Shoebridge heard her voice say - 'Leave it to me!' and

hung up the phone wondering what she would do next.

Doctor Shoebridge had already recalled her patients to her office, and they were sitting across the desk from her with the expectant look of people who thought they knew that they were in the safest of hands. And in the waiting room outside were two other people who she feared had the same symptoms that suggested the virus could be already spreading – unchecked - on the base.

Shoebridge excused herself from the surgery, went into the outer office, and called the secretary of the Base Commander.

'Hi Shirley – could I speak to the Boss for a minute?'

'Oh – I am sorry Amy – the Colonel is tied up at the moment. Is it urgent? I can patch you through to his cell phone if you like!'

That would be nice! Shoebridge realized that this was the day when the United States Air Force Colonel David Eaglin would be playing golf and he certainly would not welcome a call from one of his Lieutenants. Especially if his game was not going to plan – which it usually wasn't. Stoically she persevered.

'Thank you, Shirley! – if you could do that, I would be grateful.'

As it turned out the call was not too bad.

'Good afternoon, Sir. Lieutenant Shoebridge here. I am afraid we have a developing situation on the base. We have a couple of people who are already diagnosed as having a virus and I am afraid it will not get any better. The protocol requires that we inform the World Health Organization because it is a notifiable disease. I thought that you should know straight away and maybe that action would be better coming from your office.'

'Shit Amy – how bad is it?' was the Colonel's response.

The Lieutenant held her breath before continuing. Careers could be made or broken on what happened next.

How bad was it? Or more importantly – How bad could it get? And – more to the point – Were the test results that she was basing the call on false positives?

'Bad Sir!' She replied – cursing herself when she realized she was standing at attention while the Colonel was probably sitting on his trundler drinking a beer.

'Ok – I will need to pass this upstairs. I know you will do what you have to do to keep everyone safe. Don't worry – just do your job!'

Shoebridge returned the phone to its cradle with some difficulty as she was shaking uncontrollably. But she had a job to do.

She had to pass through the waiting room on her way back to her surgery. The number of people waiting to see her had increased by four in the short time that she had been in the office talking to the base commander.

The stress of all this was beginning to take its toll. She just sputtered an apology to those waiting, before turning back to the outer office. She was hoping that no one saw the tears. She had another call to make.

The Lieutenant called Doctor Kartal.

'Mirac - I need to get my people into the Adana hospital – we cannot handle them here without causing a panic. We are only dealing with about five thousand potential infections in Incirlik – you have near five hundred times that number in Adana! The Colonel is taking care of the WHO and I guess we will hear more from them very shortly – that is assuming the message gets through the drones that we have back in Washington!'

Doctor Kartal realized that the young Lieutenant was stressed. But he now had a job to do. So that would have to wait. Before long politicians would get themselves involved and then the blame game would start. Relations between the two countries were fine at the level it was at present being played. It was a very different matter at the higher level.

'Amy – I have talked to the Turkish Ministry of Health and our local hospital. The hospital is not equipped for this, and it will take them at least a couple of days to get organized. The Ministry does not want to help at the minute because they need to have it confirmed by someone from World Health. In the meantime. I suggest that you plan on isolating your patients at the base until we have a decision. At this stage, we do not know who the index patient is. It may be that the outbreak is traced to Incirlik. In which case that is the best place to isolate your patients rather than moving them to Adana. And you can imagine the reaction either from our Ministers or yours if we start moving people around before we know!'

If Shoebridge was stressed before the call, it was nothing to the way she felt now. She had never cared much for politics and now she realized why. While Kartal was a friend that she had trusted, even he was being controlled by politics. It was now a battle between Turkey and the United States as to who got the blame. While she understood the reasoning behind Kartal asking her to contact the World Health Organization, there was more at play than just the influence. If the US raised the issue with the WHO, then the initial attention would be on Incirlik. World attention would be focused on what the major players were going to do about the crisis, and the World would more readily accept US involvement than they would of the unknown city of Adana.

Still – her responsibilities were to look after her patients. Someone else would have to worry about collateral damage. She was only a Lieutenant.

Amy Shoebridge walked back through the waiting room. There were now too many people for the eight chairs that had been provided for patients and her assistant was scrambling to supply some more.

At least the junior aide had recognized that something was not as it should be. All the people in the waiting room were now wearing masks.

Air Force Colonel David Eaglin knew that dealing with this problem would be tricky. Military people do not, as a general rule, deal very well with matters of a medical nature. Show them something to shoot at and something that they can kill, and they are in their element. Tell them that there is a virus that they can neither shoot at nor kill - nor even see - and they have difficulty understanding or even accepting it.

Tell them that the existence of this tricky little bugger is based on an unconfirmed report from a very junior, female Flight Lieutenant and you are pushing shit uphill with a fork.

He knew that the US had a responsibility to report the matter to the World Health Organization and their own CDC – Center for Disease Control – in Atlanta Georgia which was itself a worldwide operation. But as base commander, his first responsibility was to his people and the US Air Force. Eventually, word would get out to the press, and then all hell would break loose. In the meantime, he would follow the normal protocols and hope that attention would soon shift from the messenger to the message.

In the US Air Force that meant pushing the matter upstairs for some else to worry about.

Colonel Eaglin put a call through to his headquarters at the Pentagon where their day would just be getting underway, not knowing what reaction he would get to a non-military event. And knowing that he was still relying on the word of the lowest-ranked officer on his staff.

'We have a developing situation here at Incirlik…'

Chapter 34

Drugs

Mark was beginning to think he was getting more paranoid. Nonetheless that feeling that something was not right had served him well over the years. And now was not the time or the place to tempt fate by making a change in his reactions.

Although his team had only been for a short tour of the city of Kandahar and they had only been away from their base for a few hours, he was convinced that someone was following them. Having four almost identical MaxxPro armored fighting vehicles had made the task of countersurveillance relatively simple once they had first spotted a vehicle that appeared to be on their tail. It was clear from their observations that the major focus of the following vehicle had been on the whereabouts of the MaxxPro that held Mark and Dusty. This was made clear when Dusty took a couple of diversions from the route being followed by the other three vehicles in their group.

Sure enough - a vehicle followed them wherever they turned. Based on his earlier experience in this war-torn country it would not pay to ignore the occurrence.

Marks' first thought was that it could be the British MI6 since they had seemed keen to interfere. But that thought was quickly discounted that because of the sheer ineptitude of the following vehicle. The second thought was that it could be the Russian SVR which was still active in Afghanistan and seemed intent on interfering on both sides of whatever conflict they came across wherever they could. Or it could be even their own CIA doing the surveillance because something was happening on what they regarded as *their turf* by a team of Americans with doubtful credentials.

These thoughts of professional involvement were dismissed. Unless they were being extremely clever, the people following them were just too amateurish. For one fleeting moment, Mark thought it could be the Afghanistan Intelligence agency NSD – previously known as KHAD. That idea seemed to be a little far-fetched given that the NSD had far more serious problems to worry about. And in the present political climate, it was extremely doubtful that they would risk tangling with people who had obvious connections to one of the few countries that seemed to be on their side.

The next thought was that it was the Taliban, but that theory was also debunked for two reasons. Firstly – what possible reason would the Taliban have for following Mark after he had only just arrived in the city and had shown no interest in anything remotely connected to them?

Secondly – the Taliban never wore business suits.

The dilemma resulted in a conference between all nine members of the team. Mina was away tending to her daughter, but her absence did not matter because she was not involved in this part of their plans. It was in such discussions that Mark was pleased with his decision to have Elliott Shannon as part of his team. Elliott was the only member who had the depth of experience in intelligence matters having previously worked with the CIA as a spook. And he brought a degree of sanity to the discussion, sufficient to at least convince Mark of the difference between paranoia and good fieldcraft.

'Ok - We will maintain our present distribution of people to vehicles, except that Ben and Elliott will operate independently of the other three.' Mark summarized what the meeting had decided.

'Our group of vehicles will continue as if nothing was happening. Elliott – you have the most experience in this sort of thing – I want you to tail them and find out as much as you can about what they are doing. And if possible – where they are from. If they look likely to threaten us in any way, then we can decide what to do about that. In the places where we are about to go, we cannot afford any trouble but if any of them become a real nuisance I would have no hesitation in taking them out.'

That comment brought a huge grin from Dusty. The thought of making their own rules of engagement appealed to him despite his day-time job in civilian life as a lawyer. Apart from suggesting that they could simply crash the following vehicle and end the issue, he still made a significant point.

'This is the same thing that we saw in Sudan – someone was following us and in particular, it was Mark who seemed to be their main focus of attention. In the Sudan case we assumed that it was Haji's men, but to be fair it could have been any one of several other groups. As far as we know, we left Sudan while Haji was still in prison. So - it is unlikely to be him. If it was someone from Hajis team that would suggest that they, or whoever they worked for, has followed us to Afghanistan. Or they already had resources in this country who have been alerted to our presence here.'

Mark had to think about that before commenting.

'It is all a part of the same problem! From the very start in this mission - and by that, I mean starting back weeks ago in Mozambique – someone has been one step ahead of us. Certainly, they seem to have been able to anticipate with remarkable accuracy what we are going to do next. For the time that we were in Africa that would point to a leak in our communications. That would have to mean someone aboard the USS Carl Vinson and someone aware of our mission at that time. When we moved to Afghanistan and were no longer under control of anyone from the Carl Vinson that should have been the end of that. So, that is the bit that scares me. The only people on this side of the world who knew that we were shifting to Kabul was our Embassy in Khartoum. Then there are the people in Washington DC who I spoke to in arranging our trip to Afghanistan. If the problem is in Washington DC, then we are in real trouble. However. there are so few people involved and I would have to exclude them! So – that would point to the US Embassy in Khartoum. Ambassador Luxton seemed a straight guy. I am not so sure about his Deputy. Even so, I do not think she would be that stupid as to try to compromise a mission. As for what happened after that – only the people who we met at Bagram would know where we went from there. And that means the CIA, DEA, the US military, and I presume the US Embassy in Kabul. And then there is the British MI6. So that means a shitload of people, all of them supposed to be on our side, could know.'

Marks' analysis of the problem was surprisingly correct.

He just could not connect the dots.

The task of finding the drug laboratories in the city

of Kandahar turned out to be a lot easier than they expected thanks mainly to an unprecedented level of cooperation between the local Central Intelligence Agency head of station and the Drug Enforcement Administration. The evening before, Mark had called Karen Marshall at DEA headquarters in Washington DC, more to report on the meeting that he had attended at Bagram where he had not exactly covered himself in glory. He need not have worried about Marshall's response. She had already had a report from the meeting which was as negative as Mark had indicated. And she seemed to agree with the conclusion that he had reached that nothing productive would come from that source. But she did suggest that he contact Sean Dunne – a long-serving CIA agent who held the dubious position of local Chief of station in Kandahar. Since Mark and his team were no longer on a mission that could be seen as in conflict with the best interests of the CIA, Mark's initial reluctance soon dissipated.

On the earlier mission to Afghanistan Mark had been responsible for gaining evidence that would convict the CIA Assistant Deputy Director of Intelligence who would have been one of the men that Dunne reported to at Langley Virginia. And, in the earlier part of his current mission, Mark had been carrying out a job for which the CIA should have been employed, and for which they nonetheless got all the credit.

Sean Dunne turned out to be a cranky old man, five feet seven in height, overweight at about two hundred pounds, and an old friend of someone in Marks team - Elliott Shannon. In the absence of any DEA agent in Kandahar, Dunne assumed the role of the local reference in their area of expertise.

There was plenty to keep him busy in this region of Afghanistan. And, of more value to the team, he also had an excellent working relationship with the Afghan police.

In Kandahar, the existence of laboratories for refining opium into heroin had increased in recent times for a variety of reasons. There had been a spate of recent instances where problems were getting a consistent supply of opium to the more sophisticated laboratories in Pakistan. Whether this was a consequence of activity by the Taliban, or another group of insurgents was not known. The facts were that shipments had just vanished in transit along with the people who were supposed to guard against such events. They could have gone anywhere. There were suspicions that they had been *diverted* to the northern border where there was now a flourishing market for the drugs in China.

This was annoying for the local distributors in Kandahar who did not have contacts in the north of the country. Nor could they project the same influence that they could in the south, so it was becoming impossible to control shipments. Or the people doing the shipping. However, the local drug lords had finally cottoned on to the fact that it was more profitable to export the finished product than the raw materials. And they had also realized the fact that it was much easier to transport small packets of heroin each worth many thousands of dollars and each of which you could carry in your pocket than to try to transport huge bundles of raw opium over some of the most inhospitable roads on the planet.

The person who controlled the drug activity in this part of the country was a man named Ahmed Karzai. He was the brother of Hamid the President of Afghanistan. From previous experiences, it was known that he was not a man to be trifled with and that was not simply because of his brother. He was known to be quite ruthless in his dealings with people both within and without the drug business. And he was in the trade to make money.

However, he was motivated as much by money, as he was by the power and influence that came with that. He kept his position by using physical violence. Where he could not directly control people by such means he resorted to bribery.

And that usually meant the Afghan police.

After months of trying, the Afghan police were no closer than they had been at the start of their investigation into solving the murder of a drug lord named Wakil Hekmatyar. He had been the drug boss in the city of Marjah – about one hundred miles to the west of Kandahar. Mark Taylor could have solved that dilemma for them by pointing out that a CIA officer would have been convicted in the US of various crimes including the killing of Hekmatyar, Unfortunately, this CIA man – Stephen Rodriguez – was now dead - well he had been murdered – before he could be brought to court. But both men were inextricably tied up with the problem of the missing shipments.

All of these factors came together to make things work in favor of Mark Taylor and his team.

The Afghan police wanted to solve a crime on which they had made no headway since the death of Wakil Hekmatyar had first been reported. Well – in all fairness – the death wasn't *reported* to the police. The local police simply observed that Hekmatyar was no longer around, went on a search, and found a body. They – erroneously - believed that Ahmed Karzai had been involved in this murder, and Karzai had been the chief suspect. But the police either had no proof or had no real leads.

Or the police were so riddled with corruption that it would not have mattered anyway.

This whole scenario led to a theory that was being formed in Marks's mind. Ahmed Karzai was the only person in this part of the world with sufficient influence and control of the drug trade to be able to do major deals. That would include any deals with foreign governments. Also, he was the only one with sufficient control, influence, and motivation, to force deals on the local people.

And that meant the Taliban.

The CIA knew - or at least thought that they knew - that Iran was shipping weapons into Afghanistan. These weapons they knew – or thought that they knew - were ending up in the hands of the Taliban. The Taliban would have to pay for those weapons and ammunition. The CIA believed that the only way that they could do that was by trade rather than by cash. And the only thing that made any sense in any such a trade pointed to drugs. However, the CIA did not have control of any resources to be able to do anything about that.

The British MI6 probably had more idea of what was going on than they had so far revealed. But they were also in the business of gathering intelligence rather than acting on it and were under-resourced. In past performance, the Russian SVR was probably active in encouraging the drug trade for no particular reason other than that it would cause trouble for the Americans. The Afghanistan National Directorate of Security – the NDS - could be involved but it was anyone guesses how effective they would be. And, left to the local Afghan police, the prospects were not great that the issue would ever be resolved one way or another anytime soon.

The meeting with the Afghan police was arranged by the CIA Sean Dunne for the following morning. It was also attended by Mark Taylor, Dusty Miller, and Elliott Shannon.

Mark did not see any point in holding back his critical

piece of information and so he immediately told the police of the theory that Wakil Hekmatyar had been killed by an American – the CIA Assistant Deputy Director Intelligence Stephen Rodriguez.

This piece of news was greeted with a mixture of shock, disbelief, and relief by the police officers, dependent on whether the officers concerned were on the payroll of Ahmed Karzai. Or on the payroll of someone else that may or may not have included the government of Afghanistan.

However, revealing that piece of information allowed Sean Dunne to suggest that the Afghan police could visit Ahmed Karzai to tell him that he was no longer a suspect in a murder.

That would give the police the opportunity to meet with the architect of the scheme that they were interested in. And allow Mark and his team to meet this horrible man.

By way of recompense, the police gave Mark a rundown on what they believed to be the size and shape of the Ahmed Karzai drug empire. Which probably explained why Karzai was so powerful. And why the Afghan police were impotent.

The meeting with Karzai in the afternoon of the same day was equally simple. Because Karzai was who he was, he was not bothered by the presence of several Americans accompanying the Afghan police. He would not have expected anything less. Although he appeared to be a little bemused by the fact that no one explained the role of Americans and why they were there. That soon became clear.

That meeting started and ended amicably enough with the chief of the police contingent simply saying that

Karzai had been cleared of the historic suspicions of any involvement in the death of Wakil Hekmatyar by these Americans. The police did not say that Karzai could continue with the rest of his illegal trade. But that would have been insensitive. And being a complete waste of time.

By way of recompense, Karzai gave them a rambling overview of how he was working for the good of his people and his country, which told them absolutely nothing that they wanted to hear. No mention of the Taliban. No mention of any deal with Iran. Yet – the police had earlier told Mark about a shipment that the Taliban had a real interest in. That shipment had been managed by this man. And there appeared to be no drugs involved.

The real problem for the Afghan police was that they could not do anything about the drug trade. There was one simple reason - Economics. The whole economy of this region of Afghanistan was dependent on the opium crop. No matter what the government in Kabul had to say about it, that was the reality. Irrespective of the existence of the likes of Ahmed Karzai who ruthlessly exploited the trade to enable the drug lords to make an obscene fortune out of it, there were thousands of peasants out there whose very livelihood depended on the poppy. What others did with opium and the drugs that were derived from it did not matter to them. Their only issue was to put food on the table to feed their children who would otherwise go hungry.

But all of this aside, Karzai could not avoid boasting about his control of anything that moved into or out of Kandahar. He proudly boasted that he had the drug trade and the drug traders coming to him. So – had Mark found the source of the information that he was after?

It was believed that a shipment of arms had recently reached Kandahar from the west. It was believed that the shipment had found its' way to one of the many warehouses that were run by Karzai. The police had no evidence of what the shipment contained and was powerless to do anything about it.

What they did know was that it had simply disappeared.

There were rumors that another shipment would head westward in the next couple of days. From the same warehouse. It was believed that this shipment would contain drugs. The Afghan police did not have the resources – or the inclination - to search every vehicle that headed west. Even if they had the resources, they could hardly search every truck and everyone on board without just cause. The size of the product was small. Its value was high. It would be well-nigh impossible to find. Therefore, there was only one way to stop the trade. Stop it at the border where the drugs changed hands. The place where someone got drugs in exchange for some form of repayment. Whether the exchange was legal or illegal – it would still occur in one of the most inhospitable parts of the country that had been the playground of smugglers for centuries.

The only real advantage that Mark came away with was that now he had a sample of heroin which Dunne assured him was from one of the laboratories run by Ahmed Karzai.

Sean Dunne did not say how he had come by this sample.

Mark did not ask.

When they were back at the Kandahar Airport, Elliott and Owen went to see the US Army procurement officer and negotiated to swap their transport for something a little less obvious than the military vehicles that they had been given. This was because, while the Maxxpro was an ideal vehicle for the terrain and would have greatly assisted the team if they got into a firefight, it did stand out like a dogs' balls. The team had decided that they needed something a bit less obvious. They returned with two trucks that were mechanically sound but were aesthetically abysmal. They also gained the keys to a couple of Humvees and a promise that they could have any number of other vehicles.

Things happened rapidly the following morning.

The APC (Armored Personnel Carriers) that Mark had been told came with the last shipment into Kandahar began to leave town heading west. The vehicles were old Russian military trucks that had been acquired by fair means or foul years before and were of doubtful reliability. Still – they did the job of supplying transport and protection in a land where the latter attribute was more important than the former.

Mark's team had to scramble. They were watching only two of Karzai's laboratories on the basis that intelligence suggested that his other laboratories were used to supply drugs for the rapidly expanding Chinese market and other markets such as India and Pakistan which between them catered for about one-half of the world population.

Because Mark felt that he knew where the APC trucks were heading, he dispatched Brent and Owen in a Humvee to get ahead of them at least as far as their first stop. He was confident would be the city of Farah. That was the place where Mina had said that she was based during her work for MI6. Mark, Dusty, Blake, and the two girls followed the trucks being careful to keep a safe distance in the rear, while Elliott and the rest of the team trailed further behind looking for anyone who would have been showing any interest in the team.

The target APCs had left Kandahar at just after ten o'clock in the morning. They had waited until the traffic had cleared. Although Kandahar had a relatively small population of just over half a million people, the residents still managed to crowd the streets of the city in the earlier hours of the day. The Taliban or whoever was driving the APCs wanted to have a clear run. And they did not appear to be in any particular hurry.

At least, for the time being, this allowed Mark and his team to have a clear view of who they were following. And it would make it relatively easy to spot anyone who was following them.

The road headed northwest and rapidly deteriorated in quality. Fortunately for the team, there was a moderate stream of traffic in both directions so that there was little chance of their being spotted by the people they were following.

There was a problem about one hundred miles to the north of Kandahar when they came across a breakdown. Mark was immediately suspicious that this was a trap, casting his mind back to the journey from Kandahar to Kabul not so long ago when he had been involved in what became known as the Battle of Ghazni. In that case, the convoy that they were in had been attacked by a bunch of insurgents. However, in this case, it turned out to be simply a matter of peasants running out of fuel. This was rectified by Owen Squires, and they continued uninterrupted for the rest of the way.

The journey should have taken about four hours but lasted just a few minutes short of six hours. Discussions with Mina caused speculation that the trucks that they were following would bypass Farah and either turn left before the town and head into the border territory or head straight past the turn-off to Farah and head towards Herat which was about three hours' drive further north. But the trucks took the turnoff to Farah and once they were in the town the two trucks dispersed to separate private dwellings where they seemed to camp for the night.

The first incentive for Marks' team was to head for the Farah military base where the team would feel more secure. While the city – really a town – was relatively small even by Afghan standards, it was riddled with Taliban and other people who would not take too kindly to their western visitors. On the other hand, being in a military base would make it more difficult to keep a track of what their target was up to.

Mark was beginning to question his judgment as he surveyed the township. While Mark had plenty of experience in foreign fields it still bothered him that being in a town or city in a place such as Afghanistan was not the same thing as being back in the States. In addition to the strangeness of everything, there were obvious differences. There was virtually no traffic nor was there the hustle and bustle of a vibrant economy given that the population of Farah was barely more than 50 thousand. Instead, there was a slowness or hesitancy about everything. It was almost as though no one wanted to be there. Whereas a group of businesspeople chatting on the corner of Times Square in Manhattan would be taken as perfectly normal, a group of men shouting at each other in the streets of Farah conjured up images of a bunch of thugs about to attack something or anything. Whereas in New York you could do anything that you like, and no one would take any notice, here everyone just stared at anyone and anything. Maybe because it was something new or different. Maybe because it presented an opportunity to steal. Or blow it up!

The current mission for Mark was to simply see for

himself – if that was at all possible – the transfer of drugs to Iran. Whether that transfer or trade was done for cash or weapons would be a secondary consideration at this stage. But he was convinced that the people overseeing the trade on the Iran side of the border would be military types and most probably would be a part of the feared Iranian Revolutionary Guard rather than the usual drug runners.

They were now close to the border and soon he would know, one way or the other, whether his theory was right or wrong.

Against his better judgment and under guidance from Mina the team checked into what could best be described as a doss house. That house simply consisted of four large rooms. Two rooms were earmarked as sleeping quarters, one was a common lounge area with nothing more than beanbags by way of furnishings, and the other was a utility room with crude cooking and washing facilities. Off to one side was another room that was assumed to hold the toilets that amounted to little more than holes in the ground surrounded by poles and blankets that gave a modicum of privacy.

The blankets could do nothing to contain the stench.

There were twelve other people already there when Mark and his team arrived, but they all kept to themselves and by and large they ignored the foreigners who had just arrived in their midst. As did the owner or manager who graciously accepted American dollars in payment at a rate of five dollars per head.

Mark got his men organized to maintain a roster to keep an eye on the people they were following and to ensure that at least one of their vehicles would be ready to continue following the target trucks should they move. Only then did he have the chance to talk to Ben and the rest of the team who had been the last arrive in Farah.

'You are being followed by two men in a jeep' Ben said with a laugh.

'They tried to keep it covert but what gave them away was when you arrived in Farah. They have not been here before, so they had little choice but to follow you. And then, when you came to this hovel, they parked across the road and waited. One thing we do know about them is that they are armed, but only one of them seems to have a clue about how to use their weapons.'

'How do you know that?' asked Dusty, who remembered the last time he and Mark had been in this country when he had seen ample evidence of incompetence in using anything even remotely technical.

Elliott answered that question.

'When we got held up by that breakdown, they both got out of their jeep to take a look. The taller of the two initially did not have a rifle, but the smaller guy sent him back to get one and then had to show him how to use it. As you did back at the breakdown – the shorter guy was suspicious that the holdup was a ruse by the Taliban or some other gang to stop the traffic and attack. So, we concluded that he is the experienced one.'

'Ok' Mark asked. 'So -where are they now?'

Ben again laughed. 'They are sitting – and I assume going to sleep – in their jeep. Do you want me to go and sort them out?'

The reply that Ben got came as a shock.

'Yes! But not just yet!'

The team waited until dusk before they made a move on the unsuspecting men who had been tailing them since they left Kandahar. Dusty and Ben crept up to the jeep from behind while Mark and Elliott just strolled up the street and passed where the jeep was parked. Owen was concealed behind a building to the right of the jeep as a backup in case something went wrong. While the two men in the jeep were concentrating on the progress of Mark and his companion, they were suddenly surprised to find that they each had beretta pistol across their necks. Dusty had little patience while the men protested their innocence. Both of the men were dragged out of the jeep where Dusty just trussed their hands behind their backs with a roll of masking tape. Mark and Elliott came back to the jeep and the two men, complete with their rifles, were dragged down the street to the local office of the Afghan police.

Again, Mark had thought of taking them to the Farah military base, but that would have involved a more complex explanation than he was prepared to give. After finding the state of the police station and the condition of the one man staffing it, he would probably have been better off taking the military option.

While Mark was anxious to keep a close watch on the people that they were supposed to be following, Blake had assured him that they had camped for the night and would not be going anywhere any time soon. Which also told Mark something else. It looked as though there was no connection between the people his team was following and these people who were following Mark.

They pulled Owen into the team at the police station to help with any language problems. Mark flashed his DEA badge, but the officer seemed oblivious to what it meant. That told Mark something else.

The rumors that he had heard about the Afghan police force were probably true. Well, more than sixty percent of the force were on drugs although what particular kind of drugs he did not know. But sixty percent of what? The force was reputed to consist of more than three hundred fifty thousand positions throughout the country. How many of these positions were filled with men was the question lcft unanswered. If the rumors were even half true Mark was quite lucky to have found a police station with someone in it!

Stoned as he was, the officer on the check-in desk could speak sufficient English to get the message. Mark and Owen were crowded into a tiny room where two Afghan police officers chatted to the people from the jeep. It was all very pleasant except that they offered nothing to the people they were interviewing while they each had a mug of hot tea.

At first, the detainees refused to say anything claiming that they could not understand either Pashto or Dari. However, such claims did not make any sense. What were they doing traveling through so inhospitable a region and being unable to communicate with anyone?

Then one of the Afghan police officers revealed that he had dealt with such intransigence before. He knocked over one of the cups of tea and at once shouted at the taller of the two men being interviewed blaming him for the disturbance. That caused the man to shout in his defense to which reaction the police officer just smiled and said something else in a language that Mark did not recognize.

'So – your guests are Iranian' he said to Mark while still smiling.

Mark nodded and pulled a Browning semi-automatic pistol from his waistband and threw it on the table in front of their guests. The pistol was of Belgian origin but was made supposedly under the license of Iran.

'This was in the jeep and is of a type used by the Iran military – so that makes sense. Do you want to ask them to explain that?'

In response to the question which the police officer

asked in Farsi, one of the men grabbed the pistol and pointed it at the policeman screaming incoherently in his tongue. Both Mark and the Afghan police officers all sat there apparently frozen by the turn of events.

And then they all burst out laughing.

The conversation between Mark and the Afghan police switched to English as they ignored the man who madly was waving the pistol around before having eventually realized that the pistol was not loaded.

'We will hold them in the cells until our commander returns next week and he can decide what to do with them. We will ensure that they will not be of any further problem to you.'

The senior police officer instructed his two assistants to bundle the Iranian men down a dark passageway and into the cells, shook hands with Mark, and wished him well. From the body language displayed Mark had serious doubts about whether the prisoners would remain in custody for much longer than it took his team to return to their accommodation. To make sure that there was no further problem, or at least make sure that the Iranians would have difficulty continuing their surveillance in its earlier form, Owen was sent to disable their jeep and ensure that they would at least have to acquire some other form of transport.

The chances of the men being released in exchange for a bribe Mark put the odds at about 90/10 in the Iranians favor. Their chances of getting transport would depend on how well resourced the Iranians were, but Mark put those odds at about zero in this part of the country.

Mark and his team made their way back down the street to their doss house only to find that they had another potential problem. Mina and her daughter had disappeared. None of the other residents volunteered any information on where they had gone.

He had Owen call Blake, who was watching the house where one of their target trucks was parked. Blake had nothing to report. Rather than break the news of Mina's disappearance over the phone, Ben was sent to relieve Blake so that he could come back to their base. Mark had formed the impression that Blake was getting attached to the two girls but, had not had the time or the inclination to rationalize that with their mission. Now he would have to while trying not to upset Blake too much.

When Blake returned, he at once noticed that Mina was not around.

Mark took Blake and Owen to one side for a chat.

'I thought it best if you were involved before we decided what to do.' Mark started. 'You two are closer to Mina than the rest of us and you may know what she is up to. But I thought I had made it clear. We cannot have members of our team wandering off – especially in a place like Farah – without telling us where they are going or what they are up to. So – what goes on?'

Blake was mortified for several reasons. He had not realized that his attraction to Larmina Meskin had been so clear that his leader would wait before deciding on a course of action. His caring attitude towards Mina's daughter was genuine but he would have to accept in retrospect that it could be interpreted differently. However, he had not a clue where Mina and Misha would have gone without having at least confided in someone. He also had conflicting thoughts about having failed Mark and having been abandoned by the girls. Consequently, he did not know what to say, other than to curse.

Mark realized the pain it would cause but he had to make a decision. Because of the earlier problems that he had

had with Mina which he had been prepared to write off as the inevitable trivial lies told by people when faced with both a difficult situation and a conflict between family and a mission. But now this looked like it could be the end of the road for that relationship.

'Ok folks. We need to decide whether Mina is necessary. I was expecting that she would be useful in finding the crossing points on the border and useful in identifying those people who could cause us harm in this part of the world. My inclination now is that we would be better off doing it on our own. Do I have your agreement?'

Owen had nothing to gain by coming to Mina's defense, but he also knew that Blake was hurting. He offered his opinion – not sure if it would help.

'I am sure that Mina has just slipped away to see friends. And I believe that her input can be useful. We have not yet got to the border territory. I am sure that Mina will have a better understanding of what is a very inhospitable part of this country. Having said that – we do not know if she will even come back!'

Mark looked to Blake for a reaction. Mark could see that Blake was upset but what was not clear was whether he was upset by Mina's disappearance or was upset that the lady who he had taken responsibility for had once again failed to live up to the expectations of the group, Mark hoped that it was the latter.

And Blake had to say something!

He let out a sigh.

'I am sorry Mark. I have let the side down. It will not happen again. If we have to decide to dump Mina from the group I will understand, and, I agree that this time she has probably gone one step too far. I genuinely believed that she could help us, but not at any cost.'

Mark hesitated before replying. He was conscious of the fact that they were in an area of Afghanistan that had been the home for the Meskin family until very recently and it would have been hard for them to come here and be camped up with a group of foreign men.

In the end, he just gave Blake a friendly punch on the shoulder.

'Ok - if Mina does not return by the time at which we are ready to leave then that is the end. You can stay here if you wish. But we have too much on our plate to have the time to go searching for her. Similarly – if she does return and we are not satisfied with her explanation then we cannot continue with her on the team.'

Blake was hurting, but he accepted what Mark had said.

And – No!

Blake would not be leaving the team with or without Mina.

The problem for Mina was that she had the same responsibilities as any mother. She had to find a balance between the reality of living in the present and the expectations of her young and impressionable daughter. Here they were in the town in which her daughter had been born and, although the recent memories of the place were not good, her daughter would also have vivid memories of much happier times. And the young, when faced with the stress of injury or even death surrounding them, tended to shut out those memories.

In the end, and to placate the endless tears that streamed from Misha, Mina reluctantly went out the back door and ran a couple of hundred yards down one of the side streets until they came to the house where her aunt had lived. Her daughter could hardly contain her excitement as she knocked on the door and it was opened by one of Misha's cousins. Greetings were exchanged between the shedding of tears until the aunt and Mina exchanged the words that each had dreaded.

'I thought you had been killed!'

And the realization that this was not the case was just too much. Having lived with the loss for so long, the grief was overcome by sheer joy. They collapsed, arms wrapped around each other, crying uncontrollably.

Misha took it all in but did not understand what all the fuss was about. She and her cousin went off to another part of the house to play, leaving the older women to get on with whatever they were crying about.

The peace was shattered when the front door burst open and four bearded men dressed in identical rags and all carrying AK-47 rifles entered the house. They knew what they were looking for. The two women were grabbed and roughly moved out into the street. None of the men used their rifles. While two of them bundled Mina into a vehicle the other two dealt with the aunt. Her throat was slit from ear to ear and the body was left on the side of the road.

Just as quickly as the men had arrived, they jumped into another vehicle and disappeared down the road at high speed.

The vehicles eventually stopped outside a rundown property on the outskirts of town. The four men manhandled Mina inside a ramshackle house and slammed the door shut behind them.

Sitting on a chair drinking tea was an elderly man who could have been anyone were it not for his headdress. He looked up as the men came in and smiled at Mina who had been thrown on the floor in front of him. Mina looked from the Iman to the four men wanting some form of explanation. None was forthcoming until the religious man got to his feet and addressed her.

'So – what have you been up to?' he asked smiling

down at the young lady. But he did not wait for a reply.

'You have caused me no end of trouble since you decided to join the infidels. Well, now you can do a small job for me. I am afraid you will not survive but at least your daughter Kaamisha will – provided that is you conduct the task that I am going to set for you. '

The Iman signaled to the four men who then grabbed Mina, crudely ripped off her dress and pants that Owen had fashioned for her back in Kandahar. Then they pinned her to the floor one man holding each arm and one man holding each of her legs. They also tore off the Kevlar vest that the Americans had insisted that she wore but noticeably kept that to one side for their use.

Mina was terrified as she struggled with the men refusing to accept that this was happening to her. She looked pleadingly at the Iman, not fearing for her life, but fearing for what would likely happen next.

She was faced with what seemed to be the probability she was about to be raped. It was a fate that she had suffered before and that experience just made the expectation that it was to occur again all the harder to take.

In desperation, she whispered to the Iman.

'No! Please! Don't do this!'

But she knew that she was wasting her time. Looking into those cold, almost lifeless eyes, she could see no empathy. A man who was supposed to preach all that was good in the world and spoke with the authority of Allah was about to oversee an act that every decent person would loathe and condemn.

However, seemingly bored with the men and anxious that they should get on with the job, the Iman just raised a hand. The men stopped wrestling with her. They just held her semi-naked body spread-eagled on the floor. Even Mina stopped struggling – from fear of what would happen next. Or was it the sheer power that the Iman displayed? No – she was not about to be raped. But the fate that was about to be meted out still had her terrified.

A small man who was well over seventy years of age and wearing glasses that looked like they hadn't been cleaned in years, entered the room carrying a contraption that consisted of a belt, shoulder straps four cylinders, and a box with various wires attached. He proceeded to tie the belt around the waist of the writhing body of Mina. Until she realized what it was that the old man had brought into the room.

Then she stopped struggling again and froze in fear.

While the contraption was crude, there was little doubt about what it was.

It was a suicide vest.

When the old man had finished strapping it firmly in place, he attached a couple of the wires to the vest although he seemed to struggle with the decision of what wire went where causing the men to retreat in panic. The Iman remained unmoved. Finally, the old man struggled to his feet, nodded his head to the Iman, and walked back out of the room. At no stage had the man uttered a single word.

The four men reluctantly, but under instruction from the Iman, dragged Mina to her feet and instructed her to put on a new set of pants, a dress that was several sizes too big for Mina's slim frame, and a Hajib.

The Kevlar vest remained cast to one side.

The Iman again smiled at Mina appearing to be satisfied with the night's work.

'Sit down my child for a moment while I tell you what you are going to do now.'

Chapter 35

The British

The British had long since lost their influence on the international stage. Gone were the days of the British Empire when the Royal Navy held sway over the vast oceans of the globe. Gone was the power and influence that came from being head of the British Commonwealth of Nations. Now the world was a much more complex place. Some would say that money and control of resources were now the major factors in projecting influence. With the rapid development of technology, especially in communications, it did not matter where you were in the world. Power could now be projected from a keyboard.

But there were other forces at play.

There was a battle going on between the United States, Russia, and China to determine which of these countries had the greatest *influence*. And it was no longer a question of who *rules the waves*. In the age of the Internet, it became a question of who rules the media. Or rather it was a question of who could make the best use of the media in all its various forms to project influence. Or to impose influence.

The British Secret Intelligence Service - otherwise referred to as MI6 and formed way back in 1909 – appeared oblivious to this changing world and carried on its role of collecting and analyzing intelligence in the interests of protecting the security of the United Kingdom.

And there was more to it than this rather insular objective. MI6 which name appeared during the second world war to name Military Intelligence section 6, had a finger in many pies. The intelligence that was gathered from numerous sources – which may or not be shared with British allies or friends – had a significant influence on how many international events played out. And that influence did not necessarily have much to do with the bigger picture. Or the bigger players in international affairs.

The Chief of MI6 – Richard Northcross – had the same kind of problem that all heads of intelligence service departments had – *When do I acquaint my boss with the latest information that has been brought to my attention?*

That boss was the British Foreign Secretary (equivalent to the US Secretary of State), but it would not end there. If a matter was raised by MI6 at that level, it would inevitably be mentioned to the Prime Minister either formally by the weekly briefing by MI6 or informally from a confidential chat. Either way, the Chief (affectionately known as C – and not M as used by James Bond movies) would then face the very real risk of the story being leaked – to the media or elsewhere. Then anything could happen. It was a sad fact that the MI6 motto *Semper Occultus (Always Secret)* did not appear to apply to politicians.

MI6 had been concerned about the antics of Iran and in that context had followed the recent events that had occurred in Africa with some interest. The fact that the United States CIA had received the credit for their role in protecting the President of Zimbabwe and in avoiding a diplomatic incident in Sudan was laughable given that the CIA had nothing to do with either event. But this masked what the real problem was.

There was a noticeable increase in the availability of drugs to the diplomatic communities throughout Africa and the middle east. Intelligence gathered by MI6 field officers suggested that that was being organized by people who had strong ties to Iran Intelligence. Added to that, someone was causing trouble which seemed to be particularly aimed at US diplomatic staff. And it could be no coincidence that some of the people targeted were suspected as being CIA operatives. Of course, MI6 could not be certain of that. But it did not take a rocket scientist to work out that something was going on.

What MI6 had been unable to do was to fathom out why.

The latest intelligence had the Iranians shifting their resource north to Turkey and that added a whole new set of issues. Although the United Kingdom had a somewhat fractious relationship with Turkey, that country was a member of the European Union. In addition to that, Turkey was a member of NATO as well as had various agreements with the Americans. Which meant that they were all meant to be on the same side. The move to Turkey meant that Iran would now be in reach of continental Europe.

And now things had taken a further step.

The British had known for some time that Iran – as everyone else in the international community knew - was supporting various groups of terrorists. Now they had evidence that they were even supplying weapons to the Taliban in Afghanistan and doing so in direct contravention of various UN directives arising from US sanctions against Iran. MI6 was also aware of an attempt by the US Drug Enforcement Administration to solidify that evidence by having a team in the theatre. Now that attempt was under threat.

Most recent information received by MI6 - as a consequence of a mole deep inside the Iran Ministry of Intelligence - had indicated that an attempt would be made to destroy that team.

The obvious solution to the dilemma – in normal circumstances – would be for the British Chief of the Security and Intelligence Service to call the United States Director of the Central Intelligence Agency to resolve the issue. If the situation required it, C could have his Foreign Secretary call the Secretary of State. If it was looking like the situation was about to balloon into World War III, he could get his Prime Minister to call the US President.

But none of these options were open to him - were they? As far as the MI6 knew, the CIA had been compromised in at least two countries in Africa.

Who knew where else the trouble had spread?
And who knew whether the troubles had spread to the CIA headquarters in Langley Virginia.

Then there were the problems with the US Department of State to consider. Apart from the relatively minor problem that had occurred when their Ambassador to Kuwait died – by suicide according to State, murdered by agents of Iran according to MI6 agents on the ground in Sudan – there was also the issue of what was happening at the diplomatic headquarters at Foggy Bottom in Washington DC. MI6 was convinced that Iran, or another country with firm links to Iran, had a mole somewhere within the US diplomatic service.

So – that left the only option of contact between the two allies occurring ahead of the government level as a very risky proposition. That would have the effect of causing the US President to immediately summon his advisors for a Please Explain session which would mean *trouble at the mill* to use an English working-class term. And have the effect of revealing the very source of information that MI6 was anxious to protect.

Instead of taking this risk, C asked Neville Chesterfield the head of his South Asia section in London England to call Reginald Smith the MI6 Head of Station in Kabul Afghanistan on an encrypted link for a quiet chat.

'Hi, Reggie. C wants you to do something for him. You reported earlier that a bunch of yanks was poking around the south of where you are - looking for the connection between Taliban drugs and Iran weapons. We have had information from sources with connection to IRGC that suggests that an attempt will be made to take them out. Richard would like an immediate report on how vulnerable you think they are. And what we can do to prevent that. If you could have that to him by close of play today, he would be grateful. Can you do that?'

Smith hesitated for a few seconds. How the hell was he going to find out in the time that he had been given what the hell the yanks were up to? He did not even know where they were but could more or less guarantee that they would be well to the west of any place that he could get any help to them. Fortunately, he had a satellite phone number on which he could call Mark Taylor. But what notice would Taylor take of anything that he said or asked, given their most recent conversation? Still – Neville outranked Reggie by a considerable margin. He could not be sure that C knew anything at all about the request but was he in any position to doubt that. He decided to take the easy way out and asked a question, the answer to which would tell him whether his call to Taylor would be received well or not.

'Neville – all we know is that they were heading west towards the border with Iran and as you well know that is a bandit country. I will have to call them and find out what their position is. Do I warn them? Or if not – what do I tell them?'

Now it was the turn of Chesterfield to hesitate for a few seconds. That hesitation told Smith that the instruction had to have come from C.

'Yes – I think you have to!' Chesterfield finally answered.

Chapter 36

Last Chance

Mark was organizing the men for the night watch when his satellite phone vibrated. He had instructed everyone to switch the call option to vibrate rather than a ring to avoid disturbing young Misha. However, realizing that a call could be a fatal distraction at other times they left them in that mode. He glanced at the screen and seeing that the caller was from MI6 in Kabul almost chose to ignore the call.

Fortunately - he did not.

'Hello, Reggie – To what do I owe the pleasure of this call?'

'Mark – cut to the chase. We have it on good authority that someone is out to kill you. That has come from our sources in Iran. Now – I have been instructed by my boss to render any help that we can. Well - it is a little more complicated than that – I have to advise London on what we can do to help – but I do not know how I can get any help to you given you may be well to the west of where I am at the moment.'

Mark had to laugh.

'Reggie – if you mean the two Iranians that we have had locked up in the Afghan jail in Farah – we have dealt with that. As for your agent that we were supposed to have helped us – she has disappeared and, on her performance so far, I only hope she has gone for good.'

Mark was about to hit the kill switch, but the tone of Smiths' voice caused him to pause.

'How do you know the two men were Iranian? We have no information to confirm that there is an Iranian hit squad in this country!'

'Reggie – if – and it's a big IF – this was a hit squad – I do not know what they could hit. Hit squads do not normally go around with fifty percent of their team unable to handle a simple rifle. And where I come from, they do not go around dressed for dinner. I have never seen a pair of would-be assassins who were so inept. So – unless you have something else to tell us – this conversation is over.'

Again - the tone of Smiths' voice caused Mark to pause.

'Mark – you may not realize this, but you are playing a very dangerous game here. I do not know who the people are that you had locked up – but I doubt that they were the kind of people connected to Iran Intelligence or the Iran Revolutionary Guard. These people are ruthless and would not think twice about killing you and your friends. And you are playing in their territory, not yours. Now let me help you. Let me propose to my boss that we send you some troops for support. Just stay put until I get back to you.'

Smith did have a point. Being in the west of Afghanistan Mark had realized that his team was vulnerable. Even traveling the relatively short distance between Kandahar and Farah they had moved from the security of an area with massive allied military presence to the insecurity of a Taliban-infested area where help would be non-existent should they get into trouble. Mark had yet to contact the military base at Farah, but he had heard that it was set up more like a fortress than a simple base. Their state of readiness was off the scale compared with that which applied at the other places that Mark visited. While that was good, there was a reason for it. They were expecting trouble at any time. While it was true that Mark had a team of experienced men, he had to admit that they could easily be overwhelmed by sheer numbers if some group decided to attack them. Mark was about to answer Reggie when the Smith continued.

'You may also not be aware that you Americans have a couple of other problems. Firstly - your CIA is in the shit. Secondly – the US diplomatic service has been compromised. So – for all the power that you people project – we do not think these two organizations would be of much use to you. They have bigger problems to worry about than a group of ex-Special Forces guys wandering about trying to get themselves killed in one of the most dangerous places on the planet.'

Again – the MI6 representative in Afghanistan did have a point.

Mark sighed. Decision time again.

'Ok, Reggie. We will increase our countersurveillance procedures. But we need to continue to observe the people we are following. This group is too small to be a threat to my team. If that situation changes – then we will review our next move.'

Now it was Reggie's turn to sigh.

'Ok – I have done the best I can. I will recommend to London that we assign a British SAS squadron from Kandahar to help you. But, even if that is approved, it will take a couple of days to get organized. Meanwhile Good Luck. You sure as hell are going to need it.'

When Mina returned to the doss house it was late in the evening and most of the residents had already turned in for the night. Elliott and Owen had just been relieved by Dusty and Ben to keep an eye on the Taliban trucks. For the night ahead Mark had arranged a roster so that everyone, including himself, had a stint at this boring task. Given the dire warnings from the British MI6, he had chosen to advise his team and to let them make their own decisions. Mark simply stated his view that they should not let this opportunity to follow the Taliban slip by – they should just be more aware of their surroundings - and at this stage, every member of his team agreed.

Then Mark had to consider what to do with the MI6 member of the team.

He decided that he would not tell her of this new threat to their safety because of the source of the information.

Mina had changed clothes, but she still appeared to be wearing the Kevlar vest evidenced by the cylindrical shape of her body, so she was intent on going ahead with the mission. She had discarded a few other things – the main one being – there was no sign of her daughter Misha.

Mark chose to let matters take their course as Mina went straight to where Blake and Owen were seated and started an animated discussion with raised voices on both sides of the conversation. Eventually, a frustrated Blake got to his feet and motioned that Mina and Owen should join him as he moved towards the table where Mark and Elliott were seated.

There was an awkward silence as the rest of the team sat down and looked at each other before Blake opened the conversation addressing Mark - an angry and frustrated tone in his voice.

'Larmina has something to say!' as he glared at the young lady.

Mina burst into tears and muttered something in Farsi that only Owen could have interpreted before she composed herself and managed a few words.

'I am sorry! My daughter Misha asked to go to see her cousins and I did not have the heart to refuse her wishes despite what you had said about us all staying together. It was only just down the road, and I did not see that it would cause much harm. And you all seemed so busy. And now...' the tears started to flow again.

Mark was as sympathetic as he could be. But it had been a long and tiring day and he did not need this shit. He launched into a rant that, on reflection, he should not have done.

'So - Misha has decided that she wants to stay here in Farah, and I can understand that. But have you thought this through? Mina – it would have helped if you had decided not to come with us if for one moment you had thought of this possibility! As it is now, you are no use to the team in your present state, and quite frankly we would be better off without you. Is that a fair assessment of the position? Or do you think I am being unreasonable? In case you haven't caught on yet – our mission is a serious one and lives could be at stake here. That is why we must have discipline and strict rules that we all abide by. I cannot have – I will not have! – part of the team wandering off doing their own thing – especially without having the courtesy of telling one of us where they are going and why. I thought that I made that crystal clear. I thought that you would have got the message. However, that message wasn't clear enough and you haven't got it. So – Let me put it to you this way. Can you give me any reason why I should take the risk of keeping you in the team?'

Mark bit his tongue as he looked at the young lady. She was distraught and conflicted between her role as a mother and her responsibility to the team. And she had taken his words to heart. But Mark was more aware of the effect his words had on the men – particularly Blake. And to be fair, he was talking about an understanding that existed between the male members of the team rather than a set of instructions that he had issued.

It was Owen who tried to be the peacemaker.

'The fact of the matter is that we need Mina to take us to the crossover point on the border, or at least to a position where we can see what goes on. There are official border crossings that are manned by forces from both sides. They are easy to find. Numerous crossings are not so easy to find. We will be headed for one of these. And we have to do that without others knowing that we are there. This part of the country is amongst the most inhospitable places in Afghanistan and one false move on our part could result in an outcome that doesn't bear thinking about. Therefore, if we go ahead without help from Mina, then we face very serious risks and I think we can all agree on that. We need to balance that against the risk we take if we cannot rely on all members of the team to do their job.'

Owen then turned so that he was talking directly at Mina. He spoke in Farsi and then immediately translated into English.

'I have seen Mark operating in this country is extremely difficult circumstances and I know him to be fair and reasonable in both what he does and what he expects of other people. I can conclude that your actions were foolish and unreasonable, and I think we are now in a position where only you can answer for yourself. You must know your value to the team. You must also know the potential cost to the team if you let us down again. So – the choice we have is *Last Chance* or *No Chance*. The choice for you Mina is much simpler. Can you be trusted? Are you part of this team or not?'

To be fair, Mina put on a brave face. And she did not burst into tears. Nor did she try to hide the mortification that she felt at having let down the team.

Mina looked at Blake but there was no eye contact - he was just staring at the table. That caused a lump in her throat as she realized that Mark and Owen had simply expressed what all the men felt. And Blake would not make eye contact because he was feeling the hurt more than the others.

She turned to face Mark, with tears trickling down her cheeks.

'I know I deserve this, and I would understand it if you decided to go on without me. I cannot change what I have done, and I agree that I was foolish. I should have told you – No! – I should have asked you. But in my defense – you were all so busy and there was so much happening. Misha was an added complication that I realized you would not need going into the border region with all the issues that you may not know of until you get there. If you decide to continue without me, I will understand, but I believe I can make a valuable contribution. I beg you to let me prove that I can do this. I will not let you down again. I am sure you want to discuss it with your friends so I will leave you to make your decision. Thank you for hearing what I had to say.'

And then the tears began to flow as Mina left the group and rushed into the room that had been assigned for the women.

In the silence that followed, Elliott decided that he should say something. Mark was pleased to let him have the floor. And what he had to say did make sense.

'Many years ago, when I was training at the CIA Farm to be a spook, we had a guy come along to tell us about a scheme used by the FBI for assessing whether criminals were telling porkies. Their problem had been that in many criminal investigations they would end up with tons of paperwork much of which contained various statements where the stories varied depending on who took the notes, who the interviewer was, the state of mind of the person being interviewed, and all manner of other factors. They needed a method of pulling that all together to find out the actual truth. Some bright spark came up with a method which they referred to as SCAN – which stood for Scientific Content Analysis – although it was not of course particularly scientific. Some referred to it as Verbal Veracity Assessment. Never mind about the fancy words – it aimed to assess deception. By analyzing all the factors and who said what and when, they were able with a reasonable amount of success to work out whether people were deliberately trying to mislead the investigation – in other words - who was not telling the truth. It was not quite the same thing as a lie detector – it was just another tool. It does require a specialist to understand all of the quirky parts of such a technique, but it was surprising how often in later years that came in handy.'

'Now. How does this affect Mina? Listening to what she had to say – on the positive side there is no doubt that she regrets what has occurred and is genuinely sorry. She knows her value. And she is keen to stay with the team. On the negative side, there is something that she is not telling us. Whether it is pertinent to our situation I just don't know. For what its' worth – in my opinion I think the advantage of having Mina on the team outweigh any disadvantages. After all what - harm can it do?'

He would regret that analysis even though his assessment that Mina was holding something back was spot on.

The following morning there was a frustrating interlude when nothing was happening. That was caused by the Taliban trucks and their drivers simply staying where they were with no sign of any movement. Mike and Hamish were watching one of the trucks while Brent and Ben had the other one under surveillance. They called Mark on a monotonously regular basis to provide their reports.

They had nothing to report.

The delay meant that the rest of the team just sat there with nothing to do except speculate on what was not happening. And the delay probably worked in favor of Mina. Mark had a dilemma to resolve. The discussions of the night before had been tense. But the emotion had drained from all the parties as the new day at least had the offer of action.

Mina had been talking to Blake and Owen. And it was Blake who approached Mark with her theory about the delay.

Mark did not know what his final decision was going to be about her future with the team and he did not want to preempt that at the moment. She was seated at a table with her hands resting on her lap. Everyone noticed that she had changed out of her earlier clothes. She now had a blue outfit which in true Afghan-style meant that the only part of her body that was revealed was her face.

And Mark had to admit that she looked beautiful.

Mark smiled at Blake.

He had a look on his face that would have made a dead body look quite appealing. But Mark was not about to distance himself from anyone in the team. Either they were all in this together or they were not. As gently as he could he suggested to Blake that he should start to demonstrate that.

'Why don't you bring Mina over so that she can tell me herself? And we can get the other matter out of the way at the same time.'

The three of them came over to where Mark was seated talking to Dusty and Elliott and sat down across the table. At first, the body language said that Mina would rather be somewhere else. But eventually, she relaxed and told them what she was thinking.

'The border country is rugged and very inhospitable, and there are patrols by border guards on both sides. The Taliban would not want to get too close to their meeting place until they are certain that the people they have come to see are also in position. They would not have satellite phones like you do and are probably relying on a much slower form of communication. One that would be both extremely reliable and extremely cautious. Also, the actual place they meet would depend on many factors the more important being the border guards who are probably oblivious to the exchange irrespective of the apparent semi-official nature of these transactions. And there is also a risk that there is other traffic going on at the same time.'

Mina smiled, gaining confidence, before continuing, realizing that she had got the undivided attention of the whole group.

'The Taliban take great care in arranging these exchanges. I believe that on the Iran side of the border, they are dealing with the IRGC – that is the Iran Revolutionary Guard Corps. On the Afghan side of the border, many other terrorist organizations or groups are not necessarily aligned with the Taliban. There are guns to be had and that is all that they would care about. I guess that the people we are following are waiting for word from someone closer to the border that it is all clear. The IRGC wants the drugs so they will wait. The Taliban want the guns, but it is probably not as simple as that. There are groups of people in this part of the world who may be aligned with the Taliban, but who would not know that the deal was being made on their behalf back in Kandahar. This is Afghanistan and not everyone wants to – as you Americans say – sing from the same song-sheet.'

This time she laughed.

And this time Mark reached a decision. How could he not keep Mina on the team given her knowledge and understanding of the situation that they faced? It was one thing to be a fully trained United States Marine with all the confidence and arrogance that came with that. It was another thing entirely to be in a foreign country like Afghanistan where local knowledge could mean the difference between success and failure.

In the end, his decision was lost in the chaos that followed when a call came through from Mike.

The Taliban trucks were on the move.

Elliott, Blake, and Mina scrambled to gather their bits and pieces and loaded them into their truck while Mark, Dusty, and Owen tidied up the doss house to eliminate any sign that the team had been there and shuffled out into the street to await a pickup. It was not quite the distribution of resources that Mark would have preferred but that would soon sort itself out.

The Taliban trucks headed north towards the town of Shindand on a road that had not seen much maintenance in recent times. Then they turned west on what could best be described as a goat track and the rate of progress slowed considerably. The goat track presented the team with a major and seemingly insurmountable problem. It would be impossible to follow the trucks without revealing that they were there because of the amount of dust that the vehicles were generating. The only solution was to stop and discuss what they could do now.

And once again it was Mina who showed her experience by outlining the kind of territory that they were facing.

Wherever this track led to, they could make a few assumptions. This track was likely to be the only road between here and the part of the border where they were headed. Also, the track was so narrow that there was just nowhere obvious where the Taliban would be able to turn around presumably until they reached their ultimate destination. This scenario of course meant that at some stage the Taliban trucks would return. Which in turn meant that Mark's team would become the followed rather than the followers.

Therefore, at some stage, the team would need to get off the track and hide while the Taliban passed. According to Mina the track which was winding its way in a seemingly endless climb into the hills – mountains would be a more accurate description - would eventually overlook the valley that marked the actual border where it was assumed that the IRGC was waiting. From this point, the team would have a bird' eye view of both sides of the border and be able to see the exchange of goods in all its glory. Therefore, there would be no need to follow the trucks down the other side. That was assuming, of course, that the Taliban intended to return the way they had come. However, there was one assumption that could be relied upon. The Taliban would be making their way back to Kandahar and to do that they would need to go through Farah.

If the spook business had one norm that everyone should adhere to it was that there are no such things as coincidences. But a rule that was drummed into all spooks is that they should never make assumptions. Now Mark was being asked to make several assumptions about the terrain that lay ahead of them, and to make assumptions about what the Taliban would do. And there was another assumption. Well - it was not so much an assumption as a question. Would the team be able to hide in an area that was about as featureless as the surface of the moon?

Dusty supplied the rest of the solution, probably out of sheer boredom at the time it was taking to get all these factors reconciled.

'Since we are proposing to only go halfway, why don't we just let the Taliban go ahead and then follow at our leisure? We can see what happens and then if we cannot hide our trucks, we just hightail it back down the track. Or am I missing something here?'

Mark patted Dusty on the back. 'If that is what happens then so be it. But I had something else in mind for the return trip.'

The groan from Dusty was quickly followed by a grin.

'Let me guess – you want to get a closer look at what is in the trucks when they return?'

It was Marks's turn to grin.

The rest of the team did not understand what that conversation had been about. They just shrugged and got back into their vehicles.

Through his high-resolution binoculars, Mark had occasional glimpses of the two trucks of the Taliban grinding their way up the mountain road. Well - that was not strictly true. He could see dust trails and had to assume that they were being caused by vehicles. And he had to smile. As a general rule, drivers in Afghanistan had only two speeds – stationary or flat-out. Going uphill would present a few issues but on the winding road that would not stop the drivers from getting the maximum speed no matter what the terrain. The reason why the drivers had their eyes wide open was out of fear but that did not stop them from driving as they did. The philosophy seemed to be that the quicker they went then the sooner they had passed another opportunity to die. The person in the passenger seat on this particular leg of the journey would also need to have nerves of steel. He would be on the side of the vehicle closest to the edge of the road with the prospect of plunging several hundred feet down the side on the mountain. Mark did observe that the second of the two trucks were getting increasingly further behind the leading vehicle but could only guess on why that should be so.

Maybe it was to get out of the dust cloud.

Maybe the following driver was more sensible than his leader.

But there was good news for Mark and his team. It was doubtful that any member of the Taliban would be looking behind them.

The team proceeded up the mountain track at a more leisurely speed, carefully ensuring that they generated only the minimum of dust. Because of the admittedly unlikely event of a vehicle coming down the mountain towards them, Blake and Owen took the lead in the Humvee. They began to have regrets for having gotten rid of the original MaxxPro vehicles because in this part of the country they were unlikely to meet any vehicle that could compete with the MRAP (Mine Resistant Ambush Protected) features. However, the APC trucks that they had ridden well even though it was at times difficult to see the track.

The team eventually arrived at the top of the track and started down the other side of the mountain. Laid out below them was the huge valley that was the border between the two countries and beyond that further to the west was Iran. They did not need binoculars to see the dust created by the Taliban trucks and could see that it would probably take them at least another hour before they reached the bottom.

They were informed by Mina that the most likely event was that the Taliban would cross over into Iran territory based on what had happened on previous visits, but she offered no reason.

They came to a clearing on the track from which they had an excellent view of all that was below them and Mark decided that they had gone far enough. Although there were still no materials in the terrain that they could use to hide their vehicles there was a narrow gully where they could at least get off the track and unless someone coming up the road from either direction stopped, they were unlikely to discover the company they were in.

Irrespective of that, a scheme had been forming in Mark's discussions with Dusty, which seemed to negate any problems that might be caused should they get discovered by the returning Taliban.

The team had more than enough firepower to deal with two trucks that probably were carrying no more than eight people in total. They had the massive advantage of surprise and what did it matter if just one more load of Iran-supplied arms did not make it?

The team made certain that the position they were in was below the skyline as seen from down in the valley, shuffled the three vehicles into the gully and then spread out below the ridge and assumed positions from which they could see anything that occurred in the valley and beyond.

Everyone took the opportunity to have something to eat and drink. The food consisted of US Army MRE (Meal Ready-to-Eat) packs and bottled water which was warm.

But at least it was wet.

And then, due to an unusual set of circumstances, an event occurred that threatened the entire future of the mission.

The rule that was applied to any force on patrol or anything else where US soldiers are in a position that is remote from their base was that no one would go anywhere alone. In the case of any women serving in the military that was just hard luck if they wanted to have a moment to themselves – for example, to attend to matters of personal hygiene. Typically, there were few other women available. In such cases, they just went and did their thing and hoped that their man standing guard was discrete. And, when appropriate, would look the other way.

It was a problem that Mina had experienced throughout her short career working with MI6 and she took it in her stride as she went to relieve her bladder behind one of the trucks hidden in the gully. In this case, Blake and his M16 rifle in tow were appointed as her guard.

Everything would have been fine were it not for the cumbersome dress that got caught on one of the cylinders. And that would have been fine as well if she had not let out a curse in Dari. That caused Blake to react – more fearing that Mina may have been in trouble.

Which of course – she was.

At first, Blake could not believe what he had just seen. And then he quickly raised his rifle and yelled out *'Do not move'* before realizing the stupidity of it all.

What was the point of aiming a loaded rifle at someone who was wearing a suicide vest?

Blake yelled to Mark to come into the gully, but at a

loss to know what to do. Meanwhile, Mina once more burst into tears,

At least she did as she had been instructed. She sat there rigid and petrified as she realized that Blake was unwavering. His M16 was pointed directly at the of her head.

Mark entered the gully closely followed by Dusty and found that Blake pointing the M16 in the direction of Mina. His aim never varied as he explained that she was wearing an explosive vest.

The automatic reaction of Mark was to go forward towards the lady who had caused nothing but trouble since she joined the team, but he was retrained by Dusty.

'Let's find out what this is all about shall we? Blake – What's the story?'

Blake was about as mad as Mark, but for different reasons. He almost choked up when he replied.

'She is wearing a suicide vest that she must have got when she went walkabout last night in Farah. Because she hasn't made any attempt to explore it my conclusion is that either it will be set off by a remote device or she is waiting for the opportunity to set it off herself when circumstances are right. I doubt whether it can be set off remotely - at least not here - because there is just no way a device would be able to reach up into these mountains. I don't *fucking* know! We will have to ask her.'

The three men were partially shielded by the body of the truck and there was little doubt that the armor of the vehicle would be quite capable of absorbing any moderate explosion. They could quite easily have been completely hidden if the vest were to explode now. That is provided Mina stayed where she was. And that was on the assumption that the explosive device would not be sufficiently powerful to endanger the truck.

And to be fair, Mina appeared to no attempt to reach for a detonator.

Mark hated moments like this. He was the one in charge. He had to show leadership. And there was one simple solution. Mina had to die. Right here. Right now. Blake was the one who had her in his sights but, if he wasn't going to shoot, then Mark had no choice but to pull the trigger himself.

Mark decided to at least try to get at the truth.

'Mina! Do you want to explain?'

Based on what Elliott had rambled on about the previous evening concerning the SCAN technique, he was not sure that he would be able to believe her reply. Once again, his initial response was one of heartbreak as Mina turned to the men with a look of horror and anguish on her face. Body language said this would be the truth. But Mark just did not trust his instincts anymore.

'The man said Misha will die if I do not follow their instructions. Now I do not know what to do! They said that I was to wait until I was well away from Farah so that the vest could not be traced back to them, find the opportunity to get alongside as many of you as I could, and explode it. The only stipulation was that I had to make sure that Mark would be amongst those killed. I do not want to do what they said – but what can I do! I have to choose between Misha and Mark! Help me please!'

The tears started to flow again. She still did not make any attempt to reach for the detonator.

But that did not help Mark. If what Mina had said was true, she was going to die anyway, and the only question was whether Mark or Misha would join her in the afterlife. As Dusty watched he had formed the clinical conclusion that this was the end of the Meskin family – sad though that may be.

That was unless there was a way that both Misha and Mark could be made to disappear until the team could get back to Farah and go and kick some ass.

The three men looked at each other and shrugged. The glances they exchanged said it all. The part of this dilemma that Mina had not counted on was that the insurgents, Taliban, or whoever had supplied the vest to Mina most probably had no intention of letting Misha live irrespective of the outcome. All three of these men had dealt with similar situations before and they knew how these things usually worked out.

And the results would not be good.

It was Blake who had, at last, calmed down and tried to get sanity into the situation. He had reached the same conclusion as Dusty.

'Mina – we can solve this for you if you can trust us one more time. Please – let me remove the vest. When we get back to Farah we will go and find Misha. All we need to do is to blow up the vest without you in it and keep you hidden until we get Misha back.

She looked pleadingly at Blake as he calmly rested his arm on the side of the truck. Still holding the M16. Still pointing it directly at Larmina Meskin.

Despite his calm demeanor and the clinical manner in which he had explained the position to Mina, Blake was still grappling with the conflicting thoughts that went through his head. On the one hand, he had a duty to the members of his team. On the other, he realized the shocking truth. He had fallen in love with this girl.

Mina recognized the hesitation. And recognized the conflict in the eyes of the man behind the rifle. In this moment of madness, she recognized the signs and that broke her heart. She turned towards Mark, unable to keep eye contact with the man who, in such a small period she had come to respect. And – Yes – it was love.

None of the men had the heart to tell her the horrible truth - that Misha probably would be already dead. In a more practical sense, they probably would not say so anyway. They knew that had they done so the probable result would be that she would detonate the vest out of sheer frustration and grief. Worse still - she could run towards the men to take them with her into whatever afterlife she envisaged as the only means of being reunited with her daughter.

'Let Blake disable your vest and then we can talk about what happens next' Mark said – not knowing whether Blake had the necessary skills to do that. 'Do not let these insurgents win! You are better than them! Just trust us – we can do this!'

The next few minutes seemed to last for hours as Mina sat there just staring into space. In the confines of the gully, the atmosphere was electric. Nothing moved and there was no sound.

Mina slowly stood and faced the man she was to kill. The man who had befriended her and shown so much understanding and patience over the past few days. And then she started to speak again in a tone devoid of any emotion and caused the men she faced to gasp in disbelief.

'You think that Misha is already dead – don't you!' as she stumbled to find the words. "Thank you for keeping that from me. I understand why you did that. But – you are right! We must not let them win!'

She struggled with the hijab and threw it on the ground. She removed the dress and pants and stood there displaying the suicide vest the rest of her body covered only by her underwear. And then there was a transformation. Mina seemed to straighten her back and a defiant expression took over her face.

'Please take this vest off me. I only ask for one thing. Let me kill the man who did this to me! And let me kill the man who has taken my Misha.'

Blake was trembling as he handed his M16 to Mark and said that he and Dusty should stay behind the protection of the APC truck.

He approached Mina and began to examine the vest conscious of her watching his every move. She was a very beautiful lady and Blake had to concentrate hard to avoid any distraction.

The belt was fairly crude and small compared to other vests that he had seen. As far as he could tell there was only one detonator – a simple switch to the left of one of four cylinders that he assumed held the explosives. There did not appear to be any method of causing an explosion using a remote device such as a cell phone so that meant that whoever had set it up either trusted the wearer to carry out their mission or he just did not have the skills to rig it that way.

That was the good news.

The bad news was the trigger. That was part of what appeared to be a circuit and there seemed to be no way that it could be bypassed safely because there was no way of knowing which part of that circuit would activate the trigger. Blake smiled at the diminutive figure of Mina who by this stage was sweating. He realized that they were both sweating.

'Ok – just a few more minutes. I need to go get a few tools. Just stay still. Do not touch anything!'

He went to the door of the APC and opened it, shielding him from Mina and the bomb, and reached inside to get the toolbox. As he did so he whispered to Mark. 'I don't think there is any way I can do this! The vest is so *fucking* crude – it will blow up if I try to disarm it!'

There was no need to say anything else. But Blake had to do something!

'There is one thing I can try. Remove the vest without

activating the trigger. But that will be dependent on Mina doing exactly as she is told. And I will need help. You Ok with that?'

Mark had been in the position before when he had to get his men to move into situations that could be fatal. But never before in circumstances where he was not also in the same amount of danger as the men under his command. Momentarily Mark thought of getting Ben Chapman to help. He was the most qualified member of the team to deal with explosives. But – What right did he have to ask a man to place himself in danger in these circumstances? As Mina had explained – the bomb was to kill Mark! He took a deep breath and got up from his crouched position.

He had insisted that all of his team wore their IBA gear (Interceptor Multi-Threat Body Armor System) throughout this mission. What good that would do if the suicide vest exploded was anyone's guess.

'Ok – I am coming with you. Let's do this.' and Mark stepped out from his cover and walked towards the bomb. Blake was too shocked to intervene. Dusty just called out 'No!' And then let forth a stream of profanities before leaping to his feet and rushing after Mark. Normally, if the officer wanted to get himself killed that was fine – sergeants just did as they were ordered. But to be honest, Mark was more important to the completion of this mission than a mere sergeant.

Blake asked Mina to turn around while he examined the shoulder straps. Mark heard Dusty protesting, but it was too late now. He got Dusty to hold the trigger device and resisted the temptation to just rip the thing off.

Now they were all sweating!

'Ok!' Blake said in as calm a voice as he could muster. 'Tell me how you were to activate this thing.'

Mina was scared but answered.

'He just said to this flick this switch. '

She moved her hand towards the trigger.

All three men involuntarily ducked, before a nervous laugh eased the tension.

'Ok – there must be something that is triggered if you attempt to remove the vest. What did he say about that?'

The tension returned at Mina's reply.

'He just said I would explode!'

Blake just shrugged and began tracing the wires from the four cylinders to the switch. And there it was. Two wires went up into each of the shoulder straps and that made sense. The best place to put a pressure switch was at the point where the vest carried the most weight, and at the point where there was less chance of anybody's movement setting the explosives off accidentally. But it appeared that the designer of this vest did not care too much about that.

It was now too late to protect Mina or anyone else from the truth. Blake delivered the news

'We have two pressure switches – one in each shoulder strap. All we have to do is to remove the belt around Minas' waist, undo the shoulder straps, and then we can hold the point where the pressure switches are and tape them in place. Or we simply fling the vest and hope that there is a delay mechanism built-in,'

Nobody said a word. Blake shrugged 'You want my opinion? This thing is so fucking crude anything could happen!'

Mark had to say something.

'Just fling the vest!'

The shoulder straps were undone, and the belt was

untied so that as far as Blake could tell it was now free. Now the only thing preventing an explosion was the weight on the straps.

Although the bomb looked to be small, it would be contained in the gully which would amplify the effect.

Consequently, the explosion would shatter the eardrums of three members of the team who were trying to disarm the vest. Meanwhile, the rest of the team, who had been watching the activity in the valley below, would be oblivious to the drama that was unfolding meters away.

Elliott was closest to the entrance to the gully where a cloud of dust appeared, followed by a muffled explosion.

'What the hell was that?'

Chapter 37

The Brits

The head of the South Asia desk in MI6 was used to receiving a bollocking from the Chief of SIS over something over which he had no control. Neville Chesterfield had simply delivered a report that C had asked for. That report had now come in from the head of station in Kabul Afghanistan. And now Chesterfield was expected to justify the report and its' recommendations having had very little to do with its drafting or its conclusions.

However – he had read it. And although the recommendations seemed a little on the extreme side, he would probably agree with them.

'Is Reginald completely off his trolley?' the head of MI6 demanded of his underling. 'You were supposed to ask for a report of what we could do to help a bunch of Americans avoids being killed, not come up with a plan for starting World War III!'

Chesterfield was patient. It was perfectly normal in the security and intelligence business to have to deal with a situation where a decision had already been made at the highest level. But where it was necessary to obtain a report that justified that action so that the boss could cover his ass if things did not turn out as he had intended. The situation was further complicated by the fact that Chesterfield could not know whether politicians were involved in any original decision. All that he could do when faced with an angry boss was to try to support the officer in the field. He would attempt to embellish the recommendation with what little he already knew of the situation in the chaos that defined the happenings in the hellhole of Afghanistan.

'I understand that Smith has been in contact with Taylor. He is concerned that Taylor does not appreciate the danger that he is in. Smith at first thought that the matter should be left there. But he has reasons why he is anxious to keep him alive. Apparently - Taylor is something of a security expert and could be useful to us. That has its origins back when Smith lent a couple of satellite phones to Taylor on a recent visit he made to Afghanistan. You will recall the stink that caused for our friends in the CIA – but that was neither Smiths nor Taylors fault. And you will never guess – Taylor loaded some software into the phones that blocked our normal backchannel that would have enabled us to check on what he and his team were up to. According to Taylor, the system has yet to be adopted by the US military and Smith thinks that there is a good chance we could acquire it for our use.'

Chesterfield knew then that he had got the full attention of his boss. For years, the British had tried to get ahead of their allies and enemies alike in developing a secure means of communications. That goal was elusive. Which meant the expenditure of billions of pounds just to stay where they were. For the major communications systems, various encryption methods had been developed since the famous Enigma machines of World War II (which were broken by Polish – not British – mathematicians) which keep most security systems secure most of the time. But with smaller devices in more general use, the problem was the operating systems. The Taylor modification did not appear as an APP (application) so it could not be copied, did not appear as a simple EXE (Executable) file, and did not appear as a more complex – but still routine – DLL (Dynamic-Link Library) file. So – what the hell was it?

While the Chief was pondering this question, Chesterfield pressed on.

'Smith has recommended deploying one of our SAS squadrons for the simple reasons that there is an RWW wing currently located at the Kandahar base pending redeployment to heavens knows where. Meantime, they need something to do to keep them occupied. Smith has had a preliminary chat with the commander, and he is keen to treat it as a training exercise.'

Even Chesterfield thought the deployment of an elite Special Air Service squadron consisting of sixteen highly trained men was a bit overkill. And one trained as a Revolutionary Warfare Wing was just plain silly. However, the deployment of such a wing was under the control of the SIS and the Foreign Office so he had to give Reginald Smith, way down the pecking order in MI6, full marks for being aware of this special relationship.

And C had to laugh at the audacity of the recommendation.

'Ok – I will need to consult the Foreign Secretary and meanwhile, nothing goes out to anyone including Kabul. Are you quite clear on that Neville?'

The CIA had long since abandoned the office in

downtown Kandahar and had moved into the airbase. There was just no point in trying to keep a foothold in a city where there was the constant threat of the Taliban taking over the whole place. Even the US military had moved to the base, so the CIA had little choice but to follow them. In the relative peace that the base provided the agents were still able to perform their role while pretending to be something else.

They still expected to be kept informed of matters that concerned the movements of military personnel and they were both miffed and confused when the British SAS squadron just up and left without a hint of what was going on. It had been expected that the RWW wing would leave by air to return to the United Kingdom for rest and recreation. Instead, they had left the Kandahar base in four armored vehicles heading west and with the obvious intention to harm someone.

The senior CIA agent contacted the executive officer of the US Army contingent and politely asked what the hell was going on. From the reaction that he got it was obvious that the US military people had no clue and a call to a friend in the British base administration got the same result.

The only person who did know was the MI6 head of station in Kabul. Reginald Smith smiled to himself as he got on his satellite phone to give Mark Taylor the news that he had managed to convince the British government that the deployment of a SAS squadron was called for.

Unusually, Mark did not answer the call.

He left a message for Mark to call him back. There was no point in giving him the good news. Much better to tell him directly.

Chapter 38

Revenge

Of the other six members of the team who were not involved with the suicide vest, Elliott Shannon was the closest to the explosion. He was spread-eagled on the ground scanning the valley through his binoculars and because of the angle of the gully he could not accurately judge where the noise had come from. Owen and Brent were further up the mountain road on point checking that no one would come from that direction, Ben, Mike, and Hamish were doing the same job further down the mountain.

They all heard a more muffled noise but still, the disturbance was obvious.

The first thing that happened was that all three groups called Dusty had been given the job of coordinating communications.

None of them got any response which they thought was unusual but not particularly concerning. Nothing was happening at the moment down in the valley. The Taliban had stopped in a position concealed by bushes just to the east of the border and apart from one of their men sitting on the roof of one of the trucks with what looked like an AK-47 rifle and presumably acting as the lookout. There was no movement on the Iranian side of the border.

Elliott told the other two to stay where they were while he went to investigate what the noise was all about. He contacted the other two groups and told them to remain in their positions while he went to find out what had happened. And why Dusty had not responded to their calls.

As Elliott entered the gully, the first thing he saw was Dusty slumped down beside the second of the APC trucks with his left arm covered in blood. He rushed over to him and quickly assessed that he was alive but hardly aware of where he was or what had happened. Then he peered around the side of the truck and saw the heap of bodies in a strange position. Blake had his arms wrapped around a semi-naked body. That was Mina. Just to the side lay Mark.

There was no movement and no sound.

Blood was everywhere and there was no sign of life.

Elliott looked around to find out where anything could have come from to cause this carnage – but nothing was obvious.

There was just a deathly silence.

Elliott called Mike, Owen, and Ben.

'You had better get down here – there has been some kind of accident – quickly! Everyone else stays in position.'

The three men came running into the gully and stopped dead in their tracks as they viewed the carnage – and unsure what had caused it.

Dusty began to show signs of life. Owen got down on the ground next to him and tried to get him to talk.

'It was a bomb! I just turned around to call Elliott and there was an explosion said Dusty as he tried to get to his feet. That did not work as he slumped back down obviously concussed by the blast.

It was Ben who rushed to the three bodies entwined further down the gully. He did a quick check on the three bodies and yelled over his shoulder as he got down to the ground.

'They are still alive! – But only just. They need help!'

The attempt by Blake, Dusty, and Mark to remove the explosive vest from around Minas' waist was almost successful. Blake had loosened the shoulder straps while Dusty had ensured that the switch would not be triggered by accident or by design during that process.

The problem came when Blake went to unwrap the ties that held the vest against her shoulders. Mark yelled that he had found the pressure switch on the shoulder strap that he was responsible for but had also located some other wires that suggested another trigger. So - the designer wasn't quite so stupid after all! And Mark could see the irony of it. The insurgents who had attached the vest had told Mina that she should not try to remove it, but that was hardly meant to be for her safety. Apart from the implied threat - they hadn't bothered to say why!

Knowing that a pressure switch would need to have a built-in delay to allow for random movement, Blake knew that he would have a couple of seconds to complete his task. What he did not know was just how many seconds had already elapsed and how many more seconds were to pass before the bomb exploded and achieved what the bombers had intended – to kill Mark and Mina.

In desperation, he yelled to Mark and Dusty to let go, get down and hurled the vest with all his might further down the gully. Mark and Dusty both had the same thought – to get away from the explosion. Mark tripped over a rock and virtually went straight to the ground. Dusty dived for the cover of the APC but did not make it far enough.

Blake only had one thought. He wrapped his arms tightly around Mina and sank to the ground covering her as best he could.

As the bomb exploded in mid-air shrapnel fired off in all directions.

The next thing that Mark could recall was the face of Elliott yelling something into his face.

But he could not hear anything.

At least he was still alive.

What had saved the life of the three men was the Kevlar IBA vests that they each wore under their uniform fatigues. Mina, who astonishingly did not have a Kevlar vest, was hardly touched by the explosion having been protected by the body of Blake.

Mark and Blake had suffered concussion and had taken the brunt of the shrapnel blast in their arms and legs. That is where all the blood came from.

The gully took on the appearance of a field hospital as the four injured people were dealt with. Surprisingly, it was Dusty who had the worst of the concussion probably as a consequence of the shockwave traveling over the bodies on the ground but hitting Dusty with full force in his standing position as he had turned to run. The shrapnel wound to all four of the victims turned out to be largely superficial once the blood and dust had been wiped away.

And the team realized how fortunate they were that the US government stores procurement system was as bizarre as it was. Some store's procurement committee back in the Pentagon, in yet another brain-dead moment, had decided that the cost of removing and accounting for the stores from surplus vehicles was more than the cost of replacing them. The APC trucks were expected to, at some stage or other, be around when bombs were exploding. And both trucks had enough medical supplies to treat a whole regiment.

The concussion finally wore off and Mark could consider the cost to his team. On the physical side, his first assessment had looked bleak. As the day wore on, he realized they had been very lucky.

It was on the mental side that he would have a problem.

Mina could not be consoled as she faced the prospect of returning to Farah after having failed to carry out what she had been instructed to do and has had her life saved by one of the very men she was supposed to kill.

Now she faced the prospect that her daughter was already dead, or would die, as a consequence of her failure.

At first, Mark ignored the vibration of his phone for the simple reason that he was already shaking as he slowly recovered from the shock of the explosion and did not notice it. When he finally did notice the person calling terminated the call. Mark checked his call log to find out who that caller was and was at first surprised and then angered when the log revealed there were several unanswered calls from Reginald Smith of MI6 Kabul.

His initial reaction was to just ignore the call. But then he had to let off steam at someone. And who better than the man who he blamed for this mess.

He hit the call-back button.

Smith answered at once.

He barely got past the word 'Thanks' when Mark cut

him off.

'Are you calling me to make sure I am dead – Are You? Why I ever got involved with you Brits I will never know. But – God help me – never again!'

While Mark paused for a breath, Smith took the opportunity to get a word in.

'Mark – what are you talking about?'

'Your agent – that's what I am talking about! Not content with her earlier lying and then going walkabout in her hometown – now we have just removed a suicide vest from her that nearly crippled my team. We have just had a major explosion in our ranks. Two of my men are badly injured and I am not much better. I have yet to decide what to do with your agent – that is if she doesn't bleed to death meanwhile! So – thanks very much for your help!'

He ended the call.

Mark called Mike in to deal with the casualties as he was the most experienced at attending to injuries of this type. There were plenty of sets of gear to replace those that had been shredded by the blast. Mina would just have to accept a set of fatigues that were several sizes too large.

After being bandaged up a redressed Mark limped off back to the road to turn his attention to the reason they were here.

There was still a mission to complete.

Dusk was settling over the landscape and still, Elliott could detect no movement in the Taliban camp other than the occasional change to the man atop the truck. There was still no sign of any movement on the other side of the border. The only significant event had been a patrol vehicle traveling from south to north slowly along the bottom of the valley on the Afghanistan side of the border. That caused the Taliban lookout to lie flat on the roof while it passed but he did not seem to be overly concerned probably because the Taliban could easily have wiped out the patrol if they chose to. Mike remained with Blake, Dusty, and Mina in the makeshift sickbay in one of the APC trucks while the rest of the team were hidden up and down the road. Mark was left to conduct the communications function previously assigned to Dusty.

His satellite phone chirped again. He answered it in a normal voice assuming it was a call from either Owen or Ben. He was wrong.

It was the interfering head of MI6 Kabul.

'Mark – please listen to me for a couple of seconds then you can ditch the phone for all I care. We have a squadron of our elite SAS forces on their way to join you. They will still be a few hours away, but they will provide all the protection you need.'

This was getting bizarre. Mark was calmer than he had been as he replied to this lunatic from Kabul.

'Reggie – we are in the middle of nowhere. How does your SAS intend to find us even assuming that we need them? Despite being attacked by one of your own we are still functioning as a unit and are hopefully at the point of achieving what we set out to do. So – unless you have some good news for us - I am rather busy!'

Mark may as well have been talking to himself. Reggie just continued.

'Major Ross McKinnon assures me that he knows how to find you and will be with you as soon as possible. I cannot tell you how he knows – otherwise, I might have to kill you!' Smith ended with a sardonic laugh.

'You haven't had much luck so far!' said Mark as he again terminated the call.

And then things started to happen in a hurry.

The Afghanistan patrol vehicle slowly made its way in a north to south direction and immediately after it had disappeared to the south the Taliban began to move towards the fence-line.

At the same time, there was movement on the Iran side of the border. There was a convoy of vehicles moving straight towards the place where the Taliban APCs were positioned. The trucks on the Iranian side eventually stopped a hundred yards from the actual border and two of their trucks continued straight up to the border fence directly opposite the Taliban.

It was an amazingly efficient operation. It all happened so fast that Elliott barely had time to take photographs of the deal. The border fence just opened as easily as passing through a well-used gate. One of the Taliban supervised the handing over of a couple of small parcels and the Iranians just dumped twelve cases which were rapidly uplifted and divided equally between the Taliban trucks. The gate was closed, and the Iranians turned around and headed back to the west. The Taliban turned away from the border and headed to the east. The whole exercise was completed in under five minutes.

Both sides in the transaction disappeared leaving no sign that anyone had ever been there.

It was then that Mark realized what was to happen next. It was not what he had expected would happen as the sunset in the east and darkness descended. He did not predict that the Taliban would try to return up the road in darkness. And it was going to seriously tax his depleted manpower if he were to achieve what he knew he had to do.

The Taliban turned away for the border and started their slow climb back up the mountain.

The team could follow the progress of the trucks up

the mountain track as their lights bobbed and weave along the winding road. They were going much slower than they had previously probably due to the extra weight from their cargo and the sheer practicality of driving at night on a road that even in the light of day would have tested the most experienced driver. Things slowed even further when the second vehicle first stopped causing Elliott to switch to his night-vision glasses to see what was happening now. The truck had started to roll back down the hill – only to come to a halt when it was slowed by scraping it along the cliff on the side of the road. The Taliban must have had a form of communication because after a few minutes the leading vehicle also stopped and then started a hazardous journey in reverse down the hill until it reached the stranded truck. There was a period where everyone was on the road and the Taliban seemed to be engaged in an argument about what was to happen next.

Mark counted eight Taliban involved in the discussion and that seemed to be their total manpower. So – at this point, the two sides in whatever battles were to follow were evenly matched in numbers if not inability. The deciding factor could be whether Dusty and Blake could overcome their injuries and take part in the ensuing battle.

Eventually, the Taliban seemed to reach a decision. The disabled truck was somehow manipulated away from the cliff, prevented from rolling any further down the mountain, and the rear doors opened. They then unloaded the six boxes and struggled up to the leading vehicle and loaded them on aboard. There was then another argument among the Taliban which told Mark a couple of things. Firstly, it was obvious that there was no clear leader among this group. Or no discipline. Or both.

Secondly, it was obvious that there was now insufficient room for all the men in the remaining truck. In the end, they manipulated the crippled truck around so that it was now facing down the hill, and the driver and one Taliban passenger set off back down the mountain. The rest of the men were still arguing as they boarded the other truck with three men crammed into the front and the other three crammed into the back with the boxes that were assumed to hold the arms supplied by the Iranians.

That set the odds very much in favor of Mark and his team – only the three men in the front seats would have any idea what struck them.

Mark had Owen maneuver one of their APC trucks so that it was just uphill from the area where the gully was and facing downhill. Such was the size of the truck and the width of the track that the Taliban would have no choice but to stop. What happened after that was really up to them. They could either try to fight their way out of an ambush or accept the inevitable.

In the end, they did both.

As the Taliban truck came around the corner Ben put the headlights on full beam blinding the Taliban driver. At first, nothing appeared to happen as the driver struggled to gain control and then he slammed on his brakes and veered to the left.

Immediately the passenger door opened, and two men tumbled out waving AK-47 rifles and looking for targets. One of the men focused on the headlights shining down towards the driver but that was a waste of time. The lights of the truck were protected to withstand an IED explosion and the 7.62 bullets from the AK-47 would have no effect. It did however result in the shooter being shot dead by Hamish who was crouched at the edge of the gully. Meanwhile, the rear doors of the truck were flung open. Three men tumbled out onto the road also waving AK-47's and looking for targets. They hesitated momentarily, confused by the command issued by Owen in

Dari to put down their weapons. Two complied, one didn't so another one of the Taliban died as he was shot through the head. The whole exercise had lasted less than a minute.

The remaining four of the Taliban were spread-eagled face down on the ground and had their hands tied behind their backs and feet bound with masking tape before Ben blindfolded each of them. Only then did Mark appear out of the gloom.

The driver was the only one of the four Taliban prisoners who said anything and that was in Dari. Owen went over to where Mark was standing to provide a translation.

'He is saying that someone is a *gholona* or a *shithole* and he is asking *in chist?* or *what is this?* Owen laughed. 'He is a bit pissed-off.'

Mark could see the funny side but was in no mood to put up with any nonsense.

'Inform the driver that he should shut up or he gets tape over his mouth. Now let us see what we have in the Taliban truck.'

Marks' satellite phone started to vibrate. It was Elliott.

'Looks like someone is coming towards us from the east – I have seen at least three vehicles coming up the hill. I cannot tell how many men there are, but it looks like quite a few. And they are moving fast.'
That was the last thing that Mark needed right now! His depleted team had been able to handle things adequately due to the element of surprise and the fact that the Taliban forces had lost one of their trucks. But that was then. This was now. They no longer had the benefit of surprise.

Owen and Ben went to examine the contents of the truck while Brent and Hamish took up station to check on the road up the hill from the west. Mark went further up the hill to join Elliott to get a better read on what was happening on the hill to their east. He found Elliott in a state of near panic.

'They have disappeared!'

Marks' phone chirped again. It was Ben.

'I do not know what is going on – but we have got a shitload of new machine guns that look like the Heckler & Koch MP5 made under license in Iran and even a box of Russian RPG anti-tank weapons – but there is no ammunition with any of them. The only stuff that is any use to us would be the Iranian-made Akhgar machine guns because they use the same 7.62mm as we do – but they are no fucking use without bullets!'

Mark had a decision to make. Leave his limited force spread out and therefore vulnerable to their being picked off one at a time or consolidate his force in one area that he could defend. He reluctantly decided on the latter even though that would rob him of information on where any attack may come from.

Their APC trucks were loaded with the weapons from the Taliban truck and then the whole team withdrew from the road back into the gully. That left the Taliban truck, two dead bodies and four prisoners trust up in the center of the road. Mark then positioned his team around the gully to wait for the coming battle. Dusty was starting to show signs that he was recovering from his earlier blast. At least he was starting to swear again which Mark took to be a good sign. Nonetheless, Mark took a position at the back of the gully where he could keep an eye on both Dusty and Mina, Blake who was still suffering from the wounds to his legs from the earlier blast insisted that he was good to go and took a position with Ben at the entrance to the gully. Owen and Elliott assumed positions on each side. Mike and Hamish got themselves settled atop the two APCs where they could cover all angles. Because of the configuration of the set up they were well hidden. The moonlight did not filter into their hiding place – so Mark was as confident as he could be that they could withstand any attack. The team was as ready as it could be.

The only risk they faced was being overwhelmed by sheer numbers. Mark was not concerned about the ability of his team to fight because he had with him some of the best-trained men on the planet. What he was concerned about was - what would happen if they ran out of ammunition? So - it was a numbers game and there was not much else he could do about that.

They waited. No one moved. No one may a sound. And then the first sign of any movement on the periphery of the gully came thirty minutes later. Mark had not expected an attack to come from the back of the gully, but he detected a slight movement. Well - that was not quite true. He detected that the shape of one of the rock outcrops had changed. He had Dusty focus his night-vision goggles on the spot and he confirmed there was a man. Creeping ever so slowly along the northern wall of the cliff.

Suddenly they were back in Special Forces mode communicating by hand signals. The shape that Dusty had seen was not right. The man – whoever he or what it was – was wearing a military uniform and was certainly not a Taliban fighter. Then the question was – Was he friend or foe? Had the advice from MI6 been correct and they were about to be attacked by an Iranian special forces team? Could Mark take the chance of shooting first and risk killing someone who was there for other reasons?

On the spur of the moment, Mark decided that he had to find out in a hurry because if one man was creeping towards them from the rear the odds were that others were also doing the same thing from other directions. The

Taliban he felt that he could manage. Professional soldiers were entirely another issue – whether they were friend or foe.

On the assumption that the guy would also be wearing night-vision gear, Mark suddenly stood, made a very deliberate move to slowly place his gun on the ground, and then just walked towards the shape of the man with his hands held above his head to show that he was un-armed.

And the reaction that Mark got could have been quite comical in another place and at some other time. It was not quite the same as the famous words of Henry Morton Stanley's *'Doctor Livingstone I presume'* statement from the wilds of Africa back in 1871.

The *'Major Taylor I presume'* was greeted with relief as Major Ross McKinnon of the British SAS squadron introduced himself.

McKinnon put his fingers to his lips and issued a piercing whistle which resulted in nothing that Mark could see. However, as he walked the SAS officer towards the entrance to the gully three more men in SAS uniform appeared from the same direction as their Major had come from and immediately headed to secure their position behind the Taliban truck. Two jeeps – each with four soldiers appeared down the road from the east and these men set about forming a perimeter around the area without a word coming from their commander. The lights of the jeeps told the visitors all they needed to know.

Mark signaled to the rest of his team to stand down as he turned to McKinnon with a grin on his face.

'Yes – you can see we had a little fun before you arrived. There are two more of this group who we believe went back down the hill – some problem with their vehicle we think – and we don't know where they have gone or if they intend to return. We were a little concerned when we saw lights coming up the road from the west, but we can now assume that was your people. Still – we could not take any risk and that was why we were hunkered down in in the gully.'

Mark would have expected a reaction from McKinnon but there was none. His attention was focused on the people who had appeared from the gully. He was staring in disbelief at Larmina as she walked out to join the men.

'Meskin! What the hell are you doing here? We thought you had been killed back in Farah! Good to see you are still alive! How are you? And what the hell happened to you now?'

Despite being protected by Blake during the explosion, the lady still had several dressings where the shrapnel had ripped her skin, although most of them were covered by the male fatigues that she was wearing.

The reaction of the SAS Major had Mark confused. There was nothing but the utmost respect in his attitude towards Mina. And he had greeted her like a long-lost friend.

'Do you two know each other? How come?' Mark asked.

Larmina Meskin walked up to the Major and formally shook his hand with a smile on her face. 'Excuse my dress – the lads insisted that I wear this to be one of the team. The bandages – well Mark will tell you what happened!'

She then turned to Mark, with the smile still on her face she said.

'I saved his ass back in Farah is all.'

She walked away to deal with Blake who was still having problems with the dressings on his shrapnel wounds, while the two Majors (one active and the other one retired) settled down on the far side of the road for a serious chat.

'Major – I don't know how to tell you this now' Mark began – not sure how this would turn out. 'I may as well be straight to the point. Half of our problem here was that Mina had a suicide vest on her which my men had to dismantle. They were successful but there was collateral damage as you people like to say!'

McKinnon was disturbed by that.

'You are not saying that Meskin deliberately tried to explode a suicide bomb! Or are you? That would be totally out of character!'

Mark could only shrug.

'She *got* the vest from the Taliban during our stopover in Farah. The blood and bandaging that you can see on Blake - the man that Mina is attending to now – and Dusty who is somewhere around, and also on my arms and legs - was caused when the vest exploded – and not by any scrap with the Taliban. You can imagine – it was a close call, and we are very lucky to be here having this conversation.'

'So - you think that this was the attempt on your life that our people would have been talking about?' McKinnon asked.

Mark had to think about that. He had assumed that it was the Taliban trying to disrupt his team from getting a handle on their drug trade. However – the Taliban were dealing with the Iranians. And the Iranians would be equally concerned since they would not want the Americans getting evidence of their breaking international law by exporting weapons.

What if there was more to it than that?

What if the Iranians had asked – or even ordered – the Taliban to take Mark and his team out? And it all had nothing to do with the drug trade.

Mark had to laugh.

'Yeah – it is called making assumptions which we all

should have learned in Spooks 101. I have been involved in chasing drugs too long and had not thought this thing through. You arc probably correct and maybe I should concentrate on where this all started.'

Mark told McKinnon of their experience in Africa following the man that they knew as Mohamed Haji. Following him to the point that he ended up in a Sudan jail – which Mark had *assumed* was the end of the matter. But it was not the end – was it?

Haji had escaped and he could not do that without having powerful friends. The US Ambassador to Kuwait had been murdered and it would have taken the resources of a nation-state to carry out that kind of event. Haji had solid links to just the kind of country that would be involved in such action. And according to British Intelligence, one such country was scheming to take Mark Taylor out. Which was the very reason Mark was having the conversation with McKinnon. There was one country behind everything.

Iran.

Mark had been too dumb to make the connection.

And now Haji had gone to Turkey probably plotting and planning further misery confident that his nemesis was miles away in Afghanistan where he could be easily disposed of by people who were one of the few cultures that were more brutal than the Iranians.

Mark gave McKinnon a bitter smile.

'I think I have misread the Iranians every step of the way. We have been followed at every stage of our trip around Africa and now into Afghanistan. I thought they were just keeping an eye on what we were doing and where we were going so that we did not interfere with their various activities. But – What if the whole plan was to make sure that we were distracted? What if the whole ruse was to make sure we did not know what they were really up to? What say they have other plans that involve the Turks? And they have happily gone along with our diversion here for a couple of reasons. Firstly - we are miles away from where the real action is. Secondly - just to make sure we are out of the way; they get the Taliban to take us out. And what is more – they planned to use one of our team to achieve that. How could I not have seen that!'

It was now McKinnon's turn to smile.

'Don't be so hard on yourself Major. No one could have foreseen all the twists and turns. And you are not the first to underestimate Iranian intelligence. They have the habit of being unpredictable and you must remember they are more ruthless than even the Israeli Mossad. At least you are still alive and have worked out where they are going. The questions you need to answer are - What are the Iranians really up to? And then - What are you going to do about it?'

'Yeah!' Mark replied. 'The job I was given by our President was to prevent Robert Mugabe being killed – and we did that – albeit more by good luck than by good judgment. The man Mohamed Haji is the problem – but we have no authority to take him out now that the original threat is over. We are only here in Afghanistan courtesy of our Drug Enforcement Administration. And we have no support from either the CIA or the State Department. We intended to find a link between drugs and the Iranians – and we did that – to answer part of the question as to why and how drugs are finding their way into US diplomatic offices. In addition to finding the answer to that riddle, we have proved that Iran is also contravening the UN rules that ban exporting weapons to the Taliban. Now we have to find someone who cares!'

Both men stood in silence absorbing the truth of what Mark had said. In Mark's case, it was a matter of repetition of his experience when he was in uniform – the men on the ground knew that something was not as it should be and were unable to do anything about it. For McKinnon – in the uniform of another country – here was a situation in which it was simply not his problem. But he could sympathize with his American friend and resolved to do something about that.

Mark shook his head and came to a decision.

'Ok – we have to get moving and deal with what we have. The first thing we need to do is get back to Farah and sort out the Meskin business one way or the other before we move on to other things. Larmina told us that she was given the vest by people back in Farah with instructions to try to destroy our mission. She says that she was told that if should does not explode the vest and destroy us her daughter will die. We believe that Misha will be dead already. But we have Mina holding on to the hope that she will still be alive.'

McKinnon looked confused.

'Misha is her sister, not her daughter!'

Mark shook his head. So - Mina had been trying to protect her daughter even by misleading her masters at MI6. It was only by pure chance that Mark had been able to find out the truth – a chance conversation between Misha and Blake. That made Mark determined that someone would pay for that irrespective of whether Misha was alive or dead.

'No Major. Misha is her daughter. Now, are you going to help me sort out the people who put her through all this shit?'

McKinnon was upset by the news.

'My team was sent out to protect you from an attempt on your life organized by some foreign power you have impressed someone in our high command! Now it looks as though that attempt was to have been carried out by a suicide bomber which, I must say, you have managed to defuse somehow. However, the danger is not over yet! You still have to get back to Farah before going on to Kandahar - which is the most Taliban-infested region in Afghanistan. So -our job is not yet done. Meanwhile, I am sure that we could find the time to help you, Major – so let's do it!'

The two Majors shook hands.

Brent drove the Taliban truck with Ben and Owen riding shotgun. The four prisoners were bundled into the back together with the two dead bodies. Ben and Owen had simple instructions to conduct – Any problems caused by the prisoners? Shoot them. And they had a massive advantage in sensing any problems. Although the Taliban did not know it, Owen spoke their language like a native.

The small convoy took off for the slow trip back down the mountains and into Farah. The SAS vehicles were interspersed throughout the convoy. The split of the team between the APCs had to change with Mike taking the three patients – Blake, Dusty, and Mina. Mark insisted on driving their Humvee at the head of the convoy probably more out of ego than anything else, leaving Elliott and Hamish driving the other APC.

There was no hurry. Mark did not want to risk having any accidents in the dark and on a road that would require his men to concentrate. He had ensured that Mina was kept busy assisting Mike but mostly caring for Blake, to keep her mind occupied. The convoy was going directly to the US military compound to get rid of the Taliban scum before they could try to find Misha.

The US military compound in Farah is based at the airport. The airport is primarily used by the military. Because of the increasing prominence of the Taliban in the province, it was more a fortress than a base.

To get to the airport from the north the team had to travel through the town and then turn east towards the mountains. Fortunately, it was early morning when they made it into Farah so that there was no traffic to impede their progress. Mark was aware that some of his old mates from the US Special Forces may be in residence at the base having been dispatched to assist their Afghan allies with *training.*

That they were there for *assistance with training* was far from the truth. They were there because the Taliban had made several attacks on Afghan military and government resources over the last couple of years and they would have been expected to shift the balance of power back to the Afghan government forces. So, Mark turned up with a bunch of Taliban prisoners was well received even if it did require the completion of an extraordinary amount of paperwork.

In the safety of the compound and surrounded by men from the same background as himself, Mark felt reasonably secure. He did ask that his visit to the Farah base would be handled with the utmost secrecy for the simple reason there were Afghan forces on the base that outnumbered the US contingent, and he did not want news that he was not dead to leak out. He also ensured that Mina was kept hidden for the same reason.

The colonel in charge – Jim Cranston – had been a Major at the time when Mark and Dusty had been with the US Special Forces. He remembered them both and that made the process a little bit easier. However, it did raise the question of what Mark was up to in this neck of the woods and bringing in four Taliban prisoners and a shitload of very new weapons sourced in Iran and destined for the Taliban in Kandahar. It did not make sense to Mark either. He just hoped that something would arise from this. Either through the military waking up to the significance of the drug trade in their war on the Taliban or through diplomacy which should surely raise questions about Iran interfering in a war by supplying weapons that sanctions said that they were not supposed to have.

Mark did not know at the time why he kept a copy of the film of the cross-border exchange. It was a good job he did – otherwise nothing would have been said about the matter by the United States diplomatic service!

It was early afternoon when the team left the base and left behind the Taliban truck and their smaller run-about which they had no further use for. Dusty and Blake had been able to see the base doctor while they were waiting for Mark to complete all the paperwork and apart from cleaning the shrapnel wounds and changing the amateur dressings, they were both pronounced alive and well – if a little lucky.

Now their focus could switch to the part they all dreaded.

Finding out the fate of little Misha.

Initially, there was disagreement over who should be involved in the search. There was a risk that with Larmina involved she could be seen and blow the whole thing before they got to Misha. That is if she was not already dead. And if that was the case it was not seen as appropriate that Mina be the first to receive that news. For different reasons, Marks' appearance could tell the Taliban that their plot had failed and brought about a similar result. And then there was Blake. Whether it was from a feeling of guilt that he felt from their brush with the Grim Reaper or the simple fact that he cared, no one could tell. Either way he had become almost irrational in his thinking and his goal now seemed to be confined to ending the lives of the people responsible for the problem. With this attitude, he may kill the Taliban before they had a chance to talk. Like – to allow them to tell them where Misha was!

In the end, Mark made the only decision that made any sense. He could not exclude anyone from the search because that would be too cruel. Mark, Blake, and Misha would go with the team but would take no active or visible part in the search. The presence of Mina could be necessary to provide directions around the streets of Farah. With Blake in attendance, Mina would at least have someone to settle her down if things got rough. Mark would be there to hold Blake back in case he decided to take things into his own hands. None of the three would reveal themselves until the team was back at the base.

That having been decided, there seemed to be little point in employing any subtlety or finesse in how they went about it. With Ben and Elliott in the front seats of one of the trucks and Dusty and Owen driving the other one they drove down the street that Mina had walked on that fateful night – no more than two nights prior. Dusk was fast approaching as they slowly moved down the street waiting for word that they had arrived at their destination.

Mina identified the house where she had first met the people who had outfitted her with the explosive vest. The tension in the truck was palpable but Mina and Blake did as they had been told and stayed well hidden in the back. Mark, while keen to watch what was happening, also stayed out of sight, but kept a watchful eye as Mina and Blake craned their necks to get a better view.

It was not as though they risked any interference. The two APCs were each flanked by two jeeps each carrying four men from the SAS squad plus another jeep that held Ross McKinnon and two of his senior NCOs.

Everyone in Marks team had been fitted with communications devices provided by the SAS. These were similar to those used by the US secret service with a small earpiece connected to a microphone that was attached to the sleeve. They were short-range but good enough over the distances that they expected to experience. More importantly, they would enable everyone to know what was happening.

Some said that this may have looked like overkill for the task at hand.

Neither of the two Majors could have given a stuff about that.

Ben and Mike walked up to the door and made enough noise to awaken the dead while Owen stood behind them. Four of the SAS troops stood five yards behind Owen with their M16 rifles pointing at the door, loaded and the selector switches were all set for automatic fire. Four other members of the squad with similar weapons had disappeared behind the house to cover for anyone foolish enough to try to escape.

A lady dressed in a typical drab grey dress and pants outfit but with no scarf covering her head answered the door.

Mina instantly got on her communications device. She was the lady that Mina had referred to as an aunt and who she had visited two nights earlier.

This time the lady looked scared shitless.

'Where is Kaamisha?' was all that Mike asked.

The lady shook her head and muttered something in Dari that neither Mike nor Ben could understand.

But Owen did. He stepped forward and with not an unkindly look on his face let out a string of words in Dari which caused a few tears to start to form in the lady's eyes.

Owen turned to Mike and translated what he had said.

'I simply told her that we are here to collect Misha. My reading of her reaction is that she does not know where she is. Which either means that Misha is not here, or it could mean that the worst we suspected has happened – that Misha has been killed.

Mike did not see any point in being polite, knowing that Mina was being held in a bearhug in the back of the truck to prevent her rushing out, having heard, and understood the entire conversation in both English and Dari.

'Where is she?' he asked towering over the diminutive figure in the doorway.

Owen stepped forward again. This time his words were not so kindly and also in Dari, and this time the lady responded by pointing down the street, tears streaming down her face and screaming incoherently.

'Ok – she now says that her cousin took her and that he lives down there. Let me just check on something' and Owen went to the truck where Mina was waiting. He did not want to risk any sighting of Larmina. He got in and closed the door and addressed Mina in English so that Blake and Mark could understand what he was saying.

'Your aunt says that her *cousin* took Misha and she pointed down the street. Do you know what she is talking about?'

'Is she alive?' was the only stammered response he got.

Owen did not know where to look and it was Blake who pressed the issue.

'We have no reason to suspect that she is not. Just

answer the question so that the lads can do their job. We will find her – but we need you to stay calm and try to help.'

Mina could hardly speak. Her words were barely audible.

'It could be that is the man – and he is no longer a part of my family! Not anymore!'

She almost spat out the words.

'I know where he will be! He will be with the Imam. It will be the Imam's house that she was pointing to.'

Owen got out of the vehicle and returned to the doorway. Now his attitude had changed. He addressed the lady in Dari and what he said caused the lady to attempt to get back into the house. He grabbed the lady's arm and spoke in English/

'Ok – you are coming with us.'

Mike grabbed the lady's other arm and propelled her towards the vehicle that Dusty was in and threw her inside while Owen climbed back. Mike made a signal to the following vehicle which said to remain cool. There was no way the woman could recognize Mark, but they were not going to give her a chance to warn anyone of their next visit.

The Afghan psyche was at play. It was one thing to be a member of the same family. It was another thing entirely to need to stay alive in this dog-eat-dog world.

They traveled little more than a mile down the street before they turned off the main thoroughfare and into a street that had what looked like an industrial site on the right and only a couple of ordinary houses on the left. They were directed to the largest of the two houses. The SAS troops spaced themselves out to form a perimeter around the building so that there would be no way out or in.

Ben and Hamish immediately went around the back of a building while Mike, Dusty, and Owen went straight to the front door. All the men were armed with M16 rifles and Dusty used the butt of his gun to smash in the door and rushed inside. Almost simultaneously Ben and Hamish came in through the rear door leaving the rattle of gunfire echoing behind them. Ben smiled at Dusty.

'There are some mop-heads hanging around in the rear garden. The SAS has that under control.'

They found themselves in a large room where three men were sitting on the floor taking tea. Dusty recognized the Imam as the man wearing a white headband and more formally dressed than the other two. The second thing that Dusty noticed was that there were four cups – so who was missing? The third thing that he noticed was the man to the left of the group. The sudden interruption had startled the men but the one on the left made the mistake of reaching for a rifle that was leaning against a chair. Dusty launched himself across the room splattering the tea and the cups over the other people and pinning the man who had gone for the gun to the ground. He thought of saying something like 'Go on – make my day' but instead just glared at the man and then kicked the gun to one side.

Owen ignored all that. He addressed the Imam in Dari and simply asked the question.

'Where is Kaamisha?'

What surprised all the men was the arrogant attitude of the Imam, as he answered in English.

'Who are you talking about?' he asked. 'And why do you expect us to know the whereabouts of the girl?'

Dusty was almost as good as Mark in reading body language. Despite the difference in cultures, he could recognize when someone was lying. And he did not have the respect for a prayer leader that someone of the Muslim faith would have shown.

Dusty stood and reached down, picking up the Imam by the throat and lifting him clear of the ground. All the anger from their near-death experience the night before welled up. But the lawyer in him told him to be calm. And to play his cards one at a time.

'So - you are the one who caused Larmina to blow herself up and take my friend with her into the afterlife. Well, now we have come to at least make sure you keep your side of the bargain. Larmina said that she had to do this on your instructions to save the life of her daughter. She did what you asked of her. Now let's see if you are a man of your word. Where is the girl?'

The Imam smiled.

At least he tried to smile.

His eyes shifted to the doorway to the left-hand side of the room.

Owen opened the door and stopped dead in his tracks. Turning around his face ashen he spoke to Dusty in a voice that could have come from the depths of a grave.

'Can we get Blake in here? He has to see this. But definitely – no one else.'

Although Owen had not been trained in the Special Forces, he had cottoned on to the unspoken words that Mark and Dusty had exchanged. Dusty just nodded his agreement. And tightened his grip on the throat of the Imam.

Owen spoke into his mike. 'Blake! You will have heard that exchange. Best if you come in here. Alone!' Screams were coming from outside but no way of knowing what that was about.

Blake rushed into the room and saw that Dusty was holding the Imam by the throat.

'Is that the man who set this whole thing up?'

'Yes – but don't worry about that for now. The room on the left is where you want to be.'

Blake made his way past Owen to enter the room and stopped in shock in the doorway. There was a bed of sorts. On that bed lay the body of a young girl - what he assumed was Misha. She was strapped down with some rough ropes, blindfolded, and had her mouth taped. A man was sitting at the far side of the bed. He held an AK_47 rifle. The rifle was pointing directly at the young girl.

There was a pregnant silence as the two men eyed each other. Neither flinching.

Blake switched off the mike and then broke the silence.

'Ok – What happens now? We do not want any trouble. We have just come to collect the girl.'

A strangled reply came from the Imam. Dusty loosened his grip so that the man could at least speak.

'We are not surprised that the survivors came looking for her. Now we have to do a deal. Our lives for hers.'

The Imam looked at Dusty with a victorious smile on his face.

'So let me down and withdraw your men. A large force is on its way to escort us out of here. We will leave the girl for you to collect. Of course, we do not know if we can trust you. Therefore, we have rigged a bomb to explode if anything should go wrong. We will tell you how to dismantle the bomb when my men are clear of this place. Is that not a reasonable deal?'

Dusty tightened his grip.

He wanted to kill the Imam here and now. But how could he do that if the result would be the death of the young girl that they were supposed to rescue?

'You are lying – Aren't you?' Dusty said through clenched teeth. 'You were just waiting here for confirmation that Mina had carried out her task. And then what were you going to do with the girl? The *large force* that you talk about coming to your rescue is just the men returning from the border - isn't it?'

Blake stared at the body on the bed as he signaled to Dusty that the situation was still not resolved.

There was no sign of movement from the girl and for all that he knew, Misha could already be dead. He assessed the angles between himself and the man with the AK-47. Because the man was sitting down, there was just no way that he could take the man out unless he fired a shot so low that it would probably hit the inert body on its way through.

It was too big a risk. If there was even the remotest chance that Misha was still alive, he had to take it. That meant that they would have to trust the Imam.

But - Could they trust the Imam? A man of God. Was he a man of his word?

Probably not.

Chapter 39

Iran Special Force

The Iranian Special Forces, known to Iranians as the Takavar Brigades, are probably not up to the standards of the US Special Forces. But they are nonetheless regarded as ruthless and efficient at what they do. Like most of the Special Force units around the world, the Takavar had their origins in copies of the British SAS – Special Air Service – which despite its name is a part of the British Army. There have been many variations over the years since the SAS was formed in 1941 during the second world war. The most noted would be the United States Navy Sea Air and Land (SEAL) teams, formed during the Presidency of JF Kennedy and now regarded as the very best in the world.

There is a common theme - all teams formed and defined as *Special* are the elite units of their country's armed forces. They conduct covert operations including counterterrorism activities and hostage rescue where direct and decisive action is seen as the only means of achieving a result. They are often involved in operations that are personally ordered by their Commander in Chief and have little regard for the normal niceties of international diplomacy. They define their own Rules of Engagement.

Perhaps the one factor concerning the training of such troops that could come into play was aptitude. Well – that was not quite true. The training was pretty standard. And a ruthless attitude and aptitude in such forces were a given. But one thing that the British and the United States had built into their training was the ability to think on the fly. It is probably a matter of culture.

In years gone by the Navy attitude – *if it moves, salute it – if it doesn't, paint it* – was the norm in many armed forces, and in some cultures it still is.

At times, the military discipline that requires the troops to follow the orders of their superiors at all times does have advantages. At other times it can be disastrous. It is also often unrealistic to expect that all people will take the same action having received but not necessarily understood the same instructions. Consequently, the simpler that an operation was the more likely it was to succeed. Or – to put it another way – the less likely it was to fail.

Which is not necessarily the same thing.

On the other hand, the complexity of some operations was decided by their very nature and there was nothing that could be done about that.

This was one such operation where the Iran forces had been ordered to carry out this mission by the Supreme Leader of the Islamic Republic of Iran - Ali Khomani. Except that the plot behind the operation was extra-ordinarily complex and any one of several things could go wrong.

And usually did go wrong.

Getting into Turkey had been straightforward. The

Iranian Special Forces squadron of sixteen men could have crept across the border from Syria where they had been previously stationed. Then the trip would have involved a stroll of no more than eighty miles west. However, this mission was supposed to be covert. And it was important. So - the team had first traveled to Teheran for a briefing and a blessing for their mission. Then they had been flown to Istanbul under the guise of being part of an Iranian trade mission. From there they had the problem of ceasing to be assigned as delegates for Iran's struggling machinery industry, which did very little trade with their Turkish neighbor and traveling to the southern city of Adana in the guise of tourists. At least they did not need to carry any weapons for this early part of their mission. Which had the effect of making the men feel naked in a heathen land.

Once they had arrived in Adana, they were met by some undercover Iranian intelligence agents who had been in the city preparing for their mission. The agents had found a couple of trucks and arranged tenancy of a large warehouse in a quiet backstreet about ten miles east of the city. There they could hide the team and various other bits and pieces.

The group had busied themselves removing all markings from one of the trucks. This was done to ensure that any witnesses would be unable to remember anything specific about what they had seen. The other truck was spray-painted white and then began the laborious process of signwriting in red and fitting various lighting features to the front and the back. The warehouse also contained a forklift truck, a couple of jackhammers, an assortment of shovels, and two dozen bags of ready-mix concrete

The members of the Special Forces unit were reacquainted with their weapons which paradoxically had been smuggled by lesser mortals across the Syrian border.

The men were then divided into three teams. The first team of six men changed from their civilian clothes into different uniforms very similar to the dark green worn by Turkish paramedics and were directed to a side room where they were to receive further instructions. The second team of four men dressed in casual clothes was instructed to assume guard duty. They were to remain inside the warehouse which made their job complex. There was only one small window at the side of the main roller-door to the warehouse, and two frosted glass windows in the kitchen and toilet areas. The final team of four men wore normal fatigues. They were directed to an area on the left side of the warehouse where the floor was marked out as a three-yard square. There they grabbed the jackhammers and shovels. They began removing the concrete floor.

This whole exercise was overseen by an insipid little man who claimed to be a member of Iran Intelligence. No one spoke to him, so he just sat down on one of the piles of concrete bags.

Mohamed Haji was quite used to being ignored by the arrogant men of the Special Forces.

It was then a matter of waiting.

The immediate mission was to take control of another vehicle and use that to get into the nearby base of Incirlik. The complexity of the operation left the Special Forces men stunned. But the entire plan had been dreamed up by the Iran Intelligence people, with some input from the clerical side of their administration and so it was accepted by the specialist troops for what it was. Cursing and the use of foul language are forbidden under Islamic law. Within the Special Forces unit, which was acting under the direct instructions of the Supreme Leader, the law was strictly observed and enforced.

Except when the men of the Special Forces were alone.

The ambulance and the following truck made their way from the Acibadem Adana Hospital heading east out of the city a little later than had originally been planned. There was such a heavy demand for their services since the World Health Organization (WHO) had agreed that this Hospital rather than the University Yuregir Hospital would be the one that held the isolation units for patients suspected of being involved in the current epidemic.

Of course, the matter was political and practical rather than purely medical. Originally the WHO had insisted that any infected personnel from the Incirlik Air Force base should be isolated in the same facility as the Turkish peasants. The United States ambassador had lobbied the Turkish Government to use Acibaden because of security considerations and that was accepted. The WHO could not have cared less just so long as people were held in isolation and the Turkish government did not want a diplomatic incident to add to the problems it already had in trying to deal with the conflict about which country had introduced the virus in the first place. However, the Turkish Ministry of Health was insistent on administering to Turkish citizens before worrying about their uninformed guests from Incirlik.

Then came another complication.

The number of people who turned up infected at the Incirlik airbase far exceeded the number of infected from the local population of Adana and surrounding areas. Whether this was a statistical fact or was merely a consequence of a stricter testing routine at Incirlik was beside the point. The Turkish Ministry of Health insisted that the Americans should be isolated at Incirlik. At that stage, the WHO gave up. They said that they would deliver vaccines to the Acibadem Hospital and the Ministry of Health would have to organize the distribution from there. The two vehicles which left Acibaden were each crewed by two paramedics. The lead vehicle had all the lights and sirens normally associated with the ambulance service. However, the driver did not see much point in inactivating them, given that there was very little traffic heading east and this trip was not an emergency. All that they had to do was to get into the Incirlik airbase. Once there they had to set up a couple of tents at someplace that was remote from the base administration facilities and administer vaccines and take swabs from whoever turned up. Then they would return to the Hospital at the end of their shift, leaving someone else to decide whether the exercise had been a waste of time or not.

They almost made it.

A couple of miles west of the base they came across another ambulance that was parked at the side of the road with its hazard lights flashing and obviously in some kind of difficulty. The lady driver of the lead vehicle decided that, since they were only on their way to Incirlik, she would stop to at least find out what the problem was. All four of the Turkish paramedics got out to give help.
And that started a chain of events that they would come to regret.

There was not that much to distinguish the two sets of paramedics – apart from the fact that there were eight of the Iranians in the stricken vehicle and only four of the Turks.

The Iranians had decided that this was the better of two evils. One theory was that they should try to infiltrate the hospital staff and through that get control of the allocation of the ambulance to Incirlik. For fairly obvious reasons, Larijani rejected that theory. His grounds for the rejection were that it was far too complicated to arrange an infiltration and it would involve a far greater chance of exposure of the plot. He preferred instead to simply take over the allocated vehicle leaving the only problem of how to do so without attracting too much attention. Having three ambulance vehicles involved in this scenario would of course attract the attention of every other motorist and passenger who the world over would slow and gawk at the prospect of seeing the blood and guts of any injured or dead people. And that is where training and skill came to the fore.

The Iranians stood aside to have the four Turkish paramedics deal with the inert body lying in their ambulance and then, since the Iranians each had a Swiss SIG Sauer semi-automatic pistol and two of them were also carrying Heckler & Koch MP5 submachine guns, they rapidly overpowered the Turkish paramedics.

The paramedics were bound and gagged on the floor of the ambulance that had previously been parked and disabled. The paramedics who then exited the ambulance were identical to the people who went in, so no alarm was raised by the dozens of people who saw the scene unfold. Well – that was not quite true – but a paramedic uniform was just that and few people would remember the gender of the people they had first seen.

Two of the Iranian *paramedics* climbed into their ambulance and with four Turkish paramedics safely hidden in the back, immediately left the scene. They headed west and then turned left off the main road, headed into an industrial area, drove straight into a large warehouse, and closed the door.

The remaining six Iranians split into two teams, climbed into the Turkish ambulance and truck, and continued west on the short distance to Incirlik.

As far as the residents were concerned normal service was resumed.

The ambulance and the truck pulled up at the barrier gates which blocked the entrance to the Incirlik Base. The Iran Special Forces Sergeant Haslam Ghorbani presented his papers to the US Air Force Sergeant Isaac Neffinger. Ghorbani was thankful that the gate was staffed by someone who had been briefed on some aspects of the visit. Otherwise, he may have had a problem.

An Iranian whose first language was Persian or Farsi as it was known, masquerading as a Turk whose language was Turkic, speaking to an America whose knowledge of languages other than English was very limited, was a sure way to confuse.

This was another area in which the plot could fail. A few days earlier Mohamed Haji had a chat with Colonel Samuel J Henning from the US Ankara Embassy and told him what his expectations were. And based on the threat that Haji would release an incriminating film of Henning if he did not get his way the assumption was that that the Americans would be compliant.

At first, Henning had been reluctant to comply. Letting a group of Iranians into a US airbase was bad enough. Letting them into a base where nuclear weapons were held was even worse. Eventually, Henning had acceded to the request because Haji said that the aim was to simply embarrass the Americans. Also, Henning felt that the nuclear arsenal was safe given the protection that was afforded to the nuclear codes and the fact that Iran could not have any hope of unscrambling them even if having done so they would know what to do with them.

However, Haji was nervous because the three earlier attempts to compromise people had been not exactly successful. In the case of Lawrence Johnson – the Kuwait Ambassador – that would have succeeded except that he was dead. Well – the truth of the matter was that Johnson had failed to follow instructions and had talked to the CIA – so the Iranians had to kill him. In the second case, compromising Checksfield in Harare had been very easy but of no use to Iran because nothing had happened in Zimbabwe to make it worthwhile. In the third case – Wallace Perriott – the Deputy Chief in the US Khartoum - had got himself recalled to Washington and was no longer any use. Sure – the Iranians could release compromising details of Perriott's misdemeanors but that would be petty and would cause more problems than it solved. Now they had Henning in a similar trap. Could they depend on this one?

Ghorbani was at least thankful that he did not have to say much. He had been told by Haji that there was a phrase he had to say in English which would confirm his identity, and so he repeated it in the hope that he got it correct.

'The sun will rise again tomorrow'

He did not know what it meant. He then held his breath waiting for the American sergeant to respond.

Neffinger, who was not the brightest person on the planet, had to think. What was the fucking response that the Colonel had told him several days ago? Something about *'Yes!'* but it was more complicated than just a single word and something about both of them seeing it. Rather than wait he just said the first thing that his mind could come up with and muttered.

'Yes - We will both be there.

Ghorbani looked relieved. The fact that Neffinger was supposed to say the words *'Yes - God willing we will both see it!'* did not matter. In any case, the papers that Ghorbani had presented were perfectly in order. Neffinger was not too sure about other things.

'Have you got the wrong name tag?' he asked Ghorbani with a smile on his face.

Hasham Ghorbani looked at the tag which displayed the name Yaren Durmaz. He gritted his teeth as he realized that was not his name. Sergeant Ghorbani would have been even more mortified if he had been able to recognize that Yaren was a girls' name.

The ambulance had been expected although it was a little late and, according to the Hospital paperwork, the driver was supposed to be a female. But this would only be typical of Turkish bureaucrats, especially under stress when there was an epidemic going on. The fact that it had a different driver to the one that had left the Hospital was the reason why Neffinger needed to be on duty because he was the one who had been told to ignore any minor inconsistency. It was still touching and go whether he had the duty on the inward side of the gate.

There was supposed to be a plan B, just in case the sergeant was not on duty, but no one had been briefed on that. The driver of the ambulance was relieved that this was not necessary although he was sweating as he waited to be waved through. What the Iranians could not know was whether this was an elaborate plot by the crafty Americans to embarrass Iran. But they had to assume that Neffinger was on their side and that they would not have to fall back on their insurance policy – the four paramedics that were being held as hostages in case anything did not work out as planned. But – so far it looked hopeful that this part of the plot would be successful.

Ghorbani looked in his rear-vison mirror to see that the truck loaded with isolation tents and vaccines were still there. The World Health Organization had insisted that these vaccines be sent to Incirlik as a test of the ability to immunize people against a virus and to try to develop some kind of herd immunity. Again, the paperwork appeared to be in order. He just hoped that the guards did not inspect it too closely because there were a few things added to what the paperwork said – like an extra couple of men and they were carrying weapons. If these discrepancies were discovered, then they would need to fight their way out – he was confident that they could overcome the guards at the gate - but that would be the end of their mission. He held his breath but again he did not have to.

Of overriding importance to the staff at the gate, was that the Turks were coming to the base simply to vaccinate the US personnel and that is all that they cared about. After all, they were more scared of the virus than they would ever be about an ambulance driver who was wearing the wrong badge.

It was only a couple of days earlier that a viral infection had broken out in the city of Adana which was the closest town situated only a few miles to the west of the Incirlik base. It was a viral infection similar to the SARS – severe acute respiratory syndrome – a strain of coronavirus that had broken out in Chine in 2003. It was a very unusual occurrence in Turkey but there was a procedure for this which the authorities had followed. It appeared to be localized so there was no need to panic, but WHO - the World Health Organization - was taking no chances and quickly established an isolation unit in the Acibadem Hospital. What nobody knew for sure was whether the virus had struck first in the city of Adana or the Air Force base at Incirlik. And, because this tricky little bugger had a vastly different effect on people, everyone at the base had been told to *assume* that they were infected until they were told differently or until they had received the vaccine.

When the first suspected case was identified by the medical staff at the US base the World Health Organization immediately recommended that the patient be transferred to the isolation unit for further diagnosis and that was done. As part of the strict routine for containment, they also said that *anyone who had been in contact or in proximity* should also be isolated. In the case of an Air Force base, the size and complexity of Incirlik meant upwards of eight thousand people – which was quite clearly impractical.

Therefore, to a man, everyone on the base was scared shit-less.

Then came the other problem. There was an inadequate supply of vaccines. There were no vaccines approved by the US Food and Drug Administration and a quick run around proved that those that did exist were untested. The only solution was to assess what vaccines could be found on a control group to make sure that there were no side effects and - hopefully – that they did in fact work.

No one thought to contact the Iranians but that would have been silly. Iran was under so many sanctions that it was most unlikely that it could have developed anything.

However, the Incirlik airbase offered a solution. They had a team of people who were identifiable as a group who could be kept isolated on the base for the two or three days necessary for what would be a trial. The fact that the work of this group was secret only appealed for such a trial more relevant in the present circumstances.

Having successfully dealt with the contingent at the gate now came the most difficult part of thc mission for the Iran Special Forces personnel. The Iranians were not certain where they were expected to go having gained access to the base because they had been unable to do anything other than to rely on what they could find on Google maps. They also did not know whether anyone at the Gate would expect the two vehicles to go to the base headquarters before heading for the parking space on the south side of the base? And would anyone be watching from the base administration office and expecting that at least the delivery truck would call into the loading bay? The whole mission was now entirely dependent on Sergeant Neffinger getting his story straight. And him being able to convey the message to the visitors in such a way there would be no mistakes and no misunderstandings that could prove fatal.

The Iranians were still uncertain whether they could trust the Americans and there was still the horrible suspicion that this was all a ruse. Once they were in the base there would be little chance of them fighting their way out – sure they were a team of six Special Forces troops and fully trained and armed ready for battle. But the US forces on the base numbered more than five thousand, not to mention other nationalities none of which would have much sympathy for what they were about to do. The intelligence officer who had set it all up had been extremely confident as people in his business tended to be. But Haji, or whatever his name was, was not the one who had actually to carry out the mission. And Haji was probably ready to leave Turkey the instant there was the slightest hint that things were turning pear-shaped.

And he would have plenty of time to come up with a

plausible story for his masters in Teheran of why the elite troops had failed in their mission due to their incompetence.

The American sergeant directed the ambulance and the truck towards the designated park on the south side of the base and close to one of the bunkers that lined that area.

The base covered a large area most of which was solid concrete and that suited the Iranians just fine. They unloaded the poles from the truck and erected the structure over which they would mount the tent covers. Anyone who was watching would have assumed that this was the first time that the men had made such an erection which would not have been the expected outcome. But they were in the middle of an epidemic, so these things were to be expected.

And then waited for their patients to come to them.

That is what the people at the base were supposed to see. What would happen was technically similar, but very different in its detail. To implement the plan would require speed and it would require many parts to come together. And a certain amount of luck.

The base administration had prepared a list of people who should receive the vaccine and in what order. At the request of the Hospital, they had been divided into groups of a maximum of twenty because that was the number that could be accommodated in the holding tent at any one time. And it made the management of the process fairly simple. People were to be delivered to the inoculation point in a couple of buses except for a maintenance group that had its transport. The only thing that concerned the Iranians was the position on the list of this latter group - the Army aviation maintenance group identified as Ag6416. That group was correctly placed on the list at position seven within the first one hundred forty. Correctly placed by an admin clerk who had been paid a suitable sum to ensure that this was done.

After receiving the vaccine each group had to wait for between twenty and thirty minutes in case anyone suffered a reaction before being released back to their normal duties. It did not require a rocket scientist to work out that at that rate it would take about two weeks to vaccinate the entire airbase personnel. Something should be done about that. The USAF base commander Colonel David Eaglin would probably need to talk to someone at the hospital and that someone would need to talk to someone from the World Health Organization.

The Colonel did not know it yet, but he would have more serious things to worry about.

The call was finally put through to the base administration office. The paramedics were treating group five on the list and the bus carrying group six was about to begin the short journey across the airfield.

'We have enough vaccines to do one more group of twenty, then we can do a group of ten which will be number seven on your list. Everything is going well, and we have proven the system is working. We will finish with group seven, leave our tents here and return tomorrow.'

'Thank you so much. Your work is appreciated!' came the reply from the clerk who took the call.

Further to the east of the parking area, a United States Army maintenance crew of five men and one woman were working on the contents of hardened aircraft shelter number 57. The work simply involved checking the serial number of a B61 nuclear bomb, checking that the storage area was dry and clean and that was their job complete for another day. Having conducted this boring job countless times in the past, the crew were quite pleased to be greeted by another officer although they were bemused by his arrival in an ambulance. However – speaking in perfect English – well as perfect as someone born in Teheran but educated in the Bronx could speak – the driver patiently explained that they were worried about the outbreak in Adana and even more worried that it was suspected of having spread to Incirlik, and therefore they had received authorization from Colonel David Eaglin to vaccinate this small group as well as providing vaccinations to everyone who wanted one. The maintenance crew had of course been briefed on the procedure but appreciated the medics taking the time to explain what this was all about.

Having been assured that there would be no ill effects, the six people agreed to have the vaccine and came into one of the tents. A second officer got out of the ambulance to help the man. Not that he needed any help.

While the first man was injecting the woman with neutral saline, the second man sprayed an aerosol can in the face of all five of the men and promptly rendered them immobile. The drug in the aerosol can had nothing to do with the SARS-like illness that was taking its course in Adana. It was a drug very recently developed by Georgetown University Hospital, stolen by Iran, and was used in this mission without any knowledge of its effectiveness. But it seemed to work.

Time was now of the essence.

The truck was quickly backed up to the storage area while the men poured out of the rear of the ambulance and the six unconscious Army personnel were pushed inside in their place. The visitors outnumbered the residents, but the odds were that it would not matter. The ambulance was backed into a parking space while the truck was parked alongside. One of the men armed with a Browning semi-automatic pistol escorted the lady to the fork-lift hoist that was parked outside the shelter. Sitting beside her with the pistol held against her ribs he instructed her to drive directly into the nearest bunker, use her code to gain access through the door, and load the nearest bomb onto the hoist.

There was a moment of panic as a Lockheed C-141Starlifter transport plane roared into land not more than a hundred yards from where they were. The leading trooper signaled to his man to quickly get the bomb on board the truck and signaled the other men to get set to leave. He smiled at the fear that had temporarily gripped his men. There are very few windows in the aircraft so no one would be looking. It looked as though their mission would be a success.

The co-pilot of the C-141 nearly jumped out of the seat. He scrambled to interrupt the pilot who was talking to the control tower. 'Shit! Did you see that? Someone just loaded a bomb into that truck!'

The pilot looked to his left.

'Are you sure?'

'Of course, I am fucking sure – I will call it in!

'Tower this is Lockheed C-141 landing on runway 1. Something is happening to the south of the perimeter. It may be routine – but it sure as hell don't look like it.'

'Ok flight – checking it out. You can continue to gate 4'.

'Security – Tower here. We have just had a report of unusual activity at the southwest end of the base. Recommend you check it out.'

'Ok – Roger that. Confirm disturbance at southwest.

Inside or outside the perimeter.'

'Not certain. Report by landing aircraft. Sounds serious.'

'Ok – I am onto it.'

'Mobile unit 13. Disturbance at location parking area west of bunker 57. Check and report. Over.'

'Mobile 13 to base. Going over there now.'

There was a moments' hesitation, then he was back on the radio.

'Mobile 13 to Base – there is a truck heading west from that location. Looks like he is heading out the main gate. Recommend you warn the Gate and have it checked. We are heading for bunker 57 – there is something wrong!'

'Roger that.'

'Gate number 2 – you have a truck heading your way. Recommend you detain and check. I am activating the alarm. Repeat alarms are active now.'

The base alarm started to sound as the truck rushed towards the gate. Sergeant Neffinger was still on duty but what was he to do? All had seemed fairly straightforward when he had let the truck in. Now alarms were going off everywhere and he had been instructed by his base to check the truck.

Now that was not part of the plan.

He could see the truck thundering towards the guard post.

It looked unlikely that the truck either would or could, stop before hitting the gate. He was confident that the gate was strong enough to stop a truck. The truck was the one that he had cleared earlier, and he had not followed the correct procedure. So - he would be in the shit anyway. But he did not know what to do!

What made his mind up for him was the sight of two armed guards taking up positions on either side of the gate. Sergeant Neffinger had never been the bravest in this Army and so he leaped for cover fearing what would happen when the impact came. The two brave soldiers were shot dead by people leaning out of the truck before they could raise their rifles. Then the front window of the truck on the passenger side was pushed out and a shoulder rocket launcher appeared which looked similar to the US Javelin anti-tank weapon. That caused an explosion that blew away most of the barrier gate.

The next rocket was aimed at the guard hut and the hut disintegrated and ended the life of the man who was responsible for letting the truck into the base in the first place. Before any of the base personnel could react, the truck screeched to a temporary halt as four heavily armed men leaped out and stormed towards the remnants of the barrier.

That is where the plan almost failed.

While two of the men struggled to remove the debris and the other two scanned the surrounding area for any signs of opposition, base security managed to shoot both of the lookouts. One of them had his right leg shattered and was in so much agony he would take no further part in the afternoons' events. The second one was hit in the head and was probably dead before his body had crumbled to the ground. Had Americans shot the two men clearing the debris first there would have been a very different outcome. As it was there was now just enough space for the truck to squeeze through the gap. And it did, to the annoyance of the two who had cleared the way, as they were pounced on by the gathering security detail.

Armed men scrambled into two armed vehicles that had been positioned by the entrance to the base for just such an event. Well – not quite. The MRAPs had been positioned inside the gate to pursue anyone who broke into the base, so it took a few extra seconds to get them facing the right way. They crunched over the remnants of the barrier gate and set off in hot pursuit of the truck.

The Iranian truck was three hundred yards ahead but would be no match for the pursuing vehicles once they got up to speed. Both of the following trucks were similar to the RG 33 MRAP – Mine Resistant Ambush Protected vehicles with a top speed of around seventy mph, but with a brute of an engine. On the road leading to Adana, the drivers of the MRAPs were confident that they would soon overhaul the truck.

The driver of the Iranian truck could see the Americans coming through the rear-vision mirrors and was aware of the relative speed. It would not be long before he would be overtaken. He could not do anything about it because there was no position from which they could fire their weapons. And he was down to himself, and one other having left two behind and seen two of his men shot and probably dead.

The truck took a high-speed right-hand turn, then a left and a final left turn hoping that his memory had not failed him.

The American MRAPs tried to follow but were delayed picking their way through the vehicles and people who had crashed or been scattered avoiding the Iranian truck. They had seen the truck take a corner to their right. They suspected that it had then turned left because, if it had gone straight ahead, they would have been able to see it.

They turned left.

The Iranian truck had vanished.

Chapter 40

Checkmate

The United States military services are not equipped to search for stolen nuclear weapons probably because it is not a situation that arises very often. No one at Incirlik airbase had a clue what they should do next other than to seek help from the Pentagon. The Base Commander - USAF Colonel David Eaglin - saw his dreams of promotion disappear before his eyes. He had done well for a working-class kid from the Broncs albeit that his career path had been blocked by something as simple as an eye test. The test had somehow concluded that he was color blind. So – Eaglin's flying days were over. He faced the choice of becoming a desk puke in the Air Force or trying his luck in private enterprise. In the latter case that would have meant becoming a bus or truck driver which was the Air Force definition of civilian pilots. He had opted to stay in the Air Force and had only recently been asked to take command of the Incirlik Airbase. Up until the last couple of weeks that had been going well. And he had even improved his golf handicap.

Now he faced a couple of problems that no one could

have foreseen, but for which he would be blamed for the simple reason that they had both occurred on his watch.

The first task that the Colonel faced was reporting to his superiors in Washington DC the loss of one of the US strategic weapons. Well – that was a bit of a laugh. The weapons had been stored at Incirlik years ago as part of the nuclear strike force in pursuit of the cold war with the Soviet Union. That had no relevance to present-day conditions. It was inconceivable that they would play any part in any NATO or US field operations that were planned for the future. For years many had suggested that they be moved considering their proximity to the middle east conflicts, but nothing had been done. Still – they were still classified as strategic so that meant that someone would be interested.

Of much more importance to Eaglin was that three of his men had lost their lives in just simply performing their normal duties. Who would remember that when all the dust had settled? The answer was that no one would. No – they would remember the name of the Base Commander.

In the end, to fulfill his first task – he sent a message to his commander in the Pentagon with a copy to the Turkish Ambassador in Ankara.

Classification: Secret – Eyes Only
From: 39 ABW Incirlik Turkey
Report at 1714 hours TRT. Incident at Incirlik Airbase. Three air force fatalities. Two people are in custody believed part of the raiding party. One B61 is unaccounted for.
More details follow. Request instructions.
Col. D. Eaglin USAF

The second task was much simpler. Eaglin gathered

together his senior staff to find out what had happened. Despite the loss of life, the focus of immediate attention had to be on security and why it had failed. While he felt sorry for the head of the 39th Mission Support Group which managed security on the base, the man who did the work was a non-commissioned officer of Master Sergeant rank so he would take instructions rather than requests.

'I want all the people who were on duty at the main gate at the time those two vehicles entered the base placed in custody. I also want those who were on the gate at the time of the truck's departure also in custody. From now until further notice the security at all points is to be doubled. And no one gets into or out of this base without written authority from God himself. Is that understood?'

It was.

'Now – where are we keeping our guests?'

Squadron leader Simon Tolley who headed the support group had to answer that having sent his Master Sergeant to carry out the boss's earlier instructions.

'We are holding them in the detention facility under guard,' came the reply which Tolley knew would be inadequate. Everyone was in trouble with the Colonel in this mood and they would just have to take it.

'What language do they speak?' Eaglin next asked. He got no reply.

'Ok – I want the two of them isolated and we will try to see if their stories are the same. Have them examined by Shoebridge – just to make sure they are fit and healthy you understand. She speaks a bit of the local language as well as can understand a bit of Arabic. I want to know if these men are Hezbollah – and quickly. If they are not, this may be a bigger problem than we think.'

Tolley used his cell phone to issue instructions. It was going to be a long day for the squadron leader. There were still questions about the security and how the hell people had got into the base. And they had still to get to the real issue.

Where the hell had the bomb gone?

As an Air Force officer, Eaglin had flown a variety of US aircraft bombers that were meant to deliver death and destruction to whoever lay in his flight path. But he had little idea of the technology involved.

The next thing that Eaglin did, before he rang the Pentagon to offer his resignation, was talking to one of his senior engineers in the hope that he could shed some light on the dilemma. Like how do you find a lost bomb? That resulted in the Flight Lieutenant calling in one of his E6 Technical Sergeants for the simple reason that she had recently been on a course back in the States which had included a session on Nuclear Quadrupole Resonance or NQR. Not that either the Lieutenant or the Colonel would have any idea what that was all about. But it at least gave them some confidence that there could be a solution.

The sergeant got as far as patiently explaining that NQR was a radio-frequency technique that could be used to detect the presence of quadrupolar nuclei prevalent in many explosives. At which stage Eaglin had a much simpler question.

'Is there a device or a sensor that can be used to detect a bomb?'

Without knowing what had triggered the question that had been asked, the sergeant began to explain the work done by the National Reconnaissance Office in their endeavors to detect nuclear weapon sites that were not so obvious by their physical characteristics – like to find mobile launch sites versus silos. The fact that they had given up on any hope of being able to do that from a satellite using NQR technology was what she thought the boss needed to know. She was probably the only person on the base who did not know that a bomb had gone missing

– after all, it was beyond anyone's ability to keep secrets on a base like Incirlik.

That caused Eaglin to take the sergeant into his confidence.

'I don't give a rat's fart what they might want to do. This is for your ears only at this stage. Someone has stolen one of our bombs. How do we find it? Is there a device that we can get that can read the fucking thing before it gets too far?'

The sergeant was about to say that the course she went on did not cover that. But she was now starting to think about her promotion. So – she took the easy way out.

'Yes, Sir – I am sure there is. But it is not a device that we have here,'

'Ok – find out all you can, and report back inside one hour. Whatever you engineers have got in your toolbox – I want one! And I don't care where it comes from!'

'Ok – next subject – tell me exactly what happened when we lost sight of the bomb. It is not the kind of thing that can just disappear so easily – is it?'

Tolley did not have all the answers to that question, but he tried. He was only too well aware that the Security Force Squadron (SFS) was under pressure, and it did not help that his boss was absent from the base – summoned to Ankara to attend yet another course in security management – which he needed about as much as he needed a hole in the head! He was also aware that the airbase had a code of conduct that said *See something – Say something*. That had happened in this case. It was just that they still could not find the bomb!

'We had our security force following the truck out of the base after they crashed through the gate. It was decided to use a couple of M-Gators because they can get into places where other vehicles cannot. But we never expected that someone would break *out* of the base. So - our vehicles were on the wrong side of the gate which caused some delay. They followed up the road to Adana but lost track momentarily due to the carnage caused by the truck. Reports say that they knew the direction that the truck was headed. But it just vanished in the industrial area, and they could not regain contact. My men radioed back to the base for help and that was sent immediately. They have so far been unable to find any trace.'

Eaglin eyed Tolley for a moment unsure what to say. What he wanted to do was bark in frustration which was the usual military way of responding when something went wrong. But – it wasn't Tolley's fault - was it? Something did not seem to be quite right. Was it a coincidence that this had occurred at the precise time when Lieutenant Colonel Prescott had been absent on a nonsensical course? And who would have arranged that? US Army Colonel Samuel J. Henning. And who decreed the security arrangements for the base? Henning!

'Could you please get for me a copy of the personnel appointments to the schedule for the western guard gate for the last few days? I want to see whether anything has happened that could be described as unusual. I am not saying that anything is wrong. It just seems to me that there could have been an error and I want any chance of that eliminated.'

While his staff struggled to get the information that the base commander had demanded, it was time for the stakes to be raised. He was about to pick up the telephone to make a call when it rang anyway.

'Yes – Amy. We are rather busy here. So - it had better be important!'

Amy Shoebridge was petrified. The last time she had to contact the Base Commander was to deliver the bad news about the SARS outbreak. She wasn't sure that today's news would be any better.

'I had a call from the Acibadem Hospital querying why their paramedics had not returned. So – I drove over to the site where they were doing their vaccinations to find out how long they would be. What I found was that the ambulance and tents were still there but no sign of the paramedics. However – in the tent I found six of our maintenance staff suffering from a drug overdose. I have them in the sickbay and it looks like they will be Ok.'

Then she lost it.

'I am sorry!' she sobbed. 'I have been so busy; I did not know what happened at the gate. Is this something to do with why you are having a meeting?'

'Ok – It is not your fault Lieutenant! We are all having a bad day! Have one of your staff call back the hospital and tell them – we have a problem and will get back to them soon. You come in here and join us. I am about to have a heart attack.'

The day would not get any better for the colonel.

Eaglin rang Brigadier General Ian Corbin who was the Defense Attaché at the US Embassy in Ankara. At least the Brigadier was Air Force, and that should count for something.

'Hi, Ian. How was your day?'

'Better than yours – I guess!'

That told Eaglin something important – The Ambassador had little respect for the security classification of eyes only!

'Yeah – well shit happens! There are two things that you could help me with if you can. Firstly – I believe Colonel Prescott is on some course or other in Ankara – I would like him back in a hurry. Secondly – I have to have some help in sorting out this mess. I know that there are a couple of FBI guys at your Embassy. Could you use your influence to have them released to us for a couple of days? There are a couple of things they can do for us. We still do not know how these people got into the base. It looks as though they either came from the Adana Hospital or they somehow replaced the paramedics. And we have other fatalities to investigate.'

Corbin could have been more sympathetic but, in all fairness, he had other more important issues to deal with. Like how to avoid being tainted by what could become an embarrassing situation.

'Prescott I can manage. I will talk to Henning and have Prescott released at once. As for the FBI – that is a little outside my area. You could talk to James Bayer. However, I do not know if the CIA is up the play on this one. At least not yet.'

That told Eaglin something else. Bayer was the spook in Ankara.

Since Eaglin and Corbin had once been friends (which in Air Force terminology meant they had been of equal rank on the same base – admittedly as Captains) they did at times speak frankly to each other. But someone at Langley would have a fit at the clear lack of security in discussing matters of this nature.

Eaglin decided to push his luck. He was in the shit anyway.

'I thought it might have more effect if you were to have a quiet word with the Ambassador. While I have still to hear back from the powers that be at the Pentagon, I cannot afford to wait. At the same time – I don't want it to appear that I am jumping the gun. But – you know how these things work – Damned if I do, Damned if I don't. We can always send them back!'

More out of annoyance than anything else, Corbin agreed. And that worked. A secretary from the Embassy staff rang a secretary at the Incirlik airbase to confirm that two people should be expected to arrive by air shortly and required accommodation befitting officers of the FBI.

Any satisfaction that Eaglin may have felt from his discussion with Corbin was quickly dashed by his next call. That came from Brigadier General Terry Grant at the Pentagon – someone who had not crossed the path of the Colonel before this evening.

'We were expecting a full report on your incident. I have been asked to check on where you are at!' came the question from the arrogant punk whose only job in life was driving a desk.

Eaglin was seething and his response was hardly proper.

'I haven't had time for that, and to write out my letter of resignation as well! We are a little busy here!' Was the best that the Colonel could deliver.

'Oh – spare me the drama, David! We can get around to talking about your future later. Meanwhile, I have a report to provide for the President and he wants that yesterday. Can you at least give me a verbal rundown on what the fuck happened and then maybe we can all avoid early retirement! For now!'

Peter Fairfield - the Director of National Intelligence - was not happy that he had all the facts. The only thing in his favor was the fact that CNN had not yet reported the problem that this meeting was all about.

Fairfield had spoken to the Presidents' Chief of Staff - Nicolas Harrison - earlier in the day to try to find a spot in the President's busy schedule. He had stressed that he had matters of extreme importance that he had to bring to the attention of the Commander in Chief while trying not to cause too much panic. The real trouble for Fairfield was that - no matter how he spun it – there was one certain fact.

The United States had lost track of one of its nuclear bombs.

What he could have done is pass the buck to Barry Crammer who, as Secretary of Defense, was ultimately responsible for taking care of such strategic assets. He was just unsure whether Crammer would know anything about it. The original message had been addressed to the Pentagon. But someone in signals had realized the importance of the message and copied it to his office. And then he had to decide what to do with it. The Secretary of Defense would certainly have to be informed, as would the National Security Advisor and the Chairman of the Joint Chiefs. The State Department would need to be involved because at least one other nation would be implicated. And possibly two if his briefing from the CIA was to be believed. And he was just as certain that the Attorney General would have to be involved since there were dead bodies to worry about. Unfortunately, he would also have to inform the Vice President although that was a political decision that someone else could make.

The Oval Office in the White House is not the largest room in the building and all these people would not fit in. Consequently, Harrison decided that they should use the Situation room which was located in the West Wing basement. The DNI was fearful that this was a little over-dramatic but was past caring by the time they all got together. At least the added drama meant that what he had to say would be taken seriously.

The President thanked everyone for coming. But – having no idea what the meeting was all about - he then turned to the DNI.

'Well Peter – you called this meeting – I understand

you have something to tell us. Must be more important than a change in the brand of toilet paper being used in the Kremlin!'

No one laughed. This President would soon learn that meetings in this room were not the place where you could make jokes. Especially ones that were so old.

Fairfield chose to ignore BJ's flippant comment.

'Mister President! We have a report from the commander of one of our military bases in Turkey that they have lost one of our strategic weapons. We are still awaiting full details, but the preliminary reports are suggesting that the bomb was removed during a routine medical check on-base personnel.'

He had no choice but to pause. The babble of noise and gasps from the attendees stunned Fairfield. He demurred to the President.

'How could that happen?' was the inept question from the President. But it was a good question since it reflected what everyone else was thinking. And a question to which nobody had an answer.

'We just do not know yet Sir. The Base Commander has sought instructions because there would be repercussions from the Turkish government. And the issue for us is – on the assumption that the bomb was stolen by a foreign power or by someone acting on behalf of a foreign power – they will try to cross the Turkish border which we cannot control. We can hardly ask the Turkish border control people to be on the lookout for one of our bombs!'

A better question would have been – Who would have the balls to try?

Peter Fairfield and Bruce Aderholt – the National Security Advisor – were the only two people in the room who were privy to a source of information that the CIA had developed to provide them with information from within the Iranian administration. That source was so secret and so closely guarded that its very existence was known only to a few. Which *few* did not include the President. The source was so delicate that no attempt was made to verify the information that came from it for fear that such an act alone could cause their source to be compromised. The real scary thing was that the CIA was concerned about a possible leak within this administration. Such was that concern that, in case of the prospect of a compromise, arrangements were in place to shut down the source.

Unaware of the minefield he was stepping into, President Thomas felt he should lead the discussion. So - he asked another question.

'Ok – so what are we doing about it?'

Crammer, who could see that his department of Defense would be under threat sooner rather than later, felt inclined to say something.

He should have remained quiet.

'There are procedures to follow on this!'

That brought an instant response from Admiral Mullen.

'When was the last time we lost a nuclear bomb, Barry?'

The stunned silence that followed caused the Chairman of the Joint Chiefs of Staff to continue before someone in the room came up with the answer to his question. Half a dozen nuclear bombs had been lost in the past and, what was more significant, they had never been recovered. But the facts were that the bombs were useless to someone who could not gain access to the firing mechanism and whoever had them had – probably - long since abandoned whatever sick plan they had. For now, someone had to bring the meeting back into the real world.

'Ok – we have *lost* a bomb. It is not the kind of device

that can be easily triggered by a bunch of terrorists. The particular devices stored at Incirlik are shaped like traditional bombs. And they have to be dropped from an aircraft that can both carry them and release them. That is no trivial task. The codes to activate a nuclear bomb are probably the most guarded secret in the world. If those codes had been stolen - or compromised in any way - I feel sure that we would know about it. I, therefore, assess the risk of someone – or some nation-state – threatening the United States with a nuclear bomb as very low. What we should be focusing our attention on is - Who carried out the theft? And - Where is the bomb? I am not qualified to comment on the intelligence assessment – but if you want my opinion – whoever orchestrated the SAR's epidemic in southern Turkey did it with the clear intention of using it as a cover so that they had the opportunity to raid the base and steal the bomb.'

The comments put the pressure right back where it belonged – between the DNI and the NSA. Peter Fairfield was the first to react.

'We assess that it is the Iranians. They have been a source of many of our recent problems in the middle east. The CIA has been alerted to the presence of their agents in Turkey since the shambles in Sudan.'

President Thomas turned deathly white and almost shouted.

'What shambles?'

Aderholt had to own up to that one.

'Sir! We were waiting until we could clarify the facts. The people who were arrested by the Sudanese police following the problems at the meeting of the African Union in Khartoum escaped. Our information now is that they are probably in Turkey.'

Vice President Roger Warren had remained silent during the meeting. Although he knew that he was not the most popular member of the presidents' inner circle, he nonetheless had excellent sources of information. He could not resist the temptation to take part.

'Do I read you correctly? You are now saying that your friend – Mohamed Haji is the name that I seem to recall – went from Sudan to Turkey. And all you can say is that you understand that he is probably in Turkey. That is even though he is on your *most wanted* list. What happened to the team that BJ had authorized to follow him? And we were given to understand that they succeeded in doing that – were we not? At least you had your CIA take full credit for their success. And now you can neither confirm nor deny where Haji is. Well – what happened to the non-CIA team that seemed to be the only people in your organization that is capable of following him? Where are they now?'

Fairfield fielded that question.

'We understand that they are in Afghanistan.'

At that point, the President lost the plot.

'Why does everyone in this government always pre-empt their comments with – *'We understand'* Peter! You either know or you do not know. Now – where the fuck are they?'

Chapter 41

Reorganization

During the time that the Imam was making his statement about what he expected to happen, Blake had reached his hand behind his back and rested his fingers on the trigger of his pistol. It was then a matter of getting the man with the AK-47 to rise just far enough out of the chair to give Blake a reasonable target to aim at.

The fact that the likes of John Wayne could pull a six-shooter out of a holster and shoot a man with deadly accuracy one hundred yards away - and in the blink of an eye - was fanciful at best. Especially with a gun that was lacking in the balance characteristics of modern weapons. Even so, the best shot in the world would be lucky to hit a target that was more than twenty feet away. Blake estimated that the man was about twenty feet away, so he was reasonably confident he could hit the target. The question was – where would he hit? And he had to be sure. His target was holding a semi-automatic AK-47 and an injured target could spray the room with bullets in seconds. So – he had only one chance. And that shot had to be fatal.

He spoke in a calm voice -which did not reflect the way he was feeling.

'Dusty – How about you bring the Imam to the doorway? I want him to see what happens now!'

Dusty only knew that he had to trust his instincts. Blake had a plan, and that was good enough. With enormous strength in his arms, Dusty lifted the diminutive Imam and carried him to the doorway.

And it worked.

The man sitting at the side of the bed involuntarily rose from his chair muttering what must have been the Farsi equivalent of 'What goes on?' and raising his rifle towards Dusty. Well – actually towards the Imam, who was between Dusty and the man holding the AK-47. That caused the man to hesitate. That gave Blake the only opportunity he needed.

In such a confined space the bark of the pistol was shattering. The man with the AK-47 looked shocked as the bullet hit his spleen, then confused as the rest of his body refused to accept any instructions from his brain. With a final realization that he was about to die, he collapsed in a heap on the floor.

The noise affected the body that lay on the bed.

It moved.

Blake threw the pistol to one side and rushed to the bed. He tore the blindfold off her eyes and ripped the tape from her mouth. Tears streamed from his eyes. Misha started to cry as he tore at the ropes that held her down until she was free. And when she was, she just clung to Blake and sobbed.

Dusty had other things to do. Still holding the Imam, he punched him in the mid-rift and then hammered him in the head knocking the guy out cold. He then tore strips of cloth from the Imam's dress, bound his hands and feet, added a blindfold, and gagged him. Ben and

Owen, taking the cue from Dusty, quickly did the same thing to the other two men and the lady who claimed to be Mina's aunt. All three of them had been cowering in the corner. Suitably bound that is where they were returned together with the immobile Imam and the dead body of the man from the bedroom.

A group of four members of the SAS squadron assumed positions guarding the prisoners, while the rest were surrounding the house to ensure that no one left without a valid reason. And that no one could get in.

Only then did Dusty say anything. He lifted his left arm and spoke into his communicator.

'Mark – I think it is safe for you and Mina to come in now.'

Mark entered the front door holding on to Mina. She looked scared with tears streaming down her face and looked barely able to stand. The first thing she saw was the bundle of bodies thrown into the corner. There was no reaction at all.

She looked at Dusty, wondering why he was dripping with sweat. She would have no understanding of the exertion necessary to hold that weasel by the throat for so long. Dusty for his part, simply pointed towards the bedroom door and stood to one side. Despite the energy that he had spent he had a reassuring smile on his face.

Blake was sitting on the bed with Misha hung around his neck like a ragdoll. At first, Mina rushed towards the bed. Then she stopped before quietly sitting beside Blake and trying to put an arm around his huge shoulders. And then a strange thing happened. Blake lifted his arm to cradle Mina and then offered and was rewarded with the most heartfelt kiss. Misha must have sensed something for she turned to see what was happening. And then all three of them clung to each other and burst into tears.

Mark and Owen sat on a couple of chairs while Owen quizzed the old lady that they had brought to the house. There was no hurry. To make sure that there was no misunderstanding Owen spoke in Dari and then translated it into English. What he wanted to know was what had been her role in organizing this group of thugs. Seemingly having got the answer he expected, he turned his attention to the remaining two tea-drinkers. That told him nothing. He then turned his attention to the Imam, although there seemed to be the little point since he was still out cold.

Or was he?

The frustration that Mark felt at the lack of progress began to take its toll. So - he asked Owen to speak to the inert body of the Imam in Dari.

'Since the Imam is unconscious, we may as well bury him as is. There is no point in our wasting ammunition or dirtying one of our knives on that scum!' That got a reaction.

So – the Imam was alive and probably would have heard all the discussion with his associates. That had been a one-sided conversation. Mark decided that there was no point in repeating what had already been asked of the other men.

The next move was to get Major Ross McKinnon to join the conversation. Although Mark and his team could work independently of the SAS, he felt that he owed them something, and so he was inclined to include them in whatever decisions he made now.

'Ok - All of them deny any knowledge of the explosive vest blaming it on the man who has mysteriously disappeared. The lady appeared to be mortified by the death of Mina but at the same time does not seem to be surprised' he said with a smile. 'Both of these men seemed satisfied that they had achieved something and so I think they were part of the original deal. But – we will not shoot them yet! We need to have a further conversation in front of a Judge. My original opinion was that we leave the lady here but now I think she is guilty by association. Therefore, we take them all off to the dock at the US base where they can rot in hell. I don't think we want to take them to the police because anything could happen – like they could be back out on the street the instant our back is turned. We had better take the body of the dead man with us as well because of the way that these people operate - they will want to parade him as a martyr in the street for everyone to see. As for the Imam – he is the leader of the group. So - he will be sentenced to death. All in all – a good day's work! Any comments?'

Nobody had anything more to say – except Dusty.

'I thought the Rules of Engagement were of your choosing? Why don't we just finish them all off now? Why go to the trouble of transporting them anywhere?'

Mark could understand why Dusty was intent on ending the lives of all four people in the house – and having them join the one who had already departed this life. They would probably be let out again whichever place they took them to. It was not that even the Americans in this country seemed to accept the inevitable. It was just that, if you locked up everyone who had been involved in a misdemeanor, that would account for more than half the population of the country.

The final decision was made for them by the wonders of modern technology. A strange beep sounded in the room which took everyone by surprise. This was followed by a robotic voice in Dari which Owen translated.

'You have mail'

The sound came from behind the couch.

And there it was. A laptop computer of indeterminate age was sitting on a small table behind the couch. It was connected to a router and the telephone network. What would the Imam want with a laptop? Although Afghanistan only had 4G communications, that could still connect to the internet. It did seem a bit of a stretch, but it could supply the answer to the puzzle that had been bugging Mark since this whole mission had started – Why did the people he was following always seem to know where he was?

The answer could be that they were communicating over the internet.

With an air of anticipation, Mark got onto the keyboard and fired up Outlook. There was no password needed so the screen was soon displaying the most recent email message. Mark would have expected a message that made sense and indicated where the message had come from. He was disappointed on both counts.

The email message in English read:

'You have mail!' followed by gibberish that read *NM10V25*.

That could only mean that – Yes there was a message – But wherever that message was, it certainly was not in this email.

The *'Sender'* name however was printed in a language which Mark could not recognize and Owen had no clue. He right clicked on the message, got the Find *Related* option, and clicked on *Messages from Sender* option. That produced nothing helpful. In frustration, he disconnected the laptop and packed it up. He decided that he would take it with them. Then he would get Brad Morgan from his office in New York to connect and download the entire system.

Mark did not know how close he had come to find out

how the Iranians were communicating with each other. And their friends in the Taliban.

Mark went into the bedroom where Blake and the Meskin girls were. They had to get moving but he was still anxious that Mina should stay hidden until they had resolved the question of what to do with the Imam and his friends. Dusty and Owen, with help of the SAS force, got their prisoners out of the house, together with the body of their dead colleague.

It took a bit of fiddling to get all the parts in a place so that they could maintain the illusion that Mark and Mina were not amongst the living. It simply meant that their prisoners would be held in one of the trucks while Mark and Mina would travel with the SAS. When the two teams arrived back at the Farah airport base the prisoners had to be locked away before the team would be satisfied.

Mark had decided that the team should stay at the base overnight having had enough excitement for one day.

Despite the problems that they had along the way Mark was content that they had successfully proven what was happening on the border. Drugs were being supplied by the Taliban in exchange for guns. And they had fingered Iran as a primary player in this deadly game. He now had photographs of the various transaction. He had samples of the drugs. He had a supply of new guns captured from the Taliban. And the guns were of Iranian manufacture.

Now he had a laptop that seemed to be part of the system of communications but, despite his knowledge of computers, he was dependent on others to decipher the riddle. But could he rely on the antiquated Afghan telephone system to be secure enough to enable that?

Probably not.

So - all that was left for him to do was to get the hell out of Afghanistan and get this information to someone who could do something about it.

McKinnon came to see Mark just before they both turned in for the night.

'I have been talking to the people that pull our strings. When we get back to Kandahar my team is due to be rotated out of this hellhole for some R and R. I have asked if we can give you and your team a lift because I understand we will have a stop-over in Turkey. Just a thought.'

Mark had yet to talk to anyone in Washington so he may not have been up with the play. But McKinnon had been talking to someone – probably in London – who knew far more about what Mark and his team were going to be asked to do next than he did.

The smile on Marks' face could have been misinterpreted by the SAS officer as one that signaled that he was trying to hide what he knew. If it was an attempt to hide something, it was wide of the mark. Mark was just amused by the British ability to always manage to be one step ahead of their American colleagues. And he was also very much aware that he was not part of the diplomatic and intelligence services that made an art form out of keeping secrets. When it suited them. So - he would be the very last to hear of any plans made by his masters.

Instead of pursuing the subject with McKinnon, he just said 'Let's get some sleep. Thanks for the offer. We may take you up on that depending on the instructions I receive when we get back to Kandahar.'

The trip from Farah to Kandahar was achieved without much fuss. The British SAS forces were evenly spread through the small convoy and their presence would distract any attention from both the Taliban and any of the other terrorist cells that operated in the western provinces of Afghanistan. There were several hold-ups on the road caused by mechanical breakdowns of civilian vehicles rather than any conflicts. They simply detoured around the problem areas and there was minimum disruption to their journey.

Mark had deliberately not made any contact with the DEA or any other US people who may have had an interest in their progress. He used the time while others did the driving to think of what he was going to say and do once they were safely back in the Kandahar airbase. He was anxious to move but he had some logistics to worry about and, while he now had a clear idea of the next move, eight other men had to have a say in any decisions he made now. And there was a couple of ladies that had joined his group who would need to be considered.

He had thought of calling MI6 in Kabul and telling them to come and collect Mina and Misha and that would have been the end of that.

But – could he do that?

That Mina had not carried out the instructions that she had been given by what could only now be assumed to have been the Taliban acting on the wishes of the Iranians was one factor that caused Mark to pause. It was the primary factor that tipped the balance in favor of his considering something else. Then he had two other questions to find answers to. Of some importance was - What did Mina want to do? But of paramount importance was – What did Blake Whittaker want to do?

In the cold light of day personal opinions and feelings had no place in making decisions that would affect a mission. At least that would have been the position five or six years ago when Mark was commanding a company of US elite troops doing the bidding of the government of the

United States. Now he had a group of men who looked to Mark Taylor as their leader and who would respect any decision that he made.

But it was not as easy as that in the present circumstances - was it?

Blake had been dealt a cruel hand when his wife had been killed. He did not complain. Just did his job. As well as could be expected of any man. And better than most. That was not sufficient to explain why he had been the first to go to Misha's aid when she was upset by the conflict that she had been thrust into the middle of. The explanation was that the man cared for the little one probably because he could relate to that through his own experience. The girl was the same age as his daughters. And she was at an age where she was vulnerable. Also - the girl was partially blind and anyone who was even half-decent would desperately want to help. But beyond that, there was another reason.

Blake had fallen in love with their mother.

After they had settled into the Kandahar base Mark instructed his team that he would need to talk to the whole group about what they were to do next. He could only give them an hour to consider their position.

He had a message waiting for him in Kandahar. And it was a message that he could hardly ignore despite its simplicity.

When you return to Kandahar – call the office of the Director of National Intelligence. Priority – Immediate. Subject Operation Steel Tiger.

In ordinary circumstances, a team would receive instructions through the local US representatives. That would have meant the Kandahar base commander for the simple reason that the Ambassador was unlikely to travel to the south of Afghanistan to deliver a message to a Major.

Mark called Washington on his satellite phone confident that the security would be better than any official communications device that the base could provide. The DNI was part of the Department of Defense so calling the Pentagon was the first step. When he said who was calling and the subject Mark was immediately patched to one of the Assistant Directors – for Policy and Strategy – a gentleman who said his name was Roy Sherman. Mark was relieved that he was a civilian. And one that seemed to know what he was talking about, even if he was reading from a set of instructions passed down the chain of command. He did not say how long that chain was. At least he never mentioned the President by his title or his name.

'We have had indications that there is some trouble in Turkey, apparently caused by someone who you will be familiar with – Mohamed Haji. We want you to go there and see if you can put a stop to it. We understand that you have a team of eight men. We will leave it to you to decide how many of them you will need and how you get there. And as before – you can decide on the rules of engagement. Now, do you have any questions?'

Yes – Mark did have some questions. Like – Why should he care? He tried to be as polite as possible.

'I will have to discuss what you have said with my team. They may not be so keen to get involved. I will call you back when I have done that.'

Sherman was not so polite in his response.

'Taylor – you must understand that this order comes from your commander-in-chief. You do not have the choice!'

Mark was still polite in his response.

'Then you have better ask the Commander-in-chief to call me himself.'

Mark had the intention of calling Washington when he had returned to Kandahar. It was just not what he had expected.

Deep down Mark now believed that the team would be dragged into yet another episode in this curious mission. But he was not going to be bulldozed into it by some lowly bureaucrat. And not without a clearer message of what was expected. While Sherman delivered the bad news to whoever was pulling his strings, he would have to talk to the DEA in Washington before they embarked on an excursion to the west. He would also be talking to Ross McKinnon of the SAS about any options that they may be able to provide. And, maybe, find out some more about what he knew of what had been planned for him. Maybe that would require a chat with MI6 in Kabul which office had demonstrated an amazing ability to be well ahead of anything that he knew. He would also need to talk to Brad Morgan but would wait until they were somewhere that had reasonable security before he did that.

He would not be taking to the CIA agents in Kandahar.

To the more observant members of his team that should have given them a clue of the way, he was thinking. The rest would soon catch on.

It would be a busy hour.

The first call was to Kabul. Mark felt that he at least owed MI6 that courtesy.

'Hi, Reginald – We are now back from our trip west, and thanks to you we have made it in one piece!' was his opening statement.

Mark could almost feel the relief that Smith felt. And to be fair, while he would have expected MI6 to take full credit, Reggie was much more contrite and dismissive of any role that he might have played.

'Yes – a nasty business!' Smith responded. 'I have been in touch with McKinnon, and he has filled me in on the details. Glad to help in getting the SAS to ride shotgun on that little escapade. You can thank my boss for that. So - what is your plan now?'

'Yes! Please convey my thanks to your boss. But now we have another problem. The Meskin ladies are in grave danger if they stay in Afghanistan. The Taliban will not forget what happened and frankly, I doubt whether you or anybody else can provide the protection that they will need. The fact that Larmina failed to execute the Taliban plan would be sufficient to make her forever marked. And - of course - I must owe her one for that. With your permission, I intend to do something about that. I have to talk to my team first – but are you Ok with that?'

Reggie actually laughed.

'Since I don't suppose that you intend to get rid of the Taliban the next best thing is for the Meskin's to disappear and if you can do that you will have my full support. Now one more thing we must talk about is – Have you given any thought to letting us in on your comms package? I know you have plenty of other things on your mind, but C was especially interested.'

And that summed up the whole business - didn't it? The British were friends. But friendship only went so far. The British had asked an otherwise unemployed SAS company to come to the aid of their American friends on the basis that the gesture could be of benefit in any subsequent and unrelated negotiations with an American

software company about the rights to a package. Sure –
the American government should have the first call on a
product developed by one of their own. If they did not
want it then all bets were off, and it went on the market.
Business was business.

It was now Mark's turn to laugh as he decided that
a harmless lie was called for.

'We will see how my negotiations go.' Mark replied.
'If the US doesn't want it, they could have no objection to
my selling it to one of their allies. For sure we will not be
trying to sell it to the Chinese or the Russians!'

'Fair enough. Good luck and be sure to let me know
what you decide.' and the call was terminated.

Mark next called McKinnon of the SAS.

'Hi, Ross. Its' Mark Taylor. How are your plans for
getting out of dodge?'

'You need a lift?' was McKinnon's immediate answer.

Mark had to like the no-nonsense approach from Ross.

'Well - that depends – When? And where to?'

'Ok – the timing is flexible.' McKinnon replied. 'We
have a Globemaster currently undergoing an engine
change – should be ready by noon tomorrow. There is
plenty of room if you want to come. As for where to.
Ultimately, we are heading home which is Credenhill
Herefordshire but have several stops on the way mostly in
friendly countries. The first stop will be Incirlik Turkey.

Now that just left the Drug Enforcement Agency
and that would be the hardest call to make. Not because
Mark would need to talk to his potential future mother-in-
law. But because he was not certain that she would be
receptive to what he had in mind. And that was presuming

that he could get the team to go along with his plan.

To try to make this easier he explained in an email what had happened since they departed Bagram, glossing over the difficulties they had with the attempt to blow them all up. It was not a very long email, so it did not take long to encrypt and transmit.

He called on Karen Marshall's secure line.

He got a surprisingly good reception.

'Thanks for the email – you seem to be enjoying your time in Afghanistan?'

'Yes!' Mark responded. 'Except that we seem to be in the wrong country. What we have discovered is that the Iranians are trading weapons for drugs which seems to contravene a couple of regulations around sanctions. However, more to the point – our friend Mohamed Haji appears to be now in Turkey. What I want is your permission to go into Turkey and find out what he is up to. That would mean you're extending our mission which was to trace the drugs in Afghanistan. Can you do that?'

There was a pause on the line while Marshall considered the question. There was no doubt that she was in a position where she could. The question was – would she?

A very cautious Karen finally replied.

'Mark – Are you sure that you want to do that? There is currently an outbreak of SARS in east Turkey. I understand it is not yet contained. I also understand your wish to get to the bottom of this business, but you don't want to go risking your life with something that you cannot see.'

Mark had to think about that for a second before he committed.

'We will be careful. We will be largely in the company of British SAS troops and should be Ok. The more important thing is to find out if Haji has been up to his usual tricks like he did in Harare and Khartoum. The difference is that Turkey shares a border with Iran. In any case – Turkey is a NATO country and a large one at that. An outbreak of disease should be relatively easy to avoid.'

Again - the cautious reply.

'Mark – I will support you if you think that is what you believe is the best approach. Just be careful!'

'Ok – I just need to convince the rest of the team. That should be a done deal. I will let you know within the hour.'

'Fine – just be sure to tell them about the outbreak,' Karen warned him.

Mark would do that, but first he had to ask.

'Whereabouts in Turkey is it?'

'Mark – it is at the Incirlik airbase!'

Then came the call that sealed it.

Mark certainly knew who Peter Fairfield was but had never spoken to him. His satellite phone chirped and, because so few people had access to the number, Mark assumed that it was one of the team. So, he answered as 'Mark.'

'Major Taylor! – it is Peter Fairfield – Director National Intelligence. I understand that you and your team are in Afghanistan.'

Mark had long since lost any inhibitions at being addressed by people in positions of power. Ok – Fairfield was a member of the President's inner Cabinet. This was the first time that Mark had spoken with one of these powerful men. So, he assumed that the call must be important. What he did not know was whether the DNI had any idea of what his team had been up to. All that Fairfield seemed to know was that they were in Afghanistan. Where he had got that piece of information from was anyone's guess.

Mark decided to play it safe and let the DNI tell him.

'Yes – we have been trying to figure out how the Iranians get hold of drugs – and I think we have solved that part of the riddle. We are about to head elsewhere'

Fairfield seemed stuck for words. When he did speak his tone had the effect of irritating Mark.

'We are talking on an unsecured line so I will be brief.'

'Excuse me! Which end of this link is unsecure?'

'Why? Your end!'

Mark was about to give the DNI a brief outline of Taylor Software's app that he had insisted on installing on all the phones that were used by his team when he could almost hear the bell going off inside the head of the DNI.

'Ok, Taylor – I know what you are talking about. The Brits have been trying to get information from my people on what you have done. I will talk to you later about that – because our NSA people are equally puzzled. For now - we have more important things to talk about. But first – Where are you headed to and why?'

The reply that Mark gave seemed to stun the DNI, although a trip to Turkey to find out what Haji had been up to since his escape from Khartoum did seem perfectly logical. And had been the subject of the earlier chat that Mark had with Sherman.

'What the fuck is going on here? Taylor! The information about the whereabouts of Mohamed Haji was only recently brought to my attention. How the hell did you know?'

Mark could not resist the temptation to turn the screw on the head of the largest security organization on the planet. Apart from the fact that it had been implicit in his conversation with a member of the DNI's department. Which told Mark what he had suspected. He was not being told the complete story and no one had yet figured out which parts he should, or should not, be told.

'I heard that snippet of information some days ago

from Ibrahim Mustafa.'

He did not think that he needed to tell the DNI that Mustafa was a member of the National Intelligence and Security Service of Sudan.

Maybe he should have.

'Who is Mustafa?' came the response from Washington.

'He is the gentleman who helped us get Haji arrested when we were in Sudan. Your CIA got all the credit for that little escapade so I would have thought you would know. You are not going to tell me now that the CIA had anything to do with Haji's escape – Are you?

Fairfield laughed.

'Ok, Major – you make your point. Let us talk about the reason for my call. The President wants this Haji business ended. You seem to be the only one who can recognize this villain. He would like you to take your team into Turkey and track him down. It seems that everywhere he goes there is trouble.'

Now it was the turn of Mark to pause. He suddenly realized what the concern was in Washington. He did not know whether to mention that to the DNI that he had spoken to Karen Marshall. He decided that this bit of news may overwhelm the DNI, so he just repeated the news that he had gained from that conversation.

'You mean that you believe the Haji is involved in the SARS outbreak?'

'Major! Is there anything that you do not know?'

There was. And it was another piece of the jigsaw that the DNI was aware of. Still armed with what facts he did know, Mark had still to get agreement from the rest of the team. And he could only tell them what he knew.

Mark gathered his team together with less confidence than he had previously envisaged would be the case. He was surprised that Larmina Meskin was not present. He did not know whether that was because she did not regard herself as a part of the team or whether she just did not know what she was supposed to do. Either way, her fate would be decided at this meeting – one way or the other.

Mark wanted to keep the team intact for what he hoped would be the last part of this mission that had covered Africa and now the Middle East. He was not expecting any trouble in the NATO country. Just a quiet trip to find out what Haji had been doing. From their trip into Afghanistan, they had all the proof that would be needed to show that Iran was in contempt of the restrictions that the United Nations had imposed – admittedly at the insistence of the United States and their western allies. They had got a fair idea of how Mohamed Haji – with the obvious sponsorship of Iran – had tried to set up a drug distribution network through the United States diplomatic staff in Africa. And now all that they needed to do was to ensure that Turkey would not be subjected to the same nonsense.

'Ok people' Mark began. 'We have to decide where we go from here. I will tell you what my objective is, where I think we need to go, and how we can get there. After that, it is up to you to decide whether you want to come along for the ride.'

At this stage nobody said anything. Mark had been in many such meetings during his years with Delta Force. He knew that the reactions of all the participants would be critical. Reading the body-language Mark thought he had their undivided attention. Then there were people in the room with as much experience as Mark. And that experience included the ability to hide their feelings.

'We need to find out what happened to Mohamed Haji after he escaped from Khartoum. The information I received before we came to Afghanistan was that he was in Turkey. From the information that I have received from Washington, I believe that is still the case. I suspect that he will be trying the same tricks that he was up to in Africa – namely finding a weak spot in one or more of our diplomats and then getting them to distribute drugs to their peers. But – as you all know – it can do irreparable damage to the US interests if that is allowed to get out of hand. Now we get to the crunch. We have been following the Taliban in Afghanistan and we have seen the exchange of drugs for weapons. And those drugs are being supplied to Iran and from there I suspect that the same drugs are being supplied to our friend Haji. For the first time since we have been on the road, Haji is now in a country which shares a border with Iran.'

Mark had a drink before continuing. Still - nobody spoke. Not even Dusty.

'Now what do we do? I have a request from the Director of National Intelligence – which means our President - to go to Turkey and track down Mohamed Haji and put a stop to his antics. To do that we have a British Globemaster waiting outside on which we can hitch a ride. The SAS troops who helped us on our recent exercise will be on board but will not be a part of what we need to do. The first stop will be the Incirlik airbase in eastern Turkey. I mention that because I have information that there has been a SARS epidemic breakout at the Incirlik airbase, but our attention would be further west than that. So – that is the plan. Now, comments please.'

There were a few. Apart from Dusty enquiring about the availability of McDonald's in Turkey, Owen checked that he would be needed on this part of their trip concerned that his knowledge of the Turk language was not as good as his command of Farsi and the other languages of the Afghans. Ben wanted to know whether they would have access to decent transport once they were on the ground. Elliott had nothing to say. Blake waited until they had all absorbed what had been said and then raised the issue that Mark had been waiting for.

'What are we going to do with Mina and Misha? They cannot stay here.' Blake asked in a quiet but level tone.

Owen Squires was the one who recognized the difficult position both Mark and Blake were in. He knew what Blake wanted for the girls and himself. He knew that Mark would want them all to be happy with the outcome. But would Mark be prepared to take the risk of compromising the mission because he went with his heart instead of his brain? So – he tried to lighten the mood in a room that had become suddenly tense.

'Misha would like to go to England and meet the Queen. After that, she would like to go to the States and visit the White House.'

That brought a smile to the face of Mark. The man who had saved his life and that of his friend Dusty Miller not so long ago in this very country was once again displaying the kind of loyalty to his friends that money could not buy. However, Mark still had to decide – and that was hard.

He turned to Blake very much aware of the pain that the man was feeling. Here was a man who had also shown loyalty over many years but was now grappling with emotions that seemed curiously in conflict with their mission. The man was asking his leader – and his friend – to agree to effectively offer protection to a lady who not two days before was committed to blowing Mark into the next world. Could any of them be sure that this would be sure that this would be the end of that phase in Larmina Meskin's life? All because Blake had stepped up and protected the daughter when someone needed to. And Mark was the only one in this group who thought that he knew the reason why. Misha was the same age as Blakes's twin daughters who had lost their mother in a violent crash caused by a drunken idiot. Even so, there had to be more to it than that.

'What does Mina want to do Blake? Mark asked as gently as he could.

Blake shrugged. But body language said that he was determined.

'She wants out of Afghanistan. She doesn't want Misha to be bothered by any more stress. She wants a life free of conflict. To be honest – I have promised that I will do all that I can to help her. As you know Misha needs medical help that she could not get in this country. I have friends in Washington that can help. Misha is too young to know what she needs but she does know where she wants to be. Mina does know what she needs and that is Misha's only chance to live a full life. I have promised her that there is a home for her and Misha if that can be arranged. I want them to be safe!'

Mark realized – probably belatedly – that the group had already discussed the fate of the new female members of the team. It was akin to addressing a bunch of school kids and about to tell them that Thanksgiving would be celebrated on the fourth Thursday in November.

Elliott stepped in and saved Mark from the trouble of responding.

'I have had a chat with Ross. Why don't we arrange for Mina and Misha to go with the SAS to their home base in England? Because of the earlier connection between Mina and MI6, McKinnon says they will have no problem justifying the move and they can take care of them until Blake gets his shit together.'

'Do you think traveling by Globemaster is proper? It is Ok for a bunch of hardened troops. Not so good for a couple of ladies!' was all that Mark could think of to say. Even that was a waste of time.

'It is not that bad! The Air Force supply earmuffs!'

Mark admitted defeat.

'Ok – since everyone seems to agree – let's get moving!'

Chapter 42

Analysis Of The Dead

With the sun just rising in the east as Azra Fatma took her black Labrador cross dog for his usual early morning walk. On this particular morning, it was raining Neither of them seemed to notice and it did not stop her from following their usual routine. Her dog had not yet figured out that he was no longer a pup and so he strained at the leash anxious to find something new. He was named Kiri - a name that Azra had adopted from her friend without knowing it was a female name. But Kiri was only a dog. He could not have cared less. He also could not have cared less whether it was raining or not. Devoted though he was to his owner, he had two other priorities which overrode everything else in his micro-world – food and walks.

If pressed to make a choice, then food was probably the most important.

Azra had a routine that placed the walk first. And so - Kiri would get that done. Then have a feed. And then probably sleep for the rest of the day.

But this day was going to be very different.

This part of the city of Adana in the south-eastern part of Turkey had seen better days. There were many abandoned houses in the industrial area. But to be fair, they had not been up to much even when they were relatively new and had been occupied. In the streets that Azra and Kiri walked along most of the fences separating the houses were in a state of disrepair to the point that it was difficult to figure out where one property ended and the next one began. And the area was littered with rubbish which people dumped there because no one cared.

Still that suited Kiri just fine. Out of the chaos came plenty of new rubbish. On every new day, there were new smells to explore. And, in the dog world, if something smelt Ok, that usually meant that it was at least edible. To find that out, of course, you had to eat it. And, being a Labrador, the taste was a secondary consideration.

Azra let him run and it took her a while to realize that he was spending an unusual amount of time in one patch of his patrol area.

At first, she just called his name because that would signal to Kiri that they were heading closer to home and then meant closer to food. But this time Kiri did not respond.

She backtracked down the street looking for him.

She found him frantically digging away in the ground and he seemed oblivious to anything else.

At first, she was going to scold Kiri for making a mess, even though no one appeared to live in the house by the Kiri excavation site.

But, on closer inspection, she at first gasped and then let out a scream that would have woken the dead.

He had uncovered part of a body and from what she could see it had not been in the ground for more than a few days. With tears from shock and fear streaming down her cheeks she reattached the lead and dragged Kiri away from the awful scene and rushed to her home.

Her parents had been killed in a motor car accident several years ago and Azra was being raised by her grandparents. Consequently, they were very protective of their granddaughter and their attitude was that they should not get involved in the events that she was screaming about. They were very skeptical about what Azra had to say and was inclined to write it off to her vivid imagination.

In frustration, Azra ran out of the house to the shop on the corner, still crying, and tried to get help.

As luck would have it, a US military police vehicle from the nearby Airbase at Incirlik was passing by and the driver stopped to find out what all the screaming was about. The driver did not speak Turkic and so could not understand what the girl was saying. But he could see the terror in her face, and he followed her down the street and into the yard where in halting English and with hand signals she had claimed to have found the body.

With the rain and the poor light of the early morning, the sight of an arm did not seem to call for the girl's reaction.

But it was – or had been - a human being.

While this was a local matter over which the US military police had no jurisdiction, the driver felt that he had to do something and so he reported the matter to his base office. That caused the duty officer to simply call the local Adana police station and alert them to a potential homicide on their patch.

That got a response.

Why the Adana police force needed to arrive with sirens wailing was a question few could ever answer. There would have been serious doubts that a perpetrator would be found within a hundred miles of the crime scene. But it was a potential murder!

The first two police cars did arrive within minutes of their station receiving the call. Having quickly identified the area where the body had been found they taped the whole property and then commenced their initial questioning of their only witness. In the absence of any other clues, Azra was detained and placed in a police wagon pending the arrival of their senior officer.

A third police car arrived moments later, and Senior Sergeant Jerry Burak immediately took charge of the situation. He had spent most of the last couple of weeks scurrying around the city trying to get a handle on something he could not see – a mysterious virus called SARS – as well as controlling traffic, neither task having excited his normal police instincts. Now he had the potential to do real police work!

He quickly arranged a tighter cordon around the actual grave to prevent any further disturbance on the scene until he could get assistance from a forensic pathologist.

When the pathologist eventually arrived, she took charge of the site. She supervised the careful uncovering of the whole body. She made a first assessment of the corpse and then had it paced into a black plastic body bag for it to be transported back to the morgue.

At least she was able to reach preliminary conclusions.

The body was that of a white female in her early thirties. The only clothing with the body was a hospital-type gown although it was not clear whether that was being worn or had simply been cast into the shallow grave. It was splattered with blood and other human material. It was not clear whether that was a result of the crime or the burial. The lady had been in generally good physical shape. That is – apart from the bullet that had entered her forehead and then made a mess of the back of her head as it exited the skull. Therefore, proving the cause of death was relatively straightforward.

Death appeared to have been caused by a single bullet to the forehead.

There was no evidence that a bullet would be retrieved from the corpse.

Further examination would be needed to determine whether she may have already been dead before the bullet had been fired. There did not seem to be any evidence of a struggle. Certainly, there was nothing under the nails or on the hands to indicate that the Jane Do had been in a fight or had made any attempt to fight off her attacker. Although the body had only a flimsy hospital gown as cover and the body was otherwise completely nude, there was no evidence of any sexual motive for this crime. But it was too early for that possibility to be discounted.

The body was placed in a black plastic body-bag and carried to the pathology van where it would be transported to the morgue for further examination.

The officers and the pathologist then returned to the graveside relieved and puzzled.

All that was known so far was that a serious crime had been committed. But there remained a few unanswered questions. Like – Where had it occurred? Who had pulled the trigger? When had they done the deed? And then the critical question – Why did this beautiful young lady have to die?

The first thing to focus on was - Where had the murder been carried out?

Because the grave had been dug in close proximity to the rear door of a house, Burak decided to knock on the door to see if anyone was home. Getting no reply, he used his cell phone to tap into a database to find out who the owner of the property was. That told him that the property had been abandoned by the owners some time ago. It was then placed in the hands of a property management company which had an office in the city of Adana.

The Sergeant contacted that company and spoke to a receptionist who was the only person on deck so early in the day. There was a delay of several minutes while the lady from the property company searched through her records. It was finally revealed that the property had been rented to a couple of businesspeople for a period of three months. Rent had been paid in advance for the full period – and according to her records it had been paid in cash. And - Yes – she did have a telephone number where she could contact her clients.

Burak thanked the lady for her help and instructed her to place the papers into a sealed bag which one of his officers would collect from her shortly.

He then rang the number that he had been given as the point of contact for the people who were supposedly residents in the property of interest.

He got a message to say that the number was either invalid or it was not currently active. He was told by the moronic voice to try to re-enter the number correctly.

That required a repeat call to the property company where the lady confirmed that she had provided Burak with the correct number. The lady was instructed to try calling the number herself without having any confidence that she would have any more success than the police. Which she didn't.

He thought of pressing the lady on why they would have a number that was useless and why it took a police enquiry to reveal what should have been obvious to any half-decent property management company. He decided not to bother and instead asked her to have the Manager call him on his cell phone whenever he or she decided to turn up.

Having given up on that line of enquiry, Burak went back to the rear door of the house.

It was not locked.

He went inside and immediately got an answer to the question – Where had the murder been carried out?

Right here!

There was dried blood splattered on the floor and on one of the walls. No attempt had been made to clean it up. And the perpetrators of this crime did not know about criminal investigations. Or they just did not care.

A bullet was lodged in the wall and from the residue spattered around it this was obviously the one that had caused the mess to the lady's skull.

So - they had evidence of a crime. They had a body and a bullet that had caused the death. An extensive search of the property did not find any weapon. The police bagged the bullet for forensic examination which they were confident would soon reveal what type of weapon it was. Just no evidence of who had been holding it at the time of the time of the murder.

Now came some real police work. They had to find out who had fired the fatal shot. Sergeant Burak called in more police resources to conduct a thorough forensic search of the house. In particular they needed to take prints off any of the admittedly few surfaces that the perpetrators may have touched. He did not hold out much hope of getting any evidence from this source. Well – he knew that he would get fingerprints. But finding a match could be difficult. So – while they may have prints, it was only on rare occasions that they would match any that they had on their files. But they did it anyway, because that was the only way to answer the question of - Who had pulled the trigger?

What they needed to do now was to find the gun and get fingerprints off that and match them to prints that they found in the house. That would consolidate their evidence but otherwise achieve little.

The police now focused their attention on the outside of the house, conducting a grid search of the grounds.

That revealed two areas of interest.

In one hole that had been dug close to the shallow grave, they found some clothing. These garments were definitely for a lady. But there was nothing yet to confirm that there was a link to the body. The forensic analysis would decide whether there was any link. It could reveal whether the clothes would fit the body and further DNA analysis would soon put two and two together. Although it was too early to make any assumptions it seemed either a fait accompli or an extraordinary coincidence that the clothes should be buried next to the body. And in an area where the ground had been disturbed

The same applied to the second area which was on the far side of the plot. And it proved more interesting than the first.

That hole contained only a purse. Again, there was nothing definitive or conclusive, except that the bag appeared to be in remarkably good condition. Careful examination of the contents of the bag revealed only an aerosol can that had nothing written on the outside to say what was in it. The police officer who found it was about to test the can to find out what it contained before being stopped by a scream from Burak. The sergeant screamed because the aerosol can could be evidence. And every little piece of information was only tagged as relevant when you knew what it was. Although he had no idea how that was connected to the body. He did not yet realize that the can in fact held evidence of a far more serious crime.

And had the police officer gone ahead and tested it he could have started his own cluster in this pandemic.

More out of frustration than anything else, Burak then went to talk to the only *witness* that they had.

Azra had been sitting alone in the back of the police wagon during this whole process and was not really in a mood to talk.

But she tried.

No – she had no idea who the dead body was.

No – she had no idea who else had been at the property.

No – she had not buried anyone in her whole life.

No – she had no idea where the tools were that had dug the holes.

And – No – she did not own a gun.

Having shed no light on the crime, Azra was told that she should not talk to anyone about what she had seen. Friends because the police did not want to start any gossip that may attract any attention to their investigation. Enemies because their enquiries could lead to an attempt to subvert the course of justice. Like - they could look to kill Azra. could alert or casual acquaintances and to call Burak if she recalled anything that she had not so far been able to reveal. With that instruction came a clear warning – The perpetrators could return to the scene of their crime.

Kiri would not be walking in this area of town – ever again!

At the end of a frustrating day the police bundled all the bits and pieces that they had collected into evidence bags and left to return to their headquarters. Probably no wiser than they had been when they arrived.

Sergeant Jerry Burak and his officers had no clue of what they had found. There was no reason for the lady having been buried in this particular property. They had no idea who she was or who had been responsible for placing her there. And, more importantly, what possible motive could someone have for causing this brutal murder.

And without any obvious motive it was going to be a difficult crime to solve.

Basically, the body was that of *kim oldugu nerede oturdugu bilinmeysen kimse* – someone whose identity and place of origin were unknown.

However, there was one thing that Burak could do.

The US FBI had sent a couple of experienced investigators to the Incirlik Airbase.

While they were farting around trying to get a handle on a security breach which had occurred at the base, maybe they could spare some time to help with a real crime!

Chapter 43

CNN

Mark had found that getting from the southern Helmand province of Afghanistan into Turkey was far easier than he had expected, although he had arrived in a different place than had been his original intention.

Despite struggling for years to reduce the US presence in the hellhole that was Afghanistan, suddenly the US had decided to shift at least some of its front-line battle-hardened troops out and relocate them at a base in eastern Turkey. As a consequence of that, the Kandahar airbase was a busy place and there were several Globemaster means of transport being loaded up for the relatively short trip west. And based on pure mathematics, there would have been room for Marks team irrespective of the offer of a lift from the British SAS contingent.

They had been running around in Afghanistan for about a week and had heard very little news from the outside world. If they had been up with the latest news, they may have had a different understanding of the forces at play. Consequently, they did not recognize the increased military activity that surrounded them. But, there again, it would turn out that they were not the only ones who were unaware of what had happened before their landing at Incirlik.

The Royal Air Force C-17 Globemaster was not the largest transport aircraft in service – the C-5 Galaxy is a monster by comparison – but it still had a very intimidating presence especially to the two ladies who were joining them on this flight. And the facilities provided for the passengers were not particularly well suited to transport people. There were very few windows in the plane and none of them were in the area where the passengers were housed. The aircraft supplied few amenities and seats that were not the most comfortable. Nonetheless Mina and Misha were just too excited to care – Misha because it was something new and different, Mina because she was heading to a new life in a country that was not continually at war with itself. Even so, their attitude would be tested by the five-hour flight time in the noisy and uncomfortable environment.

The mess hall at the Incirlik Airbase was busy at this time of the day – people coming off shift and people just starting theirs. The television was tuned into CNN, as it was in most overseas military camps when senior officers were around. There was little truth in the rumors that troops when away from home exclusively tuned in to porn sites – well, at least, not in mixed company.

Mark and his team were having a rest and just watching the comings and goings before planning on what they would do next. It was assumed to be just a normal day in a normal overseas mess hall.

Except that everyone was wearing a mask and there was tension in the air that is hard to miss!

The team had met up with a couple of FBI personnel who were on the base investigating some misdemeanor that someone had got up to. The FBI agents – Mike Delaney and Hector Swarbrick - would not say who or what they were investigating. Which was good because neither Mark nor the rest of the team were interested. What they were interested in was the CNN commentary which just so happened to be talking about events that had occurred very close to where they were now.

With what limited knowledge they already had of the situation they knew that the CNN report was wide of the mark.

The CNN article had started with a picture of headlines from the Daily Sabah, a recent addition to the Turkish pro-government media which stated *Iran female Diplomat shot dead at Incirlik Air Force Base*. CNN then went ahead to bemoan the fact that there had been a virus outbreak at the Incirlik base in recent weeks and that would probably mean the end of life on earth as we know it.

The facts were that a body had been found in the city of Arana and, at least at this stage, there was no link either to the virus or to the Incirlik base. Well – that was unless the virus delivery mechanism method had changed to a bullet.

Because CNN was a US-based broadcaster the difference between Adana and Incirlik was irrelevant to the vast majority of their viewers. As it was, the epidemiologists on the case were still undecided on where the virus outbreak had occurred. The original infections that had occurred in Arana and appeared to have been efficiently managed by a couple of doctors at the local hospital. In a similar way the infections at the US Air Force Incirlik base appeared to have been contained. If it wasn't for the involvement of the World Health Organization, the matter could have ended there.

But the WHO had a change of mind which was puzzling. They had originally instructed that all infected patients at the airbase should be transferred to the Arana Acibadem hospital and held in isolation for a few days before making a full recovery. And that would have been the end of this apocalyptical event.

However, a brain-dead member of the Turkish Ministry of Health, had decided that there was a threat to the local population. And so - the decision had been made by the World Health Organization that there would be two clusters with the consequent complications that arose.

CNN was not the only one of the many organizations that misunderstood what the hell had happened.

The FBI agent Delaney let out a sigh, and under his breath muttered to his partner 'Thank God what *really* happened at Incirlik hasn't got out yet!'.

That comment attracted the attention of Mark and Dusty. Since muttering seemed to be the normal mode of conversation, Dusty turned to Mark and muttered under his breath.

'That could explain the military shipping in Special Forces troops from Afghanistan. So – What the fuck happened?'

The FBI agents both heard Dusty's question. They exchanged a knowing glance and seemed to agree on what should be said.

'There was a raid on the Incirlik base a couple of days ago. A couple of people on both sides were killed. The present theory is that the raid was carried out by an ISIS group with possible links to the Hezbollah. That is all we know at the moment.'

Mark and Dusty knew when they were being told porkies.

However, what had attracted the attention of the FBI agents was the statement on CNN that the body had been identified as Iranian and a female diplomat. This was because the last they knew of the investigation, the Turks had no clue of who the deceased was, how the body came to be where it was, or who had been responsible for its demise. Certainly, they appeared to have no idea of a possible motive. All that they knew was the gender of the body.

Delaney got on his cell phone and ended in a heated conversation with someone named *Jerry* conducted in both English and Turkish – most of the English did not extend beyond words with four letters and starting in 'F.' Eventually, Delaney slammed the cell down on the table and turned to Swarbrick.

'Ok, he has agreed to meet. So - finish your drink and lets' go!'

Then, almost as an afterthought, he turned to Mark and said 'Do you guys' care to join us? The Adana police station is located in a rough part of town, and we could use some backup!'

Mark hesitated. That hesitation occurred because he thought that two young, extremely fit, armed, and fully trained FBI agents would be more than a match for whatever the *rough part of town* could throw at them. Therefore, there had to be some other reason for this invitation. What if there was a link between these apparently unrelated events? What if there was a link between the description of the body given by the CNN report – identifying the body as that of an Iranian – and the FBI comment that the raid on Incirlik could have been carried out by ISIS or Hezbollah? In this part of the world *Hezbollah* meant Iranian influence. Mark and the team were tasked with finding Mohamcd Haji – a known troublemaker. And known to be associated with the intelligence organization of one country. Iran!

Mark was troubled by this realization. Could it mean that Haji was embarking on a very different strategy that was not limited to sex and drugs? Could it mean that he was taking things to a whole new level?

'Yes – Dusty and I would love to join you!' was all that Mark said, apart from asking the obvious question.

'Who the hell is Jerry?'

The Adana police station was nothing like what Mark had expected, having seen far worse *rough parts of town* in New York City. The atmosphere in the station was friendly and the Turkish officers, most of whom spoke almost perfect English, seemed only too pleased to share their information with their visitors.

While at the level of their respective Presidents, relations between the United States and Turkey were not exactly cordial, that did not seem to have filtered down to this level. And police officers were cops the world over.

The room that they crowded into was small and had no furniture except a table, six chairs, and the obligatory mirror on the wall. Jerry Burak, the Turkish police officer who Delaney had spoken to earlier, assured the visitors that no one was sitting on the other side of the mirror. This piece of information was received with some skepticism by the FBI agents which caused a mere shrug and a laugh from their host. Yes – their meeting was being observed – probably by a higher-level officer. Yes – the FBI would not be volunteering any information at this particular meeting. And - No – Mark and Dusty would not be making any comments.

Burak started the meeting by also assuring the visitors that what they had heard on CNN had not come from him.

That was probably true.

What Burak did not say was where he thought that the CNN information had come from.

That was probably because he had absolutely no idea.

The FBI was used to such a situation.

The CNN network of informants was the same everywhere and was probably far superior to anything that the CIA or other international intelligence gathering organizations could muster. However, there was an important difference between the objectives of newsgathering organizations and intelligence gathering organizations.

The former wanted a story. The latter wanted the truth.

'We got lucky!' Burak informed his guests to get the meeting underway. 'We have found a guy who is a waiter in a local restaurant. He posted on a Facebook chatroom that he recognized the girl whose body we found as our *Jane Doe* as someone who he had served a few days ago. So – we got one of our guys who spends time on social media – to befriend him and try to get any further information. That did not tell us much, but another person got into the post and added that the girl was Iranian. At least she had spoken in Farsi when they met in the restroom at the same restaurant that our waiter works in. We later interviewed this waiter. We are holding him in custody more for his protection than anything else. We have had a forensic artist work with him to produce sketches of the girl and the man that she was with at the restaurant. As with all such sketches they are not very dependable. But they are a start.'

The FBI agents had kept quiet to this point. But the looks on their faces spoke volumes. Mark and Dusty had no idea of the significance of Burak's comments. But they were about to find out.

Burak continued.

'We keep a close eye on what goes on back in Ankara, especially at foreign embassies. When the hint came through that the deceased could be an Iranian that caused us to focus on the Iranian Embassy to see if we could trace her from there. In the case of the Iranians, we have a higher level of surveillance we employ facial recognition technology. Checking back through a couple of weeks of film, someone looking very similar to our victim was seen going into and out of the Iranian Embassy regularly. That means that - if it is her – she either works for the Iranian government or was a close associate of someone who does. Further investigation had the lady at various times accompanied by a man. We do not yet know who he is. However, the last time we have the lady on film, she was leaving the Embassy with another man. We showed that piece of film to our waiter friend and he confirms our suspicions. That man was the one who was with the deceased dining at the restaurant in Adana. We have no idea who the man is. We then checked with our National Intelligence Organization. They confirm our assessment that this man is at least a person of interest in this investigation. At best we have a prime suspect, and that - as you people say – good enough to take to the bank.'

For some reason, Burak turned to Mark to explain the significance of what he had just said.

'You may know of our Intelligence service - but as MIT – they get that acronym from the Turkish Milli Istihbarat Teskilati. I think they are similar to your CIA, in their structure if not in their performance. They are not a military group, so we tend to get better cooperation from them. They do share our feed from the cameras, and they confirmed what we thought. The girl is Iranian although in their opinion she probably has – or should I say *had* - a lowly clerical job and she is almost certainly not a spook. The man is also Iranian but is not known to be a player. The MIT then checked through their sources whether there were any Iranians that had recently turned up missing but have got nothing so far.'

The look on the face of the Sergeant showed what he thought of the Iranians.

'The Iran Embassy also confirmed that they do not know the girl. They claim that she is nothing to do with Iran and that as far as they are concerned there is no missing person who fits the general description that we provided. Our assessment of all this is that the Iranians are lying. We believe that we have found exactly where the girl came from, and we are mystified why the Iranians are in denial. We still do not know why she turned up dead. Nor do we know what was she doing in Adana? We think that we have a picture of the last person to see her alive. We have no idea of what the motive could be

A look around the faces of his guests confirmed that he now had their undivided attention.

'Now comes to the interesting bit. The World Health Organization had been trying to trace the origins of the recent SARS outbreak which occurred in Adana and at your base in Incirlik during the last few weeks. Because the outbreak was unusually localized, and it had not appeared anywhere except originating from one case in Adana and a few cases that were reported from your base at Incirlik, they speculated that it could have resulted from an isolated incident in which only one or two people were involved. So – they checked from the dates that the occurrences were reported and considered the likely incubation period for a virus such as SARS. Then they checked where the people who were infected were on those few days on either side of the likely date of first being infected. And guess what? They all ate in the same restaurant on or about those dates. And by a strange coincidence – that was the restaurant in which our friend the waiter works.'

'At first, we were a little confused why the first people with symptoms were all female. We rationalized that they must have met, or touched, or simply breathed the same air in the ladies' restroom. Armed with this theory we sent a blood sample from our dead body to the lab for testing for the SARS virus. This came up negative for SARS! That means that, although she was in the same environment as the others, she did not become infected.'

Burak looked up from the papers that he was reading his notes from. Three of the four men looked stunned.

Mark Taylor had a grim look on his face, but his eyes showed that his mind was elsewhere. Was the man in the sketch someone that he knew?

Delaney broke the mood.

'Thanks for your report - Jerry. Let me now guess where you are coming from. You want some help in trying to tie up the WHO study, and you want us to speculate on what happened. Right?'

The nod of the head told Mike that that was exactly why Jerry had asked them to come down to the police station.

But there was more to it than that.

Originally Burak seemed to have assumed that Mark and Dusty were with the CIA but now he seemed not so sure.

He addressed his next remarks to Delaney.

His attention was focused on Mark and Dusty.

'Have you spoken to your CIA people to find out what they are thinking?'

That question got a laugh from Delaney.

'Err – you know how it is. The MIT has probably got the better deal. The FBI and the CIA do not exactly share information the way the security services can in Turkey.'

Although they are supposed to, he did not add.

'So – No – we are not privy to what the CIA is thinking.'

'As I thought!' replied Burak. 'So – let me tell you what our MIT says that your CIA is thinking. This is pure speculation you do understand. Although relationships between your CIA and our MIT are very good, they do not necessarily know exactly what the CIA is thinking. But then, who does?' he added as an afterthought.

'We understand that they believe that the lady either heard or saw something, at the restaurant. She may have overheard something at the Iran Embassy but that would not fit with the facts. So - they think that, either before or after she arrived in Adana, she did something or saw something, that got her killed. They originally thought that the man who the lady was with that evening was the carrier of the virus. Now they have discounted that theory because that also does not quite make any sense. Neither the CIA nor MIT knows who this guy was. They have a lead on the gentleman that the lady was seen with on earlier occasions, and they are trying to follow up on that. They now think that the lady was killed to prevent the source of the infection from becoming known and involving Iran in an embarrassing situation. That man who went with the lady to the restaurant has disappeared. Speculation now is that he must have been important. They think that he was working for VAJA – the Iran Intelligence outfit. If that is so – he could be difficult to trace.'

Burak then reached into his pile of evidence bags that he had brought into thc room. He pulled out a bag one holding an aerosol can and the other bag containing what was a lady's purse.

'This information is not known to anyone outside this room. These items were found at the same location where we found the body. They were in a separate place from the grave and are not necessarily related to the crime – but as you people say - their presence was a strange coincidence. They were sitting in a girls' bag - buried at the site – but evidently of very recent origin. We have not tested the contents of the can because we frankly do not have the expertise necessary to do a thorough enough analysis. We are hoping you could help us there. We have consulted Doctor Mirac Kartal who is something of an expert in infectious diseases and he confirms that it could be the source of the outbreak. Which would mean – the SARS outbreak in Adana was a deliberate attempt to start some form of an epidemic.

'Ok' said Delaney. 'Do I gather that there is some doubt on a possible motive for the killing? It is difficult to pin it to the virus because we know so little about what occurred. There could have been a much simpler explanation. The guy tried to get his rocks off, the girl refused, so he killed her to protect his honor! You know how these things work. The Iranians do not share our respect for females and human life!'

Mike Delaney wished he had not said that. The Turks had almost as bad a reputation as the Iranians had when it came to dealing with such things as respect for females. In western society, especially with the recent prominence of the Me2 movement, men were being held to account for their treatment of women and their mistaken assumption that women were mere objects to do their bidding. But even that did not envision that those men would kill to protect their egos.

Burak held his hands out in front of himself in mock surrender.

'I am just a simple cop trying to solve a murder. I am not one of your profilers trying to get my head around what a man may, or may not, have as his motive – his raison d'etre as our French friends would put it. That she was killed by a single bullet to the forehead is a fact. That the bullet came from a pistol of Iranian origin is only a possibility. That the lady was an Iranian is probable. That her partner on that fateful evening is the probable carrier of a deadly disease is a possibility. Now this whole business is getting beyond my scope. I have a cause of death. I have a probable perpetrator who is at best unknown, at best identifiable as a member of the Iranian Embassy. If you want my opinion – the lady simply delivered the virus under instructions from her partner and was then disposed of having completed her task. It is now up to other people to decide what happens next. What I am unable to explain is how CNN came up with their theory that the deceased was an Iranian diplomat, even though there has been no mention of a missing person by Iran. And there has certainly been no mention of Iran by us. However - I have one more piece of the puzzle.'

Burak reached down a retrieved a couple of evidence bags which he placed on the table.

'These are items that we found at the property where we found the body. The first one is an aerosol can the contents of which are undetermined. All the other items found at the site were clothing and our forensic pathologist has confirmed that they belonged to the body. The can was found in the other item - a purse on the same site, which we believe also belonged to the deceased. It was buried some distance from the body but was with the vicinity. We do not have the technical knowledge to be able to analyze the aerosol can. Well – let me rephrase that. We could analyze it. But may destroy evidence in the process.'

Delancy was the first of the team to catch on to what Burak was alluding to.

He let out a low whistle.

'Holy shit! If I am reading you correctly – You think that this aerosol can could be the source of the virus! I don't know enough about viruses – whether they can be transmitted in that way. But – Why not? You want me to do something about that?'

Burak was disappointed that the fabled FBI could not do something right here and now. He reluctantly accepted Delaney's instruction to package the can off to the FBI Laboratory in Quantico Virginia. That would take a couple of days, although given that they would know exactly what they may be dealing with, it would not take long once the FBI had their hands on the can.

Burak delegated the task of getting the package organized to one of his officers, then returned his attention to what was bugging him.

He thought that the Americans were not being entirely truthful.

'What I am struggling to understand is how you people knew that Iran was involved at all. I thought you may be able to shed light on this part of the puzzle.'

That comment caused Delaney to pause.

'I am sorry! The first we heard of Iran being involved in any of this was when we saw it in the CNN newscast. What are you suggesting now?'

Burak looked offended by Delaney's response.

'Come on Mike! It was CNN that broke the story. And they did not get that piece of information from our Polis!'

That summed up how foreign intelligence agencies thought of the CIA, or other parts of the United States security services and their relationship with the media. Especially the American media. And they applied the same logic to the FBI. They assumed that all media reporters and investigators were agents of their government. This was understandable for countries that had such strict control over their press that they could not see it any other way. Because Mike Delaney did not have these components in-built into his thought process he was lost. Recognizing this, his only possibility was to talk to CNN and try to solve the riddle that way. Meanwhile, he would try to placate his host as best he could.

'Jerry – we do not have that kind of control of our media. I will talk to them and try to find out where they got their information from. But I don't hold out much hope! They are very protective of their sources and would probably not say anything that would be useful. The best I could do is to tell them that their information is incorrect. But can we say that? I could try the angle that their mention of Incirlik as being the center of the SARS thing was misleading. But that risks the possibility that they would question why I am so sensitive about Incirlik. That may lead to them inquiring into matters concerning the raid on the base – and we do not want that – not at this stage anyway.'

Mark was stunned by that.

Why would he be so sensitive about a raid on the Incirlik base?

On their way back to Incirlik Mark and Dusty were sitting in the rear seats of the car and exchanged a couple of signals that said that there was something else that they needed to know.

Whether their newfound friends from the FBI would enlighten them they could not know.

But it meant that Mark would need to re-think his plans.

Chapter 44

Plans

Mark knew that he had only an hour to get his act together. The SAS Globemaster was due to leave for Ankara's Esenboga airport very shortly and he was determined to get his team sorted by then. Before that, he had to find out what had happened at Incirlik. He suspected that something had happened during the raid on Incirlik that was significant. He did not know what had happened. All that he knew for sure was that the FBI knew more about it than he did.

On the journey back to Incirlik he had studied the sketch of the Iranian man who had been complicit in going with the girl in the Adana restaurant. While there were many forms of disguise, he was not aware of anything that could be done to make anyone look significantly younger or to change the shape of the head except the use of copious amounts of make-up. And he was as near certain as he could be that the waiter would have mentioned that if it had happened. So, Mark reluctantly admitted that the sketch was not of Mohamed Haji. At least he had a clue of where he could start looking.

The group split upon their arrival back at Incirlik but shortly afterward Mark tracked down Mike Delaney for a chat. As it turned out he was just as anxious to talk as Mark – for different reasons.

Delaney was well versed in FBI techniques of profiling. He had noticed Mark's reaction to the things that had been said during their informal meeting with the Turkish police. And he knew the difference between surprise and shock.

They settled for a corner table in the mess area and at this time of the day, the place was quiet. It was noticeable that both men were anxious to speak first but Mark was the one in a hurry. He cut off Delaney and went straight in.

'I don't know whether you are aware of what I do for a living and what I am doing in this part of the world. You can ring your boss Mike Fisher and he will tell you. But I do not have time for that now. Just tell me – What has happened at Incirlik in the last few days that causes you to be here? If you do not want to tell me then I will have to go over your head. But I must know. And I am more than happy to tell you why if you will level with me. Fair enough?'

Delaney smiled. He had already frantically checked with his headquarters who this mysterious American was, and that was why he had invited Mark on his visit to the police in Adana. He did not previously check what Mark was specifically up to in Incirlik for the simple reason that it was none of his business. But Delaney had got the clear message that he should cooperate. And that message had come from very high up the Washington totem pole.

Now – if the guy wanted to talk – Delaney knew enough to know that he could safely tell Mark virtually anything concerning the FBI's interest in Incirlik. And he could gather possibly very useful information that would in turn help his investigation.

'Ok – for your ears only at this stage. There was a group of people who got into the base two days ago. We are assuming that they were from Hezbollah, but we have no proof of that. They got into the base as a team of paramedics ostensibly to provide vaccinations to the base personnel to fight the SARS epidemic. It appears that they intercepted a couple of vehicles coming from one of the Adana hospitals to Incirlik and took them over. The police are still trying to figure out what happened to the original paramedics. Personally - I would have to assume that they are dead. However, that is not my case, and I cannot interfere with the local police. Of more concern to us is what the group was here for. They did give vaccinations to a hundred or so base residents and everything looked on the level. But then all hell broke loose. They over-powered a base maintenance crew whose job was to check the contents of the bunkers on the southern side of the base and took off with what they were checking. And that is what I saw you react to when we were talking to Jerry, although you could not have known the seriousness of the situation.'

Mark was stunned.

'You mean they ....?'

'Yes – they got away with one of our nuclear bombs?'

Delaney shrugged – more in frustration than anything else.

'And they have just disappeared! Our forces have failed to find any trace of either the bomb or the people who stole it. I will get back to that. Now – tell me. When we were talking with Jerry earlier today – I noticed that you went very quiet when he was talking about tracking the source of the recent epidemic. Do you want to tell me what that was all about?'

Mark thought carefully before he replied.

'A few weeks ago, my team set out to prevent the assassination of Zimbabwe President Robert Mugabe. We did that, which resulted in a gentleman called Mohamed Haji being locked up in Sudan. We were very pleased with our efforts. But I think we have been fooled. I am beginning to think that from the very start the Iranians had a much bigger goal and the involvement of Mugabe was just a diversion. And now that I know what has happened in Incirlik my thoughts of what that goal was, have got me scared. Do you want to hear my theory?'

He may as well not have asked – Mark just continued talking.

'The Iranians have been feeding the US diplomatic staff in Africa with drugs as well as compromising our officials. Our recent trip out east has provided ample evidence that the Iranians are exchanging weapons for drugs with the Taliban in Afghanistan. We thought that was simply something that supported their effort in Africa and that they were just expanding the operation to include Turkey. We have been tracking the leader of their group since he escaped from prison. We know that he came from Sudan to this country. Where exactly he is now, we do not know except to say he was not the man who was in Adana. But what say Haji has been orchestrating this whole thing? But organizing drug deals and compromising US staff wasn't their main aim - Was it?'

'Shit! I know what you are going to say next' Delaney interrupted.

Mark continued as though he was talking to himself.

'So - they follow the same pattern in Turkey as they had in Africa. They use drugs and other means to compromise people and get them to do their bidding. But then it turns nasty. Somehow - they infect people with the SARS virus. They are clever. They plant the virus outside of the US Air Force Incirlik base but make sure it is in a place where people from the base would visit. Because the base is self-contained the dutiful World Health Organization decrees that the virus can be contained in that area. WHO officials instruct the Turkish health authorities to go in and vaccinate everyone on the base. That gives the Iranians the perfect opportunity to get in and cause mischief. It must have taken months of meticulous planning to come up with a plan to steal a nuclear bomb. And such an audacious scheme must have had help from inside. That was their objective from day one. The garbage about killing Mugabe was a distraction. The garbage about drugs was simply misleading. That resulted in our going on a trip to Afghanistan chasing shadows. I am not saying that we could have prevented what has occurred. But it does seem that the Iranians have made us look like a bunch of amateurs.'

Delaney looked at Mark for a moment not sure what to say. He knew the story that Mark had told him was logical. He also knew that for it to be close to the truth there had to have been a whole ton of help from US personnel or from people who were closely allied. Which meant that the Iranians had been lucky. Or they had been able to keep it tight with few people knowing the full story. And they would need to have extremely good intelligence.

It was going to take some investigation to get to the real truth of what had happened. He was about to start by asking Mark to elaborate on several points of contention when Mark surprised him by standing up and heading off.

The body language should have warned Delaney that other matters were troubling Mark. But to be fair there was just too much going on. He had only met Mark earlier in the day and had only gained limited knowledge of what he had been up to recently.

Mark was seething with rage.

Why had he not been informed by the DNI of the extent of the problems at Incirlik? It was inconceivable that Fairfield did not know. Was this yet another case of some brain-dead bureaucrat in Washington deciding that the men in the field did not need to know? Or had they failed to connect the dots linking the pursuit of Haji with the present problems? Or was the situation worse than that? Had the decision to say nothing about the theft of a nuclear weapon been made by Fairfield?

'Sorry, Mike – I have to go. I guess I am leaving you with a problem to solve. I must get my team organized then I have a plane to catch. I will leave a couple of my men behind to tidy up and maybe they could help with your investigation.'

'Where are you going? I agree with your analysis so I thought this would be the place you would want to stay?' Mark gave a bitter laugh.

'No – I think the architect of this is probably in Ankara – as usual hiding away from the real action like the coward that he is.

I must go and find Mohamed Haji!'

Major Ross McKinnon intercepted Mark as left the mess hall and made his way out onto the tarmac where his team was waiting.

'Mark – we are leaving very shortly. Are you coming with us or not? Is everything Ok?'

'Ross - can you just give me ten minutes to get organized. The brief answer to your questions is Yes and No. Yes - I will be coming. No – Things are not Ok.'

McKinnon was astute enough to know when he should keep quiet.

All the team was gathered by the gate waiting expectantly

to reboard the flight. As Mark approached, they all stood and automatically began picking up their phones and other bits of personal gear assuming that they were about to leave.

Mark ignored the chaos.

He gathered the men around him.

'Things have changed a little since this morning. I will fill you in with the details as we move on. Elliott and Owen – I want you two to stay here and help Delaney and Swarbrick of the FBI as best you can. And I want you to keep me informed of anything that they uncover. I will send you a text letting you know what is going on. The rest of us are going to Ankara. I just need to send an email to our friends in Washington!'

To: [Redacted]@nctc.gov
From: Mark Taylor
Attention: P. Fairfield DNI
Moving team from Incirlik base to Ankara Turkey. Two people will remain behind to help the FBI. Prior knowledge of the situation at Air Base would have been useful. Will advise IDC.
Taylor.

There did not seem to be any point in encrypting the message since Mark did not doubt that the full implications of the situation would be clear when CNN or some other media organization caught up with the news – probably very shortly.

Having a meaningful conversation in the fuselage of a C-17 Globemaster transporter was difficult. By using a variety of techniques ranging from yelling to hand signals Mark managed to convey to Dusty the gist of his most recent conversation with the FBI and the news that came out of it. He would leave the organization of what they would do when they got to Ankara until they were on the ground. Mark had no idea why the British would need to have two stops in Turkey since Incirlik and Ankara were only about three hundred miles apart.

He did not ask.

The flight had no sooner settled at its cruising altitude than it began to descend. After a flight time of just over two hours, the Globemaster landed at the Etimesgut Air Force base ten miles to the west of Ankara. Once on the ground it offloaded the seven American passengers. Also offloaded was one British official. The latter carried only a small black satchel. He was whisked away by what looked to be a courier from the British Embassy - on the basis that the courier was dressed in a business suit. And the vehicle had diplomatic plates.

Mark watched, but said nothing, as Blake was the last member of his team to vacate the aircraft. He had said goodbye to the Meskin girls. But it was more than a farewell. As the Globemaster made its way back onto the runway to continue its journey to the west and home, Blake bit his lip. Would this be the last time he would see them?

From the tarmac, Mark made two calls on his satellite phone. The first was to Karen Marshall of the DEA in Washington DC. The second was also to Washington. This time to his father at CIA Langley. And that call was not for a quiet family chat either.

Once they had extricated themselves from the makeshift terminal they settled into a nearby café while Mark explained what he was now expecting. He first outlined his discussion with Delaney of the FBI which surprisingly was received with little more than a narrowing of the eyes and a clenching of jaws. Which indicated to Mark that his team understood the implications. And they were ready.

'The first thing we need to do is to get out of these clothes and into something a little more comfortable. Then we will hire three ordinary cars and split into three teams – Dusty will come with me. We first need to go to the US Embassy, make our presence known, and try to get some sign of what has been happening in this part of the world. Blake and Ben – I want you to cruise the streets around the diplomatic community in particular the Iran Embassy. Mike, Hamish, and Brent – I want you to get us a couple of motel rooms which we will use as our base and then await further instructions. We want to find out whether Mohamed Haji is still in town. If he is, then we have a job to do finding out where he goes. I hope the people in our Embassy will cooperate. But I do have an alternative. I know that the Turkish police have a form of surveillance on the Iranian Embassy. I may have to contact the Adana people to arrange something. But first things first. Let's find out what our Embassy has to say.'

Mark and Dusty fronted up to the US Embassy on the Ataturk Boulevard and were pleased to note that their visit had been expected due to the earlier calls to Washington. They were escorted to the office of the Deputy Chief of Mission more as a courtesy. Then they were moved to an office at the back of the building where they sat down with the head of the Political section – a nervous young man called James Bayer.

This was what Marks second earlier call to Washington had been about. Although Bayer would not of course confirm it, he was the CIA representative at this Embassy, Mark needed to be certain who he was dealing with.

There was no point in delaying the inevitable.

'We are trying to track down a man by the name of Mohamed Haji' Mark began, knowing full well that his statement would get no meaningful response from his host. He continued as though it did not matter whether he had any reaction or not. But with a twist that would make certain that he got the attention of Bayer.

'You are no doubt aware of the problems at the Incirlik airbase. We have no evidence at this stage that there is any connection between those events and Haji. Also - we are not certain that the Iranians are involved. However, with Haji in town and a Hezbollah group suspected of involvement in the problems at Incirlik there are just too many coincidences. The President would expect that we follow through on that as a possibility during our mission. Now – Haji – who is likely to have used any one of several aliases to get into Turkey – has been responsible for a few events in recent weeks that have seen various US diplomats in Africa and elsewhere compromised. He was recently arrested in Sudan on immigration issues. Haji escaped from prison shortly after his incarceration. That could only have been with the help of the Iranians. Our information is that he made his way into Turkey over a week ago. Therefore, we have two things to worry about. Firstly – Where has he gone? And secondly – Has he adopted the same modus operandi in Ankara as he has in other places where we have been following him.'

Mark thought of waiting for Bayer to respond but quickly thought better of it.

'Just in case you are thinking to demure – we know that you are the CIA Chief of Station in Ankara. That is why we are here talking to you. We are here to ask for your full cooperation.'

To his credit, Bayer knew when there was no point

in trying to conceal who he was or the position he held at the Embassy. He did not know who Mark Taylor was or who he represented. But the message had come from the Ambassador that he was someone important. And someone who obviously had contacts in high places. Bayer was young enough, and ambitious enough, to realize that how he managed this situation could make a big difference to his future in the organization that he represented.

Bayer's immediate problem was that he had not a clue of where an Iranian called Mohamed Haji might be.

'I can put the word out to my network of informants and find out what we can' he offered. But even that did not satisfy his visitors.

Mark let his voice drop to almost a whisper.

'You will need to do better than that. Haji is on the CIA terrorist watch list. He is marked as a man with a high priority for notification. Now - it is not for me to tell you how to do your job. But the last thing we want is to have every one of your informants blabbering about the elusive Mr. Haji and the fact that someone is looking for him.'

That comment did have a noticeable effect on Bayer. Mark could see the beginnings of the effect that bureaucracies had on the early career of many young men. Bayer had a job to do but was surrounded by people and systems that fitted everything into a series of boxes. Trying to think outside this concept of the order of things was difficult for a majority people. And those who couldn't think outside the box were destined to remain at the bottom of the bureaucratic pyramid with a career that could be limited to straightening paper clips.

Fortunately, Bayer recovered.

He just said 'ok,' got out of his chair and went to the safe which was built into the wall and hidden behind an indoor plant. Mark was pleased to see the safe was locked.

Well – that could mean that he had simply had no reason to have opened it on this day! There was a tendency in most offices to leave a safe open until the end of a working day. The instructions carved in stone by the security people were that it should be opened only to retrieve something or to put something away. And then locked.

After rummaging around Bayer eventually returned to his desk carrying a bunch of papers. And to be fair he quickly pulled out a photograph which he slid across the desk.

'Is this your man?'

Mark shuffled the paper across to Dusty for confirmation.

'Yes – that is Haji.' Dusty confirmed then added 'The picture is a little out of date.'

Mark pulled another photograph out of his pocket. It was far clearer than the picture that Bayer had produced, and the face was devoid of facial hair which projected an image of a very different man.

Why the CIA did not provide their people with alternative images of people who had a habit of constantly changing their appearance as well as their names is a constant riddle!

'I suggest that you make some copies of that.' Mark said – the frustration very evident in his voice. This job could be more difficult than he had envisaged!

'Now – how many men can you spare to do surveillance on the Iranian Embassy? There are seven of us in my team with three vehicles. Can you find another eight men and four vehicles? That way we can cycle people through and cut down the risk of them being spotted by anyone from the Embassy.'

It was all happening too fast for Bayer. But he seemed to agree with what Mark was proposing. Apart from his theoretical training at the CIA Farm back at Camp Peary Williamsburg Virginia, he had zero practical experience at surveillance and countersurveillance. He realized he was out of his depth. As a last effort to get some authority into what he had to say, he suggested that they mix their teams. That way he felt that they would have a better chance of spotting Haji since the men in Marks team had eyeballed Haji in Khartoum.

Mark agreed with this suggestion. But for another reason. If the rest of the CIA contingent were as obviously inept as their head of station, they would struggle if they were left to their own devices! Mark changed tactics.

'Now – how are your relations with the local police and with the MIT? I understand that they have some form of surveillance that we could tap into. We are anxious to know whether and when our friend Haji has visited the Embassy in recent weeks. We have been talking to the police who have seen some of the take but that was not focused on Haji.'

To be fair Bayer did not act as surprised as he was at Mark's knowledge of the local scene.

'I can get us into that feed. The Turks have a series of cameras around the area of the Kugulu Park which is alongside the Iranian and other Embassies. They claim that the intention is to protect property as well as to monitor traffic. But we know that they also provide good information on who comes and goes. We do not believe that the cameras are aligned with any one Embassy. And the pictures are not always that good. But, if you already know something about the people you are looking for, they are good enough. Now – because we can – we have recently tried to get the intelligence types to try our special gear for facial recognition. And some of our equipment is color enabled which improves the image by some magnitude. We would not trust the local police with that kind of information, but their MIT guys are pretty switched on and keen to give it a go. You understand that

MIT is primarily a civilian organization. But they are still well disciplined. What is more, the Turks – especially the intelligence people - do not particularly like the Iranians.'

Mark was beginning to like this young man.

'Ok – so how do we get to look at the take?'

Chapter 45

The Prospects Of War

Why anyone would want this job was a mystery to any sane person who had an idea of what the job entailed. Just getting finally confirmed in the job had been a marathon. And then, when you had to do it, you would wonder whether it was worth it.

There were un-told millions of dollars spent first fighting against people in your own party just to get the chance to stand for them or their interests on the final ballot paper. And then many more millions of dollars spent when you went one-on-one with someone from the opposition party that wanted the same job. Sure, if you won that fight, you got to sit in a custom-made chair. You became the leader of the free world, and you were allowed to drink your morning coffee out of a cup that had gold writing on it. That writing proclaimed to anyone who bothered to read it that you were now the President of the United States of America.

But it came with its costs. The President was hog-tied by a schedule that dictated what he could and could not do and when he could or could not do it. The choices that made up the schedule were made by someone else. So, despite the position of power, you did not even get to choose what did, or did not, go onto the schedule. And changes would periodically be made to the strict schedule at the whim of someone, or some group, who applied whatever logic appealed to their sense of duty. Either with, or without, regard for what the subject of this schedule thought or wanted.

All that President BJ Thomas knew about this mornings' change to the schedule was that Peter Fairfield – the Director of National Intelligence – had asked for an urgent meeting. He had also asked that Barry Crammer – the Secretary of Defense – should be present. And he had stipulated that he would be accompanied by the Deputy Director of Intelligence from the CIA.

Whether the subject of this urgent meeting would be about the re-allocation of toilet paper in the Pentagon or about the declaration of the start of World War III was unknown even to the Secret Service people who job it was to rearrange things such that the Presidents time was not wasted.

The President was of course the effective chairperson of any meeting held at the White House. Nicolas Harrison – the Presidents Chief of Staff – would always be there to make sure BJ kept his foot out of his mouth. After all – it was HIS house – at least until such time as someone else was sufficiently insane to win this job. But, when his guests arrived and were seated in chairs arrayed before his desk, the President still felt like asking - *What the fuck was going on!*

Instead, he said 'Good Morning, Peter – I understand that you have requested this meeting so what is it that you want to talk to us about?'

Fairfield shifted uncomfortably in his chair and then simply demurred.

'We have a situation in the Middle East. I have brought Jonathon Gibbs a Deputy Director from the CIA to explain what has happened.'

Gibbs was new at this job and was not used to meetings at this level. Although everyone else in the room was hyped-up, they were at least comfortable in the environment. The Deputy had to get his presentation right, or this could be his first and only chance!

But how did you deliver bad news?

All that BJ could be thankful for was that the presentation was to be delivered by the Deputy. The Director of the Central Intelligence Agency had been a political appointment by the previous administration and, in the opinion of the President, was both incompetent and too old for the job. He made a mental note to get rid of the Director, and in doing so almost missed the opening lines.

'There was a raid on the Incirlik Air Force base in Turkey a few days ago. We have yet to confirm the number of the Air Force security staff that were killed...'

'Incirlik? That is where we store nuclear bombs for the B52 bombers?' the President interjected, keen to show that he had been listening to earlier briefings.

'That is correct sir.'

'Ok – please continue.' said BJ having established his credentials.

'The raiders are believed to be a group attached to the Lebanese terrorist group Hezbollah which you will know is financed by Iran. Our intelligence tells us that they were acting under specific instruction from Teheran.'

'Wait a minute!' This came from Secretary of Defense. 'We know Hezbollah are a front for Iranian interests – so, they would end up following what Teheran tells them to do. But – what were they doing in Incirlik? And how did they get in?'

The Deputy turned to the DNI for guidance. He knew

that he was not going to take a hit because of someone else's incompetence.

The DNI realized that having the Deputy deliver the message was a bad idea. He sighed and decided that he had better come clean.

'Mister President – we believe that the group stole a nuclear bomb from our Air Force base in Incirlik Turkey. We have kept it very quiet until now because we were carrying out a recovery operation and did not believe it would turn out this bad. However, the recovery failed and at present we have no idea where the stolen bomb is. We suspect that the bomb will end up in Teheran. So far no one has claimed responsibility for the raid or the theft. You understand that these situations are fluid, and you could not be briefed on this until we had all the facts.'

Well - that was a laugh, the DNI thought. The fact was that they had just run out of options! The DNI had deliberately requested the opportunity to brief the President on a day when the Secretary of State would be out of town. And who was the dumb-ass that appointed John Scott as Secretary of State – you Mister President! The President had done that against the advice of your Vice-President (although that advice could not really be trusted!) and most of the support staff (which could be trusted). Appointed because of some mistaken belief that he deserved a reward for getting you elected. But – Secretary Scott was susceptible to compromise because he did not know how to keep his dick in his pants! That was the problem – wasn't it? There was nothing specific that had occurred so far that would suggest that he was in danger of revealing intelligence within the orbit of the Secretary of State. However, revealing *sources* of intelligence that he would know of from beyond that orbit was another matter entirely.

The CIA had relied on a source in Iran – in fact, their

only source of reliable intelligence at the present time from that country – and they could not afford that source to be compromised. That source had alerted the CIA to the Iranian governments involvement in a plot to steal a bomb and had confirmed that the bomb would make its' way to Iran. But where in Iran? The guess had been that there were three possibilities – the Sharif University of Technology, the Rudan nuclear research center, or the Natanz enrichment plant. The fact that the *source* did not know which of these options was the most likely meant two things. Firstly - there would be intense competition within the Iran nuclear fraternity to get their hands on the bomb. Secondly – the source was obviously not close to the Iran Revolutionary Guard Corp because that was where the ultimate decision on where the bomb would end up would undoubtably be made.

For their part, the CIA was scrambling to deal with problems within its own ranks at various overseas posts as well as within the US diplomatic community. In addition to that, a number of the US *ambassadorial* staff had recently been compromised and God only knew how far that had spread. They had ample evidence that they had problems in Kuwait, Harare, Khartoum and probably now also in Ankara. Fortunately, the United States government did not officially have any representation in Iran so at least they were in the clear there. But they had contacts in the Embassy of Switzerland and the hope was that this was safe. They could - and did – seek confirmation of things that happened in Iran from those sources. That was not the same as having US representatives on the ground but was nonetheless all part of the normal functions of the US diplomatic service. But it left the CIA out on a limb and vulnerable.

And almost entirely dependent of the diplomatic service.

And – who was responsible for the United States diplomatic services?

John fucking Scott!

The President was unaware of this dilemma. He slammed his fist down on the desk with such force that the cups of coffee crashed to the floor, and he screamed. 'Who is the incompetent that decided to keep this secret from me until now?'

The crashing of cups caused Secret Service agents to rush into the room reaching for their pistols and assuming that someone was attacking their charge.

The President, for all his faults, held up his hands in mock surrender.

'Sorry Archie!' he said to the Secret Service details lead agent.

But he remained standing – demanding an explanation from his DNI, who tried one last time to protect his source.

This President had not been here long enough to know how the system worked. Fairfield had taken a major risk in revealing anything, even without the Secretary of State present. But this dumb-ass President was just as likely to reveal too much when in casual conversation with his friend.

'Mister President – this information is still not confirmed!' Fairfield began. 'Our sources are a closely guarded secret and, in these circumstances, we need to be careful how we go about verifying what we have learnt. We had to be as certain as we could be that the information that we had was correct before we could present it to you. If you do not believe that then I will offer my resignation now. But before I do that you need to understand the reason for this meeting. The situation has now escalated to have become a very serious matter. We need your agreement on what we decide to do now.'

BJ resumed his seat, somewhat chastened by the offer of resignation. Sure – he had inherited this DNI from the previous administration. But Fairfield seemed to know more than anyone else about what went on in the world of spooks and he did bring a degree of professionalism to this inexperienced team.

'Ok – Peter – sorry for my outburst. But why in heavens name would the Iranians do that?'

'The CIA is still considering that.' Fairfield replied. 'There is one theory that the Iranians had a problem with proximity fuses on their ICBM design and want to find out how we did it. The other theory is that they stole the bomb as part of a terrorist plot to threaten someone, or to actually explode the bomb at a place and time yet to be established.'

The Secretary of Defense had to step in before things got out of hand.

'Your first theory does not make any sense - does it Peter? Why would anyone think that reverse engineering the fuse on a bomb that is designed to be dropped from an airplane would have any bearing on the design of a proximity fuse for an ICBM. The physics involved are miles apart. And surely, the Iranians could not be intending to drop a bomb from an airplane! They do not have any planes with that capability, and we would know if they tried to acquire one. And we should not lose sight of the facts – those bombs and the bombers that carry them were designed in the 1950's. You cannot be telling us that the Iranians are that far behind! Therefore, your second theory is the only one that is plausible – isn't it?'

The President had accepted Crammers' interruption for what it was – an attempt to bring a degree of sanity into the discussion. But he was missing the whole point. And BJ had had enough.

The President fixed the CIA Deputy Director with his

icy stare. He did not have the confidence to take on Fairfield again so Gibbs would have to take the load.

'What you are saying is that the CIA does not know shit! I was told last week by your people that the CIA has the best analysts on the planet! Well - what do the twenty-odd thousand analysts that you employ do all day? I know that they are not out there gathering information. I know that they are not managing spies because you told me that one agent can only manage one or two sources. Now do the mathematics – there are nearly two hundred countries in the world, there are say five hundred CIA agents most of which are, or should be, watching major countries like China and Russia. I am told that you have sources, but I am not allowed to know who or where they are! Now you tell me that these secret sources are unable to do more than guess on the intentions of a bunch of amateurs. Your organization is broken!'

The Director of National Intelligence had to step in because his President was beginning to lose the plot.

'Mister President – we have not got time to wait until the CIA has sufficient information to make a call. We may never get that information for the simple reason that we just do not know what the Iranians are up to. I recommend that you have a chat with the Iran President and ask him to function as an intermediary with Hezbollah in the interests of world peace.'

'Do you care to elaborate on that? Would it not be more proper for our Secretary of State to make the first approach at his level?'

This President may be dumb, but he was learning! Or was he just looking to pass the buck?

The DNI did not know. But he certainly did not want John Scott involved. For reasons that he could not justify. At least in present company.

'Scott is presently away from his desk – in fact, he will

not be back in Washington for some days. In any case, we need to stress that this matter is extremely serious so head-to-head talks would be more appropriate Mister President.'

To demonstrate that he had a least a grasp of who was who, BJ had one more diversion.

'In that case should I not talk to Ali?'

Ali Khamenei was the Supreme Leader of Iran and a cleric. That meant that Khamenei would be only too aware of what was going on in the world. He would almost certainly be aware of the Iranian acquisition of a nuclear bomb. However, although he was a cleric, he would be very unlikely to admit such a thing. He would almost certainly refer the matter to his minions in the Iran foreign ministry who were more adept at dealing with the leaders of other countries.

And who did not feel at all restricted by the need to tell the truth.

Fairfield had another problem.

How do you tell the President of the United States that world leaders were not the best people to convey messages between nation states? But the Islamic State of Iran was different – wasn't it? They had two leaders and it did not take much imagination to realize that the leader of the free world would need to talk to a man who was not at the top of their ladder.

'No!' the DNI replied. 'I would not recommend that. It would just result in your exchanging pleasantries for no result. Khatami, on the other hand, would be more likely to at least listen to what we have to say. He will be in his office for another hour. It is just after 10am here – 6:30pm in Teheran. We expect he will be there until 7pm Teheran time. So – if we are going to call, we would need to do so now.'

The DNI had gone as close as he dared go without

revealing the source of that piece of information. Iranians did not have the same reputation as their western counterparts for playing around with the girls in the office which resulted in some women getting pissed-off with their leaders and seeking vengeance through turning into spies for whoever sympathized with them. But there are other ways that women could get pissed-off and be turned to useful sources of information.

The President paged his secretary and calmly asked her to get Mahmoud Khatami in Teheran on the telephone. That she achieved in double quick time and with a minimum of fuss.

The telephone was switched to speaker so that everyone of the six people in the room could hear. The recording system was automatically activated. Consequently, everyone else in the world who was still alive at the end of the conversation could hear and in fact have a word for word transcript if the President so decided.

'Mahmoud! So good to hear your voice again! And how are things in Teheran?' BJ began the conversation.

'Bernard! Well - this is a pleasant surprise. And what would you be calling me for so late in our day?' President Khatami replied in passable English, ignoring the question. And asking one of his own.

The fact that the two men had never met – well they had once been in the same room at a United Nations conference a few years before but had never actually met – and BJ hated people to use his first name even at international level – made for an awkward start to their discussion.

They had spoken when, on his first election to the job of US President, BJ had received countless calls from everywhere on earth. Most of these calls came from people who he barely knew. Some of them from people that intelligence reports suggested he would not want to know. Most of them came from places he had barely heard off. All of them from people wishing him well. Very few of them meaning it.

It also told the DNI that someone in the Teheran intelligence community had a little more research to do on his President.

'Well Mahmoud - I will get straight to the point and not delay your dinner. My staff have informed me that your friends from Hezbollah have stolen something of ours and we would like to get it back. I am sure that you are aware of the circumstances that I am referring to and I thought that before this thing escalates to an international incident, we could settle this amicably by your interfering on our behalf.' The President of the United States said to the President of Islamic Republic of Iran.

There was a pause on the link, which the DNI interpreted as someone in Teheran scrambling to get someone else involved.

Then President Khatami replied.

'No – I do not know any such circumstances. Can you tell me a little bit more of what this is about? You must understand that we have no control over the Hezbollah, and it will take me some time to gather the facts. That is - unless you can be more specific what has been taken, and from where?'

BJ looked to the DNI for guidance and got it in the form of a throat-cutting motion. It is hard to read body-language over the telephone, but it was not hard to read when someone was telling porkies.

'Ok Mahmoud – I have to believe that you have not yet been brought up to date, but my people here are quite clear in what has occurred. So - what say I will call you at this time tomorrow and that will give you time to get the facts. This link is not secure at your end so I cannot go into details. If you do not have the facts, or are unable to get them in that time, then I give you notice that the United States will take all measures to recover our property wherever it may end up. Do I make my position clear?'

Again, there was a pause on the link, and then Khatami came back.

'Mister President you cannot speak to me this way. What you say is tantamount to a declaration of war.'

'Then that is what will happen.'

And BJ cut the link.

The Chief of Staff was pale as he struggled to contain himself.

'Mister President – do you think that was the wisest thing to say?'

The National Security Advisor came quickly to BJ's defense.

'Well – he would have got the message loud and clear. And it was good that you did not mention anything specific.'

The Secretary of Defense thought he was relieving the pressure.

'It is unlikely – possible but improbable - that they could make use of a nuclear bomb. They are more likely to blow themselves up trying to get around the safety features built into all our nuclear weapons.' And then he continued to elaborate which destroyed his whole purpose in trying to calm things down.

'Of course – there is a chance that they have someone with the codes – and we need to prepare for the worst.'

Now wouldn't that be a hoot?

The Defense services all had their own 'Intelligence' organizations and not all - in fact most of - their own intelligence did not make it into the CIA for a two main reasons. Firstly, military intelligence was just that – how good, where, what weapons, what detection, et cetera had the enemy - or perceived enemy - in place and was less likely to be involved with the broader picture of which country was about to fuck another. Secondly, military intelligence people were probably more adept at keeping secrets and did not believe that sharing information for the sake of it – in this case with a non-military organization like the CIA – would achieve anything that could further their cause. And this view was fully reciprocated by the CIA. Consequently, while Defense was not aware that the nuclear weapons codes had been compromised, the CIA may know differently.

Before things got completely out of hand the Chief of Staff leaped in again.

'I think we need to prepare for what happens next' Nicolas Harrison cautioned. 'Probably have Kelly draft something up for a press release – in fact, several alternatives in case the shit hits the fan. Iran will probably protest their innocence. They are probably angling for our trying to keep this whole business quiet – after-all while it is information that is freely available to anyone who cares to look, the America public is probably not fully aware that we have nuclear bombs so far from home. And of all places in East Turkey which has neighbors that are not exactly friends of ours. If CNN finds out what has happened, then we will be in the shitter.'

The White House has a whole array of media staff. Some of the staff were there to counter the hordes of media reporters who were forever pestering to know stuff before it leaked out to the public and thereby gain on their competitors. The staff that really mattered to the White House were those who wrote the speeches for the President and others in the inner circle so that a consistent story came out. Not always the actual truth. At times miles from it. But at least consistent.

One of these was a gentleman who had the nickname of 'Kelly.' He was the son of a polish immigrant Korneli Zalewski who had been christened his first and only son born in America as Ned. Hence the nickname. Kelly was the speechwriter used when no one at the White House knew what was going on.

The American public could be forgiven for not taking everything that was issued by the White House press as gospel as presented to them by reporters who also did not believe what they were told. The reporters of course had a view that if something was announced after the fact that they should have known before, so that whatever the executive did was always not enough, too much, too early, too late, an over-reaction, or an under-reaction. It was always wrong. So, they got particularly pissed if their inevitable questions were ignored.

Some of the media people viewed this as a game.

And it takes two to play.

Within twenty-four hours of the Thomas conversation with Khatami all US businesspeople in Iran or bound in that direction would have been warned to get out. The US Ambassador to Iraq and most of his staff would be recalled to Washington for consultations. This was mostly a symbolic gesture since, at least officially, there were no US diplomats in Teheran. The US President called a press conference which was timed to coincide with the evening news. That was the problem with western news. It was dictated by the demands of television. And the dissemination of the news itself was decided by factors that even the most experienced observers could not agree on.

If the Iranian Ali Khomeini spoke and raised his forefinger his pronouncements were taken as though Allah himself had spoken. If the President of the United States did the same thing he would be described as an arrogant son-of-a-bitch. As it was, the press briefing was announced without any preamble so that media both visual and print were scrambling to get organized. Some would broadcast the speech live irrespective of what the speech might contain – if it was worthy of a place it would continue, otherwise it would be instantly replaced and only monitored by a producer in case someone got shot live on television. Their only interest was in the share of the channel-switching public. Others avoided this dichotomy by waiting until they had the opportunity for their own experts to mull over the speech.

In the case of this press briefing, the latter regretted that decision.

Accompanied by the Secretary of Defense, the Director of National Intelligence, the National Security Advisor and his Vice President, the President strode to the rostrum in the White House Press Briefing Room as though he were on a mission.

BJ did not wait before plowing into his short speech.

'My fellow Americans – my officials have spent the last twenty-four hours ensuring that any American citizens in the Islamic Republic of Iran are safe. We fear that recent actions by Iran have once again brought the world to the brink of conflict in the Middle East. I have already approved a range of sanctions that will be imposed on Iran. We have called an emergency meeting of the UN security council to endorse their implementation. We are immediately placing our forces on high alert and stand ready to move to defend our citizens and our allies against any provocation. We are placing Iran on notice that any attempt to threaten the well-being of American citizens, wherever they may be, will be taken as a declaration of war, and we will respond with due force. That is the end of my statement. Any question you may have can be directed to the Vice President.'

That said, the President picked up his briefing papers and left. Leaving the press speechless. That would not last.

Roger Warren adjusted the microphone and surveyed the assembled press and then asked the inevitable question.

'Are there any questions?'

The howls from the reporters were almost deafening.

Warren held up his hands in mock surrender.

'Come now – lets' try to keep order! I cannot answer you all at once – so if you want to ask a question please raise your hand, and we will deal with it as best we can. If you could state your name and who you represent that would be good.'

That did not exactly go down well with the senior reporters present. Did this pompous ass not know who they were? Were they not the leading jockeys in the crowd of important people? And were not they the representatives of the great unwashed public who had put the punk in a position where he could serve them?

Undaunted by his flippant insult Warren tried to take control of the situation by picking out one of the few reporters that he knew.

'Brenda your question please.'

Brenda Simpson was the reporter for Fox News who Warren had picked out as one who would, at least normally, be on the side of the administration. He was disappointed.

The press, often regarded by many as hard-nosed ruthless sons of bitches, were nonetheless very astute at reading body language, and the Vice President's reaction was well-read by all present. Or was there something else bothering him?

'Mister Vice President – we had no idea that this briefing would be virtually a declaration of war. Can you please tell us what gave rise to this crisis?'

And there in a nutshell was the issue, wasn't it? No one had the least inkling that there was a problem with Iran, apart from the ongoing arguments over sanctions, the almost childish nonsense concerning Iran's nuclear ambitions, and the usual to-ing and fro-ing that went on between two countries that were poles apart in ideology. Nor was it a *Crisis* just because Brenda had said so.

'There have been several issues with Iran in recent weeks that have caused us some concern. The situation has recently escalated to the point that the President will be increasing sanctions on Iran and how they may react to those is a further cause for concern.'

'Mister Vice President - Jerome Weisman from CNN. Has this got anything to do with recent events in Turkey?'

Warren cringed at that question. It was amazing that CNN had not picked up on the events that had occurred at Incirlik. Or had they – and they were waiting for the opportunity to embarrass the administration. There was only one way to find out.

'Yes – the events in Turkey are a part of a broader range of activities that are of concern to us.' Warren replied with the accompanying shrug.

Weisman persisted. 'I am sure the public would like to know what exactly happened. They have a right to know. Is it true that there was a raid on our Air Force base at Incirlik in which several of our men were killed?'

'Yes – that is true. And we are still awaiting full details on that before we can make any further comment.'

'Is it not also true that you have nuclear weapons stored at that base?' Weisman turned the knife.

Barry Crammer – the Secretary of Defense - came to the rescue of his Vice President. Not that he helped much.

'It is a well-known fact that we have stored nuclear weapons overseas, for example in Turkey and Italy as part of our strategic force to combat the Soviets during the Cold War. In the case of Turkey, they have been there since 1961. That is not exactly news – is it?'

'Excuse me – Dave Dunn from the Washington Post. The Soviet Union as we know it ended in 1991. I can understand that you would have wanted to be closer to Moscow but really! Why have these weapons not been returned to the United States years ago? Considering the tensions in the region I would have thought that eastern Turkey is the last place on earth you would have wanted to store such valuable and strategic assets!'

And there was no answer to that – was there?

'Next question?' interjected Warren, wondering about the wisdom of ever agreeing to be Vice President.

'Michelle Glazmuzina from the New York Times. Are you saying – or rather not saying – that the raid of the Turkish airbase was carried out by Iran – and that they could have gained access to our nuclear weapons?'

'No!' blurted out Crammer. 'The raid we believe was carried out by Hezbollah – a terrorist organization from Lebanon.'

Michelle went red in the face but carried her line of questioning.

'I do know who Hezbollah is, Mister Secretary! But isn't Hezbollah a quasi-Iranian organization? And what exactly did the raid achieve? Are you saying – or not saying

– that they took one or more of our bombs? Is not that something that would require a reaction which was a little bit stronger than imposing further sanctions on Iran?'

And that of course was the whole point.

'Steve Rivenski – Fox News. What are you doing to protect US interests in the region and what are you doing to ensure that US personnel have a clear passage out of there in case this situation escalates?'

The Vice President stepped forward to answer, more confident that the question had come from Fox News.

'We have recalled our Ambassador in Iraq to Washington and issued a travel advisory that should avoid people traveling to or through Iran, and we are confident that our citizens will be safe should the situation escalate.'

Rivenski sat down perplexed. He knew that there was no Ambassador in Iran and hadn't been for many years. But - What had the Iraq Ambassador got to do with anything?

Jerome Weisman could not resist putting the boot in.

'Mister Vice President – I am sure you do not want a repeat of 1979 and the Iran hostage crisis. Would it not have been wise to have given our people time to get organized before the President issued a threat to declare war on Iran.'

'There are also plenty of Iranians in the United States at the moment who are in a similar position!' blurted out the Vice President.

The Director of National Intelligence stood at the back of the group and groaned, while the political appointees struggled to handle what should have been relatively straightforward questions. The Chief of Staff stepped forward indicating that he had heard enough and called the press conference to a close by saying,

'This situation is very fluid. I am sure that you will appreciate that we are busy trying to get clarification on several issues We will provide you with an update at nine o'clock tomorrow morning.'

His final comments were followed by a mass exodus of reporters anxious to get to their desks. In the case of the print media to start writing the morning headlines. In the case of the video, channels get their producers to reschedule their news updates.

The exception was Jerome Weisman – the reporter from CNN.

He just sat there watching some of the most powerful men on the planet exit one of the craziest press conferences he had ever seen. He finally got to his feet shaking his head.

Perhaps he should go to the middle east and find out what was going on.

'What a God-almighty fuck up!'

Chapter 46

Ankara

Mark and Dusty had got into the US Embassy in Ankara just before nine in the morning and were waiting in an anteroom until the Ambassador was free to receive his guests. The message that they had to attend a meeting had been conveyed to them by James Bayer. No reason was given. Mark had the distinct impression that Bayer was annoyed about something. Probably, Mark speculated, that was because Dusty Miller had been asked to also attend as well, rather than Bayer. Yes – racial bias was still alive and well in US diplomatic circles!

There was an unusual air of anticipation around the place and Mark remarked to Dusty that something was going on that they needed to know about. As was usual, Dusty simply replied that if there was something to know, they would find out in due course.

Mark was not so sure.

There had been something that was not right about this whole situation from the very beginning when they had first started to follow the trail of drugs. They had clear evidence that Iran was active in the drug trade. And that they were not averse to trading with the Taliban that saw drugs traded for weapons. But – what had that to do with the United States diplomatic community in Africa and the middle east? They also had evidence that it was Iranian agents who had tried on more than one occasion to gain access to diplomatic personnel through crude attempts at setting up honey traps. One such occasion had resulted in the death of a US official which had been written off in some quarters as suicide. However, that was more likely to have been because of action by foreign agents. Chief among the suspects were the Iranians, for the simple reason that Mohamed Haji had been in the same town as the body. On another occasion, the officer concerned had admitted to an affair before returning to the States a broken man with his career over. But that man was too scared to reveal what he knew about the people who had been responsible for his demise. The question now was – How many more events had occurred or were still current, that they did not know about?

And then there was the Incirlik affair!

Mark had come to form a theory that beggared belief. That was because his training with the US Delta Force had taught him not to make any assumptions and to not ignore coincidences. That meant that if you planned any mission everything was covered, and you allowed nothing dependent on luck.

But would the Iranians do and think the same way?

Mark had formed the theory that Iran agents were behind the whole sorry affair starting with the apparent attempt on the life of Robert Mugabe. They had uncharacteristically involved themselves in the drug trade as a smokescreen for whatever the aim of the exercise was. Forget Mohamed Haji for the moment. He was just an agent. It was the Islamic Republic of Iran that had looked to discredit US diplomats.

Maybe Mark was paranoid. Or it may have been by pure chance. But - the focus had been on people who were involved with the CIA. So - was that a lead-up to their real purpose?

And then there was a change of tact. Was it Iran that had engineered the SARS outbreak in the city of Adana? If so, they had chosen a location that would most likely involve people from the Incirlik airbase and there were likely to be victims from that base. The World Health Organization, in the true spirit of international cooperation, had quickly responded to what could have become a major pandemic by rapidly localizing treatment to the hospital in Adana which meant that patients would be transported from Incirlik. But then they had a change of mind. This meant that health officials would need to visit Incirlik with test kits and front-line treatment. And that had been how the terrorists or whatever they were had been able to attack US personnel on the airbase.

As the facts unfolded no one would tell Mark what was stolen. He was later able to join the dots. What had convinced him that his theory was correct was the body located in the city of Adana. Whether the body was that of a diplomat was irrelevant. Why this person had been killed was irrelevant. That the body was that of a woman was also irrelevant. Now that the body had been traced to the Iranian Embassy *was* relevant.

It did seem to be a bit of a stretch that Iranian Intelligence would go to all this trouble to achieve nothing. So – this last event had been a mistake. It was the one event that tied the outbreak to Iran. Therefore - the raid. Therefore – the theft of a bomb. So – why then steal a bomb the technology of which was many years old? And what were they going to do with it?

Mark had still not connected all the dots.

But he was closer than he thought.

All this had nothing to do with the Embassy in Ankara except for one overriding fact - Someone with connections to the US military must have had a hand in the raid on Incirlik.

The Ambassador finally signaled them to come into his office and apologized for the delay.

'I am sorry. I have been on the go since 2 o'clock this morning. We are having a bad day. And it won't get any better!'

'Is that something that we need to know about?' Mark asked the harassed diplomat.

At first, the Ambassador seemed reluctant to share his thoughts. Then he just shrugged his shoulders and muttered something about the President which appeared very undiplomatic. He used a remote to turn on the television, selected a recording, and pressed play. It was a recording of the entire press conference from Washington. The three men sat there in stunned silence before the tape ended with a picture of the White House Chief of Staff - Nicolas Harrison - urging the most powerful men in the land out of the press briefing room as though escorting tiny tots into the bathroom for a toilet break.

Mark could only stare at the now blank screen before turning his attention to the Ambassador.

'So – are we saying that it was the Iranians that stole a nuclear bomb? Someone must know the truth! And is this their endgame?'

Ambassador Neil Ziegler was from the old school. He did not like to share his thoughts with two guys who he could only regard as people well outside his normal circle of confidants. But his real CIA Head of Station Ankara was in Washington DC and Ziegler could not trust anyone else on his staff. The Iraq Ambassador had also been recalled to Washington and the Kuwait embassy was still reeling from what had happened in their neck of the woods. The Ambassador in Saudi Arabia was an arrogant prick and regarded himself as a cut above the other peasants in this region. The Ambassadors in Lebanon, Syria, and Israel had more than enough to deal with to care about what was happening in neighboring Turkey.

But that wasn't the real reason why he had no one to talk to - was it?

The earlier administration had handed itself a major problem with its position in this part of the world. Because Turkey was a member of the North Atlantic Treaty Organization it had been favored by successive US administrations. All the important military appointments covering US interests in the middle east were in this very Embassy. That was even though over the years – mostly for political reasons – the respective governments had drifted apart to the point where it would soon become an embarrassment to both sides.

Zeigler started the discussion with a question of his own while ignoring the questions raised by Mark.

'I understand from James that you are trying to get a handle on an Iranian gentleman named Haji who may be moving around under one of several aliases. Do you care to fill me in on the background?'

Mark was quite happy to do that and told him the history of their association before he got tired of this diplomatic dance.

'We will find Haji – if he is still in Turkey. However, we believe that his presence is inexorably tied to recent events in the south. What we are interested in is how he could have got information concerning the security arrangements at Incirlik. As I have told you, his pattern has been to have compromising information on some individual and use that to both introduce drugs and to get information. Since all the military in Turkey is controlled from here – who could he have talked to on your staff?'

Zeigler was shocked at the bluntness of the question. For a moment Mark thought that he had gone too far or gone too early. Body language told him a different story. The Ambassador was hurt.

Mark could have sworn that there was a tear in the eyes as the Ambassador stared out of the window and then turned back to Mark with a sigh.

'Yes – that is the question that I have been asking myself. But it goes further than that doesn't it. The raid on Incirlik – while it may have been very simple in its execution – had to have some inside knowledge to pull it off.'

The Ambassador paused causing Mark to prompt him gently.

'So - someone could have arranged that. Someone who has knowledge and authority. That is the person we will need to find.'

'Yes – You and me both! But who is it? There are at least a dozen people in this Embassy who have ample knowledge of what goes on at Incirlik. Colonel Sam Henning is the guy in charge of security. He has control of all security arrangements throughout the middle east. He tells me that he has talked to all his people in my Embassy and is adamant that none of them are responsible. That leaves the base personnel at Incirlik. I guess we must wait while the bloody FBI finishes their investigation. But - they will face the same problem that we have at any of our military bases. The base will close ranks to protect their own. Nobody will talk.'

Of course, Zeigler had just summed up the situation throughout the whole bureaucracy. The FBI would be pushing shit uphill with a fork.

Since the conversation with the Ambassador had drifted away from the reasons why Mark and Dusty had been summoned to the Embassy it was time to raise the real issue. Zeigler sat forward in his chair and eventually had to deliver his message.

'The President has requested that you do one more thing for him.' Zeigler smiled for the first time before continuing.

'You have impressed him! Let us hope you continue to do so! His advisors in Washington have concluded that the bomb is still in Turkey and that your friend Haji will be the one who will take it out of the country. Now – we cannot alert the Turkish border forces to prevent that – for obvious political reasons. And we cannot use our forces - because we just do not have either the necessary people or sufficient authority to mount such an operation. He has therefore asked that you find, and then follow, Mohamed Haji. Should you detect the man and the bomb, he wants them both followed to whatever destination he may choose. And he wants that information sent to the White House immediately it is known.'

Mark and Dusty looked at each other in disbelief before Mark spoke.

'Surely – he does not plan to take Haji out – with the bomb!'

Zeigler shrugged.

'I am just the messenger.'

Once they had left the Embassy Mark did what he realized he should have done many days before. He called Brad Morgan at Taylor Software.

'Hi, Brad! Can you tell me whether we can deploy the Sandbox system to help us with problems of tracing someone here in Turkey?'

The name 'Sandbox' was the name of a project that Mark and Brad had been working on for the last six months. Mark knew that he would need to come up with a better name. It had been called Sandbox because every time they had thought they were making progress they got slowed down by a bagatelle of issues – like the experience of running through sand or mud. Despite that, the project had advanced to the point where they could pinpoint the location of a cell phone. And right now, that seemed the best way of finding Mohamed Haji.

The more obvious way would have been to get hold of a Stingray device. But that would have caused a storm in Washington security circles. Their concern would have been letting the knowledge of that technology out into the wider world than was deemed wise. Turkey may be a NATO country but that did not mean they were trusted! And Mark and his team were not exactly a recognized part of the US security and intelligence services. Mark had only been spoken to by people at an executive Director level in the administration. But he had not spoken to anyone in the bureaucracy. So – that was that! That is even though, the last he had heard, he was acting under instruction from the President!

Brad was only interested in matters that he could control. And those matters did not include his boss. He just answered the question.

'The system seems Ok under test. But I would not want to load it directly onto a satellite phone. There is too much excess code. You could load it onto your laptop and use your phone as a send/receive device. That would work.'

Mark was used to dealing with Brad. He probably only told the bare minimum necessary to confirm he was still alive.

'Ok – I will connect to the internet when we are back

at our base. I want you to download onto my laptop whatever I will need. I will connect my satellite phone and you can load that with what is necessary. Then you can show me what I need to do. Can you do that?'

Brad started to outline the problems which Mark could expect from what he regarded as a Beta system. Mark cut him off.

'I do not have time for this. Get yourself organized. I will connect to you with an hour.'

He disconnected the call, ignoring the protestations coming from New York.

The issue that was exercising the minds of Elliott Shannon and Owen Squires, having been left behind in Incirlik to *help* the FBI was – how come nothing had been seen or heard of the people or the bomb virtually since they were last seen heading away from the base on that fateful afternoon? It did seem incongruous that an ordinary truck that was being pursued by a couple of superior military vehicles could vanish in so short a time. And - more surprisingly - the search, despite the initial setup of an extensive perimeter and subsequent extensive searching of everything and everywhere within that perimeter, had failed to find any sign of the truck. There was no sign of the men. There was no sign of the bomb.

From his earlier experience with the CIA, Elliott believed that the Turkish authorities together with their US allies would have been able to find and detain a group of Hezbollah terrorists – if indeed that is what they were. Surely, they would be able to recognize the people who were dragging a package weighing twenty-five hundred pounds along the road heading east towards the Iran border. And at the border itself – it would have been unusual for anyone to be allowed to simply declare he had approval to export a nuclear bomb. Especially one that was not made in Turkey.

The role of the FBI in all of this was to establish how a couple of men had died at the base. It was not really focused on how people had been able to get a bomb out of Incirlik although that had been the event that had caused the deaths. And it was certainly not focused on how these people had managed to get into the base in the first place. So – that really left it to the military to investigate their own security and to find their own bomb.

Elliott Shannon was not a police officer, but he had enough experience to investigate something from the beginning by asking the right questions and see what he could turn up. At least the investigation thus far had turned up nothing, so there was nothing to lose.

He first task was to find out what had in fact been stolen.

Together with Mike Delaney, he and Owen went to have a look at a bomb. They were stored at the western end of the base in hardened bunkers – usually two bombs per bunker - and were likely to stay there since the 39th Air Base Wing had no means to deliver them. There were over fifty B61 nuclear bombs held at the site, and they were guarded by US troops, except apparently when someone decided to steal one.

A bomb was not an easy thing to steal. Each bomb weighed at least 715 pounds – depending on how each was configured. They were almost twelve feet in length and had a diameter of over of thirteen and a half inches. As the saying goes – if it walks like a duck and quakes like a duck – it is a fucking duck! It would therefore be hard for anyone to claim one as anything but a bomb.

All that aside - the public would reasonably assume that a bomb would be recognizable through basic surveillance techniques. After all - having been fed a diet of sci-fi flicks over many years there was nothing that was not possible. But the truth of the matter was that a bomb would not register as anything different from any other man-made object. Of course, an exploding a bomb could be spectacular and would certainly get attention. But a more docile package be it a bomb or otherwise would be just too small.

Armed with the piece of near-useless information the US NRO - National Reconnaissance Office – which operates satellites on behalf of the Intelligence and Security services - developed a gadget that could find such objects. Well not quite. Essentially it was able to identify the fuse mechanism. Then the only problem left to solve was how to get this gadget close enough to said bomb to do its thing. On the assumption that such an operation would normally need to be covert, the scientists came up with a solution that had the gadget attached to a drone and, as everyone knows, flying drones at night is a piece of cake just so long as nothing gets in the flight path. None of this helped the satellites circulating at anything from ten thousand to thirty thousand miles above the Earth. At this point the NRO abandoned the technology. But the technology still found its way into the commercial world and is used for such mundane tasks as finding mines or bombs of which there are several million scattered around waiting to be found.

Starting at the beginning Elliott decided that he needed to first find out where the bomb had gone at the time it had left the base. He knew from Mark that the Iranians had got a safe house for the suspected murder of one of their accomplices in an earlier part of this plot. Therefore, had anybody checked whether they had gotten another place in which to hide the bomb?

He was not the least bit surprised that no one had.

He asked Delaney to talk to his contact in the Adana police. Although Jerry Burak had no idea why the question was being asked, he said that he would speak with the lady at the property management office whether they had done any other deals with the same people. That produced an unusual response probably because the manager was fearful that she could be in trouble. Not that there was anything wrong with doing cash deals. There wasn't. But she had been caught with her fingers in the cookie jar – two deals where cash was paid with zero paperwork at the client's request, and therefore no need for the firm to tell their customer that their property was being used for so short a period.

On the assurance from the police that they would turn a blind eye to the error, the Manager agreed to meet Burak at the second property and bring a key to deal with the possibility that the client was not in residence.

They turned up at 12 noon in the Sokak industrial area – a place that was halfway between the city of Adana and the Incirlik base. Neither the police nor the manager expected to be in the middle of a warzone but apart from the Elliott/Owen and the Delaney/Swarbrick vehicles there were two US MRAP vehicles plus two military trucks each carrying a platoon of fully armed Air Force personnel from the 39th Security forces squadron.

The building they had come to visit was a large warehouse the front of which was almost totally taken up by a roller door, except for a small access door on the left. Burak and the lady went to this door and pressed the buzzer. That drew no response the first time. They tried again with the same result.

The next thing that Burak did was to bash the door which, being of corrugated iron echoed through the building and would have got the attention of the dead. Still no response, so he indicated that the lady should now use the key. On entering the building, she pressed the activation on the roller door which slowly climbed up to the top – about fifteen feet from the base.

The warehouse was bare apart from two small offices on the left and what looked like a lunchroom on the right. The warehouse extended a good fifty yards to the back, but there was no other access or egress points. The offices, the lunchroom and the warehouse were completely empty.

There was no sign that anyone had even been there.

Delaney turned to Elliott looking for answers but all that he could do was shrug as the force from 39th Security looked on.

Owen was not convinced that all was lost. He had ventured to the back of the warehouse and was seen frantically waving to his colleague. Both Delaney and Elliott joined the mad Welshman and soon realized what had attracted his interest.

The floor of the warehouse was concrete that had been poured in blocks that were about fifteen feet square. The block that Owen was standing beside was of the same size but looked to have been poured much more recently than the rest. So recent that the concrete was still damp.

Elliott summoned the senior staff sergeant from the security force over to where they were standing and summed up the confusion of them all.

'I might be crazy – but do you think that our friends could have simply buried the bomb here?'

'There is only one way to find out!'

The sergeant called his base and arranged some help before ordering the men from the two trucks to surround the building and for no reason – other than that he could - ordered everyone else out of the building. By this time, the lady from the property management company was a burbling mess and Burak saw little point in staying. So - they both left.

The four people who had started the original gathering took shelter in one of the MRAP vehicles simply to get out of the rain and await developments. An MRAP maybe a Mine resistant ambush protection armored vehicle but, if a nuclear bomb exploded, it would probably be vaporized along with everything else.

Within fifteen minutes a maintenance team arrived from Incirlik and with two jackhammers they started to break up the concrete pad. This job took a little longer than planned paradoxically due to the concrete being soft and not having solidified. Eventually this work was completed and then the crew carefully prodded the underlying ground to find what was beneath.

The first thing that they found was a metal object. That discovery caused those men to vacate the building to be replaced by a bomb disposal group. Well – that was their official job description.

The bomb disposal team seemed to take forever to carefully dig around the metal until they had uncovered sufficient to make a diagnosis. The leader came out of the building and walked cautiously towards the MRAP where Elliott and his friends were waiting expectantly.

He was not in the military, but a civilian who just contracted his services to the US military, so he saw no need to wait until he found out who was in charge. He poked his head into the MRAP and delivered the news.

'Do you want the good news or the bad news?'

The look on his face told a story all its own. His expression was both serious and incredulous. Since no one said anything, he decided to deliver the bad news first.

'We have found a black plastic bag holding a body – the clothes suggest he or she was a Turkish paramedic - and we think that there may be more bodies. The good news is that we can find no sign of your bomb. There are several pieces of metal, paint tins, gas cylinders, bags, and all sorts of other rubbish – none of which is anything like the length of a B61 bomb. Unless they decided to cut it up into smaller pieces!'

Delaney was the first to react.

'Well - what is the metal?'

'The largest piece is a concrete mixer!'

Delaney was still basically a police officer. His first job was to ensure that all the evidence was preserved. He made a call Jerry Burak and asked him to return to the warehouse and bring a forensic pathologist with him. While he had been talking to the Bomb Disposal guy his people had uncovered another black body-bag. And there could be more. The only evidence in the building apart from the contents of the hole was the telephone. That did not have a number written anywhere but that was soon solved. He made one further request of Burak.

'Can you ask one of your staff to ask the telecom people to get a list of all calls made in or out of this building in the last few weeks. I don't know which network they are on but that should not be too difficult.'

Elliott was retired. But he still had a job to do. He made a call to Mark.

'We have found the site where the bomb was taken after the raid on Incirlik. It looks as though we missed catching them by a whisker. Sadly – we also found the bodies of a couple of Turkish paramedics and there may be more. What are you wanting me to do now?'

Mark hesitated for a moment. This was getting beyond being a matter between Mark Taylor and Mohamed Haji. Now it was a matter between nation-states. He had often joked about starting a World War III. But this went a little beyond that. Now you were talking about a potential nuclear conflict which required someone way above his paygrade to have to manage. Elliott was as clued up as the next man in his team and could be expected to analyze and solve most problems that he was faced with. But he could not be expected to solve this one. Neither could Mark.

'Does the base commander at Incirlik yet know what you have discovered?'

Elliott looked at a very harassed Sergeant who was in deep conversation with his group commander back at the base. The language was interspersed with four-letter words beginning with 'F,' but the message was clear – Someone had to tell Washington in a hurry.

'Yes – I think Washington will know shortly!'

'Ok – I will talk with the Ambassador. Talk to you soon.'

The Iran Revolutionary Guard was well known for its almost brutal approach to discipline. Even so, the Iran Special Forces unit had a characteristic common to all Special Forces – they were trained to think. And, to a man the unit thought that their instructions for this mission were crazy.

They had performed the first part of their mission according to the plan. They had successfully taken over the Turkish vehicles and captured the paramedics. More by good luck than anything else they had managed to gain access to the Incirlik base. There they had done what they were required to do - acting as paramedics - and then stolen a bomb. While they would have preferred to escape from the base without casualties there was always a price to pay. They had lost two men and that would make the rest of the plan more difficult to implement. But they were soldiers and the elite of their nation. And no one said that it would be easy. But who was the idiot who had dreamed up the rest of the plan?

From the Incirlik base with a couple of US vehicles in hot pursuit they had managed to find their next location and that had been timed to perfection. The roller door that gave access to their hideaway was open and they had managed to drive straight into the warehouse and have the door closed before the Americans had the chance to spot them. But that was close and almost brought the whole plan to a premature end. Perhaps the only thing that saved them was the fact that they were in a part of the town where there was very little activity so there were no witnesses to this madness.

After that scare things turned bizarre.

All the equipment and resources that they would need were supposed to be provided by the support team. What was not provided was a realistic time scale to get everything done on the valid assumption that that all would not go according to the plan.

On paper, the task was simply summarized.

1. Get the bomb locked away disguised as a piece of equipment.
2. Reload the now disguised bomb into the truck.
3. Bury any evidence and any equipment used at the site.
4. Dispose of the bodies of the captured paramedics.
5. Move to site B and await further instructions.

The first part was the only one that was done relatively easily. The plan was to disguise the bomb by attaching it to a piece of equipment designed for water treatment based on the assumptions that the bomb was round and water pipes are both empty and round. A simple

Google search would have revealed that a B61 gravity bomb was about 141 inches long and a diameter of 13 inches (depending on which model it was). However, the equipment selected to attach the bomb to only had a length in the output port of 120 inches. No one suggested that they cut off part of the bomb. Therefore, it was necessary to fabricate an extension. However, while the diameter of the port was 15 inches which meant that the bomb would fit snuggly into the tube, the fins on the end of the bomb would not. This was not necessarily a bad thing because the piece had to be fabricated in any case. It was just that anyone who knew anything more than 101 Engineering would be puzzled by the appendage.

Having solved this engineering problem, it was then a matter of shifting the contraption using the more than adequate lifting gear built into the warehouse onto the truck. The problems then were that the truck had a roof, and the length of the deck was about 3 feet short of what would be required. The simple answer was to get another truck and dispose of the Turkish wagon. That meant that the people who had the job of disguising their original vehicle for the trip east had two more tasks – hiring a more suitable truck and then painting, and then disposing of, the other.

Getting rid of the evidence was rather simplistic in principle. The best way to dispose of evidence was to bury it. The problem with this was – How did you dispose of the gear that you used to bury things? And how did you disguise the burial site? And what did you do with the soil that you took out of the hole that was to hold new stuff? The result could be that you ended up chasing your tail! But Special Forces personnel were expected to think. They came up with a plan. They would remove a complete concrete pad from the floor of the warehouse and dig a hole large enough to take all the unwanted gear. Then they would replace the concrete pad with a new one. The concrete mixer that they were to use would be the last thing thrown into the hole and the last mix of concrete would have to be done by manual labor. Any remaining soil and other rubbish which could not be scattered on the grounds around the building would need to go into the truck and be disposed of somewhere on their trip to the east as would any shovels and other gear used to make the concrete pad appear smooth and permanent. They would need to hose down the area when the job was finished – but any excess water would dry and that would be the end of that.

As for the disposal of the four Turkish paramedics – or rather the disposal of four bodies – that was made much simpler by their method of getting rid of the other evidence. When the paramedics had first been brought to the warehouse the instructions that the Special Forces personnel had received were to keep them secure for use as a bargaining chip in case that the raid on the Incirlik base did not go according to plan. Well – the raid did not go exactly as planned – did it? They had left behind two of their men and they wanted them back. However, the Turkish paramedics had now seen their truck drive into the warehouse much the worse for wear after the skirmish at the base. They had also seen the coagulation equipment – a large dust collector. That was sitting in the warehouse looking totally out of place but would be used to conceal the bomb. So – there would be no bargaining. They would have to take the chance that the Iranians that had been left behind at Incirlik would not talk. They were reasonably confident that the Americans were not as brutal as Iranians and would not resort to drugs that could make anyone give up their mother. They could not afford to take the same chance with the Turks.

The major concern for the Iran Special Forces contingent was the speed with which the Americans would react. The theory was that, because they were not on American soil, they would not launch an all-out assault. They would spend a few days having what little information they had analyzed to death by an army of bureaucrats. Then they would descend with all the fury that they could muster. But – what on?

There was a plan for that because the Iranians had one major advantage. They had a person who would tip them off. He was not a spy. That title would have shown too much respect for his lowly ranking in the Incirlik security system. But he had been involved in their gaining access to the base – albeit that he had very nearly screwed up the entire operation by being unable to recall a simple code phrase. All he had to do now was to make a call on a cell phone that had a number locked in when he had something to say. Which he did at 11:20 in the morning.

'They will be at the warehouse within the hour. It is time to leave.

Then all he had to do was dispose of the cell phone which would be done on his way out to the gate to begin his next shift.

In the warehouse they had a plan for this – albeit that they had been lulled into a sense that they had completed this part of their mission and nothing else could go wrong. The fact that the concrete pad had not yet dried was unfortunate but could not be helped. The force collected all the remaining bits that provided evidence that they had been there.

They then left the building.

They headed north to the next warehouse where they would wait for a couple more days while the dust settled. They assumed that the Americans would descend on all points to the east.

Which was almost correct.

Chapter 47

Covert

The United States had a serious problem. The normal mechanism of international diplomacy did not quite work in their relations with the Islamic Republic of Iran. And to be fair the situation was not exactly new.

In 1979 when the people in the American Embassy in Teheran were taken hostage by a group claiming to be college students, it took the Iranian authorities over a year to secure their release. Whether the Iran leadership sponsored the event or whether it was just the spontaneous reaction of people who had their knickers in a twist over some obscure misdeed does not matter. What did matter, and still does matter, is that the event soured relations between the two countries for decades. And still does.

In the present-day climate, any relatively minor happening stirred up memories of the hostage-taking and resulted in events such as the recalling of Ambassadors or the declaration of people being persona non grata on both sides. The whole shemozzle was escalated by the United States imposing sanctions which resulted in a situation where the two countries could barely talk. Consequently, the Swiss government acts as the 'protecting power' for the US in Iran. Pakistan performs the same function for Iran in Washington DC.

Despite these being the facts, diplomacy still had to go on. At present, the US Ambassador in Ankara Turkey was tasked with also overseeing events in Teheran. To keep the Swiss informed of what the US was up to, couriers regularly traveled between the two capitals with diplomatic bags. This was generally respected by Iran for the very simple reason that, if they had not done so, the United States and other countries would have immediately retaliated in kind. And would most probably have immediately imposed further sanctions which would have been impracticable for Iran to replicate.

At a more practical level of course the situation meant that the CIA could not have the usual agents in place. So, the United States was restricted to whatever information could be gleaned from satellite coverage or the agents of other countries. They had some success with agencies such as the British MI6 or the French DGSE, but the take was not quite the same – was it? There were a few Americans who were already in the country and who could be relied upon to provide information. But the risk of them being revealed was generally too high.

Therefore – if there was an urgent need to find out first-hand what the hell was happening in Iran – the CIA had to try to get agents into and out of the country under some other guise.

Mark was not too pleased to receive a phone call so late in the evening. However, given who was calling, he had little choice but to take the call.

It was quite rare for Admiral Arthur Mullen to get

himself involved in operations but even the head of the Joint Chiefs of Staff could at times wield whatever power he had if circumstances so dictated.

'Major Taylor. Excuse my call so late in the day. You must be tired of this whole business – and being harassed by Washington instead of being allowed to get on with your job?'

The question was asked but the politeness of the Admiral caused Mark to pause, and then give a vague response.

'We are getting on with our mission. We are in a bit of a stalemate at present waiting for something to happen. When it does – anything could happen!' Mark replied.

'Well – you have no doubt heard what has happened at Incirlik. What we do not know is where the Iranians have gone to. It is important that we track them down. I know that you may have other priorities. However, I wondered if I could ask for your help. We need to find out which border crossing they use and then track which of their nuclear facilities they take the damn bomb to.'

Mark did not know what to say in answer to that. For certain he would need to have access to greater manpower than he had available to him if he were to cover all the border crossing points. And following a vehicle in hostile territory was not exactly a walk in the park. Again - he hesitated, and Mullen was not surprised by the response.

'I will try if you so wish – but I will need access to more people. And – is there something going on that I need to know about?'

Mullen had to smile. Taylor was every bit as smart as he had been told.

'Yes - there is. There is disagreement here in Washington about it. The NRO has admitted that for all their fancy toys they are unable to help unless they can get a primary location on the bomb. From a political point of view, we are also encumbered by the Turkish government. We could have asked them to put a dead stop on all border crossings until the bomb is found but as you are probably aware our relations are not too good at the minute. Basically – we do not want them to know for several reasons. First – knowing that we have lost a nuclear weapon in their backyard would cause serious problems politically. Second – we are not sure that they would be all that cooperative and may side with Iran. Third – security within the Turkish administration is not the best and we cannot afford this to leak out to the press – or, even worse, to the Iranians. The Iranians know that we know they have the bomb. What they do not know is that we have no idea where it has gone.'

'And...?' Mark asked.

That caused first a sigh, then another smile.

'You are everything that your father described! Well good on you! I know that I can tell you this and know that it will be treated with caution. What we want to do is to let the bomb travel into Iran without any interference from us. Then find out exactly where the bomb is going. When it is in position, then we will inform the Iranians of what happens next.'

'You don't mean?' Mark was lost for words.

This time Mullen did not smile.

'No. It is not quite what you are thinking – although I wouldn't discount it entirely. What we want to do is to have all options on the table. If you agree, could you get down to the Embassy and talk to Ziegler. He will have details of the kind of resources we will provide.'

'The Embassy will be closed. How do I get hold of the Ambassador?'

'You will be expected. You are not the only one who

works long hours. Good luck.'

The line went dead. Mark had no opportunity to decline.

The only senior person in the United States administration that had not spoken to Mark in the last twenty-four hours was probably the President himself.

The Sandbox system seemed to do what was expected of it. It had found several cell phones that were in the Embassy of the Islamic Republic of Iran Ankara and was reporting regular traffic. The ID of each phone was logged and dutifully recorded each time it was activated. That gave Mark a series of numbers which he then reported to his contact in the Polis. They in turn passed the information to their contact in the Turkish ICTA – Information and Communication Technologies Authority – to find out who the owners of the devices were. That quickly resulted in the identification of several diplomatic officials of Iran as well as several local people who were either visitors, or who had jobs at the Embassy. It would have made life so much easier if the rest of the cell phones that could not be tied to an individual numbered one. There were three.

The theory was that one of these three phones belonged to Mohamed Haji. The reliability of that theory was dependent on a few factors. Mark had assumed that Haji had a cell phone – which was by no means certain. He also assumed that he would be using his cell phone to communicate with his friends or associates.

And then there was the over-riding factor.

Mark had assumed that Haji was at the Embassy.

Mark and Dusty got down to the US Embassy by

10:15 pm. Ziegler was there apparently not very pleased at having been summoned back to his office and away from a dinner at the British Embassy. Bayer was nowhere to be seen. The Embassy communications guy was – holding on to a bunch of papers that had been printed, de-coded, and reproduced. He was not about to let them go anywhere outside this room.

Ziegler tried to lighten the conversation but his attempts at levity did not hide the fact that he did not agree with what was being arranged. Or was it that it was the intended result that he was unhappy about?

'Mark – it looks like you have friends in Washington who believe that you can work miracles! We have received instruction that we are to provide you with every assistance in finding this bomb. I can tell you details of the resources that someone in Washington decreed you can have. I will leave it to others to decide whether they are adequate.'

Then Ziegler added an afterthought.

'I am assuming that you have agreed to all of this?' he asked.

Mark had to be careful how he answered that. No! He had not agreed. The Admiral had just assumed that he would. But – what had he assumed? If the thinking was that Mark would agree with a plan that would let the Iranians steal a bomb and then take it away someone's thinking was a few slices short of a sandwich. And had Mark correctly understood the implication? Was one of the *options on the table* to explode a nuclear bomb in Iran? That might sound like poetic justice. It might appeal to some of the right-wing lunatics back in the States. But – *fuck!*

'That depends on the resources' Mark replied. 'If they are inadequate and the job is impractical, then you have to tell the JCS that it cannot be done. At this stage, I do not know why I have been asked to do this – unless you can shed some light?'

Ziegler's day was going from bad to worse.

'Well – I can answer that for you. Your CIA friends are compromised and there is a risk that any move they make will be immediately known to the Iranians. There just isn't time to bring in more intelligence resources from elsewhere. The bomb is on the move. We need to find it! Your team is the only group that we can use!' he concluded with a shrug.

Well – that was worth a laugh - wasn't it?

From the day that Mark and his team had started on the crazy odyssey he had been suspicious that they had been tracked every step on the way. That was apart from sources within his own country that were anxious to find out what was happening – probably as a means of protecting their own self-interest. He was about to point out that simple fact when the look on Dusty's face gave him cause to pause. Yes – Mark and his team appeared to have been followed every step of the way.

Apart from the CIA in Harare Zimbabwe, the Iranians in Farah Afghanistan, and probably MI6 throughout the world, who else had been involved he could only speculate on. And - who exactly had they been following?

Mark Taylor – that's who!

'Ok – so tell us the plan!' was the best that Mark could come up with.

Ziegler shuffled the papers and found the piece that he was looking for.

'A Company of Special Forces troops were due to land at Incirlik about three hours ago. They have come from Kandahar Afghanistan – and they have their transport with them. Another Company is due in the morning – giving you a total of about three hundred men. Once they get settled in, they are to spread out along the border with Syria.'

He looked up from the papers that he was reading from.

'That border is five hundred sixty-five miles long, but the areas that would be accessible to anyone trying to cross it are much shorter. So – they will go to a few strategic locations. The idea is that their presence will deter the Iranians from going south and cause them to head north and east and take a crossing directly into Iran. We don't think they will try to get into Iraq. That would present them with a whole bagatelle of problems, the main one being that the area is populated by the Kurds. And we have forces in Iraq.'

Ziegler then returned to his papers, before continuing.

'On the flights from Afghanistan, there should be ten or eleven support officers on their way back to the US on rotation. These are in fact from military intelligence. We have asked that they be made available to us to watch the border crossings and that has been agreed upon. It is left up to you to decide how and where they are to be deployed. There are four crossings and we do not think that the Iranians would want to risk not using one of these. Of the four, one is closed so we can forget that. The remaining three – Gurbulak, Kapikoy, and Esendere – are all likely points but our analysis suggests they would use Gurbulak. It is, by far, the busiest crossing, and we assume that the Iranians would want to get lost in the crowd. According to these notes, you have eight men that you could make available plus one that we have a slightly different task for. We want one of your men to go to Teheran to work with our representative and to make sure the bomb gets to where it is supposed to go. If you do manage to find the bomb when it passes through the border, we envisage that you could try following the truck into Iran. That involves a risk, but it is an acceptable one. We will give them diplomatic cover so they would be relatively safe. That would leave you with four that you have in Ankara looking for Haji.'

He glanced up from the papers, looking more worried than he did at the start.

'You are both very quiet! Do you want me to continue?'

Mark and Dusty exchanged a look, and it was Dusty who commented as well as asked the obvious question.

'It sounds like a plan. But – How are we expected to recognize the truck?'

And Ziegler did not have a satisfactory answer to that question. But he tried.

'All the National Reconnaissance Office requirements are that your team finds any vehicle that could carry the bomb. Armed with that information, they will then watch each vehicle and follow it to its destination. They tell us that they do not have the capability of tracking the bomb as such, but they can track any number of vehicles. They are telling us that they know the likely destinations. They're at the most three of them. So, by a process of elimination, they will eventually know where the bomb ends up. We are dealing here with an organization that is run by the Department of Defense so we can be reasonably confident that they know what they are talking about.'

'Ok – How do we know what to look for?'

Ziegler could only let out a sigh because that was exactly what he was thinking. Again, he continued referring to the sheaf of papers.

'The bomb is at least 12 feet long. Judging by the evidence that we found at the warehouse where the bomb was first taken, it has been disguised as something else – but it cannot have been cut-up – someone would need to have rocks in their head to try that! So – we are looking for something with packing probably fifteen feet in length. The bomb itself is little more than one foot in diameter and with packaging say two feet square. However, the odds are that it has been packaged up with other equipment to disguise it further. Some genius over at Langley has come up with the idea that it will be part of a shipment of the water treatment plant. The reasoning is that eastern Turkey has several manufacturers of such equipment and export to Iran is not restricted by the current sanctions.'

Mark and Dusty were not sure that anybody knew what they were talking about. It was all very well to assume or conclude anything. But the facts were that Iran had people who could use the same assumptions and reach the same conclusions and for those reasons alone choose to do something completely different. The whole scheme seemed daft. As far as Mark was concerned the proposed job was certainly of a much lower priority than the task that they were currently assigned to on the instruction of the DNI. So – the real question was – could they spare a couple of days on the far eastern side of Turkey playing vehicle spotters and leave Haji to run loose. And the answer to that question was definitely – No.

The only conclusion that Mark could come up with was that there must be some disagreement in Washington. The Chairman of the Joint Chiefs of Staff was on the side of those who felt that Iran had achieved whatever had been the objective of Mohamed Haji. The DNI was on the side of those who felt that the task that Haji had been assigned to had still to run its course. Or – someone had convinced the President of this course of action.

It took just an exchange of glances for the two ex-Special Forces guys to come to a decision. Mark as the officer had to convey that decision to the Ambassador.

'I am afraid that the Admiral will have to find someone else to do this job.'

Mark stood up to leave.

Ambassador Ziegler did not look surprised, but he had a job to do.

'Can we reach a compromise?' he asked the retreating form of Mark. 'Admiral Mullen said that you would say that. He also commented that you had left two of your team at Incirlik. I suppose that they are working with the FBI and their principal role is to try to solve the same problem. So – you care.'

Mark had to give credit where it was due! They had thought through the plans. And there was equally obviously major problem in Washington. Again - the exchange of glances. All it took was a nod and it was decided.

Mark sat down again. The compromise that he was prepared to make may not satisfy the powers that be. But there was a need to keep someone else out of the picture.

'Ok – We will allocate five of our team for no more than a couple of days – after that, we will pull them out. We were asked by the Director of National Intelligence to keep an eye out for Mohamed Haji – and that is what we are committed to doing. We can manage with four people for a couple of days but after that, all bets are off. Elliott Shannon is our man out east so he will be the one in charge. We will need cover for him and his associate Owen Squires in case they need to travel to Iran. I hope not – but we take no chances.'

Ziegler seemed quite pleased with himself.

'Ok – we can organize that. We have a Consulate in Adana. They will arrange for your men to have visas as members of a group known as ERFO. That is a charity that supports kids in Iran who had struck bad times. It will be good enough to get them over the border. We will want one of your men to go to Teheran as insurance. He can direct things through our representatives there in case things turn pear-shaped.'

The two couriers boarded the Lufthansa flight at Ankara's Esenboga Airport bound for the Teheran Imam Khomeini Airport. Although the CIA liked to keep things simple, they had in this case to adopt a certain degree of subterfuge. Under normal circumstances, Lufthansa would not be visiting Ankara, but the airline was one of the few from an allied country that did have landing rights in Teheran. However, in this case, a flight out of Frankfurt had been diverted on its' way to Teheran with a minor technical issue. The next Lufthansa flight out of Teheran was in three days and that would give the two *couriers* at least two days' free time in Iran. This arrangement did require a frantic negotiation with the German Bundesnachrichtensienst – the Federal Intelligence Service – or more simply the BND. German efficiency ensured that this was quickly agreed upon.

It also needed some negotiation with the CIA Head of Station in Ankara, but at the end of the day, it was agreed that Brent Shannon would be one of the two couriers. The other one was currently employed by the CIA.

When the flight landed in Teheran the couriers, having diplomatic immunity which bypassed all the drama involved at the airport, were quickly transferred to a waiting limo, and were whisked away to the Swiss Embassy.

That is where the work began.

The CIA analysts had speculated that the stolen bomb would find its' way to one of two nuclear enrichment plants at Fordow or Natanz both of which were to the south of Teheran. The reason for this assessment – which contradicted the intelligence that had been received from their source within the Iran administration - was that the bomb would need to be stored somewhere. That *somewhere* would need, for simple practical reasons, to be underground. And because the bomb was a nuclear device, it would need to be contained so that in case of some error there would be no threat to the surrounding countryside. Since this whole affair was believed to have been a spur-of-the-moment operation, the Iranians would not have had the time to build a facility specifically for this purpose.

The US National Reconnaissance Office had convinced the CIA that it could, and would, be able to track the bomb to whichever of these facilities it was headed. However, this came with a proviso. The CIA would need to find out the mode of transport and would need to be a little clearer on the timing.

The logical expectation would have been that the Iranians would look to cross the border into Syria as the best means of getting into territory that was sympathetic to their cause. It was certainly the most direct route out of Turkey. And it would maintain the illusion that the Hezbollah had stolen the bomb.

However, that border was full of dangers. The Turks had for years had a very fractious relationship with Syria and had set up several areas along the border – in fact covering both sides of the border due to the influence of the Kurds - where Turkish troops controlled everything. In those areas where they were not actually in control, there was still random surveillance by the Turks and the Kurds. Coupled with the deployment of US forces, the risk of trying to breach the border was just not worth the effort.

Mark was therefore convinced that the point of the crossing would be to the north and east and directly into Iran. But first, he had to organize his troops. He did not have much time. The main border crossings were open 24 hours per day. For all that he knew, his team could be already late. So – they were reliant on intelligence the origin of which was a mystery

He called Jerry Burak in Adana on his cell phone. Burak did not seem to be particularly upset at the late hour and Mark got the answer that he wanted to hear.

Mike and Hamish were dispatched by military transport to Incirlik and then onto the Esendere border crossing. That was the southern-most crossing and the second most likely crossing point. Elliott and Owen were flown by helicopter from Incirlik up to the Gurbulak crossing. The people who had been assigned from the group arriving from Afghanistan were scattered between the Kapikoy and the other two as they became available.

All of them were given clear instructions. They were officially part of a polis operation - Looking for stolen cars making their way to the Iran underground economy.

They had another far more serious job to do. They were on the lookout for trucks that were carrying large pieces of equipment. The calculation of what size qualified as large was simple. Any truck which carried a load that was larger than twelve feet in length was of interest. Then the NRO swung into action. A message was sent to a number that performed a function little different from a normal help desk. They were given a code that showed which crossing they were calling from, the registration number of the truck, a priority code (1 to 5 – I meaning highly probable, 5 meaning don't lose too much sleep), and the color predominant on the top of the vehicle. That information was sent at once to the National Security Agency in Fort Meade Maryland where the truck was allocated the next number in sequence for that crossing. Then, that information was encrypted and sent twenty-two thousand miles out into space to link up with a geosynchronous NRO satellite that was parked over Iran. There was no need to de-encrypt the message. The satellite simply noted the information. From the alpha code, it knew where it had to zoom in. The onboard computers could not have cared less about the priority – that was a task the mere mortals at Fort Meade had to worry about. From the color (satellites produce pictures in black and white – shades of grey – but can still see things in color) the truck in question was quickly found and the track began. The memory chips on the satellite could manage several million tracks simultaneously so there was no need to worry about overload. This whole process took nine seconds – ample time for the truck in question to have moved a couple of feet.

The truck carrying the bomb had headed towards the Gurbulak border crossing. This crossing had been chosen because it was by far the busiest. The move had been well planned by the Iranians. The theory was that the border crossing between Turkey and Iran would be so crowded that a simple piece of equipment would be seen as light relief by the harassed border guards. It was something that would not contravene any of the UN sanctions that were in place - and which were supported by Turkey.

The normal way of operating would be for the Iranians

to simply bribe the Turkish border guards and that would have been the end of that. However, in this case, that would be both impracticable and risky. The Iranians did not know if the guards had been alerted to look for something the size and shape of a nuclear bomb. Although their intelligence sources showed that the Americans were reluctant to share their bad news with their ally, they did not trust the media to respect that reluctance. Fortunately – despite its' massive explosive power – the bomb was relatively small and so it was just a matter of hiding it in plain sight.

Several engineering firms located in the city of Adana produced a range of biochemical sewage treatment units and pumps and these products were not on the extensive list of items that were prohibited for export to Iran under the UN sanctions. This was for the very simple reason that treating shit was about as far removed from the art of nuclear fission as you could get. Yet even the Iranians needed this type of equipment to stop them drowning in their effluent. And the Turkish firm had a regular trade going with their neighbors to the east and another shipment of such goods would barely be noticed if all the necessary paperwork was in order. And there was another good reason why the Iranians had selected this type of equipment. A nuclear bomb, to the untrained eye, looked remarkably like a biochemical sewage treatment pipe. Except, maybe, by its color.

For this shipment, the bomb was hidden in one of three coagulation devices and because of the extra weight of the bomb, it was stacked with another unit on either side. The three were painted in the same shade of green and wrapped in plastic which had the added advantage that the extra bits that had been added to conceal the fins of the bomb were hardly noticeable. So – provided the border guards did not have a masters' degree in sewage treatment, and all the paperwork was in order, it would be expected to pass muster.

The distance the truck had to travel was about twelve hundred miles, so the trip was expected to take at least three days and a good deal of that was on the Turkish side of the border. But there was no hurry. The driving was shared by two men but still, they were careful to observe the Turkish road rules and they took an overnight break at Diyarbakir before recommencing their journey the following day. The rest of the Special Forces would travel in two vehicles ironically with papers that said that they were paramedics sent by Iran to help with the SARS outbreak.

The leading truck arrived at the border late in the afternoon of the second day. The border management guards managed the paperwork well and it took several minutes for the sewage treatment equipment to pass inspection. The drivers, the equipment, and the truck were allowed to pass through the border on the Turkish side. The stamped papers were subjected to no more than a cursory glance as the truck reached the entry into Iran. Even the Iranian border guards had no idea what had just passed through.

At least two of the Iran Special Forces officers were back in Iran!

And Iran was now the proud owner of its' first nuclear weapon.

The truck was tagged as a vehicle of interest and annotated that it was a priority of 1.

That rating was established because one of the men who had joined Elliott on traffic cop duty at Gurbulak knew something about sewage treatment equipment. It was mostly a throw-away comment brought about by the truck having to change lanes to avoid an accident and strayed into the lane that contained a weighbridge. The weight was duly registered as it moved towards the gate being taken no notice of by anybody except the traffic cops. The truck was already being reported by Elliott as meeting their criteria of a load with a length of more than twelve feet. He was about to give a priority when his colleague noted that the shipment was approximately seven hundred pounds heavier than it should have been. A B61 nuclear bomb, depending on the configuration of the fuse and the fins, was approximately seven hundred pounds.

With the volume of trucks passing through the crossing, a fair number of which had been tagged as of interest, Elliott thought that they had at last found a real prospect. He was so certain that he felt he should do more than just leave it to the NRO.

Elliott called Mark Taylor.

Although Elliott could get over the border and into Iran using the diplomatic cover (provided by the US Ambassador through the Adana Consulate and with the cooperation of their Swiss hosts) he was not certain that it was a good idea. There seemed to be too many people involved. Getting into Iran would be simple. Following the truck would be problematic especially as it got closer to a destination. Getting out of Iran could be well-nigh impossible.

The difficulty for Mark was that he just wished the whole problem would go away. And he had already used up half the time that he had given. As was usual with Mark he could not leave the decision to one of the team. Nor could he miss the chance to conduct a mission through to a conclusion no matter that he did not agree with it.

But where was Haji? The best intelligence estimate that the analysts in Washington had been able to come up with was that he would accompany the bomb into Iran. Against his better judgment, Mark had to ask.

'How confident are you that Haji is not in that truck?'

No offense was taken by Elliott.

'We are looking for a bomb and we think we have found it. As far as we are aware no one is strapped to it! So – the answer to your question is that we have no clue on whether the man you are looking for has left.'

Mark knew then that he should not have asked. Elliott was as aware of the search for Haji and would have informed Mark had he been sighted. But he could not be expected to do everything – could he? The truth of the matter was that, if Mohamed Haji was in the truck, the mission was at an end. It had fizzled to an end while Mark was chasing shadows. And the only action left would need to be conducted by the oldest man in the team.

'Ok – you need to keep an eye out for Haji. You know that your son Brent is already in Teheran. If you could contact him and find out what he is up to. He should be able to monitor what is happening. Between the two of you, we should be able to follow the truck. Take Owen with you. He understands these people better than we do and he could be helpful. Remember – you only need to confirm which facility the bomb is headed to. While the NRO says that it can follow anything on the ground – I have my doubts. However, if you can confirm where it ends up then we have done our job. When you have confirmation – get the hell out of there and bring Brent with you!'

Elliott had to ask.

'So – how are things going in Ankara?'

Mark again had a feeling of guilt.

Nothing was happening in Ankara!

Before receiving the call from Elliott, Mark was certain that Haji was still holed up in the Iran Embassy. He and his reduced team were conducting round-the-clock surveillance to make sure that he stayed there. At least he hoped that he was. But there was unrelated another problem for Mark to worry about.

Why had the Washington authorities stressed that they would allow a B61 bomb to make it into Iran without a fight?

He could assume that they were so confident in their assessment of Iranian capabilities that the bomb would be useless in their hands. Then the game could be that they wanted to demonstrate the American prowess at tracking. They would then be able to offer a threat of their own – as they had done not so long ago during the Gulf War with Iraq - *We can find you and put a bomb through any window in any building!*

But wasn't that a very risky business? And what about the collateral damage? Or did they not care? Were they prepared to risk many thousands of casualties - be they Iranians or anybody else? The casualties were still human beings most of who had no part in this brinks-man-ship. Sure – Mark was only responsible for a couple of men and those were men who had proposed that they drive ever closer to a bomb rather than opting for the only sane alternative! What if all the intelligence stuff was wrong. What if the Iranians were quite capable - having gone to all the trouble of stealing it – of exploding it?

Owen had the job of driving. Elliott had the job of trying to locate the truck. They had the registration plate number. They knew what the truck looked like. They did not have the oversight or the multi-processing capability of the NRO satellite. There was a steady stream of traffic heading south-east and assuming that most of it would be heading for Teheran they had about ten hours to sort that out.

They finally caught up with the designated truck after fifteen minutes into their journey. By this time, they noticed a slight difference in the way their target was presented. It was obvious that the vehicles in front and immediately to the rear of the truck were in convoy. So – Elliott assumed that the Special Forces team was back together, and the cars were now escorting the bomb to its destination. That did not particularly worry Elliott and Owen too much. However, it did present them with a minor problem. The truck seemed to have a top speed of about 50mph compared to the speed limit on the road of 70mph. Which meant that their presence tagging onto the back of the convoy would not go unnoticed for long.

Elliott called his son Brent Shannon earlier than he had expected to get help. They need more eyes. And they needed more vehicles if they were to achieve anything. There was plenty of time. There was also plenty of space in which the truck could disappear despite assurances that the NRO had things under control.

The office of the NRO was tasked with reconnaissance of all things and to fulfill this obligation to the US Intelligence and Security services it tended to share as much information as was possible to enable it to pass meaningful intelligence that is gathered from satellites. The surveillance included borders throughout the world and most of the information collected was useful to no one. However, it did store all pictures locally initially on SSD (solid-state drive) storage and later backed up to cloud-based storage (which also meant SSD storage). Consequently, if a problem should occur in an obscure place on the planet, it was possible to back-track. And it was possible to link the data to anything else that might have been gathered.

A particular area of interest over the last five days was the Turkish borders to the east of the country – be they into Syria, Iraq, or Iran. The NSA had been tasked with tapping into the Turkish border control software. The data from every person and package that passed both into and out of Turkey through the three crossings at Gurbulak, Kapikoy, and Esendere were recorded and stored. While most of this data would be useless, it was easier to take the lot and discard what was unnecessary, rather than install software that would screen the data at the source. This was simply because some Turkish bright spark might have noticed a slight drop in performance and chose to investigate. Anyway, the NSA was confident that the CIA with over twenty thousand staff who had nothing better to do than analyze the data, would soon sort out the useful from the useless.

All this effort amounted to what would be the most repetitive and boring task invented by man.

Until, that is, something happened to change that.

And it was only the tiniest flaw in what had been an almost flawless extraction operation by the Iranians coupled with a chance comment by an NRO officer that started a back-track that made the boredom worthwhile.

'Now where is he going?' was all the NRO officer asked of no one in particular. With the magic of modern computer technology and in the space of a few seconds, he was able to trace the image back to the place and the time that it had entered Iran. That was the border crossing of Gurbulak, and the time was 17:20 on the afternoon of the previous day. Armed with that the exact time he contacted the tracers at CIA headquarters at Langley who was able to check what trucks had gone through border control at, or around, that time. There was only one entry that had an approximate match to the other criteria. A truck carrying a load of sewage treatment gear manufactured in Turkey and headed for the Iran city of Hamedan. All that he wanted to know at this stage was *where was that truck supposed to be going?*

The truck had been identified as G739 at the time it had crossed the border and had a priority rating of 1. It was now forty miles east of Hamedan.

Then things got interesting. The CIA reported that they expected that, if the sewage equipment was the package that they were looking for, the truck would be headed for Teheran – a further one hundred thirty miles east of its present location. By the time, this information had been processed, the NRO said that the truck would bypass Teheran. It was now heading south.

Repositioning orders were issued by the NRO officer so that the surveillance cameras could keep a closer watch on this truck.

Messages were put out by the CIA so that their assets on the ground were alerted to the suspicious truck.

The satellite phone that Elliott Shannon carried in his overnight bag startled him when it first chirped. And he did not recognize the number that was calling other than it had to be someone who knew his number. It was the CIA calling from Langley.

'We believe that there is a truck traveling south on highway seven from Teheran and that could be our target. We cannot tell you the license plate but is a flatbed with a green-colored load. It looks as though it could be headed for Fordow. Please acknowledge.'

Elliott was used to the tone of this message. It was CIA for sure. They would never miss a chance to make the point that this is exactly what they had predicted. The fact that the truck could easily by carrying anything and go anywhere never have occurred to the man.

It also would not occur to the man half a world away from that Elliott could see the truck.

'Ok – we are on our way' said Elliot and ended the call.

Brent Shannon was twiddling his thumbs waiting for the call to the number that Elliott had been given to contact the *couriers* at the Swiss Embassy. He was the only person in the office, so he took the call. After a brief chat with his father, he rushed down to the parking area collecting their Swiss minder on the way. The two of them then headed south with his host behind the wheel of a Mercedes with diplomatic plates. The time of the day did not help with the roads crowded with traffic but eventually, they made it onto highway 7. Once there the traffic eased off and the Swiss official was able to show his competence as a driver by going well above the speed limit. He cited diplomatic immunity.

It was then a matter of how Elliott could organize the surveillance. Both Elliott and Brent had to travel at the speed of the traffic which meant that neither of them could sit behind the vehicles that they were following for any length of time. They would eventually be spotted by the RGC troops. They adopted a complicated plan that had them alternating. One of the cars would pass the truck and then pull into a gas station and let the convoy pass. Then the second car would pass the truck while the second car then fed in behind. The same process continued for many miles so that it became part of the boring routine.

It was so boring and monotonous that Elliott almost missed the fact that they were being followed.

At first, he thought that the helicopters were on another mission. However, it soon became clear that this was not the case. There were three aircraft that were flying behind them in formation. And they followed the road. The closest of them looked like two older Bell 214's. They were marked as belonging to the Iran military although Elliott could see no sign of any armaments. The third helicopter in the flight resembled a CH-47 Chinook which also appeared to be unarmed. All three were of American design and manufacture. They must have been acquired on the second-hand market because they would not have been sold directly to Iran. Or they were even older Elliott first thought. The Chinook was flying behind the two Bell Helicopters but having the capacity to carry more than three dozen troops (CH stood for Cargo Helicopter but troops were cargo, weren't they?), Elliott feared that their antics had been rumbled. And there was nowhere for them to go. Their chances of evading even one helicopter in the flat and featureless Iranian countryside were remote. When the convoy began to slow and looked intent on stopping, he knew the game was up.

Owen who was driving had seen Brent waiting at the side of the road. He had no choice but to overtake the truck, maintain their strategy, and hope for the best.

The Mercedes had only just rejoined the chase when they approached the convoy which was parked in a layby area just south of a gas station. One of the Bell helicopters landed on the road and a man dressed in the uniform of an army Colonel alighted and became involved in a conversation with the truck driver. Then the situation became even stranger. The Colonel waved to the pilot and all three helicopters left the scene heading in the same direction that Elliott and Owen had taken.

Elliott watched in his rear-vision mirror as the helicopters roared overhead. He cringed at the noise as they came directly overhead. But then they did not slow down as he would have expected. They altered their course and headed towards the grey buildings that they could see in the far distance.

They were headed directly to the Natanz nuclear facility.

The sigh of relief was brief. What was now happening to the convoy which Elliott would have expected to follow them?

He called Brent on his satellite phone.

Brent could hardly contain himself as he explained to his father what was happening to the Iranians in the convoy. The Colonel who had joined them from the Bell helicopter had the men from the three vehicles lined up on the side of the road. There they were practicing their parade ground drills. Appearing as satisfied as he could be that his requirements were met, the men were busy sorting out their best uniform dress from what little they had with them. Then they tried to polish their shoes as best they could. Then they lined up for a final inspection by the Colonel. This whole exercise had been completed in under ten minutes.

From the body language, it was obvious that the Colonel was far from happy with the performance of the troops.

At the same time, it was clear that the troops would rather have been somewhere else.

Brent called Elliott.

'I do not know what is going on, but I suggest that

you come and join us. My best guess is that this small convoy has been taken over by a choreographer and they are about to reboard and continue their journey. From what we have seen we can confirm one thing – there is no sign of Mohamed Haji. Whether he was onboard one of the helicopters I cannot say.'

To say that Elliott was confused by his son's report did not do justice to the way he felt. He already had the feeling that Haji would not be appearing with the group. What he did not understand was the mention of a choreographer in their midst!

'Ok – we will be with you in five minutes. I think it is time we quit. The helicopters have all headed towards Natanz and you can be sure that is where the truck is now heading.'

Owen turned the car around and returned along the road towards the spot where Brent and his Swiss driver were waiting. Meanwhile, the convoy that they had been following from the Gurbulak border crossing passed them, going noticeably faster than they had previously as they neared their destination.

When Elliott arrived at the position where the Mercedes was parked, he was introduced to the Swiss driver. However, Elliott had no intention of including the driver in his discussions or any subsequent communications. The Swiss were supposed to be neutral in dealings with their hosts. This was why they also looked after US interests in Iran, in the absence of any direct US representation. But that did not mean that they could be privy to any US tactics which may or may not be inconvenient to their hosts. And they could not be expected to have the same attitude towards security.

Brent was having similar thoughts. He exited the Mercedes and crossed the road to talk to Elliott.

'That was quite a performance! I guy with insignia

that showed he was an Army Colonel got out of one of the choppers and proceeded to but the troops through a parade ground drill. The troops did not seem to be overly impressed. What do you think that was all about?'

Elliott had to laugh.

'I don't think they were putting on a show for our benefit. The three choppers have gone to Natanz. I reckon that the Chinook had a team of dignitaries on board – probably from the RGC. So – there will be a welcome ceremony at the nuclear center when the troops with the bomb arrived. Therefore, they have confirmed what we suspected. Of more interest to us now is – How confident are you that Haji is not among them?'

That was the question that Brent could not be certain of his answer. He had seen all the troops standing on the side of the road going through their drills. He was certain that Haji was not there. But he had no clue of whether he was being transported to Natanz by some other means.

Elliott called Mark.

'We have followed the truck as far as Natanz. We have done our job and propose to come home. As far as we know – Haji is not on board any of the vehicles that crossed the border. We do not know if Haji was in the team who arrived helicopter to oversee the bombs arrival. Now where would be going?'

Mark had to laugh – more from relief than at Elliott's implication that he did not know where to go next.

'Well done - Elliott. Now get yourself, Owen and your son to the Teheran Imam Khomeini airport and get the hell out of there. The Embassy will have tickets waiting for you at the Emirates counter and they will take care of your vehicles. We need you in Ankara as quick as you can.'

'Ok. What is the hurry?'

The NRO was now confident that they had truck G739 in the expected location. It was close to Natanz. The expectation would be that the bomb would soon find its way into the underground storage at that facility. They had checked with the ground-based sources, and they confirmed that conclusion. That done, they were confident enough to confirm that with the DNI. What happened next would be a political decision.

The Presidential Secretary was left in no doubt that the call was urgent.

'Mister President. I have the DNI of the line.'

'Ok – put him on.'

'Mister President – We have confirmation that the bomb is at the Natanz nuclear facility. Our information is that we have a window of the next ten minutes before it is out of reach. If you are going to decide and convey the message to Iran, it has to be done now.'

'Peter – we have already discussed the options and we agreed on the course of action we would take. So – get on with it!

Fairfield looked at the silent telephone he held in his hand and then shrugged. What was it with politicians? As Commander-in-Chief, the President had to give his authority for any action that could commit the United States to anything of this nature. And as such he was also entitled to change his mind. Get on with it did not exactly meet the criteria for such a decision. But – they had only one opportunity – and time was of the essence.

The Chairman of the Joint Chiefs Admiral Arthur Mullen was the person who had been appointed to call the head of the Islamic Revolutionary Guard Corp - Major General Mohamad Jafari.

It was not going to be an easy call to make.

'General – it is Admiral Mullen calling with an important message from our Commander-in-Chief. Commencing immediately, I am to inform you that we have activated a B61 nuclear bomb. It is on a seventy-two-hour count-down. We are sending you images of where the bomb was last located – just outside your nuclear facility at Natanz. If the bomb is moved to your underground storage, then I am instructed to inform you that we may not be able to disarm it should circumstance require that action. Those circumstances would require a commitment from your people that you have the bomb and that it will be returned to our control. I was instructed to contact you in the hope that you will be able to convince your leaders of the folly of their actions. I would like your assurance that my message is understood and will be conveyed to your leaders without delay.'

There was not much that the General could say. But – he tried to stall before realizing that the Admiral had said that the count-down had already started!

'How do we know you are not bluffing?'

The Admiral misunderstood what the General meant. Jafari was referring to a bluff about the US ability to have remotely triggered a countdown. Mullen thought that he was talking about the location. But that did not matter – did it?

'Well then, the bomb will explode somewhere else. And you do not need to worry about it!'

Chapter 48

Frustration

At last! Mark and his CIA accomplice were just about to vacate their parking space and make room for Blake and Bayer to take over the spot. Boring though it was, Mark had established the procedure for the whole team to follow so that he at least knew where everyone was. And with the team having to cope with the inclusion of CIA members he did not want anyone taking any risks in their surveillance patterns.

Mark was sitting in the drivers' seat of the vehicle and had a perfect view of the front of the Iranian Embassy which was forward and to the left of where they were.

A car had pulled up directly in front of the building. It had barely stopped when a man rushed out of the Embassy and began a rapid and animated conversation with the driver.

There was no doubt in Mark's mind that the man standing on the sidewalk was Mohamed Haji.

The man was the same height and build as man they had met in Khartoum. He had not shaven for a couple of days. His complexion was right. And so was the limp.

This was the first physical sighting that any of the team had of Haji since they had left Africa. Which seemed like it was a long time ago.

There were hurried calls to Dusty and Ben who had been rostered off the afternoon surveillance which told them to get moving. The distance between the Embassies of the United States and Iran was measured in yards rather than miles. So - the plan from here was quite simple. Now that they had actual proof that Haji was in the Embassy, they had to have all the exits covered.

Now – if Haji left the Embassy - they would quickly know which of the cell phones used was his.

The gentleman who had driven up to the Embassy was directed to the basement gate and disappeared into the building. Meanwhile, Haji went back into the building the same way that he had come.

Then it was a matter of waiting.

There was no chance that they could look to detain Haji even if that had been Marks preferred option. Although Turkey was supposed to be an ally of the United States, the friendship did not go that far! And the problem now was – would Haji emerge though the same door? Or would he be driven somewhere by one of the Embassy staff? If he did the latter, there were two vehicle exits to cover. In neither case, could the surveillance get in a position – without making their presence obvious – where they could reliably identify everyone who exited in a vehicle. The only hope that Mark had was that Haji was totally unaware that they were there.

They did not have to wait long.

There were several exits to check. Marks team had four vehicles involved in the surveillance. They could cope by having one car moving and swopping places with one on a rostered basis to avoid the risk of having one car in the same place and therefore at risk of being spotted by anyone looking out from the Embassy. The problem was that they had only four people who could positively identify Haji and that was assuming that he did not radically change his appearance.

But what else could they do?

It was while the team were executing one of the changes that Haji did emerge. And they very nearly missed him. The complication was that three vehicles came out of the door to the underground garage one after the other, the first two turning left as they exited and the third turning to the right. Haji was in the third vehicle wearing what appeared to be a cap. And he was driving which took the observers by surprise. It was Dusty who recognized Haji. He immediately called Mark with the news.

'Ok – we have him, and we will follow. He appears to be headed south-west. Could I suggest that one of you try to position a car between Haji and my car so that he doesn't get used to seeing us in his rear-vision mirror.'

Blake was the nearest vehicle and in the crowd of traffic on the streets of Ankara at the time of day it would be difficult to achieve. However, the chance came at the next set of traffic lights. Blake was able to sneak his vehicle into a gap with a little help from Dusty.

That help was short-lived. Having gone through the first intersection, the Haji vehicle turned left and then right too quickly for Blake to react. Dusty was about to follow Haji when a call came through to go ahead and Marks' vehicle took up the following position. They continued this crazy mixture in the order of their vehicles for a couple of miles before it became clear what Haji was doing.

Mohamed Haji was not trying to avoid the following vehicles. He was simply trying to avoid the bottlenecks that occurred in the Ankara traffic. He obviously knew this city well. And trying to get to his intended destination in the shortest possible time.

Haji was headed to the Ankara Esenboga Airport.

That presented the following team with a dilemma.

Was Haji going to the airport to leave town? – and if so - What would be his destination?

Or was he going to meet someone – and if so, Who?

These various combinations were partially resolved when the car arrived at Esenboga. Haji simply pulled into the departure drop-off area, the person in the passenger seat jumped out and handed him a carryall, and while Haji went onto the terminal his passenger got in the drivers' seat and drove away.

While Mark was trying to get in a position to follow Haji on foot his sat phone chirped.

It was the Ambassador.

'Mark – it has started. I have just heard from Washington that they have given notice to the Iranians that the bomb has been activated. I do not know if that has anything to do with the move by Haji.'

That at least told Mark one thing that he did not know. The Embassy was monitoring the radio chatter. Not that it mattered now.

Mark felt a feeling of panic start to set in and that had nothing to do with the games that the politicians were playing. He had to take some action and he had to be decisive. He called all four of his surveillance team with one very clear instruction – Get into the terminal and find out where Haji was headed. He had to rely on the four CIA officers because they were the only ones that Haji would not recognize – meaning that his best three sets of eyes were relegated to the background.

The crowded terminal was both a hindrance and a blessing. Hindrance because they needed to track Haji using people who only had a photograph to aid them. A blessing because Mark, Dusty, Ben, and Blake could at least hide amongst the crowd.

The feeling of dread got worse as Mark scanned the terminal. It was unlikely that Haji would be heading bank to Iran because it was far easier to simply drive across the border rather than going through the hassle of air travel.

But where else could he go?

The answer to that question was – anywhere!

And the other question was – why?

Mark called Mike and Hamish to change their travel plans. When he last heard from them, they were driving from the border crossing to Incirlik. That is where he located them. He just gave them instructions to get some form of airborne transport and to get to Esenboga as quickly as was possible. It was no use trying to call the other three members of his team. As far as he knew they were in the air and heading to Ankara. At least he hoped that their flight had left Teheran before the Iranians decided to get shitty with any American visitors. He had to settle for a text message. None of which would help with the present problem.

One of the CIA agents was the first to report anything that could give them a clue. Haji had checked in with the Anadolujet airline and was now making his way towards the customs and immigration area. So – they now knew that Haji was booked on an international flight. The agent followed him through the crowd while the other members of the team converged on the departure area.

Then they watched helplessly as Haji entered the secure area and disappeared.

There it could have ended.

Mark had other ideas.

He was wary of using what documents he had to try to bulldoze their way through immigration. But he had to do something to ensure that Haji was followed. On the departure board there were two flights listed under the Turkish airline that Haji had appeared to check-in with. The first one had the destination of London England. The second one indicated that it was bound for Munich Germany. That meant that, to cover both possibilities two of Marks team would need to check-in. There was just no point in using any of the CIA agents because they would not be quick enough in recognizing a man who had so far eluded some of the best in the business. In the end Mark decided that Dusty Miller and Blake Whittaker were the most likely to be able to track their target.

And the least likely to be spotted.

Blake was only too keen to be involved, although his reason had nothing to do with Mohammed Haji. He hoped that he would be checked in on the London flight.

Dusty was worried that he would be leaving Mark with an even bigger set of problems. He did not like the idea of splitting the team. That was one of the problems of just being a sergeant. And on reflection there were still other members of the team scattered around Turkey who the officer would need to get organized – sooner rather than later.

On the positive side, both Dusty and Blake were the same size. And they were both very capable of taking care of themselves – and anyone else who just happened to get in their way.

There was another advantage in this crazy world. Very few people would remember much more about them than their prominent feature.

They were both colored.

Money was not a problem.

Getting organized in the limited time available was.

Dusty and Blake rushed to the Anadolujet customer service desk to try to book seats on the two flights. Blake opted for the flight to London England via Frankfurt Germany. Dusty settled for the flight to Munich.

While they both waited impatiently in the queue at the desk, Mark. rushed into the shopping area and bought two medium-sized travel bags. He then went to a couple of shops that sold various items of clothing and shoes, bought two complete sets, and stuffed them haphazardly into the bags. Again, the CIA agents that were accompanying them were of little use in this activity. It would make no sense to have a thin guy who was less than five feet nine buying clothes for people who were built like proverbial brick shithouses and were more than six feet in height. They were useful though in standing in the check-in queues. Their only fear was that they would get to the front of the queue without any tickets and without any knowledge of where they were going.

With not a moment to spare Dusty and Blake got there in time. There was something of a hiatus when some passengers in the queue appeared to object to their pushing in ahead of them. Dusty, who had by now had about as much as he could take of the Esenboga Airport, settled that problem by grinning down from his full height and jabbering at them in a language that even he did not understand.

All that Dusty and Blake needed to know was that they could get through the security and immigration areas and that they could do after checking in for the flight. Dusty turned and thanked the following passengers for their patience and then rushed towards the departure gates minus their pistols.

They were still armed with their satellite phones.

Immigration proved to be straightforward. That could have been a problem because of their recent, rapid, and poorly documented transit of various countries, their very recent visit to Afghanistan, and their somewhat unusual entry into Turkey. That turned out to be no problem. Apparently, the Turkish authorities were not overly interested in someone who was leaving. However, they would need to get their stories straightened out should they go ahead with the flight because the British or European officials would take a far greater interest in where they had been. And why.

The boarding card said that Dusty should proceed to Gate 5. Meanwhile, Blake headed towards his departure from Gate 3. That, however, was not their priority. According to the departure schedule displayed on the board, the first of the two flights to leave would be the Munich flight at Gate 5 and they both headed in that direction confident at least that plane rarely (if ever) would leave early. As far as possible they both kept to the busiest part on the concourse surrounded by people who were trying to find their way and not really interested in what was going on around them.

Dusty and Blake covered separate zones to make sure that they searched as best they could the departure gate waiting area and the various eateries that surrounded it. At separate times they went into the men's rest room to check who was in there.

There was no sign of Mohamed Haji at Gate 5.

Mark tapped into his satellite phone and checked into the Sandbox app. Someone was calling on one of the cell phones that they were checking. And the location had shifted from the Iranian Embassy to the Esenboga airport.

He proceeded to send the information through the Polis, who in turn would send it onto to the ICTA. But Mark knew that they had identified one of the three mystery cell phones. They now knew the phone ID for Mohamed Haji.

Mark and the four CIA agents had joined Ben in the departure viewing area and they were able to assign three sets of eyes to each of the two Gates which would be the focus of their attention. It was difficult because the viewing area only really had visual access to the actual departure Gates and about one third of the seating areas. They had very restricted sight of the region where most passengers would be having a last coffee or whatever else people did before placing their lives at the mercy of a one man driving a small cylinder with enough flammable material on board to incinerate the lot of them.

The task was harder for the CIA agents who had not previously met their target and had only seen a crumbled photograph of a man who had a variety of disguises. Mark tried to handle that by moving between the people watching and constantly reminding them of the small clues that could identify their prey.

It was difficult and it was frustrating.

It was the limp that gave Haji away. In the movies Haji, or whoever was the villain, would wait until the final call for the flight and then dash to board at the last minute, leaving those following him with no chance to get on board. But in this case Haji just followed instructions and boarded the flight in the sequence of seat allocations called by the flight crew. Mark called Blake and advised him of what they had seen.

The good news for Marks team was that he was boarding the same flight as Blake had booked for at Gate 3 and that the seating arrangement meant that Blake could get on board with minimum risk of his being spotted by Haji from the back of the plane.

The bad news was that Mark had less than eight hours to organize a reception committee to meet Haji when he landed.

Worse news was that the flight would make a stopover in Frankfort Germany where anything could happen – like Frankfort maybe the ultimate destination for Haji.

Mark was faced with a mammoth task to get his team organized and that would need to take things out of his control. However, those were the cards he had been dealt, and while he hated making assumptions, what choice did he have?

The scary thing was that Mark had to assume that Haji was heading beyond Europe.

Could Haji be headed to the United States?

There followed a feverish period of activity in which Mark was on the phone.

The first call was to the remnants of his team to gather up what few belongings they had with them in Turkey and get themselves organized. Mark would arrange payment for the tickets courtesy of the US Embassy. The men would need to confirm the times and present passports and then check in - Elliott, Owen, and Brent when they arrived from Teheran - Mike and Hamish when they arrived from Incirlik. Whatever else happened they would all be headed for London.

The second call would be the most difficult. He had the choice of using either the US CIA or the British MI5 – the domestic equivalent of MI6. That choice would be based on which organization he could trust the most.

Throughout this mission he had been dogged by what could only be explained as breaches of security. The only people who knew enough about what his team was doing were in the US security and intelligence services. It may have been unfair to place the blame on the CIA since they were only one of as many as sixteen organizations that could have been responsible. But what little evidence he did have had suggested that, whenever he had encountered problems, the CIA was never far away. And so was someone else who had a close association with the Iranian intelligence service!

Looking at the potential of using MI5 in London - or even the German BND (the Federal Intelligence Service or *Bundesnachrichtendienst*) if something should happen in Frankfort – the only method that Mark could contact anyone useful would be through the overseas branch MI6. There was a chance that he could make contact through Ross McKinnon of the SAS since they worked so closely with the security and intelligence services in the United Kingdom that they may as well be joined at the hip. However, he thought that would be asking too much of a man who was merely a soldier and probably would freak-out at being asked to involve himself in politics. Because that is what it was rapidly becoming!

He knew from discussions with the Major that 'C' had already helped Mark and his team so he was both aware of what they were up to and would be sympathetic to their request for help. But that did not mean that Mark could quite simply call Richard Northcross, and it would be a done deal. Sure – Mark was almost on a first-name basis with the US DNI and the US CJCS, but he would be pushing his luck to expect the British Chief of MI6 to even remember who he was!

The logical alternative would be to call the Chief of

Station in Kabul and ask for his help. Reginald Smith had helped him in the past and would probably do so again. The thought was that Mark would need to offer a sort of incentive.

Although it would be late in the evening in Kabul Mark decided to call Smith.

Surprisingly, Smith answered straight away, and he could not avoid the chance to show that the British were up with the play.

'Hello Mark! And what's the weather like in Ankara this evening?'

Mark groaned. Maybe it wasn't the CIA after all that had haunted his mission!

'Yeah – I see you are keeping up with the play! But we have a problem. We deployed our Sandbox system and managed to find and track Haji through his cell phone. And now that we know his ID, we have an excellent chance of being able to locate him wherever he goes. However, Mohamed Haji has just left Turkey on a plane bound for London. We have a man on the same flight following him and the rest of my team is about to go the same way. We could use help in tracking where Haji goes from there until such time as we can organize our surveillance.'

Mark could almost hear the wheels spinning in Smiths' brain. Smith answered almost at once with a question of his own.

'Is Sandbox part of the Stingray system? Or is it something different?'
Mark knew then that he would get whatever assistance he needed.

'Sandbox is a beta copy of the system developed by my company. We took the opportunity to trial it. And so far, so good. But we have talked about that already - It is too early to get excited. In the meantime, we need help on the ground in London.'

Mark could almost predict what would happen now. Reggie would call MI6 with the news that they had a potential alternative to the Stingray system. It did not matter to the Brits if the Harris Corporation bought out Taylor Software and incorporated that into their systems. The British technicians had worked it out. The Taylor system had a solution to the countermeasures to Stingray. In making that call, he may even have the time to mention that Mark had a problem.

'Ok – we can do that. Do we know your man? We would not want to shoot the wrong guy!'

Smith did not have time to even say goodbye. He just ended the call.

The next call Mark had to make was to the United States and the decision of who to call was surprisingly difficult. He could call any one of several government officials. Or he could keep it in the family.

He had started out on this mission with the authority of the President and presumably with the full backing of every federal agency on the planet. Now Mark felt like he was on his own. He had used the CIA in Ankara because he had little choice. In the normal course of events, that action would result in a mundane report being sent up the chain through the CIA station chief in Islamabad to Langley and would hopefully be filed away as irrelevant. There was the chance that Mark was just being paranoid. Paranoia brought on with his experience on earlier missions. Paranoia that had saved his life on more than one occasion.

Mark decided to call the office of the CIA Assistant Inspector General.

This office was not involved in the day-to-day operations

of the CIA. But it was headed by Harold Taylor whose only son Mark Taylor had done clandestine work for him in the past. Mark was relying on family ties being stronger than whatever else may have been at play. He was certain that his father would know at least some of the details of his recent excursion to Afghanistan. That was unless something drastic had recently occurred in Harold's relationship with Karen Marshall - the DEA Director of Intelligence.

'Hi Dad. Just giving you a heads-up on what I am up to. We are following a gentleman named Mohamed Haji to London. I suspect that he will be ultimately travelling on to the US. The problem is – I do not trust the CIA to track him. Is there any chance that you can use your influence to have the FBI follow him if or when he arrives in the United States? And, without alerting your friends down the corridor?'

Although the senior Taylor was not surprised by the request, he felt an obligation to defend the organization that paid his salary.

'Mark – you are sure that you are not being overly cautious? Haji is on the CIA watch list and would be known to both CIA and the FBI. Both organization and Homeland Security would be on the lookout for him. The chances of him escaping that lot would be slim, irrespective of what I might do. Don't you think?'

Mark expected that response. He had already thought of how he would reply.

'Dad! – I know that it might seem a bit of a stretch. But our friend Mohamed Haji seems to get around the world with remarkable ease despite being on everyone's watchlist.'

It would have been something about the intense nature of Mark's statement that triggered the reaction.

'Ok. I will see what I can do. I presume you are using your friends in MI6 again in London. Just don't go starting World War III!' Harold ended with a laugh.

'That is exactly what maybe Haji's game!' was Mark's comment before terminating the call.

The next call was much easier.

Mark called Brad Morgan at Taylor Software.

'Hi Brad! Just listen. For your information, the Sandbox system worked fine – so thanks for all your help with that. Now we are about to leave Ankara bound for London following the man we were trying to locate. I want you to follow up on the earlier problems we were having. I am still convinced that someone has been following our travels through the middle east and is probably now following our move to London. What I need to know is – are messages being passed to someone in Washington? Harping back to our earlier experience in Africa where there was definitely something going on, could you find out who had access to our movements.'

Morgan, in an earlier life, was a part of the CIA Science and Technology Directorate and was probably one of their leading professional computer hackers. Since coming to work for Taylor Software he had used his skills to help Mark develop software that could prevent hacking as well as dealing with scams and viruses. He was also responsible for the Sandbox project which meant that he was the key person in the company. However, the recent appointment of Mark Taylor as a consultant to the DEA, CIA, and other intelligence agencies to *help* with the security of their computers, had given Taylor Software access to many systems that few even knew existed.

This latest request from Mark would take Brad Morgan back to his earlier life where he could poke around in someone else's system. And he would love every minute of it.

Brad responded with 'Ok' and terminated the call.

Chapter 49

Home Run

Khatami hoped that this series of events that he had set in motion was coming to an end. Sure – his aim had been to increase pressure on the President of the United States. And - hopefully - to cause a mental breakdown in the man that he loathed.

But his plans were getting too complicated.

While his two chief protagonists – Hormuzd Larijani and Mohamed Haji - were more than happy with their progress, the President of the Islamic Republic of Iran felt that they had quite simply gone too far.
However, it was another thing entirely for him to admit that a plot which he would claim responsibility for was anything but a great success.

If his plotting did not have the desired result, Khatami would lose face with his people. And that he could not allow to happen in a country where so much depended on perceptions. Worse still – he had expended a good deal of political capital in getting his Supreme Leader Ali Khomani to go along with his plans. And that was fine – to a point.

It was only a matter of time before the Americans had had enough of his dismissive comments about the whereabouts of their bomb. They would start to hassle his Leader. They would start to bring pressure to bear through the United Nations. If they did these two things, the mood of Ali Khomani would rapidly change. The Supreme Leader was well renowned for making fiery speeches denouncing the Americans. However, if he himself was put under pressure, he would back down rather than have explain to his people why they had to live with further sanctions.

And then it would be the President of Iran who would become the victim of his own intrigue.

So – the aim now was to either bring things to a successful conclusion - or to find a way in which someone else could be blamed for the impending failure.

Of course, Larijani was unaware of his Presidents doubts.

Full of confidence, he strode into the Presidential office armed with all the latest information which would demonstrate what had been achieved.

It did not take too long for his confidence to diminish.

Khatami's first statement seemed pleasant enough.

'Welcome back to Teheran. I understand that you have been busy. So – tell me what progress has been made since we last met?'

'Well – the exercise at Incirlik all went according to plan. We now have in our possession one of the American nuclear bombs. There was a problem getting away from the Americans – we lost a couple of our men but that was within our loss parameters. At this stage, the Americans think that Hezbollah conducted the raid, and we will leave them with that thought. Overall - it went well, and now we can move on to the next stage of our plans.

Khatami did not seem to be convinced.

'I was surprised that I was not informed earlier.' he replied in a sarcastic tone. 'You may well have informed your masters in the VAJA, but I would have thought in view of the importance of the event I would have been personally advised or are there things that I am being excluded from?'

Now there was the thing!

How did Larijani - who was just a mere servant of the state - inform Khatami who was President of the same said state that there was a serious leak somewhere in the organization?

The latest information that had come from the Ministry of Intelligence was that the leak had been narrowed down to the Presidents' own secretariat.

What Lajani did not know was whether the problem was personal or simply technical.

It had been known for the CIA and other foreign intelligence organizations to hack into selected computers as a way of getting information. By the very nature of the technology employed, that was difficult to trace. The Americans were very clever. They hid their files in the operating systems. Worse still was the fact that any software downloaded as a part of a system upgrade could have all the same attributes as a more conventional hack. The same process could just as easily be erased without leaving any trace. And without anyone being any wiser.

On the other hand, the problem could be an individual and even with a ruthless organization that the Iranians were well known for, it was hard to justify the mass execution of an entire team as a means of elimination. Especially one so close to the President. And which, in all fairness, could include President himself.

For now, Larijani's answer was to avoid the question.

'No that would not be allowed. Our military was insistent that the utmost secrecy is maintained and that we wait until the bomb was in Iran and secured in one of our nuclear facilities before we wanted to inform anybody of the success of our mission. And I have only just been informed that has now been achieved' Larijani concluded.

'You still have not answered my question!' the President sneered.

'Our plans involved getting away from Incirlik and then immediately going *covert* as our American friends like to call it. During the time between stealing the bomb and getting it into Iran we were able to disguise it as water-treatment equipment. Yes – we had a contingency plan by bribing Turkish border guards to let the package through but that was not necessary. With the bomb now secure it was then a matter of my waiting so that I could advise you in person of our success.'

Larijani thought that he had done a reasonable job of explaining what had happened even if the truth had been bent a little in the telling. At least he had raised the matter as a security issue and the simple mention of the involvement by the military should be enough to placate Khatami.

However, the negative line that the President seemed set on following continued.

'So – how come the Americans now know that we, and not Hezbollah, have the bomb?' Khatami shouted. 'And what is more they have threatened to explode it!'

Larijani froze before trying to recover.

'They cannot do that! They may be clever but what you are talking about is just not possible!'

'Ok – then we will send you out to Natanz and you can sit there while their countdown expires. And for once in your miserable career, you will see first-hand whether your theories work!'

Khatami was enjoying himself. He sneered again as he asked his next question.

'I understand that your plans to have Taylor and his team of CIA goons taken out did not work. So – tell me – what happened there?'

That was a subject on which Larijani was far from happy. He was not happy that the attempt had failed. But he was thankful that he could easily shift the blame onto someone else. Especially since the method of execution of that part of the plot had been suggested by the military and not by VAJA. Again, he felt that he should try the cautious approach and see how that transpired.

'You never can rely on the Taliban to carry out what was really a simple plan!' he offered. 'The intention was to infiltrate the Taylor team with a suicide bomber and that was done. The bomber was to wait until the team was well away from any US forces probably in the lowly populated area to the west of Afghanistan. But two things went against us. Before the bomb could be exploded, a group of British SAS special troops turned up apparently on a totally unrelated mission. In the confusion they somehow got the bomber isolated from the Taylor group. It was just unfortunate timing.'

'And so – what happens next?' Khatami again sneered. 'It does not give me a great deal of confidence when a bunch of amateurs can wander around interfering with our plans with apparent impunity!'

This time Larijani decided that he should get tough.

'Is that not the whole point of your plan? The fact that the Americans have not dispatched one of their top teams suggests that they are not taking us seriously. At present they are confused. That is exactly how we want it. By the time that we implement the final stages, they will be too late and too slow to react.'

Khatami seemed to relax.

'As long as you are sure that there are not further *unfortunate timings* which seem to be something that this Taylor team seem to be rather good at engineering!'

Now it was Larijani's turn to sneer.

'We have other plans for dealing with Taylor and his team.'

Chapter 50

Home

The decision to leave could not have been a particularly easy one for the two girls. Debbie Petersen and Estefani Rodriguez had discussed it long into the night until finally, they had both reached the same decision.

Now they sat in their tent dreading what had to happen next. They had spent several tumultuous months in this place, far from home and in an environment that was alien. It had been a profound experience for people who were not used to having even simple things such as clean water available. They had now seen in all its abject reality the terrible conditions in which these people lived. No! That wasn't true. They did not live. They survived. And now these two young ladies, coming from a country where people squabbled over the *haves* and the *have nots,* had seen the real world. Where people who had nothing had to try to share that.

Debbie had volunteered to go with her young friend on this mad trip after Estefania's mother had been killed in that horrible event in Washington DC. She had agreed to go with the fragile daughter on a trip to Africa – really to get away from Mark Taylor - the man she loved. It was not that she no longer felt love for this big brute of a man. If the truth is known, now that they had been apart, and she had the time to think, she probably loved him more for his determination to do what was right for his fellow men. But - could she stand by and watch as he seemed to put himself in situations without any apparent thoughts of the risks to his own life? That of course meant there was a danger to those around him. But then – off on yet another of his missions in the never-ending fight against all that was evil – Mark Taylor had just dropped into the Pugnido camp as though taking a stroll Central Park. And his reason for that?

Battling the contradictory thoughts that flooded her mind she could not shake the truth. He had come to make sure that she was Ok!

When he had walked into the camp, and just stood there with that stupid but caring grin on his face, she really wanted to just hug the man and never let go. And it was clear from the body language that he wanted to take her in his arms.

But this place at Pugnido was a refugee camp. It was neither the place nor the time for visitors to show affection for each other when there was so much pain and suffering everywhere you looked. That is when the reality hit home. While the people in the camp had nothing other than hope to cling to, there were serious limits to what the minuscule contribution of the two girls could make to their plight. The cost of that contribution was massive.

So – the decision had finally been made. They would return home.

Debbie would return to the apartment that she had once shared with Mark in New York City. If that is, he would want her.

Estefani would resume her studies to become a lawyer. And maybe at least begin a journey that would right some of the wrongs that befuddled the world.

On a personal note - Mark had come to the camp in the middle of nowhere without any notification just to see Debbie. Almost oblivious to the circumstances – two people reunited in the middle of nowhere. That had to mean something. Wouldn't it be ironic if she could surprise Mark in the same way that he had done to her? Just turn up at the New York apartment unannounced. There they would be finally reunited in an environment where they could just be themselves.

To do that Debbie would need to plan.

First, she had to leave Pugnido.

Getting people to volunteer to come to the refugee camps was difficult at the best of times. Some came out of dedication to a cause. People were desperately in need of help and despite the huge risk that the volunteers faced amongst people with who they could barely communicate they came in their droves. And even though they could see no end to their labors, these people still came, some of them for years knowing that their mission was hopeless.

But others – like Debbie and Estefania - had come since turning their backs on problems at home. Theirs was a form of escapism rather than because of a higher calling. They still worked hard for long hours, uncomplaining and dedicated to at least the hope that they could improve the lives of those they served. They really cared for the people who were patently worse off than anything they could have ever imagined. But always there was that pining to return home. And to a life where things could return to a more normal existence.

It was not as though by turning away they were letting anyone down. Except themselves. They had volunteered to come to the Pugnido camp for a cycle of six months and they had done more than that. During their stay, they had learned many things. They had made many new friends. And lost just as many. They had attended their share of funerals. Shared in the agonizing horror of watching mothers unable to feed their children. Even unable to prevent the deaths of their children. Then they could only watch as the mothers withered away heartbroken by it all. And it was all so unnecessary – wasn't it?

All of this had been created by men fighting for power and influence and not caring about the chaos and mayhem that they caused to the lives of those who had no means to care for themselves. As with many things in this world, the fighting for power between the few had a massive impact on the life and death of millions. Very few of those affected by the fighting would ever see any benefit. Theirs was just a struggle to stay alive. And every day the situation got worse.

Doctor Lino Ernest came into the tent and apologized for keeping the ladies waiting. Ernest was a humble man. He was a native of southern Sudan, who had spent over three years fighting to squeeze funds out of the administration. He had succeeded at least in getting them to supply tents for a hospital. That gave his patients shelter from the relentless sun. As a doctor he had to do more than that. But – where were the doctors, nurses, medicines, and equipment necessary to meet the needs of his people?

He had no other place to go. He was trapped in this foreign land, with his own people.

Debbie burst into tears as the doctor sat down. It was the young partly trained lawyer from Washington DC - Estefania - who had to deliver the news to the man. A man who had become their friend.

'We have decided to go back to the United States at the end of this week. Thank you for the opportunity to come here and serve your people. We will forever remember the experience and we will continue to support your cause through charities that we will sponsor in the US. This decision has been hard, but we are not really qualified to supply anything like the care that these people need. We honestly believe that we would be more useful by raising awareness of the refugees' plight and lobbying our politicians to raise funds to meet the needs of your people.'

And then it was Estefania who broke down in tears.

The doctor reached across the table to comfort the two ladies. Despite all the pressure that he was under he smiled.

'We are just grateful to you both for having taken your time to come here and spend it with our people. You can still do a lot for us by spreading the word in your home country. Although this is a problem that Sudan has made for itself, the world must come to our aid and must prevent this sort of situation from ever happening again. If you can do that, we will be forever grateful. Thank you for all your help, and good luck in whatever you do in the future. I thank you from the bottom of my heart.'

The doctors' words were not meant as an attempt to make the girls change their minds but came very close to achieving exactly that. Doctor Ernest recognized the hesitation as they sat across the table with tears streaming down their faces. He rose from the rickety chair that he was sitting on and gave them each a hug and said a final word.

'You are young and have your whole life ahead of you. Go with our best wishes – and thank you, thank you. I am sure you will remember this experience. All we ask is that you also remember us in your prayers. Travel well and take care of yourselves and each other.'

He gave them another hug.

'Now I must get back to my patients. Perhaps you could accompany me on my daily rounds and assist raise the spirits of these people for one more day?'

The two girls were both a blubbering mess, but they went with the doctor anyway.

As darkness descended on the camp, Debbie Petersen made a call to one of the secretaries on the US Khartoum Embassy who she had befriended during her time in Ethiopia. That call was just a courtesy call on the face of it to let someone at the Embassy know of their impending departure. The call enabled Debbie to find out what flights would be available for her return to the United States with a large selection of stopovers since none of them would be a direct flight. But, despite the significance of the flight details, it was really an attempt to find out if the secretary had any information on the whereabouts of Mark Taylor.

All that the secretary could say was that Taylor had gone to Afghanistan. She qualified her comments that the information was several days old and could well have been superseded by later events. Probably because she sensed that the mere mention of Afghanistan had brought a tenseness to the conversation. And she was not wrong. Debbie had left Mark shortly after he had returned from his earlier trip to the land of the Taliban. And was she tempting fate?

Undeterred by that, Debbie pondered whether she should call someone in United States. She finally decided that she would risk making the call even though it may result in Mark being warned of her intentions. It was more important to know where Mark was, or Mark would be in a few days' time.

Afterall her plan would fail if Mark was still overseas when she arrived back in the United States.

Then it was a question of who she should call. Debbie had the cell phone numbers of Harold Taylor – Marks father and a very senior official in the CIA, Elizabeth Taylor – Marks mother, and Brad Morgan – an ex-CIA officer who was managing Taylor Software in Marks absence. Her choice was really the only one that she could make. While members of a family could be assumed to keep information on other family affairs confidential Harold Taylor was first and foremost a public servant and would do whatever his job demanded. And Elizabeth Taylor - his wife of many years who was likely to be dumped in favor of another women - would say or do whatever annoyed her ex-husband the most, without worrying about how that may affect their only son.

'Hi, Brad! It's Debbie'

Brad could hardly believe it!

'Wow! First, I get a call from Mark out of the blue. And now you call! How are you? Where are you?'

Debbie had to laugh. Brad Morgan was one of the nicest people she had ever met. And that was the reason why she had decided to call him.

'I am good – thanks for asking. And I am still in Ethiopia. So – if you have just heard from Mark then you must know where he is.'

'Yes – well I think I do.' Brad answered. 'As far as I know he and Dusty, and a bunch of others are about to board a plane headed for Washington DC – but that is all I know.'

'From where?'

'Well - He was - In Turkey.'

'What was he doing in Turkey?'

'You know as much as I do!'

Doctor Ernest came back to his office after dark. There was a ton of work to be done apart from looking after the more than sixty thousand refugees that lived in the Pugnido camp. Much of the paperwork related to the needs of UNHUR – the United Nations Refugee Agency – who needed to know the coming and goings of staff as well an almost daily demographic of the resident population. In addition to their other requirements, the Doctor also had to let the US Embassy in Khartoum know that two of the volunteers – both American citizens - were about to depart. Although the Pugnido camp was in Ethiopia the US still required advice to go through to its Khartoum office for reasons best known to, but not revealed by, the bureaucracy.

At least there were no forms to fill in. A simple email was all that was needed, although sending messages via the internet did present its challenges in this part of the world. The message was not particularly important, so it was sent to the Embassy web site for the attention of Brian Thorburn who was the current Deputy Chief of Mission in Khartoum. The message simply stated that Miss Deborah Peterson and Miss Estefania Rodriguez would be leaving the camp shortly and would be returning to the United States - their country of origin.

The message was received that evening in the Khartoum consulate office and immediately passed down to a lower level consular official to deal with. This official scanned the email so that it would find its way to the appropriate department and then closed her computer for the day.

That would have been the end of this little piece of

bureaucratic nonsense if the message had not been noted by another lower-level official named Simon Maude, who noted that his earlier discussions with his handler had made no mention of the two ladies. But that discussion had mentioned the name *Mark Taylor* and that name had been noted as a reference for the forwarding of any resultant correspondence concerning Ms. Peterson. Even though, as far as Maude could tell from what little he knew, the mysterious Mister Taylor was a resident of New York City the handler had asked for any information concerning said Taylor and so he forwarded a copy of the email to the internet address that he had been given. He then removed all the relevant files and closed his computer for the day.

Leaving no evidence of any involvement in a matter that he knew nothing about.

Chapter 51

Catch Up

The plane carrying Mohamed Haji and Blake Whittaker landed at Stansted Airport, forty-two miles northeast of London at 4:30pm. The airport was not as busy as would have been the case if they had landed at Heathrow but there was still a flurry of activity inside the terminal. Blake tried to keep Haji in his sights as they struggled through customs and immigration.

In the end, he gave up his near-impossible task and concentrated instead on trying to identify any MI5 or MI6 agents who might be around.

He failed at that too, until he was accosted by a lady who appeared old enough to be his grandmother.

'You must be an associate of Mr. Taylor – please come with me!' was all that she said before scurrying through a side door that was clearly marked 'AIRPORT STAFF ONLY!'

They went down a corridor that gave access to all manner of offices and storerooms before coming to a garage area which held several police and ambulance vehicles. Off to the left side was a desk where two men in black suits were standing and were engrossed deep in conversation. As soon as Blake and grannie appeared from the corridor their conversation ceased. They turned their attention to the newcomers.

'Thank you, Beth - That will be all for now!' one of the men said and the old dear went back into the corridor without another word.

The other man stretched out a hand to Blake and introduced himself.

'Good evening. I believe I am talking Mr. Whittaker of the Taylor squad. I am Richard Northcross. I believe you people erroneously refer to me as 'C'. I run a small organization known as MI6.'

Blake was just too tired to have any reaction. If the Northcross style of introducing himself was meant to be either intimidating or reassuring, he could not tell. What was certain was the fact that he was in serious company! Blake had heard about the British way of doing things. That usually meant over-dramatization, lots of flowery words and not much else. But often with an almost cynical or sadistic treatment of anyone and anything that was foreign. Mark was far better equipped to deal with situations like this. But he was still either in Turkey - or on a plane somewhere - wasn't he?

Blake was initially intimidated by the gentleman but decided to play along and hope that Mohamed Haji, or whatever alias he was now using, was still somewhere in the United Kingdom.

'I am sorry – You cannot blame me for all the misconceptions that our intelligence people have. From what I hear they have trouble remembering names, but they can remember letters. I am a simple soldier. And I have a mission to complete, or I get a kick up the backside. So – can you help me find the elusive Mohamed Haji?'

That brought a smile from C.

'You don't have to worry about that for the moment. We have him under intense surveillance and the chance of him slipping away is close to zero. Our information is that he is booked to fly out of Heathrow later this evening bound for Washington. Or to be more accurate – a gentleman traveling under the name of Abdul Nadir who we believe to be Mohamed Haji– is booked to fly. Our question is – do you want us to stop him here and now?'

'Ok!' Blake responded. 'So - what are you not telling me?'

Without another word from either of the two British agents, Blake was ushered into a small office that looked as though it had been built to withstand a nuclear blast. There was virtually nothing in the room except a half dozen chairs, a small table, a whiteboard, and a row of telephones of different colors. As they went into the room four police officers took up positions by the door and sealed off the corridor. Once the door was closed not a sound could be heard which meant that the room was fully sound-proofed.

Both British men removed their jackets and had just seated themselves when a tap came at the door. The assistant opened it and let in a man who made even Blake look up. He was as thin as a rake. He did not bother to say anything other than to introduce himself to Blake as Neville Chesterfield before striding up to the whiteboard. He then addressed the three men like a teacher talking to his kindergarten kids.

'Ok – this is what we know so far. Haji is responsible several operations over the last few years all of which can be linked to Iran but none of them have been on our patch. However – lately he has been involved in operations in Africa. Those have involved drugs and the compromise of certain diplomatic staff in Zimbabwe and Sudan. A similar operation in Kuwait resulted in the death of the US Ambassador – Lawrence Johnson – which we were able to link to the Iranians. We have been unable to associate Haji with that one. But the modus operandi and the result are scarily familiar.'

Without a pause, he turned to Blake and addressed him as though he were talking to an errant pupil.

'We understand that your CIA claims to have prevented the death of Robert Mugabe – first in Harare and then in Khartoum. Now we don't believe that is correct. Your team under Mark Taylor did that.'

He then turned back towards the whiteboard, still not have writing a single word on it.

'Now things get interesting. Haji moved to Turkey. They are a member of NATO and therefore, on our patch. There has been a certain amount chaos that has erupted in that country. But again, the chaos seems to have been directed towards the Americans. Several people died in or around the city of Adana and the Incirlik airbase. We understand that someone almost caused a very dangerous epidemic in southern Turkey - which was controlled more by good luck than by good judgement. Now we learn that someone raided the base at Incirlik and managed to the steal a nuclear bomb. We will leave out the question of why you Americans chose to have part of your nuclear arsenal so far from home. And why you didn't make some attempt to prevent it finding its' way into Iran? Overall - not bad for a couple of days' work!'

Blake knew what was coming next.

'Now we understand that your Commander-in-Chief has told Iran that the US has activated the bomb. Not a very bright thing to do if you want my opinion but we have to live with the threat that we may be headed for a conflict – and a nuclear one at that!'

There was an almost imperceptible nod from Northcross which caused Chesterfield to continue. Blake had to wonder why they were so keen that he should hear this. Unless they had grossly overestimated the role that he had to play. Or – unless they wanted his influence to convince Mark of some other course of action.

'Now your friend Haji he is in England. However – as I have said - we believe that he is headed to Washington DC. Why exactly? We do not know. Except to say that with his recent track record, he will be up to some mischief.'

The head of MI6 took over.

'So – what can we do to help our American friends? Our analysis is that Haji, or whoever is pulling his strings, has a problem with the Americans. And he will not let up until some goal is achieved. Whether that involves merely causing chaos or involves a threat to any individual we do not know. But one thing is clear. He has friends in high places. Whether those friends are within or above the intelligence and security services, the US diplomatic service or the Department of Justice we do not know. Therefore, we have a problem. Well – two problems. Firstly - we cannot pass the information that we have to the Americans through our normal channels because that could reveal our sources to the very people who are the cause of all the trouble. Secondly – what is the point of stopping Haji when he is only one of the people involved? He just so happens to be the only one that we know of. It looks as though he is the chief facilitator. But we do not know who the other players. Or what other resources he can call upon.'

Blake sat through the talk without saying a word.

He had just sat there to the end probably out of shock.

Not because of what Chesterfield had said as being the joint opinion of Her Majesties secret services.

Rather, because he had heard it all before.

From the mouth of Mark Taylor.

Northcross finished the briefing – if that is what it was - speaking very quietly as though he was almost talking to himself.

'We think that this whole business should end now. We can hold anyone for fourteen days under the Terrorism Act without charge. The same applies in the USA. But we think that it would be better to keep him here. We do not think it is a good idea to have a guy this dangerous travelling. So - What do you think?'

Blake knew what he felt like saying in answer to that question. Although the Brits were old-fashioned in the application of their laws - and they were lenient in their treatment of criminals - they were more likely to deny access to legal counsel. But the decision was way above Blake's paygrade.

'I think you should refer that question to Major Taylor.'

Chapter 52

Arrivals

The arrival of the flight from Frankfurt into Heathrow airport was met by officers of the London Metropolitan police. They escorted Mark, Dusty, and Ben off the plane to the amusement of the three men. And to the annoyance of everyone else on the flight.

It had been a journey that had started in chaos as Mark and Ben had scrambled to get on board the flight out of the Ankara Esenboga airport and had ended by them transferring to stone cold efficiency of a Lufthansa flight across the channel.

The time was now 11:30 in the evening and they were about to cause further annoyance to departing passengers.

This time on American Airlines flight AA791 bound for Washington DC.

In his discussions with Northcross, Blake had finally managed to convince the British that they should wait until Mark Taylor joined them before they made any decision about detaining Haji. That meant that they had two choices. They had to either find a way of delaying the flight that Haji was booked on or find a way of having someone travel to Washington with Haji, and hope that they could keep him under surveillance. The resources necessary to achieve the latter would have been prohibitive as well as being nigh impossible to organize at such short notice. Consequently, the Airbus A321 had to develop a technical problem which was a minor lie, a major problem for the airline, and a huge annoyance to the passengers.

A representative of MI5 delivered the message to the flight crew that a warning light in the cockpit that nobody was aware of would need to be rectified before the aircraft could leave Heathrow. The Airbus was backed off from the gate and parked. The passengers were then offered free drinks and snacks if they wished to stretch their legs back in the terminal which most, including the man known to be Mohamed Haji, availed themselves of. This meant the somewhat inconvenient problem of unloading the passengers via temporary steps which required them to exit the aircraft from the left front and walk around the beneath where the aircraft nosecone was open and two engineers – well one engineer and one MI5 agent – were busy changing a circuit board in the flight tracker radar system that did not need changing. But it would give the passengers an excellent view of engineers hard at work on their behalf.

This would result in a bill being sent from American Airlines to the UK Civil Aviation Authority – the equivalent of the US FAA. That would be passed on to MI5 which would in turn send an account to the United States Embassy. From there it would be referred to the US Drug Enforcement Administration. Once there it would get lost in the bureaucratic jungle.

Unfortunately, the discussion with Mark Taylor would take far less time than it took to set up the subterfuge.

When presented with the MI6 proposal Mark immediately called Washington. After being passed around various offices and a delay of several minutes he was eventually connected to Bruce Aderholt – the Presidents' National Security Advisor.

The first question that Mark would seek an answer to was: Where had the suggestion come from that Haji should be held in Britain at her majesties pleasure? And, having got an answer to that question, the next issue would be – What steps were being taken to have that implemented?

Mark was of the same view as Blake. The last thing they wanted, now that they had Haji under surveillance and contained, was to allow him to continue to Washington DC. And the reasoning was quite simple. Although they had no concrete evidence to tie the Iranian to the chaos that had happened in Turkey, they nonetheless believed that he had orchestrated the whole thing.

The only conclusion that they could make was that Iran Intelligence had somehow established a means of communication that the National Security Agency had been unable to penetrate. This was despite claims that the NSA had maintained an elevated level of surveillance of Iran Intelligence communications. Especially since the debacle that had occurred a few years previously when Iran had originated a compromise of the CIA communications system. Now the NSA claimed that it could read a fair amount of Iran's communications traffic. So – while they would have at least expected an increase in the volume of traffic and that would have indicated that *something* was happening, they knew nothing. Mark had raised the issue several times in an endeavor to find out how the Iranians could have followed his team. He had even had his own sources checking into it.

With the same result. Nothing.

That was the problem with communications systems. Every country on the planet had its own unique communications which was heavily encrypted. Add to that the different languages and the nuances of expression, what was picked up on the airways was a nightmare for those tasked with reading and then translating it into their native language. But – there was another side to this. People used their communications system in full confident that it was secure. And no one said that they could read it if they didn't have to.

In the present circumstance there was an even more deception at play. The NSA had a suspicion that the British GCHQ – the organization responsible for supplying signals intelligence to government agencies in the United Kingdom – had not only compromised Iran communications but was listening in to American communications. In the former case the NSA and the CIA would have expected some form of reciprocity as would be from their foremost ally.

And then there was the respective jurisdictions to consider. Although the British may not know it, there was the death of a British agent Banga Matsikenyeri which still had to be resolved. The British would be keen to hold onto Haji if he was confirmed as the main suspect in that death. But it was Dusty Miller – an American lawyer – who had made that connection. Matsikenyeri was only one victim. He was not a British national and he had been assigned to aid a US operation. There were more victims including the US Ambassador to Kuwait, several US air force security personnel at the Incirlik base, as well as four Turkish paramedics, and numerous US and Turkish nationals who had been exposed to the deadly SAR's virus.

With all these conflicting issues to consider, it was very quickly decided by the NSA – for all the wrong reasons - that Mohamed Haji or whatever name he was travelling under should be allowed to continue his flight. There was a risk. But that was overridden by the overwhelming desire to deal with Haji in the US justice system.

It was agreed that Haji would be accompanied in the adjacent seat by an MI6 agent who was familiar with Washington DC.

A couple of rows further back Haji would be observed by Ben and Blake. They had been allocated the seats by rearranging the passenger loading at the last minute. Two passengers would now travel first-class on a later flight in upgraded seats and at the expense of the US Drug Enforcement Agency

Mark and Dusty would now travel first class on the same flight as Haji – simply because they would be able to exit the cabin at Washington DC before Haji was able to see them.

The aim was to ensure that that Mohamed Haji could not go anywhere without being followed.

The team did not know it yet.

The whereabouts of Haji would be the least of their worries.

Chapter 53

End Game

Mark and Dusty did not normally go visiting people who had been providing the support services while they had been on a mission overseas. But this case was very different, in two respects. Firstly – the person that they were going to visit did not know who Mark and Dusty were – at least not by sight. Secondly – there would be nothing particularly social about the meeting.

It had taken extensive research to track down the person that they wanted to talk to. That was even given the extraordinary access to information that Mark, and his team had. courtesy of his daytime job with the DEA. Mark, or rather his associate Brad Morgan who was far better equipped to poke around in obscure databases, had to find out who could have been the liaison officer right back at the very beginning of their mission to Zimbabwe.

There was no doubt that someone had, wittingly or unwittingly, passed information to the people that they were following. This activity could have been occurring from a time before Mark's team was even involved in the mission judging by the timing of the demise of Banga Matsikenyeri. He had been murdered by the time the team had arrived in Mozambique. There was a very limited number of people who would have known of the relationship between the two groups. And most of those people would have been onboard the US warship.

Trolling through the messages in the various databases, but those that which involved the USS Carl Vison during her deployment off the east coast of Africa, Brad was able to establish the organizations that were central to communication for operation Steel Tiger. What this told Brad was that the communications had been overseen by the CIA. Messages would have been received from the office of the DNI by a CIA communications specialist on board the Carl Vison. He could also trace messages going back to the DNI but there was no sign of any of these messages were being passed to another party. Brad also had a suspicion that somewhere in the bowels of the CIA there had been another mission somewhat parallel to Mark's. Lacking the name of the sponsor or the name allocated to such a mission, Brad just did not have the time to follow that lead. There were very few people who were cleared to have access to the information but, as was normal in intelligence services the world over, the people who had access to the routine traffic were often over-looked. If only he could find a link.

Nothing was overlooked as Brad trolled through the mountains of data. He finally found what he was looking for.

He had a name.

Julius Perriam.

And for once in this convoluted mess things looked as though they could be turning in favor of the team.

Julius Perriam was forty-one years old. A thin man of average height with a black moustache and a goatee. His wife of no more than two years had left him to escape the arrogant and self-centered prick. Even though his recent assignment with the Navy would mean he was rarely at home anyway, she had decided that there were more important things to do in life than spending shore leave with a man who was rarely - if ever - not drugged up to his eyeballs. So, in the absence of any companionship, he had taken to doing something else to keep himself entertained when he was not at work in his role as a CIA communications specialist.

Escorts.

His most recent posting had been on the USS Carl Vison. He was back in Washington DC on leave. This evening he had a regular visitor at his apartment number 515. Crystal – at least that was the name she used - was a girl of vast experience, and little or no feelings. But she knew how to entertain. Perriam had asked for two hours, which was what she was paid for, so that is what she did. Although Perriam had satisfied himself within five minutes of the girl arriving at his pad, he continued to fondle her breasts as she occasionally checked to see whether there were any signs of life in his organ. Apart from that, they had nothing of mutual interest. Julius Perriam wondered what she did during the day butt never bothered to ask. He presumed that she was secretary to some asshole lawyer who spent her evenings earning real money doing what she enjoyed.

The truth of the matter was only slightly different. She did not have a day- time job. Yes - she worked in the evenings to pay for her drug habit. And she had to concentrate on the job to make sure that she earned the pleasure of her clients. Using her skills that she had learnt pandering to the wishes of such men, she encouraged Julius one more time as she rode on top of him, pretended to reach an all-consuming orgasmic climax at the same time as he whimpered and ejaculated. And then she waited for the inevitable offer that he always made. They shared a second joint, and then after precisely two hours she said goodbye with the promise of another meeting later in the week. Regular customers were essential. Meanwhile, off she went to a more pleasant encounter, even if the financial rewards would not be quite so good.

Even the truth of this matter was slightly different.

Crystal worked for some foreign gentleman who had simply told her that she was to deal with the wishes of this horrible little man and if she did that, and kept him happy, then she could keep all the money. The only thing that she had to worry about was what would happen if he did not call her – but that wasn't really her problem was it?

The people controlling Crystal knew precisely when Perriam was back in town and then the rules were quite simple. She would be told to expect a call. If the call did not eventuate, then she had to call a cell phone number and a member of some foreign embassy would either visit or call Perriam so that normal service could resume. Or, she suspected, Perriam would be made to disappear and be replaced with someone else.

The two gentlemen stood to one side as Crystal left the building, exchanged a pleasant smile as the harassed drug fueled lady fumbled with a cigarette and staggered into a taxi. After the taxis had pulled away from the building and were lost in the traffic the men eased their way inside the apartment block.

Mark ran up the stairs to the fifth floor so that he

could look out of breath and then strolled along the corridor until he found apartment 515. He tapped gently on the door. He knew that someone would be home because Dusty Miller had telephoned earlier and apologized for having called the wrong number. They had seen the girl come to the apartment and correctly predicted what she was, and that her stay would only be temporary.

Julius Perriam answered the door having first viewed his visitor through the spyhole, and although a little disappointed that it was not Crystal come back to further ravish his body, he decided that Mark posed no threat. Mark tended to impress people with his innocence. Many others had made the same mistake.

'Hi! I am your new neighbor from Unit 517. I have somehow managed to lock myself out while I was moving my gear. I am sorry to trouble you – could I use you phone to call my partner?' Mark looked like someone who would be suitably embarrassed by his predicament.

Perriam laughed. He had difficulty focusing, but he was in a mood to be as helpful as he could be. He had a very satisfying couple of hours and shared a couple of joints and was now tired but content.

'Sure - come on in. Where have you moved from?' he asked as he pointed to his landline on the kitchen wall.

Mark smiled. 'We're from New York. I have to call my friend on mobile – I'll pay for the call,' as he held out a five-dollar bill.

'Don't you worry about the cost. My boss picks up the tab!'

Mark dialed the number. He had to read it off a piece of paper on which he had scribbled it down only moments before. He had never used that number before and never would again. Neither would Dusty Miller.

'Hi – I have locked myself out. Could you come up and let me in?'

'Ok.'

Whether Perriam was expecting a man to appear he did not show any reaction. However, he did react when Dusty entered his apartment and locked the door.

'What's going on?' he asked.

No one answered. Both men held pistols. Dusty quickly checked the apartment while Mark told Perriam to sit down on the couch beside a coffee table. When Dusty had completed his check, Mark pulled a plastic bag from his pocket, tipped the contents onto the table, and offered the insipid man a straw.

'Who are you?' Perriam asked, his voice a mixture of what? Fear and guilt?

Mark smiled. 'All in good time. Take the drugs. It is high grade Heroin.'

'I don't ......'

'Sure, you do!' as Dusty forcefully pushed his head down towards the table. It was quite comical to watch. Perriam both did, and did not, want the drugs. But faced with these two men what choice did he have? Well – it did not really matter, did it? He sniffed up the drugs and felt the rush of adrenalin through his body, adding to his already euphoric state.

'Now – let's have a chat.' Mark began.

'You were recently involved with monitoring communications for an operation code named Steel Tiger off the coast of Africa. Is that correct?'

'I can't talk about that!' Perriam responded which a surprising amount of control and dignity.

'Ok – we know that you were recently on board the USS Carl Vison. We have established that you were involved. Now – we don't need to know what the operation was about. You see we were both involved in the operational side of that mission.'

A look of alarm started to appear on the face of Perriam.

It was almost as though someone were revealing the eighth wonder of the world, except that everything occurred in slow motion.

'What do you want from me?' Perriam asked.

Dusty was not as patient as Mark and his meaning was clear.

'We are not interested in your official role. What we need to know is what information was being passed to others. And in what format.'

Perriam was about to protest again but quickly realized it would be a waste of time and effort.

He had suspected that the work that he had been doing for Iran, innocent though it seemed, would eventually be discovered. And it was all his own fault. Prior to his recent marriage, he had gone out for a last fling with some of his associates from Langley. That had got a bit out of hand. He had ended up in bed with a girl who he neither knew nor cared about. But someone did know, and someone did care. Then it was a matter of his wife-to-be being given some bad news or Perriam had to agree to assist with passing information to an account when requested to do so. Since passing information to an account was a seemingly innocent affair, he chose that option. Now, the sooner these guys were out of here he would need to disappear – his career over – and his relationship with Crystal. At least with his life intact.

'Ok – What do you want to know?'

Mark took over the discussion.

'We know that you have been feeding messages sourced from somewhere other than the US Navy and sending them to somewhere other than normal US military links. Before you protest that you were simply the go-between you can save your breath. We do not expect that you would necessarily understand the messages. But what we do know is that you would have understood their format and sequence. Therefore, all we want to know is how the system works. Is that fair enough?'

Perriam laughed.

'Had you fooled, eh?'

Again, Dusty was not quite so patient. He reached across and picked Perriam up by his collar.

'Enough of this dicking around! We haven't got time for this!'

A subdued Perriam grabbed a pen and paper.

'It works like this. The first message includes a couple of codes that indicate who it is referring to and it also has a biblical reference that points to the content of the second message. The second message appears as a random collection of alphanumeric characters. The biblical reference indicates where a string of characters begins to have some meaning. I will show you.'

He drew a string of characters which had in their midst a string that read Lk followed by C6 followed by V19 which translate to New Testament Luke Chapter six Verse nineteen. Then underneath that he drew a string which consisted of alphanumeric characters in random order.

He smiled at his work.

'In the second string take the sixth character and the next group of characters has a meaning. Then you can take the nineteenth character and the next group has a meaning. Within the string there may be other codes – for example there may be 'dca' which is the code for Washington DC. That is roughly how the messages are structured. You must believe me that I have no idea what this all means other than it is telling certain people to be in a certain place and perform a particular task at a specific date and time. That is all I know.'

Mark and Dusty looked at each other and nodded.

'So – how does anyone know where to find the messages? Surely there is a risk that someone would figure out the pattern if there is some consistency in the format!'

Again, Perriam smiled.

'Facebook! They have several accounts and various pages. We just post them. The account appears as a group of religious nut cases. Occasionally someone stumbles into the messaging but that we can just ignore that. The main message has a biblical reference which is enough to keep the religious nuts happy. The surrounding data looks like meaningless mumbo-jumbo which you find on all internet traffic. The smart thing is that this part of the message contains the stuff that is useful if you know what to look for. The intriguing thing is – it is set up by Islamists so you would never think of associating the Facebook accounts of an apparently Christian group with having anything to do with Iran.'

'As simple as that! No wonder we could not make any sense of it. We were looking for something more complicated!' Mark commented. This was critical information – now he had to something with it!

'Ok Julius – thank you for your honesty.' not sure if he was or he wasn't being honest – but at least what he had told them made sense. 'Now I am going to tell you what you can do next. We can either pass the information on to the authorities about who you were working for and allow you to take your chance with the US justice system, or we allow you to go away from here and start a new life in somewhere like outer Mongolia where neither the US nor whoever you were working for will never find you. To earn the second option, you just need to tell us who it was that set this up. Or to be more precise – who were you working for?'

Perriam just shrugged.

'I do not know exactly who we were working for. Messages came and went under a variety of names, and I never actually met anyone. The only name that I had any direct contact with was a guy who called himself Mohamed Haji.'

Mark was not surprised by that. Perriam was both surprised and appeared more than a little scared at Mark's next comment.

'Yes – we know all about your friend Haji. We have just followed him from the United Kingdom to Washington. As far as we know he is currently hiding in the Pakistan Embassy, and you can guarantee he is up to nothing good. I would imagine that, based on what you have told us, you may well be on his hit list!'

Mark knew then that Perriam was telling the truth. Whether it was the fact that he just did not care, or whether it was the effect of the drugs he could not tell. But now was probably the only chance to get to the bottom of the riddle that had been bugging Mark almost from the start of this mission.

Sure – there were probably other things at play.

But the simple system that Perriam had outlined could possibly tell him what was to happen next.

Without a word to either of the other men present, Mark pulled out his cell phone and keyed in the number.

The call was answered straight away by Brad Morgan who could hardly contain his pleasure at hearing from his boss who he would expect to be back in the US.

'Brad! Shut up and listen. We have that guy who was the CIA communications man on the Carl Vinson that you tracked down for us. He has told us how the system works, and you almost had it spot-on. But all of us failed to see where it was happening. Can you fire up one of your machines and go into Facebook. I will put the phone on broadcast so that you can talk to me and Perriam.'

Perriam fired up his laptop and under instruction from Mark went into the Facebook account reading off the path so that Brad Morgan could follow.

Mark knew that Brad would have preferred to simply connect to the machine that Perriam was using but there was the danger that a CIA trained communications guy would be able to interfere with that link. So, Perriam talked through the process and then read off a couple of the latest posts.

Although Mark by this stage had a fair idea of how the messages were structured, he could not compete with Brad when it came to following trails of data and arriving at a rapid analysis of them. Dusty had even less idea what the conversation was about. Both of Mark and Dusty sat up rigid when the conversation between the two communications specialists reached a shattering conclusion.

'Mark – according to these posts – something very serious is about to happen and it looks like the final event in a long list over the last couple of months. Something big is going to happen in Washington DC.'

'Do you have any idea when?'

'Yes – that is quite clear. The next event will happen tomorrow!'

Mark sat bolt upright.

'How do you know that?'

Brad had to hide his pride at having done a bit of research on the fly while trying to figure out the various messages.

'Apart from the numbers pointing to tomorrow, I have

an editor looking at the text of the messages and that includes a peek at the Islamic Hijri calendar. There is the word *Ashura* hidden in the message. Tomorrow is a significant day for Islamists being the Day of Ashura. That is the date of the martyrdom of Husayn Ibn Ali. He was the grandson of Muhammad. The text also mentions *John*. Whether that is part of the biblical references or refers to someone or something else I don't know. But it is unusual based on other messages to mention anyone by name. So, from this we can assume that something is to happen to *John* – whoever he is!'

Mark could not dispute the logic. Assuming this was not a *John Doe,* the only *John* in Washington of any real significance was the Secretary of State – John Scott. Surely it was not part of the Iran strategy to make an attempt on the life of so senior a member of the Presidents team. The secretary had recently been in Khartoum around the time when Mark had been in Sudan. And he would not have pleased the Iranians by travelling onto Saudi Arabia for what would have been friendly talks with the United States closed ally in the middle east. But the head of the United States diplomatic missions could hardly be blamed for just doing his job. This may have been an extraordinary coincidence.

However, while it may be a coincidence, something else was already happening in Washington DC.

Mohamed Haji was in town.

Chapter 54

Communications

The NSA very rapidly completed their analysis of the communication messages that Mark had sought their help to interpret. The encryption system used by Iran Intelligence turned out to be crude and it did not take long for the Cray computer to spit the messages in plain text and then provide a translation into English. The pattern that Mark and Brad had identified was confirmed as being relevant - at least there was a clear link, in most cases, between the first and second messages. The first message in the sequence appeared to be the text of some event that had occurred, or which was to occur. The second message simply named a date and an individual or organization for the first message to be carried out. So, they now had the messages in plain text. The problem was that no one could make any sense of it.

The first message that Brad looked at took the form *11911xnebNtJc8v19* surrounded by what appeared to be random characters. The second message that it was linked to, took the form *21911x92678019468dca93421estJavidzim.* The interpretation of the second message was that it simply represented a reference to the first followed by date, time, and the name of someone and/or somewhere, and pointed to Washington DC via the code DCA. That presented another problem. If the theory that the message contained dates and/or times was correct and that it either represented a date or some numerical concoctions, it was necessary to know the base of the numbering system. Did it have a start point or was it calculated from some known source?

Another message had the two words that Brad had found intriguing – among the string of numbers and letters were *Ashura* and *John*. These words were inexorably linked to the date of tomorrow – provided the logic that Brad had adopted was correct.

Back in the year 1999 everyone in the computer business – and therefore the bulk of the world population - was apparently very worried about what would happen overnight on December 31st and the changeover to a new century. Those worries - which cost business and Government a small fortune in *consulting* costs - turned out to be groundless for a variety of technical, and some not so technical, reasons. Meanwhile, in the real world, people had already catered for this perceived problem by assigning a number instead of storing dates in the format month/day/year. So, when the end of the century turned up, they added 1 to the number, and life as we know it did not end.

The only remaining question was – what date was day one?

It was clear to the NSA that the message structure pointed to a system that was meant for use by unsophisticated people. And paradoxically that simple fact made it extremely difficult to work out. The NSA's Cray computers could manage the most complex of algorithms and break the most complex encryption, yet they could not break something which was so simple. It looked like a system which in concept was very similar to a system used by the British during the second world war for maintaining communications with their agents in Europe. By knowing the order of things, it was possible to hide dates and codes for places, and even peoples' names in an apparently random collection of numbers and letters. Then it came down to the difference between assumptions and coincidences. The NSA training taught its members never to assume anything. While they struggled to understand the message, they made an even bigger mistake. They did not assume any relationship between the coincidental use of two words. *Ashura* and *John*.

After speculating about the inclination to use the Iran Revolution date as a place to start, Brad decided that he would be wasting his time, and chose to speculate on the meaning rather than the timing of messages. And there he drew another blank. But for a chance conversation with Daniel at the office the investigation may have ended there.

He rang Taylor Software on the off chance that Dan would still be in the office and could send him a couple of emails that had been inadvertently sent there addressed to Mark. The emails contained attachments that would have been messy had they been transferred to his cell phone. Daniel Smith had joined the company recently having been recommended to Mark by his father Harold based on his experience in New Zealand. He was older than most people in the computer game, but he had a wealth of knowledge especially in the areas that Taylor Software operated. However, Brad did not expect him to shed any light on his immediate problem.

He was wrong.

'Are you pulling my tit?' was Daniel's reaction when Brad described the format of the first message. 'That takes me back to my days in the Royal New Zealand Navy. We had a Rear Admiral in charge back in the 1960's that used to love taking the piss out of the Treasury guys that sat on our requests for funds. Instead of writing long and pointless replies to their many ill-informed questions, he used to just quote chapter and verse from the Holy Bible. His favorites were passages that said *'Jesus Christ – the same yesterday, today and tomorrow'* and another that just said - *'Jesus wept.'* I cannot remember the chapter and verse but, your message points to the Gospel according to Saint John chapter 8 verse 19. If you read the passage, it may have some obscure meaning, but most probably it is meaningless mumbo-jumbo. If, as you say, NSA had little problem deciphering the messages, then the odds are you are being fed a load of bullshit. If it were me, I would concentrate on the second message. Now, I will send the email through to your laptop. Talk to you later.'

And with that he disconnected the call.

Brad could sense the shake of the head at the other end of the link.

He had to feel embarrassed but could not help laughing at his own stupidity. As with all things in the computer business as well as in the security and intelligence game, he had *assumed* the code was complex and therefore he had missed the obvious. Hence the basic rule of the intelligence community - *'Never Assume!'* The *hb* pointed to the Holy Bible. The *nt* pointed to the New Testament.

The group that was being used for the messages was described as a religious group and, although Brad knew that the users in the group were Muslim, the religion that was the subject of the posts was Christianity. At least the aspect he was concentrating on used the Holy Bible for reference. But he was no longer interested in the message. What he was interested in were the numbers. And he no longer cared what the base number was.

Working backwards from the numbers in the message that Julius Perriam had shown him, he had a reference point. All he had to do then was check the numbers in the messages that were logged into the Facebook account and find out if they tied in with the Julian dates of the messages that were posted. It was as simple as that.

The whole exercise took him less than two minutes.

Chapter 55

Repetition

The Boeing 767 made a smooth approach into Dulles International Airport and all on board breathed a sigh of relief – they were back home! Well – that was not quite the situation for one of the passengers. On the way through transit at Frankfort Germany Debbie Petersen was faced with the choice of flying on direct into New York City or going with Estefania into Washington DC. Fortunately, she was in no hurry. Her thinking was that Mark could still be wandering around Washington on his return from the middle east and she had plenty of time to pluck up the courage to admit she had been wrong to embark on a mission of her own. She decided to spend a few days in Washington and that gave her the chance to talk to Brad Morgan about how she could get to return to Mark without feeling like a complete wuss.

Little did she know that while the two ladies strolled through Dulles Airport customs and immigration, Mark and Dusty were landing at the same airport and would be following a similar path through the formalities. The fact that Debbie and Estefania's journey had originated in Sudan meant that the customs people held them up with their questions about what they had been doing, exactly where they had been, and what checks had they made to make sure they were not carrying any diseases, Marks passage through the same process, with the benefit of being assigned as a Drug Enforcement agent meant that Mark and Dusty were well clear of the airport by the time the girls were finished. Maybe at a smaller airport....

Then came the shock. Two gentlemen dressed in identical dark blue suits, white shirts, red ties – looking very much like the FBI agents that they were not - approached Debbie.

'Miss Petersen – could you step this way please – we have transport waiting for you outside.'

It had been a long day and a half since they had left Khartoum. First by Egypt Air which got them as far as Cairo Egypt. Then Lufthansa into Frankfort Germany. And then over the Atlantic with United Airlines and into Dulles. The girls were tired from the travel and lack of sleep. Whether that was due to the idiosyncrasies that came from flying east to west or simply because they were excited at being home from a place that had few comforts, it did not matter.

They had blindly followed the two men outside the terminal building before Debbie suddenly realized that there was no reason why she should be met.

And no reason why anyone would know where she wanted to go next.

'Where are we going?' Debbie asked, as she came to a sudden halt.

'Mister Taylor asked us to meet you. I presume you would like to meet up with him. He is downtown on business and apologizes for not coming to meet you and his daughter in person' replied the taller of the two men. He just smiled and took hold of Debbie case and started to usher the girls in the direction of a plain black SUV that had pulled into the curb.

Tears welled up in Debbie's eyes.

Not again!

Her thoughts went back to the apartment which she shared with Mark in New York City. Mark had been overseas at the time on a mission in Afghanistan, when she had been abducted by two men. Now it looked as though a similar thing was about to happen and she did not know why. What she did know was that – at least as far as she knew - Mark had absolutely no idea that she would be in Washington at this time. Also – who was Mark's daughter? It would have been funny if things were different. Estefania – the daughter of Stephen Rodriguez, a man who Mark hated – now someone had assumed that she was Mark's daughter!

Debbie gathered herself together.

'I am sorry – there must be some mistake. We will make our own way into town!' and went to grab her luggage. It was then that she recognized the bulge in the man's pocket – it had to be a gun pointing at her friend.

'Now don't be silly, or the daughter dies. Get into the car now, and do not make any attempt to attract attention, or you will both die!'

They were bundled into the SUV and no sooner had the doors been slammed shut than they accelerated towards the airport exit. Once they were clear of the airport one of the men who had been waiting in the vehicle reached over and offered them masks which he indicated they should put on. This man did not appear to speak any English and seemed to be speaking in a language that seemed middle eastern in origin. After a bewildering journey through the streets of Washington they finally stopped outside a non-descript house in a suburb that could have been anywhere. The girls were led up some steps to a door that was opened by two men who like the two men in the SUV were of middle eastern origin. Once inside the building, they were taken up the stairs, along a corridor, and then pushed into a room. The door was slammed shut behind them and locked.

They took off the masks and looked around the room. There were two single beds separated by a table which had a light but nothing else. There was only one access point but there was a curtained off area which apparently contained a rudimentary bathroom. There were no windows. The room itself was in a poor state of repair but at least it was clean. Their suitcases had been thrown onto one of the beds which had a blanket and a cushion.

They looked at each other in dismay.

But Estefania had to smile.

'Do you think what I am thinking?' She whispered. 'These guys are not very clever. They have not removed our cell phones and I got a look at the registration number on their SUV.'

Under instruction from Estefania, Debbie switched her cell to vibrate and then sent a text message to Mark asking for help. Much as she was desperate to talk to Mark or someone that would help, she was also anxious that she did not alert the men on the other side of the door. So, she began an exchange of text messages assuming that she was communicating with Mark. It seemed so impersonal!

Debbie – 'Hi – we have been picked up by two men and taken to a house.'

Response – 'What are you talking about?'

Debbie - 'We have been picked up by vehicle FN 9713 – Help'

Response – 'Where are you?'

Debbie – 'Washington!'
Response – 'How come?'
Debbie – 'We wanted to surprisc you!'
Response – 'You certainly did that! Who is WE?'
Debbie – 'Estefania is here too'
Response – 'Well that is a surprise! Hang on.'
- A couple of minutes delay, then -
Response – 'Can you tell me where you are? And why are you able to text?'
Debbie – 'We don't know where. Our capturers have left us with our cells.'
Response – 'Sounds dumb! Are you both ok?'
Debbie – 'Yes and Yes – but we want out of here!'
Response – 'Hang on.'
- A couple more minute's delay, then -
Response – 'Keep phone hidden and on mute. Fully charged. GPS On.'
Debbie – 'Ok'
Response – 'Good. Talk later & don't worry. Love you!'
Debbie – 'Love you too!'
- No response. -

The two girls looked around the room to see how they could hide a cell phone. There was just nowhere to hide it and there was no power point where they could connect to a charger. In the end Debbie just stuffed it under the mattress while Estefania went to open her bag to retrieve her cell phone. Just then there was a rattle of the doorknob and the two men – one apparently named Hashom who spoke passable English and the other one who had no name and did not apparently speak any English – entered the room.

The four men really had no idea how to conduct a kidnapping, but they were rather pleased with themselves for having gotten this far without incident. When they had locked the girls in the room, they rang their controller to report their progress.

'We have the two ladies at the address where you told us to bring them. They are both locked in the designated room. We now await further instructions.'

'On moment please' was all the voice at the Pakistan Embassy International Court Washington DC said.

A minute later the line was patched through to an officer who was more familiar with the mission.

'Are you sure that they are secure? And are you sure that no one saw you pick the ladies up from the airport?'

'Absolutely – on both counts!'

'Ok keep locked in the room and await further instructions.' And then the controller asked as an after-thought.

'They are isolated? And you have taken their cell phones?'

'Certainly! Yes Sir!' and the link was cut.

Hashom screamed at his junior.

'Get their cell phones you fucking idiot!

'Give me you cell phones!' one of the men barked while the other one stood guarding the door.

Estefania, being a trainee lawyer, was quicker that Debbie.

'My cell phone is no use to you. I haven't used it for over six months, so the battery is probably flat.' And with that she threw the device across to him. He caught it deftly and then demanded the charger unit which was similarly thrown in his direction. Satisfied with that, he then turned his attention to Debbie.

Debbie just shrugged.

'I do not have one. I did not see any point in taking my cell phone to Africa. If you want it, it is up in my apartment in New York City.'

He did not believe her.

The man grabbed her suitcase from the bed, ripped it open, spilled the contents out and proceeded to fling bits of clothing in all directions in his search. Eventually he came up empty-handed, and both men left seemingly satisfied that they had belatedly met their controller wishes with no damage done.

Estefania could hardly prevent herself bursting out laughing as she pulled a slim device from the pocket of her jacket. 'That is just plain dumb!'

By using sign-language she got Debbie to put Marks cell phone number into her spare phone and then she sent a text message to that number.

'Hi DAD – we now have two means of communication!'

They then removed all text messages from both cell phones.

Mark was grappling with problems of his own and this latest set of events had caused him no end of concern. His first reaction had been to abandon his previous plans and concentrate on getting back to the lady that he loved.

Not so long ago, Debbie had been kidnapped by trolls of that bastard Stephen Rodriguez and Mark had never really forgiven himself for letting that happen. Now history was being repeated although Mark had absolutely no idea how or why. The latest message which had obviously come from Estefania – was even more confusing. He showed it to Dusty who simply asked the obvious question.

'What the fuck is that about?' which just produced a shake of the head.

Mark got on the phone to his office in New York.

'Brad! Its Mark. What are you doing at the moment?

Brad Morgan was sitting at his desk at Taylor Software in New York City, and an explanation of what he was doing would have taken more time than the boss would have had time to hear. History was again being repeated. So, he simply replied. 'Ok – What do you want me to do?'

Mark was likewise brief with his response.

'Get down to Washington as fast as you can. Debbie is in trouble. And is there any chance that you can get Shania to come with you? We may need help from the FBI!'

'Ok – leaving now. Where do we find you?' said Brad.

'That was a quick decision!'

'I don't need yo ask permission from the boss! And Shania is right here if you want to ask her yourself! Now where are you?'

Shania had been Brad's girlfriend for some time and had recently been promoted to Senior Special Agent with the FBI. She had a couple of days off work and had been sitting on the couch across the room from the desk waiting from Brad to finish whatever he was doing, before going out to dinner and then contemplating how they would spend the rest of the evening together.

Chapter 56

Decision

Brad Morgan had been working on the riddle that Mark had posed after his discussions with Julius Perriam. He had got into the messages that were scattered around the Facebook pages that he had gained access to. They appeared to indicate that something important was to occur in Washington within the next twenty-four hours. The problem was that he did not know who would be involved in the *event* or where the event was to occur. There was nothing in the messages that he could decipher which told him who the agent was or who the target was. That is, on the assumption that there was a target.

When he finally sat down with the team to discuss what choice they had, he had a feeling of inadequacy – which was unusual for someone who came from his background.

Brad had the view that computers could solve anything and having access to a wealth of knowledge through the many databases – official and not-so-official – available through Taylor Software. When that failed, by hacking into systems where he did not have access, he could solve any remaining problems. However, this situation was different, and the pressure was on - while the subjects of their present discussions were not exactly pertinent to his employment with Taylor Software, he felt an obligation to help an obviously harassed Executive.

'Ok – let's deal with this kidnapping!'
Brad started on the subject that he was more confident about resolving and that he knew would keep Mark occupied while he continued to puzzle over other things. He fired up his laptop computer that had more power than most similar devices and logged into an AT&T account.

'We have the cell phone number, and as long as the cell is active, we can track it down.'

His fingers moved too fast over the keyboard for Mark or Shania to follow what he was doing. Within seconds he had logged into the Sandbox application. He keyed in Debbie's cell number and had the location isolated down to within an area of a couple of blocks in the suburb of Annandale. To confirm the finding he keyed in the cell phone number of Estefania and was rewarded the same location.

It was then a matter of getting feet on the ground in the same area and matching signals to pin down a more precise location. Brad left Shania to organize an FBI SWAT team. That would take time and while Mark was anxious to get to Debbie, it was more important to get this right.

Brad had a funny feeling that nothing much would happen until tomorrow and Debbie had not indicated to Mark that she was in imminent danger.

Surprisingly, it was Mark who took the initiative in dealing with the other issue, satisfied to leave the location and rescue of Debbie in the capable hands of Shania and the FBI.

'**Let us** start with the fact that we have Mohamed Haji in town. From what we know of him, he seems to rarely get directly involved. He is the planner and the man who pulls the strings. So – sitting in the Pakistan Embassy – he is orchestrating someone else to do all the work. Now we do not know who he has to do his dirty work. So - let us look at the other side. Who, what and where is the most likely target?'

All the people present had a view. Mark, Dusty, Blake, and Elliott who had been following Haji in Turkey after wandering around Afghanistan and Africa and had seen the kind of events that this conductor could create. Brad who had been diving into and out of websites and various official government databases where possibilities and theories abounded. Shania who from her experience with the FBI was used to the analysis and profiling of all sorts of scenarios where they could turn what little was known into cold hard evidence. The conclusion – who was the likely target?

It had to be someone in the inner sanctum. It could be the President of the United States – BJ Thomas, but evidence pointed to one of his chief advisors.

Whether or not it was the President who was the target, that presented Mark and his team with a major problem.

How to advise the President, or his minders, or both – that there was threat?

The team had arrived at the theory after careful consideration of all the facts. But how would that analysis translate when presented to officials? They had the analysis of messages posted on social media which was rife with conspiracy theories. Theories that they had somehow related to a man who was currently holed up in the Pakistan

Embassy. At least, they thought that he was! And that man could not be related to anyone that was even remotely connected to the President.

Sure – they had gotten some information from a US Navy chief who had been involved in messaging in the early days of this affair which led them to the Facebook accounts. So – good luck with that!

If someone tried to make any sense of what the drug induced chief had to say about messages that appeared to be religious rantings that would take the NSA many hours of work to figure out, the President or whoever the real target was would have died of old age before they had a solution!

The only person that Mark could think of to call was Bruce Aderholt – the National Security Advisor. His logic was that Aderholt had previously talked to Mark so he would be aware of his role, and he would surely be concerned of any attempt to target anyone in the Presidents inner circle of officials. Getting through to Aderholt turned out to be a mission, but eventually he was connected.

'Major Taylor! I did not expect you to call. What can I do for you?'

Mark thought of recounting his experiences over the last couple of days but realized the man would have other priorities. He delivered a shortened version. That turned out to be a mistake.

'We have analyzed the data that we have.' Mark began, unsure how he was to deliver the bad news. 'That points to an attempt to assassinate the Secretary of State, and that looks likely to occur tomorrow.'

For a moment, Mark thought that Aderholt was no longer on the line. There was silence, before Aderholt responded.

'Has this analysis come from the NRA, or has this come from elsewhere?'

That question caused Mark to pause. No – it had not come from the NRA. It had come from Brad Morgan who, although having been at one time being employed by the CIA, was not exactly an analyst. And his name would mean jack shit to the National Security Advisor and several other millions of people in government service. Mark decided to persevere knowing that he was digging himself into a hole.

'I haven't heard anything from the NRA – but they have the same information that we have. Whether they have connected the dots in the same way that we have I cannot comment, but the facts speak for themselves.'

Again, there was silence before Aderholt responded. This time Mark knew that his call had been a waste of time. He listened to the inevitable put down by a public servant hiding behind the bureaucracy.

'Taylor! Thank you for your advice. I will need to verify what you have to say with my department.'

With that said he ended the call. Body language transmitted via his tone suggested that he thought Mark Taylor was crazy.

Mark shrugged. He knew what he was about to do sounded even crazier.

He called his father at the CIA offices at Langley.

It was early evening in the capital when the Assistant Inspector General of the CIA – Harold Taylor – decided he had enough for one day. He packed the bundle of files on his desk into the safe, checked that there were no other papers left lying around that could give anyone a clue of what he had been working on, and prepared to leave his office.

In recent times it had become almost obligatory for him to make one last telephone call before he left.

'Hi Karen. I am leaving now. Should be home within half an hour. I am looking forward to a quiet glass of wine before dinner. It has not been the easiest of days. How about you?'

'Yeah – me too. See you soon!'

The lady who he had called was Karen Marshall, Director of Intelligence of the Drug Enforcement Administration. The home that Taylor had referred to was Marshall's house since he had moved in some months before. They were not married. But the word around the corridors of power in both of their respective organizations was that it was just a matter of time before the matter was resolved.

It was quite normal for them to relax with a glass of wine at the end of each day and exchange anecdotes of recent events.

This day would be slightly different.

Harold had no sooner arrived at the house when his cell phone chirped.

'Hi Dad - - Mark here. How was your day?'

It was not unusual for Harold Taylor to receive calls after hours, but he was initially relieved that it was a personnel call rather than an official one. He was soon disappointed.

After a brief exchange of pleasantries Mark got to the reason for his call.

'Do you happen to know the movements of the Secretary of State tomorrow?'

Harold answered the question before realizing it.

'He will be tied up in meetings with the President. He is apparently going to deliver an important address to the United Nations on a matter of national significance. Why do you ask?'

That question was ignored.

'Ok - Can you get me a meeting with the President tomorrow?'

The hesitation in the response was taken to mean that Harold was getting senile in his old age.

'You are joking?'

'I wish that I was!'

'Mark! You cannot just waltz up to the White House and get an audience with the President. His schedule is set for months in advance! And while you may think that you are important – you are talking about The President of the United States!'

'Father! Hear me out. We suspect that there is a threat to the Secretary of State, or the President, or to someone very close to the inner circle. If I were asked to present the facts, I would be laughed out of court. But it is very real and the only way I can prove it is to be there tomorrow. I thought that you could get me in there.'

The elder Taylor was a very powerful man in Washington. But no one had that kind of power in a city where lobbyists were everywhere. Effective lobbyists were very rare. However – Mark Taylor had been recently commissioned to do a job authorized by the President. And Mark Taylor had proved to have that uncanny ability to be correct in his assessments. Harold Taylor had a reputation as a maverick who could make things happen despite the odds. But this request?

Harold sighed.

'Leave it with me!'

Harold put down his cell phone and looked at Karen. She was the one person who he could discuss anything with.

But this request had certainly come out of left field.

'Mark wants me to arrange a meeting with the President!'

Karen Marshall just laughed. She had earlier experience with Mark, and she thought that she could both relate to him and could understand his logic. She was not too sure that the father had the same intuition. But it was worth a try.

'That should require a little bit of initiative on your part!' she said with an impish smirk and returned to opening the bottle of wine.

'Hi Nicolas. Harold Taylor here. How was your day?'

Nicolas Harrison – the Presidents Chief of Staff – was also used to receiving telephone calls at all sorts of weird hours and from all sorts of people. He knew Harold Taylor from when Taylor was the CIA Head of Station in Wellington New Zealand and Harrison was the Deputy US Ambassador to New Zealand. The tranquility of those posts was well behind both men. But they still shared an affinity for jobs well done in an environment that fostered solid friendships.

'Harold! So good to hear from you. And to what do I owe the pleasure of this call?'

'Not such good news I am afraid. You will recall that BJ had planned on making a presentation to my son – Mark Taylor?'

'Yes – he has probably filed that in the *too hard to fit into my schedule* basket, but I believe he did plan on doing that sometime. So – what is the problem?'

'Well - he had better hurry up! I have just had some bad news. Mark had been diagnosed as having a brain tumor. The medical reports suggest that it is malignant, aggressive and it is in-operable. He has just arrived back in

Washington from an overseas mission which started out as a job sponsored by your boss. Mark does not know I am doing this, but it would be good if you could find a slot in your schedule to fit him in to receive that award. I am sure that BJ would appreciate it if you did!'

Harrison had to think about that. The schedule was full – especially with all the problems with Iran. But Mark Taylor had been amid trying to resolve those exact same problems. And, as his father had alluded to, Marks' efforts had been ordered by BJ himself.

'Ok – I will look at the schedule when I get back to the office in the morning. Probably try for something within the next few weeks.'

Harold's voice gave nothing away as he responded.

'That may be too late.'

'That bad – huh? Give me a few minutes and I will call you back.'

There was silence in the room as Karen Marshall sat down beside the Assistant Inspector and held his hand. He looked into her eyes – looking and hoping for approval.

He had just taken an enormous risk. His career was on the line. He had just instigated an act that would be unforgivable in any sane democratic organization. He had just asked probably the only man on the planet who would be able to do it - to arrange an audience with the most powerful man on the same planet.

All based on a lie.

Before either of them could react, the cell phone shrilled.

Karen just squeezed the hand that she held and gave an encouraging smile.

'Good evening – Harold Taylor.'

'Harold – its' Nicolas. Ok – the best I can do is try to

fit him in tomorrow afternoon. The President is going to be at Camp David getting ready for a meeting at the United Nations. BJ himself is not planning on going to the UN, preferring to leave the details to the Secretary of State. But you never know. Anything can happen in the current situation. That is the best I can do, I am afraid. I will arrange for the Secret Service to expect him around midday – and I presume you will be going with him?'

Now that was a question that Taylor could not easily answer. The tone of the request had suggested that Mark had very definite plans for the meeting, and he figured that whatever that may entail, it probably did not involve his old man.

Taylor gave a nervous laugh.

'Mark would not want a fuss made, and he does not know why he is meeting the President. I will suggest to him that the meeting is to discuss his recent exploits in Africa and that would seem plausible. In any case, my presence would only complicate things. I think he would want to be accompanied by one of his team. I will check.'

'Ok. Talk to you later.'

'You have a lot of faith in your son Mark!'

Taylor looked up from his cell to find his other hand still clasped by Karen and she had a look on her face that was at least supportive. Or was it sympathetic? Or was it a look of resignation?

Harold gave a sigh and a shrug.

'I hope I know what I am doing!'

He thumbed the speed dial. The call was answered at once.

'Ok – can you be at Camp David by noon tomorrow? The President will be there with his usual team. That is the best I can do – the rest is in your hands!'

Mark sounded as though he did not believe what he was hearing.

'Dad – How did you arrange that? I didn't think you had that kind of influence in this town!'

The response suggested that he did not.

'I don't. And you have probably just cost me my job!'

Chapter 57

Camp David

There was a certain peaceful serenity about Camp David that belied its real purpose. How could people feel at peace in a place that contained some of the most powerful men and women on the planet?

Of course, the serenity was an illusion. There were hundreds of marines on the premises. Most of them could not be seen. But they were there. And they were armed with sufficient firepower to defend the place against the most determined assault. It would only be someone who was stark raving mad who would try to attack the Presidential entourage in this environment.

The President had decided - irrelevantly as it turned out - to get away from the White House and retreat to Camp David to prepare for what would probably be the defining moment of his Presidency. There was just too much risk staying in the middle of Washington DC where he lived and worked in an office that was recognized the world over.

The major problem was that someone – probably the Iranians – seemed to know enough about what was happening in Washington to make the security of the President questionable.

And until someone could get that under control people had every reason to be scared.

President BJ Thomas did have another problem largely of his own making. The United States was due to address a full meeting of the United Nations Security Council at which Thomas was committed to a course action that would either impose further crippling sanctions on the government – and therefore the people – of the Islamic Republic of Iran or he was taking his country beyond the brink of war.

The reason that he had a problem was quite simple. If he decided to impose the type of sanctions that the press was talking about and he managed to convince the other members of the security council to adopt them, then Iran would have little choice but to go to war anyway.

Most of the Presidents inner circle of advisors were there having been in an intense session trying to get a handle on a situation which was spiraling out of control. Attempts at diplomacy had apparently once again failed and the United States was facing the prospect of another war in the middle east which had arisen seemingly out of nowhere.

And that would turn into a nuclear conflict very quickly.

Bruce Aderholt – the National Security Advisor - summed up why the meeting had been called.

'I think we should make one last attempt to reason with President Khatami. We have previously given him an ultimatum which he has ignored. However, he must see that the result would be a nuclear conflict and his country would be the loser. From our sources of information, we know that the bomb that was stolen – whether by Iran or by their friends in Hezbollah - is still in the Islamic Republic.

Whether Khatami or anyone else in Iran knows that we know is debatable. Whether there is any truth in Khatami's claim that they have access to the codes to detonate the bomb, doesn't matter. If we act now any explosion will occur in Iran. However – if we delay - then that bomb could end up anywhere and then all bets are off! He will know from CNN and press reports that we are to address the Security Council in the morning and that the purpose of the address will be to explain what you intend to do about Iran. If that address says that you have solved the issue that will place the US of A back in the position that we used to be in – a world leader and a voice for peace. If on the other hand you must impose further sanctions, then we are admitting failure and we have lost - haven't we? So – my advice Mister President is call Khatami!'

The Secretary of Defense – Barry Crammer – spoke up before any of his military chiefs could butt in.

'Bruce! It is turned mid-night in Teheran. There is no one you can talk to at this late hour. We should place our forces on the highest alert level now. That way we can be ready. No one said in my book that you must declare war on anyone before you can get ready! And no one said that you need to wait for the other side to acknowledge any message before you do anything. Have we not learned anything from history? Remember Pearl Harbor? In that case we may have known the Japanese were about to attack but we were just too dumb to tell the people who mattered. Let's not make that mistake again. My recommendation Mister President is that you authorize our forces to go to DEFCON 2 so that our forces are ready to deploy immediately. You can always reduce the alert level later tonight or tomorrow. But you do not want to start a war when you don't know whether a nuclear bomb is hanging over you for fucks sake!'

BJ felt like he had to say something.

'We have not been at DEFCON 2 since the Cuban Missile crisis. Don't you think that recommendation is a little premature?'

Crammer was not about to back down.

'What is the difference between the Soviet Union pointing missiles at our country in 1962 and Iran threatening us with one of our own nuclear weapons today, Sir?'

John Scott - The Secretary of State - looked appalled.

'No! We should talk to Khatami first. Or even Khomeini. There must be a diplomatic solution to this!'

Nicolas Harrison – Chief of Staff – was feeling left out of it and felt inclined to say something.

'This is beyond diplomacy John. How many more times do we have to put up with the arrogance of Iran. Why do we always have to appear conciliatory when dealing with these vermin. Most Americans would say – Just Nuke the bastards.'

For once the President stepped in and made a decision safe in the knowledge that he had the majority behind him – given that he had the four military Chiefs, plus Secretary of Defense and Roger Warren the Vice President who always went with the majority.

'Barry – on my authority our forces will move to DEFCON 2 at once. I will talk to Khatami in the morning Iran time and inform him what I have done. What he does because of receiving that information is over to him. But our priority is to recover that nuclear bomb before they can do anything with it that may harm us or our allies. Now I believe you may have work to do Barry!'

With that the Secretary of Defense and his Chiefs took off heading for the helicopter pad. The rest of the Presidents men sat their somewhat stunned by the speed with which things had happened. The Chief of Staff busied himself organizing the Presidents secretary to get on the phone to the Iran ambassador, get him out of bed, bring him up to speed, and then get him to find Khatami and let her know when he would be available to take a call.

The President had other things on his mind.

'Gentlemen – I have taken the opportunity while we are all together to make a presentation to someone that we owe a lot to. You recall some time ago we had a small group of our people investigate something that needed a covert operation in the middle east. The man who led the group was a man called Mark Taylor. I have since been informed that Mr. Taylor is terminally ill and does not have much time left. I therefore invited him to come to Camp David today. I did not realize that it would be quite so dramatic a day, but Taylor is quite used to that kind of drama I suppose!' he finished with a grim chuckle.

'Archie would you please ask Mr. Taylor and his support person to come in?'

Archie was not he real name. He was called Franklin Williams and picked the Archie tag in an earlier life as a Delta Force sergeant after his athleticism brought back memories of the Olympian of the 1930's 'Archie' Williams for some wag in the same unit. And this time he greeted Mark like a long-lost friend since he was the joker who had come up with the name. He then introduced Mark to his fellow Special Service agent Asif Fisk before opening the door into the room that contained some of the most powerful men on the planet.

Mark Taylor and Elliott Shannon came into the situation room, shook hands with the President and the various other people who were seated around the table. They were invited to sit down on a couple of chairs facing the doorway and to the left of where the rest of the men were assembled.

At the time when Mark had asked his father to get him into this meeting, it had seemed like a simple request. Then all Mark had to do was turn up, assess what was a clear threat, and defuse it.

Now that he was here it was a very different story. The power in the room was patently obvious and everywhere you looked there were people whose lives seemed dedicated to ensuring that the lives of all the people present would be protected at all costs. It seemed inconceivable that anyone would be sufficiently insane to try anything that came close to what Mark had envisaged.

For a moment Mark began to relax. If he had been wrong in his interpretation of the messages that he had read, then so be it. On the other hand, the analysis of all the confusing messages over the last few months had pointed to an *event* on this day. Based on the other *events* that had occurred the dates at least were dependable. The actual events were variously successful or not successful. But they did occur. So – would the next *event* happen or not?

Maybe.

Mark had convinced himself that following his whole mission back to the days travelling through Zimbabwe in that crazy attempt to protect President Robert Mugabe, the whole trend had been a focus on the United States. Uncle Robert had merely been a distraction. Underlying everything that had occurred the focus had been on America and that usually meant people. Those people, or that person, had to be someone important otherwise what was the point? And in the way that the world worked that really had to mean that the President of the United States of America, or someone very close to him, had to be the target.

Maybe.

In the tranquil setting of Camp David, the theory that Mark had come up with seemed to be just that. A theory.

How could someone penetrate the protective detail that surrounded the President and his men? There were only two Secret Service agents present each guarding one of the doors that gave access to the situation room. They were in this room for the simple reason that it was the only space at Camp David that was sufficient to hold the number of men who were there. Otherwise - they could have just as easily met anywhere on the premises. What other agents were around would be pure speculation on Marks' part, but it was inconceivable that the risk assessment would be anything but the most thorough and the implementation of protective measures absolute.

So - there was another question that Mark had to ask. What if the threat came from within the Presidents own security detail?

A steward who was dressed in a Navy uniform served coffee without asking what anyone wanted and then retired.

The President waffled on about what a tremendous job Mark and his team had done for his country. And, being a politician, BJ could not resist the temptation to remind anyone who was listening that it had been his decision to assign Mark Taylor to the latest mission.

A couple of the presidential press teams were set up to record the event and that was the only reason why the President was still talking. He was a politician, so he was in his element although Mark detected some tension in his body language. Mark was not really listening to the bullshit, concentrating instead on the other people in the room. Trying to decide which of these men could possibly want to kill anyone. He began to think that he had been mistaken in his analysis. And if he was mistaken then that could prove to be a huge embarrassment for someone.

Busy thinking through the random thoughts in his own little world Mark almost missed the action.

The Secret Service agent who was standing by the west exit had the sun behind him so that he could not be seen clearly by the President or by the other Secret Service agent who was on the opposite side of the room. But Mark Taylor had been trained to look for movement and his eyes were drawn to the movement as the agents' hand reached behind his back. There was only the flicker of a reflection of the shiny black surface but that was enough to confirm what Mark had seen.

It was a gun.

And it was pointing into the situation room.

Asif Fisk had waited for this day for a long time. And now he was about to achieve his ultimate dream.

All those days – weeks, months, years - that he had spent training to be the very best that he could be, learning to think and act like an American while retaining his Islamic faith. Knowing that – one day – he would be presented with this opportunity. It was not as if the man that he was about to kill was necessarily bad. In fact, when he had started out on the path that would see him rise through the ranks of the elite US Secret Service, no one had been identified as a specific target. Now that the man had been identified and the day that he should die had been specified, Fisk had to admit that he did not know what the man had done to incur the wrath of his leader.

But that was not his role – was it? He was merely the

instrument. His job was to kill.

For just a split-second Mark hesitated. Maybe the agent was reacting to something else not even remotely connected to Mark's daydreams. He was in an area that was unfamiliar territory. But it was better to be wrong than sorry.

All that Mark knew was that this was the day that something was to happen. He hadn't got a clue of where that was to come from. Nor did he know who the target was although there had been speculation that it was the Secretary of State.

All that he did know was that he was the closest to the danger.

Mark yelled the word 'Gun!'

He hoped that others would react.

He leaped from his chair diving towards the agent, hoping that that single word would get a reaction from the other agents and everyone else. He did that because in an earlier life he had dived towards the shooter. That is what his training said that he should do. His earlier experience had not ended well. Still, his training kicked in.

He could not be certain who the intended target was in this case. Or if indeed there was a target. All that he knew was that a man with an exposed gun. The gun was pointed into the room while logic said it should be pointed outwards. There was no clear reason for it. And a gun was not normal in this company.

At least Archie Williams, the lead agent in charge of the Presidents detail yelled at the President to get down.

And then he yelled at the other agent.

'What the hell are you doing Fisk?'

That caused the shooter to hesitate.

And this time Mark was lucky. A shot greased his

shoulder as he tumbled into the agent smashing him to the ground and wrestling for the gun. He was within a whisker of being hit by a shot from Williams which missed everyone and thudded into the wall. Mark realized that since he was now lying on top of the agent, he was preventing anyone from having a direct line of fire. And belatedly realized that his life would be a secondary consideration for anyone trying to protect the President of the United States.

But he still clung onto the hand that held the gun wrenching it upwards and away from the table. Fisk was the younger of the two and despite Mark being fit and strong he felt his grip on the wrist beginning to ebb. So - he decided to try something else and hoped that Williams would understand.

He called out one word.

'Knee!'

Williams reacted at once.

He shot Fisk in the kneecap.

Fisk immediately let out an agonized scream. Giving Mark all the time that he needed to overpower the young man, knocking the gun loose, wrenching him onto his stomach, and pinning him to the floor.

The whole episode had lasted no more than five second.

Chapter 58

The Dear Girl

Dusty was in no mood to put up with any nonsense and he was anxious to get into the house without delay. It was almost beyond Blakes ability to control the rage that was going on inside his head, but he had to try while he patiently waited for the team to get themselves organized. The house had been identified and there were sufficient people to surround the place, so what was the hold-up?

The man in charge was leaning over the hood of his car studying a map and pointing at various features in the surrounding area. Eventually he seemed to come to a decision and a contingent of his team left the scene rapidly dispersing in all directions leaving just four men by his side.

Brad Morgan had been the one responsible for tracking the cell phone by triangulating the signal and had finally decided on this house. It was a very ordinary and had obviously been selected by the occupants at short notice without any thought to security or other considerations that would normally be applied when selecting a safehouse in a place like Washington DC. Probably because the occupants did not think that they were in any danger of detection and would be unlikely to have to use it again.

With the aid of the powerful people that Mark had contacted to resolve this issue it was now just a matter of getting an FBI SWAT team to blast through the front door. There were probably more agents in the team than was necessary, but it was just being treated as an exercise. Since the circumstances had been fully explained to the team there was a determination as the men went about their work and it was unlikely that this exercise would end up with a very good outcome for the perpetrators. Kidnapping was always frowned upon by the professionals in the FBI and would nearly always result in a successful rescue. Kidnapping a couple of young ladies that were related to someone who worked for the US security and intelligence services was just plain dumb.

Finally, the SWAT team moved in.

The front door was crashed off its hinges and four men in tactical gear with full body armor including helmets and goggles burst into a room. Sitting around a table playing cards were three men in shirts sleeves each with a shoulder holster that held a pistol.

They never got to draw the pistols.

The first two FBI agents who entered the room trained Heckler & Koch MP5 submachine guns on the men while the other two rushed to the rear door and smashed it open to let four other members of their SWAT team enter the house. These four quickly and efficiently checked the remaining rooms on the first floor. There was no one else to be found.

That caused the lead agent to bark a question at the men seated out the table.

'Where are the others?'

The three men looked at each other in confusion and then answered all at the same time. Only one of the men used English but the look on their faces all said the same thing.

'What others?'

The agent just smiled. Body-language said there were no others. He still had to be certain, but he was confident that they had only to find their hostages. He brought his weapon to a position that was at waist height and pointing directly at the men. His instructions were casual but firm.

'Ok - Remove your weapons and place them on the table in front of you. Then stand up facing the wall. Do that now. There will be no second warning.'

One of the men started to protest but was quickly advised against it by one of his colleagues.

'Do as I say now, and we can resolve this matter quickly. Any attempt to refuse my instructions could result in your being shot. As at this moment you are all under arrest on terrorism charges. You have no rights. So do not test my patience!'

The men complied. Curiously, they did not appear to the least bit concerned. Whether that was due to cultural differences or whether there was another factor at play, the Swat team had no idea.

The arrival of Dusty and Blake made for a very crowded room. Two other members of the SWAT team cautiously moved up the staircase their submachine guns pointed up and ready to fire. Dusty had been eager to follow them but was signaled that he should wait until they had checked out the upper floor of the house.

Meanwhile one agent patted down the three men removing their cell phones placed them on the table on the table. He then pushed the point of his gun into the back of the taller of the three men and then surprised Dusty by speaking in Farsi and then repeated the words in English.

'I am now going to remove the knife and the gun that you are concealing. Any attempt to resist or to use them will result in your being shot because those are the rules. Do that you understand the rules?'

Dusty moved forward to help the FBI man feeling that he had to do something. The Afro-American was a big man and he towered over the others. Even so, the men did not exactly look scared, but they had no choice but to comply.

They had the attitude that they were only the hired help and just following orders – so someone else would carry the can for this one. Then Dusty bound their hands and feet with tape and sat them down back-to-back on the floor and completed the job by wrapping a length of tape around the three of them so that they were completely immobilized.

Dusty was just finished his work when one of the men came back down the stairs and summoned Dusty.

'Excuse me sir – I think you had better come and have a look at what we have found.' He then turned around and rushed back up to the second floor.

At first Dusty was paralyzed with fear. He looked at the three men who he had just trussed up and then looked at the other SWAT team members looking for an answer. The only reaction that he got was a shrug from the FBI. Nothing at all from the other three men. He made his way to the bottom of the staircase before he turned to address the three men, his face set as though in stone.

'If those ladies have been harmed in any way you are all dead men!'

Dusty did not rush. He had to keep himself under control as he stoically mounted the steps. When he reached the top, one of the SWAT team was standing in a corridor lazily hanging his gun pointed to the floor. There were obviously no perpetrators on this floor. He just nodded towards the open door ahead and stood back to let Dusty pass.

Despite his size, Dusty was almost knocked over as the two ladies leapt up at him.

'What gives?' he asked the grinning FBI man who had summoned him from the floor below.

'Sorry sir! The ladies were hiding under the bed and refused to come out unless for someone who they knew. I guess you have met the ladies before?'

Neither of the ladies could talk, tears streaming down as they grappled with their mixed emotions. They just clung to Dusty. And then Debbie had to ask.

'Where is Mark? Is he Ok? When can I see him?'

Now how did he answer those three questions? Would she believe his answer to the first question – *Oh he is with the President of the United States of American!* He did not know what Mark would want him to say. Yes – the last time he had seen Mark he was Ok. When would Debbie be able to see him? Well - that would depend on forces beyond the control of the two friends. Dusty sighed.

'Mark is fine. He is just up town sorting out a couple things and then he will be back. The first thing we have to do is to sort out this mess here. Just give me a few minutes while I talk to the FBI, and we can get rid of the vermin down below. You have nothing to worry about now – I promise. It might get a little bit rough downstairs so just stay here until we tell you it is all clear.'

Debbie and Estefania were reluctant to let him go, but he finally managed to escape their clutches as he went back down the stairs.

Dusty had no sooner arrived back down the stairs when a loud ringtone came from one of the cell phones sitting on the table. Everyone in the room tensed.

The FBI agent levelled his gun at the three men and said, 'Who owns that phone? – and be sure you get it right! Any mistake and you arc dead!'

The tall guy with the ginger hair claimed that he was the owner of the cell phone that was ringing. The agent cautioned the man to acknowledge the call correctly and then reached over the table and activated the device and set the sound to broadcast. Carrot-top answered.

'Yes Sir.'

The voice on the phone was in a tone that showed an affinity to giving orders and having them carried out. Whoever the man was he simply said what he wanted to happen next,

'Kill the dear girl and get rid of the body!'

Then the caller just ended the connection without any further comment.

Dusty looked up the stairs to where Debbie was waiting, and she would have heard the message. Considering that she was the subject that the call was about, there was no reaction.

Dusty turned to Carrot-top and in almost a whisper asked.

'Who was the caller? The one you referred to as Sir!'

As expected, the answer he got was evasive – and a lie. 'I have no idea.'

Dusty realized that the man had critical information – but what could he do?

'Come on! That gentleman was obviously an American and you called him Sir. So – you must know who that is!'

The man merely shrugged, a look of arrogant disregard on his face.

Blake had already picked up the cell phone and was already shaking his head. 'It is obviously a call from a burner phone, so there is no help there.'

Dusty just gave the three men a look of absolute disgust.

'Ok – we will leave that to the FBI to deal with. You may be lucky and escape with your lives. If my boss had any say in the matter, you would already be dead. As it is – our justice system does not take to kindly to the crime of kidnapping no matter that you are acting under instructions from someone else. If you refuse to say who those instructions are coming from then you get to carry the can. But quite frankly – I don't give a fuck!'

Chapter 59

The Mole

The situation room at Camp David was in a mess – papers and cups had been scattered everywhere as two things happened simultaneously. The members of the Presidents inner circle were trying to exit the room ushered by navy staff. At the same time Marines and Special Services personnel were trying to get in as a show of force and to secure the area. There was only one person injured and paradoxically everyone seemed to ignore him. At this early stage after the shots had been fired the scene was one of chaos. But still there was order amongst the chaos.

As though it had all been planned, the President was whisked out of the door by two members of his detail as Marine One – the presidential Sikorsky VH helicopter - spooled up on the pad. BJ was closely followed out of the door by the Secretary of State who was almost panicked as he tried to contact someone on his cell phone accompanied by two other members of the Secret Service detail. There were six of them running towards the helicopter with the President being virtually carried without any apparent thought for anything other than his absolute safety as they scrambled the couple of hundred meters from the cabin. The rest of the people in the presidential party who had not already got out were almost instantly surrounded by marines.

Mark was still sitting on the floor nursing his wounded shoulder. He was pleased with his efforts in preventing the assassination of the Secretary of State – if that was the intended target. But no one else seemed to care.

Agent Asif Fisk who had caused the chaos was still on the floor where he had fallen. He had been dis-armed and bound so that he could not move and presented no further threat. It still seemed strange that no one paid any attention to him. Even stranger that they paid no attention to Mark - the man who had brought Fisk to the ground and had prevented a fatality. All the staff were interested in was getting the President and his men to safely. They made sure that everyone else was under instant surveillance and treated with the utmost suspicion. And then it dawned on Mark what was happening. The Navy stewards who were the custodians of Camp David could no longer trust the Secret Service personnel!

Mark had to smile at that. He had come to Camp David because the security and intelligence service did not believe his theory about what was going to happen. Now that it had happened – well, it had resulted in an agent being apprehended during an attempt to kill John Scott – the security system at Camp David had been thrown into chaos. Now – no one trusted anyone!

Mark had his cell phone in his right-hand pocket, and he felt the vibration as a call came through. His first thought was to ignore it. Then he thought that it might be some more good news concerning Debbie.

It was.

'Mark – Dusty. It is Ok – Debbie is safe. And we will get her out of here shortly. But you should know – a call just came through to these creeps from some Boss who they will not name, and his instruction was clear. His exact words were *Kill the dear girl and get rid of the body.*'

Mark initially froze, and then leapt as best he could to his feet.

'Shit!! Dusty. Get out of there now. I know who it is! Got to go.'

Mark rushed to the door and yelled towards the helicopter pad.

'Archie! Stop that helicopter! Do not let the President get on board. Move!'

Archie Williams, for the second time this day, did not move.

'Mark – what the hell are you talking about?' he shouted.

Mark looked at his old friend without realizing what he had said. Then with his voice ice-cold, he implored the head of the Presidents detail.

'Archie - If I am wrong then you have my permission to shoot me and you can have all my money. But – just this once trust me. I now believe that the I know who the mole and he is about to kill the man you are sworn to protect.'

'Shit – I can't do this! Shit! Oh Fuck!' Williams yelled into his communicator.

'Do not let Marine One leave! I am on my way to explain.'

The six men who had rushed out of the door and had headed towards the landing pad were just about to climb on board the helicopter. The President was the first to mount the steps into the helicopter as Williams and his group ran towards him. Although Williams was yelling, his message was incomprehensible to the men who were boarding the helicopter, drowned by the noise from Marine One's blade rotation. Unable to get any reaction from the group who he was trying to contact Williams pulled his pistol out and fired a couple of shots into the air.

That got their attention.

It was a choreographed response.

The President and the Secretary of State sank to the ground and the four secret service personnel sprang in front of them. The area was suddenly full of Marines who had appeared from everywhere, guns at the ready.

Time froze.

Everyone appeared stunned by the enormity of what had already happened, and now there was another issue to contend with. Having heard several shots, the marines switched their safety levers to fire mode. It was then a question of who they would shoot.

Everyone's attention turned to Mark Taylor who had rushed from the situation room and was now positioned himself at the base of Marine One between the President and the Secretary of State.

'So – it was you after all!' Mark said through clenched teeth. 'Now empty your pockets and do it slowly! I do not want to shoot you, but I will if I must.'

John Scott bristled with rage.

'What is the meaning of this. What is this nonsense? And who do you think you are? Can't you see we are trying to get the President to safety?'

Both the President and Williams who was supposed to be in charge of the Presidential detail, also looked at Mark awaiting an answer. But Mark was certain and pressed ahead.

Mark raised his gun and pointed it directly at Scott, ignoring the massive array of weapons in the hands of Marines and were now pointed in his direction.

'I will give you five seconds to comply. If I am wrong, then you can lock me up for life. But meanwhile just follow a simple request and prove your innocence.'

A vicious sneer appeared on the face of the Secretary of State as he whispered so that Mark who was closest to him barely heard.

'You obviously do not care that your dear lady friend is dead.'

Scott pulled a syringe from his pocket and laid it on the ground. The sneer remained on his face. 'That is all I have. And that is what is needed because for my earlier sins – I am a diabetic.'

Now Mark had a sneer on his face.

'Ok – then there is no problem if you inject yourself with it now. And I will help you.'

Both men grabbed for the syringe. Because of his injured arm Mark was the slower of the two and Scott grasped it.

And then the Secretary of State did the inexplicable.

He lunged at the President.

There was a short sharp crack. The bullet that had been fired by Williams shattered the Secretaries hand and destroying the syringe and its contents. Marines rushed to grab their Commander in Chief and bundled him into the waiting helicopter. Within seconds the helicopter designated as Marine One was in the air leaving further chaos on the ground including a severely injured Secretary of State, and several men shakings their heads in absolute disbelief.

Mark turned to the Secretary of State.

'It is lucky for you that your goons were unable to follow your last order. The *dear girl* is alive and well and your men are in custody as we speak. If they had succeeded in carrying out your orders, I would have no hesitation in killing you here and now, and to hell with the circumstances.'

Mark then turned his back on the man who had almost succeeded in fulfilling the wishes of the Iranian Prime Minister Mahmoud Khatami by murdering the President of the United States, and previously had almost talked the US President into embarking on a conflict that would have had catastrophic consequences for humanity.

What insane logic could cause a man to do such things?

The head of the Presidential detail tried to stop Mark as he walked away. 'How the hell did you work that out?' was what Archie Williams asked.

Mark was grim as he replied.

'I will talk you through that later. Right now, I have to go and see a lady who doesn't deserve to be involved in any of this crap!'

But before Mark had gone far, he heard a helicopter flaring before it landed on the pad. Because there were always two helicopters available to ferry the President around it was not clear whether this one was Marine One, but it turned out to be the same Marine One that had left Camp David only moments before. The helicopter was barely on the ground when the President jumped out, ignoring the Secret Service protestations, and started after Mark.

'Mark! Could you spare me a moment?'

Incredulously John Scott climbed off the ground while everyone was distracted and grabbed a rifle off a shocked Marine. He began to raise it in the direction of the President yelling incoherently as he did so. Fortunately, he was hampered by his injured hand. He never got the rifle into a firing position. He was cut down by a fusillade of shots that seemed to come from everywhere.

The traitor and mole John Scott - the US Secretary of State - was dead.

BJ sat down on the closest bench visibly upset and shaking his head in disbelief, just as he reached Mark.

'Sit down please Mark. This is all getting too much for me!' the President said as he stared in disbelief at the body of the man who had very nearly killed him.

'What I wanted to ask is - if you could spare a moment to give me your thoughts on where this all came from. I realize now that you were here today for a reason, and you know more than I do about what happened. And I owe you a debt of gratitude for saving my life. I never realized when we set out on your mission to prevent the death of an African leader that it would end up being me who was the ultimate target. Thank you!'

BJ was close to tears, but he recovered himself before he continued.

'My Secretary of State – John fucking Scott – was to represent me – us if you like – to attend a meeting of the United Nations Security Council tomorrow to talk about imposing further sanctions on Iran. Now I think I am going to do that myself and I may have something more to say than we had originally planned. I want you to come back to my office and fill me in on what the hell is really going on!'

BJ was the President.

When the president asks for something, it is not so much a request as an instruction. He expects the people to comply.

Mark thought long and hard before reluctantly complying.

In any case, what easier way was there to get to Washington DC than as a passenger in Marine One. Washington DC was where Mark was headed in any case to catch up with his mates Dusty, Blake, and the rest of his team. And particularly to be with his girlfriend Debbie.

'Yes - Mister President – I will do that. Can we give Elliott Shannon a lift at the same time?'

Chapter 60

Choices

The President's presentation to the reporters who had gathered outside the United Nations headquarters in New York could not have had a greater impact both nationally and internationally. Word had leaked out. What was not clear was whether that had been a deliberate move by the administration to ensure that there was maximum coverage.

It was known that something serious had happened the previous day at Camp David. It was also known that at least one person was now dead although the media were yet to be told who that was. That the *one* who had died was not the President had initially been slightly disappointing to the headline-hungry media. Now they were lusting for the facts.

A good deal of the credit for the formal address by the President was due to his speechwriter and the work that Mark had done over the previous sixteen hours. However, it still needed a firm, articulate and confident delivery to be certain that the message was heard and fully understood.

Everyone in the crowd of reporters and camera operators also knew that President BJ Thomas was on his way to make an important address to the United Nations Security Council. But they also had a strong suspicion that he would say things at a pre-address briefing that he could not perhaps say in the politically charged atmosphere of the council.

They were not disappointed.

The President had his people erect a large screen that he stood in front of. As his address began the display simply showed a picture of a desert and its complete lack of detail in and of itself suggested that this would be an interesting morning.

BJ Thomas was nervous as he faced the largest crowd of reporters that few had ever seen outside the United Nations. However, once he started talking, he forgot about the crowd.

'Over the previous several weeks our security and intelligence service have been following a group who were looking to cause harm to the government of the United States and its' allies. Initially, that was believed to have ended when an attempt was made to assassinate one of our friends at the meeting of the African Union.'

The picture changed to show an aerial view of Khartoum, and then quickly changed to show a picture of oil wells.

'My investigators quickly proved that the attempt was orchestrated by a foreign government. At approximately the same time as that government sought to assassinate the leader of sovereign power, one of our overseas diplomats was murdered. Our investigations have revealed that the murder was conducted by the very same people – from the very same country.'

As the picture behind the President changed to an overview of the Incirlik airbase in Turkey he continued.

'In the city of Adana in Turkey someone deliberately infected some of our people with the SARS virus and I should not need to tell you what effect that could have had, had it been allowed to spread unchecked. During the chaos that the virus epidemic created, a group of thugs – apparently belonging to Hezbollah – raided our base at Incirlik under the guise of medics and stole one of our strategic weapons.'

The picture changed to show what looked like blood-splattered bodies and then zoomed in to show just one – a close-up of a hand clutching what appeared to be a smashed circuit board against a blood-covered stomach. And just to make the impact would be more effective the view panned back to reveal that the hand belonged to a young female dressed in a lieutenants uniform writhing in agony on the ground. Then the picture zoomed out to a broad view of an airbase. BJ paused while the message sunk in. This part of the address was pure fiction, but it was doubtful whether anyone in Iran would know that.

'This young lady is a hero. The circuit board that she is holding in the picture is the difference between Hezbollah having a bomb that can be exploded and them having a pile of junk that is no use to anyone. Nonetheless, we believe that Hezbollah, or whoever they claim to be, were working for the same foreign government that our men were following, and the same foreign government that was responsible for the SARS virus in Turkey. And that foreign government has now threatened the United States and the whole of the free world with nuclear war.'

The picture now changed to show a picture of Teheran. Although nothing was said by BJ or written on the screen to confirm that it was or it wasn't, the reporters would be familiar with the picture and no further explanation was necessary.

Now the President adopted his sternest voice.

'Last evening, I authorized our forces to move to alert level DEFCON 2. That is the highest level we have been at since the Cuban Missile crisis of 1962 – showing how seriously we are taking this threat from a government that is clearly out of control.'

The picture started to slowly zoom in getting a view of the palace where the Supreme Leader of the Islamic Republic of Iran lived.

'While there is no way that the threats of using our weapons against us can be seriously implemented, what we do view seriously is that a foreign government would look to threaten the United States in this way. They will be aware that we can strike at them at anytime and anywhere. They may not be aware that the removal of that circuit board from a nuclear weapon would make that bomb susceptible to sympathetic detonation. And my forces will be authorized to make that happen unless they come to their senses.'

The picture changed to show the Iranian nuclear facility at Natanz and began to zoom in on the part of that facility where it was believed the bomb was being stored.

'The government of the Islamic State of Iran is put on notice that we will retaliate if there is any hint that the Iranians are about to launch an attack against the United States or any of our allies. As we speak, I have asked the Chairman of the Joint Chiefs of Staff to contact the appropriate people in Iran and inform them of the specific nature of our response. The countdown starts now!'

Admiral Arthur Mullen did not like what he had to do but, being a man who had spent his life serving his country, he would do it. Mullen had been given clear instructions by his Commander in Chief to deliver a message to the head of the Islamic Revolutionary Guard Corps. The fact that the IRGC was regarded as a terrorist organization did not mean that it did not have Major General Mohamad Jafaris' telephone number. Although they had not previously spoken, Jafari would probably be unaware that Mullen spoke passable Farsi. Mullen was aware that Jafari spoke fluent English having been to military schools in the United Kingdom. So – the task would be quite simple. The message would not be. Mullen had cringed at his Presidents' use of the term *countdown* – but that could not be helped now.

'General I have a message for you from our government. I am delivering it as we will understand more clearly than our political masters the full implications of what I have to say. As I have told you before, we have reason to believe that your government has taken possession of one of our nuclear weapons.'

'I know nothing of any such thing!' the General interrupted.

'General – that maybe so. As I have said before - I am only delivering a message. If there is no bomb – then there is no reason to be concerned is there? The bomb is missing – that much we know. The decision has been made to detonate the bomb because we cannot risk it falling into the hands of terrorists and the risk is just too great that they would try to explode it at the time and in a place of their choosing. You will understand that any bomb can be triggered by a series of codes. We are unsure whether whoever stole the bomb also has access to those codes. We believe that the bomb is being stored underground and my staff advise me that the damage from an explosion should not be too great. Anything within an area of say ten miles from the blast will probably be destroyed and that area would be contaminated for the next fifty years. So – if you know where the bomb is – we recommend that you evacuate that area now. We cannot delay any longer. The bomb will explode in thirty minutes from now.'

There was a stunned silence before Jafari recovered a semblance of composure and managed to stutter a response.

'You cannot do this!' he shouted. 'The US threatens us with nuclear weapons! This is unprecedented.'
Mullen waited for a few seconds before responding.

'General – there is no threat either implied or intended. You say that there is no bomb. Our information was that a bomb was originally stolen by Hezbollah, but we have since tracked that bomb to your Natanz nuclear facility. If it is not there, then you have nothing to worry about – is there?'

Again – the stunned silence, before the General had to ask.

'How do we avoid this mess?'

President BJ Thomas received a thumbs up from his Chief of Staff. The message had been delivered. He confidently raised his head to finish his talk with the press. No mention would be made of the conversation between his Chairman of the JCS and the chief of the Iran RGC. He just hoped that common sense would break out in Iran sooner rather than later.

'I am about to address the United Nations Security Council and I am going to recommend the imposition of further sanctions which will target the people in power in that country. I do not doubt in my mind that those sanctions will be adopted. I thank you all for your attendance. I will speak to you after the session, and keep you informed of any further developments.'

The reporters were so stunned by the frankness of

the statement that the President had made earlier they were initially stuck for words, except for one of the ladies from the Washington Post. And, as usual, she missed the point entirely.

'Mister President - Can you tell us what happened yesterday at Camp David?'

That question seemed to annoy the President. Maybe because it was a distraction from the purpose of this press conference. Maybe because BJ had himself still to come to terms with what had happened.

'You will have to address your questions on that subject to the FBI. All I will say is that the same country was responsible!'

BJ stormed off.

When they had recovered, they were too late to ask any other questions of the President as they watched him disappear inside the United Nations headquarters. That was probably just as well.

A lot of what had been said was factual, but that discourse omitted several key points that a President would normally be expected to comment on. In particular, the absence of his Secretary of State – the late John Scott. But mentioning the demise of his secretary would have alerted the Iranians to that fact and they may have not yet heard of the happenings of yesterday. BJ had also made no mention of the attempts to compromise various consular staffs in the Middle East because that would have cast doubt on the competence and reliability of his staff and distracted the media from the point that he was trying to make. Not to mention the extreme embarrassment that would cause both inside and outside his administration.

The other area of contention was just how valid were his claims that the bomb,which had been the subject of a complex plan to steal, was inert? No one was certain of the origins of the circuit board which had been so spectacularly displayed for all the world to see. The only way to find out the truth of this matter was to mate it with the bomb, and that did not seem likely to happen any time soon. In any case, according to the theory now put forward by Mark Taylor, the entire plot had been just a cover for an attempt on the life of the US President himself. It would have been nice to reveal that this part of the plot had failed by the simple fact of BJ still being in the land of the living. But the President had insisted that there were more important things to worry about than that at the present.

BJ felt the same pangs of apprehension as he sat down to make his first address to the members of the UN Security Council since he took office. While the media could be a pain up the ass at times, that was nothing compared with what he faced at this table. The five permanent members – USA, China, Russia, France, and the UK – probably gave him a 3-2 advantage when it came to the vote. But the ten non-permanent members could react in any number of ways – usually dependent on political considerations rather than any sense of what was right or what was wrong. And that was why BJ had chosen to address the media first. If he had done his job correctly, the international opinion would have already been formed before this council could make a statement on the issues.

The United States had submitted a Draft Resolution to the council months earlier to increase worldwide sanctions on Iran based on their failure to keep their nuclear ambitions under control. Using this resolution as the excuse, and since the UN was already in session, he had created the opportunity to call an urgent meeting to consider the latest set of events. In any case, this was a situation where world peace had been threatened, and what elsc was this esteemed body there for if it wasn't to at least pretend that it could influence the outcome. At the end of the day, it did not matter whether nine members of the council – the number needed to pass a resolution - voted in favor of what the United States would now propose, or whether one of the permanent members would veto it.

The President of the council for this month was a Frenchman so that would help.

The US representative opened the proceedings, aware that she had to address the President of the council in the presence of her boss.

'Mister President. The United States of American moves that this council adopts a new resolution in terms of resolution 1737 previously passed by the body concerning the threat to world peace, and further that it condemns the actions of the Islamic State of Iran in ignoring earlier resolutions that would restrict its acquisition and use of nuclear weapons.'

The opening statement at least got a nod from the chair and a renewed interest from Russian and the United Kingdom. No one in the meeting would have heard first-hand BJ's address to the media, but the news would travel very quickly. At the best of times meetings of the Security Council were like having a meeting in a busy railway station with people coming and going oblivious to what was occurring in the session. That included the people who were leading their particular delegations, so the actual council meetings were more or less run by a committee.

The evidence needed to support the US resolution was as much hearsay as anything else although it would be delivered by the President of the United States rather than the US Secretary of State or the head of the United States delegation. And so, it carried more weight. That did not stop other delegates leaping to the defense of their Islamic friends, or in the case of Russia, defending them just for the hell of it.

Thankfully, a message came into the hall which caused BJ to excuse himself while the debate continued. He was escorted to a side room where he was simply handed a telephone and told that Iran was at the other end.

'Good morning to you Mister President. Let me first apologize for the trouble that we have caused you.'

It took BJ a minute to work out who was talking, before realizing that it was the Iranian Supreme Leader Ali Khomani.

'Yes, Ali – good afternoon to you.' BJ replied in a defensive tone. 'You are no doubt aware that the United States is ready to defend against any attack on our territory or its citizens.'

'No! No!' Khomani interrupted the President. 'It has all been a terrible misunderstanding. Even as we speak, I have arranged for Mahmoud Khatami to be removed from his office and he will face the full wrath of our justice system for his unspeakable crimes. I have taken steps to rectify the harm that he had caused and have instructed my people to allow the United States without hindrance to immediately collect the weapon that the Hezbollah deposited in our hands. If there is anything else that we can do to bring this unfortunate episode to an end, then we will do it. You have my word.'

The President was about to let rip at Khomani venting all his anger and frustration. Then he thought better of it. That Khatami was to be removed from office was some compensation since, according to intelligence reports, he was the chief instigator of all the troubles. And the fact that he was to face the Iranian version of a justice system meant that he would probably not remain in this world. But Khomeini's offer to do *anything else* was what rankled. Nothing that the Supreme Leader Ali Khomani or anyone else could do would bring back the dead. Nothing that he could do would ease the pain that was still being felt in Turkey where there was an epidemic in progress thanks to the stupid Iranian plot. Elsewhere, the threat of a nuclear conflict had hung over the world at a time when most sane people believed such a threat had ended years before with the termination of the Cold War between the Soviet USSR and the United States.

But the real issue was that the ultimate target in all this nonsense had been the US President himself – BJ Thomas. And it was inconceivable that such a plot could have existed at all without the knowledge and authorization of the Supreme Leader who is the commander in chief of the Iranian armed forces, is the head of state, and is the most powerful man in Iran.

A sobering factor in all of this was the role that had been played by the late John Scott – the US Secretary of State – an American for heavens' sake! If the Iranians had managed to corrupt an official at this level and do so with the help of a member of the Presidents security detail what else could they do?

And - What else were the Iranians up to?

The President chose his world very carefully.

'You will know that our forces are on high alert and ready to strike anywhere and at any time against anyone who would look to cause us harm. They will remain at that level until we see conclusive evidence that steps have been taken by you to end this crisis. You will also know that I have today addressed the United Nations Security Council and asked that body to agree at once to increased punitive sanctions against Iran. You should know that this will result in a resolution later today which enables the United States and many other countries to take steps that will cripple your economy from which it will take a long time for you to recover. You can take these two issues as threats but let me say they are only threats if you wish to make them so.'

Now it was the Iranian Supreme Leader Ali Khomani who had to control his reaction.

'You have my word. Iran will honor my commitment to you!'

BJ thought of saying something else but thought bitterly that he had better not. He thought of saying that this could depend on who the next President of Iran would be! But – that would be pointless - wouldn't it? Khomani would respond with criticism of the American way of appointing the next President of the US who could on a whim undo everything the BJ had said and done.

'Very well Ali. My people will be in touch with your people to see what must be done. I thank you for your call. Let us hope that we can restore peace before matters get out of control.'

Instead of returning to the hall in which the Security Council was meeting, BJ with his entourage of Special Service officers headed for the public area outside the confines of the United Nations Headquarters. There were so many diplomats and other officials around that it would have been impractical for the public to have access to any meetings and judging by the snails' pace of decision making there were not likely to be too many interested anyway. But there was a small coffee bar that at this time only was populated by one small group of people. Mark and Elliott were there waiting for the President to confirm that the matter was at an end. They had been joined by Dusty and Blake who had brought with them, Debbie Peterson, and Estefania Rodriguez.

The ladies were somewhat taken aback when the President of the United States walked up to Mark with his hand outstretched and thanked him for all the work he had done on behalf of a grateful nation. As the President then turned to leave, he felt as though he had to say something else.

'Mark – I realize that there is nothing I can do or say to ease your problem – if there was I would do it in an instant. But good luck and thanks again!'

As BJ walked purposefully towards the exit door to return to the Security Council meeting it was Dusty who was the first to react.

'What the fuck was he talking about?' Dusty asked in his inevitable manner.

'I haven't got the faintest idea!' was Mark's honest reply.

'Why don't we get out of here and away from these politicians before we all go mad.'

Chapter 61

There was just one more thing that Mark Taylor had to do before he could turn his back on this affair.

Mark had to answer the riddle of what had been the role of the illusive Mohamed Haji. He was convinced that Haji had been responsible for all the troubles that he had encountered during the entire escapade. He had to admit that at times he had held the upper hand. Mark had thought that in Sudan they would put a stop to the troubles when they had seen Haji locked up. How the man had escaped he had no idea. But that had been merely a blip in an otherwise flawless mission that had resulted in chaos everywhere he went.

Now Haji had been in Washington DC where an attempt had been made on the President of the United States. And Haji could reasonably claim that it had nothing to do with him.

Since the recent arrival of Haji in Washington DC, the FBI agents assigned to the task of following him, with the help of Owen Squires, Ben Chapman, Brent Shannon, Mike Gilroy, and Hamish O'Dea, had simply seen him once only. On that occasion Haji – under whatever name he was using - had been seen in a taxi driving from Dulles International Airport to the Embassy of Pakistan which was located in the International Court in central Washington. From that point onwards Haji had not been seen by anyone.

So - it had been assumed that he was still in the Embassy.

The Pakistan Embassy is the de facto consular representative of the Islamic Republic of Iran giving the Iranians a form of presence in the capital city of their arch enemy. The other fact that Pakistan was supposed to be allied to the United States in the war on terror was just one irony in the game that was known as international diplomacy.

Every vehicle which left the Embassy was followed by the FBI to learn where it went and who the passengers were. Having eventually decided that Haji was not one of the passengers the FBI returned to their boring surveillance outside the Embassy.

Except on the day following the United States presentation to the Security Council the FBI sensed that something different was happening. A man alighted from the Embassy vehicle at Dulles International departures. Nothing about this man looked anything like Mohamed Haji. He was clean-shaven. He had a number one haircut. He was dressed in a formal dark business suit. To all intents and purposes, he was just a normal businessperson going on his legitimate travels.

Except that the man had a limp.

Owen Squires accompanied the FBI agent into terminal.

Salman Sharif presented himself at the Emirates

check-in carrying a smart black briefcase and a matching hold-all. He placed the hold-all on the weighing machines and handed over his ticket together with a new Pakistan passport to the smiling attendant. The lady had a cursory look at the passport, asked Sharif to confirm that he was bound for Dubai, gave him the resultant boarding pass, and wished him a pleasant journey.

Sharif quickly made his way to the international departure gate. There was a brief delay at the entrance where a group of passengers were having difficulty understanding instructions. He tried to push his way past claiming to be in a hurry. The security guard noted that Sharif had two hours to go before his boarding call and told him to wait.

By the time Sharif got to the security area, he was agitated and sweating. That made the attendant staffing the body scanner suspicious as Sharif walked through and so he was stopped for a physical pat-down. The two airport police officers who had been watching all this unfold then stepped forward, checked the boarding pass, and asked Salman Sharif to go with them to a room for a chat. He was followed into the room by two men who claimed to be FBI agents.

Sharif became more agitated when one of the FBI agents seemed to mimic his limp which caused the two police officers to intervene and bundle the hapless man into the interview room, sat him in a chair and then stood by the door waiting to see what happened.

The FBI agent smiled at Sharif.

'Could I see your passport please Mr. Sharif?'

'What is this all about?' Sharif asked in a quiet and reasonable tone,

The FBI agent replied in the same tone of voice.

'You have been selected at random for further examination for this flight. If you could just bear with us and let us do our job, this will be all over shortly. You did seem to become a little agitated back at the security gate, but I can assure you that you have nothing to worry about. Now could I see your passport please.'

'Then why did your associate need to mimic my limp.' he asked indignantly. 'I find that offensive and demand an apology!'

It was now the turn of Owen Squires to smile.

'I am sorry that you should take offence. If you must know I was injured in an accident when the Pakistan Taliban blew up the Hospital that I was working in Peshawar some years ago. Like you I have a permanent limp. I see no need to apologize to anyone.'

Sharif handed over his passport, suitably chastened. But that did not help him.

'When did you arrive in the United States?' the FBI enquired.

That question brought a shrug.

'A couple of weeks ago. If you are concerned at my new passport with no entry stamps on it – my passport was stolen by one of your criminals and my Embassy was kind enough to issue a new one. You will find that everything is in order and the passport is legitimate.'

'Ok – just allow me a couple of minutes. This will not take very long.'

The FBI agent got up to leave and was halfway through the door when he turned around with another question.

'Excuse me. It would save us both a good deal of time if you could be more specific about your arrival – like what airline did you use, what was the port of entry, what date did you arrive – that kind of stuff?'

The hesitation from Sharif would have told the FBI all that he needed to know but the agent could not resist twisting his tail.

'That is Ok. If you cannot remember, it will just take longer to check!'

It was not Sharif could not remember. The problem was that he had used a passport naming him as an Iranian Abdul Nadir to enter the United States and it was a pointless exercise to try to convince these people that he had magically become a Pakistan national. Sharif's problems were made more finite when the FBI agent stood aside and let another two men enter the room.

It was Mark Taylor and Dusty Miller.

'Hello Mohamed. So – we meet again!' Mark said as he sat down facing his nemesis.

Haji had to smile. He had no complaints about the job Mark Taylor had done following him through Africa and the middle east. He had concluded that Taylor was just a soldier. Admittedly an efficient one. But for all of that, Taylor had never really caught him. Well – apart from that incident in Sudan. Had Taylor been aware of the chronic state of the Sudanese system he would have expected that Haji would not be held for long. But – what could you expect if the US employed amateurs? And, although he had come close, Taylor had never had any evidence that he had done any wrong. All Haji had to do was talk his way out of the current immigration problem of identity – maybe spend some time being delayed by these bureaucrats – then they would have to let him go.

It was Mark's turn to smile, as he sat facing Haji across the table. Dusty did not even address Haji directly but turned his attention to the two men on his side of the table. Now Miller was back in his role as a lawyer.

'Have you read Mister Haji his rights?'

When he received a shake of the head, he then focused his attention on the Iranian.

'You do understand that under United States legal system we need to advise you of your rights before stating what you have been charged with? Do you understand that?

Haji looked confused and just blurted out.

'What is this? These gentlemen have got some issue with my passport. That is not an offense. It will soon be cleared up and I am on my way! The passport has been issued by the Pakistan Ambassador and I have diplomatic status.'

Dusty was enjoying this.

'Well - just listen to your rights and we can get on with the formalities.'

The junior FBI agent read off the rights of a person detained by the authorities. He read them because they differed from what he would normally say to a United States citizen in similar circumstances. It did not matter whether his rendition was correct because the probability was that Haji would not face a US court. He could be extradited to Turkey where the chain of evidence was not so critical as it was in the US and the Justice system did not bother too much about the rights of the accused. Or he could deal with the Americans and whatever terms they had to offer.

The smile on Haji's face disappeared when Dusty produced a package from his pocket and unwrapped the knife that he had recovered from the bush back in Mozambique. It had not been cleaned and was still coated in dried blood. The color drained from Haji's face as Dusty began to speak.

'This knife was recovered from the site where you murdered Banga Matsikenyeri. Do you recognize it?'

His body language said that he did. His voice said something different.

'Who is Banga? I have never heard of him. And why would I want to kill him?'

Now it was Mark's turn.

'He is the man you murdered in the hills to the east of Machinpanda Mozambique. Unfortunately for you, Banga Matsikenyeri was a CIA agent and whether you, or one of your thugs, killed him it does not matter. You were at least a witness and that is all we care about. It is now just a matter of matching the blood on the blade of the knife and the fingerprints on the handle and we have you at least as an accessory after the fact.'

Dusty then took over the conversation.

'Now – as you are probably aware – the United States has you on our terrorist watch list. Actually - you are listed under several names, but as we know each other well we can dispense with all that and concentrate on your real name – Mohamed Haji. Because you are suspected of taking part in terrorist activity you can be held for fourteen days without charge. And – by the way – the fact that you have been identified as an Iranian and not as a Pakistani your diplomatic cover is null and void. You have the right to call the Pakistan Embassy, but I think that you will find that they have suddenly lost all interest in their recent guest.'

It was now Mark's turn to deliver some bad news.

'Let us talk about Asif Fisk.'

There was a noticeable change in Haji's body language at the mere mention of the name which caused Mark to momentarily change tack.

'Do you know him?'

Initially Haji hesitated which was all the response that Mark needed.

'I thought so! Well – let me tell you about what Mr. Fisk is up to now. He is at present in hospital suffering from an injury to his right knee which he incurred while trying to kill one of the Americans he was supposed to protect. Unfortunately for him he got a bullet through the kneecap, and so - like you, and if he lives – he will be walking with a pronounced limp. Because of the drugs he is on to deaden the pain he is singing like a canary. He has so far given us your name as the person who recruited him for what he describes as a Jihad. We cannot use what Fisk has to say as evidence because of the circumstances in which he finds himself. However, we predict that when he becomes more lucid, he will see the error of his ways. If you get my drift.'

The FBI agent who had earlier left to check on something came back into the room and resumed his seat at the table. He did not smile.

'We have now cleared up the riddle of how and when you arrived in the country. Emirates Airlines have confirmed that an Iranian citizen arrived at this very airport five days ago. Our own sources confirm that you were followed to 3517 International Court Northwest here in Washington DC which just so happens to be a place occupied by the Embassy of Pakistan. That Embassy has no record of the arrival of the person who claimed to be named on the Emirates flight. So – in the absence of any evidence to the contrary, we must assume that the arriving person was not who he said he was. We now believe that the person in question was you. Do you have any comment at this stage?'

The problem for Haji was that this was the first time he had realized that he had been followed. In fact – it was the first time he had realized that his movements in the United States were known and had been recorded. He only had one possible answer.

'I demand to speak to our Embassy. This is outrageous!'

Now the FBI agent smiled.

'You obviously do not see the problem! According to my information you are an Iranian and the last that I heard,

Iran do not currently have an ambassador in this country. We could try the Pakistan Embassy. But they have already said that they do not know who you are. We could try the Turkish Embassy since Turkey is the point of origin of your latest journey. In fact – we could hand you over to the Turks who we understand have outstanding issues concerning unexplained deaths that they would like to clear up. Or we could hand you over to Sudanese authorities where you are believed to have escaped custody. They assure us that you would not escape again if they got their hands on you. Or we could simply had you over to Zimbabwe. We understand that your uncle Robert is quite anxious to renew acquaintances. But then we also have issues that would take precedence – such as the murder of our Ambassador to Kuwait, which we believe you can shed some light on. Not to mention the killing of our staff at our military base in the middle east. On balance, with this long list of matters that are outstanding, I would say that you will spend the rest of your natural life locked up. Or is there something that I missed?'

Haji had nothing to say. He just sat at the table – a look of defeat on his face.

'Ok – It is my job to inform you that you are now under arrest under the terms of the USA Patriot Act 2001. You will be moved from here to the District of Columbia jail Anacostia awaiting the presentation of the charges under which you will appear in court.'

Turning to the two police officers he said 'Officers – hand-cuff him and take this scum away.'

Mark and Dusty got up to leave at the same time.

'We will leave you with these gentlemen. I sincerely hope we don't meet again – because if we do you are a dead man!'

Mohamed Haji knew that he was trapped. He could have got away with it! The fact that the plans that he had been responsible for orchestrating on behalf of Iranian Intelligence officer Hormuzd Lajani, who claimed to be working under the direct authority of President Mahmoud Khatami had largely failed due to bad luck. Some of the parts of the plan were just plain daft and the plan overall was just way too complicated. That was to be expected when you had a civilian calling the shots. And now what would happen? Haji had heard the comments coming out of the American media machine but had not heard the reactions of Khatami or from Iran. Worse than that – What would be the reaction of the Supreme Leader?

Whatever else happened now – one thing was certain.

Haji would no longer have a job with the Iranian Intelligence services and, if he ever returned to Iran, he would probably be as good as signing his own death warrant. While he used to have the full support of Iranian Intelligence and no less a person than President Khatami, the failure of the plot would guarantee that everyone involved would scatter and try to pass the blame on to someone else. And in true Iranian style Haji would bear the brunt of the wrath together with Hormuzd Lajani and probably the President as well. That was why he had abandoned his various aliases that had been used so successfully in the past and look to get future employment with the Pakistan Intelligence. On reflection, what he should have done was to just to disappear into the vast metropolis of America.

During the hours, days and weeks that followed, the interrogation took what would be regarded as normal in negotiation between a terrorist and his capturer. Haji offered to provide the FBI with a vast amount of information about the Iranian Intelligence service in exchange for his freedom. The FBI accepted the offer in exchange for an offer of their own. They would make his stay in an American penitentiary as pleasant as possible by allowing access to the exercise yard for two hours instead of one hour per day.

Or he could take his chances in Turkey, Sudan, or Zimbabwe where there were a number of warrants outstanding for his arrest. In those countries the legal systems did not care too much for his civil rights. Or at least about as much as he had shown in his treatment of his fellow human beings during his short but brutal career.

It took several weeks for Mohamed Haji to realize what was happening.

The Iran Affair was over.

Epilogue

The aftermath of such events as had occurred would go unreported as is the way with all things. When people stop firing guns and stop trying to kill one another the public rapidly loses interest and return to a more normal life. That is – if they had such a thing as a normal life in the first place.

Benjamin Chapman had a life that was as simple as it could be. He was a single man who lived in Philadelphia where he had a job as greenkeeper at the Applebrook Golf Club. His boss was an ex-marine sergeant who had lost his right leg to a road-side bomb in Afghanistan. They looked after each other and few would ever know that they lived together. Whenever Ben had to go off on a mission the boss had his misgivings. More so because he realized that he could never go himself. But he always had Ben's back. The good thing about the game of golf was that it was as much a game against yourself as against opposition. It was unfair to blame the equipment, the greens, the weather, or anything else. And that would have to do.

Brad Morgan was also living a simple life. Sure – his job was highly technical and involved fairly complex logic to ensure that the systems he developed at Taylor Software were always a step ahead of the opposition and the competition. But – to Brad it was interesting and challenging rather than difficult. The only difficult part of his life had been getting to grips with his lady-friend Shania. She was an FBI special agent and had a career to think about. Some day she would have to also think about raising a family and right now that looked likely to involve Brad. Which was cool!

Owen Squires, the likeable Welshman, would return to Peshawar to be with Halah the lady who used to run a safehouse on behalf of the CIA in Kabul not so long ago. Now the two of them were doing work with the Afghanistan refugee camps in Pakistan supplemented by the odd clandestine job that they did on behalf of the US government. And that was cool as well.

Elliott Shannon, the likable Irishman who had more than his fair share of excitement in an interesting life that had spanned over four decades would return to his life as a recluse. He wandered down to the marina and spent a few hours making his yacht ready for sea. After stocking up on provisions he eased his boat away from the berth and out into the center of the Potomac River and turned to the south for a slow and peaceful trip to his home out in the Chesapeake Bay. Once there he would return to his life of reading, occasionally fishing, most often just sailing. But only when he felt like it. There would be no hurry. If he awoke the following day, then that would be a bonus.

The three members of the team who were recruited from the ranks of US Special Forces – Brent Shannon, Mike Gilroy, and Hamish O'Dea - returned to the Joint Special Operations Command at Fort Bragg. To them it was just another mission and one about which they nothing would be said - as is the way with men of their trade. These three had supplied the grunt of the group. Many would think they were just there to make up the numbers. But – without them, without the quiet unassuming role that they played, the outcome of the mission could have been an entirely different story. And they would now wait patiently for their next mission which would see them once more look to defend their country.

Archibald Miller – known as Dusty to friends and foes alike – would return to his office in downtown New York, where he would go back to being just another lawyer in a city that had more people in his profession pre head of population than anywhere else on planet earth. It was not as though he had *foes* or enemies as such. There were just some people who pissed him off and they had a long way to go to restore any trust. And he would not be alone, nor would he be a recluse. Dusty had a friend who he never talked about to anyone. This was because he had been left in the lurch in the past and did not want to go through that again. When the lady was ready to commit Dusty would know. In the meantime, he was just grateful to have someone to love and to be loved by. At least that was the way it was supposed to work.

With Blake Whittaker things would be different

this time. He had called his parents before leaving Washington DC to tell them that he was heading home. And warning them that, this time he would not be alone.

Blake was not without friends in high places but was too proud to use those contacts for his own benefit. He was therefore committed to make the life that he could for him and his extended family as best he could. That was until Mark Taylor decided to intervene.

Mark intended to pay for a visit to one of the leading Opthalmology Doctors at the John Hopkins University hospital for the simple reason that he could afford it. Then things got out of his hands. Marks soon-to-be mother-in- law, Karen Marshall of the DEA, decided to contribute and forced the Assistant Inspector of the CIA to get on board. It snowballed from there. So – very soon Blake would be back up the road to Baltimore. And now Mark had a fund that he could use to get girls like Jamal at the Pugnido Refugee camp the treatment that they deserved.

Blake was not certain of the time of his arrival and that was fine. His house was only a block down the road from his parents' place and that had provided a semblance of stability for his two daughters. The young were always more adaptable than their elders. Sure – the loss of their mother at so young an age was heartbreaking, and it was too early to tell what the longer-term effect that would have. But for now, they just got on with living their lives as best they could.

As Blake drove down their street, he saw them playing at the park not more than a hundred yards from their home. His parents were sitting on a park bench watching the girls at play – forever vigilant least one of the girls should fall – which the never did.

Blake exited from the car with Mina. The younger Misha was immediately nervous and rushed to grab Blake's hand as they walked towards the bench. Once there, introductions of the Meskin girls to his parents were over before the two Whittaker girls even noticed that their father had arrived home. And then children did what children always do. They rushed over and gave Blake a hug. And then turned their undivided attention to the other person of their own age group who had entered their bubble.

Then children did what they always do when faced with a critical situation. It took the Whittaker girls a few seconds to realize the girl that their father had brought with him was visually impaired. Then just as quickly the three girls rushed off to recommence the game. Now there were three of them to race each other on the monkey bars. And Misha seemed to always win. For now!

Blake turned his attention to the lady that he was more concerned about. Mina sat on the bench and watched the girls at play. She hoped that this was the end of a life on the run.

Mark and Debbie chose to drive north to New York City and had a stopover before they crossed the border between New York and New Jersey, turning east off the interstate 95 and checking into a motel by the Monmouth University.

In the morning Mark was up early and was relieved that the sun was just beginning to appear over the horizon. He rushed Debbie into their car and drove a short distance towards the sunrise and stopped by a section that was in the early stages of a major development.

He gazed at the rising sun, realizing that elsewhere in the world people were looking at the same sun setting on another day. But there were other things on his mind at the moment.

Mark then seemed to be stuck for words before blurting out an ill-prepared speech.

'Debbie – this is where I am planning to build a new office and a home. I want out of the rat-race that is New York city. My business does not need to be in any place really – we can work from anywhere. So - I am planning to move here where we can enjoy the sunrise and avoid the rush hour.'

Debbie could not understand why Mark was so emotional this morning.

Mark surprised himself.

Tears welled up in his eyes as he stumbled through the last of his prepared speech.

'I want you to join me as my wife – if you will have me.'

Debbie looked at Mark and burst into tears.

'Of course, I will - you idiot!'

And that, as they say, was that.

Author's commentary:

Having gone through the marathon of writing and publishing my first two books – *Covert Decisions* and *The Gatekeeper* – I felt the urge to continue the life of the central figure – Mark Taylor. A mix of personal experience working alongside the military, then with computers, and a vivid imagination, meant that the story lines flowed easily. Another story resulted.

If life has taught me anything it is that life is full of unpredictability, surprises, twists and turns, success, and failures. Features such as these should be reflected in any and every story.

My original concept of Mark Taylor was of a man with principles similar to my own – Accepting his fellow humans irrespective of race, color or creed - But intolerant of those in our society who have bigoted ideas of their own importance. A man who could be a good and loyal friend – but one who you would not want to make your enemy. A man who would fight against the odds in doing his very best for people who, through no fault of their own, need help and support. But he would never be a man who could singlehandedly solve all the problems of the world.

The result is – ***The Iran Affair.***

Visit Website on <u>www.donaldpetersbook.nz</u>

COMING SOON!!!

The Phoney War

The fourth book of 'The Mark Taylor' Series

www.ingramcontent.com/pod-product-compliance
Lightning Source LLC
Chambersburg PA
CBHW071953190726
48293CB00001B/8